Jackie Collins brings t
alive. Her phenomen
famous as the movers and
stars she writes about with an insider's knowledge. With 200
million copies of her books sold in more than forty countries, Jackie Collins is one of the world's top-selling writers. In a series of sensational bestsellers, she has blown the lid off Hollywood life and loves. 'It's all true,' she says. 'I write about real people in disguise. If anything, my characters are toned down – the real thing is much more bizarre.'

There have been many imitators, but only Jackie Collins can tell you what *really* goes on in the fastest lane of all. From Beverly Hills bedrooms to a raunchy prowl along the streets of Hollywood. From glittering rock parties and concerts to stretch limos and the mansions of the power-brokers – Jackie Collins chronicles the *real* truth.

By the same author

The World is Full of Married Men
The Stud
The Bitch
Sinners
The Love Killers
Lovers and Gamblers
Hollywood Wives
Lucky
Hollywood Husbands
Rock Star
Lady Boss
American Star
Hollywood Kids
Vendetta: Lucky's Revenge
Thrill!
L.A. Connections
Dangerous Kiss

JACKIE COLLINS

Lucky

&

The World is full of Married Men

PAN BOOKS

Lucky first published 1985 by Collins.
First published in paperback 1986 by Pan Books.
The World is Full of Married Men first published 1986 by W. H. Allen.
First published in 1968 by W. H. Allen.
First published in paperback by Pan Books 1984 .

This omnibus first published 2006 by Pan Books
an imprint of Pan Macmillan Ltd
Pan Macmillan, 20 New Wharf Road, London N1 9RR
Basingstoke and Oxford
Associated companies throughout the world
www.panmacmillan.com

ISBN-13: 978-0-330-44666-2
ISBN-10: 0-330-44666-5

1 3 5 7 9 8 6 4 2

A cip catalogue record for this book is available from the British Library.

Printed and bound in Great Britain by
Mackays of Chatham plc, Chatham, Kent

Lucky

In memory of Kimberly.
You are not forgotten.

Prologue

May 1984
Los Angeles

The jury filed silently into the courtroom. The judge made his entrance a moment later, and a hiss of expectation raged through the packed room.

Lucky Santangelo stood tensely in the dock. She stared straight ahead. Impassive. Wildly, darkly beautiful. In spite of everything.

The judge took his place, adjusted his heavy horn-rim glasses, and cleared his throat. 'Ladies and gentlemen of the jury, have you reached your verdict?' he asked tersely.

The foreman of the jury stepped forward. He was a sallow-faced man with a facial tic. 'Yes, Your Honour,' he said indistinctly, causing the judge to bark an irritable, 'Speak up!'

'Yes, we have, Your Honour,' the foreman repeated, his nervous tic becoming distractingly obvious.

'Then pass your verdict to the court clerk, if you please,' snapped the old judge waspishly.

The foreman did as he was bade. The clerk accepted the folded verdict form and took it directly to the judge who peered at it intently.

An expectant hush hung over the crowded courtroom. A silence so heavy that to Lucky it seemed more like an accusing roar.

She did not look at the judge, but she saw him read the paper, saw him pass it back to the court clerk, and she closed her black opal eyes for one brief moment of secret prayer. She, Lucky Santangelo, was accused of murder, and the next few minutes would decide her fate.

She tried to breathe evenly and deeply. Tried to remain calm, to concentrate, to think only positive thoughts.

The court clerk began to speak.

Oh God! This couldn't be happening to her. Not to Lucky Santangelo. NOT TO HER.

She held her head high. She was a true Santangelo. Nothing could get her down. Nothing.

After all, she was innocent.

Wasn't she?

Wasn't she . . .

BOOK ONE

The Summer of 1978

Chapter 1

Lennie Golden had not set foot in Vegas for thirteen years, even though it was the city of his conception, birth, and first seventeen years of life.

He looked around as he stepped off the plane, sniffed the air and took a deep breath. The place still smelled the same.

The airport was doing a roaring trade in visiting gamblers, tourists, and middle America out to have fun. Fat male butts waddled alongside peroxide plump ladies in polyester pant suits and fake jewellery. Small children whined and complained. Travelling hookers in halter tops, hot pants tightly outlining their crotches, arrived to do business. Swarthy foreigners clutched black leather attaché cases and breathed garlic over accompanying yellow-haired mistresses.

Jess was there to meet him. Startlingly pretty, five foot tall, she still had the air of a tomboy about her, which is what she had been at school. She had always preferred to hang out with the boys. Especially Lennie. They had been best friends since first grade, their somewhat unexpected and platonic relationship surviving and getting stronger every year – even though they didn't see much of each other since he had moved from Vegas to New York.

They made an ill-assorted couple. Lennie, so tall and lanky, with dirty blond hair and ocean green eyes. An overgrown Robert Redford with more than a touch of Chevy Chase. And Jess, petite and wide-eyed, with a mop of orange hair, freckles, and a *Playboy* centrefold body in miniature.

She hurled herself into his arms. 'It's *so* good to see you! You look fantastic. For a guy who spends his life screwin' around I don't know how you do it!'

'Hey –' He swung her in the air like a rag doll. 'Look who's talking!'

She giggled and hugged him tightly. 'I love you madly, Lennie Golden. Welcome back.'

'I love you too, monkey face.'

'Don't call me that!' she screeched. 'I'm married now. I'm respectable. I got a kid, the whole bit. So c'mon, Lennie – treat me like a lady.'

He burst out laughing. 'If *you're* a lady *I'm* Raquel Welch.'

She grabbed his arm. 'You got great tits!'

Laughingly they strolled towards the exit.

'So how was the flight?' she asked, trying to grab his battered suitcase.

He wrestled it away from her. 'Long and boring. If God had meant us to fly he'd have given us more stewardesses.'

'Didja score?' She winked knowingly.

'Affirmative.'

'Really?'

'Would *I* lie to *you*,' he dead-panned.

She laughed. She had a maniacal guffaw which caused people to turn and stare. 'You'd lie to the Pope if you thought it would get you through the day.'

'And there she goes . . .' he sing-songed.

'Who? Where?' Automatically she turned to check out his conquest. A nun walked serenely by.

'I told you my tastes are changing,' he said gravely.

'Very funny!' She aimed a punch at his stomach.

He held up a protesting hand. 'Lay off. I just had surgery of the tongue.'

'Huh?'

'Remember the taping of the Lee Bryant show? The one I told you I was doing?'

'Yeah.'

'They cut my four minute spot to thirty seconds. If you fart you miss me.'

She frowned. 'Schmucks. They know from nothin'. Anyway, you're back in Vegas now. Your kind of comedy schticks gonna kill 'em here.'

'Oh sure, in the lounge of the Magiriano Hotel I'm really going to cause a riot.'

'It's a change of scene. Could be just what you need. Who knows *what* it'll lead to.'

'C'mon, Jess. You sound like my agent. Do this shit – that piece of crap, and before you know it you'll have a regular spot on Carson.'

'Your so-called agent is a New York jerk-off artist.' She wrinkled her nose. 'You're a *great* comedian. *I* should be handling you. I mean I got you this gig, didn't I?'

'What do you want – ten percent?'

She laughed wildly. 'You think I wanna give up the title of best blackjack dealer in Vegas? You think I'm crazy or somethin'? Stick your commission where the sun don't give you a tan!'

They were passing a ladies room. 'Wait a sec,' she said. 'I'm so excited to see you I gotta take a pee.'

He laughed, and leaned against the wall while she dashed inside. Jess was a friend indeed. He had called her two weeks ago and said he had to get out of New York.

'No problem,' she replied without hesitation. 'Matt Traynor, the entertainment director of the hotel I work at has the hots for me – send me a tape and I'll get him to hire you.'

He had sent the tape. She had come through with the gig. Some good friend.

Idly he watched a dark-haired girl in black leather pants and a red shirt stride by. She cut through the crowd as if she owned the place. He liked her style, not to mention her body.

Jesus! Was he free yet? He and Eden had split six months ago, yet every time he saw an attractive woman he couldn't help comparing them. He was *still* doing it. Eden Antonio and he were unfinished business, why didn't he just face it?

Jess emerged from the ladies room and squeezed his hand. 'It is *sooo* great to have you here,' she said. 'I want to hear all about everything.'

'Hey – everything is a career going nowhere and a fucked up sex life.'

'Sounds exciting. So what else is new?'

They were outside now and the desert heat enveloped them.

'Jeez!' he exclaimed. 'I forgot how hot it is here.'

'Aw, stop bitching. You could do with a tan. You look like nightclub Charlie.'

They approached a dented red Camaro waiting in the parking lot.

'I see you're still an ace driver,' he remarked dryly, throwing his suitcase in the boot.

'*I* didn't do that,' she replied indignantly. 'My old man can't drive around the block without gettin' into trouble.'

He wondered what kind of man took on crazy Jess for a wife. Someone special he hoped.

'C'mon,' she said, sliding behind the steering wheel. 'Wayland is makin' lunch. The baby's makin' noise, and Lennie, *you* are gonna *love* it here. It always was your kinda town.'

He nodded grimly. 'Yeah. That's what I'm afraid of.'

*

Lucky Santangelo stood out as she strode briskly through the crowd at the airport. She was a strikingly beautiful woman of twenty-eight, with an unruly mass of jet curls, black gypsy eyes, a wide sensual mouth, deep suntan, and lean loose-limbed body. She wore soft black leather pants, a red silk shirt casually unbuttoned to the limit, and a wide belt studded with silver. From her ears hung plain silver loops, and on her right hand was a square cut diamond of such size and brilliance that one would be forgiven for thinking it was not real. It was.

No conventional beauty, she had a style and bearing all her own. Confidence wafted from her like the exotic scent she drenched herself with.

'Hey, Boogie.' With affection she greeted the skinny, long-haired man in army fatigues who stepped forward to greet her. 'How's everything?'

'The same,' he said, low-voiced, slit eyes darting this way and that, observing everyone and everything as he took her black leather tote bag and the check claim for the rest of her luggage.

'No exciting news? No gossip?' she questioned, grinning, delighted to be back.

He had gossip, but *he* didn't want to be the one to give it to her.

She talked excitedly as they walked toward the stretch Mercedes limousine parked on a red line.

'I think I put it all together, Boog. The Atlantic City deal is ready to fly. And I did it. Me! All I need is an okay from Gino and the record'll spin. I feel *great*!'

He was pleased to see her in such a good mood. He nodded and said, 'If you want it you'll get it. I never doubted you.'

Her eyes gleamed with excitement. 'Atlantic City,' she said. 'We'll build a hotel to beat everything!'

'You'll do it,' he agreed, opening up the rear door.

'Hey,' she complained, 'you know I always sit up front with you.'

He switched doors, settled her in the passenger seat, and loped off to get the rest of the baggage.

•

Gino Santangelo awoke with a start. For a moment he was disoriented, but only for a moment. He might be old, but he certainly wasn't senile, thank God. Besides, seventy-two nowadays was not exactly fertilizing oranges time. In fact, last night, in bed, he had felt like a kid again. And why not, with Susan Martino for company.

Susan Martino. Widow of the late great Tiny Martino, a multi-talented veteran of television and the movies. A comedian whose name ranked alongside Keaton, Chaplin and Benny. Tiny had died of a stroke two years previously. Gino had attended the funeral in Los Angeles, conveyed his respects to the widow – and not seen her again until she turned up in Vegas three weeks ago at a charity benefit. Now he was waking up in her bed for the fifth morning in a row, and feeling no pain.

As if she knew he was thinking sweet thoughts about her, Susan entered the room. She was an attractive, well-groomed woman of forty-nine, who looked at least ten years younger.

Her eyes were pale china blue, cheekbones high, skin white and smooth. Her silver blonde hair was neatly drawn back in a chignon, even though it was only nine in the morning. She wore a white silk peignoir on her understated but perfect body, and carried a tray with a glass of freshly squeezed orange juice, a soft boiled egg, and two pieces of lightly buttered toast cut into thin slices.

'Good morning, Gino,' she said.

He struggled to sit up, pushing his hands through his unruly black hair, which although greying at the temples, was just as thick and curly as it had been in his youth. He was still a man to be reckoned with. Age had by no means dulled his vitality and ceaseless energy – although a nearly fatal heart attack a year ago had slowed him down a mite. Like Susan, he did not look his age.

'What's all this?' He indicated the laden tray.

'Breakfast in bed.'

'And what did I do to deserve it?'

She smiled. 'What *didn't* you do.'

He grinned, remembering. 'Yeh. Not bad for an old man, huh?'

She placed the tray in front of him, and sat on the edge of the bed. 'You're the best lover I ever had,' she said gravely.

He liked that. He liked it a lot. Susan Martino was no tramp, but she'd had a reputation of sorts before marrying Tiny Martino twenty-five years earlier. The Aly Khan, Rubiriosa, even Sinatra were rumoured to be in her past. Enough for Gino to feel more than flattered by her compliment.

Not, of course, that he had ever questioned her about her past, just as she had never asked him about his.

'I wanna know somethin',' he said, interested enough to start finding out.

'What?' she replied, carefully peeling the shell from his egg.

'When you were married to Tiny – you ever cheat around?'

She did not hesitate. 'Never,' she replied firmly. 'Although *why* I should tell you . . .'

He suddenly felt possessive of this woman. This classy

blonde *lady*. And how many of *them* were there around today?

Women. Love 'em an' leave 'em had been his life's motto. With very few exceptions. In the last year taking them to bed had become boring. Another body. Another pretty face. Another thousand dollar bill for a trinket because he didn't like to dismiss them empty-handed. When they left Gino Santangelo's bed he wanted them to *know* they had been somewhere. Not that he had to pay. Never. The very thought was crazy.

'Can we spend the day together?' Susan asked, dipping a sliver of toast into the egg and feeding it to him.

He was just about to say yes, when he remembered. Lucky was coming back today. His daughter. Beautiful wild Lucky – with *his* eyes and *his* deep olive skin and *his* jet hair and *his* zest for living. How could he have forgotten? She had been away for three weeks on a business trip to the East. He would be missing her badly if it weren't for Susan.

'Why don't we make it tomorrow. I got things to do today,' he said, pushing the spoon away.

'Oh.' She looked disappointed.

He wondered how Lucky would feel about Susan joining them for dinner, and knew instinctively that she would hate it. He could understand. After all, it was her first night back, and they would have a lot to talk about.

There was time enough to introduce Susan into their lives, and he fully intended to. Susan Martino was too much a lady to be just a one week stand.

*

During the drive from the airport Lucky continued to fill Boogie in on her trip. He was more than her driver and sometime bodyguard when the climate indicated she was in need of protection. He was her friend, and she trusted him implicitly. In times of trouble Boogie came through. As he had proved in the past he was loyal, smart and usually silent, unless he had something worth saying – which suited Lucky just fine.

He drove her to the front of the Magiriano Hotel on the Strip. She got out of the car and stood for a minute feeling the usual thrill of coming home to *her* hotel.

The Magiriano – a combination of her parents' names – Maria and Gino. Gino's dream, put into being by her while Gino sweated out a seven-year tax exile in Israel. She would always be proud of her achievement. The Magiriano was very special.

In the lobby there was the usual mêlée of tourists and noise. The casino was crowded with morning gamblers. No windows. No clocks. Twenty-four hours non-stop fun.

Lucky did not gamble. Who needed to play the tables when it all belonged to her and Gino anyway? She strode across the lobby to her private elevator concealed behind an arrangement of potted palms, and inserted a code card to gain entry.

It was good to be back.

She couldn't wait to see Gino. She had so much to tell him.

*

Jess did not live in luxury, but the small tract house she stopped the car in front of at least had its own tiny swimming pool. 'This place is okay, but we're movin' on soon,' she explained airily, opening up the front door. 'We've seen a development in Lake Tahoe we're lookin' to buy into.'

'Yeah?' said Lennie, and wondered who was looking to buy into it. From the small amount of information Jess had divulged about her husband, it seemed he didn't do much at all except look after their ten-month-old baby while she brought in the money.

'Anyone around?' she called out, as a scruffy mongrel dog appeared and wagged its sorry looking tail. She bent to pet the animal. 'This is Grass,' she explained. 'Found him dumped in the garbage when he was a pup. Cute, huh?'

Wayland appeared, or at least Lennie presumed it was he. From the look of him Jess had found herself another stray.

He was dressed in grubby white chinos, a loose embroidered shirt, and his dirty feet were bare. He had shoulder-length yellow hair with a centre part, and a long pallid face. Jess – who wrote wonderful letters – had mentioned that he painted. Exactly what he painted she hadn't gone into.

'Greetings, man,' said Wayland, stoned to the eyeballs. 'Welcome to our home.' And he extended a thin shaking hand.

'Where's the baby?' Jess demanded.

'Asleep.'

'You sure?'

'Go see.'

For a moment her pretty features clouded over and Lennie sensed all was not well in this year old marriage. That's just what he needed, to be stuck right in the middle of some miserable scene. He had enough problems of his own.

Lunch turned out to be a large bowl of brown rice and some wilted lettuce coated with stale yoghurt. Jess tried to conceal her aggravation – she had been at work all night and left instructions for Wayland to fix something special – but she did it with difficulty. Lennie knew her well enough to realize she was pissed off.

The baby – a boy named Simon – woke briefly, and accepted a bottle.

'I wanna take Lennie over to the hotel,' Jess said restlessly, when the baby was asleep again.

Wayland nodded. He didn't have much to say about anything.

Out in the car she lit up a joint, blew smoke in Lennie's face, and said aggressively, 'I don't want to talk about it, okay?'

'Who's asking?' he replied calmly.

She gunned the car into action and sped all the way to the Magiriano, where she drew up to the entrance without cutting the engine. 'I'll meet you here in a couple of hours,' she said. 'Ask for Matt Traynor. He's the guy who booked you. He'll get someone to show you around.'

'Where are *you* going?'

'I got an . . . er . . . appointment.'
'Screwin' around already?'
'Give me a reason not to.'
Having met Wayland he couldn't think of one.
Matt Traynor was a fifty-five-year-old silver-haired fox in a three piece beige suit. Apart from being the best entertainment director in Vegas, he had points in the hotel. Lucky Santangelo had personally pursued him to take the job, and only the lure of a piece of the action had persuaded him.
He told Lennie he loved the video tape Jess had shown him of his work, and then proceeded to fire off questions about her as if hoping to find out every detail of her life.
Lennie made a stab at a few answers, but when Matt started asking about her marriage, Lennie felt the time had come to move on. Quickly he said he wanted to check out the lounge he would be appearing in, and generally get the feel of the place. Matt Traynor agreed, gave a few vague directions, and waved him on his way.
Las Vegas. The heat. The special smell. The hustle.
Las Vegas. Home. From birth to seventeen.
Las Vegas. Youthful memories crowding his head. The first time he got laid, drunk, stoned, busted. The first time he fell in love, ran away from home, stole his parents' car.
Mom and Pop. The odd couple.
Pop, an old-fashioned stand-up comic. Jack Golden. Dependable, a real hack. But a name everyone in show business knew – everyone except the general public. Dead thirteen years now. Cancer of the gall bladder.
And mom, Alice Golden – formerly known as The Swizzle – one of the hottest strippers in town. Good old mom, fifty-nine-years-old and living in a condo in California. From Las Vegas to Marina del Rey in one fell swoop with a used car salesman from Sausolito. Alice was not your average Jewish mother. She wore short shorts, strapless tops, dyed her hair, shaved her legs, and got laid a lot after the Sausolito salesman skipped town with ten thousand dollars worth of her jewellery.
Alice . . . she was something else. He had never felt close

to her. When he was a kid she bossed him around, sent him on endless errands, and used him as a lackey. She never cooked a meal in her life. While other kids took neat brown bags to school with home-made meatloaf sandwiches, cookies and cheese, he was lucky to scrounge an apple from a tree in the garden.

'You gotta learn to be independent,' Alice told him when he was about seven.

He had learned the lesson well.

Living with Alice and Jack *was* exciting. Their untidy apartment was always filled with dancers and singers, casino people, and general show-biz. Life was fun if you forgot about childhood.

Alice. A real character. He had learned to accept the way she was.

Las Vegas. Why had he come back?

Because a job was a job was a job. And as he'd told Jess, he had to get out of New York. The police were on his case after he'd punched out a fat drunk who was heckling him during his act at a Soho club. The fat drunk turned out to be a shyster lawyer, who, when he woke up the next morning with a black eye and split lip, decided Lennie Golden needed to be put away, and set about doing so. The aggravation of a law suit was not something Lennie needed in his life. Leaving town seemed the best way to deal with it. Besides, Eden was on the West Coast, and for months he had been thinking about following her. Not that they had parted friends.

After Vegas he planned to move on to Los Angeles.

Not just to see Eden.

Yeah. To see Eden.

Admit it, schmuck, you're still hooked.

*

Lucky entered the pool area, and paused for a moment until she caught the eye of Bertil, the Swedish head honcho of all pool activity.

He spotted her immediately. She was impossible to miss

in a one piece black swimsuit covering a supple tanned body with the longest legs in town. He jumped to attention, remembering she was the boss, and hurried toward her, greeting her with just the right amount of deference and enthusiasm. 'Welcome back, Miz Santangelo.'

She nodded briefly, scanning the mass of bronzed bodies. 'Thank you, Bertil. Any problems while I was away?'

'Nothing to bother *you* with.'

'Bother me,' she said softly. 'I like to know everything.'

He hesitated, then launched into a short story about two lifeguards who had been hitting on female guests.

'Did you fire them?' she asked.

'Yes, but they're planning to sue.'

'Have you talked to our lawyers?'

'Yes.'

'Then it's all taken care of,' she said, satisfied.

He escorted her to a poolside lounger, and she settled back to observe the action.

'Bring me a phone,' she requested.

He did as she asked, then left her alone.

She tried Gino for the third time. He was still out. Where the hell was he? Why wasn't he awaiting her arrival?

Chapter 2

'Olympia. You are a Princess. A Goddess. A Queen.'

Olympia Stanislopoulos' golden rounded body quivered with delight. 'More Jeremy, tell me more.'

The English Lord shifted position on top of the Greek shipping heiress's nubile naked body and continued his litany of praise. 'Your eyes are the Mediterranean. Your lips ruby jewels. Your skin the smoothest velvet. Your . . .'

'Ahhhhhhh . . .' Her loud cry of ecstasy silenced him. She spread her legs wide, then brought them tightly together, scissoring him in a painful embrace. While doing this her long talon-like nails scratched a lethal trail across his back, drawing blood.

His yell of pain joined her shout of ecstasy. 'For God's sake, Olympia!'

She was uninterested in his complaints. Casually she pushed him from her.

'I haven't come,' he complained.

'Too bad,' she retorted sharply, and rolled off the bed.

Olympia Stanislopoulos had never been known for her warm and compassionate nature. She bounced quickly into the bathroom, slammed the door and confronted her reflection in a full length mirror.

Fat! Rolls of unwanted cellulite-dimpled fat! Angrily she grabbed a fold of flesh around her waist and squealed with fury. God*damn* that phoney French doctor who had given her three months of treatment, a few lousy fucks, and charged her thirty thousand dollars. He'd certainly seen *her* coming – in more ways than one. She stuck her tongue out at her reflection, hating what she saw.

What she saw was a twenty-eight-year-old, five-foot-three, very curvacious woman, with great bouncy breasts, an abundance of thick blonde curls, and a pretty face. Her eyes were small and blue. Her nose nondescript. Her lips pouting rosebuds. Men loved her. She looked very sexy. A regular sex bomb. Only a sex bomb with a difference.

On her twenty-first birthday Olympia Stanislopoulos had inherited seventy million dollars. Wisely invested the millions had made her now worth more than twice that.

She had been married three times. First, at seventeen, to a fledgling Greek playboy of twenty whose family had lineage but little money. They were married aboard her father, Dimitri's, yacht, conveniently moored beside his private island. The occasion had been more than festive; two princes, a scattering of princesses, a deposed king, and most of Europe's idle jet set. The happy couple honeymooned in India, lived for three months in Athens, and divorced in Paris when Olympia discovered her new husband on all fours being roughly serviced by the butler. She was no prude, but there *was* such a thing as decorum. Dimitri consoled his petulant daughter with a magnificent apartment on the Avenue Foch – two blocks away from the family mansion.

Soon she met an Italian business tycoon. Or at least that's what he *said* he was. A man of forty-five with charm, smooth lines, a reputation as a womanizer, and a great wardrobe. He courted her through the discotheques of Europe and married her on her nineteenth birthday. They stayed together a year. She bore him a baby daughter, Brigette, while he spent as much of her money as he could. His indiscretions hit the newspapers and magazines once too often. Olympia was furious to discover he had been dancing the night away while she was screaming the night away delivering their child.

Dimitri arranged the divorce for her. She settled two Ferraris and three million dollars on her second mistake. He never had time to enjoy it. Three months after the divorce, he stepped out of a car in Paris, and was blown to pieces by a terrorist bomb. Olympia had no time to mourn, she was too busy making mistake number three, an impoverished Polish count. Take out the O and you had his number. He lasted sixteen weeks and left her with a title and all his debts.

Olympia decided marriage was out, and indulged in a great many affairs, none of which satisfied her. She began to travel frequently, dividing her time between her Paris apartment, a pied-à-terre in Rome, and the Connaught in London. Summers she spent in the South of France. Gstaad at Christmas. Acapulco when she felt like it. She went through men fast. Most of them bored her after she had sampled their bodies. She needed more than sex, she needed an added thrill.

Married men were fun. And famous men. And powerful men. The more unobtainable they were the better.

Laying them was the kick. After the initial encounter what was left? She needed a challenge. For she discovered something she had known all along – most men were easy lays. And who needed easy?

Olympia's first lover had taken possession of her body when she was a mere sixteen. The setting was Southern France, in a villa she and her girlfriend, Lucky Santangelo, had 'borrowed' from Olympia's aunt. They were on the run from boarding school, two adventurous little girls with time on their hands, money to burn, a white Mercedes, and inquisitive natures. Often Olympia looked back on those illicit carefree days as the happiest time of her life. No pressures or sneaking photographers behind every bush. No great expectations.

Warris Charters. She remembered him well. Handsome, with corn-coloured hair and slitted green eyes. An older man. A film producer. A broke hustler with an exceedingly active cock.

Sometimes she wondered what had happened to him. Warris Charters, caught with her sixteen-year-old golden curls between his legs giving him a blow job. Caught by her father and Lucky's father when the two men travelled to the South of France in search of their errant daughters.

The last she had seen of Warris was a nervous figure scurrying into the storm-ridden night clutching two Gucci suitcases and an earful of threats from Dimitri.

She had never heard from him again. Understandably so.

She had never heard from her best friend Lucky Santangelo again either. Not so understandable. After all the experiences they had shared she would have expected at least a phone call. It never occurred to her that Lucky had been forbidden to contact her. What *did* occur to her was that Lucky might have betrayed them. Summoned the two fathers to come and collect them, because she, Olympia, was having all the fun.

Who needed Lucky anyway?

'*Olympiaaaa*.' The plaintive cry was accompanied by a sharp pounding on the bathroom door. 'My beauty. What are you doing in there?'

What did the fool *think* she was doing? Playing with herself?

She flung open the door impatiently.

Lord Jeremy's naked erectness faced her.
She sighed.
It was a rainy afternoon in Paris.
What else was there to do on a rainy afternoon?

Chapter 3

Bikin'd bodies, oiled and gleaming, lay in various stages of undress beside the Magiriano pool. Lennie sauntered aimlessly among them, and remembered the countless times he and Jess had crashed out beside many of the better hotel pools while playing hookey from school. It had become one of their most interesting games, along with cruising the casinos, feeding the slot machines without getting caught, and trying to sneak into the lavish shows. In the end every security guard in town knew their faces, which kind of cramped their style – but certainly not their energy.

Leaving Vegas for New York, at seventeen, was easy. Leaving Jess behind was not. But New York beckoned, and who was he to argue? He looked at least twenty, and was six feet two, with a great body and a tousled handsomeness. A variety of jobs kept him going while he made up his mind what he wanted to do. He had no trouble getting by. A room in Greenwich Village became his home, and there was never a shortage of girlfriends as he coasted along for a couple of years just enjoying the freedom of being in the big city. To survive he did everything from slicing lox in a Sixth Avenue deli, to selling watches in Bloomingdale's. And the summers he spent in the Catskills, doing busboy duties at one of the busier hotels. It was there he learned that there was more to comedy than pie-in-the-face, drop your pants, Jack Golden style. He discovered the records of the late great Lenny Bruce. (He fantasized for a while that his mother had named him after Lenny Bruce. Just a fantasy. She had named him after a dumb cousin of hers in Miami.) He discovered political humour, irreverent humour, and the straight monologue. At last he realized what he wanted to do with his life, and he set about it with a vengeance.

Writing came first. Routines. Schtick. Brief sketches. Then he found himself an agent who began to sell some of his stuff. Not enough to give up working – but it was a start.

He had a flair for pithy original material. Sometimes it was a little too wild, but gradually his agent developed a steady market of buyers for anything he came up with. By the time he was twenty-four he was able to concentrate full time on creating. He wasn't making a fortune, but things were moving along nicely, lots of girlfriends, and plenty of good times.

Being back in Vegas was strange.

He passed a slavic blonde with cheekbones that could cut butter. She threw him a long slow look as she suggestively rubbed suntan oil on her thighs. He was not in the mood for a pick-up. Now that he was thirty there had to be more than just getting laid. She did look a little like Eden though. The same high cheekbones, icy blondeness, and cool narrow eyes. Cat eyes.

Eden Antonio. He would never forget the first time he saw her. He was living with a girl named Victoria, a photographic model who looked like Miss Prom Queen – all long lean limbs and whiter than white teeth. He had thought they had a pretty good thing going for the two years they were together. She adored him and gave him all the home comforts he had never received at home. Then one day she introduced him to another model, Eden Antonio.

When he first set eyes on Eden he knew Victoria had merely been the hors d'oeuvre. Eden had just returned from a successful working trip to Europe, and was as feline and sleek as a cat. Unlike Victoria, she did not look like Miss anything. She was pale and exotic looking, with finely etched porcelain features, and a startling bone structure. She was also making more money than him, but things were getting better all the time. He had gotten himself involved in the pilot for a new kind of television show – aptly titled 'Off the Wall' – and for the first time he was actually performing, and he loved it. Audience reaction was a charge he had never thought would turn him on to the extent it did. The show was given a weekly spot on a local station. He was twenty-seven and running on all cylinders. Not bad for a boy who had survived in New York without a pot to piss in.

Eden was neurotic, ambitious, and just about the most exciting woman he had ever met. Although she was four years younger than him, she seemed to know so much about life. She had travelled around the world, been with numerous lovers, and struck Lennie as being incredibly sophisticated. Of course, that was in the beginning. After three and a half years of a love/hate relationship, he knew her supposed sophistication for the sham it was. Eden Antonio was the most insecure person he had ever met. At times he felt sorry for her, other times she made him so jealous he could kill.

Eden! What she had put him through. He had physical as well as mental scars from their intense volatile relationship. And yet . . . still he wanted more. They might have fought constantly, but the making up was always worth it.

'You are what is commonly known as pussy-whipped,' his friend, Joey Firello, had told him on many occasions. 'She fucks up your head, and you come back for more. Dump her, Lennie. She's just a user. A classy tramp.'

Sure she was. He knew that. But he couldn't help himself.

'She's got you by the balls,' Joey said.

'No way,' Lennie replied. But it was true.

Eden adored being seen. Every night she liked to go out on the town. Weekends she attended some half-assed acting class. She wanted to be discovered and become a movie star. She already thought she was a star of sorts. When Lennie's television show was cancelled after one season, her only comment was, 'Jesus! And I was just about ready to do a guest shot for you.'

She thought his career was a dead end and often told him so. Not that she gave a damn. Eden never cared about anyone except herself.

She was a terrible actress. Lennie saw her in several class productions and found her embarrassingly inept. As a model nobody could beat her. 'Why don't you stick to modelling?'

he asked one Sunday afternoon, having watched her murder a scene from *Cat on a Hot Tin Roof*.

'*Fuck you* – you sonofabitch!' she screamed. 'Are you telling me I'm no good?'

'I'm telling you you'd be better off doing what you do better than anyone around.'

'You *bastard*!' A bottle of scent came flying through the air. 'You *cocksucker*!' Followed by a hefty glass ashtray. 'You jealous *asshole*!'

Two months and many fights later she had taken off for California with an actor from her class. A long-haired jerk named Tim Wealth.

Lennie missed her. Even though he was into performing at small off-beat clubs. Even though he loved every minute. Even though audience reaction was very positive, and gradually he began to build a small but hard-core following.

Reviews – when he got them – were excellent. The money was nothing to get excited about – but he supplemented his salary with writing assignments. His material was always in demand.

In the back of his mind he knew he would follow her to California. Las Vegas was the starting point. If he could make an impression there, then he could head for LA with a real shot. Eden was impressed by success. If he ever made it she'd come running . . .

The slavic blonde beckoned, and he realized he must have been staring. Quickly he moved on, skirting the pool, looking around. A girl lay on a lounge chair in a black one-piece swimsuit. He remembered seeing her stride through the airport earlier. There had been a lot of women since Eden, none of them helped. Each time he thought the next one would be different. They never were. Without pausing he was beside the girl in the black swimsuit, mentally zeroing in on which of his many successful lines he should go with. He decided safe was best, and besides, it always worked. Turn downs were something Lennie Golden knew little about.

'You,' he said, 'are too beautiful to be alone. So what's it to be? A drink? Breakfast? Or how about diamonds? I give great heist!'

Usually they responded one of two ways. They either laughed, or made a quick request for diamonds. Whatever they did a dialogue was created and from there it was all the way home. Make 'em laugh first, *then* move in for the kill.

Lucky raised her shades slowly and stared at him coldly.

He fell into her black opal eyes and almost gave up blondes forever.

'You've got to promise to respect me in the morning,' he said quickly. 'I'm *very* sensitive.' He grinned in what he had been told countless times was an irresistible way, and waited for her comment.

'Back off, schmuck,' she said disinterestedly. 'Try the cupcake posing under the palm tree, she looks like she could use a little of your corn syrup. More your style, y'know what I mean?' She lowered her shades dismissively.

'Wait a minute, who's writing your script – me?' She was a touch icy, but nothing he couldn't thaw.

Before he could continue further a hand descended on his shoulder, and a burly Swede in blue swim shorts said, 'This is not a pick-up joint, mister. Please leave.'

He tried to shake the hand off, but Bertil's grip was firm. 'Hey, c'mon man. I'm a guest here,' he objected.

'Show me your room key,' said Bertil, propelling him away from Lucky.

He didn't like being strong-armed. Nor did he like being made to look a fool. 'Do yourself a favour,' he exclaimed in disgust. 'Take your hands off me. I'm appearing here in the Bahia lounge. My name's Lennie Golden. I'm *talent* for crissakes.'

The scream of a distraught mother distracted everyone. 'My little girl, she can't swim!' yelled the hysterical woman.

Bertil loosened his grip. Two lifeguards and Lennie leaped into the pool. He reached the child first, pulled her up by a mop of hair, and hauled her to the side where Bertil lifted her from his arms and handed her, unhappy but unharmed, to the grateful mother. Lennie pulled himself out and stood dripping in ruined white pants and a shrinking sweater, not to mention water-logged tennis shoes. The two lifeguards shot him filthy looks. Bertil ignored him. The mother was too interested in her rescued offspring to even glance in his direction.

He looked for the girl with the black eyes. How could she resist him now?

She was long gone.

So much for heroics.

*

'I thought,' said Lucky, 'that I would come over and bring you up to date on everything. I have so much to tell you.'

It was past noon and she had finally located Gino. They spoke on the phone.

'I'm tired, kid,' he said. 'Gonna take a nap and get myself in shape.'

She was away three weeks and he was too tired to see her. What was going on?

'Where were you? I called four times,' she said lightly, knowing that with Gino it was best not to push.

'Around,' he replied.

Shacked up with some sleazy show girl, she thought. *Seventy-two and still out getting laid.*

She gave him a little silent disapproval.

'I'll pick you up tonight,' he offered. 'We'll have a quiet dinner, just the two of us. Does eight o'clock suit you?'

An edge of sarcasm. 'You're sure you won't be too tired?'

'Come *on*, kid. When am I ever too tired for you?'

Now, she wanted to say. But she didn't. She agreed that eight o'clock was fine, and spent an impatient afternoon waiting to tell him all about her trip, and the deals she had in the works. He would be so proud of her. She couldn't wait!

*

'What happened to you?' demanded Jess.

'I wanted to see if this sweater was shrink-proof,' replied Lennie sarcastically.

'It's not.'

'Oh, really? Then remind me never to go swimming in it again.'

He climbed into the car and she sped off. Her eyes glittered dangerously as she gunned the red Camaro down the Strip at full speed, narrowly missing a lumbering tourist in an I LOVE CHICAGO T-shirt.

'Shit!' she muttered.

'What's the matter?'

'Haven't had a hit in years.'

'You could have fooled me.'

She whirled the car into the parking lot of a supermarket and killed the engine.

'Gotta get dog chow,' she announced. 'And baby stuff, food, things like that.'

'Doesn't your old man take care of the shopping?'

'You experienced lunch. What can I tell you?' She grimaced.

'I think we've got to talk,' he said.

She nodded. 'We will.'

He followed her into the market. A six foot red-head in pink spandex pants and a crocheted boob tube smiled at him. He smiled back.

A short bad-tempered man in a wrinkled white suit whacked her on the ass. 'Quit it,' the man said tersely.

The red-head tossed long swirls of hair and pouted.

'Vegas is full of hookers,' Jess remarked.

'Tell me about it,' replied Lennie.

The groceries came to sixty-three dollars. Lennie insisted on paying, but Jess fought him all the way.

'You're broke,' she said.

'Not at all.'

'It's unnecessary.'

'Says who?'

'Me.'

'Take a walk, monkey face.'

'Don't call me that!'

The line behind them applauded when she finally allowed him to pay.

They fell into the parking lot laughing.

A fat boy with long greasy hair was trying to gain entry to the Camaro.

'Hey!' yelled Jess indignantly.

The boy continued his assault on the passenger window with a wire coat hanger.

Jess dropped two paper sacks of groceries and charged.

Lennie followed suit. Together they dragged the fat boy from his task. Stoned eyes signalled venom. He lumbered across the parking lot and set to work on a Ford.

'I don't *believe* it,' Lennie said.

'You're a New Yorker now, you should believe anything,' Jess responded sagely.

They retrieved scattered groceries and made it to the house in record time.

Wayland floated on a blue striped mattress in the pool smoking a joint.

Simon cried wildly on a dirty Navajo blanket.

'Shit!' muttered Jess.

It appeared to be her favourite expression.

Lennie wondered if he should have booked into a hotel. It looked like Jess had enough problems without a houseguest to complicate matters.

Chapter 4

'Hey, you're lookin' good, kid. Atlantic City agreed with you, huh?' He winked at his daughter.

'You know something, Gino, for an old man you're looking pretty good yourself.'

She never called him daddy. Only sometimes, in her mind, when it was late and she was tired and the memories came creeping back to haunt her . . .

'Cut out the old,' he snapped.

They grinned at each other, linked arms, and proceeded to her private elevator.

How alike the two of them were. The same smouldering eyes, dark olive skin, jet hair, and wide sensual mouths.

They enjoyed the perfect relationship. So similar in every way. From food to movies to books to people, they almost always formed the same opinions. Gino would say, 'I don't trust that guy – not with my left ball I don't trust him.' And Lucky would add, 'Lock up your right one – that dude is bad news.' Then they would break up laughing, black eyes locking fondly with black eyes.

They maintained separate penthouse apartments atop the two hotels they owned. Gino lived at the Mirage. And Lucky resided in the Magiriano. Together they shared a house outside New York in East Hampton. A white, old-fashioned mansion filled with so many memories . . . so much of their past . . .

Once they had lived in the house as a family. Gino and his wife Maria, with their children, beautiful dark Lucky, and her blond brother, Dario.

Now there was only Gino and Lucky. The two of them against the world. There existed a special bond between them no one could break.

It hadn't always been that way . . .

*

Gino Santangelo was born in Italy, and in 1909, at the age of three he travelled to America with his parents, a young, strong couple, filled with ambition, and a desire to capture the great American dream. But jobs were not easy to come by. Too many immigrants, all with the same idea, all brimming with energy and enthusiasm.

By the time Gino was six, the great American dream had soured. His mother ran off with another man, and Paulo, embittered and disillusioned, embarked on a life of petty crime, drink and loose women.

When Paulo was in jail, which was often, it didn't bother

Gino. He found himself shuttled between foster homes, and it taught him to be fast and smart, a true street kid with big ambitions. At fifteen he was caught stealing a car, and sent to the New York Protectory for Boys – a tough home in the Bronx for orphans and first-time offenders. The brothers in charge were a hard bunch. Discipline was the order of the day, and messing with the boys the order of the night. Gino was able to protect himself, but some of the younger boys were not so fortunate. A scrawny kid named Costa Zennocotti was hit on constantly. His cries for help went unanswered, until one day Gino could stand the agonized screams coming from a back room no longer. Unthinkingly he picked up a pair of scissors and slipped into the room. Costa was bent across a table, his trousers and shorts around his ankles, while one of the brothers plunged his erectness into the skinny child's ass. Gino lunged with the scissors.

The result was a stay in the Bronx County jail, six months' probation, and a friend for life in Costa, who, as a result of the publicity, was adopted by a well-to-do family in San Francisco.

By the time Gino hit the streets again he was older and sharper, with a strong urge to make money and beat the system. He had no desire to live with his father – still in and out of jail and now married to a prostitute named Vera. So he looked around and observed the heroes of the day. Men like Salvatore Charlie Luciano (later to be known as the notorious Lucky Luciano), Meyer Lansky and Bugsy Siegel. They were the guys with the money, the sleek cars and beautiful women, the power and the respect.

Gino saw. Gino wanted. Gino got.

His rise to the top was long and hard but eventually worthwhile. After starting off small, he went into business for himself, operating a thriving bootleg racket. By the time he was twenty-two he had a pretty girlfriend named Cindy, and a rich society mistress by the name of Clementine Duke, whose Senator husband introduced him to the world of investments and real money. Senator Duke made Gino's money legitimate. When the great stock market crash came in 1929 he was prepared, and thanks to the Senator walked away unscathed.

Along the way he had acquired a business partner, Enzio Bonnatti, and by 1933 their interests included gambling, loan-sharking, and the numbers racket. Gino refused to touch prostitution and drugs, in spite of pressure from Enzio. Because of this conflict they split their interests in 1934 and went their separate ways.

For recreation Gino opened a nightclub, called it Clemmies', and became a minor celebrity. Clementine Duke was delighted. However she was not so delighted by his amazing success with women. She persuaded him to marry Cindy – in the hope that this would take him off the market. But women to Gino were a fatal attraction. He truly loved to make love, having been initiated by one of his foster mothers at the age of twelve, then led to new levels of accomplishment by the very versatile Mrs Duke. Now his conquests were many, and often.

Cindy soon became as angry and jealous as Mrs Duke. She plotted revenge, slept around, and threatened him with exposure to the Internal Revenue Service for tax evasion.

In 1938 she fell to her death from a window in their penthouse apartment. An unfortunate accident. Gino gave her a magnificent funeral.

By 1939 rumblings of a war in Europe were shaking America. Senator Duke sat down with Gino one day and worked out ways to benefit from the situation. Gino went along with everything the older man suggested. The Senator had never advised him badly.

Gino often wondered how he would be involved if the war spread to America. He needn't have worried. On New Year's Eve 1939 he found his father in a tawdry hotel beating up Vera. She was just a cheap whore, but she had been kind to him over the years, and in return he had helped her when he had the means.

As he came upon the sordid scene, Vera raised the '38 she was holding and blew Paulo's brains out. Gino wrestled the gun from her – and later that night was accused and arrested for his own father's murder. He spent the war years behind bars. Punished for a crime he never committed.

His old-time friend and now lawyer, Costa Zennocotti, managed to extract a written and witnessed confession from Vera just before her death seven years later. Gino got a pardon and a paltry offer of compensation. What amount of money could possibly compensate for seven years of his life?

In 1949 he decided he needed a change of scene, new interests. Las Vegas was an appealing prospect – and an old friend of his, Jake the Boy – was bugging him to invest. He put together a syndicate, and they financed the building of the Mirage Hotel. Las Vegas was just beginning. Bugsy Siegel had already opened up the Flamingo Hotel and casino (later he was murdered for skimming money), and Meyer Lansky had financed the Thunderbird. Gino wanted in. It was an exciting time. He wanted to enjoy it, have fun, and forget the dark years of being locked away.

And then he met his wife to be, Maria. She was young, innocent, only twenty – with pale gold hair and the face of a fragile madonna. They were married almost immediately. And in 1950 Lucky was born. Even as a baby she looked just like him.

They lived in a large white mansion in East Hampton, with eucalyptus trees in the garden and the smell of peace and tranquillity all around.

To make their world complete, Maria gave birth to a son eighteen months later. They named him Dario. He looked just like his mother.

•

The elevator ground to a halt, and Lucky stepped out into the milling crowds filling the casino. She had planned the location of the elevator so that it delivered her right into the centre of action. Unlike Gino, whose own private elevator in the Mirage took him straight to a basement garage where his limousine and driver were on call twenty-four hours a day.

Gino hung back for a moment, his eyes ever watchful. Once a street kid, always a street kid. You could have all the power and money in the world, but it was never enough to protect you one hundred percent.

He felt the slight pressure of his gun carefully concealed in a hidden shoulder holster, and reassured, stepped forward.

Lucky turned to him with a wide grin. 'Business is booming, huh, Gino?'

'Yeah, kid. Things are hot.'

Things were always hot in Vegas. The suckers were always on parade with their quarters and dollars, ready and willing to take a gamble, run a risk, win or lose, it didn't really matter as long as they got their shot.

They ate in the hotel at the secluded Rio restaurant, just the two of them. Lucky spoke of her trip non-stop, her eyes shining with enthusiasm, her cheeks flushed.

'I've set up exactly the deal we've been looking for,' she said. 'The right property on the boardwalk. The right investors. I've even got architects and builders coming up with bids. If we move fast we can start work within the next couple of months. It's all set. All you have to do is give the go-ahead.' She paused for breath. 'Of course we'll need building permits, licences. But everything's in hand. I have it covered.' She grinned triumphantly.

Gino listened carefully. She was smart, his daughter. Smart and fast. Beautiful and bright. Tough and wild. Daddy's little girl. She made him proud. Her business acumen was as sharp as his.

He had never thought a woman could equal him – but his daughter could. His Lucky.

*

Right from the beginning Lucky Santangelo was a bright-eyed excitable child. Her younger brother, Dario, was smaller, more delicate. There were only eighteen months between them, but even when they were young, Lucky took charge.

Maria was a wonderful mother. Gino spoiled them rotten. All the time it was presents and kisses and hugs. And special hugs for Lucky, who responded to him far more than Dario.

On her fifth birthday they threw her a fantastic party for fifty children. Clowns. Donkey rides. A huge chocolate cake. And Gino on hand to sweep her up in his arms and smother her with love. Lucky remembered it as the happiest day of her life.

A week later Gino left on a business trip. Lucky hated it when he went away, but there were compensations, such as taking his place in the big double bed he shared with mommy, and all the wondrous presents when he came home.

Only this time there were no presents, or kisses, or laughter. This time there was only the pain of her mother's sudden and brutal murder, her naked body left floating on a raft in the centre of the swimming pool for Lucky to discover when she got up in the morning.

Memories, for a while, were a blur. Policemen. Photographers. Guards. Then a plane trip to California. A new house with bars on the windows, alarms, and guards with dogs patrolling the grounds. Life changed completely for Lucky and Dario. Maria gone forever. And Gino. So different, angry and sad. No more laughter and playing, or hugs and kisses. In fact he was hardly ever there. He was either in his New York apartment or Vegas hotel. It was almost as if he didn't want to spend any time with them. They were cared for by nannies and tutors and maids.

The pain hardened inside Lucky, while Dario withdrew into a world of make-believe. They had everything money could buy. But all they really had was each other.

When Lucky was almost fifteen a decision was made to send her to a boarding school in Switzerland. She was both excited and fearful at the prospect, but the thought of getting away from the Bel Air mansion was certainly tempting.

L'Evier turned out to be a strict private school run by a thin nosed woman who demanded 'respect and obedience' from her girls. If it hadn't been for her friend, a classmate, Olympia Stanislopoulos, Lucky would have hated it. Olympia's attitude was 'screw school. Let's get out and have fun.' And Lucky did not argue. Together they obeyed the rule of lights out at 9.30 p.m. And at 9.35 Lucky and Olympia were climbing out of a convenient window. It was only a ten minute ride to the nearest village where waited boys, booze and fun. It took them exactly two semesters to get expelled.

Gino arrived to collect his rebellious daughter, his face a mask of thunder. He flew her back to New York and promptly enrolled her in an even stricter school in Connecticut. It did not take her long to contact Olympia in Paris, and together they planned an escape. With a little help from a couple of credit cards she was able to get a flight to France, where Olympia met her. Then it was a fast drive in a white Mercedes convertible all the way to the South of France, where they broke into Olympia's aunt's villa and took up residence. The memories were sweet. Even when Olympia moved in her boyfriend, 'Warris the hustler', as Lucky christened him.

The memories were not so sweet the night their fathers arrived. Gino Santangelo and Dimitri Stanislopoulos. Then it was back to the Bel Air mansion – Dario was now away at school.

There were times when she hated her father. A furious blazing hate which burned deep. Other times she loved him more than anything else in the world. And she wished it could be like it once was. Desperately she craved his attention, but that seemed the last thing he was prepared to give her.

On her sixteenth birthday he surprised her by flying her to Las Vegas. Once there he arranged for her to have her hair styled, bought her a designer dress, and gifted her with exquisite diamond ear-studs. Then he said she was to accompany him to an important charity benefit he was giving for Mrs Peter Richmond – Senator Richmond's wife. Lucky was thrilled. Things were looking up. Only at the dinner he sloughed her off at another table next to Mrs Richmond's creepy son, Craven, and ignored her all night.

Later, she sneaked away, changed into jeans, cruised the Strip, and ended up fighting off a drunk in the parking lot.

Gino was waiting when she arrived back at 3 a.m., her clothes torn and dirty.

He came straight to the point. She was a little tramp whose only thought in life was to screw around, so he was marrying her off and that was that.

If she didn't like it . . .

Tough.

*

Gino had not thought of Susan Martino all night. Nor had the moment been right to mention his involvement to Lucky. So it gave him a jolt when Susan entered the restaurant with a man, smiled, waved and sat down at a nearby table.

Lucky said, 'Who's that?'

'Hey,' he stalled for a moment. Had somebody told her already? 'Don't you know Tiny Martino's widow?'

'Not the woman,' Lucky replied dismissively. 'The old guy with her, he looks familiar.'

Gino squinted – his eyes were going, but pride prevented him from wearing glasses. 'Yeh,' he agreed. 'I think I know the face.'

He began a slow burn. The man was over six feet tall, impeccably groomed, with bushy white hair, and hard but handsome features – marred only by a prominent nose. And the sonofabitch was sitting down next to Susan.

Gino scowled.

She couldn't possibly be his date.

Could she?

He signalled for the captain. 'Who are the people at that table?' he demanded.

'Guests of Mr Traynor's,' the captain replied.

'Where the fuck *is* Mr Traynor?'

'Coming in now, Mr Santangelo.' The captain backed away nervously.

'What's the matter?' said Lucky calmly, used to her father's outbursts. 'Is he someone we shouldn't have in here?'

'I'll find out soon enough,' replied Gino grimly. 'Hey – Matt. Over here,' he yelled, ignoring the other diners who turned to stare.

Matt Traynor bore down on them, all smiles, his silver hair gleaming in the candlelit room. 'Lucky. Welcome back. You look beautiful. And Gino. It's a pleasure.'

'Who the fuck is that asshole with Susan Martino?'

Matt Traynor blinked rapidly while he tried to figure out what he'd done wrong. He had heard rumours of Gino Santangelo's interest in Tiny's widow, but he hadn't figured it to be anything serious, so why was Gino bellowing like a jilted lover?

'Susan's not *with* anyone,' he explained quickly. 'I thought she might enjoy a little company, so I asked her to join me and some of my friends.' He paused, threw in the punch line with sad sincerity. 'Tiny was like a brother to me, you know.'

Gino was untouched. 'Who's the prick?' he growled.

'Am I missing something here?' interrupted Lucky.

'If I thought it would upset you, Gino –' Matt said solicitously.

'Who the fuck's upset!' screamed Gino. And he stood up.

'Dimitri Stanislopoulos,' Matt said hurriedly. 'He arrived this evening. He's here for the Francesca Fern tribute dinner. We're comping him in the Presidential Suite. Usually he stays at the Sands, and *loses* at the Sands – if you get my drift. But I met him in Monte Carlo last month and persuaded him the Magiriano would be more to his taste. The guy has more money than Onassis. And loves to play baccarat.'

'Of course!' exclaimed Lucky. 'Olympia's father! No wonder he looks familiar.'

'Olympia?' said Gino blankly.

'You remember,' Lucky continued excitedly. 'Olympia was my best friend at school – we ran away to the South of France and you and Dimitri tracked us down. It's him all right. I could never forget *that* face.'

Gino gestured impatiently. He was in no mood for the past. 'Matt,' he said brusquely, 'you'll join us.'

It was more command than invitation.

'I'm sure we'd love to,' Matt replied easily, although he was aggravated at being treated like hired help. Still, when Gino Santangelo spoke – everyone jumped.

'My date will be here in a minute with a girl for Dimitri. You want us *all* to join you?'

'Sure. Bring Susan and whatshisname over now, and the others when they get here.'

'Good idea,' said Matt, thinking it was a lousy idea.

As soon as he left their table Lucky said, 'Why do you want *them* to come over? We have so much left to talk about.'

'Why not?' replied Gino, sitting down again. 'You'll like Susan Martino, she's a lovely woman.'

Like hell I will, thought Lucky. It was becoming increasingly clear that while she was away Gino had been at play. And this time not with some two bit showgirl. She could tell she had lost his attention and it infuriated her.

'Have you been seeing her?' she asked lightly.

'Once or twice,' he replied, equally casual.

Once or twice, my ass. You've got a hot nut the whole room can see.

Inexplicably she felt jealous.

Why?

Why not?

He was her father.

Daddy.

Gino.

•

The wedding invitations, hurriedly printed, invited guests to attend the wedding of Lucky Santangelo to Craven Richmond.

Craven Richmond. Tall, skinny son of Senator Peter Richmond and his athletic wife, Betty.

Craven Richmond. Attentive, polite, boring.

Craven Richmond. A husband chosen by Gino for Lucky without her approval or consent.

She dared not disobey her father. So she and Craven were married one week after her sixteenth birthday. It was a marriage doomed to failure. They honeymooned in the Bahamas. A big joke. Although Gino thought she was some hot little nympho and married her off to protect the great Santangelo name, she was actually still a virgin in the technical sense, never having done more than a lot of heavy petting. Craven, at twenty-one was totally inexperienced, and unwilling to indulge in more than three fast minutes of sex a night.

Before their honeymoon was over Lucky took her first lover. And from then on she never looked back. How else would she have gotten through four years of being married to a man who had been paid to marry her? Yes, paid. A sad fact she had found out from Betty Richmond one day during the course of a family fight. Gino had paid Craven, and blackmailed Betty and Peter to allow it to happen.

So, she was stuck in a loveless marriage to a man she couldn't stand. And her future seemed bleak. They lived in a Washington apartment not five minutes from the Richmond palatial spread. Craven had no job. He spent his days playing tennis with his mother and hung around his father's campaign headquarters getting in everyone's way. Lucky filled her days with shopping, reading, and drifting up and down the freeways in her red Ferrari – a wedding present from big daddy. It was not the way she wished to spend her life.

Once, she had indicated to Gino that she wanted to follow him into the family business, but he had looked at her as if she were mad, and said that only boys went into business, girls got married, stayed home, and had babies.

She felt trapped in a life Gino had forced upon her. She hated him with a passion. Yet she desperately wanted to please him.

Staying married pleased him.

Fucking around pleased her.

So she did.

A lot.

Until one day, four years into her marriage, came the phone call summoning her to New York. Gino wanted to see her, and for once without Craven. She was delighted. Anything to get away, and it had been months since she'd seen her father – maybe he was missing her.

In New York she discovered that Dario had also been sent

for. The brother she had once been so close to was now a secretive stranger. He attended an art institute in San Francisco, and never communicated in any way.

Gino presided over the family dinner, which dragged until he made the announcement they had both been waiting for. It seemed he was in trouble with the tax authorities and faced an upcoming subpoena and chance of jail. He had to get out of the country for a while.

'As a precaution,' he said, 'I'm signin' over a lot of things to you two. Nothin' to bother yourselves with – you'll just have to put your signature on some papers occasionally. Costa will have my power of attorney, he'll take care of everything. And Dario, I want you to move to New York. There's a lot of things you should know about. Costa'll start teachin' you.'

'Move to New York!' Dario cried. 'Why?'

'You're a Santangelo, that's why. And you've been pissin' around at that dumb art school for long enough. It's time you came into the business.'

'What about me?' Lucky demanded.

'What about *you?'*

'If Dario's going to learn the business, I *want to as well.'*

'Don't be a silly girl,' Gino said mildly.

She felt four years of frustrated rage boiling up inside her. 'Why not?' she demanded. 'Why not?'

'Because you're a married woman who will stay by her husband's side and behave like a proper wife. And *it's about time you had a baby. What are you waiting for anyway?'*

'What am I waiting for?' she exploded. 'I'm waiting to have a life *first – that's what I'm waiting for.'*

Gino threw up his hands in mock despair. 'She wants a life. It isn't enough she's had the best money can buy –'

'Including a husband,' Lucky yelled angrily. 'You bought me a husband with your lousy money. You –'

'That's enough.'

'It's not *enough. I want more,' she screamed. 'Why should Dario get a chance and not me?'*

'Cut it out, Lucky.' His voice was ice.

'Why the fuck should I?'

His black eyes were as deadly as hers. 'Because I'm tellin' you. And watch your language. Ladies don't talk like you.'

She put her hands on her hips and arrogantly faced him. 'I ain't no lady,' she mocked. 'I'm a Santangelo. I'm just like you – and you ain't no gentleman.'

He stared at his wild daughter and thought, Christ! What have I raised here? I've given her everything. What more does she want?

'Why don't you just shut up and sit down?' he said wearily.

This made her even angrier. 'Oh, sure! Shut her up, marry her off, and who cares whether she's happy or not? You're a fucking male chauvinist who thinks women are only good for screwing and cooking. Keep 'em in the kitchen or the bedroom where they belong. Is that what you did with mommy before she was murdered? Did you lock –'

He cut her words off abruptly by slapping her across the face.

Desperately she tried to control the burning tears. 'I hate you,' she hissed. 'I never want to see you again.'

She stormed from the room. Behind her she heard him say, 'Kids! What can you do? You try your best . . . A woman in business . . . you gotta be nuts . . . Emotional . . . Jeeze, they're all so goddamn emotional . . .'

Lucky wasn't emotional. She was full of a hard cold anger.

Gino left the country shortly after. He settled in Israel for an undetermined period of time. A few weeks later Lucky heard from Costa. There were papers to be signed and he would be sending them to her.

When she received the documents, she studied them carefully in spite of a note from Costa that read – 'Don't bother reading – just sign by the pencil mark, purely a formality.'

If she was signing, she was reading.

She then decided why bother sending them back if she could deliver them personally?

Within hours she was on a plane to New York.

•

Susan Martino was groomed from the top of her perfectly coiffed head to the tip of her Charles Jourdan gold pumps. She wore a simple little Adolfo, and a few hundred thousand dollars worth of blazing sapphires. They matched her eyes, so delicately made up – nothing obvious.

She was the sort of woman, Lucky decided, who looked like she never went to the bathroom. The thought of Susan and Gino in bed together was laughable.

'I'm so pleased to meet you, dear,' she said to Lucky. 'Your father mentions you all the time.'

Lucky manufactured a smile, and wondered what had happened to the cosy evening for two she and Gino had been enjoying. Susan Martino, Dimitri Stanislopoulos, and Matt Traynor, all joined them at their table. With difficulty, Lucky controlled her impatience.

Dimitri and Gino recalled their previous meeting. They laughed about it. So long ago and far away. And now the two delinquent daughters grown women.

'Say hello to Lucky,' said Gino with a grin. 'She sure remembers you.' Once he had established Susan was not Dimitri's date, he had calmed down. And why not? With Susan beside him, so womanly and such a lady in the true sense of the word.

'My pleasure, Lucky,' said Dimitri, taking her hand and bringing it to his lips where he brushed it with a kiss.

Old-fashioned bullshit artist. She remembered him on his Greek island the summer she had vacationed there with Olympia. He had been sleeping with one woman, a soignée brunette, and making it on siesta afternoons with another house guest – a long-haired actress with horny eyes and an easy-going husband. According to Olympia, if it moved, her father felt obliged to fuck it. Not so different from Gino, Lucky had thought at the time.

Two showgirls approached the table. All teeth, tits and hair. One was Matt Traynor's date – he had the taste of a tom cat, and the other a fix-up for Dimitri. Both girls were visibly impressed by the group they were joining.

Lucky thought about leaving. But why should she? She decided to sit it out and observe Susan Martino in action.

The blonde woman did not disappoint. She handled Gino expertly. Every move was the right one. A practised courtesan who had found someone she wanted and had every intention of getting him.

Lucky was not fooled by the act.

Gino was.

Why am *I* concerned? Lucky thought. It's his life.

Like hell it is.

It's *our* life. And has been for the last year.

*

New York was exciting. So was being away from the Richmond family. Learning about Gino's business interests was the most exciting of all.

Lucky found a ready teacher in Costa, who fell for her wide-eyed interest, although he knew Gino would not approve. Day after day she appeared at the office and he began to explain the workings of the various companies. 'Of course, you're only a figurehead,' he said. 'You'll never be called upon to get involved.'

Oh no? That's what he *thought. Like a sponge she absorbed every bit of information. When Craven called angrily from Washington demanding her return, she told him their marriage was over. It was easy to make the move without Gino looking over her shoulder.*

And when Dario arrived reluctantly from San Francisco, and found his sister doing what he should be doing, he was relieved. Business had never interested him, now he could concentrate on his social life, and do all the things Gino would never have allowed. Dario's main interest was boys not girls.

Within a year Lucky knew everything there was to know about the various Santangelo operations. Like Gino before her she was a quick study.

Gino had set up a syndicate of investors to finance the building of the Magiriano. Construction on the hotel had just begun, and the weekly payroll was vast. Since Gino's exile from America, some of the investors were stalling on paying out.

'Don't we have agreements with these people?' Lucky demanded.

Costa shook his head. 'No. It was all done on a handshake basis.'

'They gave Gino their word, didn't they? What would he do if they didn't come up with the money?'

Costa cleared his throat nervously. 'He had his own . . . methods.'

'You're supposed to be running things for him. Why don't you use his methods?'

'Certain things are best left alone until the moment is right. We must wait for Gino.'

She stared at him hard. 'We can't wait. We don't know how long he'll be away. Even you say it could be years. If they gave their word, they have to be made to keep it. I want a list. I think I can work something out.'

He laughed in disbelief. 'Don't be a silly girl, these are hard men –'

Her eyes were ice-cold. 'Don't ever call me a silly girl again, Costa. You understand?'

He remembered Gino at the same age. And he knew there was no way he was going to stop her from taking over while her father was away.

*

'There's a new comedian opening in the Bahia Room tonight,' Matt said to Lucky. 'Why don't we have our coffee in there and catch the second show?'

'Is he funny? I need a laugh.'

'Would I hire a comedian who isn't funny?'

She glanced at his date, an overmade-up nineteen-year-old Barbie doll. 'There's a lot of things you do that make me wonder, Matt.'

She was fed up with the entire evening. It pained her to see Gino making such a fuss of the groomed-to-the-eyeballs Susan Martino. Dimitri Stanislopoulos was loud and overbearing. And the two showgirls an embarrassment.

'Shall I suggest it?' Matt indicated Gino, lost in the azure blue of Susan's eyes.

'Do what you like,' snapped Lucky. For a year nobody had come between her and Gino. Nobody got closer to him than an hour or two in his bed. And what did that mean? A quick physical act with some undemanding bimbo. For a man of his age he sure liked to indulge. But indulging was one thing – becoming involved another.

What did he need it for? She frowned. It would be different if Susan was a warm and wonderful person, but she wasn't. She came across as an icy, controlled bitch, with a thin veneer of saccharine charm. And Lucky wanted the best for her father, not some ball-breaking Beverly Hills widow who probably saw him as an ongoing meal-ticket. It was obvious she liked money. Judging from her jewellery the more the merrier. Why didn't she turn on to Dimitri who probably crapped gold bars?

Contemplatively Lucky lit a cigarette and blew perfect smoke rings while Matt got the party together for the move into the Bahia Room. She hadn't slept with a man for months. The urge just wasn't there.

Lucky Santangelo, celibate. The thought amused her.

There had been a time when she might have bedded one or two different men a week. If they were attractive, appealed to her, didn't want any entanglements, and were prepared for her brisk, 'Don't call me, I'll call you.' Sexually she had always lived her life like a man, and why not? As long as she wasn't hurting anyone. Sexual hypocrisy outraged her. Who thought up the double standard anyway? Why did society call a man who slept around a stud, and a woman a nymphomaniac? To hell with that rhetoric. She just liked getting laid when she felt like it without the hassle of a relationship.

Of course, there was always the exception. In Lucky's life there had only been one exception. Marco.

*

Marco entered Lucky's life when she was a mere fourteen and he was around thirty. Dark and brooding, he was, she thought, the most attractive man she had ever seen. Unfortunately the feeling was not mutual. He regarded her as nothing more than a dumb kid, and treated her as such. He worked for Gino, and sometimes did duty as a bodyguard/chauffeur when either Dario or Lucky went shopping or to the movies. Which wasn't often. Gino did not encourage outings. After Maria's death, he liked his children safely behind the gated security of the Bel Air mansion.

When she went away to school it was Marco who accompanied her to the airport. When she returned on vacations he was always there. When Gino took her to Las Vegas for her sixteenth birthday and announced he was marrying her off, she had thought for one wild and wonderful moment he meant to Marco. But that was not to be, and it was Craven Richmond, Washington, and Marco out of her life – perhaps forever.

Occasionally, along the path of an annihilatingly boring marriage, she met a man or two who reminded her of Marco. Maybe it was the dark eyes, or the way his hair curled over the back of his collar, or perhaps just a gesture. Whatever. It was enough to send her into their beds. But Marco clones were never the real thing.

With Gino out of the country, and her marriage behind her, she tried to forget him and threw herself into solving the problem of the reluctant investors. Costa was a nice man, and a brilliant lawyer, but obviously not a man of action. It was imperative that work on the Magiriano continue and she had to make sure it did, so she went to see Gino's old business partner, Enzio Bonnatti. Costa had taken her to meet him months before, and they hit it off immediately. At their first meeting he had declared himself her Godfather, and as such she felt she could go to him for his advice and help.

'Costa will not act,' she said, after explaining the situation, 'but I am prepared to do whatever my father would do.'

Enzio chuckled. 'Gino never took no shit from no one – excuse my language. You want to be like him, why not? I lend you a couple of soldiers. You frighten the crap outa number one on the list, you ain't got no problems with the rest. You want I should take care of it for you, my pleasure.'

She shook her head. 'Just let me have the assistance.'

She started off with the biggest investor, paying a visit to Rudolpho Crown, a slick-haired 'investment banker'. He sat behind a massive desk in his office and leered insolently while she discussed the money he had promised but failed to put up.

'You gave your promise, Mr Crown,' she said coolly. 'You are part of a syndicate. If you try to drop out, others will follow, and then work on the hotel will have to be stopped.'

'I gave my word to Gino. And when he comes back I'll honour it.'

Her voice was very soft. 'It makes no difference where Gino is. You gave your promise. He wants it honoured – now.'

Rudolpho grinned. 'He's hardly in a position to want anything. Word is out he won't be back for a long long time – if ever.'

She smiled sweetly. 'Risk it, Mr Crown.'

A week later he was wakened at midnight by the touch of cold steel on his balls. He opened his eyes, panic-stricken. Two men were holding knives to his shrivelled penis. He started to scream, to cry, to beg.

He saw a shadow by the door and a woman's voice said, 'This is only a dress rehearsal, Mr Crown. If your money isn't forthcoming immediately, opening night will be next week.'

Rudolpho Crown put his money up – fast. Other investors followed equally fast. The Magiriano was back in business.

Shortly after settling the business of the reluctant investors, Lucky flew to Las Vegas to see for herself the building progress being made on the Magiriano. Naturally enough she stayed at the Mirage. And there was Marco to greet her. She hadn't seen him since her wedding day.

'You look sensational,' he said.

'You look a little ragged yourself.' Quickly she worked out how old he must be now: forty-one. His exceptional good looks had not faded at all. He was still the most attractive man she had ever seen, and she burned to go to bed with him.

'How long are you staying?' he asked politely.

Just as long as it takes me to get you into bed. She gestured vaguely. 'A few days, maybe a week.'

'Good. I want you to meet my wife.'

His wife! *'How long have you been married?' she asked, hardly able to catch her breath.*

'Exactly forty-six hours. You just missed the wedding.'

It took time for Marco to sense the heat of her desire. She stepped back and treated him just like any other employee.

'I want the Mirage renovated,' she told Costa. 'It looks tacky.'

Marco was furious. 'What's going on here?' he screamed at Costa over the phone when the decorators descended. 'Get Lucky off my back. She's disrupting everything.'

'I can't,' Costa replied simply. 'She's the major shareholder. She can do what she wants.'

Wild with fury, Marco noticed her all right. By the time he noticed her enough to want her, she was businesslike and remote. She had no intention of sharing him with his wife.

Their relationship simmered. Lucky was in and out of Las Vegas watching the work on the Magiriano. There were problems – then more problems. Nothing she couldn't deal with.

Marco was always around to greet her.

'Still married?' she would ask lightly, although her stomach churned with the anticipation that he might have gotten a divorce.

'Sure am. And you? Still screwing around?'

'Give me a better hobby and I'll try it,' she drawled jokingly. She knew her casual sex life pissed him off.

One night, when his wife was out of town, he finally made a move. They had dined together, discussed old times, and when she was at the door of her suite, he said, 'I'll come in.'

He was so close she could feel his breath on her cheek. She desired him more than she had desired anyone in her life. Sweetly, she said, 'Good night, Marco. Sleep warm,' and closed the door before she could weaken.

When she had him she wanted it to be for keeps. That's the way it had *to be.*

As time passed, Lucky worked hard and played hard. She

was a resolute businesswoman, demanding and getting the best from the people she employed. She flew back and forth to Las Vegas constantly, noting that Marco remained firmly married. She still wanted him, but it had to be on her terms.

Very rarely she thought of Gino, whose empire she was taking over. She was building his hotel, realizing his dream – yet they had not spoken or been in touch at all. And that's the way she liked it. It would suit her if he never *returned to America.*

In 1975 the Magiriano was finally completed. Opening night and Lucky glowing in a black Halston dress, Marco resplendent in black tie – the electricity charging between them like firecrackers. The time was right. Somehow the fact that he still had a wife didn't seem to matter anymore.

Lucky got through the evening in a heightened state of sexual anticipation. Marco felt the same way.

Later, they came together in exultant ecstasy. A wild ritual of incredible sex, followed by the release of being with each other at last. It was a joining of soulmates. A fusion of energies.

Plans were made. He would tell his wife immediately, and arrange a quick divorce. There would be no more separations. Now that it had happened it would be forever.

When he left her bed in the morning, Lucky knew she had finally found what she had been searching for. A man she could look up to, live with, and love. Marco was everything and more. Marco was her world.

At 2.30 p.m. that day, as Lucky sat with Costa in the Patio Restaurant waiting for Marco to join her for lunch, she noticed Boogie – her bodyguard – heading swiftly across the room towards her.

As he approached she felt a chill of apprehension.

'There's been a shooting,' he said.

She knew it was Marco.

She knew it was her future.

She closed her eyes to pray, but with a feeling of foreboding she knew it was too late.

*

The Bahia lounge was crowded, but a table was made immediately available for the Santangelo party.

Lucky found herself seated beside Dimitri Stanislopoulos. 'How's Olympia?' she asked. Not that she cared, over the years Olympia had never once tried to get in touch with her. They had not spoken since that fateful night in France thirteen years before. Sometimes Lucky read about her in the newspapers, and was bored by the antics of the puffy-looking blonde with too much money and too many husbands. They might have been best friends once, but they were total strangers now.

'She's divorced again,' Dimitri said shortly. 'For the third time.'

He had extremely penetrating eyes, steel grey, and a deep Mediterranean suntan. His eyes lingered on the wildly beautiful Lucky for a moment, then his showgirl friend-for-the-night tugged on his sleeve and asked him some inane question.

Lucky turned to Gino, but his attention was on Susan. She thought she might leave, but decided to stay for the comedian who was adjusting the mike and opening with a few dead-pan comments on the day's news.

A ripple of laughter drifted through the room. He was quick to grab the audience's attention; an audience more attuned to discussing their losses and/or wins rather than listening to a stream of jokes.

He didn't tell jokes. He commented on life.

He was cutting, satirical, and painfully truthful.

'What's his name?' Lucky asked Matt.

'Lennie Golden. You like him?'

'Not bad.'

Matt smiled. Jess had come up with a winner, thank Christ. He had taken a risk booking the guy just because she wanted him to. But he had the hots for little Jess, and now he'd done her a favour, wasn't it about time she returned the compliment? It was funny really, he had never liked short girls, always gone for the statuesque type. However, five foot nothing Jess had him under her spell. He wanted to get her into bed in the worst way.

Halfway through Lennie Golden's performance Gino leaned over to Lucky and said, 'Susan's tired. I'm taking her home. I'll see you tomorrow, kid.'

He helped Susan from her seat.

For a moment Lucky was speechless. *Her* evening with *her* father, and he was taking Grace Kelly home. Shit!

'Goodnight, dear. So nice meeting you,' said Grace.

Was it her imagination or was there the glint of triumph in Susan's icy blues? Lucky manufactured yet another smile. Better to charm the enemy than to kick them in the teeth. 'Nice meeting *you*.'

After they left, Lucky was too restless to sit still. She was annoyed *she* hadn't made the first exit. Let Gino see how much it mattered if he wanted to ruin their evening together.

She glanced at the comedian, still getting laughs; noted Dimitri's strong hand on the thigh of his date; hated the way Matt Traynor waved the front of his silver hair.

Fuck 'em. What a dull group.

'I'll be back,' she whispered, although she had no intention of returning.

Outside the lounge the huge casino rocked with action. She cruised around for a while, greeting staff, watching the pit bosses keeping a sharp eye on the croupiers, noting the paying customers in their weird and wonderful outfits. Where else would you see bermuda shorts beside Balmain? Halter tops next to Halston tuxedos? Hookers and housewives, playboys and punters.

I want to get laid, she thought. *Oh God, do I want to get laid.*

She went to the front desk and selected the keys to an empty suite. Then she started to cruise. It couldn't be just anybody. There had to be a certain sexual chemistry. After all, it had been a long time.

There was a man playing alone at a roulette table. He was dark, moody-looking. He reminded her of Marco.

No!

Abruptly she turned away.

She felt lonely. What she needed was anonymous sex with an anonymous lover who would give her what she wanted, then just quietly disappear.

A hand gripped her by the arm. A voice said accusingly, 'You walked out on me. What's the matter with you? Don't you appreciate exceptional talent when you see it?'

She turned, hesitated for only a second, then smiled dazzlingly. 'Lennie Golden,' she said. 'You're just the man I'm looking for.'

Chapter 5

New York in the summer was not Olympia's favourite place. Too hot, crowded, and dirty. She tried to visit as little as possible, but there were times when she had to make the trip. And her mother's third wedding was one of them.

She travelled by Concorde from Paris with her nine-year-old daughter, Brigette, and the girl's English nanny, Mabel. Brigette was a pretty child. She had inherited her mother's thick blonde hair and blue eyes, and her father's patrician features and lithe body. She had also inherited Olympia's wilful streak.

Nanny Mabel was a frustrated fifty-year-old woman, who after thirty-five years of 'service' considered she had wasted her life looking after other people's children. Olympia was the latest in a long line of wealthy employers, and although she had only worked for her for six months, she had grown to loathe the capricious blonde heiress. The child was not much better. Spoilt, selfish and destructive. A miniature version of her mother. Fortunately, the money more than compensated, and Nanny Mabel also enjoyed the limousines, private planes, and first-class service. When in Paris, Olympia rarely visited what she referred to as the 'nursery floor' in her duplex apartment on the Avenue Foch, so Nanny Mabel hardly had to put up with her at all.

Olympia was more than a little aggravated that she had

been forced to bring Brigette and Nanny with her. But her mother had insisted the child be flower girl at the wedding, and Olympia was unable to summon up a suitable excuse.

Her mother, Charlotte, was a chic American society matron. She had married Dimitri Stanislopoulos at the age of twenty against violent parental objection, given birth to Olympia nine months later, and divorced her husband after a year. Then she had returned to America, and within a year remarried, this time to a Wall Street banker with her parents' full approval. For the first twelve years of her life Olympia had lived with them in America, but when puberty struck, she became unmanageable and screamed to be allowed to live with her father who flitted between his Greek island, his yacht, and his mansion in Paris. They compromised, and sent her to a series of boarding schools – all of which she managed to get thrown out of. Eventually she got her wish and moved in with Dimitri, who treated her as just another houseguest.

Charlotte's banker husband, a stepfather who Olympia never warmed to, had passed away a year previously. Now Charlotte had a new prospect ready for the altar. A film producer whom Olympia had no desire to meet.

'Mama,' said Brigette, as they were escorted out of customs. 'I see the men with the cameras.' At nine she spoke three languages fluently.

'Head down, eyes straight ahead,' warned Nanny Mabel sternly. 'Never acknowledge their presence.'

Olympia touched her golden curls, fluffed them out a little. She hated the paparazzi, but if they were going to catch you – well, one may as well appear at one's best. It wouldn't do to be seen looking like Christina Onassis. She adjusted her dark glasses, and smoothed down the skirt of her Saint Laurent suit.

The cameramen leaped into action.

It wasn't easy being one of the richest women in the world.

*

Dimitri Stanislopoulos was not interested in the showgirl Matt Traynor had arranged for his pleasure. She was young and not even all that pretty. He was sixty-two years old. He did not need the boring conversation of a woman forty years younger. He preferred to play baccarat, so Matt set him up at a private table with several other high rolling guests. There was a male singing star wearing a bad toupee; an Italian Contessa with skin the colour and texture of baked mud; two Japanese electronics kings; and the English girlfriend of an Arab munitions dealer.

Dimitri knew the woman. He nodded at her. She nodded back. He found her a far more interesting proposition than the vacuous showgirl.

'Where is Saud?' he asked, swooping to kiss her hand.

'LA,' she replied. 'He'll be back tomorrow. I'm keeping his seat warm.'

And more than that, Dimitri thought. He liked English women. In bed, they had a certain whore-like quality. Very appealing. And he should know, his mistress for the last eight years was a world-renowned English stage actress. Francesca Fern, an immense talent and flamboyant personality. She was fifty years old with flame-red hair, piercing eyes, succulent lips, and a beaky nose to rival his own. Francesca. What a woman! He loved her power, her dramatic presence, and her passion.

Ah . . . her passion. She was the most exciting woman he had ever bedded. And that was saying something, since he had slept with many of the most beautiful and cultured women in Europe.

Dimitri liked expensive women who knew all about the finer things in life. He liked them clad in sable, with jewellery from Cartier and Aspreys and Bulgari. He liked them in Dior clothes with designer underwear and five hundred dollar shoes. He liked them to know all about good food, fine wine, classical music, opera, and the ballet.

He liked breeding. And he did not mind paying for it.

During their affair, he had gifted Francesca with a king's ransom in jewellery. She accepted everything he gave her with a knowing glint in her eye and a husky 'thank you, darling' as if the prizes he found for her were no more than trinkets.

He admired her tremendous style. He did not admire her husband, a puny little man called Horace whom she resolutely refused to divorce. They had enjoyed some of their hotter fights concerning Horace.

'Leave him!' Dimitri would bellow.

'I can't,' Francesca would reply dramatically. 'It will kill him. I am his life.' And tears would fill her heavily outlined eyes.

'But I want to marry you,' Dimitri would shout.

'One day,' Francesca would husk vaguely, 'we will be together forever.'

In the meantime, Horace did not interfere with their tempestuous affair. He put up with it, as he put up with most things in life, and stayed quietly in the background of his wife's volatile life. Once a year they rendezvoused on Dimitri's palatial ocean-going yacht. Francesca and Horace, accompanied by her personal maid, her own hairdresser, and sometimes her two ancient Pekinese dogs.

Dimitri always invited other guests for the August cruise. It was a time he looked forward to, because he had Francesca to himself – well almost. She spent every night in his stateroom. He never *had* found out how she explained this to Horace. He never really cared. Horace must know. Horace was complaisant.

Occasionally they met in other parts of the world. New York, Paris, Rome. Even when he married for the second time they continued to meet. His second marriage lasted no longer than his first. Dimitri Stanislopoulos was not an easy man to live with.

The baccarat game was starting. 'What's the limit at this table?' Dimitri asked one of the steely-eyed croupiers.

'Six thousand dollars, Mr Stanislopoulos,' replied the man, expressionless.

'Give me two hundred thousand dollars worth of chips.'

Deftly, the man piled gold five-hundred-dollar chips in

neat stacks and pushed them in front of him. Unobtrusively a marker was produced for his signature.

Dimitri liked to gamble. It relaxed him. And he needed to relax, for Francesca was arriving in two days' time to attend a televised gala evening in her honour, and he had finally decided. Eight years was long enough. One way or another Horace had to go.

Chapter 6

'Hey,' said Lucky. 'What's the matter with you?'

'What's the matter with *me*?' replied Lennie, outraged.

They faced each other warily in the opulent luxury of the darkened hotel suite. She had said, 'You're just the man I'm looking for.' Then she had taken him by the hand, added mysteriously, 'Come with me.' And led him to the nearest elevator. Once inside the suite she had pressed against him, kissed him long and hard, then groped him intimately.

He was not yet in a gropable state. In fact he was trying to figure out what the hell was going on.

'Are you selling it?' he asked.

'Are you kidding?' she had replied, and proceeded to remove her dress.

He had said, 'Hold it, I don't want you to do that.'

Now they were ready for battle.

'You got a problem?' she sighed.

'Yeah. I think I got a problem.'

A shrug of impatience. Obviously she had picked the wrong guy.

'What is it?' she asked disinterestedly, zipping up the soft leather dress she had been about to step out of. May as well end *this* scene. And fast.

Lennie stared at her in amazement. He did not believe what was happening. Here was this woman – this strikingly *beautiful* woman whom he had first spotted at the airport, spoken to by the pool – and been insulted for his trouble.

Then she had appeared in the Bahia lounge and *walked out on his act*. Now she was coming on to him like a steamroller, and expected instant action. What did she think he was – a travelling stud with no feelings? She could be the most gorgeous woman in the world, but sex with no communication was just not for him. He wasn't sixteen and desperate to get laid.

'My problem is I don't even know your name, let alone what's going on,' he said tightly.

'Oh, and if I tell you my name will that make everything all right?' she mocked, all zipped up and ready to leave.

'You know what I mean,' he said angrily.

'No. I don't know what you mean.' Coolly she strolled toward the door. 'It's simple really. I saw you. Liked you. Thought that maybe the two of us might equal great sex. Obviously I was wrong.'

'How come you didn't think we equalled great sex this afternoon?' he said quickly.

'What are you talking about?'

'This afternoon. Out by the pool. When I spoke to you and you gave me the icy treatment.'

'Was that you?'

Jesus! She didn't even remember him. And he was supposed to get a hard-on?

'Look,' she said impatiently, hand on the doorknob, 'I'm sure we've all made mistakes before. Why don't we just forget the whole thing?'

Lennie had been through a lot of women in his time, but this one took the prize. Even Eden would never behave like this.

He wished she wasn't so goddamn horny looking. How could he let her walk out when she was offering a trip he'd probably never forget?

He decided to put a little charm back into his act. 'You know what I think,' he said. 'I think that maybe we should start from page one, go downstairs, find a bar, have a drink, and get to know each other. Hey – at least exchange names. And then, beautiful lady, we can have *really* great sex. What do you say?'

She was bored with Lennie Golden. The entire incident was a mistake. She opened the door and headed for the elevator. 'Let's just forget it,' she said off-handedly.

He followed, grabbed her by the arm. 'Let's not.'

Now that he couldn't get it up he was not going to be easy to shake. Masculine pride or some such crap. 'Hmmm . . .' she said. 'That's not a bad idea.'

He had her. They were all easy. One drink, maybe two, *then* they would go to bed with *him* calling the shots.

'You go on down to the Bahia, order me a Bloody Mary. I just want to freshen up.' She smiled. 'Five minutes, okay?'

*

Lennie leaned across the green baize of Jess's blackjack table. She dealt like greased lightning, her eyes never leaving the shiny box known as the shoe, which held the cards.

'Don't bother to wait, I won't be coming home tonight,' he said.

'Why not?' she muttered out of the corner of her mouth.

'Why do you think not? The Golden charm works again.'

'Really? Who'd you score with this time?'

'Are we playin' or talkin',' demanded a belligerent blonde in a sequinned tank top. 'Gimme a card.'

Jess grimaced, pulled a three from the shoe, with sleight of hand magically turned it into a nine – thereby putting sequinned tank top over twenty-one and out.

'Aw, crap!' the woman exclaimed loudly.

Jess allowed herself a secret wink in Lennie's direction. 'Call me,' she mouthed. She didn't usually play God with the cards, but sometimes she just couldn't help it.

Lennie grinned and strolled away. Now that his evening was set he felt pretty good. They had loved him in the Bahia lounge – given him a great reception. His two week gig was going to be a big success – he could feel it. Now he had this wild-looking female to deal with – and she looked like more than enough to occupy him for two weeks. Maybe even make him forget Eden, although he doubted if she could do that. He wondered what her name was, what she was doing in Vegas, what she would be like in bed . . .

Yeah . . . a two week relationship would suit him fine. He had had it with heavy involvements. First they stayed the night, next the weekend, finally they took over everything, until taking a shower was one long obstacle course strewn with panty-hose and bras.

He hurried into the Bahia lounge, ordered himself a beer and a Bloody Mary for her . . . whatever her name was. He would know soon enough. He would know more than her name.

*

Matt Traynor's apartment was decorated in early nouveau-riche. A lot of ornamental gilt, black fur, fake marble, and damask couches. A sign behind the bar read 'Matt's Place', and his lead crystal glasses were embossed with his initials, as were his shirts, socks, undershorts, sheets, towels and pyjamas.

'Wow!' exclaimed his date, six months out of Ohio and impressed. 'What a *fabulous* place.'

He poured her undiluted Scotch, switched Sinatra on the stereo, and adjusted the pink lighting to low.

'Wow!' said Miss Ohio. 'What a *fabulous* singer. Who is it?'

'Are you jesting with me, young lady?'

'What?'

He wondered if she gave blow jobs.

'Sinatra,' he said.

'Oh. *Fabulous!*'

'*You're* fabulous.'

She giggled inanely, and sucked suggestively on an ice-cube.

'In fact,' he continued, 'you're the most fabulous girl I've seen all year.'

'Really?'

'Really.'

He reached for her left boob and circled the nipple with his thumb.

She took a swig of Scotch, put the glass down, and leaned back on the couch.

He kept his thumb twirling, and bent to kiss her.

She responded nicely while Sinatra crooned 'Strangers In The Night'.

He manoeuvred her boob from the confines of her scoop necklined sweater, and bent his head to the erect nipple.

'Fabulous!' she murmured.

He unzipped his fly allowing what he considered to be a healthy hard-on to escape. Then he took her right hand and placed it where it would find gainful employment.

The phone rang. He had forgotten to put on the answering machine.

'Goddamn it!' he said.

'Don't answer,' she said.

His hard-on deflated. He picked up the offending instrument. 'Yes?' he snapped.

'Matt. This is Lucky. I want you here. Now. There's something I need taking care of.'

'Can't it hold until tomorrow?'

'No.'

For the second time that night he was more than pissed off with the Santangelos. First Gino, now Lucky. The pair of them were a pain in the ass.

'If it's important –'

'It is. Come to my apartment.'

'I'll be there.'

'Fast.'

He banged the receiver down and stood up. His penis hung out of his trousers, a sorry reminder of what might have been. Quickly he zipped it from sight.

'I've got to go out,' he said.

'Oh, what a shame!'

'Can you wait for me?'

'Well . . .'

'There's television, and you can have fun in the jacuzzi. I won't be long.'

She wasn't hard to persuade. 'Fabulous!' she said, and Sinatra crooned on.

*

Lennie glanced at his watch. Half an hour had passed and she obviously had no intention of showing up. Bitch! They were all the same. And this one was a whacko anyway, it was better she *didn't* show.

But still . . . he was mad – at himself more than anything. If he thought she was so horny looking why hadn't he taken her up on her offer? *Wham Bam thank you ma'am.* And goodbye, Charlie.

For Christ's sake, what was so threatening about a woman instigating the proceedings? He could deal with that.

She had probably not shown because she figured him for a jerk. And rightfully so. No doubt he had turned down a great experience. Jesus! He couldn't wait to tell Jess about it. They would at least get a few laughs out of Lennie Golden – the reluctant fuck! Hey – he might be able to work it into some great comedy schtick.

He thought he might call her. What did he have to lose? And maybe it wasn't too late.

Suite eleven twenty-two – the memory never let him down. He hurried to a house phone. No answer. Maybe she was out cruising, busy finding a replacement for Mr Reluctant.

Why was he feeling jealous of someone he didn't even know?

Why could he see her face, that beautiful face?

And why could he feel her lips, full and sensual and . . .

Knock it off, schmuck. You blew it. Don't sweat it. Forget it. At least his routine had been a smash.

Tonight the Magiriano.

Tomorrow the Carson Show.

Why not?

He had worked his balls off for it.

Chapter 7

'Fire the comedian,' said Lucky.

Matt frowned. 'What?'

'Lennie Golden. That's his name isn't it?'

'You mean Lennie Golden who went on tonight in the lounge?'

'Do we have two Lennie Goldens working for us?'

'I don't understand. He opened great. The audience loved him. Even *you* said he was good.'

Coolly she lit a cigarette and stared out at the spectacular view over the Strip. 'I never said he wasn't good. I just said I want you to fire him.'

'Is that what you summoned me for?'

'Yes.'

'Jesus Christ, Lucky.' A vein throbbed angrily near his temple. 'Jesus Christ! I'm not some lackey you can jerk around on a string. It's two o'clock in the morning. Why didn't you tell me on the phone?'

She wondered if he would dare speak to Gino like that. Decided he wouldn't.

'Do you like your job here?' she asked mildly.

'It's not a job. I got points in the place. I'm a director of the company.'

'Sure. *I* made you a director, and I can move you out any time I want.'

'So do it,' he snorted.

'Maybe I will.'

They glared at each other. He broke the stare first. Working for the Santangelos gave him more power than he'd ever had in his life. He didn't want to blow it. 'So what is it you want me to do?' he said sourly.

'Pay him. Fire him. Get him off the premises.'

'May I at least ask why?'

'Because he's *too* good for the lounge. He makes people

think. He makes them laugh. He stops them drinking and playing the tables. I want you to fire him tonight and get him out of here.'

'If that's what you want.'

'It's *exactly* what I want.'

After he left she finished her cigarette, then went to the bureau and fished out a joint. She would get high instead of laid. Probably more satisfying in the long run.

How nice to phone Gino now, have a father/daughter chat.

Ha! She laughed aloud. They had never had that sort of a relationship. Not since she was five years old. Not since her mother was murdered . . .

Flashes of white hot pain. She could still picture the scene as vividly as if it were yesterday. The pink pool . . . Maria's naked body floating on a raft . . . her long blonde hair fanning out in the water . . .

Abruptly she closed her eyes, but the image became even more vivid. For a year she and Gino had been wonderfully close, but never close enough to discuss what had happened to Maria, never close enough . . .

She began to cry. But she didn't know she was crying until the tears rolled down her cheeks.

Lucky Santangelo crying. Never!

Angrily she wiped her face. Goddamn it! Gino found himself a girlfriend and she went to pieces. She hadn't even missed him when he was seven years in exile. Hadn't given him so much as a second thought when she took over his empire. Now he was shacking up and she was breaking down. What *was* this crap?

*

In 1977 Gino returned to America. A six-million-dollar settlement with the IRS plus pulling a few strings made it possible.

Lucky awaited his return with trepidation. He needn't think he was taking over. She had worked hard, made her mark, and now she planned to stand firm. Of course, it would mean returning to Vegas, a city she had stayed away from since Marco's murder.

Enzio Bonnatti had been wonderful. He had tracked the assassin, dealt with the slime, and taken over the running of the Magiriano until she wished to go back.

With Gino's imminent re-entry into America the time had come.

Costa arranged a meeting two days after Gino's return. They met at the Pierre Hotel in New York. Father and daughter. Seven years apart. Seven years of silence. Lucky was hostile and uneasy, although Gino seemed friendly enough. He could see at once that this was not the spoiled girl he had left behind. This was a woman, self-assured, confident.

He smiled and held open his arms. 'Lucky.'

She was taken aback. Did he honestly expect it to be that easy?

He stared at her quizzically and tried to turn his arms into a gesture, a shrug. 'Well, well,' he said, 'look at you. All grown up.'

She regarded him coldly. 'I thought I was all grown up when you married me off at sixteen.'

'So it didn't work out. But it kept you out of trouble, right? You goin' to hold a grudge forever, kid?'

She spotted a bottle of Scotch and poured herself a hefty glass.

Gino did not take his eyes off her. 'I guess we better talk,' he said at last.

She was unnerved by his steady stare. 'Yes,' she said defiantly. 'A lot of things have changed while you've been away. I'm involved now, I'm part of it.'

'So I heard.'

She turned to face him, her eyes blazing. 'I can tell you this – no way are you shoving me out. No way. *Vegas is mine, and I'm going back.'*

'A little late in the day.'

'What do you mean?'

'Come on, Lucky – you seem like a smart girl. You gave *Vegas to Bonnatti* – handed *it to him. You think he'll just step down with a smile?'*

'I know how to handle him.'

He laughed aloud. 'Don't you realize Bonnatti is no longer our friend?'

Yes, she knew. Although she wasn't about to admit it to Gino. Earlier that day, Boogie had flown in from Vegas with stories of betrayal that made her cold with fury and hot for revenge. It seemed she'd been taken for dumb pussy. Bonnatti had arranged Marco's murder. He had wanted her out of Vegas – and getting rid of Marco did the job. She had fled, just like the bastard knew she would. And now he had control. But not for long, she had her plans. And Gino was not going to screw them up.

Before they could discuss the matter further, Dario arrived.

Lucky wasn't pleased. This was supposed to be a business meeting and it was turning into a family reunion.

Dario did not stay long. He was a jumpy nervous wreck, and after ten minutes of stilted conversation he ran from the room like a thief.

'What the fuck is the matter with that kid?' Gino stormed. 'Get him back, Costa. I think it's about time I straightened the little pansy out.' Much to his chagrin Costa had relayed his son's sexual preferences to him.

'Oh,' said Lucky. 'I think you've left that a bit late. If you had paid more attention to him when he was a teenager –'

Gino whirled on her. 'And who do you think you're talkin' to?'

She didn't back down. 'When Dario and I were little we had *no family life. Shut up in that Bel Air mausoleum like a couple of lepers. No wonder Dario is screwed up today.'*

He glared at her. 'Terrible life you had. A beautiful home. The best money could buy.'

She raised her voice excitedly. 'Money. Who cares about money? I wanted you *when I was growing up. I wanted you* to care *– to be with me. I wanted you to be a proper father.'*

Her words cut into him. 'I always did the best for both of you,' he growled. 'The best I knew how –'

'Well, it wasn't enough,' she said triumphantly.

Police sirens wailed in the street outside. Costa went to the window and tried to see what was going on.

'Get the fuck out of here and bring Dario back,' Gino screamed. Costa left hurriedly.

'I'm going,' Lucky said. 'You and I – we can't communicate. We never could.'

'You talk about me bein' a proper father,' he steamed. 'How about you bein' a proper daughter? Runnin' away from school. Screwin' anything in pants. Goin' from –'

'I didn't, *' she interrupted – incensed with fury. 'And even if I did, so what?'*

'So what? she says. So what.*' He shook his head sadly. 'You're right, Lucky. You an' I – we just aren't on the same wavelength. Why don't you go. Seven years an' not even a lousy postcard. That's a* daughter.*' He felt suddenly tired. Someone was pounding on the door. He opened it and Costa burst in, white and trembling. 'Dario's been shot,' he gasped, 'outside the hotel. He's dead.'*

'Holy Christ!' Gino cried out. 'Holy mother of Christ!'

Lucky stood transfixed.

Suddenly Gino clutched his chest and staggered towards the couch. A low moan escaped his lips.

'What is it?' Lucky asked urgently. 'What is it?'

He moaned again, his face gray. All at once he looked every one of his seventy-one years.

'I . . . think . . . it's . . . my . . . heart . . .' he mumbled. 'You'd . . . better . . . get . . . me . . . a . . . doctor . . . fast . . .'

It took her father's near death for Lucky to realize how much she really loved him. He had his faults but he was still daddy . . . Gino . . . And when he whispered from his hospital bed – where he hovered between life and death – for her to take revenge . . . honour the family name . . . She knew at once that she would do as he had asked with no question.

Enzio Bonnatti.

Friend.

Godfather.

Assassin.

Betrayer.

She drove to his mansion out on Long Island, filled with an icy calm.

Revenge. Why not?

Revenge for the Santangelos and for Marco. There was no son to do the job – it fell upon her shoulders, and she did not flinch from family responsibilities:

The shooting of Enzio Bonnatti was a clear-cut case of self-defence. Apparently the man had tried to rape Lucky Santangelo, and she had shot him with his own gun. The case never even came to court.

With Lucky by his side, Gino recovered quickly, and gradually they rediscovered the closeness they had once shared before Maria's death. They moved back to Vegas. 'You take the Magiriano, kid,' Gino said. 'I'll have the Mirage. One of these days we'll build a place together.'

It was a dream. But Lucky always knew it could become a reality.

For one year they had been inseparable. Now there was the widow Martino to contend with.

*

An old Clint Eastwood movie played on television. Lucky finished the joint and watched it for a while. She liked Eastwood, he had a sort of silent eroticism that appealed to her. He was probably a great lay.

Gradually she drifted off to sleep, only to be jolted awake at dawn by a forgotten nightmare.

She got up, pulled a silk kimono over her nakedness, and watched the sun rise over the desert. It was a beautiful sight. Once, she might have phoned Gino, woken him, and allowed him to share it with her. But in the morning light she realized it was okay if he'd found someone to spend the night with. She could be a lot of things to him, but she could never be his lover. And perhaps he needed the closeness of a woman to hold.

Maybe Susan Martino would be good for him.

Maybe.

Chapter 8

Once in a while Olympia decided she should play the perfect mother role. Not often. It was hardly a part she relished. However, a meeting with her own mother required that she make the effort.

Charlotte intimidated her. She was so annoyingly correct. She did not smoke or drink. She certainly did not do drugs. She was slim, active, and an utter bore. She was also very rich. Although that was one area where Olympia beat her out. It would be hard to top Olympia's massive fortune.

Unfortunately, being in Charlotte's presence always made her feel like a child again, so before leaving, Olympia sat in the luxurious bathroom of her father's Fifth Avenue penthouse and snorted three lines of coke. The insidious white powder made her feel marvellous. A deep breath, a glance in the mirror, and she was ready for anyone and anything.

Nanny Mabel and Brigette waited by the front door. The child gazed up at her mother, huge saucer eyes in a picture-pretty face. 'Mama,' she said, 'please can I have a hot dog?'

'What?' snapped Olympia, adjusting the collar of her sable jacket in the hall mirror.

'An American hot dog,' the small girl repeated patiently.

'Certainly not,' scolded Nanny Mabel. 'Wherever do you get such ideas?'

'Mama?' questioned Brigette, ignoring her nanny. 'Can I?'

'Hmmm . . .' Olympia replied vaguely, licking her lips and sucking in her cheeks. 'Whatever Nanny says.'

'Nanny says no,' whined Brigette.

Olympia's voice rose slightly. 'Then *listen* to Nanny. Do come on.'

She marched out of the apartment, followed by the two of

them. Into the elevator, onto the sidewalk.

The chauffeur leapt out of the waiting limousine and held open the door. Two idling paparazzi raised their cameras.

Olympia manufactured a condescending smile, and reached for Brigette's hand. The child suddenly stood stock still and screamed, 'I *haaate* everyone!'

'Brigette,' exclaimed a furious Nanny Mabel, 'stop this behaviour *at once*!'

The two photographers, sensing something more than the usual polite picture – began to snap in earnest.

Brigette, now the centre of attention and enjoying it, yelled even louder.

Olympia wanted to jump in the car and distance herself from the whole embarrassing scene. But how could she? The screaming brat was *her* child – unfortunately – and she was playing perfect mother for the day.

'Do something,' she hissed at Nanny.

'I can't, madam.' Her attempts to pull Brigette towards the car were unsuccessful.

'Oh God!' exclaimed Olympia. A flash exploded in front of her face. 'Go away you stupid little man,' she shouted at the photographer.

An amused crowd was gathering. Olympia could stand it no longer. She turned on Brigette in a fury, smacked her across the face, picked the surprised child up, and flung her in the car.

The cameras captured every moment.

*

A day later Dimitri viewed the photograph of his grandchild being set-upon by his daughter with a mixture of annoyance and anger. The annoyance was because he had constantly implored Olympia to avoid publicity. And the anger was because she was striking his precious little Brigette, a child he doted upon.

He flung the newspaper to the ground and picked up the phone. Within seconds he had Nanny Mabel on the line.

'Madam is resting,' she said.

'Wake her,' thundered Dimitri.

'I'm not allowed to.'

'Do it!'

Grumbling to herself, the woman did as she was told.

Olympia hurled abuse and picked up the phone. 'What is it?' she demanded. She had long ago stopped being in awe of her father, ever since she had inherited her fortune at twenty-one.

He complained for a while.

She listened fitfully.

He gave orders on how she should conduct herself publicly.

She ignored him.

'Why are you in Las Vegas?' she asked, when he paused for breath.

A moment's silence, then, 'Francesca Fern is being honoured. As I am such a close friend, she and Horace begged me to attend.'

Olympia stifled a rude laugh. God! He made her so mad. He honestly believed no one knew about his affair with prima donna Fern. The whole world knew. They had fucked their way from one end of the globe to the other.

And he had a nerve complaining to *her* about the paparazzi. They had captured *him* doing everything short of actually making it with one of his society whores.

'Who on earth gets honoured in a dump like Las Vegas?' she sneered.

He changed the subject. 'I want to see Brigette.'

'We're staying in New York until Monday.'

'I'll try and fly in on Saturday, then we can return to Paris together.'

'Good.' She was pleased. Better than travelling on a commercial airline. She liked Dimitri's Lear jet with all its luxuries. When she found the time maybe she'd buy one for herself.

Once off the phone she stretched out on the bed and decided New York was turning out to be a fun place after all, if one ignored the paparazzi – and they were everywhere since the now famous photo had appeared on the front of the New York *Post* that very morning.

Tea with Charlotte the day before had gone well. Brigette, after her outburst, behaved perfectly. And Charlotte was so preoccupied with her impending wedding she hardly found time to criticize, although she did mention that Olympia was ten pounds overweight and needed a good facial.

Later, Olympia met with friends and had a perfectly wonderful time, ending up at 2 a.m. at Studio 54 – which she loved.

That day she had lunch at 21, shopped along Madison, and now she was resting before another evening on the town. She wondered if she would meet Mr Wrong, and hoped so. Two days without sex was two days too many.

Chapter 9

Jess presented herself in Matt Traynor's office at noon the day after Lennie's dismissal. She was full of righteous indignation.

'Why did you fire Lennie?'

Matt stared at the angry girl confronting him across his desk. She was so pretty, so stacked, so *short.*

'Jessie baby –' he began.

'Don't call me Jessie, and don't call me baby. Just give me an answer.

He knew what he would like to give her, she made him uncomfortably hot. Instead he shrugged noncommitally and said, 'House policy.'

'House bullshit. I hear he was great.'

'Yes he was, and I told him so, but he stopped people from playing the tables.'

She snorted disbelievingly. 'Well, if *that's* the reason, why don't you fire Ann Margret, Diana Ross, Tom Jo –'

He held up an authoritative hand and wondered if she gave great head. He was sure she did. 'Okay, okay. I don't need a list. Why don't you have dinner with me tonight and I'll try to explain it to you properly.'

'I'm working.'

'Tomorrow night?'

'Ditto.'

'When's your night off?'

'I'm also married. Remember?'

'How about a late supper after your shift tonight?'

'Where?'

He had been asking her out for two months. This was the first breakthrough. 'My place,' he said quickly.

She laughed loudly. She had a laugh like a hyena and eight thousand freckles and crazy orange hair. He thought she was the most attractive girl he'd seen in months.

'What's wrong with my place?' he asked belligerently.

'Nothing. Except that every showgirl in town knows its location, size, even the colour of your sheets.'

'I give a lot of parties,' he said defensively.

'That's not all you give. I'm surprised you're not riddled with the clap.'

He managed a laugh, quite flattered she knew so much about him. As a matter of fact he had never had the clap, but the rest was accurate. And why not? He was making up for lost time. Married for twenty-four years, he had been divorced by his wife five years ago. *She* divorced *him*. The woman was mad. Nobody could have been a better husband. For the first six months he missed her, and then, like a revelation – the joys of being an affluent, powerful *single* man hit him. And then he found out that while he was married things had changed. The sexual revolution had taken place, and you no longer had to fight and scheme, promise and declare undying love to get a girl into bed. From that moment on Matt lived every second to its fullest. And when his ex-wife – a retarded feminist – decided they should get back together – he told her exactly where to stick the idea.

'Will you have dinner with me or not?' he asked.

Jess chewed on her thumb for a moment – a childhood habit she was unable to break. She really wanted to find out why Lennie had been so unceremoniously dumped. But dinner with Matt Traynor . . . ugh! With his silver waved hair, and his gold chains, and his perpetual leer . . .

At least if she went to his place nobody would see them together. It would be too humiliating for people to think she had been added to his list of conquests. She couldn't understand why he wanted her anyway. She was hardly his style. But he had a very obvious yen for her – one she had taken advantage of by getting Lennie the job in the first place. All she'd had to do was show Matt a video tape of his work and a few key reviews – one a rave from *The Village Voice*, and Matt had said, 'Sure. We'll book him. If *you* say he's good – that's enough for me.'

Lennie being fired like that had made *her* look a fool. He had hired a car and stormed off to LA in the middle of the night with – 'I don't *need* this shit. Thanks a lot, Jess.'

She knew that as soon as he calmed down he would realize it was not her fault, and she hoped by the time he called to apologize she would know exactly what *had* happened.

So dinner with Matt it was.

'Okay,' she said.

He looked pleased. 'Later?'

She sighed, 'I guess.'

'Don't look so thrilled about it. Who knows – you might enjoy it.'

'I'm a vegetarian.'

He wondered if that meant she didn't give head. Decided not to pursue it. 'Tonight,' he said. 'I'm delighted.'

'I'm glad someone is,' she muttered.

'What?'

'Nothing.'

•

The rented Chevrolet got Lennie into Los Angeles at eight o'clock in the morning. Not bad considering he hadn't left Vegas until three-thirty a.m.

The city was already hot, a steamy smoggy heat which promised a long and sultry day.

He came off the freeway at the Sunset Boulevard exit, turned left, and realized he had no idea of where to go or what to do. He had only been to LA once before, and that was on his thirteenth birthday with mom and dad. They had stayed with an aunt in the valley for five uneventful days – the highlight of the trip being a visit to Disneyland – memorable because mom got stoned on excitement and sang *The Star Spangled Banner* to a wooden indian.

So – he did not exactly know his way around. However, he did know that getting out of Vegas immediately was an absolute necessity after the silver-haired-smarm had told him he was out.

He, Lennie Golden, was out.

OUT.

Dropped.

Bounced.

Fired.

Shit!!

He pulled over to the side of the street and groped in the pocket of his faded workshirt for the infamous Golden black book. It was his lifeline and he carried it everywhere. There were two pages crammed with LA numbers. Friends. Contacts. Friends of friends. Agents. Clubs. Connections. And dear old mom. Feisty Alice Golden – the Jewish mother who would *not* cook him chicken soup or ask about his love life. More likely she would offer him a joint and tell him about hers!

Alice. Maybe he would crash at her place for a couple of days while he considered his next move. But then he thought about her new boyfriend – the one she had brought to New York last year. A total jerk with false teeth and an uneasy laugh. Lennie was not in the mood for *his* company. He moved down the list.

There was Jennifer. A perfectly delectable sugar-lipped blonde who had abandoned acting class in New York to try her luck in LA.

There was Suna and Shirlee. The twins. Would-be singers and actresses now doing commercial voice-overs.

There was his friend, Joey Firello. A fellow comedian who had arrived in LA several months earlier, and was already a regular on a weekly TV show.

And then of course there was Eden. They had not parted friends. She had stormed out of his life bad-mouthing him at full volume.

Ah . . . Eden, the queen of all bitches. A beautiful, mean, fucked up, difficult *cunt*.

He wanted to see her.

He needed to see her.

Maybe she'd dumped her actor friend and was ready for a reunion.

Without hesitation he searched for a dime and a phone booth.

A male voice answered on the third ring. An unfriendly, 'Yeah?' Was this the actor? Or a new guy? Or maybe just an answering service.

'Eden Antonio,' he said briskly.

'Who wants her?' growled the voice.

'Uh, tell her Lennie.'

Why did he feel like a twelve year old trying to make out? And why was he calling her anyway? What was he going to say? I'm here. Just like that. No job. No place to stay. I'm here. Eden would tell him to shove it.

'She ain't around,' said the voice, and cut the connection.

*

Eden Antonio was not a star, nor even close, but she worked occasionally on a daytime soap, and she knew that eventually it would lead to more important roles.

She sat in the middle of her queen-size bed painting her toenails, and said to her current boyfriend – a short bald man wearing an expensive custom-made dark suit – most un-Californian, 'Who was that, sweetie?'

Santino Bonnatti shrugged dismissively as he dumped the phone down. 'Some jerk.' His beady nugget eyes darted around the room. This Eden broad was something, but her apartment was not. 'I bin thinkin',' he said. 'How about if I move ya out of this place an' set y'up in a decent joint. Would y'like that?'

Eden concentrated on her toenails. She had known Santino Bonnatti for six weeks, and she had been sleeping with him for five. He was hardly Paul Newman, but according to her girlfriend, Ulla, who had introduced them, he was loaded, and might not be averse to investing in a movie if the right deal came along.

'What business is he in?' she had asked Ulla.

Her friend looked vague. 'I'm not really sure. Commodities, I think. Import. Export. Important stuff.'

That had been enough to pique Eden's interest. For once in her life she wanted a rich boyfriend, not just a good looking bum with nothing but big dreams and a hard-on.

The fact that Santino had a wife and four kids stashed in a Beverly Hills mansion did not bother her at all. She didn't want to marry him, just use him until he got her where she wanted to be.

'Exactly what did you have in mind?' she asked coolly.

He straightened his tie and peered at his reflection in a mirrored closet. 'I dunno,' he said vaguely. 'I could set ya up in a house. It'd make it easier for me.'

'Do you mean buy me a house?' inquired Eden, never one to let the grass grow.

'Yeah,' he replied expansively. 'Why not?'

Why not indeed, she thought excitedly. I'm screwing your hairy little body, it's about time compensation was forthcoming. A house would be very nice indeed.

She stretched out a long pale leg, and admired her blood-red toenails. The black peignoir she wore fell back and exposed a glorious mound of pale blonde pubic hair. She had it dyed regularly.

'I think I would like that a lot,' she said slowly.

His beady eyes fixed on her pubis. What a horny broad this one was. A few weeks into the relationship and he was already springing for a house. He felt like slamming another fuck into her, but business called, and she would be available later. 'I'll contact a real estate friend who owes me a favour,' he said. 'We'll find ya somethin' nice.'

She smiled. She had thin lips and small perfect teeth. 'I'm sure you will, sweetie.'

'Gotta go,' he said.

'A hard day at the office?' she asked sympathetically.

'Naw. I don't like sittin' behind a desk. I got some foreign shipments comin' in.'

She had no idea *what* he did. Every time she asked he told her something different. One day he was importing olive oil from Italy, the next Colombian coffee. Whatever it was he was rolling in money.

She held out her arms invitingly. 'Do I get a goodbye kiss?'

He obliged.

She waited until the front door slammed behind him, then she rolled onto her stomach, reached under the bed, and pressed the playback on a hidden tape machine connected to the phone. If Santino thought he could censor her calls he had another think coming. Besides, taping *his* conversations was fascinating – especially when he spoke to his crabby wife with the whining Italian accent.

He had made two calls the previous evening. One, a complicated business conversation dealing with shipments and vast sums of money. And the other to tell wifey he was in San Francisco and would not be home.

Lying little shit. Well, they were all liars. And all shits. Eden knew about such things.

'Some jerk' turned out to be Lennie Golden. For a moment Eden felt a rush of excitement – what was *he* doing in town. If indeed he was. Maybe he was calling from New York. She played back the tape.

Lennie Golden. A luxury she had allowed herself. A loser. But sexy and smart and funny, with a great body. Oh yes . . . she missed their lovemaking. In a way she missed their fights. And they had had some humdingers!

Then she remembered. Lennie Golden. A one-way street to nowhere. He would always be a nothing . . . And she,

Eden Antonio, was going all the way to the top – with a little help from a friend.

*

In the underground garage waited Santino's car and driver. His bodyguard, Blackie, had already joined him at the elevator. Santino never travelled anywhere without protection. In his business he needed it. There was no reason to take unnecessary risks, and that's what Eden's crummy apartment was.

'Remind me,' he said to Blackie, 'I gotta get this broad set up in a house.'

'Yes, boss,' nodded Blackie.

Santino took a breath spray from his pocket and squirted it in his mouth. Eden intrigued him. She was beautiful and cold and a user. It would be interesting breaking her in. She thought he was a mark, ready to be fleeced. But she didn't know him, did she?

She would. When he was ready. And only then.

*

Wayland did not bother asking where Lennie was, so Jess felt no need to explain his abrupt exit.

She returned home after meeting with Matt, stripped off her clothes, and flopped out on the overgrown grass beside the dirty pool.

Wayland was in a daze – as usual, so stoned he didn't care what happened to anyone. The baby was asleep in a wicker carrybasket under a tree. Jess bit on a hang-nail and thought about her life. It wasn't perfect. Whose was? But it could certainly be a lot better.

Why had she married Wayland?

Was being seven months' pregnant a good enough reason?

Maybe. Maybe not. Plenty of people had kids without getting married. Yeah, but maybe they didn't have a mother dying of cancer in the hospital. A mother whose fervent wish was to see her only daughter married.

Funny really, for all of her thirty years she and her mother had fought over everything. Came the crunch, and she found she would do anything for the woman who had brought her into the world. So she married Wayland, who at least before they did the deed seemed like a fairly normal human being – not the stoned zombie she had ended up with.

He had *really* fallen into a soft patch. A wife who worked her ass off, cleaned the house, looked after the baby, *and* kept him in drugs. What more could a man ask for? Man. That was a laugh. He hadn't been near her in months. He preferred to get high rather than laid. The two did not always go together. Not that she cared. She would rather he *didn't* touch her. He never showered, his hair was always dirty, and his teeth were beginning to rot because of the nasty little habit he had of ingesting pure sugar – just spooning it straight from the package. Disgusting!

She gave a long drawn-out sigh. She was depressed by Lennie leaving. They had spent hardly any time together, and she had harboured the hope that once they talked – *really* talked, he would help and advise her. In fact she had been counting on him to get her out of the mess she was in. She hadn't told him about her mother, had not wanted to upset him on his first day in town. Now it was too late. He had thought she was screwing around. Ha! Who had the time, energy, or inclination? Her hours were spent between home, hospital, and the casino.

She stared at Wayland and hated him. When they first met he had seemed like a gentle, easy-going, kind person. A touch eccentric, but he was an artist. He had shown her a portfolio of brilliant drawings. Since they were married he had not put pen to paper – let alone brush to easel.

For gentle read weak; easy-going meant lazy; and kind equalled dumb. She snorted in disgust, and the baby started to cry. Wayland did not budge – naturally. Jess jumped up and scooped Simon from his basket. At least she had a gorgeous baby – the relationship had produced *something* of value.

She walked slowly into the house and thought about dinner with Matt Traynor. Not an event she relished, but maybe if she found out the truth she could persuade him to rehire Lennie.

Oh, if only she could! She needed a friend, and she needed him now.

*

So much for Eden. In a way Lennie was relieved because he really wasn't prepared to talk to her. Best to get settled first, and *then* give her a call.

While he was near a phone he decided he would check out his mother, maybe the boyfriend had moved on, one never knew with Alice. She had gotten herself an answering machine, and there she was in high spirits and gravelly voice saying – *Hi-de-ho! This is Alice. I am out. Disappointed? Don't be. Leave your name, your number, and (giggle, giggle) vital statistics. If your luck is in, I will call you back.*

Why did she make him cringe with embarrassment? Shouldn't he have learned to accept her by now? He tried Joey Firello. Also out. Then he called the twins.

Shirlee answered, screamed a greeting, and insisted he come by for breakfast immediately. It seemed like a good idea. Besides, he had nowhere else to go.

Chapter 10

In the morning Lucky felt great. She was back, the sun was shining, and she couldn't imagine why she had been so uptight about Gino and the widow Martino the night before. It was nothing. It was a lay. Someone different. A constant parade of showgirls was enough to get anyone down.

She grinned. Good old Gino. He still had it. She should be proud of him, not mad. And today they would get everything settled, it would be business as usual.

In high spirits she leapt out of bed, did a few isometrics, then threw herself under an icy shower. For a split second she saw Marco's smiling face – so handsome and dark . . .

She forced the image away, and thought instead about the casual pick-up the night before. Fortunately he had not been hot to trot, because she would have regretted it in the morning. How dumb of her to have picked an employee – she hoped Matt had done as she asked and fired him.

She stepped from the shower, shook drops of water from her glistening black hair, and slipped into a white towelling track suit. In Atlantic City she had run for the first time, and liked it. There was a jogging track on the grounds of the Magiriano, and she planned to use it.

Downstairs early morning gamblers filled the Casino. The ping of the slot machines was a twenty-four hour sound. It reassured Lucky that all was in order. She stopped for an orange juice in the coffee shop, chatted with a couple of security guards, then made her way down to the gym where she found Boogie working out with weights.

'Hey – hey – hey,' she exclaimed. 'What's with you?'

Boogie looked sheepish at having been caught. He was tall and quick and skinny. Never thought about developing a muscle in his life.

'It must be love,' Lucky crooned, and with a wave made her way outside to the running track.

*

Gino's morning progressed at a more leisurely pace.

Susan awoke him, again with a tray of goodies, kissed him lightly on the lips, and said, 'I never realized anyone could make me as happy as you do.'

He struggled awake with a grin. This sure was some classy broad. 'You don't do a bad job yourself,' he said, and decided he would buy her a present, maybe an important piece of jewellery.

She smiled, all pearly teeth and swept back hair. She looked like a million bucks in the morning.

He fingered the decolleté of her beige lace peignoir. 'Anyone ever tell you you got great tits?'

'Gino!'

'Wassamatter? No one ever told you that?'

'Not in quite such a way.'

He gave a dirty laugh. 'You're such a goddamn lady. That's what I like about you.'

'Ah . . . so that's what you like,' she murmured teasingly.

'That and your great tits!'

He dug his hands in and she imperceptibly flinched, but did not draw back.

He played with her nipple and guided her hand to his penis. Deftly she moved away. 'Breakfast time,' she said sweetly.

Obligingly his hard-on slid into oblivion.

'Hey,' he objected, 'last person who told me to eat my breakfast was a six-foot nurse with hair on her chin.'

'Eat up.'

He grinned. 'I'd sooner eat your pussy.'

'Gino! Sometimes I wonder if you're seventy or seventeen.'

'Just keep wondering, sweetheart. I like to keep 'em guessing.'

*

After running around the track for twenty minutes, Lucky took a brisk swim in the super-Olympic size pool. She managed twenty-five laps, which pleased her, considering she was out of practise. On her way back upstairs, she stopped by Matt's office, but he was not in.

She sat on his desk and called Gino. He was not there either. For a moment her face clouded over. Two nights in a row with the widow Martino? Two all-nighters when he loved his own bed? Two nights of solid fucking which was not good for a seventy-two-year-old man with a heart condition.

She frowned. Her day did not seem quite so bright. She needed answers and he was out getting laid.

'Have him call me the minute he gets back,' she said to the operator. 'Oh, and you can tell him it's urgent.'

*

By the time Gino was dressed and ready to leave the comfort of Susan's rented house, it was past noon. Susan, dressed in a crisp white tennis dress, sat under an umbrella on the patio sipping mint iced tea.

'Would you care for some?' she said.

He was still in a joking mood. 'What did you have in mind?'

'Tea, dear. Not even Superman can manage anything else today.'

'Hey –' he said. 'How about tonight? You wanna have dinner with me and Lucky?'

A tiny note of surprise crept into her carefully modulated tone. 'Do you always dine with your daughter?'

'Huh? Yeh . . . well, most times. We kinda got into the habit.'

'Doesn't she have a boyfriend?'

He shrugged. 'She was married to this guy – a real nothing. My fault.'

'Why was it your fault?'

'I married her off when she was very young. Thought I was keepin' her out of trouble 'stead of gettin' her into it. She divorced him when I was out of the country. Now she's wrapped up in the business – knows as much about things as I do.'

'And you spend all your time together?' Susan stated dryly.

'Suits both of us.'

It doesn't suit me, she thought, but did not say. Instead she beamed and murmured, 'Lovely. We'll all have dinner. Lucky seems like such an interesting girl. I shall enjoy getting to know her.'

•

Matt reached Lucky before Gino. His tone was cool.

'Are you pissed at me?' she questioned.

'Why should I be? I dig getting out of bed at two o'clock in the morning and firing a first-class comedian who didn't do a thing to deserve it.'

'Don't say dig. It makes you sound like some creep from the stone age.'

'Thank you.'

'You're welcome.' A long silence which *she* finally broke. 'Who will you replace him with?'

'A singing nun. Should send people to the tables in droves.'

'Ha, ha. Was he upset?'

'Of course the poor bastard was upset. His ego took a nosedive.'

'Tough.' She paused, then added, 'You paid him for the whole two weeks?'

'I even gave him a bonus.'

'Then that's okay.'

'If you say so.'

She put the phone down and hoped she would never set eyes on Lennie Golden again. He was the first man ever to reject her advances. Still . . . even if he *had* performed she would have fired him. He had gotten himself caught in a no-win situation. It was his own fault anyway, he had started the whole thing by the pool in the afternoon – coming on to her like stud-of-the-year. Of course, physically he *was* undeniably attractive. Not *her* type, she didn't go for the Robert Redford look. She liked her men dark and hard with a certain menace about them. Who did the creep think he was anyway? She hated guys like that.

Suddenly she saw the funny side of it. Mr Come-on couldn't get it up. The only way *he* made it was *his* way.

She hoped he had learnt his lesson.

*

The pure yellow diamond ring on the widow Martino's pinky sparkled brightly.

Gino could not wipe the grin from his face.

Lucky scowled.

Another sensational evening. Just the three of them this time. And the bitch giving Lucky digs that she recognized as major danger signals.

Naturally it was all very civilized. Susan, calm and charming. Only Lucky caught every one of the zingers that came her way.

She did not rise to the bait. She knew she was being set up, and there was no way she was blowing it in front of Gino. Susan *wanted* her to blow. Susan *wanted* a confrontation.

So Lucky stayed cool. She smiled and fended impertinent questions, and laughed and joked, while all the time her black eyes shone with fury that this grasping woman had somehow invaded their lives.

'What do you think?' Gino asked proudly, when Susan finally went to the ladies room.

I think you're getting senile.

I think she's a cunt.

'I think she's very . . . uh . . .' she groped for a suitable adjective, '. . . attractive.' Jokingly she added, 'But isn't she a touch ancient for Gino the Ram?'

She used the nickname he had carried in his youth. Costa had told her all about *that* part of his life.

Gino fingered the almost faded scar on his cheek, another reminder of far-off days, and smiled ruefully. 'I don't want the twenty year olds, they got no conversation. I don't want the thirty year olds, they're all lookin' to get hitched. Susan's just right for me.'

"How *old* is she?'

'I don't know, and I ain't bothered. Forty something. Who gives a shit?'

Forty something, my ass. She has to be over fifty at the very least.

'She must have been awfully young when she married Tiny. Weren't they together thirty years?' Lucky asked artlessly.

'Nah. More like twenty.'

'Oh. I read somewhere it was thirty.'

'Yeh?'

At least she had implanted the suspicion that the widow Martino was older than he thought.

'Excuse me, dear.' Susan returned to the table freshly powdered and lipsticked, and smelling of Estee Lauder's Youth Dew.

Lucky stifled her fury. She was not about to sit there any

longer. 'I think I'll stroll around the casino. You don't mind, do you?'

Mind? They couldn't care less if she took a running dive off the roof of the hotel.

Chapter 11

The twins greeted Lennie exuberantly. He hadn't seen them in eighteen months and was amazed at the transformation. In New York they had been two fairly ordinary looking girls. Not unattractive, but no raving beauties. Now they were traffic stoppers. Platinum blondes (previously the hair was mouse) with matching nose jobs, gleaming suntans, gorgeous bodies and pneumatic breasts (Californian silicone at its best).

'I don't believe it!' he exclaimed.

'It cost a *fortune* – but it's worth every red cent,' drawled Suna.

'Sure is,' agreed Shirlee.

'You look awful,' they chorused.

'Thanks a lot,' he replied. He really needed this.

They lived in a tiny wooden one-storey house on Keith Avenue, with dead plants hanging on the porch, along with macramé pots and baskets and a withered grape vine. The house was filled with a hodge-podge of Salvation Army furniture and junk. There was a minute back yard, and a clapped-out Volkswagen parked in front.

The two girls wore brief striped leotards and high heeled white sandals. They were identical.

'What are you doin' here, Lennie?' they chorused, settling him on a couch with busted stuffing, and sitting down on either side of him.

He laughed. 'I honestly don't know. Drove in last night with nothing in mind.'

'From New York?' asked Shirlee.

'Some drive,' added Suna.

'From Vegas,' he said.

'Vegas,' they exclaimed. 'What were you doin' there?'

'It's a short story. Boring. I thought I'd give LA a shot.'

Shirlee stood up and stretched. He couldn't get over the bodies they had acquired. She stared at him significantly. 'Have you seen Eden?' she asked.

'Eden who?' he dead-panned.

'Come off it, Lennie,' sighed Suna.

He tried to look nonchalant. 'Is Eden still here?' he asked casually.

'Yes,' said Shirlee.

'And *how*,' added Suna.

Where is she? he wanted to ask. Who is she with? Does she still look great? Does she miss me?

He managed a calm, 'Is she still going with that half-assed actor? What was his name – Tim Wealth or something?'

The two girls exchanged looks. Neither wished to tell him Eden Antonio had hooked up with a short, bald, married mystery man, and was nothing more than a kept woman.

'Don't think so,' Shirlee said, and abruptly changed the subject. 'Do you have an agent here?' she asked.

'No. But plenty of numbers to call.'

Suna shook her head knowingly. 'You need an agent. Nobody gets anywhere without one. This isn't New York where you use who you know.'

'So I'll get an agent. No hassle. What are you two doing? Apart from looking like the reincarnation of Marilyn Monroe.'

'We're *hot*!' exclaimed Shirlee.

'Well, almost,' added Suna.

'We're up for a series,' said Shirlee.

'No more voice-overs. From now on it's all or nothing,' enthused Suna.

'This house might look like a dump to you,' Shirlee said seriously. 'But it's central. One block from Santa Monica and *three blocks* from Beverly Hills. Do you realize how important location is?'

No, but he realized these two Barbie dolls were not the girls he had known and liked in New York. It was not merely their bodies that had undergone a transformation.

'Do you ever run into Eden?' he asked casually, unable to keep off the subject.

'When we first came out here,' said Suna.

'Yeah, before she got big time and stopped returning our calls,' snorted Shirlee.

'Big time?'

'She does a bit on some soap opera. Thinks that makes her better than everybody else. Anyway, I thought it was over with you two,' Suna said.

'Yeah, it's over. I just wondered how she is doing, that's all. Can I use your phone?'

'Sure,' they chorused. 'Just put the money in the appropriate box.'

Next to the phone, located in a dish-strewn kitchen, were two boxes. One was marked 'local' and the other, 'long distance'. He had no idea which Marina del Rey was – so he stuffed a dollar in each opening. Mother's answering machine was still keeping vigil.

On impulse he dialled the operator and requested the Magiriano Hotel in Vegas. For some reason he felt like speaking to the girl with the black opal eyes.

When the switchboard operator answered, he asked for suite eleven twenty-two.

'Sorry,' said the operator. 'That suite is unoccupied.'

Had she checked out? So soon?

'Well, give me the name of the person who was registered there yesterday?'

'Suite eleven twenty-two has been unoccupied for five days.'

'That's impossible.'

'I'm sorry, sir. Suite eleven twenty-two has had no guests for five days.' The operator disconnected him.

Shit! He must have remembered the wrong number. Now he had no way of finding out her name, and even though he had acted like schmuck of the decade, he still wanted to see her again. Why should *she* get to make the last move?

'What's the matter, Lennie?' murmured Suna, strolling casually into the kitchen.

She was probably checking to see if he'd deposited his money in the box.

'Nothing. I just can't get through to anyone.'

'Story of my life,' she said, sticking her finger into an open jam-pot, then sucking it.

He wondered if they were going to offer him the promised breakfast, even a cup of coffee would be welcome.

Shirlee drifted into the kitchen. 'Where are you staying?'

'I don't know. I'll give you a call when I'm settled.'

'Please,' said Suna.

'Yes, please,' echoed Shirlee.

'Goodness me!' exclaimed Suna, catching sight of the kitchen clock. 'I must rush, I'll be late for my dancing lesson.'

'Me too!' added Shirlee. So much for breakfast.

Lennie made a fast exit.

*

'Why did we have to meet in the parking lot?' Matt grumbled.

'Why not?' replied Jess, and jumped quickly into the passenger seat of his white, fifty-thousand-dollar, Excalibur, in the hope she would not be seen.

'Anybody would think,' he said gruffly, 'that you don't want to be *seen* with me.'

'Nonsense,' she answered briskly. 'This just seemed like the most convenient place.'

'Sure it is,' he said, playing with his gold chains.

'Let's go,' she said impatiently.

'What's your hurry?'

'No hurry. We'll sit here all night if that's what turns you on.'

'*You* turn me on.'

'Are we going or what?'

He started the car and drove off at show-off speed all the way to his apartment. Jess was unimpressed. Even more so when they entered his shrine to bad taste.

'This place looks like something out of *Playboy*,' she exclaimed.

He took it as a compliment and thanked her.

She stifled several more comments, deciding if she was to get any information out of him she'd better try to be civil. Frankly, she found him pathetic – an ageing swinger who wouldn't give up. If he just acted his age, got rid of the gold chains, the wave in his hair, the too-young clothes – he would be quite an attractive older man. Tom Jones pants at age fifty was not a pretty sight. He had to be at *least* fifty – the lines on his face told her that. What was next? A face lift?

He touched a few switches, and the lights dimmed to a soft pink glow, Sinatra came on the stereo, and the sign behind the bar which read 'Matt's Place' blinked on and off.

'Jesus!' Jess muttered under her breath, sinking onto a damask covered couch.

'Scotch?' Matt questioned solicitously, already behind the bar and pouring.

'Coke,' she said quickly.

'I don't have any,' he replied. 'But I do have some grass if you're interested.'

'I *meant* Coca Cola.'

'With Scotch?'

'Plain.'

'You don't drink?'

'Sometimes.'

'Not tonight?'

'Maybe later.'

The 'maybe later' made him feel good. That meant she was planning to stay awhile. Perhaps all night if he was fortunate. Or if *she* was, depending on which way you looked at it.

She obviously loved the apartment. She hadn't stopped looking around from the moment she'd walked in.

'Would you like the grand tour?' he asked, handing her a Coca Cola in an initialled glass. Wait until she saw the bedroom!

'Not right now.'

'Why not?'

'Because I'm hungry, and you invited me for dinner. Remember?'

How could he forget? He had arranged a magnificent dinner. Only it was not due to arrive for another hour. He had hoped that maybe he could get her into bed *before* the food arrived. He hated making love on a full stomach, it gave him heartburn.

'Jess,' he said smoothly, 'I want you to know that you are the most fantastic girl I've seen all year.'

He sat next to her, put his arm around her shoulders, then let his hand casually slip down to her right breast.

She jerked away. 'Cut it out, Matt. I came here for food and information – so please don't grope me while coming on with dumb bullshit lines. Okay?'

•

The twins depressed Lennie. He hated the transformation. They didn't look real anymore, more like a couple of blow-up dolls – the kind you purchased in the porno shops around Times Square. A lot of people in New York put LA down. They said it was fantasy land – all sucking and fucking, sunshine and sex.

So what was so bad about that?

Plenty. If there was nothing else. Suna and Shirlee looked like there was nothing else.

He stopped for coffee and eggs, and tried Marina del Rey Alice for the third time. She answered on the second ring.

A breathy, 'Hi, this is Alice Golden. What can I do for you?'

'You're asking for an obscene phone call,' he cracked.

'Lennie, darling! Why are you calling? Something wrong?'

That said a lot for their relationship. Not for Alice cosy mother/son chats. She came right to the point.

'I'm in LA,' he said. 'Nothing's wrong.'

'Why are you here?'

Did he detect a note of alarm? Alice did not appreciate

the fact she had a thirty-year-old son. It madc her feel ancient.

He juggled a cigarette from his shirt pocket and lit up. 'I had a gig in Vegas, so I thought I'd visit.'

Panic. 'Me?'

'No. LA.'

Why should he visit *her*? She was only his mother.

'That's nice.'

'Yeah. I thought I might get connected here.'

'Well, darling, it's a good enough place to get connected.'

'And I thought I might throw in a visit to you at the same time.'

There was a long silence. Oh, it was great to receive such a warm welcome!

He took her off the hook. 'Unless it's not convenient.'

'Darling! You're so understanding,' she gushed. 'Right now I have a new "friend". He thinks I'm forty. I don't want to surprise him. Not yet, anyway.'

'When?'

'When what?'

'When will you surprise him?'

A shriek of laughter. 'Never, I hope. He's a live one!'

'I'm glad you're happy.'

'Ecstatic.'

'Whatever happened to the schmuck with the false teeth?'

'Old news, Lennie, dear.'

'I'll call you again.'

'If a man answers – hang up!'

'Wouldn't dream of doing anything else.'

'You're such a good boy. And so talented!' A flash of conscience. Maybe she should offer *some*thing, after all, he *was* her flesh and blood, and she loved him in her own special way. She just wished he didn't look his age. 'Remember my friend, Rainbow?' she said, not waiting to see if he did or did not. 'Well she married that *meshugeneh* Foxie – you know – he owns the club on Hollywood Boulevard. Maybe they can use a funny person like you. Mention your father – she always had hot pants for him. I wouldn't be surprised if he *schtupped* her while my back was turned.' Alice laughed gaily. 'What the eye don't see the heart don't fret over. I should care? You think I wasn't having a good time myself? Lennie, I had every man in Vegas chasing after me. Every one!' A thoughtful pause. 'Of course, that's when I was at my peak. I could twirl tassles like *no*body could twirl tassles!'

He had heard it all before. Alice the Swizzle. The toast of Las Vegas. And Jack Golden. What a comedian!

She never called Lennie a comedian. She referred to him as a funny person. In her eyes he didn't do much at all. Just stood there, and talked a lot about life. When she had first seen him perform at a club in New York she had been shocked. 'You use language like that – on stage? And they let you get away with it? Your father *never* used language. He could make them laugh just by being there.'

Your father this, your father that. According to Alice the sun shone out of Jack Golden's ass. And according to Alice, Lennie could *never ever* come anywhere near the dizzying heights his father had achieved.

Bull.

Shit.

He let her carry on for a while, she loved reminiscing. And when he said goodbye she did not even ask when she might hear from him again. He was not surprised. Alice was Alice. She didn't have a motherly bone in her carefully preserved body.

Leaving home at seventeen and taking off for New York had been one of the easiest moves he'd ever made. She had handed him a bus ticket, five hundred dollars, and a kiss on the cheek. 'Go for it, Lennie, darling,' she had said, delighted to be rid of the responsibility of raising a son.

So he had done just that, even though his father had made a half-hearted attempt to persuade him to stay. Poor old Jack Golden. Alice had cut off his balls and used them for earrings. He died six months after Lennie left. Alice didn't bother to inform him until two months after the funeral.

'I couldn't find you,' was her lame excuse.

She hadn't tried too hard. He had sent her three postcards with his phone number and address. She claimed never to have received them.

Now he was in Los Angeles and she really didn't give a damn. Why had he bothered calling?

'Remember my friend, Rainbow?' his mother had said casually. Remember her? How could he ever forget her? For years she had reigned as Queen of his adolescent fantasies. Rainbow. The most beautiful stripper in Las Vegas. She had made Alice Golden look like a carthorse.

And Jack Golden was schtupping her? Really? Jack Golden. The mensch. His father. Schtupping beautiful Rainbow?

Lennie found it hard to believe, but Alice had said so . . .

He wished Jack was still alive. He imagined the conversation they might have. '*Hey dad, did you ever get it on with Rainbow?*'

'*Why yes, son, as a matter of fact I did. Anything you want to know?*'

'*Yeah. Tell me about her tits, her pussy, her skin. Tell me everything, dad, 'cos I jerked off just thinking about her a hundred and fifty times a day!*'

He was twelve years old and out on a spree with Jess. They sneaked into the back of The Hot Banana strip club and caught the girls in action. When Rainbow came on he thought he would faint.

Auntie Rainbow. She had been to their house on several occasions, Alice and she went shopping together. Auntie Rainbow with forty-three inch tits, a sweet smile, and cascades of red hair.

Auntie Rainbow in a G-string that left little to the imagination, a couple of orange sequins, black net stockings with stiletto heels, and a long feather boa.

When Auntie Rainbow took it all off he had come in his pants.

'What's the matter with *you*?' Jess had said in disgust, and not spoken to him for a week.

After that, whenever Rainbow came to their house he made sure he was around. Once, he caught her in the downstairs toilet, sitting on the john, panties (black lace – he still remembered – oh how he remembered!) around her ankles. She didn't bat an eyelash. Later he heard her say to his mother with a laugh, 'The kid caught me taking a pee.' His mother had laughed too.

Rumour had it Rainbow had arrived in Vegas many many years before, age fifteen. She had hooked up with a notorious gangster by the name of Jake the Boy. (Like Bugsy Siegel before him he was handsome and a friend of the stars.) Jake had draped her in diamonds and furs, then dumped her when she turned seventeen. That was when she started her career. By the time Lennie first saw her she must have been at least forty – but even then she was devastating.

What did she look like today? Probably fat and ugly. Certainly old. Was it worthwhile destroying the fantasy? Would she even recall the kid who followed her around with lust and devotion shining from his teenage eyes?

Did he remember Rainbow? Ha!!

He decided he'd better find somewhere to stay. It was obvious camping at Alice's was out of the question.

He called Joey Firello, who advised him to book into the Chateau Marmont – an old hotel in the Hollywood Hills that catered to show business and would not cost him his balls. Joey sounded pleased to hear from him. 'Check in, and we'll get together later.'

He wasn't sure he wanted to see Joey.

Joey Firello was on his way. Lennie Golden was stuck in the same old rut. Oh yeah, he could always get work, but where was it taking him? All around him things were happening for other people. John Belushi, Dan Ackroyd, Chevy Chase, Joey Firello. They were on a roll.

Naively he had imagined Vegas as a spring board to bigger and better things. And he had ended up with shit on his face.

LA better have something exciting to offer, otherwise . . .

Otherwise what?

Chapter 12

Preparations for the gala evening to honour Francesca Fern were elaborate. The Magiriano's huge ballroom was festooned with exotic white orchids. An intimate touch supplied by Dimitri Stanislopoulos, his way of paying homage to Madame Fern.

Lucky dropped by during the day to see that everything was being set up smoothly. No problems. She had a terrific staff who rarely – if ever – put a foot wrong. And her catering manager was the best in town, the food would be magnificent.

Throughout the day celebrities arrived – by private plane, limousine and commercial jets. Naturally there were baskets of fruit, chilled champagne, caviar and a selection of expensive cheeses waiting in their suites with a personal note from Lucky. No matter how rich or famous anyone was, they all adored getting something for nothing – a fact of life Gino had taught her.

She had never met Francesca Fern, but she sent her six bottles of Cristal champagne and a welcoming note.

Gino had already informed Lucky he would be bringing Susan Martino to the event.

'When is she leaving?' Lucky had been unable to stop from asking.

'Why?' Gino snapped. He really did wonder when Susan *was* leaving. Originally she had said she was in town for a few weeks. The subject had not arisen again. As far as he was concerned she could stay forever. She made him very comfortable indeed.

When he picked her up later that night to escort her to the Francesca Fern dinner, he broached the subject. 'I kinda gotten used to havin' you around,' he said. 'You got no plans to leave, have you?'

Susan smiled wanly. 'Life goes on,' she said quietly. 'Would that everything stopped at whim.'

'Huh?'

She patted him lightly on the arm, the yellow diamond ring he had gifted her with sparkled brightly on her little finger. 'I have a home to run, and many responsibilities. There's the charity work I'm involved with. My children . . . Of course they're not children any more. Nathan's at college, and Gemma might be married in the fall. They still need my attention though, especially as Tiny is no longer with us.'

'Yeh,' Gino muttered uneasily. It was the first time she had mentioned her kids. Somehow he liked the thought of Susan with nobody in her life but him.

'I expect I shall leave this weekend,' she continued. 'I will need an excellent reason not to.'

Wasn't he excellent reason enough? Jeez! How many women would kill to be in her place?

•

Dimitri glowered at his reflection as he adjusted his bow tie. Here he was, in Las Vegas, attending Francesca Fern's big event like an obedient puppy. She had insisted he be present. Naturally, he had complied, even arrived two days early so he would be rested and full of energy. Francesca admired ceaseless energy. She, herself, never stopped, and she expected – though never received – the same of the people around her. 'Dimitri,' she would purr in her deep husky voice. 'We are twins, the same star, the same destiny. Only *you* can keep up with me.'

They were both Geminis.

Now Madam Fern had flown in with her entourage – including browbeaten Horace – and where was her phone call? Where was her presence in his suite? Where *was* the damn woman?

Dimitri knew exactly what time she had arrived – eleven-thirty in the morning. He had allowed her the courtesy of an hour to rest, and then he had called her suite and been told by her insolent male secretary that the great Miz Fern was in the middle of an interview with *Time* magazine and absolutely could not be disturbed.

'Disturb her!' Dimitri had bellowed, used to getting his own way.

'That's out of the question,' replied the secretary.

'Disturb her!' Dimitri thundered a second time.

'I'm sure Miz Fern will return your call when she is able,' retorted the secretary and hung up.

Dimitri was so furious he called back immediately, only to reach Horace.

'Francesca's busy at the moment,' said Horace, in his usual worried whine. 'I'll get her to phone you as soon as she can.'

Dimitri had spent the day in his suite waiting for her call. It never came.

He was incensed. In all his dealings with women, nobody ever dared to treat him the way Francesca Fern did.

Now he was ready to attend her gala, and anger coursed through his veins. He was not some miserable fan. If Francesca thought she could treat him in this fashion and get away with it, she had better think again.

*

Lucky called Matt at the last minute. 'You'll have to escort me to this thing tonight,' she said with a sigh of annoyance. 'Gino's taking Grace Kelly.'

'Grace is in Monaco.'

'Someone should tell dear old Susan. Maybe she'll stop the masquerade.'

'Don't you like her?'

'Oh Matt, you're so perceptive – right on the dime.'

'She's a very nice lady.'

'Hitler only had one ball, but he could charm 'em too.'

'What are you talking about?'

'Forget it. Pick me up at six-thirty.'

Matt decided he had a problem. Escorting Lucky Santangelo had never figured in his scheme of things. He had hoped to see Jess later. Not that she ever wanted to see *him* again. She had told him so, in no uncertain terms. Just because he had tried to jump her bones.

He shook his head. The sexual revolution seemed to have eluded poor Jess. Silly girl. But he was not prepared to give up yet. Now he was supposed to drop everything and be at Lucky Santangelo's beck and call. Why?

Because she's the boss, that's why.

•

Francesca Fern clicked talon red nails. 'Emeralds,' she commanded.

Horace sprang toward her travelling Vuitton jewel case and found the requested gems.

Francesca clicked again. 'Jourdan diamanté shoes.'

Horace raced for the closet and located the size ten evening shoes. Lovingly he placed them upon his wife's large feet.

Francesca arose, clipped a huge emerald to an outsize earlobe and snapped, 'Perfume.'

Horace obliged with a liberal spray of Joy.

'Let us go,' sighed Francesca. 'The peasants are waiting.'

Chapter 13

Mr Wrong wore a white silk tuxedo, a plastic smile, and several gold bracelets. He was a Spanish recording star – who – according to his PR – drove women crazy. His accent was enough to drive anyone crazy. Had he not been halfway famous, Olympia would have disregarded him totally. As it was they were at adjoining tables in New York's Regines on Park Avenue, and Olympia knew the platinum blonde English woman he was with – a sort of international fixer-upper – who adored putting the right people together. So before long they all joined up – Olympia's group, Mr Spanish Recording Star, and his friend. His name was Vitos Felicidade, and by the time he rocked Olympia in his arms on the dance floor, he knew exactly who she was – thanks to his blonde ladyfriend who excitedly filled him in, then told him – in Spanish (good international fixer-uppers always speak more than one language) to go for it. Both he and Olympia sensed interesting but limited possibilities.

'You 'ave a wondeefool 'air,' he murmured, pressing what appeared to be his idea of a hard-on between her thighs.

Olympia allowed desire to run rampant, hoped he was better hung than he appeared, and said, 'So do you.' Although she wasn't quite sure whether he meant she had wonderful hair or a wonderful air about her. Since she had both, she didn't much care.

'I fluuuck yew beauuuutifully,' he purred with a winning smile. Pure plastic.

I hope you fluuck better than you speak English, she thought as she discreetly slid her hand down and felt for his cock. An encouraging rub and they were away.

Outside the club the lurking paparazzi jumped to attention. Olympia Stanislopoulos and Vitos Felicidade. Together! More than together! They jostled for position to capture the coupling of the two celebrities.

'This is so boring!' complained Olympia.

'Boooooring,' agreed Vitos, lifting his head so there was no chance of a bad angle. 'We take my car or yours?'

Two chauffeurs stood by their respective limousines.

'Who cares?' sighed Olympia, throwing herself into the back of his. 'Let's just get out of here.'

Chapter 14

'I hate these evenings,' Lucky confided to Dimitri. 'They make me want to scream and run naked down a beach someplace. Y'know what I mean?'

Dimitri regarded the black-eyed girl without a flicker of interest. He wished, quite frankly, that she would be quiet. He just wanted to concentrate on Francesca. Holding court at the top table like the Queen of England.

And *he* was not seated at the top table. *He*, Dimitri Stanislopoulos, was sitting at the *next* table, the grandest insult of all.

Lucky waited for his reply, which was not forthcoming. Silence reigned. Screw him. If he didn't want to make conversation she could take a hint. She was just trying to be polite because it was her hotel, he was a big gambler, and she could see he was pissed as hell about the seating arrangements. She wasn't exactly thrilled herself. Daddy and the widow at table numero uno with the star, her seedy husband, and a clutch of major celebrities. Francesca's secretary had organized the seating arrangements. Badly, Lucky thought. She wished she hadn't come – who needed this shit?

Matt, sitting on her other side, seemed to be enjoying himself. He was surrounded by friends and acquaintances from Hollywood where he had spent many happy working years. A fine escort *he* was. What had she expected – Al Pacino? She was trapped between the two dullest men in the room. Matt Traynor and Dimitri Stanislopoulos. Some winning combination.

Thanks a lot, Gino. Is this what my life has become?

She reached for her champagne glass and signalled for a waiter to refill it. Getting smashed was the only way to get through *this* evening.

*

Gino observed Susan in action. It was the first time he had seen her do her stuff surrounded by the elite of show business. She knew how to handle herself all right. Not one wrong move.

How would it be if he was married to a woman like Susan? He was too old to keep whoring around, one woman by his side and in his bed would suit him nicely.

He watched her chiselled profile as she chatted quietly to Horace Fern. After Maria he had never thought he would marry again. Dear sweet Maria . . . dead twenty-three years . . .

Surely he had waited long enough?

He glanced across at Lucky, sitting at the next table. How would *she* take it? She would hate it. But she would get used to it. She would have to.

*

It was a long night. A night of speeches, performances, and tributes. The television cameras whirred, and Francesca Fern blossomed. She played *grande dame* to the hilt. Francesca knew how to milk an evening.

Later, when the TV crew had left, and the guests began to thin out, Francesca graciously did the rounds. She stopped next to Dimitri, bent to peck him on the cheek, and husked, 'So generous of you to be here tonight. Your gesture is much appreciated.' Theatrically she posed next to him, while her personal photographer captured the shot.

He gripped her wrist so hard she almost cried out. 'What is this charade?' he demanded in a hoarse whisper. 'How *dare* you treat me this way. What game are you playing?'

She managed a fixed smile, while hissing fiercely, 'Let go of me, you filthy animal. I heard all about you and Norma Valentine. Don't think you can have us both, because you *cannot*. I *will not* be humiliated in such a way.'

Norma Valentine. He almost laughed aloud. Norma Valentine was an English film star he had met in the South of France. She had been brought to his yacht a week previously by a Greek business associate and she had stayed the night. One night only. She meant nothing to him. 'I was in her company once,' he explained. 'I didn't even like her.'

'Ah, but you liked her enough to fuck her. *And* to send her a Cartier bracelet the next day,' Francesca said fiercely.

'A gambling debt. She won at cards.'

'Please, Dimitri, credit me with superior intelligence. More than you – for I am telling you – if you can sleep with Norma Valentine, then, my God – you will *never* sleep with me again.'

'You're married,' Dimitri objected. 'Since when do you forbid me to sleep with anyone else?'

'Sleep with whom you like,' spat Francesca, her smile

finally slipping. 'Because you will no longer be sharing *my* bed.' She wrenched her wrist free, and stalked off.

'I guess the crunch is outta the cookie,' commented Lucky, who had not been able to help overhearing, and was feeling no pain due to several more glasses of champagne.

'I beg your pardon?' Dimitri glared at her.

She shrugged. 'Francesca Fern and Norma Valentine were up for the lead in "Sirrocco Sings" fifteen years ago. Norma went on to win an Oscar for the role *and* make it as a movie star. FF never did a flick. They are arch enemies – it's Hollywood trivia. How come *you* don't know?'

He was outraged. 'Were you eavesdropping on our entire conversation?'

'Couldn't help myself.'

'Really!'

'Relax – you'll give yourself a hernia.'

'You are a very vulgar young lady.'

'Cut the crap, Dimitri. I'm not your daughter's little friend anymore. And I've had it with you ignoring me like I don't exist.' She rose. 'This is *my* hotel. You have been playing at *my* tables all week – why don't you just loosen up and we'll go out and get drunk. Huh? How's that for a great idea? *I* need to, and you *certainly* do.'

He saw her for the first time. And her smouldering beauty and vibrant youth struck him as the perfect way to erase Francesca from his thoughts. Lucky Santangelo was right. No more could he dismiss her as Olympia's little friend.

His penetrating eyes held hers. 'So, you require a drinking partner, is that it?'

She returned his gaze, surprised to finally get his attention. 'Yes. And *you* have been elected.'

'Should I be flattered?'

She glanced over at Gino and caught him in deep whisper with Susan. 'Be what you like, but let's get out of here. And fast.'

*

'I had a busy life. Did a lotta things – some good, some bad. Y'know what I mean?' Gino rubbed the faint scar on his cheek.

'I realize you are not Billy Graham,' Susan replied.

'When y'come from where I do, y'gotta learn to look after yourself. Nobody does it for you.'

'I'm sure.'

'I started out on the streets. Never had no formal education. Kinda picked up things as I went along.'

'You're a true survivor. Look at where you are today.'

'Yeh. I did okay. Like I made the great American dream come true. From nothin' I made it big.'

'Quite an understatement.'

'I know Presidents, politicians, mayors, civic leaders. There's people owe me favours you wouldn't believe.'

'Of course.'

'Stick with me, kiddo. I'll show you one hell of a good life.'

'Is this a proposal, Gino?'

'Y'know somethin', I think it is.'

'I'm . . . surprised.'

'*You're* surprised? How d'you figure *I* feel?'

'It's something I'll have to think about.'

'So think. Who's stoppin' you? Think all you want. Only I'll need an answer before I go to sleep tonight on account of the fact that I might change my mind in the mornin'.'

Susan laughed softly. 'Gino, you're incorrigible?'

'Yeh? Make the most of it.'

'I must talk to my family, my children . . .'

'You see me askin' Lucky's permission?'

'It's not that easy . . .'

'Make it easy – say yes.'

'Yes,' she whispered.

'What?'

'I said yes.'

'Hey! I'll be damned!'

They were in Francesca's suite enjoying an after the event private party.

Gino leapt to his feet. 'I got an announcement to make!' The assorted group gave him their attention. 'This lady and I.

Susan Martino and I. Jeez! What can I tell you? We're gettin' married!'

*

Now she had his attention, Lucky found Dimitri an enjoyable drinking companion. He wasn't Gino, but he had that certain aura – and she liked the authority of an older man. He was also strangely attractive with his shock of thick white hair, prominent nose, and penetrating eyes. The drunker she got, the more attractive he became.

Olympia's daddy. She was having erotic thoughts about Olympia's daddy!

He was very tall, a big man. Gino was much shorter, more wiry. Physically they couldn't be less alike.

'This is fun,' Lucky said, as they roamed from bar to bar.

He was drinking ouzo, tossing it down like lemonade. But it did not seem to affect him.

He nodded. He didn't know why, but he was enjoying himself. Francesca Fern would regret tonight. He would personally see that she regretted it for the rest of her miserable life. Nobody spurned Dimitri Stanislopoulos, least of all a cheap whore actress.

At three o'clock in the morning they found themselves in a small Greek café, surrounded by waiters coming off their shifts, and other late night workers. Dimitri bought drinks all round, while a thin boy played the mandolin, naturally the theme from 'Zorba'. Dimitri danced, balancing a plate on his head, and he laughed so loud that for a moment Lucky thought he might choke. Then he smashed twenty-three plates in a row, gave the smiling proprietor a thousand dollar bill, and with unspoken agreement they retired to Lucky's penthouse apartment.

For a moment she was nervous, a kid again. She fluttered around, fixing him a drink, then going into her bathroom and holding a cold towel to her forehead.

I'm being ridiculous, she thought. *What the hell is going on here?*

She returned to the living room and faced him.

He said her name once, very quietly. Then without further ado he peeled the sensuous sheath of a black silk dress from her body with expert strong hands.

She felt like a swimmer about to take the plunge. Expectant, excited, ready to excel.

His hands were big, his fingers long and firm. Slowly he explored her body, brushing her skin until he hooked into her bikini panties – the only other garment she wore – and drew them down past her thighs, her calves, her ankles.

She was naked, but he remained dressed, merely loosening his bow tie.

With great care he pushed her down onto the couch, took his brandy glass, dipped his index finger into the shimmering liquid, and brought it first to the nipple of her left breast, and then to the right one.

The liquor stung, but only for a second. With hardly a pause, he started to suck it from her, making her sigh with pleasure. She threw her arms behind her head and stretched luxuriously. He cupped her breasts together and flicked his tongue across both nipples.

'Get your clothes off,' she murmured urgently.

He laughed. 'Such impatience!'

'Get 'em off, Dimitri. I mean *now*.'

Keeping both hands on her breasts he traced his tongue down her body.

She writhed with excitement. Maybe I'm drunk, she thought, but this guy certainly has a great touch. Or maybe it's been too long between pit stops. She smiled with secret laughter.

He opened her thighs by pushing his head between them.

'I . . . want . . . to . . . feel . . . your . . . body . . .' she murmured. 'Please. I'm . . . asking . . . nicely . . .'

His tongue, like his fingers, was thick, slow moving, and experienced.

'Ooooh . . . yes . . .' she moaned. 'Oh yes, yes, yes.' Her legs parted even more as she felt the tenseness of the past months building up, preparing for release, getting ready to explode.

He paused to flavour his tongue with brandy while his hands continued to work on her breasts.

She felt the sting of the alcohol, the expertise of his fingers, and the strength of his tongue.

'Oh, God, Dimitri! Oh God! This is soooo great. So utterly fantastic. *Ohhhhh . . .*'

She hit the plateau. Hard. And it was worth waiting for.

He buried his head between her legs and enjoyed every hot throbbing moment.

Chapter 15

Jess found out nothing. Absolutely nothing.

Oh yes. She had found out that Matt Traynor had a constant erection, talked a lot, and thought he was God's gift.

Had he honestly believed she would fall for his very thin-on-the-ground charms? Had he really imagined she would jump between his brown striped sheets like all the rest?

She actually had to fight him off. Do battle. And she was only five feet tall against this five eleven or more. It had been some struggle. If she hadn't resorted to slamming him in the balls with her elbow she would probably *still* be there.

And when she got home at some ungodly hour, she found Wayland entertaining a group of scruffy friends who were eating *her* food, smoking *her* grass, and messing up *her* house. She really let fly, and when roused she had some temper.

Wayland got excited – unusual for him, and left with his friends, only to return at seven a.m. so stoned he couldn't even speak.

They were all the same. And why hadn't Lennie phoned? Didn't he think she was worried about him? Didn't he think she *cared*?

In the morning she took the baby out beside the pool, and lay with him in the long grass. Having Simon was the only positive thing she had done in her entire life. He gave her a reason to keep on going, to get through each day and make it to that weekly pay cheque.

Wayland staggered outside. 'There's no milk,' he complained.

'Go to the market and get some,' she said patiently.

'I don't have any money.'

Reluctantly she fished a twenty from her jeans pocket and threw it at him.

He nodded wisely. 'I'll stock up.'

'Sure you will,' she muttered. 'Five bucks food and the rest on whatever you can score.'

He didn't hear her. She couldn't care less. Quietly she rocked Simon in her arms and crooned a soothing lullaby. Soon it would be time to visit her mother in the hospital.

*

Foxie was eighty-five years old, small as an elf, bald, with sharp darting cross-eyes, and ears that stuck up like something out of 'Star Trek'.

Foxie was canny, cheap, insulting, a good friend and a mean enemy.

He was also a Hollywood legend – although only to people in the know.

Foxie had a keen ear, a cruel wit, limitless energy, and no ailments.

For a man of eighty-five he was remarkable.

Lennie had never met him, but the stories he had heard could fill volumes. He was looking forward to the experience.

Foxie's the place – named after the man himself – was located on Hollywood Boulevard, and boasted a mixed clientele. People came to Foxie's to hang out and have fun. All kinds of people. From local pimps and hookers to Beverly Hills namedroppers to Sam Schmuck from the Valley and an occasional movie star or two, Foxie's was *the* place. The food was terrible, the drinks generous, and the entertainment hilarious. A mixture of new talent, strippers, working comics, and a 'discovery' night that was better than the Gong Show. Once a month was 'take it off night' – an evening where ordinary females leaped on the stage and couldn't wait to show everyone what they had. To get into Foxie's that night you had to book weeks in advance.

Joey Firello suggested they stop by. 'It's where *I* started out here,' he explained to Lennie. 'Six weeks in and I got me the TV show. Now I'm signing autographs and turning down pussy!'

Joey looked like a handsome monkey. He was thin, short, and wiry, with Rod Stewart hair and Mick Jagger lips. He was, at twenty-six, four years younger than Lennie.

'Look,' Joey said, 'if Foxie don't like you we'll go to the Improv or the Comedy Store. You'll get connected.'

'Sure. I know,' Lennie said. He felt ridiculous. Joey the Kid giving *him* advice and help. Joey the Kid who had arrived in New York three years earlier with twenty-eight bucks, some corny gags, and a lot of hustle. For nine weeks he had slept on Lennie's floor. His hustle had paid off. Now he was wearing cashmere sweaters and driving a second-hand Jaguar. Foxie greeted him like a brother.

'I want you to meet a friend of mine,' Joey said. 'Lennie Golden. Remember the name. He's funny.'

'As funny as you?' snapped Foxie.

'Give him a shot. See for yourself.'

Foxie picked at his teeth with a wooden toothpick and cocked his head to one side. 'You wanna try out tonight?'

'I wasn't planning on trying out,' Lennie said quickly. 'I've got a video of my work – I thought if you liked it we could do business.'

'You East Coast *momsers* – you're all the same,' Foxie snorted. 'Don't want to try out. Want me to waste my time lookin' at tape shit.' He bit the toothpick in half and began to eat it. 'At Foxie's you either try out or get out. I can fit you in at ten o'clock. Take it or leave it.'

Joey nodded. 'He'll take it.'

'Do I have a choice?' Lennie joked.

'No choice,' said Joey. 'Do it. He'll love you. I'm gonna get on the phone and summon up fans.'

Lennie wondered if Joey might call Eden. They hadn't discussed her all night. The silence was killing him. Why didn't Joey mention her? They must have seen each other. He was determined not to ask.

Christ! He was nervous.

Lennie Golden nervous. Christ!

He had played a thousand and one joints.

Foxie's was no different.

Except.

At Foxie's.

He had to be a smash.

Chapter 16

Vitos Felicidade was not the most exciting lover Olympia had ever had. He was hot in a different way. He was a star, and therefore a worthwhile trophy to hang on to for a while.

Brigette took an immediate dislike to him. The child was becoming impossible. Since her display of temperament on Fifth Avenue she had discovered that being difficult resulted in plenty of attention, and if there was one thing Brigette craved it was attention. When she first met Vitos she kicked him in the ankle, called him a foreign pig, and ran to her room screaming.

Olympia was humiliated. She took out her fury on Nanny Mabel who promptly threatened to quit.

Vitos suggested that Brigette should be sent away to boarding school. Olympia was tempted, but the child was still so young, and she couldn't help remembering her own unfortunate experiences in such establishments.

On the day of her grandmother's wedding Brigette refused to get out of bed. Nanny Mabel came running to Olympia in a terrible state. Reluctantly Olympia stomped into her daughter's room to deal with the situation.

'Don't *want* to be the flower girl,' Brigette kept on repeating stubbornly. 'Don't *want* to wear a silly yucky dress. *Don't want to!*'

'You have to,' Olympia admonished, trying to cajole the

child into some form of obedience. 'Your own grandmother is getting married. And if you are good – *very* good, I shall take you to Tiffany's – the big jewellery store on Fifth Avenue – and buy you anything you want.'

Nanny Mabel, standing beside the bed, snorted her disapproval. Trying to bribe a nine-year-old child with jewellery. Ridiculous!

'Anything, mama?' questioned Brigette, her bright blue eyes widening. 'Anything at all in the wholewideworld?'

'Yes,' agreed Olympia reluctantly.

'When?'

'Tomorrow.'

'Okay.' Brigette gave a happy smile and jumped out of bed.

Olympia glared at Nanny Mabel. 'All right, Nanny? Do you think *you* can take over now?'

'Yes, Madam,' sniffed the disapproving woman.

Olympia swept from the room into the sanctuary of her bedroom. Vitos was arriving in two hours, and she had so much to do.

She regarded herself in a mirror. New York was not helping with her weight problem, her face looked positively round. Angrily she sucked in her cheeks. Why couldn't money buy great cheekbones? Why wasn't she six inches taller and twenty pounds lighter?

Hah! Vitos had no complaints. *He* thought she was perfect. Latin men liked a woman with flesh on her bones, not to mention millions in the bank.

She scowled at her reflection.

Vitos arrived twenty minutes later, wearing a pink suit, dark glasses, and a perpetual sneer.

Brigette, just about to depart early with Nanny, managed a quick, 'You look *soooo* dumb.'

Vitos ignored her, and helped himself to one of Dimitri's cigars.

When Olympia made her entrance ten minutes later, he was asleep in a chair, and the cigar had burnt a hole on the polished top of a priceless antique table.

'Wake up!' Olympia screeched.

He did as she asked, and they snorted four lines of excellent coke to prepare themselves for the trip to her mother's wedding.

Olympia wore white. She knew it was incorrect, but so what? Her blonde curls were frizzed and puffed out. A professional artiste had applied her make-up. She felt she looked her best, and Vitos seemed a suitable accessory.

The paparazzi, observing the couple so dressed at noon, decided *they* must be getting married, so they followed them in a variety of cars and motor scooters, all the way to Long Island where the *real* bride's groom-to-be lived.

'How tiresome!' Olympia exclaimed, as the photographers drew alongside the limousine at every stoplight, clicking and snapping away.

Vitos raised his chin and smiled. 'Tirrrrsome,' he repeated, wondering if this extra blast of publicity would boost the US sales of his new album, not doing quite as well as everyone had anticipated.

Olympia's mother was not pleased when the arrival of her daughter (always a handful – thank God she had decided to live with Dimitri) brought with her fifteen skirvy-looking photographers and a smiling but vacuous Spanish recording star. She took Olympia to one side. 'You shouldn't wear white,' she said sternly. 'It makes you look fat. And exactly *who* is that person you have with you?'

'Vitos,' said Olympia vaguely. 'He sings. He's quite famous.'

'I don't care *how* famous he is,' admonished her mother. 'He looks like a pimp.'

Olympia giggled. 'A pimp! Mother! Where did *you* learn words like that?'

'Please, Olympia. I am getting married today. I would appreciate it if you would refrain from upsetting me.'

Charlotte's intended was a tall, thin man, with mean eyes and a limp. Olympia took an instant dislike to him, and told everyone who would listen she thought he looked like a Nazi war criminal.

The wedding took place in the garden at three p.m. Brigette

as flower girl, was prettier than any of the bridesmaids. She looks angelic, Olympia thought with a proud smile, watching her daughter trail dutifully behind the bride. She caught Nanny Mabel's eye and for once the two women were in complete tune, proud guardians of the exquisite little heiress.

This peaceful reverie was interrupted by three screaming paparazzi falling from the collapsing branch of an overhanging olive tree.

'Oh, God!' exclaimed Olympia as everyone panicked, thinking some sort of raid was taking place. 'I'll get the blame for this, I know I will.'

'You all *stink*!' yelled Brigette suddenly, jumping up and down with glee as she seized the perfect opportunity to cause trouble. 'You all STINK STINK STINK!'

'Oh, *God*!' Olympia turned to Vitos for moral support.

He was asleep, a vacuous smile in permanent position.

She kicked him sharply on the ankle. 'Wake up!' she ordered. 'What do you think this is – a rest camp?'

'Olympeea –' he began plaintively.

'Don't Olympia me. *Do* something!'

He leaped to his feet and waved an ineffectual fist at the photographers who were now scrambling for their cameras and grabbing random shots.

'You all STINK!' Brigette continued to yell.

Olympia clutched Vitos by the arm and smiled – might as well look good if one was to be splashed across the front pages of the world.

Vitos caught her message and also smiled.

All around them chaos reigned.

Chapter 17

'I want to talk to you,' said Gino.

'I already heard,' replied Lucky, trying to hide the hurt and rejection she felt.

'I've bin tryin' to find you all day.'

'So you've found me.' She shrugged. 'Congratulations. What more can I say?'

They stood by the reception desk of the Magiriano. Lucky had just returned from a drive and wore jeans, a loose T-shirt and aviator shades. Her hair was wild and she was makeupless.

'Hey, kid, y'look about sixteen!' Gino joked.

She pushed her hands through her hair and stared at him.

'You're mad at me,' he stated.

'Why should I be mad?' she replied sarcastically. 'I mean you're only my *father* – that's all. So why should I be mad that you decide to get married and *I have to hear it from Matt Traynor*?' Her voice rose. 'Why the hell should I be mad at that?'

He fingered the scar on his cheek. 'Circumstances, kid,' he said. 'I didn't plan it. Things just fell into place. I thought you were at the party when I told everyone.'

'Thanks a lot. I guess my presence is really felt.'

'C'mon, Lucky,' he soothed. 'I called you as soon as I got up this morning. It's not my fault you've bin out all day. Where were you, anyway?'

'There's a whorehouse twenty miles outside town – sometimes I help out.'

He frowned at her flippancy. 'Let's go upstairs,' he said. 'I've bin hangin' around here for an hour – does that show I care?'

'Big deal,' she mumbled.

They walked to her private elevator, the sound of the slots jangling reassuringly in the background. She was frightened, truly frightened. If Gino got married again where did that leave her?

She had driven through the desert for hours thinking about it. When Matt had phoned her early in the morning with the news, she had been utterly devastated. Dimitri had departed hours before and she was alone, hung over, and in no mood to digest such shocking information. Quickly she had dressed and slipped quietly from the hotel. In the underground garage she took possession of her Ferrari, and drove out to the desert with Otis Redding on the tape deck and just her thoughts for company.

Now she was back, and Gino was present, and *how could he do it to her*?

Inside her penthouse there were incredible baskets of mauve sterling silver roses everywhere. She looked around in amazement and turned to Gino. 'Did you do this?'

His scowl deepened. 'No, I didn't.'

She reached for one of the white cards attached to the baskets. A simple signature, nothing else. *Dimitri*.

She crumpled the card in her hand.

'Who sent them?' asked Gino.

'Francesca Fern,' she replied quickly, tossing the card into a corner.

'Nice of her.'

'Why not? It was a great evening.'

'Listen, kid.' He sat down on the couch and sighed. 'I made a mistake. I shoulda told you first – but I didn't, so let's not make a federal case out of it.'

'Who's making a federal case? I just thought you might have discussed it with me before informing the world.'

'You're my daughter, not my jailer. You think I need your permission?'

'I think you need my advice.'

He was angry now. 'Screw your advice,' he said darkly. 'Susan said you'd be jealous and she was right.'

Lucky shared the Santangelo temper. She glared at her father. 'I don't give a damn *what* Susan said. The widow Martino is your problem – and believe me – if you marry her you'll have more problems than you ever imagined.'

'My daughter – the mouth. You don't even *know* Susan – so quit puttin' her down.'

'I'm trying to save you from making a big mistake.'

'Kid, I made a lotta mistakes in my life – most of 'em before you were ever around. You know somethin' – I managed to survive *without* your advice – so stick it where the Pope don't go roller skatin', put a smile on your face – an' wish me the best of luck.'

She forced a stiff smile, hated him for a stupid old fool, and nodded. 'You're right. It's your life, and if it's what you want . . . well then . . . congratulations.'

'That's more like it.' He grinned, temper forgotten. 'An' now I gotta get a move on.' He headed jauntily for the door.

'Stop!' Lucky said urgently. 'You can't keep me waiting any longer.' The frustrations were building. 'You've *got* to make a decision on Atlantic City.'

He glanced at his watch impatiently. 'Right now I gotta run. We can talk about it when I get back.'

She glared at him. 'Where are you going?'

'Didn't I tell you?'

She shook her head and waited for the bombshell.

He didn't disappoint. 'Promised to fly to LA with Susan. She needs to tell her kids in person, doesn't want them reading about us in some newspaper.'

It was starting. She was losing him. Gino . . . Daddy . . .

'What kids?' she asked calmly, although the last thing she felt was calm.

'I think she's got a matched pair, a boy and a girl.'

Something icy clutched at her heart. 'How old are they?'

'Who knows? Nineteen, twenty.'

Susan was right. She *was* jealous. But not of the old bag – of the 'kids' who might one day regard Gino as their stepfather.

Oh God! She couldn't stand it! Why was this happening? Why had Susan Martino appeared in their lives and spoiled everything?

'When will you be back?' she asked, concealing her dismay.

'I shouldn't be gone more than a couple of days. I'll call you.'

'But I need to know about Atlantic City *now*,' she said desperately. 'I've spent a tremendous amount of time and energy putting everything together. If we don't get a lock on it immediately all my work will have been for nothing.'

He was anxious to be on his way. Susan was waiting, and right now she came first. 'Everything'll hold,' he said confidently. 'When I get back we'll sit down together and work out the way to go. I promise. You can count on me.'

Once she would have believed him. Now she wasn't sure. 'I thought we wanted to build a hotel together more than anything else in the world,' she said softly. 'Surely you can give me a yes or a no so I can put the deal in motion?'

'Two days,' he said, kissed her on the cheek, and was gone.

She walked out to the terrace and stood for a long while gazing out at nothing in particular. The sun began to slide beneath a cloud and a chill entered the hot air. Thoughtfully she bit her lower lip. Who *was* Susan Martino? What was her story? Married to the very famous Tiny for many years. But how about before that? Did Gino know anything about her at all?

On a hunch Lucky picked up the phone and summoned Boogie. It took him only five minutes to arrive at her door.

'I want a full rundown on Susan Martino,' she said. 'Everything. Birth to now. You got it?'

He nodded. Over the years he had become used to Lucky's odd-ball requests. She always had a reason for everything she did. Lucky Santangelo had style. She was one of a kind, and his loyalty would never waver.

When Boogie departed she checked with the switchboard. Dimitri Stanislopoulos had called twice, and left a message for her to call him back.

Dimitri . . . She didn't know whether she wanted to see him or not.

Dimitri . . . Olympia's father.

Dimitri . . . an interesting lover.

She looked around the room full of flowers and decided she *would* see him again. Drunk or not she had enjoyed his company *and* his lovemaking, although he was hardly the kind of man she was usually attracted to. For one thing he was too old, and too commanding. Lucky was used to calling the shots.

The thought of an evening alone while Gino flew to LA with his ladylove drove her to the phone.

'I am leaving tomorrow,' Dimitri informed her. 'So tonight we will dine.'

In a way he reminded her of Gino. A strong man who expected, and usually got, his own way.

For once she did not mind swimming with the tide.

*

Susan Martino lived in manicured luxury on Roxbury Drive. A large house, heavily mortgaged – although Susan did not reveal that to Gino.

A Swiss couple lived on the premises in a converted apartment above the four car garage. The woman cooked and cleaned, while the man looked after the garden and acted as general handyman. For these services they received two thousand dollars a month. Susan's business manager had told her she would not be able to afford to keep them much longer.

In the garage there was a yellow Rolls – leased. A brown Mercedes – leased. And a Toyota station wagon which belonged to the couple – courtesy of Tiny, who, when he was alive, spent money like it fell from the palm trees lining his driveway. Which was the reason Susan found herself in such dire straits now.

Tiny had not left a will. He had left a mess.

A month after his unfortunate death, Susan had been forced to face the grim reality. Within two years she would be broke. In spite of the vast amounts of money Tiny had earned during a wildly successful career, he had managed to dispose of every red cent – one way or the other.

When the accountant started going through the bills with Susan, she shuddered. Tiny had done things with his money she could hardly believe. Ten thousand dollars to this friend in need – twenty thousand to that one. He kept a whole family of relatives, and supported every hard luck story that came his way. Plus he seemed to have picked up every restaurant cheque in the world. And personally thought nothing of spending a hundred thousand dollars a month on gifts!

She ranted and raved for a while. Screamed, threw things, sobbed uncontrollably. Then she sat up and took stock. She was forty-nine years old, beautifully preserved (a touch of surgery around the eyes and chin, and a bust lift was all that she'd had done), elegant, charming, a delightful companion, and obliging in bed. What more could a man want? An older man. *A much older man.* For she was smart enough to realize that older men needed extreme youth – it propped up their sagging hormones, not to mention their waistlines.

So, Susan Martino made a list of suitable candidates, and set about snaring one of the men on it.

One by one she struck out for a variety of reasons. Somewhere down the list – way, way down, was the name Gino Santangelo.

Susan had never imagined she would ever come close to picking Gino Santangelo. He was a shady figure with an even shadier past. A man of mystery, who lived in Las Vegas with his pushy daughter. Some said a criminal who hid his activities behind a million different companies.

Susan did not care. By this time she was desperate. There was hardly any money left, and something had to be done quickly. She rented a house in Las Vegas for a month, hopped on a plane, and within two days she was in business. Voila!

Gino Santangelo had fallen neatly into her clutches. And her luck was in, for the pushy daughter was out of town, which gave her a clear runway for full thrust ahead.

Now she had him. And would she *ever* be able to introduce him to her friends?

Very very carefully. He was rough as a street hood in spite of the life he had led, and his impressive connections.

In bed he horrified her. He was so . . . crude. Even at his age he wanted to do so much. She was weary of him always trying to bring her to orgasm. As if she cared. For years Tiny had flung himself on top of her, heaved up and down a few times, and that was it. She really didn't want to be bothered by anything else. Sex. Ugh! It was so dirty. And

Gino was especially dirty with his fingers and tongue and constant need to have proof he was giving her a wonderful time.

Nobody could say she wasn't a brilliant performer. She deserved an Oscar for best actress in bed!

'Welcome home, Mrs Martino,' greeted the Swiss housekeeper.

'Thank you, Heidi, it's nice to be back,' replied Susan with a warm smile. 'This is Mr Santangelo. He will be staying with us for a few days. Kindly make up the bed in the blue guest room.'

Heidi nodded, and went off to do as she was bade.

'Guest room!' exclaimed Gino, pinching Susan on the ass. 'You gotta be kiddin'!'

'For show,' she said. 'The children will be here tomorrow.'

He grinned. 'Wassamatta? Don't they know mama gets it on?'

Her smile remained in position. 'Gino, dear,' she said briskly. 'Let us not create unnecessary problems. What we do is *our* business. I believe in setting an example in the home.'

He whacked her behind. 'Baby, when I'm in the home, we do what I say. Got it?'

Her lips tightened, but she didn't argue. For now, Gino was boss.

*

'I often fantasize about a man who is taller than me, richer than me, and smarter than me!' Lucky hiccoughed delicately. 'You know something, Dimi? I don't think he exists.'

Dimitri smiled and stroked her breasts. 'Perhaps you have found him,' he said mildly.

She chuckled. 'Well . . . you're sure as hell *older* than me. You are the oldest man I've ever been to bed with.'

'And the richest I presume.'

She reached across him for a cigarette. 'I guess.'

'And I am tall.'

'You sure are.'

'And smart. Extraordinarily so.'

'Except when it comes to Madam Fern.'

He frowned. 'We will not discuss Francesca.'

She sat up abruptly. 'Hey – I just had this great thought. You may – and this is only a thought, mind you – but you *may* be the perfect man!'

'I have been told that before,' he said modestly.

She climbed off the bed and walked across the room, naked. Dimitri admired the strong symmetrical lines of her long lean body. She reminded him of a young French movie star he had once had. The confidence of her aggressive youth aroused him. She was not like other young women, there was something different about her. She had a dangerous edge to her personality, a certain aura of strength and power. He found himself intrigued and certainly aroused by her. Even if she *was* the same age as his daughter, and usually a woman was not worth talking to – let alone bedding – until she was at least forty.

Lucky appeared to be the exception. She interested him in a new kind of way, *and* she managed to take his mind off Francesca – temporarily.

When he thought of Francesca he felt sweeping waves of rage. She had treated him inexcusably, and she would have to beg his forgiveness.

He knew her only too well. Francesca was a proud woman, and his indiscretion with Norma Valentine had deflated her ego. Now that he was aware of the enduring rivalry between the two actresses he could understand her fury. But there was no excuse for her dismissive rudeness. She would have to come crawling before he would even *dream* of taking her back. And she would. If he knew Francesca as well as he thought he did, she would.

Lucky selected a can of beer from her well stocked bedroom fridge, and strolled back toward the bed. She offered the can to him. 'Want some?'

He couldn't help being amused. 'Your tastes are very plebian.'

'My tastes suit me.' She grinned. 'For you it's the best Courvoissier. For me it's Coors!' With that she tipped the can, held a finger over the opening, and allowed a fine spray of liquid to cover his chest.

He was unamused. 'Lucky! Don't do that.'

Laughingly she straddled him. 'Why not, Dimi? Are *you* the only one allowed creative licence?' Slowly she twirled his nipples with the tips of her fingers. Then bent to lick the beer from them with quick flicks of her tongue. 'Sometimes,' she said wisely, 'the cheap stuff works just as well as the expensive crap.'

Chapter 18

And he was.

A smash.

They loved him at 'Foxie's'. Lennie had found a home.

Foxie offered him a three month contract with time off to do any television spots that came his way. He was not really into committing for what he considered to be a lengthy amount of time, but the new agent he had signed with seemed to think it was the way to go. The agent's name was Isaac Luther. He was young, had plenty of enthusiasm, and was a real pusher. The fact that he was black made Lennie think maybe he would try harder. He had done okay for Joey Firello – who had recommended him in the first place. Lennie liked Isaac's attitude. They both had the same long-term goal – stardom, big bucks, and hopefully creative control.

'Take the gig,' advised Isaac. 'Everyone gets by 'Foxie's' at least once a month. It's the place to be.'

So he signed, settled in, and found it to be one of the best career moves he had ever made. Foxie's was not just a place, Foxie's was a way of life. The people who crowded in night after night were the most interesting eccentric and exciting group Lennie had ever encountered. And they really liked what he did. The regulars especially, who never got tired of listening to the same old schtick, and were always on hand with encouragement and advice.

Foxie himself continually told Lennie what he thought. Do this. Do that. I like the Puerto Rican hooker bit. Drop the burglar routine. He had a sharp ear for dialogue, and a finely tuned sense of what would work and what wouldn't.

Any hecklers in the audience Foxie always dealt with personally, leaping up from his special table and showering them with abuse, or demanding that they be ejected by one of his two heavy-set bouncers.

'I never take no shit in my place,' he announced at least once a night. 'People come to Foxie's, they gotta behave like human bein's. I don't stand for no trash in here.'

Foxie was adored by the regulars. They traded insults and barbs, and once a week he took the microphone and gave them twenty-five minutes of his own particular brand of humour. He was like an old and feisty Don Rickles with flashes of Buddy Hackett and Charlie Callas.

At eight-five, his timing was still impeccable.

Rainbow was away – 'Visiting her sister in Arizona,' Foxie said in staccato tones. 'Do you know my Rainbow?'

Lennie explained the connection.

Foxie laughed, a sound rather like several short trumpet blasts. 'What a world! So you're Alice Golden's kid. *I* remember Alice the Swizzle.' A wily grin produced a spread of tobacco-stained teeth – all his own. 'I suppose she thinks I don't remember her. I *always* remember the good-'uns.'

The grin spread into a leer, and Lennie received alarming visuals of Alice and this pint-sized lech in bed together. He tried to be understanding, but come on, Alice, really! Was there no end to her escapades?

Just watching Foxie was an education in itself. And watching the resident strippers was another fascinating pastime. There were three of them. A glorious looking Mexican girl with blue-black hair down to her ass. A Swedish blonde with gravity-defying boobs. And an Oriental who performed with such delicate grace that stripper was hardly the word to describe her activities.

'My Rainbow trained every one of 'em,' Foxie boasted proudly. 'Knowin' how to take it off's a dyin' business. We're not sellin' pussy an' tits here, we're sellin' a *show*. You want pussy – go down the street to one of 'em porno places an' jerk off with the rest of the jerks. We're sellin' *art*.'

Lennie would hardly call it art. But he had to admit that whatever the girls did – they did it with style.

Now that he was settled, he telephoned Jess a couple of times, always connecting with the monosyllabic Wayland. On the third try he left his number and instructions for her to return his call. 'You'll remember to give her the message, won't you?'

'Sure, man,' replied Wayland. By the time he replaced the receiver he had forgotten.

He also called Eden again. Three times. On his first shot the same male voice picked up, so he didn't bother saying anything, just hung up. The second time the phone rang and rang. The third time an impersonal answering service asked him for his name and number. He passed. He had to talk to her direct.

Joey told him she had a new boyfriend.

So what? He didn't care. They were unfinished business, and she knew it as well as he did. It was only a matter of time before they would be together again.

*

There was always the routine to go through. Jess knew it by heart. Drive to the hospital, find a parking place, report to reception, take the elevator to the fourth floor. She could do it with her eyes closed. And sometimes, when she walked through the women's ward for the terminally ill, she wished her eyes *were* closed. Week after week the occupants of various beds changed. One down, another million to go. And the visiting relatives all with that same pained 'why am I here' expression – an expression Jess knew only too well.

She summoned a smile as she approached her mother. She

always took a little something – often only a new picture of the baby, but whatever it was her mother seemed grateful.

She sat beside the austere hospital bed for forty-five minutes every day. The doctors had told her it was only a matter of time. Sometimes time passed so slowly.

When she left she was usually soaked with sweat and shaking. Sometimes she had to sit in the parking lot and smoke a joint before she could even think straight.

On Saturday, at two o'clock precisely, she arrived for her visit. Reception tried to detain her, but she went to the fourth floor anyway.

Her mother's bed was empty, the sheets stripped off.

A black nurse put a kindly arm around her shoulder and said, 'We called you late yesterday afternoon, honey. Didn't you get the message?'

She knew she shouldn't be shocked and sad. She knew it was something she had been preparing to happen for months.

'No, I didn't get any message,' she mumbled, and her eyes filled with tears.

'Come outside,' said the nurse sympathetically. 'We keep some medicinal spirits for occasions like these.'

'No thank you,' she replied politely, fighting to control her tears. 'How can I make . . . arrangements?'

The nurse told her what to do, and she returned to reception, filled out various forms, made out a hefty cheque, and left.

She sat in her car and gazed blankly ahead. Was it possible that the hospital had phoned to report the death of her mother and Wayland had been so stoned he'd forgotten to tell her? She knew he was in bad shape, but this was unforgivable. If it wasn't for Simon she wouldn't even bother going home. Now her mother was dead, she would have to try and put her life in some kind of order. Carrying on in the same old way was impossible, she was not the kind of woman who could allow a man to continue using her so blatantly.

She sighed. If only Lennie were around. She should have

told him. If she had done so he would have stayed, not gone running off with some bug up his ass.

Damn Matt Traynor. It was all his fault.

*

To celebrate his first week at Foxie's, Lennie took a group out to dinner. He rounded up the Barbie twins, and Joey, and Isaac, and Isaac's pretty black wife, and the Swedish stripper with the great boobs. They partied all over town, and round about four in the morning he ended up in one of the twin's beds. Only he wasn't sure whether it was Suna or Shirlee, and these days it didn't really matter.

The next night he walked slowly into Foxie's, trying to take control of a monumental hangover. He felt like a ten ton truck had bulldozed his brain.

Foxie greeted him at the door with a slap on the back and a wicked grin. 'You'd better be hot tonight,' he snapped. 'Rainbow is back. An' if my Rainbow don't like you – you can be Bill Cosby and Carson rolled into one – but if she don't like you – *you're out*!'

Chapter 19

Dimitri flew out of Las Vegas in his Lear jet, and Lucky was relieved. She had no need of an involvement with a man old enough to be her father. A quick interlude was enough.

He sent her more baskets of sterling silver roses, an invitation to join him on his yacht, and a list of his phone numbers, across the world. She didn't miss him. But she did miss Gino who had said he would be back in two days, and now a week had passed.

Boogie arrived with his report on Susan. It was interesting, but contained nothing earthshaking. So she was hot stuff before she married Tiny. So what? It would probably arouse Gino's interest further instead of dampening his ardour. The Widow Perfect *never* screwed around while she was married to Tiny. Gino would love *that.* Just spent money, hosted parties, gave great charity, bought jewellery, and spent more money.

She had two offspring. Nathan, age nineteen, and Gemma, age twenty. There was no report on *their* activities. Lucky decided she needed one, and sent Boogie back for further investigation.

The only news she could use was the fact that dear old Susan was broke, and if something didn't happen soon, her Beverly Hills mansion would be snatched from right under her Beverly Hills ass. It *was* possible Gino was already paying the bills.

That's something she would have to find out, and soon.

*

The Martino children impressed Gino. They were so . . . upright. He had expected a few kinks here and there, it was only natural with teenagers. But these kids were perfect, just like their mother.

Nathan, at nineteen, was the youngest. He was of average height, with brownish hair, matching eyes, and a polite manner. He attended USC, and was studying law and philosophy. He was also on the football team, an excellent surfer, popular with the girls, and a straight A student.

Gemma, at twenty, had dropped out of college to pursue a career in interior design. She was an attractive girl with short honey coloured hair and a definite leaning towards anorexia. She was engaged to a boy she had been at school with.

Both children still lived at home.

'They like you,' Susan announced after the first family dinner.

'And I like them,' Gino replied, thinking – why couldn't Lucky and Dario have been like these two? Jeez! The troubles he'd had with his wild daughter and difficult son.

'It's not going to be easy for them to accept my getting married again,' Susan explained. 'So, if you don't mind, I think we should wait a few days before telling them. They'll get used to you in the meantime, and then it won't be quite such a blow.'

'Hey –' he objected. 'We *came* here to tell 'em.'

'And we will,' Susan soothed. 'But there's no rush, is there? Since the press don't appear to know about us, I would sooner wait. Just a few days.'

Waiting was no hardship. Susan treated him like a king, nothing was too much trouble. He luxuriated in all the home comforts she provided. Living in a hotel with room service twenty-four hours a day was one thing. But living with a woman who catered to his every need was another. He basked in her constant attention. And although he knew Lucky was waiting for his decision on Atlantic City, he did nothing about it. Hey – surely he had his priorities straight if he put business second – for once?

*

'Honestly, mother!' complained Nathan. 'The man is a low-life.'

'Yes,' agreed Gemma hotly. 'How could you bring him here? How *could* you?'

Susan gestured around her impeccable living room filled with objets d'art and expensive furniture. 'This is the way we live. And I intend to maintain our style of living . . . do you object to that?'

'But he's so crass and loud,' said Gemma.

'Well,' Susan replied calmly, 'your father was hardly quiet.'

'Daddy was a *star*!' steamed Gemma. 'I hope you're not comparing him to . . . to . . . Gino Santwhateverhis-nameis.'

'Hood,' said Nathan. 'That's what we'll call him.'

Susan flushed. 'You will not.'

'Hood.' Gemma tried the word slowly. 'Hmmm, not bad, brother.'

'*Mr* Santangelo is an American businessman,' Susan said sternly. 'He moves with the power makers. He dines with Presidents'.'

Gemma looked at Nathan. Nathan returned her stare. 'Hood,' they said in unison.

'Face it, mother,' Nathan added. 'Because it's the truth.'

*

When Gino had been away for ten days Lucky called. She had made up her mind she was not going to contact him, but the lawyers in New York were putting on the pressure. They insisted it was impossible to stall the involved parties any longer.

Furious, she placed a person-to-person call to Gino in LA. 'I think we've blown it,' she said flatly. 'The deal is off.'

He hardly missed a beat. 'Perhaps it's for the best,' he replied. 'At my age I don't know if it would've been the right move.'

Oh, Jesus! Suddenly Gino was *old* – and admitting it. What was the bitch doing to him – putting bromide in his coffee?

'I don't believe what you're saying. We always wanted this, it was our . . . our . . . dream,' she stammered.

'Yeh, kid, but dreams change. We'll talk about it when I get back.'

'When will that be?' she asked, holding her breath, trying not to explode with fury. *When, daddy, when?*

'Another day or two. Hang in there. We'll come up with another scheme – somethin' a little easier for an old man.'

She flung the receiver down with such force it smashed into two neat pieces. Old man indeed! This wasn't the Gino *she* knew.

What was she going to do? She was trapped in Las Vegas, trapped in a business partnership with her father who obviously had a case of galloping senility. She couldn't make a fucking move without him. She had been better off when he was in exile and *she* called all the shots. If he was going to go through with this marriage she wanted out.

That was a thought. And one that appealed.

Lucky Santangelo. On her own. With no one to answer to except herself.

She wondered how Gino would take the news. Especially

when she told him he would have to buy her out.

Christ! He would never do that. It would mean selling the Magiriano, and splitting the money down the middle. And there was a syndicate of investors to take care of, and no more freshly laundered cash coming in every week.

But . . . he would still have the Mirage, and all his holdings, companies, and other investments. It would hardly make any difference to him.

There was no way he would sell the Magiriano. And did she *really* want out?

Yes, she really did. There was no point in hanging around with Susan Martino in residence.

Besides, she was entitled to a life too. And a change of scene was exactly what she had in mind.

Chapter 20

Rainbow did not look old, fat *or* ugly, even though her eyes were crinkled around the edges, deep laugh lines etched their way down each side of her mouth, and her use of make-up was excessive. A ruined beauty, true. But a spectacular ruin, with a statuesque body, magnificent breasts, and a spread of pale red hair.

Lennie figured she had to be in her late fifties at least. She made him feel like a teenager as she looked him up and down with a practised eye and drawled, 'Foxie tells me you're a pretty hot tamale. Gonna prove it to me tonite?'

Oh, the times he could have proved it to her!

'I'll try,' he said, giving her the lopsided grin.

'If you're anything like your old man you'll never stop trying!'

So it was true! Jack Golden *had* indulged in the pleasures of Rainbow's fantasy-provoking flesh.

Fortunately she liked him. 'Lennie,' she told him magnanimously, 'you're about as funny as your daddy. In a different way, of course. Jack Golden had 'em splittin' their pants. But I guess it's a whole new world today, and you seem to capture what's goin' on well enough.' She swigged on a glass of brandy and milk – her favourite drink – then continued. 'Listen to Foxie – he *knows* what he's talkin' about. And in this business, knowledge is everythin'.' She tossed her mane of hair, still thick and lustrous. 'Me, I'm just an old broad who follows her gut instinct.'

He wished the old broad would quit with the low-cut dresses. Every time he saw her ample breasts his imagination ran riot. It wasn't easy beating down the early memories.

She did have a great act. Hadn't changed a thing in all the years. Same smile, hair, hooker shoes, and feather boas. Same sleight of hand that allowed you to see nothing while you thought you were seeing everything. Old fashioned illusion. The girls took it all off, but Rainbow – thank God – stuck to her old routine. A peek here. A peek there. Nothing dirty. She was a relic from another age, and the audience went wild.

'She does it once a week,' the Oriental stripper confided to Lennie. 'And they love her.'

'I can tell.'

'Sometimes, when Rainbow is on, they line up around the block to get in.'

He could believe it. Alice would be spitting blood if she knew Rainbow was still pulling them in. He phoned her on the off-chance that she might be wondering what was going on in his life.

She didn't ask what he was doing, where he was living, or anything of a personal nature. She merely said, 'Lennie, I have a twenty-five-year-old boy mad for my body. Should I let him?'

He took a deep breath, chose not to answer her question, and said, 'I'm working at Foxie's. Did you know your friend Rainbow is still taking it off?'

That stopped her in her tracks. 'What?' she said at last. 'At her age?'

'What age is she?'

'Better you shouldn't ask. Old enough to know she should have stopped doing that years ago.'

'They love her.'

'Who loves her?'

'The audience.'

'They used to love me,' Alice sighed wistfully. 'And certain people still do. Lennie, darling, tell me, is twenty-five cradle pinching?'

'Snatching.'

'Watch your language.'

'Foxie remembers you.'

A coquettish tone entered her voice. 'That old *bubkes*. He was crazy for me. He had a *schnickel* like a ten cent piece. Used to flash it at all the girls. But I never let him . . . *do* anything. You get what I'm saying, darling? *Never*.'

Which meant of course that she had screwed his brains out.

'I thought you might like to see the show one night,' he suggested. 'I could drive out to get you, and take you home later.'

'I hate freeways.'

'We don't have to go on the freeway.'

'I hate driving.'

'*I'll* drive.'

'You know what I mean. Besides, who wants to see Rainbow and Foxie? I never liked either of 'em.'

'Come *on*, she was your best friend. Besides, I was inviting you to see *me*.'

'You!' She laughed rudely. 'You, with your filthy language and dirty talk. Once was enough, thank you. If your father was alive he'd disown you.'

Disown him for what?

'Forget it,' he said shortly, hanging up.

Why did he bother? Alice Golden did not give a damn about anyone except herself.

*

Hardly anyone came to the funeral. A couple of her mother's canasta-playing friends; an elderly cousin who lived in Tahoe;

and three neighbours. Not a majestic turn out, but Jess did the best she could, and invited them all back to the house for Kentucky Fried Chicken, potato chips, and cheap red wine.

Wayland made a marvellous host. He greeted them with a casual wave, handed Jess the baby, then sat under a tree cleaning his fingernails and staring blankly at the sky.

Jess curbed her anger, entertained her guests, fed Simon, cleaned up, put Simon to sleep for the night, and headed for work. She had not requested time off. Who needed extra hours with Wayland for company?

Matt hit on her almost immediately. He sidled up to her empty blackjack table, sat himself down, and said, 'When is the most gorgeous chick in Vegas going to give me a second chance?'

'Go away,' she said hollowly.

'Are you still mad about the other night?'

'Get lost.'

'You should be *flattered* that I came onto you. What did you *think* we were going to do in my apartment – play tag?'

'I thought,' she said slowly, 'that we would have dinner and discuss why you fired Lennie Golden.'

'Firing your friend was not my idea. If you want to meet me later I'll tell you exactly what happened.'

'Sure, just like the last time.'

He smoothed back a lock of silver hair escaping from an invisible cage of hair spray, and tried to figure out what was so different about this one. Why did he want her so much? A lowly blackjack dealer – and short too.

'Jess,' he said sincerely. 'Trust me. I'll take you *out* to dinner. How's that?'

Even dinner with Matt was better than going home to Wayland.

Two would-be gamblers climbed on to stools and thrust money at her. Big spenders. One proffered a twenty, the other slid across three ten dollar bills. Automatically she stacked the chips and spun the neat piles in the right direction.

Matt stood up. 'Same time. The parking lot,' he said.

She nodded. She needed to talk. Like it or not, Matt Traynor would just have to listen.

*

'It's lovely,' Eden said.

'I told ya I'd get ya the right place,' Santino crowed, strutting around the marble terrace of the small empty house perched high on Blue Jay Way in the Hollywood Hills.

'I'll have to hire an interior designer,' she mused.

'Sure.' He puffed on a very large Cuban cigar. 'I gotta decorator broad owes me a favour.'

'It seems you have a lot of people who owe you favours.'

'It's the only way t'go.' He scattered ash on the ground.

Eden walked toward the gleaming blue pool, with the fountain at one end, and the two stone cupids at the other. 'I adore it!' she exclaimed.

Santino was pleased. The sooner he moved her in, the better. He wanted her under his control.

He took off his jacket and settled himself on a patio chair. This whole set-up was going to work out fine.

'Why doncha take a swim,' he suggested. 'Christen the joint.'

She looked at him. He was sweating. He was always sweating. Well anybody would sweat if they togged themselves out in a three piece suit every day.

She remembered the first time they went to bed. Under the suit he wore patterned boxer shorts, socks with suspenders, and a shoulder holster with an ominous looking gun nestled within. For one moment she had imagined he was a cop. A cop couldn't get her into the movies. She had almost dressed and left.

Her Swedish friend, Ulla, had told her that Santino Bonnatti had more money than brains. All her life Eden had been looking for a man with just such qualities. He would finance a movie for her to appear in. She would become a star. And then she would move on. In the meantime he was fortunate to have her.

'Go on, swim,' he urged.

She knew what he wanted and she didn't mind one bit.

His desire gave her power, and she liked the feeling.

With studied sensuality she peeled off her dress. There was nothing underneath except pure perfection. Some men considered her on the slender side. Santino liked her that way. His wife, she had found out, was a heavy woman.

She kept her shoes on, strappy white sandals which emphasized her blood-red toenails.

Santino stood up. 'Come here,' he said thickly. 'I just thought of another way to christen the joint.'

*

'There's someone from the Merv Griffin show out front,' one of the strippers confided just before Lennie went on.

He didn't drop dead with excitement. There was always *someone* in the audience. An agent, a talent scout, a producer. Once it was rumoured Burt Reynolds was sipping champagne at table number two. The Swedish stripper had been so unnerved by the rumour she ripped off her clothes five minutes before her grand finale.

Burt Reynolds turned out to be a look-alike fresh from a television contest. Miss Sweden was so furious she refused to talk to anyone for a week.

Lennie had been around long enough to know it didn't matter *who* was watching. When you went on you did your best. If your best wasn't good enough – fuck 'em.

He had some new material he wanted to try out. Some mother/son schtick, with Alice as the role model. Wouldn't *that* be a laugh if the Griffin Show saw him, liked him, and insisted he use the new stuff on their show. Alice would *love* that. She probably wouldn't even recognize herself, although he was painting a ruthlessly cruel but truthful picture.

He was restless after the show. Nobody came running backstage to tell him how great he was. Nobody from the Griffin Show materialized.

He had a drink at the bar and went home to the emptiness of his hotel room. It was after two in the morning, but fuck it, he needed her. Expecting the same male voice to pick up or the answering service, he dialled Eden's number.

She answered the phone herself. That strange, throaty voice, which sounded like she was recovering from terminal bronchitis. 'Hello.' A sleepy pause, then stronger, 'Hello.'

He waited for the curse words. As if on cue, she let forth a volley of obscenities.

He timed her perfectly. You didn't live with a woman for three years without knowing every move she made.

Just before she was about to slam the phone down, he spoke. Softly. Slowly.

'Eden. This is Lennie. Prepare yourself. I'm back in your life.'

Chapter 21

Olympia knew the moment her father walked into his New York apartment that she had made a mistake staying there. Why should she, Olympia Stanislopoulos, one of the richest young women in the world, feel like a lodger? She immediately called a friend of her mother's who dabbled in real estate and requested she find her an apartment tout suite.

'Yes,' the woman told her, 'I know the perfect place.'

'Show it to me at once,' Olympia said. She had decided New York was very much to her liking and she *should* have her own home there. Hotels were so boring, and staying at her father's again was definitely out. It was acceptable to share his plane, his yacht, even his private island when the need arose, but in New York it was surely time to buy her own place.

Dimitri immediately spotted the cigar burn on one of his precious antique tables. He roared with fury and summoned his butler. Olympia allowed the stupid man to take the blame. It constantly amazed her that her father was so into his possessions. He was aware of everything. If one book was out of place in any of his homes, he knew it.

Brigette greeted gran-pop, as she called him, with a vigorous hug and a kiss on the lips.

He picked the child up in his arms. 'How's my baby?' he sang.

'Very bad,' said Olympia ominously. 'She's been a *very bad* girl. She ruined mama's wedding.'

He ignored that piece of information and presented Brigette with several huge gift-wrapped boxes.

Olympia remembered when she was a child. Many presents. But gestures of affection were always reserved for his latest mistress. Perhaps he was mellowing. Or perhaps he liked Brigette better than he did his own daughter. She summoned Nanny Mabel and dispatched Brigette and the presents from the room.

'How was Las Vegas?' she asked dutifully. 'I hear it's a dreadful place full of terrible little people.'

Dimitri regarded her critically. She was looking plump. Why didn't the girl take care of herself?

'You are right,' he said. 'But I was merely honouring Francesca Fern, hardly sightseeing.'

'How *is* Francesca?' Olympia asked. She was always intrigued by his continuing infatuation with the horse-faced actress. Francesca was certainly lasting longer than any of the others.

'Very fine,' snapped Dimitri. He had no intention of discussing his personal life with his gossipy daughter. If Olympia knew it was over, she would make sure it hit every society column in the world. 'I saw an old friend of yours,' he added quickly, to get her off the scent.

'Who?'

'Lucky Santangelo.'

Lucky Santangelo. Ex best friend. Oh, the adventures they had shared! Once. A long time ago. Fifteen years to be exact. They probably wouldn't even recognize each other now. And they certainly would have nothing in common.

'Where did you see *her*?' Olympia sniffed.

'She owns the Magiriano Hotel.'

'Oh. Did her gangster father give it to her?'

'She built it herself while he was out of the country. She's a very clever business woman.'

Olympia was silent. *She built it herself.* Oh, really? With her own two hands. Was he trying to make *her* feel guilty because she had never done anything except inherit money and marry a series of cretinous fortune hunters?

'How does she look?' Olympia asked curiously.

Dimitri changed the subject, it wouldn't do for his daughter to have knowledge of his latest affair. 'Who notices such things?' he said dismissively. 'I wish to leave for the airport at noon tomorrow. Please do not be late.'

Olympia nodded vaguely as he left the room. She had no intention of leaving the next day, but she did plan to send Brigette and Nanny Mabel. The two of them were getting on her nerves, she needed a little time alone to recover from the trauma of her mother's wedding. Oh, the embarrassment of Brigette's outrageous behaviour. The child was becoming a monster.

Yes, she would pack them off with Dimitri at noon. He could keep an eye on them in Paris while she purchased an apartment in New York and thought of herself for once.

Lucky Santangelo a very clever business woman indeed! Ha! Olympia remembered her as a raggle taggle gypsy who couldn't even find a boyfriend. She, Olympia, had taught her about men and sex and clothes. And a fine lot of thanks she had received for her trouble. Not one word in fifteen years.

She remembered Lucky arriving at L'Evier, the boarding school they had both attended in Switzerland, a skinny dark haired kid who had registered under the name of Lucky Saint because no one was supposed to know who her father was.

As if anyone cared.

Gino Santangelo.

The first time Olympia set eyes on him from their window she had shuddered. He was so . . . sinister looking. Dark like Lucky. On the short side, but very, very sexy with thick curly hair, a strutting walk, and bad, black eyes. It was the first time she had noticed the appeal of an older man.

For a long time she had fantasized about him. Sometimes, when she indulged herself, she had imagined Gino was in the room with her, sucking on her tits, sticking it to her with absolutely no finesse but a hell of a lot of brutal energy.

She had never confided to Lucky that she harboured a wish to fuck her father. Lucky would not have appreciated the thought.

Olympia sighed and recalled the tlme Gino got himself engaged to Marabelle Blue, a famous blonde movie star. He had informed Lucky on the telephone, and she had crawled into bed sobbing. At the time Olympia was not supposed to know who she was. She did, of course. She had found out by skimming Lucky's diary two days after she arrived at school. Lucky was sobbing, and Olympia couldn't sleep, so she went to her friend and comforted her, softly at first, but the softness had turned into passion, and before long the two schoolgirls were entwined like lovers.

One night of warm wet sweetness. The next morning things were back to normal. Neither of them had ever mentioned it. It was as if their lovemaking had never taken place. Sometimes Olympia thought of it. Over the years there had been a few women. Not one of them came close to the night of illicit passion with her school friend . . .

'Mama!' Brigette entered her train of thought. 'Look!' The child thrust an expensive Cartier watch at her.

Olympia glanced at the watch. It must have cost over a thousand dollars. Why did Dimitri buy such presents for a nine year old?

'Don't want it,' Brigette whined. 'Want a Snoopy watch, mama. Want to go to Disneyland.'

'Yes, dear,' said Olympia, taking the watch and tossing it to one side. She would send the chauffeur out for a Snoopy watch and give it to Brigette just before the child departed the next day. This would circumvent a nasty scene, for Brigette would not be pleased when she discovered Olympia had no plans to accompany her.

Chapter 22

Now Lucky found it was just a question of waiting for Gino to return so she could tell him she was moving on. The only problem was that he seemed to have no intention of doing so.

She steamed in the Las Vegas heat while the days passed slowly, and the nights even more so. Eventually she could stand it no longer. Atlantic City was over . . . play the game or leave the field . . . she had been *forced* to leave the field.

Angrily she collected some of her favourite books, a tape machine, and a stack of soul tapes. Then she got on a plane to Palm Springs, and holed up in the Canyon Club Hotel where she was given her own house and pool, and complete privacy. 'Call me the instant Gino returns,' were her instructions.

The solitude was strangely welcome. She lay out by the pool all day with Bobby Womack and Teddy Pendergrass and Marvin Gaye for company. And at night she settled into bed with Mario Puzo, Joseph Wambaugh, and early Harold Robbins (always a kick to reread *A Stone for Danny Fisher* and *The Adventurers*). She turned off completely. Ordered only healthy foods. Did not smoke or drink. Wore no makeup. And treated her bronzed body to a morning spa, half an hour of vigorous exercise, and an evening sauna.

She was never lonely. She had learned at an early age to be satisfied with her own company. And although sometimes she thought about how pleasant it might be to have a sister or a brother – she could still remember the closeness she and Dario had shared as children – it was okay. She was content.

Waiting seemed interminable. But waiting *her* way was certainly more tolerable. Somehow she revelled in the peace and the quiet and the aloneness, because soon she knew everything would change. Soon she would be starting over.

*

'I gotta get back,' Gino said often.

'Why?' Susan would reply. 'You have people to run everything for you. Surely it is more pleasant to stay here with me?'

He had to admit it was. But he was beginning to feel guilty about Lucky. He knew she was angry at him, therefore he didn't even bother to call, reasoning that he would be better off to deal with her face to face.

Life in Beverly Hills was like one long vacation. Living in Susan's house he found a freedom from responsibilities. For once the phone wasn't always ringing, people weren't bothering him with minor problems, he could relax and do what he wanted.

Long ago he had surrounded himself with the best lawyers, accountants and executives money could buy. It was called taking care of business without actually having to do anything. He had learned that lesson while marooned in Israel for seven years. Delegate, but never lose touch. Besides, while he was away, Lucky would watch over everything. The kid was as smart as any man. He felt sorry about disappointing her on Atlantic City – but if he was going to get married, becoming involved in major new projects was out. For the time being anyway.

Lucky would understand. She would have to.

Susan had still not mentioned that they were planning to marry to her children.

'C'mon,' Gino complained. 'Get it over with. Can'tcha see they love me!'

She told them over dinner at Chasen's with Gino present. The two of them made polite noises and kicked each other under the table.

'Y'see,' Gino said later, 'they think it's fine. Now I gotta get back to Vegas, tie up a few things. We'll leave tomorrow.'

'*I* can't leave,' Susan said quickly.

'Why not?'

She lowered her eyes. 'It's just not possible. When Tiny passed away . . .' She paused. '. . . I didn't really want to mention this to you, but he left what my lawyers are beginning to call a financial nightmare . . . It's something I have to try and deal with myself, and since we've been together I haven't paid any attention to sordid business matters. If you return to Las Vegas, then I –'

He interrupted her, slamming his forehead with the palm of his hand. 'Jeez! Why didn't you *tell* me? Christ! We're together, aren't we? We're gonna get married for crissake. I should have asked you if everything was alright.'

'It's not your problem, Gino,' she said firmly. 'Although I do appreciate your concern.'

'Listen. From now on *your* problems are *my* problems. I'll fly back tomorrow an' send one of my best accountants to LA to meet with your lawyers. He'll get a handle on the situation, and then I'll put everything straight. How does that grab you?

'You don't have to,' she said, immediately agreeing.

He caught her in a tight hug. 'Sure I have to. And next weekend you'll fly to Vegas an' we'll be together.'

She had never thought it would be so easy. For a moment she tensed, not prepared for another of his vigorous lovemaking sessions. Then she relaxed, and endured his suffocating embrace. After they were married he would not get within ten feet of her.

His hands began to reach for her breasts. 'You're a sexy broad,' he said, laughing. 'Y'know that, don'tcha? You know that, Susie? You're one helluva gorgeous sexy broad!'

Inwardly she shuddered.

Outwardly she succumbed.

His rough touch did nothing for her. She couldn't wait until he left.

*

'Thank God the hood has gone!' announced Gemma, just minutes after Gino departed for the airport. The three of them sat in the breakfast room picking at their food.

'Thank God is right,' emphasized Nathan. 'Mother, surely you're not serious about *marrying* that gangster?'

'Don't speak like that about Gino,' snapped Susan. 'And kindly accept the fact that now your father is gone I have to make a life for myself.'

'Yes, but not with the hood,' complained Gemma, crunching a piece of crispbread.

'Certainly not,' agreed Nathan, downing his orange juice.

Susan sighed. She had raised two tight-assed WASP snobs. Tiny would be horrified.

But of course, secretly, she agreed with them. It was ludicrous that she was being forced to commit matrimony with a man like Gino Santangelo. Why hadn't Tiny taken care of his business affairs? Why hadn't he looked to the future? Thoughtless man.

She pulled her silk peignoir tightly across her breasts and eyed her two offspring. Gemma, so skinny and snippy looking. Hardly a beauty, but passable. And Nathan, a Californian boy with floppy hair and a surfer's body.

If she didn't have the two of them to support . . . And they expected every comfort. Children raised in Beverly Hills were different from the rest. Delicately she sipped her lemon tea. Thank God Gino had left, at least he would not be bothering her for a while. She had no intention of returning to Las Vegas at the weekend. There was a wedding to plan, and it would be a magnificent affair. At least she owed herself that.

If Gino wished to see her, *he* could return to Beverly Hills.

She hoped he wouldn't.

She knew he would.

*

Lucky received the message out by the pool. Gino was back.

She packed and was at the airport within an hour.

A confrontation was long overdue.

Chapter 23

They were to meet on the corner of La Brea and Sunset at 'Tiny Naylors' – a drive-in restaurant. Lennie got there first, and sat in his rented car wondering anxiously if she would turn up. It was two-thirty in the morning, hardly time for a reunion. But when he had blurted 'I've got to see you,' over the phone, Eden had replied, 'I'm busy tomorrow, but if you like I'll meet you now.'

An uncharacteristic gesture. He had expected her to scream because he was calling so late. Instead she had been surprisingly receptive, and now he sat waiting for her knowing it would be a typical Eden move for her to get him out, and then not turn up at all.

He lit a cigarette and ordered a burrito and a coke from a tired waitress. Two hookers in matching purple hot pants and open-weave tops sauntered by.

'Wanna fuck or sumpin'?' demanded one, too exhausted from her night's activity to suspect he might be a cop.

'Not tonight, ladies,' he replied civilly. Although that was a lie. He wanted to fuck Eden.

'Why not?' demanded the other hooker, a plump Mexican with a gold front tooth. 'I give you a preview, honey. You shit your pants.' She raised her open-weave top and flashed two globules of golden flesh at him.

He nodded approvingly and repeated, 'Not tonight, ladies.'

'Fag!' spat the Mexican.

'Shithead!' said the other one.

They spotted a motorcycle with two greasers astride, and went on their way.

The waitress brought his burrito and coke. He wolfed it, then glanced at his watch. She had said twenty minutes. Half an hour had passed. How long was he going to wait?

The hookers were doing business. The plump Mexican

linked arms with one of the greasers and they vanished into the shadows. The other one leaned across the handlebars of the bike and whispered promises to the rider.

Eden wasn't going to come. Why should she? She hated him. She had told him so that last night in New York.

'You're a loser,' she had said. 'A nothing, a lousy lay.'

Eden had a way with words.

But he wasn't exactly blameless when it came to name-calling. He had called her everything from a stupid cunt, to a talentless dumb bitch.

They had not parted on the best of terms.

And yet . . .

He could remember the good times.

When Eden wanted, she could be the sweetest female in the world. She could make a man feel like a king, top of the whole fucking heap. In the three years they were together, the good times outweighed the bad. And the sex was great. Eden with her thin body, long silky hair, heart-shaped face, and sly topaz eyes.

She was a killer. She had an exotic beauty that he just couldn't get enough of.

As if on cue, her pale pink Thunderbird slid into the slot beside him. She lowered her window and smiled. Her eyes were obscured by Jacqueline Onassis sunglasses, and her hair hidden beneath a silk scarf. 'Hello, Lennie,' she drawled in her best Lauren Bacall husky voice. 'I bet you thought I wasn't coming.'

•

Matt Traynor did not behave like a perfect gentleman. He met Jess in the parking lot as arranged. He took her to a Polynesian restaurant for dinner. He plied her with Scorpions and Navy grogs until she could hardly walk. And then he took her back to his apartment and tried to screw her.

She did not object.

She did not know.

As soon as they arrived she passed out on his couch. He lifted her skirt, pulled down her panties, and was just about to force himself aboard when his conscience got the better of him. What the hell was he *doing*?

Frantically, he went into action, pulling her panties back up and re-arranging her skirt. He felt like the world's worst heel. Groaning to himself, he poured a straight bourbon, and hoped to God she never realized he had almost committed a dirty act. Then he threw a leopard skin rug over her and nervously paced the apartment.

She stayed unconscious until five-thirty in the morning, when she woke, swore loudly, demanded his car keys, and rushed off into the early morning light with a parting, 'I'll leave your keys under the front seat.'

He was destroyed. He had expected, even quite looked forward to the Doris Day/Rock Hudson scene.

Doris (distraught): 'Oh dear! What happened? Tell me *now*. Did we . . . do anything?'

Rock (with a manly knowing smile): 'Did we do what?'

Doris: 'Don't torment me. You know what I mean.'

Rock (reassuringly): 'Of course not. What kind of a man do you take me for?'

Doris (relieved and grateful): 'You're *my* kind of man.'

Fade out.

Now she was gone. And she hadn't even asked. Didn't she care?

He entered his stainless steel kitchen and fixed instant coffee. His back hurt. All that bending over. His eyes ached. All that tension.

He wondered if she would ever talk to him again.

*

'I knew you'd come,' Lennie said, although he hadn't known at all. He got out of his car and climbed into the passenger seat of the Thunderbird. Eden was wearing a skimpy sun-dress, and high-heeled sandals. He reached over and took off her sunglasses. She wasn't wearing make-up but she still looked great.

'Hey,' he reached over and touched her hair beneath the scarf, 'Good t'see you.'

She stared at him long and hard. 'Hello, Lennie. You're a surprise, but a nice one.'

She knew how to push his buttons, she always had.

'I thought we might drive to the beach,' she suggested, 'and you can tell me what you're doing out here.'

Well Eden, I came to the coast so that I could make love to you again. The hell with my career.

'Good idea. Shall I drive?' He hoped he sounded casual.

She nodded.

He got out of the car while Eden slid over.

The Mexican hooker was returning from the shadows with a triumphant leer. 'Change your mind, cutie?' she yelled. 'I can take us both to Paradise for twenny bucks.'

He ignored her and got behind the wheel.

Eden moved close to him. 'I missed you, Big Man,' she murmured softly, placing her hand on his thigh.

He developed an erection that wouldn't quit.

They roared down Sunset, made Brentwood in eight minutes, the Palisades in twelve, and within twenty, they were cruising along the Pacific Coast Highway, searching for a suitable place to park.

She had been doing all the talking, telling him about her acting roles. 'I never stop working,' she confided. 'I guess I'm a better actress than you thought.'

He didn't want to get into *that*.

They parked on a bluff, and made their way to the beach. It was a beautiful night. The moon was bright and the ocean at peace. They walked along the seashore, holding hands like new lovers, and splashing in the surf. Then, they fell on the sand like old lovers, and found every secret place with ferocious familiarity.

She wrapped her long legs around his neck and rocked with his rhythm as though she never wanted it to end.

He gave her what she wanted, what *he* wanted. Slowly. Fast. Very fast. Then slowly again, keeping his control by reciting the goddamn alphabet in his head, because he didn't want to come, didn't want it to end, wanted their lovemaking to go on forever.

'You . . . always . . . were . . . the . . . best,' she said huskily. 'Jesus . . . Lennie . . . My . . . big . . . man . . .'

He felt her spasms and let rip while she moaned with untamed pleasure. When they were finished he stroked her silky hair, and said, very quietly, 'We belong together. You do know that, don't you?'

She didn't answer. The only sound was the sea lapping gently on the shore.

*

Jess raced Matt's ridiculous car to the hotel. She dumped it in the parking lot and leaped into her Camaro. Then she drove home in record time.

She could hear Simon crying as she parked. Her head throbbed. Too many fancy drinks, but getting plastered had taken her mind off the funeral, and that was something. The house looked disgusting. Wayland had obviously entertained again. Dirty cans and bottles, the lingering heavy stench of marijuana, empty McDonald's wrappers. And an unfamiliar male body asleep on the floor.

'Goddamnit!' she yelled, kicking at the sleeping form, who groaned and rolled over.

In the bedroom Wayland sprawled on the bed fully dressed. Simon cried in his crib. There was the smell of urine and worse. She scooped him up and changed his filthy diaper. Wayland did not stir. Wearily, she took Simon into the kitchen and fixed him a bottle. The crying was driving her nuts. The mess was driving her nuts. She shoved the bottle into Simon's mouth and enjoyed peace.

This week she would tell Wayland to get out.

Chapter 24

'I don't give a fuck what you want to do!' screamed Gino.

'And I don't give a fuck what *you* think!' screamed Lucky.

They had been yelling at each other for an hour. One long

hour of insults, recriminations and accusations. The harmony of their past year together had vanished, and it was back to the antagonism and ill-will of former times.

'You don't run my life,' Lucky stormed. 'I'm not your sweet little girl who has to do what daddy says. And I don't *work* for you either.' She paused to catch her breath and glare at him. He wanted it all his own way. He wanted to marry Susan *and* keep daughter dear at his fingertips, some kind of surrogate boss who would take care of business while he pissed off to Beverly Hills.

Well, daughter dear was not standing for it. No way. No fucking way. Daughter dear was getting out.

'We're partners,' she said coldly. 'Half the Magiriano is mine – and I'm cashing in and going on to do other things. So we either sell, or you buy me out. Which is it to be?'

He had to admit the kid had balls. Mad as he was, he could still admire her. She was a pain in the butt, but street smart and savvy and tough. One of life's natural winners.

'Hey,' he threw his arms wide. 'You want out, you got it. What're we fightin' over? I'm not gonna hold you back if you wanna do other things. I'll buy out your share. But you gotta remember, everythin' I own is gonna be yours one day anyway.'

Who was he kidding? If he married Susan Martino, everything he had would be Susan's.

'That's settled then,' she said evenly, weary from the argument.

'Yeh. An' if you're so sure it's what you want, I'll put it in motion right away,' he said, gruffly.

It's not what I want, it's what you want.

'There's one other thing,' she said.

'What?'

'The house in East Hampton,' she blurted. 'I'd like to own it.'

'Huh?' He stared at her, hard black eyes head-on with hard black eyes. 'Why?'

'Because I don't want you taking another woman there. It was mommy's house when we were all a family. It's the only real home I've ever known, and I want to have it.'

He was angry again. First she wanted to sell the hotel, then she wanted him to give her the East Hampton house. What kind of shit *was* this?

'Okay, okay, it's yours,' he said grudgingly.

She was very businesslike, aware of the fact that to protect herself, once he married Susan, she had to be. 'I'll have a real estate agent put a price on it and I'll buy it from you. The money can come out of my share of the hotel.'

He shook his head as if he couldn't quite believe what was happening. 'Lucky,' he asked softly, 'why are we acting like a couple who's just gettin' a divorce! Before you know it we'll only be communicatin' through lawyers.'

'Talking of lawyers,' she said crisply, 'I'm sure you've thought of asking Susan to sign a pre-nuptial agreement.'

'What kind of smart ass remark is that?' he shouted. 'Jeez! You're somethin', you really are. You hardly even know Susan, an' now you got her walkin' off with all my money.'

'I'm just behaving the way you taught me. This *is* California, and there are such things as community property laws.'

'Jesus Christ!' he spat in disgust.

Quietly she left the room. She had pushed about as far as she could go.

*

Susan Martino, Gino discovered via the accountant he sent to LA, was several hundred thousand in the hole.

He spoke to her on the phone. 'How didja ever get in such a mess?' he demanded.

'Don't you mean how did *Tiny* get me into such a mess?' she replied logically.

'I'll take care of it.' He was not exactly delighted, but it had to be done.

'I told you before, you don't have to,' she reminded.

'Call it a weddin' present,' he offered magnanimously.

'Thank you.' Her tone was appreciative, but not overly so.

He admired the lady-like quality she brought to everything. She really was a class act. 'You missing me yet?'

'Yes. But I have the wedding to plan, and it's keeping me extraordinarily busy.'

'What's to plan? You'll hop on a plane an' we'll do it here. No big deal.' He paused to light a cigar, in spite of the fact that after the heart attack his doctor had insisted he quit.

'Hey – why don't we do it this weekend? Get it over an' done with.'

She laughed pleasantly. 'You *are* joking, aren't you? My God, Gino, get it over and done with – you make it sound so trivial.'

'You got other plans?'

'I most certainly do. A wedding is a sacred occasion. Surely you want to do it properly?'

'We can do it properly in Vegas.'

'Not at all,' she chided. 'We must be married in Beverly Hills. I have so many friends here. It will be a joyous day – one to remember.'

'*My* friends are *here*,' he pointed out. 'An' we'll be livin' here. I didn't want to tell you on the phone, but Lucky's leaving.'

'She is?'

'Yeh. Gave me a whole speech about gettin' out an' movin' to New York. I gotta tell you, Susie, I'm sick about it.'

He might be sick, but *she* was ecstatic. She had never thought it would be so easy to get rid of the pushy daughter.

'I'm sure it will be for the best, Gino, dear,' she said comfortingly.

'You think so?'

'Oh, yes.'

Susan did not tell him her plans for the weekend were to stay in LA. She hung up with promises of love, and then she phoned her lawyers to find out when all the debts would be cleared. Obviously, Gino Santangelo had been an excellent choice. Old, rich and pliable. Over-sexed for a man of his age, but she could put up with that for a while longer.

Putting up with men. The story of her life. From the age of fifteen, when she was deflowered by a swashbuckling movie star of the fifties while her hairdresser mother sat downstairs swigging vodka, to now, and Gino.

Putting up with men. A series of rich, important men. While mother reaped the benefits of a pretty teenage daughter. No money ever actually changed hands, but something was always going on. A new white Cadillac for mother to drive. Three televisions. Plenty of clothes. Hampers of food. Crates of champagne.

Susan felt revulsion whenever a man touched her.

Go upstairs with Mr Whoever, Susan, he wants to show you something.

One wealthy man after another, until it became a way of life, and she played the game automatically, because *somebody* had to supply mother with life's little luxuries and perpetual booze.

When she was twenty, her mother ran a light at Sunset and Fairfax, and was killed instantly in a collision with a gardener's truck. The Mexican driver sued. Naturally Susan found someone to settle the case for her. Six months later she was smart enough to discover Tiny while doing extra work on one of his movies. He didn't stand a chance. She knew what she wanted, and she went for it with controlled dedication. He divorced his first wife with nary a protest, married Susan, and together they rose in the hierarchy of the Hollywood social scene. She became a perfect hostess, warm confidante, and mother of his two children.

After a few years Tiny screwed anything that breathed in his direction – it wasn't easy being married to one of the Queens of the Beverly Hills/Bel Air social set.

After a few years, Susan met a beefy Russian masseuse named Gloria, who came to the house to ease her neck tension. It turned out Gloria knew plenty of other places where tension could be eased, and Susan succumbed. She had succumbed a few other times. But for the last three years she had been having a very satisfying affair with a producer's wife named Paige Wheeler. The women enjoyed discreet liaisons at various venues including each other's homes when they could get rid of the servants. Unfortunately, Paige's husband, Ryder, had recently given birth to a huge hit movie, which meant Paige's time was taken up with a solid block of unavoidable social engagements. Plus the fact that she also dabbled in interior design. And of course, Susan had been busy in Vegas snaring Gino. The two women hadn't seen each other in months.

Susan's hand hovered over the phone. She deserved a treat. One little treat.

•

The morning after her confrontation with Gino, Lucky awoke sick to her stomach. She threw up, felt only slightly better, and crawled back to bed. This was not the right time to get sick. There was so much to do. She had to start packing, meet with her lawyers and get everything in order.

For a moment she wondered if she was doing the right thing. But in her heart she knew that if Gino married Susan she would be better off away from them. Maybe Susan *was* a wonderful human being. Maybe she *did* love Gino for himself.

Maybe . . .

On impulse she grabbed the phone and called Costa Zennocotti in Miami. He had retired there a year ago, and by all accounts was very happy to live the quiet life after forty years as Gino's lawyer and best friend. He was her friend too. After all, it was Costa who had nurtured her ambition, and taught her everything about business while Gino languished in Israel.

'Uncle Costa,' she greeted warmly when he picked up the phone. 'How are you?'

'I am currently mastering the art of French toast,' he replied, happy to hear from her. 'At my advanced age I have finally decided I should cook.'

She laughed happily. It was so good to speak to him. 'I thought you had droves of women around you who did that sort of thing,' she joked. She knew he was seeing a divorcee who apparently had caused him to gain fifteen pounds.

'Yes, yes,' he said quickly. 'But you know me, I hate to be dependent on anyone.'

Indeed she did know him. Uncle Costa. A quiet, well-mannered man. Married for over thirty years to Auntie Jen who had passed away several years ago. One of those rare marriages where both partners grow together and remain content and in love. No screwing around for Uncle Costa. He had been the perfect husband.

'When did you last hear from Gino?' she asked.

'Not recently. Why? Is something the matter?'

'Oh, this and that. Nothing earth-shattering. I think I might be selling my share of the Magiriano.'

'Nothing earth-shattering she says! *That's* earth-shattering. What's the matter, Lucky?'

'Can I fly in and see you? I need to talk.'

'When?'

'In a few days.'

'Any time, my dear. You know I'm always here for you.'

Yeh. Uncle Costa was always reliable. But what about Gino?

'I'll call you again.'

'Make it soon.'

'Yes, I will.'

She hung up and thought that yes, it would be a nice idea to visit with Uncle Costa. Every time he talked she managed to find out a little bit more about Gino's colourful past. Costa loved to reminisce and she loved to listen. Her mother, Maria, had been Uncle Costa's niece. And it was rumoured that her grandmother, Maria's mother, had also been involved with Gino.

She shivered. Costa would never talk about *that*.

Feeling slightly better, she got up, dressed, and ventured downstairs. The casino was a hive of activity with early morning gamblers out in full force. She bumped into Matt who looked uncharacteristically harassed. She would have to call a meeting to let her key people know she was moving on. They all considered Gino their real boss anyway. She hadn't allowed that thought to surface before, but now she realized it was true.

You'll be out on your own, kid, for the first time in your life, she thought.

It was exciting.

It was very exciting.

She grinned. And suddenly she felt *much* better. Maybe she'd go for Atlantic City anyway. Without Gino. Find another property, new investors. Hey – she could do it. She *knew* she could do it – she just had to convince everyone else.

Chapter 25

Lennie slept like he hadn't slept in a long time. One of those great dreamless sleeps where you feel cocooned by clouds and so comfortable and at peace you never want to wake up. But he did. And it was noon.

He leaped from bed, and threw himself under a hot shower where he sang 'Staying Alive' at full volume.

In the bathroom mirror he observed the scars of battle. Eden and her lethal nails. His back looked like a road map criss-crossed with thin red trails.

So what? He had her again. What were a few scars between friends?

For a moment he stopped to think. They hadn't really talked, just enjoyed great sex and each other's bodies. She was as hungry for him as he was for her. On the drive back she had fallen asleep curled up against him. He had driven to his car and suggested he follow her home. 'No,' she had said. 'I've got an early call.'

So he had watched her drive off into the dawn, for it was five in the morning when they parted company.

Now, all he had to do was get through the day without her. It occurred to him that he should have found out where she was working and met her for lunch. Come to think of it, he should have found out a lot of things, he didn't even know where she lived, all he had was her phone number.

Tonight he wanted her to accompany him to Foxie's. He would sit her at a front table, and let her get a load of the feedback he was receiving from the audience. She had always criticized his work. Once she saw him in action in LA she would realize how wrong she had been.

It was just so right that they were back together. Sure, they had their fights, but who didn't? He and Eden were an unbeatable combination.

An inner voice mocked – *Who are you kiddin,' Lennie Golden? She eats you up and spits you out. You and Eden together – forget it.*

He ignored the subliminal warning.

*

Eden had lied. Which she did a lot. Beautifully. There was no early call. The first item on her agenda was a one o'clock meeting with the interior designer who owed Santino Bonnatti a favour.

She rose late, luxuriated in a scented bath, dressed slowly, and arrived at the house on Blue Jay Way fifteen minutes late for her appointment. Punctuality was not one of her priorities.

The decorator was a woman, which annoyed her. She loathed dealing with women. They either hated her because of her beauty, or fawned over her because she was once one of the top photo models in America, before she gave it all up for her acting.

This woman was different. She was short, in her forties, with a mass of copper coloured frizzy hair, and a skirt split up to her crotch. She was also businesslike, with a gay assistant, a drawing board, and a lot of sketches and ideas. Her name was Paige Wheeler. Idly Eden wondered what favour she owed Santino, but she wasn't about to ask.

'I want a lot of white,' she said vaguely. 'White couches and rugs and everything modern and clean cut, with plentv of mirrors. I like chrome too . . . I want the place to look glamorous.'

Paige nodded, made notes, showed her swatches of material, and suggested certain ideas.

Eden agreed with most things. She was just as anxious to leave her apartment as Santino was to install her in the house. As long as the place looked sensational in *People* and *Us* layouts, what did she care? It would probably only be home for a short while anyway, because when stardom hit she was moving on. She had no intention of sleeping with Santino Bonnatti for the rest of her life. Just as long as it took.

For a moment she thought of Lennie and their lovemaking. Oh, Lennie . . . he certainly hadn't lost his touch. The guy was a great lay. A *really* great lay. And she should know . . . many men had made the trip to heaven and left without credentials.

It was a pity he was a loser. Always had been, always would be. Working at some dump on Hollywood Boulevard. Didn't he know Hollywood Boulevard was out of *town* for crissakes? Nowhere city. Just like all the nothing gigs he had played in New York.

Nobody could say she hadn't given Lennie a chance. Three years' worth of a chance. But in the sex stakes he was still something, and after Santino's ape-like attentions she needed a respite. So. She was glad he'd called. Glad she'd seen him. Just hoped that he'd go away quietly.

'Peach wallpaper will look most effective in the bedroom,' Paige said briskly. 'Perhaps we could incorporate it into the total concept.'

'Hmmm . . .' Eden agreed. 'And I'd like a fur bedspread. Something wild and sexy . . . Something . . . movie-starish.'

'I know exactly what you mean,' nodded Paige, exchanging an amused glance with her assistant.

'Good,' said Eden. 'Are we finished?' She had an appointment to have her nails done, and she was already twenty minutes late.

*

There was no getting rid of Matt Traynor. There he was again, hanging around her table, asking her how she felt, asking her out again. Jess couldn't stand him, and yet . . . at least he was there, and in his own peculiar way he seemed to care.

'I guess I made an idiot of myself last night,' she mumbled.

She didn't know! Relief rushed through him. He had another chance. 'Not at all. You told me about your mother. It did you good getting drunk.'

'Anything would do me good lately.'

'Let's do it again tonight.'

'What, get drunk?'

'Just talk.'

She had decided to tell Wayland to go. Why didn't she delay it just one more night until she felt more able to deal with it? Maybe she should ask Matt's advice. There were always legalities involved in things like this. Getting Wayland out might not be as easy as she had assumed.

'Okay,' she said, surprising both of them. 'As long as it's not dinner for two at Chez Traynor.'

*

At three o'clock Lennie was paged beside the Chateau Marmont pool where he was working on a suntan. Well, not exactly paged Beverly Hills Hotel style, more like the pool-side phone ringing and a pony-tailed blonde yelling, 'Anybody named Golden here?'

He thought it was Eden and jumped.

It was not Eden. It was a researcher from the Merv Griffin Show who said one of the producers had seen him at Foxie's the previous night, and that they had a spot open in three days' time, and if he wanted it, it was his.

If he wanted it. Did Barbara Walters give Special? Was Clint Eastwood Dirty Harry? If he wanted it. Ha!

'Yes,' he said, 'I think that fits into my schedule.' And he gave them his agent's number.

Eden was going to love this. She would come with him to

the taping, hold his hand, maybe slide to her knees in the dressing room and give him a little bit of her special luck. At last he was on a roll.

Frantically he started thinking about what he could and could not use. Television was different from playing clubs. Television demanded great visuals, clean material, no bad language, and fresh original routines. Not that all his routines weren't fresh and original. He wrote his own material, nobody fucked with what Lennie Golden wanted to say.

He didn't know whether to work on his suntan or hurry to his room. Eden had said he looked pale. 'Like a New Yorker,' she had husked.

So what was wrong with looking like a New Yorker?

Fuck it. He hurried inside. There was work to do.

*

'You went out last night,' said Santino softly.

'I did not,' lied Eden indignantly. She had no intention of answering to Santino. 'I watched television all night, and it was extremely boring.'

His voice was a cobra's whisper. 'Where did you go?'

'Nowhere. I told you. I –'

His slap jerked her head back and left the red angry imprint of his hand on her face.

She was shocked and stunned. 'How dare y –' she began.

A second slap stopped her. 'Never lie to me, Eden,' he said mildly. 'Never. This time I'm gonna overlook it, but believe me – don't you *ever* do it again.'

Santino strode from her apartment muttering to himself.

Blackie said, 'Everything all right, boss?' as they rode down in the elevator.

Santino did not bother to reply. He spoke when he wanted to speak, and only then.

He flexed his knuckles, and studied the pointed toes of his hand-made Italian shoes.

Women. Teach 'em up front who ran the show. The same applied to the people he employed.

Demonstrate strength and there would be no revolution.

*

Matt took Jess to an Italian restaurant. She found she was ravenous and ate her way through a pasta salad, a veal cutlet with a side order of spaghetti and clams, and a healthy piece of raspberry cheesecake. Tension and worry always affected her appetite, and she went on great eating binges.

She patted her lips with a napkin, stared piercingly at Matt, causing him to nearly choke on his salad, and said, 'So go ahead, shoot.'

'I thought you were a vegetarian,' he stuttered, groping for something to say.

'Sometimes,' she replied vaguely, and reached for her wine glass. It was empty.

He ordered another bottle, wondering if tonight was to be a repeat performance, and regretted the fact that they were not dining at the Magiriano where he could have signed the cheque. But who knew the non-drinking vegetarian would change course with such a vengeance?

'Come on,' she persisted. 'Tell me about Lennie. It's time you opened up. If *you* didn't want to fire him, who did?'

He decided there was no harm in the truth. And there was also no reason why *he* should take the blame. He owed her something – he would give her information. Perhaps she would be grateful enough to consummate their relationship properly.

'Lucky Santangelo wanted him out,' he said smoothly. 'Don't ask me why, because I don't know. She rousted me out of bed at two in the morning to fire him.'

'Lucky Santangelo,' Jess repeated slowly. 'Why would *she* want to fire Lennie? I hear he opened great.' She frowned. 'I didn't think she even got involved in things like that. I don't understand.'

'Nor do I. I'll tell you this though – I have all the clout in the world, but honey, if either of the Santangelos want something, I jump, just like everyone else.' He toyed with one of his gold chains. Why was he telling her all this?

He should be building himself up, not putting himself down.

Jess's mind was racing. Lucky Santangelo. The Lady Boss as she was known. What possible reason could *she* have to dump Lennie?

'Now you know the story,' Matt continued. 'And I don't think I have to tell you that it's strictly confidential.'

'What do you think I'm going to do – put an ad in the trades?'

He shrugged. 'I just don't want to be quoted on it, that's all.'

She nodded. Why hadn't Lennie called? She really missed him. And she needed him. And now she had something to tell him. 'Matt,' she said slowly. 'Do you have a lawyer? I think I want some advice.'

'What kind of advice?' he asked quietly.

'The divorce kind.'

She started to tell him about Wayland, and once she started she couldn't seem to stop – the drugs, and the weird friends and the sleeping all the time. Everything came pouring out.

'*I* pay all the bills,' she said. 'He hasn't contributed one dollar since we've been married. If I tell him to go, will he?'

Matt listened carefully. And he didn't like what he heard. She was hooked up with some spaced-out drug addict, and they were always bad news, they *never* went quietly. He remembered one girl, a singer, who was living with a heroin user. When she told him to get out he had slit her throat with a razor. She lived, but her voice didn't.

'Is he violent?' Matt asked, questioning his own sanity in getting involved in this.

'No. Not at all. In fact he's quite gentle, especially with the baby.' She sighed. 'It's not going to be easy telling him to go. He's like a big kid. In a way I feel sorry for him.'

'You have to see a lawyer,' Matt urged. 'I'll set you up an appointment. Why don't I get my man to fit you in tomorrow morning? He'll do me a favour. Call me at ten o'clock and I'll let you know what time.'

She squeezed his hand gratefully. 'Thank you,' she said. 'You're really a very nice man.' *In spite of your silly hair, and your gold chains, and your dumb apartment*, she wanted to add, but she didn't. Slowly she was changing her opinion of Matt Traynor. He wasn't as bad as he looked.

*

The girl on the answering service was getting snippy. 'Yes, Mr Golden. I have passed on your *four* messages. And no, Mr Golden, it is not my fault that Miss Antonio has not returned your calls.'

'I'm at another number now,' Lennie said edgily, giving her the number at 'Foxie's'. 'So this is message number five, and please tell her it's urgent.'

'I'll certainly do that, Mr Golden.'

'Thank you.'

'You're welcome.'

He hung up, hating the operator more each time.

Why was Eden playing games? Why was she acting like a bitch before they were even back in gear? Goddamn her. Who needed it?

He went on stage and for the first time felt lousy.

Foxie gave him the benefit of a stream of insults.

Isaac was there, and announced it was a good job the Griffin Show hadn't been in tonight.

Rainbow smiled. 'Got your period, honey?'

He tried Eden's number again and again. The answering service picked up on all calls. They refused to supply him with her address. Joey Firello, who might have known it, was out of town. Suna and Shirlee were away for the week. Tomorrow he would find it. And he would also find out what kind of a game she thought she was playing.

He refused to fuck up his life because of Eden Antonio one more time.

*

At exactly ten in the morning Jess called Matt. He had kept his promise and arranged a twelve-thirty appointment with his lawyer. She was suitably grateful, and for once did not attempt to wake Wayland, who sprawled on the broken couch in the living room, out cold.

She fed Simon an early lunch and settled him for a nap. Then she crept quietly from the house.

Wayland awoke fifteen minutes later. He was groggy, still stoned. He looked around for Jess, and when he could not find her, realized she had gone to work early without leaving him any money.

He needed money. Edge was coming by the house later with some good dope, and he had promised him a hundred and fifty bucks. Jess would scream when he asked for money. If only she would get with it, she could sell some of the stuff he scored in the Casino, and make them a solid profit. Had to talk to her about getting her act together. Had to –

He forgot what he was thinking, unzipped his pants and pissed against the living room wall. Then he popped a few assorted pills, the last of his stash, and remembered he needed money to replenish his supply. Jess was not treating him right. She shouldn't have sneaked off to work without leaving him money.

Sometimes she hid it.

He started a slapdash search, knocking things over, tipping coffee and sugar and flour out of their containers in the kitchen.

Sometimes she –

He couldn't quite grasp the thought. But he did know Edge was coming by soon and he needed to get connected.

In the bedroom the baby started to cry.

Sometimes she hid it . . .

He had the thought again.

Once she had hidden fifteen hundred dollars under the baby's mattress.

He staggered into the bedroom. Last night he had speedballed with a few friends. They had come to the house. What else was he expected to do? He couldn't go anywhere when he was babysitting.

He lifted the kid from the crib and placed him carefully

on the floor. It immediately started to crawl toward the open patio doors, but Wayland was too stoned to notice.

Frantically he began pulling at the sheets and covers. Then he lifted the small mattress and hurled it across the room.

Nothing.

Not a dime.

Not a dollar.

Not a cent.

Tiredness overcame him. He flopped across the bed and immediately fell into another deep sleep.

Chapter 26

The Snoopy watch did not bring peace. Brigette screamed like a stuck pig when she discovered Olympia was not returning to Paris with her. It was almost as if the child sensed Olympia's withdrawal, and wanted nothing to do with it.

'I want my mommy!' she yelled, jerking away from Nanny Mabel who was trying to secure her in a vice-like grip – all the better to drag her into the limousine.

'Mama will follow you,' Olympia sighed, hating the scene. 'In a day or two.'

'No you *won't*!' screamed Brigette. 'You won't! You won't!'

'I will,' Olympia insisted.

'For God's sake.' Dimitri appeared, glaring thunder. 'Why did you make this last minute decision not to come, Olympia? It *is* irresponsible of you telling the child now.' He shifted his stern gaze to Brigette, who immediately shut up. 'We will go now,' he said. 'Your mother will follow us in a few days. In the meantime you will stay with me.'

Brigette's face brightened. As long as she wasn't left alone with Nanny Mabel.

'Thank you, father,' sighed Olympia, touching her blonde curls.

He frowned. 'No longer than a week,' he said. 'I have

meetings in London and Rome, and I have no intention of taking Brigette with me.'

'Certainly not, father.'

They exchanged dutiful kisses and at last Dimitri, Brigette and Nanny Mabel were on their way.

Olympia threw herself into a soothing tub, ordered two bottles of Louis Roederer Cristal champagne and a healthy supply of caviar to be put out, then she summoned Vitos to spend the night.

He arrived with news of a party being given by a seedy English rock group called The Layabouts, contemporaries of the Beatles and the Stones.

Olympia decided she wanted to meet them as the lead singer had always intrigued her. His name was Flash.

Vitos flashed his perfect blank smile. 'We shall go,' he said, after she had told him that is exactly what they would do.

The limousine transported them to a huge loft in the Village where two burly security guards checked them out. This is what Olympia was learning to love about New York, there was always something unexpected going on.

Once inside she smiled her way through the crush while Vitos guided her past the mass of seething freaks into the inner sanctum where she set eyes on Flash for the first time. He looked like a refugee from a gypsy encampment. Long dark curls, pock-marked skin, thin cruel lips, rotting teeth, dangerous yellow eyes, and a stringy body.

She had seen him on television and in magazines for years. He was a cult figure, up there with Andy Warhol and Mick Jagger. He was also a reformed heroin addict, a dedicated cocksman, and possibly the best rock guitarist in the world. Meeting a passably pretty, plump Greek shipping heiress did nothing for his libido. He had no idea who she was. ''Ello darlin',' he said. 'Wanna snort?'

Olympia fell in love instantly.

Nobody had ever accused her of having perfect taste.

Chapter 27

Now that she had made her decision, Lucky had no desire to spend any more time than was necessary with Gino. She didn't want to risk his trying to change her mind, because she knew what she was doing was right.

He was back in Vegas alone. No Susan. The Widow Perfect had remained in Los Angeles arranging the nuptials.

'You're comin' to the wedding, aren't you?' he asked.

She did not want to attend his wedding. Why should she be present when he committed an insane act?

'Well . . .' she began, searching for an excuse.

'I want you there,' he said. An order, not a request.

'Sure,' she agreed reluctantly, wondering why she still jumped.

There was no need for her to hang around while all the involved paperwork went ahead, so she planned to leave in one week's time. First she wanted to visit Costa, in Miami, and then on to New York, which she had decided would be her base. Leaving the Vegas hotel business was going to be a wrench, no use kidding herself.

And leaving Gino . . .

They dined together one night. Conversation was stilted. Things just weren't the same. She told him when she was going, and he nodded resignedly.

Tell me it's all off between you and Susan and I won't budge, she thought.

He didn't say a word.

•

Matt heard about the tragedy on the early evening news. Another backyard drowning. This time an 11-month-old baby boy who had crawled out of an open patio door and fallen into the family swimming pool.

The newscaster, a woman who looked like she had just

come from the Miss America contest, assumed a grave expression, and informed her audience that although foul play was not suspected, the parents, Jess and Wayland Dolby, had been taken to the police station for further questioning.

For a moment Matt was stunned. *It was Jess. It was her kid. What the hell had happened?*

Galvanized into action he grabbed his jacket and hurried from the office.

*

Susan and Paige met at a Brentwood house which Paige was redecorating. The owner, a macho superstar who had appeared in Paige's husband's hit movie, was in Hawaii with another macho superstar, also male.

Susan arrived at the house first, and waited impatiently outside in her yellow Rolls. Paige only kept her waiting a few minutes before she arrived in her metallic gold Porsche. She hurried from the car and rushed over to Susan who now stood beside her Rolls, allowing the affection she felt for Paige to envelop her. The two women embraced. They made an incongruous couple. Susan so elegantly groomed in a sleek silk suit with upswept blonde hair, and Paige, with her frizzy mass of hair and slit-to-the-limit skirt.

'Sorry I'm late,' Paige said, exuding a mixture of strong perfume and musky body odours. 'I just got a new house to decorate, a rush job. Some little starlet one of Ryder's investors is setting up. She wants the usual – Monroe white, mirrors, and fur bedspreads. All the better to fuck on!'

Susan smiled. If Gino had made such a crass remark she would have reprimanded him with a look.

They entered the house. It was almost complete, a masculine fantasy of wood and leather.

'What do you think?' asked Paige, taking her through it room by room.

'Very impressive,' enthused Susan, although it *was* a little overdone.

'Ted'll love it,' said Paige. 'So will his boyfriend.'

They reached the bedroom and stood in front of the dark oak four poster bed.

'King size,' Paige said, 'to match its owner.'

'How would you know?' Susan asked quickly. She had her suspicions that Paige sometimes slept with her clients, although she never voiced such a thought.

'Because *everyone* knows,' Paige replied. 'Just like everyone knows Tiny possessed one of the biggest cocks in Hollywood.'

Susan frowned. Sometimes Paige went too far. She wished she would not mention Tiny. Now he was gone she would prefer to forget him, *and* his hateful organ, which, as a matter of fact, *had* been one of the most awesome appendages she had ever seen. She looked at Paige meaningfully, and slipped the silk jacket from her shoulders. 'Did you miss me?' she asked. 'Because I missed you.'

Paige smiled. 'But of course,' she said, stepping out of her skirt.

Susan hurriedly removed the rest of her clothes and waited for Paige's special touch. Sex with a woman was so natural. There was none of the underlying violence that always seemed to be present when sleeping with a man. Susan felt no threat or violation. It was so delightful to let herself go. To lie back and feel so totally and completely at ease.

Her orgasm, when it arrived, was the real thing. With a man she always faked it. Somehow it was easier that way.

She lay naked and content in the centre of the big oak bed and began to tell Paige about Gino.

The other woman listened intently as the story unfolded.

Susan concluded with a sigh, 'I'm marrying him,' she said. 'I'm afraid it's the only answer.'

Paige nodded. Frankly she thought Gino Santangelo sounded like dynamite. The trouble with Susan was she didn't know a good thing when she saw it. After all, a fuck was a fuck, it didn't really matter what sex it was.

'I want you to know,' Susan continued, 'it won't make any difference to *our* relationship.'

Paige rose from the bed. 'Marriage agrees with you,' she said. 'You need a man around, if only to pay the bills.'

Susan stretched luxuriously. 'You, my dear one, are what I need.' She parted her legs abandonedly. With Paige she could never get enough loving. With Gino it was always too much.

'I've got to rush,' Paige said, beginning to dress. 'I'm having twelve guests for dinner tonight. We're screening the new Bronson film.. I would have asked you, but I know how you hate coming on your own. Never mind, soon you'll be a couple again.'

'Yes,' agreed Susan, a touch irritably. She had been ready to play some more, and now Paige was rushing off. It really was too bad considering they hadn't seen each other in months. 'Can we meet again soon?' she asked.

'We could,' mused Paige, applying lipstick. 'But I don't know if I'm ready to share a bed with Ted. He's coming back tomorrow. Which reminds me – I need fresh flowers, and more cushions, and . . .' She rushed to her purse and extracted a Gucci pad and pen. 'Honestly, I don't know how I do it all. I'm like a juggler, keeping everyone's balls in the air. Ryder would fall to pieces without me, and the teenage monsters are *so* demanding. Bradford was thrown out of school last week for pushing pot. And Ricky smashed up his brand new Corvette.'

Later, driving home, Susan decided that her two uptight WASPs weren't so bad. And Gino . . . well it *would* be nice to have a man by her side again. There was a time when Paige wouldn't have *dared* to have a dinner party without her. Now it was – ***I know how you hate coming on your own*** – and that was that.

At home she called Gino. He sounded blue. She cheered him with soft words and decided to make the wedding as soon as possible.

•

Over the years Gino had learned to appreciate a relationship as opposed to just getting laid. Any jerk could get laid, developing a closeness between two people was what really mattered.

He had married twice in his life. The first time to Cindy. She couldn't be trusted.

The second time to Maria. The one true love of his life.

In between there had been few women who left their mark.

Clementine Duke – the wife of a Senator. A cool and classy lady who came upon him when he was twenty-two and guided him toward the good things in life.

Bee, who took him in when he needed her help, and waited for him while he spent seven years in jail.

Marabelle Blue, sex symbol supreme. She turned out to be a neurotic mess who tried suicide when he rejected her.

And the last permanent liaison was with an attractive widow, a woman not unlike Susan in the looks department. She had moved in with him in Israel and shared his exile. When he returned to America he left her behind.

Now Susan.

Was he making a mistake? There was always that moment of doubt.

He didn't think so.

He lit a long thin Havana cigar and gazed thoughtfully into the future.

Chapter 28

The detective had a few strands of carefully arranged greasy hair.

Jess couldn't help staring, even though she knew instinctively it was annoying him. Childishly she thought if she stared long enough this whole unbelievable nightmare would go away.

'Why didja leave him with your husband if y'knew he was zonked outta his skull?' the detective demanded. 'Ain'tcha ever heard of child neglect? If y'ask me you may well've dumped the kid in the pool yourself. Mebbe y'did. Nothin' surprises me in this screwed up world.'

His cruel words did not get through to her. She refused to hear what he was saying. She knew they had to let her go. They couldn't keep her. She hadn't done anything . . .

Except claw and scratch and kick and scream, and if she'd had a gun she would have shot the sonofabitch.

Wayland.

Asleep.

As if he didn't have a care in the world.

And their baby . . .

Simon . . .

Floating . . .

Like a toy . . .

The rush of horror. This wasn't happening, couldn't be happening.

Her breathing restricted. Reflexes slow.

She began to scream. And then she pulled her baby from the pool by his hair. A neighbour's son appeared and bent over the small, bloated, lifeless form.

Eventually Wayland staggered from the house, blank-eyed and shirtless. 'Wassamatter?' he mumbled.

She flew at him, beating his chest with her fists, raking his vile face with her nails, until her screams brought more neighbours and finally the police.

It was all a blur from then on. A blur of hate, confusion and despair. Now she was waiting to wake up from the horrific nightmare, for she was sure this couldn't be reality.

And yet . . . she had held the cold, wet flesh of Simon, her only child, and she knew – without a doubt – that life was gone.

*

It was obvious Eden had no intention of returning his calls. Lennie could not believe she would casually come back into his life, screw up his head, and then expect him to vanish as if nothing had taken place.

'Miss Antonio has received all your messages,' the girl on her answering service told him when he called upon waking at noon. 'And she will get back to you as soon as she is able.'

So fuck off. That's what the message conveyed. *Fuck off and don't call again.*

He was angry. She had wanted him as much as he had wanted her. Godammit. What *was* this crap?

He stretched for the phone again and connected with Joey Firello's answering service. Didn't anyone pick up their own phone in California?

'Mr Firello is out of town. I'll give him your message.'

'I need to talk to him now,' Lennie said quickly. 'Don't you have a number where I can reach him?'

'I'll give him your message,' the operator replied, ignoring his request.

Fucking zombie.

With difficulty he tracked down Suna and Shirlee in Palm Springs. Neither of them could remember where Eden lived, although they assured him it was near them.

'That's a big help,' he said.

'You're not going to see her, are you?' questioned Suna.

'You and she together are poison,' Shirlee added, on an extension phone.

He had not called for their advice. 'Who's her agent?' he asked quickly.

'Nobody important,' they said as one.

'I want a name, not a rating.'

They supplied him with a name. He called, and was informed by a secretary there was no way she could give him the home address of a client.

'It's urgent,' he said sharply.

'Leave a message,' she replied. Snitty broad.

He dropped the phone. It was happening already. Back in his life for one night and she was making him crazy.

He knew that if he was smart he would forget the whole thing. Dismiss her from his thoughts as she had probably dismissed him.

But who was smart? When it came to Eden he was the dumbest ass in town.

*

The imprint of Santino's hand burnt into the pale skin on her cheek. Eden stared into the mirror, her eyes cloudy with fury. Nobody had ever hit her before. Nobody would have dared.

Bastard.

Hairy bastard.

He looked like a bald ape. He should be worshipping at her feet, not lifting his hand to her.

It was all so unexpected. She had guessed Santino Bonnatti was hardly Mister Charm, but she had not been ready for such a vicious attack.

And how did he know she was out anyway? Was he having her followed?

She decided to dump him.

That decision lasted five minutes. Timing was everything, and with a new house and his possible investment in a movie, now was not the right moment to say goodbye.

She leaned closer to the mirror and studied her face. Then she raised her hand and gently felt the marks of his jealousy.

She went into the kitchen, gathered ice in a towel, and held it to her cheek.

The phone rang three times, and then the service picked up. She had no desire to speak to anyone. Lennie Golden had left countless messages. It was probably him again.

Screw Lennie. He was the cause of all her troubles.

And screw Santino Bonnatti.

Bastard.

He would not get away with such behaviour. He would pay.

Eventually.

When the timing was right.

When *she* was ready.

*

Scotch eased the rejection. Half a bottle, and when Lennie hit the stage at 'Foxie's' he was belligerent and mean, with a cruel edge to his humour.

Rainbow was standing at the side when he came off. She jerked her head toward the pay phone in the corner. 'Somebody belled you from Las Vegas. I told them to call back in ten minutes.'

'Who was it?' he slurred.

She wrapped her robe tightly around herself. 'Do I look like a secretary?'

'You look like a hot piece of ass,' he lurched in her direction.

'Aw, cut it out, Lennie.' She gave him a disgusted shove. 'If Foxie were around he'd skin your balls.'

'At least I've still got 'em.'

She laughed aloud. 'Sonny, you'll *never* have balls like Foxie.'

The pay phone rang, saving him from summoning up a smart retort.

He wondered who was calling him from Vegas, and hoped it was Jess. He needed to talk. Once and for all he had to get Eden Antonio out of his system.

Chapter 29

Matt said, 'I'd really like you to come to the funeral this afternoon. Jess is falling apart. You being there would mean a lot to her.'

'I hardly know the girl,' Lucky replied.

'She's worked for us for over two years. Can't you show her this kindness? I want her to know we care.'

Lucky wondered at his involvement. Sophisticated, jaded, Matt. When did he develop heart? 'Okay,' she said. 'I'll come.' And then she added with a sudden rush of sympathy for Jess. 'Is there anything else I can do?'

'Just be there – that's enough.'

She nodded. 'Perhaps we can arrange for her to have three months' paid vacation. Send her away somewhere to think things out . . . It's going to take time . . .'

For a moment she remembered Marco. His smile, and the way his black hair curled over the back of his collar, and the way he used to look at her.

Oh God. She still dreamed about him. On nights when she was so lonely that only *he* could keep her company.

'I know,' Matt said. 'I was going to suggest that I take her to Europe.' He paused hopefully. 'You could manage without me for a few weeks, couldn't you?'

She wondered if now was the time to tell him she wasn't going to be around. Decided it wasn't.

'How involved are you?' she asked.

He shrugged. 'I'm involved. She's not.'

'Well . . . I hope it works out for you.'

Matt wanted to talk. Quickly he said, 'I know she's twenty years younger than me and we've got nothing in common. She's not even my type, but Jesus, when I look at her it's all over. She could make me a very happy man.'

Lucky stood up. She wasn't feeling great. 'Why don't you tell *her*, not me?' She walked him toward the door, not wanting to appear rude, but also not inclined to hear the confessions of a reformed chauvinist. She almost had to push him out.

When he was gone she ordered tea and toast from room service and sat down at her desk to go over some papers.

She felt horribly nauseous. Just nerves. Once she was on her way things would be different.

*

Matt hurried back to his apartment where the maid was keeping an eye on Jess. She sat on the couch staring blankly into space.

'Guess what?' he said. 'Lucky Santangelo wants to attend the funeral. That's really something. You must have made a big impression over the years.' He walked to the bar and began pouring a hefty slug of brandy into a glass. 'A lot of people are going to show up. Most of the croupiers, some of the showgirls, a couple of waitresses. Oh, and Manny – you know – your favourite pit boss. He's definitely coming.' He handed her the glass.

'It's not a party,' she said, her voice a whisper.

'Drink up, it'll make you feel better.'

'It's not a party,' she repeated sadly.

He held her hand. 'I know that, sweetheart. But believe me, people care about you. They want to show their respect.'

She took a gulp of brandy. 'You turned out to be a very nice man,' she murmured.

He was embarrassed, thinking that he wasn't so nice after all.

'I contacted your friend in Los Angeles,' he said quickly. 'It took me several phone calls, but I tracked him down at 'Foxie's'. He's flying in today, and should be arriving about now. I've arranged a car to meet him and bring him straight here.'

For a moment there was a flicker of a smile. 'Lennie,' she said quietly, 'is my best friend in the world.'

'I understand,' Matt said reassuringly. 'You told me yesterday. That's how I knew you'd want him here.'

Since hearing the news, Matt had taken charge. It was he who had collected Jess from the police station, summoned a doctor who had doped her up with sedatives, watched her as she slept restlessly in his bed, listened as she rambled on about her life.

It was he who had arranged for the funeral, organized cars and what he hoped would be a suitable turn-out.

It was he who had fed her hot soup, and held her as she sobbed the night away.

The day before she had been hysterical. Now she was quiet, almost child-like.

'Lennie's my best friend,' she repeated. 'We grew up together, you know.'

'Yes, I do know. You told me all about him.'

He dared not ask whether that best-friendshipness had ever been sexual. What if she ran off with the guy? And he, Matt Traynor, the jerk, had brought him back into town.

No time to worry now. He had too much to organize The funeral was in three hours, and he wanted to make sure everything went smoothly.

*

Lucky decided a letter to her chief executives would be best. She drafted several, but ended up throwing them away.

Matt phoned to inform her that he had arranged for Boogie to pick her up at two o'clock. He was certainly concerned enough, making arrangements with *her* driver. Any other time she would have balled him out.

The last thing she felt like doing was attending a funeral, especially when the normally blue desert sky was turning grey, and the weather stations predicted thunderstorms. But she wouldn't let Matt down now.

She was just so *tired*, as if every ounce of energy had been drained from her body. All she wanted to do was sleep.

It occurred to her she should visit her doctor, have a physical, get a little vitamin therapy. It was no use running off to conquer New York feeling like a dead camel. She called her doctor and made a morning appointment.

Gino had returned to LA for a few days.

A few days. Sure. More like a few weeks.

Susan beckoned.

He came running.

How nice to have a permanent hard-on at his age. Maybe it ran in the family.

She laughed dryly. Sex was the last thing on her mind. She wanted to build an empire – her *own* empire – and then maybe think about her non-existent sex life. There had been no one since Dimitri Stanislopoulos. Yet she didn't care.

Sex was important when she wanted it to be.

Only then.

Chapter 30

The plane ride was bumpy, and by the time they prepared to land it was raining.

Nothing like a desert rainstorm, Lennie thought. Black clouds, tough stingy hailstones, and a humid heat that never quit. He had a hangover. And the memory of a fierce fight with Isaac Luther when he had told him he couldn't do the Griffin Show.

'What do you mean, you *can't* do it?' Isaac had yelled.

'I can't do it because a friend needs me in Vegas, and I gotta go.'

'Screw friends. This is the big break, man. If you blow this you're crazy.'

Lennie shrugged. 'Some things in life have to take priority. Maybe they can reschedule my spot.'

'They're more likely to reschedule your ass,' Isaac exploded. 'You're letting them down at the last minute. Don't do it, Lennie.'

He had gestured impatiently. 'No choice.'

Foxie had been more agreeable in his own inimitable way. 'Go. Stay there. An' don't come back until you got yourself straight. I don't like drunks, an' I don't stand for no shit acts in my place. These last two nights you've given me both.'

No arguing with that.

So here he was, back in Vegas, with the rain pissing down, and a lousy taste in his mouth.

In LA the sun was shining and he would have been preparing to go before the TV cameras.

He would also be getting no reply from the lovely Eden. A true cunt. As always. The hell with her. She was unimportant. What was going on in Jess's life was all he cared about.

Matt Traynor had called him the previous evening. The same Matt Traynor who had fired him. 'Jess needs you here,'

Matt said, and then given him a sketchy rundown on what had happened.

Jesus. Just looking at that freak Jess was married to had given him bad vibes. Wayland. A stoned creep scoring off the money she brought home. Why hadn't he said something to her? At least taken the time to find out what was going on.

But no. He hadn't done that. He had rushed out of town with a bug up his ass because he got canned, and only he, Lennie Golden, mattered.

Goddamn it.

She had needed him.

He never stayed around to care.

And now her baby was dead, and maybe he could have prevented the tragedy.

A car waited for him. An Oldsmobile driven by a retired showgirl in a purple sequinned uniform. Ah . . . Las Vegas . . . City of bad taste.

The ex-showgirl drove like Paul Newman on the track, and by the time they arrived at Matt's apartment, Lennie was a nervous wreck. Thunder and lightning greeted him as he left the car. He pulled up the collar on his jacket and ran inside.

*

Matt glanced around the assorted gathering which huddled graveside and made a mental note to repay the favours of those who had turned up. It wasn't a huge group – maybe twenty people. But it was a respectable number, and he was pleased. Lucky – God bless her – was there. She hadn't let him down. She stood beneath a large black umbrella, her head bowed as the pitifully small coffin was lowered into the ground.

Lennie stood to one side of Jess, supporting her, and Matt was on the other. He could feel her body shaking with silent sobs and he didn't know what to do. She made him feel helpless. He just wanted to protect her from the world. And if she would let him, that's exactly what he planned to do.

As the second Mrs Traynor she would have more than enough protection.

Wayland was not present. Wayland was even now hitching a ride out of town, which Matt had assured him would be the healthiest thing he could possibly do.

The rain was relentless. It would have to rain, Matt thought, adding even more misery to the pathetic scene. After the ceremony he had arranged refreshments in a nearby restaurant. It was a mistake. Everyone just wanted to get the hell out of there.

*

For a moment Lennie did not recognize the woman. Her jet hair was pulled back tightly, and dark shades covered her expressive eyes. Her body was concealed beneath a long black leather coat, tightly belted. She looked like a spy out of a Le Carré novel. Beautiful, mysterious, and ice-cold hot.

Then he remembered. The girl from the casino. The nearly one-night stand. Why was she still in Vegas?

As soon as he could he edged toward her. She stood at the bar gulping a Pernod on the rocks.

'Hey,' he accused. 'You stood me up.'

She did not remove her black shades so he could not tell if she was looking at him or not.

'Do I know you?' she asked coldly.

'We almost made history, only you wanted to start the course before I was ready. Lennie Golden. Remember?'

An imperceptible nod.

'So what happened? You were supposed to meet me in the bar.'

'Maybe someone more willing to learn came along. Excuse me.'

She brushed past him, went over to where Jess sat with Matt, said a few words and left.

First Eden, then this one. Was the famous Golden charm evaporating?

Christ, funerals were depressing. Poor little Jess seemed like a forlorn kid. He wished Matt Traynor would leave her alone, the old guy was a horny swinger, panting after her as if she were the only female in town. Hadn't he ever learned timing?

Lennie wondered what he could do to ease her pain, she looked so lost. He went over and squeezed her hand. 'How're you feeling, monkey face?' He hoped to spur some sort of reaction.

She shook her head blankly.

There was nothing to say at a time like this. Maybe just being there was enough.

*

Santino returned at seven in the morning. Eden was asleep, but he had his own key to her apartment (when he had started to pay the rent and all the bills he had insisted) so he let himself in, entered her bedroom, and sat watching her for a while. She slept naked on chocolate brown sheets which contrasted nicely with the paleness of her skin and the blondeness of her hair. Who did she think she was playing games with? One mistake was all he'd allow her. If she cheated on him again she wouldn't get away with a smack on the face.

She was a skinny broad.

After Donatella, his wife, Santino considered anyone under one hundred and fifty pounds skinny.

He could still see the mark of his hand on her cheek and it excited him. Broads like Eden Antonio needed constant watching. His father had taught him that. 'Any cunt who thinks she's hot stuff is gonna need a sharp eye on her fanny,' Enzio, his father, had announced one morning at breakfast to Santino and his elder brother, Carlo. 'To keep 'em in line you gotta buy 'em plenty, fuck 'em regularly, an' beat 'em occasionally.'

Enzio had roared with laughter at his own wit and wisdom. But wit and wisdom had not been enough to protect him from cold planned murder at the hands of a woman.

Santino scowled with fury when he thought of that fateful day a year ago. And he scowled even harder when he remembered the instructions he and Carlo received from his father's business associates. 'No more killings,' they were told. 'No more revenge. The violence has to stop.'

Just like that they were forbidden to do anything.

As far as Santino was concerned it was like cutting off his balls. Although Carlo took it calm as a fucking priest.

Santino scratched his bald pate and thought about his brother. Carlo was a shithead, a nothing. Unfortunately they were partners and blood brothers, and as such had to stick together. But not in the same city.

With Enzio gone, Santino moved his end of their operation to LA. And there he planned to stay. A wise decision. Without Carlo looking over his shoulder he was able to expand and branch out. The family business had included a string of massage parlours. Santino found that the porno magazines sold in such establishments raked in a fortune. He investigated the publishers and distributors. Reasonable men. Before long Santino was a part of the action – and with the imports he brought in from Denmark and Thailand – plus videos – he was rolling in profits. He had more money than Carlo. The shithead Carlo. What kind of man refused to act on his own father's murder?

Santino knew it was up to him to even the score with that bitch, Lucky Santangelo. And he would do it one day. *For sure*.

Eden stirred, and threw her arms above her head.

Santino's small eyes bore into her pink-tipped breasts. Small but perfect. His wife filled a 42D cup. It was like having sex with a pregnant cow. Quickly he rose and pulled down the jogging pants he wore. Then he allowed his erection to slip from the confines of patterned boxer shorts.

Eden sighed in her sleep.

Roughly Santino ripped the sheet from the bed exposing all of her. She had blonde hair on her snatch which drove him crazy. He was partial to blondes. In one fast movement he straddled her chest and thrust his erection toward her mouth.

Her eyes were hardly open before he was rocking back and forth.

'Suck it,' he demanded hoarsely. 'Take it, baby, Take it all. You know you love it. You know Santino is King.'

Chapter 31

The drug culture had always appealed to Olympia, although she had never got into it in a major way. A lot of cocaine and plenty of pot was about as far as she had travelled. She did not want to become hooked like some of her so-called friends who couldn't get out of bed in the morning without a snort. She was smart. She was a social user. And if she wasn't going out she could go days without indulging and not miss it at all. As far as she was concerned, a toot of coke was the modern day equivalent of a Scotch on the rocks. Nothing wrong with *that*.

Dimitri had asked her once if she indulged. 'Certainly not,' she had replied, suitably shocked.

'Good,' he had nodded thoughtfully. 'Because a girl in your position has to be very very careful. There are many people who would be only too pleased to discover you have a weakness. You would be exploited mercilessly.'

What did he think she was? Dumb? She had married three men, all of whom had exploited her to the limit. Why hadn't he warned her about men? They were far more dangerous than drugs.

It completely slipped her mind that Dimitri *had* warned her. Constantly.

So . . . drugs were no problem. They made her feel good, allowed her to have a fantastic time at parties, and did not give her a hangover or make her fat.

Conveniently she forgot the dawn cravings for chocolate cake, double cream cheesecake, and Häagen Daas Rum Raisin ice cream.

She was sure Dimitri was into coke. Or at least some of his jet-set girlfriends were. How could one be part of the social circle without indulging?

Flash indulged. Heavily. He might be a former heroin addict, but that did not stop him from grabbing anything else going. Uppers, downers, sleepers, quacks, grass, and of course – cocaine. The rich man's drug. Only Flash never had to pay, because he was so famous – or maybe infamous – that the hangers-on and the gofers and the groupies and the star-fucks always managed to get him everything he wanted for nothing.

Flash was looking for a place to crash in New York. He had a permanent residence in the Bahamas (for tax reasons) and in LA he stayed with a dissolute movie star (male) with stoned eyes and a grin like a sick cat. But Flash needed a New York base. And Olympia looked like she could provide it.

Enter Flash.

Exit Vitos.

Flash made a lot of money, but he was notoriously tight-fisted. Why spend when there were others to do it for you?'

The first night he slept with Olympia he had no idea who she was. They whiled away a few hours rolling around on a water bed in an apartment he was borrowing. She wasn't really his type. Too chubby. His style was usually young, tall models with stringy hair and beautiful blank faces. But Olympia was there – coming on strong, and Flash needed to get laid. He *always* needed to get laid. So he had said goodbye to his entourage, and taken her to his borrowed apartment.

Olympia told Vitos she had a very important business proposition she had to discuss with Flash. Vitos didn't seem to care. He was deep in conversation with Bianca Jagger, or was it Diane Von Furstenberg? – Olympia never could tell them apart.

Flash proved his reputation to be true. And Olympia was happy. She left by cab while he slept. And at noon the next day she let him know she was not just another little groupie. He awoke to find six cases of Dom Perignon, a healthy supply of Iranian caviar, and a small gift from Tiffany's. The gift was a solid gold and diamond guitar pin. On it was engraved OLYMPIA/FLASH NEW YORK 1978.

Even Flash knew that to get Tiffany's to engrave something in a couple of hours meant you had clout.

She had enclosed her card – OLYMPIA STANISLOPOULOS – with an address and phone number.

The surname was as well known as Onassis.

'Who is she?' he asked, handing the card to Como Rose, his manager.

Como looked at it, belched loudly and said, 'She's Dimitri Stanislopoulos' daughter, for crissake. Richer than the Gettys.'

Flash knew a good thing when it came his way. And she had come and come and come.

He grinned, revealing a full spread of dangerously loose, rotting teeth. Dentists were not an important part of his life.

'Call her,' he said. 'Have her here at five. I'm taking her to the concert.'

She turned up at five-thirty, dressed in taffeta, lace, and diamonds.

'You're friggin' late,' Flash said. 'Friggin' overdressed, and we're gonna need a couple more boxes of the fizzy stuff. Arrange it.'

Nobody had ever spoken to Olympia like that before. She liked it. A lot. A refreshing change.

They snorted several lines of coke; swigged champagne on the way to the stadium where The Layabouts were giving their first New York concert in five years; and sent the paparazzi into a frenzy.

Within a week Olympia had purchased a huge apartment overlooking Central Park, and Flash took up residence on the same day she did.

That night they stood on the landscaped terrace and surveyed the city spread out before them.

'Not bad, gel,' Flash announced, and lit up a joint.

Olympia swigged from a bottle of Dom Perignon she was holding (her new habit) and agreed. Why had she wasted so much of her life in Europe when New York was such *fun*?

She wondered what she was going to do about Brigette. So far she hadn't mentioned the existence of her daughter to Flash. Maybe she could just forget about her for another week or so. Why bring it up and ruin everything?

Flash dragged on the joint long and hard. Why hadn't he thought of shacking up with a rich bird before? It was definitely the way to go.

He wondered what he was going to do about his 16-year-old wife stashed somewhere in England. So far he hadn't mentioned her existence to Olympia. Well it was a secret wedding, nobody knew. Maybe he could just forget about her for a while. She was used to his long absences. Why bring it up and ruin everything?

Olympia and Flash were perfectly suited.

Chapter 32

The child's funeral depressed Lucky. It seemed so . . . pointless. It made her feel angry and helpless. If people brought children into the world, they should look after them. The infant's death was no accident, it was caused by human error. She had heard all about Wayland from Matt. If he were her husband she would have strung him up by his balls.

Standing by the grave in the pouring rain was a downer. But later, in the restaurant, it was even worse. One fast drink and she was out of there. She had given Matt the favour he requested, it was enough.

She was alone at the bar, drinking Pernod, when the comedian materialized. He was tall and rangy with green eyes and a killer smile. She remembered him instantly. She even remembered his name *before* he re-introduced himself. Lennie Golden. A comedian. And how.

She wanted to say, 'What the hell are *you* doing here. I had you fired and I'm never supposed to set eyes on you again.' Instead she said nothing while he fumbled for words. And when he told her his name she pretended not to know who he was, brushed past him, and made a fast exit.

The truth of the matter was she found him disturbingly attractive. He had turned her down once, and she did not plan to go for twice. What a nerve he had even speaking to her.

When she got back to the hotel she decided not to hang around any longer. There was no reason for her to stay, even Gino had left. She called Costa and told him she would be arriving in Miami the next day. Then she began to pack, urgently throwing things into several suitcases. Somehow she knew she had to get out at once.

•

In Bel Air all was peaceful. The cook prepared sesame chicken, one of Gino's favourite dishes. There was an excellent baseball game on the Advent television which he watched from a comfortable armchair, while Susan, looking ladylike yet sexy in a pale blue peignoir, attended to her needlepoint.

This is a long way from the streets of Brooklyn, he thought. The long-ago far-away mean streets where he had started out without a dime to call his own.

He puffed contentedly on a thin Havana, and dipped a silver spoon into a dish of ice cream.

Yeh. He was making the right move. This was the life for him.

Susan had set the date. He was ready.

•

Lucky took an early plane out of Vegas. She stopped at her doctor's on the way to the airport for a B_{12} vitamin shot. Her doctor, a woman – because male doctors seemed to treat female patients like backward children – insisted on running a few simple tests before giving it to her.

'I can never get you in here for your yearly physical,' Doctor Liz Turney complained with a smile. 'So I'm grabbing you while I can.'

'You'd better grab quickly,' Lucky replied, surrendering her arm for a blood test, 'because I'm on my way to the airport.'

'Always in a rush. Have you ever thought of slowing down?'

'What for? I've got things to do.'

'Well find time to give me a urine sample, if you please.'

'Just give me the shot, doc. That's all I need.'

Liz Turney handed her a small glass bottle and pointed her in the direction of the toilet. '*I'll* tell you what you need.'

The flight to Miami took forever. The plane made two stops, adding even more hours to the journey. By the time Lucky arrived she was tired out.

Costa was at the airport to greet her. Uncle Costa. She hadn't seen him for a year, and she marvelled at how much better he looked. Last time they met he was grey-skinned and weary-eyed. Now he sported a healthy suntan, and his eyes were sharp and bright behind distinguished horn-rims. He wore a snappy sports jacket, nicely creased pants and an open-neck white shirt. He presented the image of a respectable retired businessman. Which was exactly what he was.

'You look so well!' Lucky exclaimed, throwing her arms around him and hugging him hard.

He drew back and inspected her critically. 'And you, Lucky, well . . . you look tired.'

One could always depend on the truth from Uncle Costa.

'Thanks a lot!'

'Should I lie?'

'Yeh. Why not?'

'Because I never lied to Gino, and I'm not going to start with you. You'll have a good night's sleep and tomorrow you'll look as beautiful as ever.'

'I didn't book a hotel.'

'I should hope not. You're staying with me.'

They walked toward a Chrysler saloon, followed by a porter with Lucky's three suitcases. She planned to have the rest of her things sent directly to the East Hampton house.

Happily she tucked her arm through his. 'I was hoping you'd say that. I think I've had enough of hotels to last me forever. Staying with you will be wonderful.'

He glanced at her shrewdly but said nothing. There was time to talk and find out what was bothering her. He had always loved Lucky as if she was his own daughter, and anything she wanted she could have. Even if it was only his time.

Chapter 33

'You're comin' to LA with me,' Lennie said firmly.

Jess thought of all the reasons she couldn't

There weren't any.

'I'm going to LA with Lennie,' she told Matt.

He didn't believe her. He was crushed. Making plans had kept him so busy he had forgotten to tell her about their future together. He wanted to look after her, provide for her, even *marry* her.

'You can't do that,' he stuttered.

'It's the only thing I *can* do,' she replied wanly. 'I've had it in Vegas. Too many memories. Lennie was right, I have to get out of here.'

'No, you don't,' he protested.

'Yes, I do.'

He wanted to tell her how he felt. Say all the right things, and by doing so, convince her she had to stay. But expressing himself, revealing his true feelings, was not an easy task for a man like Matt. He just didn't know how to begin.

'What'll you do in LA?' he asked blankly.

She shrugged. 'I'll make out.'

He was sure she would. Girls like Jess were a rarity. She was pretty and smart and vulnerable and wise. Some guy would grab her like picking peaches. Some schmuck. While he, Matt Traynor, that well known man-about-town, couldn't even find the words to make her stay.

'Keep in touch,' he said gruffly.

'Sure,' she mumbled.

But he knew she wouldn't.

Chapter 34

Being with Uncle Costa was almost as good as the last year with Gino . . . the year before Susan Martino had entered their lives.

Lucky talked to him long into the night. All her fears and frustrations, hopes and ambitions came tumbling out. He listened patiently, never interrupting, never criticizing.

'I love Gino so much,' she concluded fiercely, as the dawn light began to creep into the cosy living room of the oceanside apartment. 'But I hate him too.' She ran a hand through her unruly black curls, a gesture which immediately reminded Costa of Gino. 'He can be so . . . so . . . stupid!' She jumped up and paced around the room. 'Susan Martino is not his kind of woman. She's just a plastic, groomed-to-the-eyeballs, ladylike bitch, who's going to grab his money and make his life miserable. Any fool can see it. Why can't *he*?'

'Lucky,' Costa said, choosing his words carefully. 'Gino is just like you. He knows what he wants and he always gets it. If he decides to marry this Martino woman he will do so. Nothing you or I do or say will make the least bit of difference.'

'I know *that*.'

'Besides, maybe you're wrong about her. Perhaps she will be good for him.' He gave a long drawn-out sigh. 'A man needs the company of a woman. It is not good to be alone.'

'He wasn't alone,' Lucky blazed. 'He had me.'

'Did you share his bed at night?' Costa asked mildly.

'He could get laid any time he wanted,' Lucky replied defiantly.

'And did it ever enter your head that a man of his age might need more than just a one-night adventure? When you get old, Lucky, companionship is what really matters. Someone who cares about you.'

'*You're* alone. *You're* happy.'

'If I could find the right woman I would marry her in a minute.'

'Shit,' Lucky muttered. She wasn't winning any wars.

'Accept it,' Costa said. 'You're doing the right thing by moving to New York. Now you can look around and do what *you* want – break the tie between yourself and Gino. Everything you've ever done has been for his approval. The time has come to live your life for *you*.'

•

Lucky stayed in Miami for three days. The weather was nice, the life style simple, and Uncle Costa an interesting and wise companion.

She flew into New York early on Saturday morning to find it was raining, hostile and alive. The streets were crowded with people. Oh God! How she had missed the pace of the city. Immediately she felt great. There was a sense of excitement in the air. New York was a challenge. Costa was right, she had to start living her own life. If she didn't, she would regret it.

She checked into the Pierre Hotel and wondered how she was supposed to start.

There were a couple of messages waiting for her. One from Costa just to be sure she had arrived safely, and another from Dr Liz Turney. What the hell did *she* want?

Lucky felt a tingle of apprehension. All those stupid tests Liz had insisted on running . . . Maybe there was something wrong with her. Oh shit. She *had* been feeling tired.

Convinced she had some terrible ailment she returned the call.

Lis Turney was cheerful and to the point. 'Lucky,' she announced crisply, 'I'm delighted to tell you that you're going to have to slow down.'

'Why?' Lucky demanded suspiciously.

'Because, my dear, you are pregnant.'

BOOK TWO

The Summer of 1980

Chapter 35

Carrie Berkeley anticipated her sixty-seventh birthday with mixed feelings. On one hand she looked great. Slim, athletic, her taut black skin hardly marked by the harsh march of time, her short dark hair cut in the latest style with only a sprinkling of silver streaks.

On the other hand, there was no escaping the fact that sixty-seven was sixty-seven, and *that* was getting up there. Dare she even think about it . . . that was definitely *old*.

Carrie shuddered at the very thought as she hurried around her Fire Island house straightening cushions and moving her collection of Art Deco silver frames to different positions.

The house was lovely. Comfortable and tasteful, a true reflection of her personal style. Every few months the editors of *Vogue* or *Harpers* would phone begging yet again for a chance to photograph her at home. 'Absolutely not,' she would say firmly. 'I no longer wish to be in the public eye.'

And she meant what she said. Three years previously she had divorced her husband, prominent businessman and theatre owner Elliott Berkeley. And by doing so given up all the trappings of being a rich man's socialite wife. *The* beautiful Mrs Elliott Berkeley, perfect hostess, perfect fashionplate, perfect perfect perfect.

Oh, if they only knew the truth . . .

Carrie Jones, thirteen-year-old prostitute. Set on the streets by her grandma and uncle. Sent to Welfare Island. Hooked up with a pimp named Whitejack who fed her drugs while she plied her trade. At fifteen she was in a mental institution, out of her mind, and completely alone in the world. Nobody cared if she lived or died.

She stayed locked up for nine long anguished years. And then came the jobs . . . everything from working as a maid to a dime-a-dance girl. Until she found herself pregnant and realized the only way to make enough money to survive with the baby was to return to the life she knew so well . . .

A whorehouse was better than working the streets.

A whorehouse meant her baby son, Steven, had a home, clean clothes, and a girl to look after him.

A whorehouse was her life, until dear sweet Bernard Dimes rescued her and four-year-old Steven.

She would always be grateful to Bernard . . . always love him . . . Even though he had been dead twenty-five years.

Bernard had introduced her to a different world. He was an elegant man with money and class. He was also a successful theatrical producer. When he married Carrie his friends and acquaintances were shocked. Who was she? Where had she come from? And how could he marry a *black* woman?

It was Bernard's private joke – his boldest production yet – that he invented a background for Carrie which suddenly made her acceptable in their prejudiced eyes. According to Bernard's story she was a beautiful African princess whom he had met on safari in Kenya and lured back to America with her baby son to marry him.

What an outrageous lie. Only someone like Bernard could carry it off.

Carrie lived the charade because it amused him. And by living it she became it – and was soon embraced by the media. Even her son, Steven, never knew the truth until 1977, when she was forced to reveal everything.

She had shattered his world, his security, his heritage. Disoriented and angry he had given up his job as a respected public prosecutor and left America for Europe where he wandered around for two years, finally returning at the end of 1979. He visited her once then to tell her that he understood. But she knew he didn't mean it. He was cold and distant. She hadn't heard from him since.

And then he had called her unexpectedly two days ago. 'I have to see you,' he'd announced.

And soon he would be there.

*

Steven Berkeley drove a black Porsche. It wasn't his. It belonged to his friend, Jerry Myerson, who had loaned it to him for the day. Jerry was one of New York's most successful lawyers. He deserved a Porsche if that's what turned him on. Frankly, Steven considered paying fifty thousand bucks for a car ridiculous. But he had to admit, it *was* fun to drive.

He played with the accelerator, secretly pleased with the surge of power the pressure produced.

Jerry Myerson was a good friend. They had attended high school, college and law school together. Jerry had officiated as best man at his 1966 wedding to an unsuitable dancer named Zizi. Bad news Zizi. Five feet two of dynamic trouble every inch of the way. He had stayed married to her for five years. The divorce was a relief. Carrie had always hated her.

Carrie.

His mother.

For a moment he felt the familiar surge of rejection and anger. Feelings he had hoped to conquer by now. Ever since she had told him . . . revealed herself . . .

All his life he had believed he had been born in Africa, that his father was dead, and that Carrie had brought him to America as a baby.

The truth was a shock.

Born in America. Brought up in a brothel. And his father could be either of two men – both of them white.

He had forced their names out of her. One of them a brief one night affair. The other a rape. Forty-one years ago he had been conceived, and Carrie couldn't tell him which one was his father. But he had to know. Then he could get on with his life.

Automatically his foot pressed down hard and his mouth tightened into a grim line. Steven was undeniably handsome. Over six feet tall with the body of an athlete, very direct green eyes, black curly hair, and skin the colour of rich milk chocolate. Age suited him. As each year passed he seemed to get better looking. Once he had been one of the hottest Assistant DAs in New York. A steely prosecutor, with an incorruptible reputation. But Carrie's revelations had thrown him off track, and for the last three years he had bummed around Europe, taking transient jobs, and trying to come to terms with the reality of his beginnings.

Carrie had brought him up believing in a dream. When she shattered it, she broke his life in two. It was taking time to put it back together again.

Now, finally, as he drove toward Fire Island, he knew what he had to do. Three years ago she had given him two names, Freddy Lester and Gino Santangelo. One of them was his father. And whether she liked it or not, she was going to help him discover which one.

Chapter 36

The hot sun burned into Lucky's body as she stretched out on a mat, beside a sea-water swimming pool shaped like a grotto. She wore only the bottom half of a miniscule bikini, and her skin glowed with oily bronzeness. Her jet hair was plaited into one thick roll, and a Sony Walkman rested beside her, the earphones firmly in place. She listened to the soulful sounds of Bobby Womack, a long-time favourite. And his voice enveloped her, leaving no room for thought as she lost herself to 'Inherit the Wind'. Only when the tape clicked off did she finally open her eyes.

It was a hot day. Blue skies, with little puffs of clouds so high they just drifted like decorations. A very slight breeze made the heat bearable.

Lucky stood up, stretched languorously, then dove into the pool. The water was cold, unheated. But invigorating and refreshing. Easily she began to do laps, cleaving the water with a stylish symmetry. She did not stop until the familiar white shoes of Dimitri appeared at the edge of the pool.

'Mr Stanislopoulos,' she said formally, treading water.

His piercing eyes met hers. She liked his eyes. They were deep, knowledgeable. He had the look of a man who had been many places and done many things.

'Lucky,' he said, equally formal. 'And how are you today?'

As if he didn't know. As if for nearly two years they had not been as close as two people could be.

Dimitri Stanislopoulos. Sixty-four years old. Old enough to be her father.

And like her father, he was a man of substance and power. A man with whom she had been able to find a comfortable companionship and kind of love. Not the white heat of Marco, but a satisfactory relationship.

*

When Lucky arrived in New York ready to start over and conquer the world she had not planned on being pregnant. Hell, no! She had never thought about having a baby. Not for her the maternal instinct. Babies were for women who wanted to sit home, change diapers and vegetate.

Coolly she had thought about abortion. She had gone to sleep thinking about abortion, and eight hours later she awoke knowing it wasn't the answer.

Of course, she knew who the father was. No doubt about that. *Dimitri was the only man she'd slept with in months.*

Oh God! Dimitri Stanislopoulos, father of Olympia. Oh God!

She hugged the secret to her for a week. She didn't have to tell anyone, not even Gino. She could have the baby and bring it up herself – she was more than capable and certainly financially independent. Then other thoughts crowded her head. The child, when it began to grow, would want to know who its father was. And surely the child was entitled to that knowledge?

The child.

Boy or girl?

She didn't care. Whatever it was she wanted it.

Suddenly her life took on a whole new meaning.

She called Dimitri in Paris, choosing from the list of numbers he had given her.

It was three o'clock in the morning there. He was asleep and short-tempered about being disturbed. 'Yes?' he snapped.

'This is Lucky Santangelo. You're going to be a father,' she announced. No point in playing games.

'What?'

'I'm having a baby. And you are the fortunate daddy.'

Dimitri sat up in bed, relieved he was alone. 'I don't understand –' he began.

'It's easy. We played the game. We scored a goal. I'm delighted now that I've got used to the idea. How do you feel?'

He cleared his throat and squinted at his watch. 'Have you any idea what time it is?' he asked sternly.

'What's the matter with you? I just told you you're going to be a daddy and you're worried about the time!'

He didn't know what to say. So he said what he always did when in doubt. 'Do you want money?'

'Huh?'

He missed the ice which crept into her voice and plunged ahead. 'Call my secretary at a decent hour. She'll send you a cheque for an abortion and your expenses.'

'You aaaaasshole!' Lucky screamed. 'Do you honestly think I called you for money? *You fucking* creep. *Drop dead.' And she slammed the phone down in a fury.*

Who did the man think he was? How dare he speak to her as if she was some little hooker looking to score. How dare he! Screw *Dimitri Stanislopoulos.* And *his stupid millions. She hadn't phoned wanting anything except his joy.*

Several months passed, during which time Lucky moved into the East Hampton house. Now she was pregnant she didn't feel ready to conquer New York. And yet, sitting around for months on end was not for her either. She saw a top gynaecologist who assured her the early morning nausea and constant exhaustion would only last a short while. He prescribed vitamins, a healthy diet, and rest.

She was fed up with rest. She needed action.

In the mail one morning she received an invitation to Gino's wedding. Immediately she called Costa. They talked it over and decided to go together. Not that she wished to attend.

And yet she knew that she must. She refused to give Susan Martino the satisfaction of not *being there.*

The wedding was a circus. Layer upon layer of movie stars, studio executives, show biz lawyers, agents, directors and producers. Gino's Vegas friends were lost in the shuffle.

Lucky felt like an outsider. Why did she feel she was at Gino's funeral, not his wedding? She exchanged only a few words with him, and sat quietly at a table with Costa, observing Beverly Hills social intercourse. She wore a simple white silk suit and emeralds she had bought for herself. Her four month pregnancy did not show yet, but the constant tiredness was causing faint circles beneath her eyes and she was still exhausted.

Gino did not comment on her appearance, but Costa was immediately concerned. He wanted to know what she was doing, and when she shrugged and said 'nothing', he frowned, because knowing Lucky as well as he did, he was aware something *was wrong. She did not have the temperament for just sitting around. He put it down to the fact that Gino's marriage was upsetting her more than she cared to admit.*

When Lucky met Susan's two offspring she loathed them immediately. A couple of snobbish rich kids with inflated ideas of their own importance.

And then she observed the entrance of English prima donna Francesca Fern, with her entourage. Five minutes later Dimitri Stanislopoulos appeared.

'Oh no!' Lucky muttered.

'What?' asked Costa.

'Nothing.' She slouched in her seat on the tented patio, hoping he wouldn't see her. Better still, wouldn't remember her. Their baby was not for sharing. He'd had his chance and blown it.

He did notice her. Later. Fortunately they were surrounded by people when he came over to the table, kissed her hand, and mouthed a few inane sentences. She noticed that his eyes flicked over her, looking for a sign, wondering if he had imagined their Paris conversation.

She was coolly polite. Screw him.

A week later he turned up at the door of her East Hampton

house. It was fall, and the trees were golden brown, the leaves scattered on the ground in studied confusion. She wore a white track suit, tennis shoes and no make-up. Her hair was piled untidily on top of her head.

'You look very young,' he said, standing on the doorstep, his limousine and driver waiting in the driveway.

'What do you want?' she asked flatly.

His eyes dropped to the slight bulge around her waist she hadn't bothered to conceal. 'I want to know if it's true. Are you having my baby?'

Voice like ice. 'No.'

He was very tall. A big man. Powerful looking with his shock of white hair and piercing eyes. 'I think you're lying.'

'I don't give a damn what *you think.'*

'If that's the case why did you phone me?'

'That was months ago,' she said coldly. 'I was testing you. You failed.'

His eyes scorched hers. World-weary eyes filled with Greek fire. 'I'll be back,' he said.

And he was. There was no getting rid of him. As if to make up for his initial reaction he pursued her relentlessly. Silver purple roses every day. Crates of champagne. Jars of caviar. Baskets of exotic fruits.

She finally allowed him to take her to dinner. He sent his helicopter to collect her, and they dined aboard a private yacht which circled Manhattan as they feasted on pâte and lobster.

Later they made love. His large hands traced her stomach gently. 'I want a boy,' he said.

'Don't be such a chauvinist,' she replied.

On July the second, 1979, in a private nursing home in Connecticut, Lucky gave birth to a son. Dimitri was present at the birth.

They named the child Roberto Stavros Gino Santangelo Stanislopoulos. He was their secret. And had remained so.

*

Lucky floated on her back and held her arms invitingly toward Dimitri. 'Come on in,' she called. 'It's wonderful.'

He did not need asking twice. He pulled off his white La Coste tennis shirt. Unbuckled his black snakeskin belt. Kicked off his shoes and removed his white linen pants. Dimitri Stanislopoulos did not believe in underwear. He had a firm strong body. An excellent physique for a man of his age. He was a big man in every way, and took great pride in his physical strength and robust health. With a roar he jumped into the water, trying to grab Lucky, who wriggled from his grasp and kicked off down the pool.

He followed her with a powerful crawl until he cornered her in the deep end. A shadow lay over this end of the pool, and a rock hewn waterfall took up one corner. Lucky swam to the waterfall and tried to shelter behind it out of his reach.

Dimitri pressed through the falling water and crushed her against the rough side. With one hand he tore the bottom of her bikini off and thrust himself upon her.

'You sneaky sonofabitch,' she objected, half jokingly, as they began to sink beneath the cool green water.

He didn't relinquish his hold, merely gripped her firmly, his thighs like steel as they rocked together beneath the water. When they surfaced she was gasping for air, but her legs were wrapped tightly around his waist and her face flushed with pleasure. Silently they finished the act, exploding with satisfaction at the same moment.

Dimitri let go of her. 'I think it's time for lunch,' he said.

'Jesus!' Lucky exclaimed. 'Sex. Food. You certainly believe in catering to your appetites!'

'Why not? Life is for living good. I worked hard for what I've got today. Now I enjoy myself. Surely you agree?' He hauled himself from the pool and wrapped himself in a terry cloth robe.

She swam to the side. 'I hope our son doesn't take after you.'

Dimitri reached down to help her out. 'I hope he does.'

'Yeh. He'll be a fat stud. Great! Can't wait.'

Dimitri roared with laughter. 'Am I fat, Lucky. Am I a stud?'

'Given half a chance,' she teased.

He smiled and passed her a robe. Then he scanned the horizon and said, 'Let's hope there are no paparazzi hiding anywhere today. I don't enjoy giving exhibitions.'

Lucky followed his gaze. The pool overlooked the sea. There were no craft in sight. Sometimes small vessels disguised as fishing boats bobbed about in the distance with hidden cameramen using long-lens cameras aboard. Dimitri's island was considered fair game. Today all was clear.

'Lunch,' Dimitri said firmly.

'You go on up. I'll follow in five minutes.'

'As you wish.'

She was glad she had relented and allowed Dimitri to share their son. He was a great father when she let him be. But keeping their secret was becoming more complicated each day. She was sure the servants in the Greek villa knew. And CeeCee, the pretty black girl who looked after Roberto. And the elderly couple who took care of the East Hampton house. And Dimitri's lawyer.

A secret is no longer a secret when shared by more than two people. Lucky sighed. Dimitri kept on mentioning marriage, but she shied away from the idea. She had tried it once and hated every moment.

Dimitri was becoming more insistent every day. He wanted to tell the world about his son. He wanted to be sure everyone knew Roberto was his rightful heir. 'If anything happens to me,' he warned Lucky constantly, 'there will be nothing but problems.'

'Why?' she asked. 'You told me you've changed your will.'

'It's not enough,' he worried. 'Olympia will want everything. She'll fight my instructions. I know her.'

Lucky had not renewed her friendship with Olympia. Dimitri thought it best they did not meet. She also had not mentioned to Gino that he was a grandfather. He had married Susan and settled in Beverly Hills like a senile old fart. She heard he had people running the Vegas hotels and had liquidated a lot of his other business concerns. She had received more than her fair share of the Magiriano, banked it, and forgotten it. Her career was on hold while she enjoyed her son. Why should she share him with Gino? He hardly ever called her. She hadn't seen him since his wedding.

Sometimes she awoke in the middle of the night and missed him. He was old. He had already suffered one heart attack. Why didn't she go to him, show him his grandson, mend broken bridges?

Because he didn't care about her.

Because he had chosen Susan Martino over her.

Lunch was served on a magnificent terrace overlooking the sea. Lucky could remember visiting Dimitri's private island as a teenager with Olympia. She had never imagined she would be back as the mother of his child. Some of the servants remained the same. She wondered what they thought. Did they remember her? Would they tell Olympia?

'Olympia rarely comes here,' Dimitri said dourly, when she mentioned it.

Lucky knew he did not approve of his daughter's high profile romance with a drugged out English rock star. They were constantly making headlines. It infuriated Dimitri. 'The girl is a fool,' he had commented. 'She's married three fortune hunters. Now she's living with this . . . this . . . degenerate.'

Lucky stifled a laugh. Sometimes Dimitri acted his age.

Not in bed. In bed he was a master. Sometimes too controlled and technically perfect. He knew everything there was to know, and used his skills accordingly.

She once asked him how many women he'd had. 'Thousands,' he'd replied, without a trace of embarrassment.

Thousands. Hmmm . . . No wonder he knew every move to make.

She wondered if Gino had had thousands.

Probably. The two shared much in common.

After lunch CeeCee appeared carrying Roberto. He looked like Lucky – dark haired and black eyed, with an infectious grin. He also looked like Gino. She knew she was being unfair keeping them apart.

Dimitri's face lit up. They had been on the island with him

for a week, and he never tired of spending time with his son. Usually he only saw him when he visited Lucky's East Hampton house.

When CeeCee took the baby for his afternoon nap, Dimitri strode restlessly back and forth across the terrace. 'Lucky,' he said impatiently, cracking his knuckles irritatingly. 'Enough is enough. My son has to have my name. Legally. I insist. We must marry.'

'How romantic,' she murmured.

'For God's sake. You know I adore you.'

Did he? They had been together on and off for a year and a half. During that time she knew he had seen Francesca Fern. She hadn't questioned him. It was not her style to cling.

'I don't know . . .' she began.

'What can I do to persuade you?'

What could he do? She had been thinking about Atlantic City again. She missed the hotel business. The excitement, the power . . .

She had money of her own, but not nearly enough. As Mrs Dimitri Stanislopoulos she would be able to do whatever she wanted.

And Dimitri was right. Roberto deserved the protection of bearing his father's name legally.

'I want to build a hotel,' she began slowly.

He nodded encouragingly. 'Whatever you want, Lucky, you can have. Just tell me, and it will be yours.'

Chapter 37

'No,' said Jess into the phone cradled next to her ear. 'Lennie Golden is booked solid for months. There's no way he can even read the script.'

'Please,' the person on the other end begged. 'If he reads it, he'll love it, and then he'll want to do it.'

'Sorry.' She replaced the receiver and yelled out, 'Vickie. Where the hell are you?'

Vickie teetered into the room on dangerously high stiletto

heels. She wore them with black fish-net tights, spandex shorts, and a lurex boob tube. Her fine brown hair was teased to the limit, and her outstandingly ugly face was carefully made-up. She looked like your friendly neighbourhood hooker, not a personal secretary, which is what she was supposed to be. Jess wanted to fire her, but Lennie wouldn't hear of it.

'Sorry, Jess,' Vickie squeaked. 'I was in the john. I got a little bathroom problem this week.'

'You've always got a little bathroom problem,' Jess complained and stood up from behind the old worn desk where she had been sitting. 'I do not expect to have to answer phones. That's what we pay *you* for.'

Vickie lowered two sets of false eyelashes. 'Sorry, Jess.'

Where did Lennie find them? The last one he had hired looked like a man in drag, but at least she/he answered phones. This one was always in the bathroom.

'I gotta go out,' Jess said, reluctant to leave her in charge. 'Can you hack it?'

Vickie grinned. She had never managed the money for a capping job, and her teeth were a mess. 'Can I hack it? What a question!'

'Take messages,' Jess admonished sternly.

Vickie nodded.

Jess left the small office in an unassuming building on Sunset, and knew without a doubt they needed larger space and two *decent* secretaries. Lennie was becoming big business and they were running a penny ante operation. Okay for six months ago, but not now. Not with Lennie rising like a meteor.

Jess rode the elevator to the underground garage and collected her car – a used Datsun. She kept on meaning to trade it in for something better, but who had the time? So much had happened, so many good things. Thank God she had listened to Lennie and left Vegas for LA. At first it had been awful. She had sat in the hotel room Lennie put her in and stared at television day and night. He had allowed her to do that for a few weeks, and then one day he had said, 'Okay, kid. That's it. You're out on the road again.' And from that moment on he hadn't left her alone – he dragged her everywhere he went. She met all his friends – Suna, Shirlee, Joey Firello, Foxie and the statuesque Rainbow, Isaac and his pretty wife. They all accepted her immediately and went out of their way to rally round. The twins took her to the gym with them. Joey insisted she sit in on several tapings of his TV show. Rainbow escorted her to Frederick's – an outrageous lingerie shop on Hollywood Boulevard, and encouraged her to buy a slit up the side purple satin nightgown. Isaac and his wife invited her to their house in the valley for Sunday Bar-B-Qs. And Foxie, whose rudeness was legendary, developed a fast crush – and whenever she was around spent his entire time regaling her with stories of his colourful life. Since he was now eighty-six years old, they never ran out of conversation.

Lennie, of course, was always there for her. Supportive and understanding. A true friend. Without him she knew she would have fallen to pieces. But he pulled her through it, and she owed him plenty.

Eventually the time had come for her to stop depending on other people. She was running out of money, and she had no intention of sponging off Lennie. But what to do? There was no way she was returning to Vegas, and jobs for croupiers were not exactly heavy on the ground in LA. She turned to Foxie for advice.

He bit off the end of a stinking old stogie, spat on the floor, and suggested something she had never even thought of. 'Go into personal management,' he said. 'You're a smart little broad with a lotta moxy. Use it.'

'Personal management of what?'

'Lennie, of course.'

'Lennie's *got* an agent.'

'Who's talkin' agenting?' He waved his cigar wildly in the air.

'If he has Isaac, why would he need a manager?'

Foxie shook his head in disbelief. 'An' I thought you was

smart. For a girl grew up in Vegas you don't know a lot.'

'Sure I do,' Jess bristled. '*Stars* have agents and managers. When they can afford them.'

'An' how do you think they got to be stars in the first place? You think some agent with thirty clients an' a mortgage to pay got 'em there?'

'I don't know.'

Foxie nodded wisely. 'Then listen.' He talked fast, a jumble of words. And what he said made sense. Sure Lennie had an agent, and Isaac was okay, he had a stable of young comedians and did his best for all of them. But his best, split among all his clients, just wasn't good enough. Foxie cited the Merv Griffin Show as an example. 'Lennie walked on account of wanting to be with you at your kid's funeral. You think Isaac's bin back to 'em with the name Lennie Golden? Naw. He's shit scared . . . thinks it might affect his other clients an' *their* shots on the show. That's an agent for you. Now, a personal manager would be in there hustlin'. Get the difference?'

She got it. And it made sense. She also heard for the first time that Lennie had given up his chance of appearing on the Griffin Show to be with her. She owed him more than she'd thought, and she was determined to pay him back.

'How do you become a manager?' she asked.

'You understand deals. You believe in your client two hundred percent. An' you go for it no holds barred. I coulda bin the best manager in the business if I'd wanted to. I coulda sold shit to a stable of horses with dysentery!'

Jess giggled. Old Foxie certainly knew how to turn a phrase. 'Teach me,' she begged.

'You're a natural,' he replied. 'An' you got the right goods t'sell. Lennie's gonna be big. I picked it when he first auditioned.'

Within a week she had re-booked Lennie on the Griffin Show.

He was delighted. 'How'd you do it, babe?'

She grinned. 'Moxy and no mortgage.'

'Huh?'

'Forget it.'

And so his climb began. Jess was dedicated, and there was nothing else on her mind. She went for it, just as Foxie had taught her to do. And Lennie was good, so everything she got him paid off and led to other things.

Isaac was pissed at first, but he soon got used to it. Especially when Jess proved she knew what she was doing better than anyone else.

The Griffin Show first. A repeat performance two weeks later because Merv liked him. A third shot a month after that because audience reaction was strong. Two guest appearances on Joey Firello's comedy hour. And then the offer of a weekly TV show in which he got to play a crazy doctor in charge of a health spa. The programme, called 'The Springs', was a cross between 'Soap', and 'Hill Street Blues'. It started off with hardly any ratings at all, until gradually it built up a small cult following, then a large cult following, and suddenly it busted right to the top of the ratings and became a hit halfway through its second season. Lennie and the rest of the virtually unknown cast developed sensational TVQs overnight.

That had taken place six weeks ago. To say that Lennie was now hot was putting it mildly.

Jess steered the Datsun into the slow moving afternoon traffic. There was so much going on, and hardly time to handle it all. She honked at an erratic driver who promptly gave her the V sign.

'Shove it up your ass, sailor,' she mouthed, and shot past him.

The first thing she had to do was get Lennie straight. Rumour had it he was drinking, although not in front of her. But then, since the success of the show, she had hardly seen him. He was either doing interviews, working, or socializing with a series of willowy blondes who passed through his life like a dose of salts.

That was all they needed. A drinking problem just when he was on the brink.

The erratic driver cut in front of her, forcing her to brake abruptly. She tried to control her temper but couldn't resist a massive blast of the horn.

Stay calm, she warned herself. She was on her way to lunch with Lennie and she didn't want to arrive flustered. It was important to maintain a cool, collected exterior. All the better to find out what he had been up to.

*

The blonde had said she was nineteen but Lennie wasn't betting on it. Seventeen more like. A sexually experienced seventeen-year-old whom he couldn't wait to get rid of. One evening of lust was enough. He wished they didn't always want to stay the night.

She was dressing. Slowly. White pants, a cutaway top, lace-up shoes, dozens of bangles.

'Can you drop me in Westwood?' she asked.

'I'm not going that way. But I'll call you a cab.'

'I don't have any cash.'

'I'll pay the driver.'

She tuned into a soap opera on television while he phoned the taxi company and told them to send someone over fast. He wanted her out of his apartment. Not that there was anything wrong with her. She was pretty, with a Californian body, and a pleasant enough personality. But she was his third blonde this week, and he was overdosing on available pussy, and not liking himself for it.

When the cab buzzed from downstairs he pressed twenty dollars into her hand, promised he would call soon, and shut the door behind her with a sigh of relief.

Immediately she was gone he stripped the sheets off the bed, dumped them on the floor, opened all the windows, and fixed himself a refreshing vodka and orange juice. It was eleven in the morning. Not too bad. His one day off and nothing to do until a one o'clock lunch with Jess at Scandia.

He had been working non-stop. Not only was he re-writing his dialogue on 'The Springs' as well as performing on the show most days, but he was putting together some new material for his act, and also trying to work on a screenplay.

Plus there was constant publicity to do, and a different party every night.

Well, why not? Didn't he deserve it at long last?

The phone rang. It was his mother. Dear old Alice had re-entered his life with a vengeance. Amazing what a touch of fame could do.

'Lennie, dear,' she said.

He reached for the vodka and gave himself a refill. 'Yes?'

'I've been thinking.'

'Yes?'

'Why can't you get *me* on the Merv Griffin Show?'

He was incredulous. 'What?'

'Don't sound so surprised. I'd be marvellous.'

'Doing what?'

'Doing what I do better than anyone. Telling about my life. Telling stories.'

'What stories?'

'About Las Vegas. Your father. Me. I've had the most interesting life of anyone I know. Someone should write a book about me . . . would they have a bestseller! I shiver to think.'

'So do I.'

'Don't be rude.'

'Who's rude?'

'Since you got on television every week you're rude. I never hear from you, never see you. How do you think that makes me feel? I'm your mother, Lennie, and you've thrown me aside like old clothes.'

All of a sudden Alice the swinger was his mother, a fact she would not have admitted six months ago. After his second Merv Griffin appearance she had written him a letter care of the show. He had called and listened to her complain. It seemed she was put out because he hadn't invited her to the taping. Shortly after that he made the trek to Marina del Rey and spent a day in her company. She had fixed him a bacon sandwich, confided all about her new boyfriend – a twenty-six-year-old musician who was 'out on the road'. And embarrassed him with an exhibition of six new exercises she claimed kept her fit, young and sexually active.

He hadn't seen her since, but she phoned him regularly – very regularly since 'The Springs' had zoomed in the ratings. He sent her money which she never mentioned, and put up with her phone calls. What else could he do? She *was* his mother.

'Well?' demanded Alice.

'Very.'

'What?'

'Very well.'

There was a frosty silence while Alice considered what to say next. She came up with a humdinger. 'I'm thinking of getting an agent.'

Lennie reached for the vodka. 'What the hell for?'

'Ha! You think you're the only one should have a career. If you cared about me at all you'd give me *your* agent. I sing, dance, tell funny stories. Why can't you get me a guest spot on your show?'

The thought of going to Isaac Luther and offering Alice as a client was too hilarious to contemplate. Lennie choked back laughter. 'Gotta go. I'm running late.'

'Think about introducing me to your agent. You won't be sorry. It's never too late to make it, you know.'

'Yeah, ma.'

'Call me Alice – it sounds better. And lie about your age. Stick to twenty-five, you don't look any older. You can get away with it.'

'Thanks for the advice.'

He hung up still laughing. If nothing else she was a character.

Harriet, the maid, arrived shortly after. She was extremely old and had trouble walking. Her cleaning left plenty to be desired, but he had inherited her when he rented the apartment – a one bedroom penthouse in a service building on Doheny.

'Morning, Mr Gold,' she said.

'Golden,' he corrected. She had only been working for him a year. She nodded absentmindedly and went into the kitchen where she took off her shoes and switched on the television.

Lennie returned to the bathroom. He stripped off his robe and stepped under a cold shower. He looked forward to lunch with Jess, and then at three o'clock he had an interview with *People* magazine. He hated giving interviews, they were an intrusion on his privacy, and he had nothing to say about his personal life.

What personal life?

Was getting laid a lot personal? He doubted it.

Towelling himself dry he wondered what to wear. Most of his clothes rested in a heap on the floor waiting for someone to take them to the cleaners. From the pile he extracted black pants and a black shirt. Jess would probably complain. 'You need to buy new clothes,' she would say.

Now he had the money he didn't have the time.

What *did* he have time for?

Working.

Screwing.

Drinking.

Working.

Little Jess had really done it for him. She was a dynamo. She had taken over his static career and shoved him up the public's ass like a rocket. And not a moment too soon. She had saved both their lives. And now he was really on his way. TV series. Good money, Christ, if *People* magazine wanted him it meant he was somebody. They were going to take photos – a day in the life of Lennie Golden. He wondered if Eden would see them, and stepped on the thought.

Eden Antonio was old news.

Eden Antonio meant nothing to him.

He reviewed their relationship. Three years together in New York. Fought like tigers. She went west. He followed. One meeting. Great sex. And that was it. She had used him because she probably felt horny, and dumped him with about as much feeling as a sphinx. Christ, how he hated her.

Bull . . . shit.

What?

Bull . . . shit. If she came to you now you'd grab her.

Maybe.

Don't give me that maybe crap.

He loathed the conversations which took place in the privacy of his head because they were true.

He knew things about her.

She was living with some married hood. The guy had bought her a house, clothes, jewellery.

The twins gave him fragments. He tried to appear uninterested.

He knew where her house was. He knew her private phone number. He had driven past the house a few times. Phoned and hung up more than once.

But he refused to contact her. If she wanted him let *her* come running.

And if she ever did . . .

Dressed in black he prepared to leave the apartment.

Harriet lolled in the kitchen, varicose-veined legs stretched before her, a game show blaring on the television. 'Just taking a lunch break, Mr Gould,' she said contentedly.

'Put clean sheets on the bed,' he instructed, knowing she wouldn't and that he would have to do it himself. Feeling sorry for the old bag was one thing, but he needed a maid desperately.

In the underground garage he collected his new black BMW. What a car! He had walked into the showroom and bought it off the floor six weeks ago. His first extravagance. It felt good. He wished he had someone to share his success with. Jess was terrific, but she wasn't around when he really needed her in the cold empty hours of the early morning when he desired the warmth of a lover, a companion, a soul-mate.

Sometimes he would reach for the blonde asleep beside him, wake her gently and make love.

No. Not love. Sex. Just sex.

Success was great. Money was great. Recognition was great. It just wasn't enough.

Something was missing in his life.

Chapter 38

Driving back to New York, Steven Berkeley tried to decide how the meeting with his mother, Carrie, had gone.

She had been thrilled to see him, overly attentive. She had wanted him to stay the weekend, but he had declined, anxious to get to the point and out of there.

'Look,' he had finally said, 'I can't lie to you, and I don't intend to. I need to get my life straight, and to do that I have to know who my father is.'

There had been a long pause, while she got up, paced the room, sat down again, and finally looked him in the eye. 'I've told you everything I know,' her voice hardly more than a whisper.

'You gave me two names,' he said harshly. 'Two names, and that's supposed to satisfy me? Well, it doesn't. Not by a long way. I have to know *which one* is my father. And *you* have to help me.'

It had not been easy. She didn't want to cooperate. She had no desire to sift through the ashes of her past. But gradually he convinced her that if she ever wanted to see him again she had no choice. Finally she had agreed to the plan he set before her.

Now, driving along the half-empty freeway, he wondered if he was doing right. Jerry Myerson had advised him against doing anything. 'What do you think's going to happen?' Jerry had questioned. 'You drag Carrie to see some guy who might – and I emphasize the might – just be your old man. Then you tell him the facts – like forty-two years ago he went to bed with Carrie – and *then* you ask him to take a blood test. Are you *kidding*? If you were white they'd kick your ass out the door. But when they take a look at you they're going to *laugh* you out. Why put yourself through it? And why humiliate Carrie?'

Jerry didn't understand. There are some things in life that had to be done.

He knew where Gino Santangelo was. Still alive. Seventy-four years old. Married to Tiny Martino's widow and living in Beverly Hills. There was no doubt he was the same Gino Santangelo Carrie had had a one-night affair with back in 1938 when he owned a night club in New York called 'Clemmies'.

Tracking Freddy Lester had not been so easy. The only information Carrie could provide was that he was from a New York society family, his best friend was named Mel, and at the time she met him he had recently left college.

Steven had found three candidates. One a judge. One a publisher. And the third a retired doctor. All three were about the right age, lived in or near New York, and shared different versions of the same name. Judge Frederick Lester. Fred E. Lester. And Fredd Lesster, MD.

Of the three Carrie would have to pick the right one.

Jerry Myerson was correct. It was not going to be simple. But as a former DA, Steven had tenacity and determination, and even more important – he knew he could do it.

With a little help from Carrie. She at least owed him that.

Chapter 39

Olympia had suspected for some time her father had a secret mistress. Not that she cared. Dimitri could do what he liked, and so could she. But her curiosity was aroused. Who was the mystery woman? And why the secrecy?

She ran into Francesca Fern in New York at '21'.

'Dahling!' they both exclaimed. 'You look divine! We must have lunch.' Kisses brushed cheeks.

'How about tomorrow?' Olympia added, interested to find out if Francesca knew what was going on.

Francesca, who had no particular desire to lunch with Dimitri's petulant daughter, could think of no quick excuse.

'The Russian Tea Room, one o'clock,' Olympia stated firmly.

Francesca nodded vaguely, planning to cancel at the last minute. But in the morning Horace annoyed her. She had a screaming argument with her agent on the phone, and lunch with Olympia seemed a welcome excuse to storm from the house.

Olympia awoke late in her luxurious Fifth Avenue apartment overlooking Central Park. Flash was in the south of France working on a new album with 'The Layabouts'. She planned to join him in a few days, but quite frankly she was enjoying the peace and quiet. Life with Flash was a series of parties, and peculiar people, late night drug trips and kinky sex. Not that she minded any of it – but the break would do him good – make him appreciate her. Sometimes she felt he took her too much for granted. He had money, but never spent a dime. He always expected her to pay for everything – which she did. 'The rich bint'll get it,' he'd say to anyone who asked. 'She's got more loot than the friggin' Queen of bleedin' Blighty.'

Olympia, remembering her lunch appointment with Francesca, hurried to dress. She put on a cream leather mini skirt which refused to zip. She discarded that and wriggled into a silk Chloe dress which made her look fat. She finally settled on a blue linen suit which hid a multitude of sins. Lately Flash had taken to calling her Tubs, which infuriated her. She, in turn, had nicknamed him Bones, which made him snigger.

Tubs and Bones. The darlings of the gossip columns. Oh, if the public only knew!

The two women arrived simultaneously, kissed each other vaguely on the cheek, and settled into a lefthand booth, whereupon Olympia ordered a Bloody Mary, and Francesca decided on Perrier. Olympia immediately regretted her decision to invite Francesca to lunch. What were they going to talk about for two hours? They had nothing in common except Dimitri, and five minutes would dispose of him.

'I have a two o'clock appointment with my couturier,' Francesca announced briskly, as if thinking the same thoughts.

'Good,' replied Olympia swiftly. 'I have a manicure at two.'

Francesca reached into her purse and produced a thin black cheroot. She placed it between brightly carmined lips, and two waiters leapt forward. She accepted their attentions with the attitude of a star, and tossed her flame-red hair. 'I leave for Paris in the morning,' she announced. 'I never stop travelling.'

Olympia plunged right in. 'Have you seen Dimitri recently?' she asked.

'Isn't he in Greece?' Francesca replied off-handedly.

'Yes.' Olympia paused mysteriously. 'Again.'

Francesca did not jump to the bait. Her hooded eyes surveyed the room, and her husky voice summoned a waiter. 'Menu,' she commanded. She looked bored.

Olympia persevered. 'This is his third trip to the island this year.'

Francesca turned toward her. 'So?'

'So . . . don't you think it's a little . . . strange?'

Francesca shrugged, snatched the menu from a hovering Captain, and studied it intently. 'Nothing strange. It's *his* island.'

'Hmm,' said Olympia. '*I* think it's strange that he hands out explicit instructions *nobody* is to visit while he's there. And that includes me. I wanted to send my daughter and I was informed I couldn't.'

Francesca dragged deeply on her cheroot, and waved to a passing producer. 'Why are you telling *me*? *I* have no wish to go there.'

'You and Dimitri are such good . . . friends. I thought you might know why he's acting like this. Does he have a new girlfriend?'

Francesca turned her brilliant gaze on the Captain. 'A herb omelette,' she requested. 'And a green salad. No dressing.'

Olympia frowned. Francesca didn't seem at all concerned that Dimitri might be shacked up with a secret new love.

'For you, Miz Stanislopoulos?' the Captain asked respectfully.

'Blinis, sour cream, caviar, apple pancakes, and a dish of strawberries on the side.'

Francesca's look said it all. 'Don't you watch your diet?' she murmured.

'No,' Olympia replied defiantly. 'It goes straight to my tits – and Flash watches those.'

Lunch, after that, was all downhill. Stilted conversation, and a rush to be the first to leave.

'Goodbye,' said Francesca graciously. 'I expect we shall see each other as usual in August.'

'I don't know about that,' replied Olympia. 'Dimitri might be otherwise engaged. He could cancel the cruise.'

'I don't think so,' said Francesca with a knowing smile, and swept out.

Olympia could not stand the woman. She decided to stay and order another portion of strawberries, a fresh Bloody Mary, and maybe just the tiniest piece of cheesecake.

She was glad she did, for who should appear a few minutes later, but Vitos Felicidade, her short term lover before Flash.

'Vitos,' she cried out, waving vigorously.

He stopped, glanced in her direction. It took him a moment to remember her, but when he did the smile was perfect, the hand kissing beautifully executed. 'Oleeempeea! So loooovlee.'

Vitos had been the victim of a huge media blitz in the past year, and was now far more famous than when they first met. He was dressed impeccably. A Savile Row blue silk suit, custom-made shirt, gold cufflinks and a not so discreet diamond identity bracelet. He was accompanied by two women. One of them was his personal PR, and the other, a fat female carrying a tape recorder and a file of clippings.

'Thees ees the New York *Times*,' he announced, indicating the large woman. 'Ana thees – Pamela.' The PR nodded curtly, as Vitos elaborately gestured toward Olympia. 'Ladeez, may I presenta you, Senorita Ol*eee*mpeea Stan*eee*zlopoulos.'

Both women jumped to attention and stared at the voluptuous puffy-faced blonde. Her affair with rock cult figure Flash had been making headlines for two years.

Olympia nodded dismissively – she hated the press unless it was *Vogue* or *Harpers* – even *Architectural Digest* passed muster.

She scribbled her phone number on a book of matches and handed them to Vitos. 'Call me,' she instructed with a knowing look. 'Later.'

His smile was still perfection. He clicked his heels in an olde worlde fashion, saluted, and departed, the two women close behind him.

Olympia pursed her lips. He might provide a relaxing interlude. The afternoon stretched endlessly before her. She did not have an appointment with her manicurist. In fact she had nothing to do at all except return to her apartment (dull without the electric presence of Flash) and her child. Brigette, now eleven, was even more of a monster. She and Flash had experienced instant hate, and a month after their meeting Olympia had arranged for Brigette to continue her education in England. Flash's manager had suggested a suitable school in Oxfordshire, and Olympia packed Nanny Mabel and Brigette straight off. Brigette attended weekly boarding school, and Nanny Mabel was installed in a house nearby so that Brigette would have somewhere to spend the weekends. It was all working out well enough – if one chose to ignore the dreadful report cards.

The major problem was vacations. Naturally Olympia had to spend *some* time with her child and there was no escaping vacations. She had hoped she could send Brigette and Nanny to Dimitri's island, but he, surprisingly, had said no. That was when Olympia realized something was up. She had thought Francesca might have provided answers, but no such luck.

It was not easy being a mother. Awesome responsibilities. And Brigette did not appreciate a thing. The older she got the more difficult she became. Did she realize that right now Olympia was giving up precious time with Flash?

No, of course she didn't.

Leaving the restaurant, Olympia dismissed her limousine and strolled along the street to Bendels, one of her favourite department stores. She browsed for a while, picking a pale beige suede outfit, and an eight-hundred-dollar pair of sequinned shoes. She ordered them to be sent.

It was a pleasant summer day, not too humid, so she headed for Bergdorfs, and dropped another two thousand dollars there. As she proceeded across Fifth Avenue on her way home, she noticed a news vendor on the corner. She observed the stand, because, displayed amidst a bunch of girlie magazines, right next to the *Enquirer* and the *Star*, was a rag called *Pointer*. And on the cover of the rag was a large picture of Flash, leering, naked from the waist up except for a long ragged scarf, with his scrawny arm around a couldn't-be-more-than-seventeen, skinny, flaxen haired doll. And the headline read: *SECRET FLASH MARRIAGE WITH TEENAGER.*

Olympia stopped and stared. She narrowed her small blue eyes. She reached into her Hermès bag and thrust a ten dollar bill at the news vendor while snatching a copy of the offending paper. And as the old man groped for change she scanned the caption beneath the picture. It was brief and to the point:

Legendary Rock Superstar, Flash, revealed in the South of France where he is working on a new album with the Layabouts that he has been secretly married to 18-year-old Kipp Hartley for three years. Kipp, a schoolgirl when they met, is expecting their first baby early in the New Year.

Chapter 40

The decision was made. Lucky was getting married. For the second time.

'No big ceremony. Let's do it here with just the staff for witnesses,' she told Dimitri.

He agreed. That way people would have no idea when

they were married, and Roberto would not have to go through life with even a shadowy stigma of illegitimacy.

They decided to have the ceremony the day before leaving the island. Dimitri's lawyer flew in forty-eight hours beforehand. He carried with him a briefcase stuffed with papers. Most of them were for Lucky to sign. She didn't mind, as long as the most important paper of all was included. This was an agreement between her and Dimitri stating he would be entirely responsible for purchasing the land, building and financing an Atlantic City hotel which would belong to her free and clear. And on her death it would pass into the hands of their son, Roberto.

'Your wedding present,' Dimitri said, signing the document with a flourish.

She added her own signature. Other than that she relinquished most of his fortune. What did she care? Roberto would receive half of everything anyway, and the hotel was a multi-million dollar investment which would be all hers.

The day of their wedding was perfect. Lucky wore a simple white dress with flowers in her hair. Dimitri chose a lightweight suit – nothing too formal.

A Greek Orthodox priest was flown from the mainland for the ceremony. The wedding guests were the staff, and Roberto, who spent most of the day balanced on CeeCee's hip, not understanding at all what was going on, but enjoying the excitement in the air.

Lucky remembered her first wedding at sixteen. Las Vegas. Five hundred guests. A big gaudy circus she had been a part of. Unwillingly.

Gino's fault. Gino's way of getting rid of her.

The sun cooled, Roberto was put to bed, and Dimitri and Lucky dined on the terrace alone. They feasted on thinly sliced roast lamb smothered in herbs, roast potatoes flavoured with garlic, small fresh peas sauteed in butter, and for dessert, a miniature wedding cake made of strawberries and meringue.

They toasted each other with ouzo, Dimitri's favourite

liquor, and later swam naked in the pool.

In bed he made love to her slowly, and she gave herself up to the ritual of his experienced-talented lovemaking.

How different from her wedding night with Craven in the Bahamas. He had burned himself to a crisp in the hot tropical sun, and spent the night bitching and whining. What a wimp!

Tomorrow we will leave the island, she thought.

Tomorrow I must telephone Gino and Costa.

Tomorrow . . . tomorrow . . . tomorrow . . .

She drifted off to sleep, one arm flung casually across her new husband.

*

Gino raised his hand and bid five thousand dollars toward yet another needy cause. Susan had needy causes coming out her ass. One thing after another. You couldn't fault Susan Santangelo. She gave great charity. With *his* money.

Susan tossed him a bountiful smile. 'Thank you, darling,' she whispered.

They were at a function at the Century Plaza Hotel. Table for twelve. His table. No, her table. He paid. She invited.

He was seated between Susan and her good friend, Paige Wheeler. He liked Paige. She had a sense of humour, which is more than could be said for most of Susan's 'good friends'.

The other guests included Paige's husband, Ryder, a film producer who had no conversation except 'the industry'. And an assortment of Susan's attendants. Her hairdresser, her interior designer, and her dentist. And of course her children. Gemma, Miss High and Mighty. And Nathan – 'mustn't-soil-my-hands-with-a-day's-work-now-that-I've-graduated-from-college.'

Once he had thought them charming, a credit to their mother. But two years in their company had taught him otherwise. They were convinced the world owed them a living – both victims of Too much too soon and What's in it for me? Two Beverly Hills brats in designer sportsclothes and matching convertibles.

Sadly Gino had to admit he could not warm to either of them, although he had tried many times.

He knew they didn't like or even approve of him.

Fuck 'em. What did he care? He had married Susan, not her kids.

Susan was determined they should all be one big happy family, and she never stopped shoving them together.

They called him Gino.

Susan wanted them to call him father.

They tried to stay out of his way.

Susan wanted him to adopt them legally.

Jeez! He had laughed in her face when she first suggested it. '*C'mon*. They're grown-ups, adults. What's all this adoption crap?'

'They're children at heart. They need a proper father. Unless you adopt them, Gino, show them you *really* care – then I'm not sure if you'll *ever* get along.'

'Horseshit.'

'No, dear. Face the truth.'

She had already discussed it with her lawyer, who, according to Susan, thought it an excellent idea.

Whenever she brought the subject up, which was often, Gino changed the conversation. 'Wouldn't it be nice,' Susan was fond of saying, 'to have children who really care about you?'

Her way of getting in a dig at Lucky.

It *was* true. He never heard from her. She attended his wedding with an uptight expression, and he didn't think she had called more than twice since.

When he first married Susan he had never really given much thought to how Lucky must have felt. *He* was getting married, what did *she* have to do with it? But in retrospect maybe he should have shown her more consideration, after all, they had been inseparable for a year – after a lifetime of misunderstandings and fights – and he had enjoyed their closeness as much as she had.

The Santangelos. Father and daughter. An unbeatable

combination! He missed her. Maybe the time had come to mend bridges.

'Methinks your mind is elsewhere,' Paige whispered in his ear. 'And who can blame you? These events suck.'

He turned to regard Susan's friend. She was an attractive woman with her unkempt frizzy hair, and what in his day had been known as 'bedroom eyes'.

She rested her hand lightly on his thigh. 'Charity balls have always bored the pants off me. Send a cheque is my motto. Don't you agree?'

He could feel the warmth of her hand through the material of his trousers, and he could also feel his cock begin to grow hard. Susan, for a variety of reasons, had not slept with him for six weeks. He might be old, but he wasn't buried. He needed regular sex.

Paige's hand did not budge. If she moved it up a couple of inches she would feel the strength of his reaction.

She didn't have to move it. She knew.

'You're a very sexy man, Gino,' she said, making sure her words were for his ears only.

'An' you're not a bad lookin' broad,' he replied, playing the game and enjoying it.

'Don't you think,' she said, very softly indeed, 'it's high time we did something about it?'

He hadn't played around on Susan. He had been faithful.

Screw faithful. He felt hotter than he had in a long while. To tell the truth, Susan was not the greatest in bed. Too damn ladylike. She was a fantastic wife if you liked tasteful parties, and needlepoint, and weekends in Palm Springs knocking a dumb golf ball around.

Paige, unobserved by the rest of the table, and cloaked by a long cloth, was moving her hand up and rubbing his hard-on. He almost groaned aloud.

'Yeh,' he encouraged gruffly.

'Call me at my office,' she responded, with one final squeeze. 'Soon. Very soon.'

Chapter 41

Lennie had not expected the cover. Not the goddamn cover of *People* magazine.

Everyone was impressed.

Except Alice.

Naturally.

She had called in a fury. 'I'm hardly mentioned,' she screamed. 'There's no picture of me. Are you trying to sabotage my chance of a career too?'

He just didn't believe her. 'C'mon –' he began.

'No. *You* come on,' she yelled. 'I've written them a letter. I want an apology. I want them to do a piece on *me*.'

There was no satisfying Alice. Instead of being proud of his success she was jealous. His own mother jealous! It was ridiculous.

The twins insisted on throwing a party for him. They were flourishing, having landed a series of highly lucrative toothpaste commercials which had made them into visible personalities. Suna was dating a plastic surgeon, and he allowed the party to take place in his Coldwater Canyon house complete with jacuzzi and tennis court.

A hundred people were invited.

Two hundred turned up.

The plastic surgeon served Mexican food. A raucous rock group played loud music (courtesy of Shirlee, she was going with the drummer). And a wild time was had by all.

Lennie found himself, at four in the morning, bombed out of his mind and naked in the jacuzzi with three girls and an assortment of drugs supplied by kindly well-wishers. He dragged on a joint as two of the girls snorted coke and the third nearly drowned while trying to go down on him.

Was this stardom?

Was this having it all?

Free drugs and too much pussy. There had to be *more* than this.

He was glad Jess had left. He knew her feelings on 'letting things get out of control'.

'Whatever you do, Lennie,' she had told him earlier in the evening, 'don't turn into an asshole.'

He knew exactly what she meant. But couldn't he be an asshole for just one night? How many times in life did you get to be naked in a jacuzzi with three hot females and as many drugs as you could handle?

One of the girls had enormous boobs. She straddled him against the side of a jet, and dangled them near his face. He caught a nipple in his mouth and went for it.

One of the other girls, equally well endowed, decided to get into the act. She crammed the tip of her right boob into his mouth.

Now he was sucking on the two of them, and the aqua baby was sucking on him.

He felt lift off.

The zoom.

The peaking.

The throb.

The landing.

Jeeeeesus!

Nothing like being a star.

He wanted to go home. He pushed away female flesh and leapt from the pool. People were littered around in various stages of undress. He picked his way over bodies, found his clothes and dressed.

His car waited in the driveway. Jess had stuck a note on the windshield. '*Asshole*,' she had written. '*Drive carefully.*'

He did. All the way to her apartment which was one block away from his.

She ushered him in without complaining, fed him black coffee, and they sat around talking until the morning sun was bright in the sky. He let it all out. His high at finally making it. The constant nagging feeling in his gut that it was just temporary – that maybe he shouldn't get too excited – it wasn't going to last.

'You'll last,' she assured him. 'This is just the start.'

'From your lips . . .'

They hugged tightly. He started to say something about Eden, then changed his mind.

Jess fixed him bacon and eggs and put him to sleep in her bed. Fortunately it was Sunday. No work. No grind.

She went into the other room and called Matt. They had kept in touch. When Gino Santangelo got married and left Vegas he had promoted Matt to general overseer of everything concerning the Magiriano. The only person Matt had to answer to was Gino himself.

He was always delighted to hear from her. Even more delighted that in a few days she would be returning to Vegas with Lennie. Only for a week, but it was better than nothing.

Six months previously, before Lennie was really hot, he had booked him to appear in the main room of the Magiriano, sharing top billing with Vitos Felicidade. What a coup! When he had booked them neither had been a big star. Now they both were.

'Want to release us from our contract?' Jess joked, as she had been doing for the last couple of months.

'You're cute.'

'Thank you.'

'What can I do for you today?'

'Just wanted to check details.'

'You've checked them a hundred times.'

'I'm meticulous.'

She liked her talks with Matt. In a funny sort of way she almost missed him. She wondered if he still weighed himself down with gold chains, blow-dried his hair, and hit on every showgirl in town. Somehow she had thought he might visit her in LA, but he never had. 'Too busy,' he'd explained, when she'd asked him once.

She knew about busy. Lennie's career kept her on the go. No time for anything else. Not even a personal life. In two years she had indulged in only one affair. A sometime actor with spectacular pectorals, amazing thighs, rock hard everything else, and the brain of a retarded teenager. Their affair lasted exactly six weeks. It was all she could take of fantastic sex and nothing much else. When they parted he suggested she become his manager. His manager! Sleeping with him was ordeal enough!

After talking to Matt she pulled on shorts and a T-shirt, checked that Lennie was asleep, and drove down the hill to Carl's Market where she picked up groceries and the papers. She couldn't help worrying about Lennie. Eden Antonio still had a hold on him. He wasn't going to feel really good about anything until he put her behind him once and for all. And how was he going to do that when he wasn't even seeing her?

Jess frowned. She had never met Eden, but she had heard enough stories to know the woman was a spoiled bitch living with some rich mafiosa hood, and ambitious as hell. A few days in her company would surely allow Lennie to see her for what she really was?

Wishful thinking.

He was hooked.

The only way he could get unhooked was to do it himself.

•

Eden stared at the cover of *People* and bit down hard on her lower lip. Sonofabitch! The bastard had actually made it. Who would have thought Lennie Golden would ever get himself on the cover of *People*? Not her for one. As far as she was concerned Lennie had limited talent. Oh sure, he was a great lay. But fine cocksmanship did not a cover make.

She narrowed her topaz eyes and glared at his picture. He was grinning. At her? Like – *listen baby, I told you I'd make it. Now what the fuck are you doing?*

What *was* she doing?

Not enough.

Not nearly enough.

She was living in the house Santino Bonnatti had bought her like a virtual prisoner. He kept her locked up on Blue Jay Way with a chauffeur-bodyguard to take care of her every need. That's what Santino had said when he installed the goon as if he were doing her a favour. 'This is Zeko. He's gonna look after ya, an' drive ya around. He's gonna take care of your every need. Okay, bunny rabbit?'

What was she supposed to say? No? It was either put up with what Santino wanted or get out of the relationship fast. And she was too smart to get out before the moment was right. Santino was the key to her future, and while it was taking time, she knew it would happen – eventually.

Now, at last, there was a decent script, an interesting director, and a legitimate producer – Ryder Wheeler. The film was titled 'My Life as a Call Girl', and she was to star in it. Santino was putting up most of the money, and he was also executive producer.

Eden was excited. It had taken a long time coming.

Zeko entered the room without knocking and stared at her. He had one real eye and one glass. It gave him a crazed look. He was six feet four inches tall and bald as a baby's ass. She was sure he spied on her when she took a bath in her beautiful marble bathroom with the glass wall and thick foliage outside. She could imagine him crawling through the prickly cactus to catch a peak. Perversely she did not install window shades. Let him look if that's what turned him on. Occasionally she would part her legs and stroke her golden pussy, give him a real show.

'Yes?' she asked haughtily.

'I'm gonna get Mr Bonnatti now,' he said.

'Go ahead,' she said dismissively.

It was past noon and she was not dressed. She wore silk pyjamas and high heeled mules. Santino always visited after Sunday lunch with his family, an event which seemed to make him exceptionally horny. In a perverse way she had grown to enjoy his attentions. He was everything the other men in her life had *not* been. He had an attitude of being able to get anything he wanted – and this seemed to make up for his lack of physical attributes. Sometimes he was a little kinky, and a couple of times he had gotten carried away and hurt her. But ultimately she felt she was still calling the shots. Santino obviously adored her, and so he should. Where else would a man like him find a woman like her?

She had found out how he made his money, and it wasn't from importing olive oil and coffee. Santino Bonnatti dealt in pornography and drugs. She shivered and glanced once more at Lennie's picture, then discarded the magazine and went into the bathroom to shower and dress. Santino liked her squeaky clean, in contrast to his wife, who, according to him, only took one bath a week.

After showering she inspected her closet. So many clothes, and so little opportunity to wear them. Santino only took her out in public once in a while, although he had mentioned that soon they might be having dinner with Ryder Wheeler and the new director at Chasens. She looked forward to the occasion, and planned what to wear. The sensational red Halston with the ruby necklace he had given her on her birthday. At times he was very generous. There had to be *some* compensations for putting up with a man like Santino Bonnatti.

Chapter 42

Vitos called. Not a moment too soon.

'Let's party,' Olympia said.

'Lasta time we party you go offa weeth Flash, you leava Vitos alone. No nice for Vitos.'

'Did *I* do that? I didn't *mean* to.'

'Now Vitos beeg star you want heem again. Why I shoulda?'

'Because you'll get your dick sucked just the way you like it.'

'Ol*eee*mpea!'

He collected her in a white stretch limo, and they partied all over town. For once Olympia did not snub the lurking paparazzi. Instead she posed for them, one arm around Vitos' neck.

He responded nicely. In America publicity was the name

of the game. And who better to play it with than one of the richest women in the world?

Not that he considered Olympia a woman. She was girlish, like an excitable puppy. She was also a lot plumper than the last time they had been together. In bed it didn't bother him. He had always liked females with meat on their bones. Olympia had more than meat, she had potatoes and vegetables too. Undressed she was roly-poly.

He enjoyed making love to her. He sank his teeth into rolls of sweet smelling flesh. Buried his head between suffocating thighs. Grazed among the wonders of her very large breasts.

She liked to climax several times. She was not easy to please, and at the end of two hours they were both bathed in sweat and exhausted.

'Why don't we get married?' Olympia suggested, bunching a pillow behind her and sitting up in bed.

Vitos smiled. Wonderful teeth. A matinee idol smile. It was a shame his hair was thinning.

'Whatta you mean, Ol*eee*mpeea?'

She squinted at him. He was handsome, but dumb. Flash – with all his drug problems – was ten times the man Vitos was.

'Married. M-A-R-R-I-E-D. You understand what I'm saying?'

She had figured it out. Marry Vitos. Piss Flash off. Serve the scummy bastard right. When Flash had learned his lesson she would simply divorce Vitos. So it would cost a couple of million to pay Vitos off. Cheap at the price.

'You lika the idea marriage?' Vitos asked, stroking her thigh and thinking what marriage to Olympia Stanislopoulos would do for his PR rating.

'I think we make a beautiful couple. Don't you?'

'Mebee we do.'

'Is that a yes?'

'Tomorrow I go Vegas. Ona week the Magiriano Hotel. You come with. We talk.'

'That's a *hell* of an answer,' she snapped. 'I don't ask people to marry me every day of the week.'

'Ol*eee*mpea,' he said soothingly. 'I beega star now. The American wimmen they lova me. I taka time, we do it. Whatta you say to *that*?'

She swallowed what she really wanted to say, and nodded understandingly. 'Sure, Vitos, I'll come with you. I'll wait, and we'll see what happens. Right?'

He smiled happily. 'Right, Ol*eee*mpeea. Right, my darling.'

Chapter 43

They sat in Judge Frederick Lester's courtroom for two days. During the luncheon recess on the second day, Carrie turned to Steven and said, 'It's not him. I'm sure now.'

Steven felt a chill of disappointment. Of all the candidates, Judge Frederick Lester was the one he had hoped would turn out to be his father.

'How can you be so sure?' he asked in a low angry voice. 'It's been over forty years.'

'I *am* sure. I've stared at the man for two days.' She was near tears, but she held them in check, not wanting Steven to see her distress.

They left the courthouse and stood on the steps outside.

Carrie gazed straight ahead and wondered what the result of Steven's quest for his past would be. She did not want to remember . . . But it was impossible to forget . . .

*

It was her friend, Goldie's, twenty-first birthday. She had a date with her boyfriend, Mel, and he was bringing along Freddy Lester. It was after show time, and the girl who had agreed to be Freddy's date had turned her ankle and was hobbling around in agony. Goldie looked beseechingly at Carrie. 'Please!' she begged.

Carrie did not see how she could say no. After all, it was Goldie's birthday. Anyway, she had to learn to trust herself sometime; she couldn't be a recluse for the rest of her life. Nine years locked in an institution was enough. 'Okay,' she agreed reluctantly.

When they emerged from the theatre, Mel and Freddy – who was quite good-looking and knew it – were waiting outside the stage door. They greeted the girls with enthusiasm.

'Hiya, fellas,' said Goldie, in her best Mae West voice.

'Happy birthday, gorgeous,' replied Mel, grabbing her in a bear hug and kissing her full on the mouth.

Carrie and Freddy stared warily at each other.

'Whoops-a-daisy!' exclaimed Goldie, pushing him away. 'You're spoiling my lipstick, you big oaf.' She grinned at Freddy. 'Hello, I'm Goldie, as if you didn't know. And this is Carrie – your dream date for the night. Aren't you the lucky one!'

Freddy's expression did not indicate that he was the lucky one at all. He nodded curtly to Carrie as the four of them set off down the alley to Mel's car. Once there Mel opened up the doors. Goldie climbed into the front, and Carrie got into the back while Mel and Freddy stood outside.

'What's the matter with you?' Carrie heard Mel ask his friend.

'Je-sus!' Freddy replied, in what was supposed to be a whisper. 'She's a fucking dinge!'

'So?' replied Mel matter-of-factly. 'Haven't you ever heard of black pudding?'

'Sure,' replied Freddy, 'but I've never taken it out in public.'

'Aw, c'mon,' laughed Mel. 'Let's get this show on the road.' They climbed into the car.

In the back, Carrie gazed miserably out the window. Their hateful words hung in her ears: Fucking dinge. Black pudding.

Her eyes filled with salty tears which slid silently down her cheeks. She kept her head determinedly turned toward the window so that no one would observe her misery.

They started the evening off in a small jazz joint on Fifty-second Street. Neat little combo playing, champagne flowing. Goldie was in high spirits, rarin' to go. And when Carrie stated she wanted to stick to fruit juice, she let her have it full blast. 'Hey, listen, chickie. It's my birthday an' I plan to have fun. If you're gonna moon around with a long face it's gonna spoil everything. Now have some champagne, for God's sake, an' put a smile on your face!'

Carrie obliged. She had forgotten the potent taste of champagne, although when Whitejack, her former pimp, was flush, he had bought it by the bucket.

One glass turned into two, then three, and on to another club, and frothy white daiquiris which were so delicious she had at least four. After all, they were such little drinks, what harm could they do?

By the time the four of them piled into Clemmie's nightclub they were feeling no pain. Carrie and Freddy were the best of friends, giggling, laughing, dancing. And when his hands accidentally on purpose kept brushing against her breasts she didn't mind one bit. She felt free and alive. It was the first time in years she could honestly say she was living.

'You are sim'ly great, y'know that?' Freddy slurred.

She responded by locking her hands around his neck and gazing into his eyes. Fucking dinge no longer reverberated in her mind. 'Thank you,' she murmured sincerely. It had been a long time since anyone had told her that.

'No, I mean it,' Freddy insisted, as if he was expecting her to argue.

'Hey,' said Goldie, nudging Carrie. 'You see that guy over there. That's the Gino Santangelo. He owns the joint. I met him once. He's a real bad boy.'

Her eyes swivelled to check him out. 'I've taken on a lotta bad boys in my time,' she boasted.

'Carrie!' exclaimed Goldie, giggling. 'I've never seen you like this!'

'Yeah. You don't know nothin'!'

Goldie nudged Mel. 'She's really bombed.'

Mel grinned. 'How'd you like to make yourself fifty bucks, Carrie?'

'What didja have in mind, big boy?'

'I betcha fifty bucks y'can't make it with the great Mr Santangelo.'

'Yeah?' Her eyes gleamed. 'You just lost yourself a bet.'

Before any of them could stop her, she was on her feet and sashaying across the crowded club.

Goldie clapped her hand to her mouth in amazement. 'Oh, my God, Mel! What have you done? This isn't like her at all.'

He laughed nastily. 'C'mon, doll, she ain't gonna do anything she hasn't done a hundred times before.'

Freddy grimaced drunkenly. 'Thanks a lot, old buddy,' he complained.

Gino sat at his usual table. Cock of the walk. A constant stream of customers trailed over to pay homage.

He wore his customary three piece dark suit, white silk shirt, tasteful tie. His black hair was slicked down. The huge diamond ring on his pinky caught the light occasionally and gleamed expensively. Only the scar on his face gave him a slightly sinister look. That and his hard black eyes, which one woman had recently compared to Rudolph Valentino's.

He sipped his Scotch and inspected the female heading his way. Black. Exotic. And breasts that would stop traffic.

She reached his table and smiled. 'Mr Santangelo?'

'Yes.'

'I hear you own this place. I just thought I'd stop by and tell you what a classy spot I think it is.'

He smiled. He liked bold women. Sometimes. 'Sit down, have a drink.'

Carrie sat. She felt marvellous. Just drunk enough to believe she could own the world if she wanted to.

'Champagne?' he questioned.

'Naturally.'

He clicked his fingers, and a waiter was instantly by his side.

'A bottle of the best champagne.'

Gino studied her. A rare unusual beauty. One glass and he would take her home.

One more glass and she would go.

Later, they were together in his apartment and the love-

making was good. When it was over he wanted her to go home. He got up from the bed. 'Hey, hey, hey,' he said, 'betcha didn't learn to do that *in school.'*

The champagne was still colouring Carrie's mind. She felt powerful and in control and oh, so good. *Gino Santangelo had not used her. She had not used him. It was a mutually enjoyable experience.*

Lazily she stretched. Her body felt reborn, as if someone had come along and hammered out all the tenseness.

'My car's downstairs. The driver'll take you home whenever you're ready,' Gino said easily. 'Oh – and here's a little present for you. Buy yourself something pretty.'

He handed her a hundred dollars. He always gave the women he took to bed money for a gift. It was an idiosyncrasy of his, and no one ever objected.

'You sonofabitch!' she screamed, leaping up from the bed. 'You think I'm a whore?'

'Hey, of course not . . .'

'How dare you! How dare *you!' She struggled into her clothes like a wildcat, glaring at him and screaming.*

'Hey, listen, if I thought you was a whore I'd have given you the going rate. This money's a present.'

'Fuck you!' she screamed. 'If I was a whore it would have cost you a hell of a lot more.' And throwing the money in his face she stormed out of his apartment.

She ignored Gino's car and driver waiting downstairs, and began to walk along Park Avenue. She was sobering up in a hurry. Fucking dinge *was coming back to haunt her. And a red hot fury was building inside her.*

What had she been thinking of, approaching Gino Santangelo like that? Who else but *a whore would go over to a man's table, sit down, and half an hour later share his bed?*

Fucking dinge. Whore. *The words flew through her head. She had tried so hard to be decent, and now – after one night – she was back where she had started.*

She walked seven blocks before she got a cab, and then the driver gave her a dubious look and said, 'I ain't goin' to Harlem, honey.'

'Nor am I, honcy.*'*

He didn't like that. He maintained a frosty silence all the way to the Village.

She paid him off and climbed the three flights of stairs to the roomy loft she shared with Goldie. Once inside, she was dismayed to find Freddy Lester in bed. Her bed. *She could not believe her eyes.*

Angrily she shook him awake. 'Get out of here,' she insisted in a furious whisper.

'Aw, c'mon, toots,' he mumbled, bleary-eyed and still drunk. He had no intention of getting up and going home.

'Will you get out of my bed?' she hissed.

'Whyn't you come in an' join me? I've bin waitin' all night,' he slurred.

'Whyn't you drop dead?'

He gripped her wrist. 'C'mon, sweetie pie, be a sport.'

'Let go *of me.'*

He was surprisingly strong. With ease he pulled her onto the bed.

'I'll scream if you don't stop,' she raged.

'Don't do that, sweetie.' And he placed the heavy palm of his hand over her mouth, stopping her from screaming and holding her down all at the same time. With his other hand he pulled up her skirt and ripped off her panties.

She went numb. The strength just drained right out of her.

He took this as a sign of acquiescence, and somehow got out his penis and began jamming it into her.

She made little choking noises in her throat. His hand prevented her sobs of anguish from emerging. She willed her mind to go blank, and when he took his hand away she did not scream. She waited until he finished, and then said calmly, 'That'll be thirty bucks, mister. Thirty big ones.'

'What?' he mumbled.

'You screw a whore, you pay,*' she said in a cold unruffled manner. 'Especially when you screw a fucking dinge.'*

'But –'

'Pay or I holler rape.'

He paid.

Six weeks later she realized with a dull shock that she was pregnant. It was a bombshell, because she had always thought she was unable to conceive. 'You just ain't fertile,' Whitejack had assured her on many occasions.

Now she was pregnant and she had no idea who the father was.

Gino Santangelo. Freddy Lester. It could be either.

She didn't know what to do or where to turn.

*

'Well,' Steven said tightly. 'I guess we go see the publisher next. I'll arrange an appointment – you can say you want to do a book on your life.'

Carrie nodded numbly. Why was Steven torturing her like this? She had been a good mother. He had never suffered because of the life she once lived. Even when she ran a brothel and sold drugs for the notorious Enzio Bonnatti, she had always seen to it that he was never involved.

'When?' she asked listlessly.

'I'll arrange it as quickly as possible.'

She nodded again, and for one brief moment hated her good-looking unfeeling son. What did he know about her suffering? What did he even care?

Chapter 44

They spoke on the telephone. Lucky and Costa.

'Uncle Costa?'

'Yes.'

'I'm married.'

'You're what?'

'I'm married again. To a very nice person, you'll like him.'

'Do I have a choice?'

'Trust me.'

'Ah, Lucky, I've always done that. Does your father know?'

'Uh . . . not yet. I'll tell him.'

'When?'

'Soon.'

A grunt of disapproval. 'Who's the boy?'

A nervous laugh. 'Well . . . er . . . he's not exactly a boy.'

The phone rattled while Costa moved his position. 'Who is he?'

She quickly changed the subject. 'I've got another surprise for you.'

'Isn't one enough?'

'You're a great-uncle.'

'Thank you.'

'No. no. A *Great-Uncle.*'

'I don't think I understand . . .'

'Yes you do. I have a baby.'

'Whose baby?'

'*My* baby.'

She could hear the shock in his voice. Costa had always been old-fashioned. '*Yours*, Lucky. What does this mean?'

'It means,' she said patiently, 'that eighteen months ago I gave birth to a fantastic little boy named Roberto, and two days ago I married his father.'

Silence.

A long silence.

Then: 'Does Gino know?'

'Not yet.'

A drawn-out sigh. 'Not yet.'

'Don't repeat me like that, I hate it!'

'What *should* I say?'

'Congratulations. Tell me it's wonderful, and that you can't wait to fly in and see me and Roberto. Because we're dying to see you.'

'Eighteen months ago you had a baby, and now you're dying to see me. Hah!'

'Don't be mad,' she pleaded. 'You know I love you.'

'What a way to show it! *I* feel bad enough. How do you think Gino is going to take it?'

'He won't care – he has his own life with superwoman.

She'll *hate* him being a grandpa. It'll remove the curl from her hair for a week!'

'Lucky. I think you'd better visit Gino. I don't recommend you tell him on the phone.'

'I'm hardly a child,' she said stubbornly. 'I don't have to ask his permission to do anything.'

'Who's talking permission?' Costa replied gently. 'You can do whatever you want, but I think it would be a nice gesture, don't you? Gino's first grandchild, his only one . . . He's not so young . . . His heart's not in such great shape . . .'

'Did something happen?' she asked quickly, frantically.

'No, no, nothing happened. But I spoke to him a few weeks ago and he sounded fed-up and bored. He said he missed you.'

'Did he really?'

'I don't make things up.'

She was thoughtful for a moment. Why not visit Gino in California? Take Roberto. Oh, she couldn't wait to see his face when he saw such a gorgeous baby. *Her* baby. *Her* accomplishment. And she could tell him about the hotel and casino she was going to build in Atlantic City. At last. Without his help.

'I'll go,' she decided impulsively. 'Will you come too, Costa? I'd like that a lot.'

He hesitated. 'I don't know if it would be a good idea. There'll be you, the baby, your husband –'

'Oh, he won't come. He's off on a business trip, and won't be back for a week.'

'I thought you said you only got married two days ago.'

'So what? That doesn't make us joined at the hip. We both lead our own lives.'

Costa sighed. 'You young people . . .'

'Uh . . . he's not so young . . .'

'How not so young?'

'I'll tell you when I see you.'

*

Paige Wheeler screamed aloud. Several times. Gino Santangelo might be old. But he was dynamite.

Susan never made her scream. Nor did Ryder. But then of course, Ryder was completely disinterested in sex, only business turned him on. One of the reasons Paige enjoyed so many lovers.

She and Gino shared a large double bed in the Beverly Wilshire Hotel. Paige had booked the suite for a client two days earlier. The Beverly Wilshire was the perfect place for an assignation. Central. Luxurious. And if one was spotted in the lobby or thereabouts, well one was merely visiting Tiffany (located right next door) or lunching in the very fashionable El Padrino restaurant, or browsing Brentanos bookstore. Perfect alibis, all of them.

'Hmmm . . .' said Paige, sitting up in bed and stretching for a cigarette. 'Now I know why Susan's always complaining.'

'What's she got to complain about?' asked Gino, reaching across her full breasts for the matches, and lighting her up.

Paige drew deeply on her cigarette. 'Your . . . er . . . enthusiasm, stamina, and staying power.'

'You gonna tell me you broads discuss sex?'

'What else is there to discuss?'

'An' she *complains*?'

'Foolish woman.'

'Jeez!'

'Susan never did know how to enjoy herself. Poor Tiny had to go elsewhere all the time.'

Gino felt like he was getting an education. Since marrying Susan she had grown less and less willing in the bedroom. The more she pushed him away, the more he tried to please. Christ! He had thought there was something wrong with *him*. Like age had finally caught him with his pants down and he no longer had what it took. He had been knocking himself out, and now her best friend calmly informs him Susan doesn't like sex. Some act she must have put on in the beginning. Jeez!

'Is this a revelation, Gino?'

'A what?'

'Didn't you know?'

He felt ridiculous, a position he very rarely found himself in. 'I guess I knew,' he said guardedly, 'otherwise I wouldn't be here with you today.'

And he had to admit that being with a woman like Paige was a relief after two years of Susan. Paige stripped off all her inhibitions with her clothes. She was no great beauty, but she was an enormously sexy lady.

'Maybe I shouldn't have said anything,' Paige said delicately.

'What would have stopped you?' Gino replied. 'A tank?'

She lifted one leg from beneath the sheet and trailed her toes down his chest. 'You . . .' she murmured huskily, 'are a very raunchy man. And I . . . am a very raunchy woman. Do we have to waste our time talking about Susan?'

He lifted her toes to his mouth and sucked on them one by one. 'Who's talkin'?' he growled.

Chapter 45

Lennie, Jess, Isaac and his pretty wife, plus a reporter from *Rolling Stone*, flew up to Vegas in a private plane, courtesy of Matt Traynor and the Magiriano Hotel. For about ten minutes they all tried to hide the fact that they were impressed.

Lennie was the first to break. 'I gotta tell you – if Alice could see me now she'd shit a brick!'

Isaac began to laugh. 'How about *my* mother, man. She used to clean other people's floors an' now her son is flyin' high. Wait until I tell *her*!'

His wife, Irena, shyly pulled out a camera and started to take snaps. 'Nothing like a little proof,' she murmured.

The reporter from *Rolling Stone* was not at all impressed. He flew in private jets with rock stars all the time. He was amused by their excitement and promised not to write about it.

'Sure,' muttered Jess, the cynic of the group. 'He'll make us out to be a bunch of hicks just off the bus.'

'Who cares?' laughed Lennie. 'All the reader remembers is seeing your name. That's what you're always telling me.'

'Just so long as they spell it right,' added Isaac, king of clichés.

Jess had negotiated the Magiriano appearance. She negotiated the money on most of Lennie's deals, but he still kept Isaac on and paid him ten percent commission.

'We don't need him anymore,' she had pointed out to Lennie months ago. 'He's taking a free ride.'

'Let him ride,' Lennie had said easily. 'He was there for me when nobody wanted to know. We can afford it.'

When Matt sweetened the Vegas deal with the private plane and other trimmings, Lennie had immediately suggested they take Isaac and Irena along. Jess agreed. She had nothing against them personally, they were a nice couple. It was only business-wise she got angry.

'I think,' Lennie said, 'tonight I am going to blow a thousand dollars at the tables. I always wanted to do that.'

'How much are they paying you for this gig?' asked the *Rolling Stone* reporter.

'He never discusses his money or his sex life – just makes funny about other people's,' interrupted Jess quickly.

Lennie fixed her with a look. Lately she was coming on a little too heavy. He could answer his own questions, and fully intended to. He needed no wet-nurse.

*

'You look so . . . so different!' Jess exclaimed. 'You lost weight. You look . . . great.'

Matt smiled. 'I dumped fifteen pounds. Cut my hair. And I jog – two hours a day. It keeps me sane.'

Gone was the Matt Traynor of old. In his place was a thin, fit-looking man, with grey crew-cut hair and a flat stomach. Instead of the fancy clothes he used to favour, he wore plain dark slacks and a white open-neck shirt.

'No gold chains,' Jess grinned.

'Had 'em melted down and sent to Sammy Davis Jr.'

'I bet he was thrilled.'

'Hasn't stopped calling me since.'

They exchanged smiles.

'And you?' he asked. 'Miss Success Story. When are they writing you up in *Forbes*?'

'When I let 'em.'

'Seriously, Jess. I'm very pleased for you.'

'Thanks.'

She had dressed especially carefully. He hadn't said a word sbout how *she* looked.

While minions were frothing about showing Lennie and the others to their suites, he offered her a drink.

'In your apartment?' she asked jokingly.

'I gave it up. I live here now.'

'Lead the way.'

*

Lennie's penthouse suite left nothing to be desired. Water bed. Mirrored ceiling. Jacuzzi. Thick pile carpet. Colour televisions everywhere – including the john. A magnificent terrace with breathtaking views.

Everything.

Except

Eden.

He had thought – only for a moment – what if Eden were here, waiting for him?

Who needed her?

There was a fully stocked bar and plenty of beautiful available showgirls downstairs. He was a star now. He could select anyone he desired.

*

Not an initialled glass in sight. No fake marble, ornamental gilt, or dimmed pink lighting either. Just a modern functional penthouse with clean lines and a masculine feel.

'Drink?' Matt asked.

'Anything cold and non-alcoholic,' Jess replied, looking

around appreciatively. 'You've changed your style of living,' she commented.

'It was about time,' he replied, fixing her a tall glass of grapefruit juice with shaved ice from behind a high-tech bar.

She accepted the drink and sipped it slowly. 'Ummm, delicious.'

'I'll tell room service.'

'Is that how you live now? All room service and never having to do anything for yourself?'

'I run the hotel, Jess. I'm on call twenty-four hours a day. I never have *time* to do anything else.'

'Nothing?' she joked.

'Well . . . this and that.'

They laughed, and neither could think of anything else to say. So naturally they both spoke at once.

'Do you think –' Jess started.

'I thought that later –' Matt began.

A buzzer sounded on one of the three phones located on the bar.

'Excuse me,' he said.

'Sure.' She sipped her drink and watched him as he took the call. They were being so polite to each other. It was as if they were vague acquaintances, not two people who had shared the tragedy of her life. She never allowed herself to think about the nightmare of losing Simon. But she would always be aware that it was Matt who got her through the first forty-eight hours. If he hadn't been there for her she would probably have gulped down the nearest bottle of pills and ended it all.

He put the phone down with a grimace.

'What's up?' she asked.

'Vitos Felicidade has added to his entourage. He's on his way from New York, and he's bringing Olympia Stanislopoulos, her child and nanny. I'm running out of penthouse suites.'

'Oh, shame!'

'Still a smart ass.'

'Yes. And look where it's got me.'

'I have to meet with my reservations manager.'

'I understand.'

'He's on his way up.'

She set her glass down and walked to the door. 'I was finished anyway.'

He hurried after her. 'Tonight I want to host a dinner for Lennie and his friends.'

'I'll check with him.'

'Call me soon. Let me know how many.'

She nodded and departed.

Once the door was shut behind her, Matt sighed with relief. He had been determined not to make a fool of himself, and he thought he had handled it pretty well. It was obvious from past experience that Jess was never going to regard him as anything more than a good friend, and even though he still wanted her as much as ever, he had decided to cool it. He was too old to start chasing after someone who didn't want him. Too old and too wise.

Jess checked her reflection in the mirrored wall of the elevator. She thought she looked pretty good. LA suntan. Jose Eber short haircut. A green cotton jump suit which complimented her orange hair. High heel shoes which added inches and made her into a grown up.

Hmmmm . . . He hadn't said one thing about the way she looked.

Not that she cared.

Why the hell *should* she?

But she *had* enjoyed his having the hots for her. Oh yes, she remembered how his hands used to shake when he was near her. The way he looked at her all the time, and quite frankly, for two years, she had missed that ardent attention.

Now he was Mister Businesslike. Charming and nice, but where were the shaking hands and the lingering looks?

Maybe he had only liked her when she was little Miss Nobody.

He *did* look good. Was it possible that now he wasn't hot for her, *she* had an itch for him.

Nonsense.

*

Being back in his hometown as a star was very pleasing to Lennie. And the timing was perfect. Cover of *People*. Local boy makes good. Jack Golden's kid – Lennie. Bigger than his father ever dreamed of being.

Briefly he thought of Alice. She would have loved coming back like a big shot. But she was so busy bitching about her own career (what career?) that he hadn't even bothered to tell her about his return appearance at the Magiriano.

Two years before he had roared out of town busted out and pissed off. He would have gladly strangled Matt Traynor then. But time passes . . . things happen . . . Jess had explained it wasn't Matt's fault. Some bitch upstairs had ordered him axed. Lucky Santangelo – whoever she might be. 'The lady boss,' Jess had whispered.

Screw *her*. Apparently she had nothing more to do with the hotel – he made sure of that before agreeing to return.

Now he was back. And they were giving him all the home comforts a star grows to love and expect. Private plane. Twenty-four hour limo and driver. A bodyguard (did he really *need* a bodyguard?) And the pencil.

Ah . . . the famed Las Vegas pencil. It was not an actual pencil, just permission to sign for anything he wanted and never having to pay. Food, drink, room service . . . whatever. Oh, the times he and Jess had dreamed of having that power. Only high rollers and big stars were given the privilege. He was more pleased about the pencil than anything else.

Jess arrived in great spirits. He had been a little worried about her returning to Vegas and the memories, but she genuinely appeared to have put it all behind her. Not a mention of Wayland or the baby.

'Well, well, well!' she exclaimed, looking around at the baskets of flowers, champagne cooling on ice, and a huge dish of exotic sliced fruit laid out on a buffet table. 'I see they welcomed you properly.'

'Hey –' he grinned, 'they're lucky to have me. If I'd held a grudge they'd *never* have gotten me back.'

Jess picked at a slice of papaya. 'Matt wants to have a

dinner for you tonight, and whoever you want to invite.'

'How *is* your boyfriend?'

'Don't say that,' she snapped, a little too quickly, causing Lennie to raise an eyebrow.

'Where's your sense of humour, monkey face?' he asked.

'Don't *call* me that!' she yelled.

He held up his hands, making a peaceful gesture. 'I come as a friend. Have mercy.'

She couldn't help laughing.

'Hey,' he said, 'I want to use the fucking pencil, only I've got everything I need.'

'It's tough bein' a star,' she commented dryly.

'Let's go to the drugstore. I have this insane urge to sign.'

'Call down. Stars have things sent.'

'You're so full of shit. Let's go.'

He pulled her by the hand and they left the suite.

The drug store, located on swimming pool level, sold everything from paper panties to three thousand dollar mink bikinis. Lennie grabbed a wire basket and started throwing things in. Toothpaste, toothbrushes, aftershave, shampoo.

Jess trailed patiently after him. 'Do you really need all this?' she asked.

'Kid – it's free,' he mumbled, filling one basket and starting on another.

'Lennie,' she suggested, 'if we're going for freebees let's go for the good stuff.' She dragged him over to the cosmetic counter. 'Stock me up with Estee Lauder,' she commanded, getting into the spirit of it all. 'And Dior. And Clinique.'

They filled the second wire basket, and a third.

'I think it's enough,' Jess said, when he started piling in a month's supply of candy.

'But I don't have everything I need,' he objected, grabbing three boxes of Tampax and a handful of tastefully wrapped Durex.

Jess began to break up, and when Jess laughed everybody noticed. Her laugh still sounded like a crazed hyena.

'Oh shit!' said Lennie, as a few stares came his way.

'Aren't you on the cover of *People* magazine?' asked a

bronzed woman in shorts which displayed large cellulite dimpled thighs.

'Oh. You're Leonard Goldman,' announced a tall brunette, as if he didn't know.

He grinned engagingly. A crowd began to form.

'Who's de jerk?' snapped a red-faced New Yorker.

'Nobody,' replied his spandexed girlfriend.

Lennie turned to Jess for help. She was bent double by the magazines.

'Can I have your autograph?' sighed a winsome little thing. 'I watch you every week. I'm your favourite.'

They were moving in on him. A wall of people. He was being crowded into a corner, and suddenly he felt vulnerable and under attack. Pens and slips of paper were shoved at him. He scribbled his name a few times. Shit! If this was what stardom was all about you could shove it.

A pregnant girl touched his face. 'For luck,' she giggled. While an older woman hissed out of the corner of her drooping lips, 'God is watching you. You'd better be careful. God doesn't forgive.'

He wanted out. He needed rescuing. Fortunately Jess got herself together and grabbed a security guard. Together they hustled Lennie through the throng and rushed him to the nearest elevator.

'That crowd weren't nothin',' the elderly guard sneered. 'Once I hadda rescue Elvis. They tore his pants off. They woulda killed him with love. Took eight of us to get him in a limo. *Those* were the good old days.'

Back in the suite, Lennie said ruefully, 'I never did get to sign.'

Jess grinned. 'What were you going to do with eight packets of Durex anyway?'

'Fuck a lot.'

'So what else is new?'

Chapter 46

Vitos had not expected Olympia to insist on bringing her child and nanny to Vegas. But insist she did. 'Brigette will be my bridesmaid,' she said. 'I cannot get married without her. What kind of a mother do you think I am?'

The truth of the matter was, Olympia did not want Nanny Mabel and Brigette in New York answering the phone and telling tales. She wanted them with her, where she could keep an eye on them. Now, when Flash called, he would get the answering service, and they wouldn't know where she was. Let the scumbag suffer. He wasn't winning *her* back so easily.

It never occurred to Olympia that he might not want her back. She sailed through life filled with supreme confidence – easy when you could buy and sell most people.

Before leaving New York she contacted her lawyer. 'Courier me a marriage document,' she demanded. 'You know what I mean – a pre-nuptial agreement.'

'You're not getting married again, are you?' he groaned incredulously.

'I might be.'

'Please, can't you wait until we can discuss this properly? Your financial affairs are complicated. It'll take time to work out.'

'I want it now. Immediately.'

She had never been to Las Vegas before, and it both fascinated and repelled her. 'All these dreadful people,' she complained to Vitos, as they were whisked through the lobby with their accompanying entourages.

He nodded like a puppet, blazing the perfect Felicidade smile at his fans.

'Everyone looks so . . . so . . . cheap,' she said in the elevator.

'These pipples buy my records,' he remarked sagely.

'They would!' she muttered under her breath.

They were placed in adjoining suites. Vitos had the more lavish one which infuriated Olympia. She decided to call Lucky Santangelo and complain. Dimitri had mentioned that Lucky owned the Magiriano. It would be interesting to see her again . . .

What did she look like? Was she married? Did she have kids?

Once settled, Olympia sent Nanny Mabel off with Brigette to explore, and then she called the front desk. 'This is Olympia Stanislopoulos,' she announced imperiously. 'Kindly tell Lucky Santangelo I wish to see her.'

'Miz Santangelo's no longer with us,' said the operator.

'Where is she?'

'I'm afraid I can't help you, ma'am.'

'Who can?'

'Perhaps the manager, or Mr Traynor.'

'Have either of them call me. Immediately.'

She felt strangely disappointed. It would have been interesting to see Lucky again. Or would it? They shared so many memories of a carefree summer, once, long ago. Lucky had been her best friend. But who needed friends? They always let you down eventually.

*

Vitos spoke heatedly to his manager in Spanish. The gist of the conversation was his marital situation. He had married at eighteen to a local girl in his Spanish home town. When his star began to rise in America, the marriage was annulled. Now he wished to marry Olympia. How legal was the annulment? There were no children. And where were the documents?

His manager grimaced. This was a great opportunity. Big as Vitos was becoming, marriage to Olympia Stanislopoulos could only mean more fame and acceptance in America – the promised land. It was not something to be rushed into and blown.

'We must obtain the best legal advice,' he warned. 'And I will order a search for the papers.'

'Quickly,' Vitos cautioned. He had a hunch Olympia was not the most patient of women.

*

Brigette eyed the busy gambling tables, the scurrying crowds, the scantily clad cocktail waitresses, the over-made-up hookers. 'This place *stinks*!' she informed Nanny Mabel loudly.

'Shhh,' Nanny admonished.

'Stinks!' yelled Brigette. 'Stinks! Stinks! Stinks! I hate it.'

Privately Nanny Mabel agreed, but she wasn't about to hear it from her precocious charge. The child became more like her mother every day.

'Be quiet,' scolded Nanny Mabel.

'Won't!' screamed Brigette. 'Can't make me. This place is *stiiiinking!!*'

'If you misbehave here I'll be forced to tell your mother. And she'll –'

Before she could continue further, a grim-faced security woman packing a gun appeared. 'Shut the kid up,' she commanded.

Nanny Mabel shot Brigette a warning look.

'I'm not going to shut up,' Brigitte yelled. '*I'm* going to do whatever *I* like. So there, you stupid fat pig!'

'Oh no you're not,' said the guard.

'Oh yes I am,' said Brigette.

'Oh dear,' said Nanny Mabel.

*

Matt Traynor presented himself at Olympia's door.

'Who are you?' she demanded, pulling a Chinese robe tightly around her.

'I run the hotel, Miss Stanislopoulos.'

'You got my message I presume.'

'What message?'

'About Lucky Santangelo.'

'No, I'm afraid I didn't.'

'Well, where is she?'

'Miss Santangelo is no longer connected with the Magiriano.'

Olympia frowned. 'Too bad.'

Matt did not appreciate being kept at the door like a delivery boy. 'May I come in?'

'What for?'

Matt decided he did not like the plump blonde heiress with the petulant expression and all the charm of a bad-tempered shop girl. 'We have a slight problem with your daughter . . .'

'How boring! What's she done?'

'Kicked a security woman, tried to dismantle a blackjack table, and –'

'Where is she?' Olympia interrupted.

'We have her downstairs in an office. She's creating a considerable disturbance. She refuses to er . . . be quiet . . . until you collect her.'

'God!' Olympia was visibly irritated. 'What about her nanny? Why doesn't *she* deal with her?'

'She seems to have no control of the situation.'

Olympia rolled her eyes heavenward. 'This is most inconvenient,' she said testily, as if it were Matt's personal fault. 'Wait. I'll have to dress.'

She slammed the door in his face and left him angrily marching up and down the corridor for ten minutes. Eventually she emerged and they proceeded downstairs in silence.

Brigette sat moodily in a small office chanting 'Las Vegas stinks! Las Vegas stinks!' at the top of her voice.

Nanny Mabel, red in the face, hovered outside, while the grim looking female security guard stood at attention.

Olympia fixed her daughter with an icy blue stare, and she shut up.

'What's been going on?' Olympia demanded.

Brigette produced a full flood of ever-ready tears. 'Mama, mama,' she cried, 'these people have been *so* mean to me. Really really *mean*.'

'Excuse *me*,' said the security woman. 'This child needs a good spanking. She's rude and spoilt and –'

'I'm not interested in your opinion,' Olympia said dismissively. 'Come along, Brigette. It's time for bed.' She glared at Matt. 'My daughter is tired, it's been a long day.'

With that she took Brigitte by the hand and swept out, a nervous Nanny Mabel trailing in her wake.

Chapter 47

Carrie Berkeley had immense style. For many years, while married first to Bernard Dimes, and then to Elliott Berkeley, she had been a celebrity. The sort of celebrity who never really does anything but is always mentioned in gossip and society columns, and is often photographed for the fashion magazines. Several years in a row she had appeared in *Harpers Bazaar* as one of the 'Ten Most Beautiful Women in America'.

When she divorced Elliott and went to live permanently on Fire Island, she retired from public life. But hers was still a well-known name, and it was no problem to arrange an appointment with Fred E. Lester of Lester and Wellington Publishers.

Steven wanted to accompany her, but she refused to let him. 'I'm quite capable of deciding whether it's him or not,' she said coldly.

Lately that's how she felt about Steven. Cold, withdrawn. He was her son, but she would never forgive him for what he was putting her through. Never.

What did it *matter* which one his father was? They were both bastards. Who cared?

Fred E. Lester sat behind an oak desk in a large, comfortable office. He was tall and broad-shouldered, with flurries of white hair surrounding a bald spot, and a healthy weekend tan. He was in his late sixties. He rose when Carrie was ushered into his office by a solicitous secretary, walked around his desk, and with outstretched hands said, 'I don't suppose you remember me, it was a long time ago, but . . .'

She felt a moment of sheer panic. *It was him.*

The blood drained from her face and a sickness filled the pit of her stomach.

'. . . a charity ball,' he was saying. 'It must have been some twenty years ago. You still look exactly the same. Lovely as ever.'

Thankfully she slumped into a chair. *It wasn't him.* Fred E. Lester looked nothing like the college boy of so many years ago. How was it going to be possible to recognize a man she had only spent one night with forty-two years ago? Damn Steven. Why was he putting her through this?

'Coffee? Tea? Perhaps a drink?' Fred Lester asked.

His secretary stood by the door expectantly.

'Tea,' Carrie said quietly. 'With lemon.'

'Make that two,' Fred said, sitting down behind his desk, and playing with a silver pen.

Carrie tried to recover her composure. She glanced around the office. There were framed covers of books on all the walls.

'My successes,' Fred said with a modest smile. 'In this business you boast about your successes amd try to hide your failures.'

She smiled politely.

'Now then,' Fred said, clasping his hands together. 'Let's hope that you and I are going to have a big success.'

'I beg your pardon?'

'You *do* want to write a book for us, don't you?'

She remembered that it *was* the reason she was sitting in his office. Steven had called and made the appointment. 'Mrs Carrie Berkeley has an interesting idea for a book,' he had said, and an appointment was immediately forthcoming.

'I have a few ideas,' she faltered.

'That's where it all begins.' He beamed.

She stared at his bald head. It shone, as though someone had polished it with a soft cloth. Whitejack's head had shone. Black and shiny. Sometimes he oiled it. 'Makes all the pretty ladies cum,' he used to say with a wicked grin, flashing his large white teeth.

'My hunch is that you would like to write a beauty book,' Fred Lester said. 'Am I right?'

'Beauty and . . . uh . . . maybe fashion, style,' she replied, picking up on his idea.

'Couldn't be better. The timing is just right.'

He had very nice eyes. Brown, kindly eyes. On his desk there were three silver frames containing family pictures.

She felt secure with him. In a funny way he reminded her of Bernard, her first husband.

'Now then,' he said. 'Why don't you tell me what you have in mind, and we can proceed from there. Does that sound reasonable?'

She nodded, and racked her brain for ideas.

Chapter 48

Costa met Lucky at LA airport. He fussed over Roberto as if *he* was the proud grandpa.

'You haven't told Gino, have you?' she demanded.

'I arrived late last night,' Costa said. 'He doesn't even know *I'm* here.'

'Good. We'll really surprise him.'

She checked into a bungalow at the Beverly Hills Hotel, and immediately called Gino.

To her disappointment he was out. Now she had decided to tell him, she was too impatient for roadblocks. It was only a matter of time before Dimitri made an announcement, and she really did not want Gino reading about her marriage in a newspaper.

'When will he be back?' she asked the maid.

'Later,' the woman said unhelpfully.

Later could mean any time. She wondered where he was. What did a person who wasn't in the movie business *do* in LA? Gino had always been so active. Didn't he miss the hustle of Vegas? Surely he couldn't spend his days strolling up and down Rodeo Drive.

She and Costa lunched out by the pool, while Roberto napped.

'Well, Lucky,' Costa asked. 'When are you going to tell me? Who is this man you have married?'

She took a deep breath. 'Dimitri Stanislopoulos,' she anounced.

'No, really, who?' he persisted.

She shrugged. 'Dimitri.'

Costa shook his head and looked grim.

'It's not a crime for crissake,' Lucky said quickly. 'So he's a few years older than me. Big deal.'

'I wish your Aunt Jennifer were alive,' he said dourly.

'We *all* wish she were alive. But she's not, and even if she were, she wouldn't be telling me what to do.'

'You've been on your own too long,' Costa said. 'You've never had anyone to turn to. When you were growing up you should have had a mother. Someone to confide in. A –'

'Will you quit with the dirge? I *like* being on my own.'

'Dimitri Stanislopoulos is an old man.'

'So are you. Does that make you a terrible person?'

'Lucky, Dimitri Stanislopoulos is a father figure. Don't you see what you've done? You've –'

'Fuck you – Costa.' Her black eyes blazed with anger. 'I expected a lecture from Gino, but I don't have to take this crap from you. I am nearly thirty years old. Will everyone stop telling me what to do.'

She stormed from the table.

•

Paige Wheeler had this little trick of holding him inside her like a vice. 'I used to go with a snatch quack,' she informed Gino when he asked her where she'd learnt it.

'A what?'

'A gynaecologist. He taught me everything I know. The man was an expert. Well, he was looking at it all day, I guess he picked up a thing or two.'

Gino liked her little trick. It meant he could go for as long as he wanted, and then she would take over, holding him, keeping him hard, until he was ready to make it again. Gino never liked to rush. He genuinely loved pleasing women. It gave him a real charge to observe their abandonment and pure lustful pleasure. That's why marriage to Susan was such a deep disappointment. Paige was right, Susan did not like sex. Why hadn't he noticed the signals *before* marrying her? Now he was stuck in a marriage he really didn't want.

Every day he thought about getting out, calling Lucky and saying, 'Hey – kid. I was wrong. Let's go take over Atlantic City, an' build our own hotel. Let's set the fuckin' world on fire!'

It wasn't as simple as that. Susan never set a foot wrong. She was solicitous and attentive. She watched his diet. Made sure he exercised. Had the cook prepare all his favourite meals.

And she looked good, too. Attractive, groomed, gowned to perfection. They attended all the best social events, including every A-rated party.

Apart from sex, Susan was the perfect wife. She was also suffocatingly boring.

He hated Beverly Hills. He hated the whole phony social bit. He hated the A-parties filled with senile geriatrics. Same people. Same conversation. Same fucking bullshit.

Gino Santangelo wanted out. He just had to figure a way to do it.

*

'Oh hi, Susan,' Lucky said. She *would* have to get stuck with Grace Kelly. 'Is Gino around?'

'Are you here? In California?'

No. I'm at the North fucking pole. Where does it sound like I'm calling from? 'Yes. As a matter of fact I am.'

'How nice.'

'Isn't it.' Beat of three. 'Can I speak to Gino?'

'Sorry, dear. He's out.'

'Will he be back soon?'

'One never knows with Gino.'

'Very true.' At least she knew that much about him.

'I'll call back later.'

'Good.'

Sure. You're really pleased I'm here. Not even a 'Where are you staying?' Or, 'We must get together.'

She prowled the bungalow. Roberto was out with CeeCee by the pool. She didn't know where Costa was. She didn't care.

Oh yes she did. He was concerned about her. How could she fault him for that? Dimitri *was* thirty-five years older than she. Costa would just have to see them together, and then he would realize the relationship worked.

*

Paige dressed. She wore delightfully whorish clothes and drove a gold Porsche, which Ryder had bought her for Christmas. Sometimes Gino puzzled about Susan's friendship with her. She was so unlike Susan's other friends – the polished Hollywood wives with their designer clothes, flawless face lifts, and narrow code of ethics.

'Susie likes me because I'm outrageous and fun,' Paige confided. She didn't add that Susan liked her because they had been having a hot and heavy affair for several years.

Paige realized she might be playing a dangerous game, bedding both the wife *and* the husband. She wouldn't mind giving up Susan. But Gino was irresistible, and great in bed.

It seemed unlikely they would confide in each other, so she saw no pressing reason to surrender either.

'Tomorrow,' Gino said. 'Same place. Same time.'

'Impossible. I promised Ryder I would go with him to Las Vegas. He has to entertain one of his investors.'

Gino threw her an incredulous look. 'You're goin' to Vegas an' you didn't tell me? You gotta be kiddin'. I used to *own* that friggin' town. I coulda got you the finest reservations, the best tables, anything you wanted.'

Paige applied a bright red lipstick to her full lips. 'Ryder spent his erstwhile youth ferrying young ladies to Vegas for dirty weekends. I don't think he'd appreciate any suggestions about where we should stay and what we should do.'

Gino shrugged. 'You're missin' out. There's only one way t'go to Vegas, an' that's with me.'

'Would we take your wife and my husband, or leave them behind?'

He ignored the dig. 'When d'you get back?' he asked.

'Wednesday.'

'We'll meet Thursday. Same place. Same time.'

'I can't. I'm working.'

'So cancel.'

'I'm doing a Bel Air estate for a bi-sexual movie star and he's *very* demanding.'

He grabbed her around the waist and rocked against her. 'So am I.'

She laughed. God! He must have been the horniest man alive when he was young. As it was, he was sexier and had more staying power than a lot of men half his age.

'Yes, I know. That's why I need a few days off from your amorous attentions.'

He narrowed his eyes. 'Who else're you screwin'?'

She fluffed out her frizzed hair. 'Whoever drops their pants for me. Just like you.'

He grinned. 'You're some broad. You don't jump. I like that.'

'Thank you. I do love compliments.'

•

Rodeo Drive was not her scene, but Lucky gave it a shot anyway. She wandered into Lina Lee and bought a deep purple leather jacket with huge shoulders. She studied the windows of Fred the jewellers, and then strolled down the street to Giorgio's, where she purchased several drop-dead dresses. Shopping was not one of her great passions, she preferred to live in jeans and shirts, but occasionally she indulged. She loved extravagant outfits. The way rock stars dressed appealed to her. They had a certain style, a freedom, a knockout approach. Recently she had watched Flash on television. He wore black leather, trailing white scarves, and gold earrings. He looked sensational.

Dimitri had mentioned that Olympia was living with Flash. What a couple they must be!

Lucky was quite looking forward to seeing her again. Growing up she had had no other girlfriends. Only Olympia, and for a while, they had been so very close . . .

What if Olympia was furious that she'd married Dimitri? What if –

Oh shit. She hated playing 'what if'. It was a stupid game. When Dimitri returned from his business trip they would announce their marriage. Olympia would either like it or not. Whatever.

•

'Lucky telephoned you,' Susan said.

Gino had been home for an hour. 'Why didn't you tell me before?' he asked angrily.

Susan gestured vaguely. 'I didn't think it was important.'

'Did she say?'

'Did she say what?'

He tried to hold is temper. 'Whether it was important or not?'

'No.'

He started toward his study.

'She's not in New York,' Susan added.

'Where is she?'

'I think she said something about being out here.'

'What's her number?'

'I don't know.'

Now he was really furious. 'Why didn't you get it?'

Two bright red spots appeared on Susan's porcelain cheeks. 'I'm *not* your secretary, Gino.'

'Then don't take my friggin' calls.'

He stamped into his study. Lucky was in town and he didn't know where to reach her. What was the matter with his wife?

•

Lucky apologized to Costa when she returned from her shopping trip. He hugged her and told her he was only concerned for her well being. They sat in the Polo Lounge and she started to confide in him about her plans.

He watched her intently. She was so like her father. Ah . . . he could remember the good old days as if they were only last week. Gino – with the same enthusiasm and bright-eyed optimism. They were both go-getters. Only Lucky had grabbed what she had wanted in a man's world. It wasn't easy. Being married to a man as rich and powerful as Dimitri Stanislopoulos could only help.

At five o'clock Lucky looked at her watch and said, 'Let's call Gino.' A waiter brought a phone to their table, and she requested the number. A maid answered. 'Mr Santangelo,' Lucky said.

'One moment, please.'

She held her breath. It was several months since they had spoken. She loved him. She hated him. Goddamn it, she *missed* him.

His greeting was deceptively casual. 'Hey – kid.'

'Hey – Gino.'

'Where are you?'

'LA.'

'Where?'

'The Beverly Hills Hotel.'

'So, you don't let anyone know you're comin'?'

'Why? Would you have sent a brass brand to the airport?'

'Smart mouth.'

She sensed a warmth that had been missing. She knew him well enough. He was genuinely delighted to hear from her. 'I've got a surprise for you,' she said quickly.

'Y'know I don't like surprises.'

'This one you'll like, love.'

'Yeh?'

'Yeh.'

'How y'bin, kid?'

'Pretty good. And you?'

'Makin' out.'

'Costa's with me.'

'Costa! Jeez! Whyn't you both come over?'

'We'd love to.'

*

Susan was sitting at her dressing table removing the day's make-up with cold cream.

Gino bounced in. 'Lucky an' Costa are comin' for dinner. Tell the cook.'

'We're eating out tonight,' she informed him.

'Change it.'

'I can't do that. We're going to a sit-down dinner for twenty at April Crawford's.'

'Call her. Tell the old bag we can't make it.'

Susan continued to tissue off her make-up. 'April Crawford is *not* an old bag,' she said calmly. 'April Crawford is a fine and respected actress, a *real* movie star of the old school. We can't possibly cancel, it's her birthday.' She crumpled the used tissue and leaned back. 'I wrote this engagement in your appointment book three weeks ago. It's on your desk.'

'Hey – my daughter's in town. She's comin' over. *That's* what we're doin' tonight.'

'Is that the same daughter you haven't heard from in months? The same daughter who never calls or writes?'

He didn't need Susan's criticism of Lucky. His eyes were hard. 'Hey – big mouth,' he said. '*You* go to April Crawford's. I'll stay here. Tell the cook to fix something.'

A moment's pause. Susan knew exactly how far she could go. She got up, went to him, and placed an affectionate kiss on his cheek. 'Sorry, darling,' she whispered. 'I wouldn't think of going without you. I'll have cook prepare something delicious. *Of course* we must be here for Lucky and Costa. Excuse my sarcasm, it's just that sometimes I get so . . . hurt for you. A proper daughter would – oh, forget I said anything.'

'Yeh. Why don't I just forget it.'

Chapter 49

Dinner was a noisy affair which took place in the Rio restaurant at the hotel. There was Lennie, high on too many shots of vodka. There was Isaac and Irena. There was the *Rolling Stone* reporter with a young female photographer mysteriously known as Mouth. There was Matt, with an attractive thirtyish divorcee. And there was Jess. Alone. Sober. And suffering from a double dose of anger.

First, she was angry because Matt had a date.

Second, she was angry at herself for *being* angry.

'Why don't you loosen up?' Lennie hissed. 'You're acting like an old maid at a wedding.'

'Why don't you butt out?' Jess suggested.

Mouth busied herself with a string of cameras. She was intelligently pretty, with spiked hair, sharp eyes, and pointed breasts, bra-less beneath a loose T-shirt.

Isaac and Lennie swapped stories, while Irena listened admiringly.

Matt's date looked out of place in a cocktail dress and mink wrap.

The *Rolling Stone* reporter watched everyone and everything.

Matt played genial host.

Jess tried to be pleasant, and did not succeed.

From the restaurant they all went up to Lennie's suite. Isaac produced some good grass which made Matt uncomfortable and he left, his date hanging onto his arm.

Everyone turned on except Jess. She wasn't in the mood.

They played music, drank a little, smoked a little. And later Lennie found out why the photographer was nicknamed Mouth. She left his suite at five in the morning with a smile and some great photos.

He couldn't sleep. Went down to the pool and did laps. Walked outside the hotel and inspected his billboard.

LENNIE GOLDEN. In twenty-foot letters. LENNIE GOLDEN. Thousands of twinkling lights. It felt unreal. He handed a passing drunk ten bucks for luck, and breakfasted in the coffee shop. It was too early for the fans. Only a few die-hard all-night gamblers and some ragged looking hookers.

Opening night tonight. Sharing the limelight with Vitos Felicidade. He wasn't nervous. Performing never gave him the jitters. In fact being on stage, communicating with an audience, was the only place he felt really secure and in charge. When he was a kid at school he could grab attention any time he wanted by telling dirty jokes – the dirtier the better. Jess used to feed him material. Jess had the filthiest mouth of anyone he knew. He loved her. She was his only real family. Count Alice out.

He finished breakfast and returned to his suite. He had a busy schedule. There was an early morning rehearsal. Lunch with the *Rolling Stone* reporter for an 'in depth' talk. Two scripts of 'The Springs' to check out. And another photo session with Mouth.

He was sorry he'd allowed her to do the things to him she did so well. Jesus! If he was a female he'd have the reputation of being the easiest lay in town. What he really needed with a woman was a solid relationship. He'd had it with one night stands. How about someone to care for him and share his success? Someone who didn't just jump into bed with him because he had some half-assed name.

Eden.

Fuck Eden.

Wouldn't you just love to?

No.

For a moment she was on his mind.

But only for a moment.

Things were getting better.

•

Olympia was bored. Acutely. She had come to Vegas to spite Flash and marry Vitos. But Vitos seemed more concerned with his stupid opening night, rehearsing, and constantly gargling with some disgusting honey concoction. Now she was stuck out by the pool with a disapproving nanny and a truculent daughter, and she had nothing to do except sulk.

Clad in a white one-piece swimsuit, with rolls of excess flesh peeping out everywhere, she lay on a striped chaise under a protective umbrella. She had purchased piles of magazines, but watching the passing parade was definitely more interesting. It had been a long time since Olympia had sat beside a public swimming pool. She could have stayed upstairs on her private terrace, but it was so hot, and besides, Brigette had asked her to come with her to the pool, and it was one of Olympia's 'I am a perfect mother' days.

'Let's take a swim, mama,' Brigette suggested. She was a lovely looking little girl. It was a shame her personality did not match her looks.

'Not right now, dear,' said Olympia. 'I need to rest. Nanny will take you.'

Nanny Mabel, awkward in an old-fashioned bathing suit, glared at her boss.

Olympia was oblivious to the baleful stare. She was too busy eyeing the bikini clad lifeguards whose bulging crotches received her full attention.

*

Lunchtime. And Lennie was safely settled with the *Rolling Stone* reporter.

Walking through the lobby, Jess bumped into Matt.

'How's everything?' he asked.

She smiled brightly. 'Fine.'

'Nothing you need?'

'Can't think of anything.'

'Is Lennie happy?'

'He seems to be.'

'What time did the party end?'

It slipped out before she could help it. 'I thought *you* were the one having a party.'

He laughed easily, and referred to his date of the night before. 'Tina's an old friend.'

Again she couldn't help herself. '*Old* being the operative word.'

He laughed again. 'How about a snack?' He took her arm, assuming she would say yes.

'I'm too busy.'

'You've got to eat.'

'I'll have something sent up. I have calls coming in from LA.'

'Diligent lady.'

'I enjoy my work.'

'You've certainly done all right for Lennie.'

'He would have done it without me. He's brilliant. You should have spotted that when you first had him here.'

Matt frowned. Sure Lennie Golden was good. But why did Jess gleam when she talked about him? Why did her whole face light up?

She was sleeping with him. He knew it for sure. And that meant he, Matt Traynor, didn't stand a chance.

He had known it all along. When she had left Vegas with Lennie he knew it. That's why he'd never pursued her.

'I'll see you later,' he said. 'Are you sure there's nothing you need?'

'Nothing.'

He's not interested in me any more, she thought. He couldn't give a damn.

Why should she care?

She only knew she did.

*

'Tell me about your mother?' the *Rolling Stone* reporter asked.

Lennie had a mouthful of hamburger. He chewed slowly. 'What do you want to know?'

'Well . . . your father was a comedian – you told me that. You don't have any brothers or sisters. You arrived in New York at seventeen and we've got the story from there. But you never mention your mother. Is she still alive?'

How tempting to do away with Alice. Kill her off in print

and never have to deal with her again. Alice would hardly stand for that. Now he was famous she found it perfectly acceptable to have a thirty-two-year-old son.

'Yeah, she's alive,' he said.

'How does she feel about your material? Your mother/son comedy routines hit a nerve in all of us. Does she love it? Get upset? What?'

Lennie hunched his shoulders. He had had enough of being interviewed. Who gave a shit *what* Alice thought. She had never offered an opinion. He had never asked. The only comment she had ever made about his act was that he should clean it up.

He grinned, stretched. 'Hey – you wanna know stuff like that you'll have to ask her.' Quick glance at his watch. 'I have to move it. See you later. You'll be at the show, right?'

The reporter nodded, and clicked off a small tape recorder.

Lennie rose, winked at a hovering waitress who had asked for his autograph earlier, and strode out of the restaurant.

•

At three o'clock Olympia left the pool so she could begin readying herself for the evening ahead. Vitos was in his suite, stretched out on a slant board practising scales. 'Oleeempeea!' he exclaimed. 'So lovleeee.'

'Vitos,' she said sharply. 'I did not come to this tacky gambling palace in the sky to sit around. What's happening?'

'Tomorrow I weel know,' Vitos said, sitting up with a big smile. He had told Olympia he needed certain papers from Spain. It was true. He had to get his annulment papers and nobody seemed able to locate them.

She picked a grape from a table laden with fruit, and pouted. 'How long do we have to stay here?' she asked.

'One week.'

'Thank God that's all! This place sucks.'

•

Lennie wore a black leather jacket, tight black pants, a white shirt open at the neck with a narrow black leather tie, and white tennis shoes. His dirty blond hair was artfully tousled.

Jess stood on tiptoe and kissed him on the cheek. 'You look gorgeous!' she whispered.

And then he was on.

Deep breath.

Get the adrenalin pumping.

Go for it!

*

Sitting in the audience Eden wondered if he would spot her. He could hardly help but do so. She was at the best table, centre front. She was with Paige and Ryder Wheeler. Quinn Leech, the director of the soon-to-be-movie, and his contemptuous plain girlfriend. Santino. Of course. And two of his Las Vegas acquaintances. 'They could be investors,' he had told her earlier. 'Be nice to 'em.'

Both men were repellent. One short and squat with a wild abundance of hair sprouting from his ears, nose, neck, hands. Eden got the creeps just looking at him. The other, big and paunchy, with small mean eyes and slicked back greasy hair. Neither had dates, whch meant that after cursory glances at Paige Wheeler (at forty plus, too old for their jaded tastes) and Quinn Leech's girlfriend (too plain for their *Playboy* mentalities) they concentrated all their attentions on Eden.

She responded with frosty looks and flat conversation. Living with a man like Santino Bonnatti was bad enough. Why should she be nice to a couple of gorillas who only *might* invest in the movie? Santino didn't need investors anyway, he had enough money to do it himself.

She stared at Lennie, centre stage. He looked great. Well, he always was a handsome son-of-a-bitch. Fortunately she knew she looked great too. A silver dress cut low and slinky. And she was wearing her ruby necklace and earrings – Santino's gift. Her hair was parted in the middle, and brushed her shoulders – a pale curtain to frame her chiselled features.

When Santino had said they were going to Las Vegas for a few days she had been delighted. It was so boring sitting in the house on Blue Jay Way – a virtual prisoner. She couldn't wait for the movie to start so she could get out and resume some kind of a normal life. When filming began Santino would just have to leave her alone. There would be costume fittings, script conferences, rehearsals – she hoped. Some directors liked to work with their actors for weeks before production began.

Naturally Santino had not given her any notice. 'We're goin' to Vegas,' he announced, and an hour later they were on their way, by car, with Zeko driving. It would have been nice if she'd had time to go to the hairdressers, get her nails done, maybe do some shopping.

But no. Santino did things his way. Eden had learned to go along with it.

Once they arrived, Santino settled her in a suite at the Sands Hotel, with Zeko in attendance, then he left, returning an hour later. 'Get dressed,' he said. 'We're goin' to an openin'.'

'What opening?' she asked.

'That Spanish singing pimp – Vitos somethin'. Here.' He thrust a wad of bills in her hand. 'Go an' buy somethin' that'll give me a stiff prick. Take Zeko.'

She had no idea Lennie Golden was sharing the bill with Vitos Felicidade. It wasn't until they were driving up to the Magiriano that she saw the huge billboards.

Paige leaned across the table and whispered something.

Eden didn't hear her. 'What?'

'Hot, isn't he?' repeated Paige. 'Reminds me of a horny Redford with a touch of Newman's heat.'

It occurred to Eden that nobody knew about her three year affair with Lennie Golden. For some obscure reason she found that aggravating. He hadn't even mentioned her in the *People* article – just vaguely stated that he'd dated a lot of models in New York.

Wasn't she part of his past? A big part.

It infuriated her to think he had made it first. *She* should be the one getting all the attention. *She* should be on the cover of *People*.

Paige was obviously waiting for an answer to her comment. 'Not bad,' she managed.

'Not bad!' exclaimed Paige. 'He is *hot*, honey. When *I* say someone's hot you'd better believe it.'

Eden quite liked Paige Wheeler, although she hadn't spent much time with her. A couple of dinners, two or three lunches with Santino's permission. Paige was fun. She enjoyed life, and it came across. Oh! Wouldn't it be interesting to see her face if she confided just how hot Lennie Golden really was!

And she missed him.

For a moment.

Only for a moment.

And only in bed.

*

The audience loved him. They were the real power who could make or break a star.

He knew he had them the minute he walked on stage. He could feel the vibes – feel that they wanted to share this evening's success with him.

His humour was deadpan, ironic, cutting.

They went for it immediately, picking up on every little nuance.

He told truths. It broke them up.

He trashed television. They loved it.

He started on family relationships. People were crying with mirth.

He hit his stride. Confident, in charge, his timing impeccable.

And then he saw her.

Chapter 50

'Where *the hell* do you think it's getting you?' Jerry Myerson shouted.

Steven and he stood at opposite ends of the living room

in Jerry's New York townhouse. They were both angry. Steven, because he wished Jerry would butt out. And Jerry, because when he was a very young man he had once harboured a secret crush on Carrie, and he hated to see what this was doing to her.

Steven gestured impatiently. 'I'll let you know when I get results.'

'And when will *that* be?' Jerry asked sarcastically.

'Don't you think I wish I knew?' Steven turned his back and stared out of the window at the snarled traffic on 54th Street. A cab driver was making obscene signals at the driver of a large delivery truck blocking traffic. Soon a fist fight would erupt.

'The best thing you can do is get back to work,' Jerry stated bluntly. 'I've told you there's a job for you with my firm any time you like.'

Steven turned around. 'That's what I *want* to do. And as soon as this thing is settled that's what I *will* do.'

'Good. Then you can pay me back the money I've loaned you.'

Steven's eyes blazed. 'Are you worried about your money, Jerry?'

'No. Asshole. I'm worried about *you* and your state of mind.'

They argued some more, but both of them knew it wouldn't make any difference. Steven had something to do. Nothing was going to stop him.

The next day Jerry took Carrie to lunch at Le Cirque. She looked tired, but she was pleased to see him and hugged him tightly. He was the only other person to know the truth about her past, and he seemed to understand a lot better than Steven.

'He's taking me to see the retired doctor tomorrow,' she said wearily. 'Who knows? Maybe the face will fit the name.'

'I hope so,' Jerry said. 'For both your sakes.'

She toyed with her martini glass, and lowered her eyes. 'Jerry,' she began hesitantly. 'I just don't know what to do anymore. When I'm with Steven I feel he hates me. It's as if he's put a steel cage around himself, and there's no penetrating it. I only did what any mother would have done – I protected him from the truth.'

'I know,' said Jerry sympathetically. 'You can't blame yourself. He's caught up in an identity crisis. There's only one way he can work it out, and that's by himself. It's not just you – neither of us can help him.'

'I'm glad you understand.'

'That's what friends are for.'

'Thank you, Jerry.' She put her hand over his and squeezed. 'And how's everything with you?'

He grinned. 'I am managing to stay single in spite of overwhelming odds. It's not easy being rich, straight and successful in New York. The ladies go right for the good old wedding ring.'

Carrie smiled and felt relaxed for the first time in weeks.

*

Fredd Lesster, MD lived halfway between New York and Philadelphia. He turned out to be eighty-five years old and half Lebanese. One glance was enough to rule him out.

Steven, once again borrowing Jerry's Porsche, drove Carrie back to the city in silence. She was staying in a friend's apartment. Her friend had gone to Europe for six months, and it seemed more sensible to be there than at her house on Fire Island.

'Why don't you come up? I'll fix you some eggs or something,' she offered.

He shook his head.

She wanted to reach out and touch him, he looked so miserable. Why couldn't he just accept things the way they were?

'I'm sorry about today,' he said, staring straight ahead. 'It was a wasted trip.'

'It doesn't matter.'

'Yes it does. It won't happen again.'

She wondered if that meant he was giving up on Freddy Lester. Maybe he didn't need him after all. Maybe Gino

Santangelo was his father. Steven knew where Gino was. Why didn't he just fly to California and persuade him to take a blood test?

She almost laughed aloud. Gino Santangelo would never remember her. He would think Steven was a mad man, a mental patient. He would spit in his face.

'What now?' she asked quietly.

Steven leaned across and opened the passenger door. 'I'll speak to you in a day or so,' he said brusquely.

Thank you very much. Shall I just put my life on hold while I wait for your next move?

'Goodnight,' she said, getting out of Jerry's car.

He roared off into the night with not a backward glance. He didn't even bother to see she got into the building safely. So much for love and concern, of which he had once had an abundance. He made her very sad.

She couldn't sleep, and sat for a while by the window watching night-time shadows and listening to the perpetual whine of the police sirens. Memories invaded her head, and when she did finally fall asleep, it was an uneasy rest.

Chapter 51

Susan was no slouch when it came to doing things her way. Within three quarters of an hour she had phoned April Crawford and pleaded a dreadful migraine; phoned Chasens and ordered a supply of their wonderful chili; applied an understated make-up, and dressed in a simple peach caftan. When Lucky and Costa arrived she was ready.

Gino was also ready. He was delighted to be greeting the daughter he found he had really missed. 'Kid!' He threw open his arms.

'Daddy!' She fell into them. Too bad if he didn't like the title, she felt like using it for once.

Susan smiled graciously at Costa. 'Welcome. Do come in.'

They all trooped into the house. A casual Californian four million dollar mansion. Nothing pretentious.

'Well, well, well,' exclaimed Gino, surveying Lucky with a grin. 'Lookin' as good as ever.' He turned to Costa, poked him playfully around the middle. 'An' you my friend, gettin' a little gutty. Too much home cookin', huh? Too many Miami widows handin' you somethin' hot?'

'Yes,' Lucky joined in. 'I've been meaning to talk to you about your weight, Costa. They're turning you into a fatso!'

They all roared with laughter, except Susan, who failed to see the humour in someone not watching their diet. She was meticulous about everything she put into her mouth, which was one of the reasons she had stopped performing fellatio on Gino a month after marrying him. He hadn't been pleased, but too bad, there was nothing he could do about it.

'What'll you have to drink?' Gino asked, putting one arm around Lucky and the other around Costa as he guided them toward the bar.

'Pernod on the rocks,' requested Lucky.

'Something soft,' said Costa.

'Something soft! The story of your life!' joked Gino, preparing to fix the drinks.

'Hans will do that, dear,' intoned Susan smoothly, gliding over.

'Forget it. I'll do it,' replied Gino, already putting chunks of ice in the glasses.

Susan motioned Hans, the houseman, away. Then she turned to Lucky with a pleasant smile. 'And how are you, my dear? It's been quite some time.'

Phony broad, thought Lucky. *You haven't changed. Still doing your Grace Kelly number.*

'I'm in good shape, Susan.' *Ha! Wait until she hears I've married Dimitri Stanislopoulos. She'll wet her panties!*

'You certainly look very well,' said Susan. 'A touch tired, but I expect it's the time difference. I'm always wretched when I do that trip. Three hours difference may not seem a lot, but believe me –'

'Hey – Gino,' Lucky said, ignoring her. 'You missing Vegas yet?'

He grinned. 'Are you?'

'Me? I've got a lot of other things to keep me busy.'

'Like what?'

'Like Atlantic City. I'm going in, before it's too late.'

'You are?'

'Why not? It's what I want. And now I've got the financing.'

'Yeh?'

'Yeh.'

'Who from?'

'I'll tell you later.'

Susan's smile was fixed. She had no idea what they were talking about. 'I've ordered chili from "Chasens", she announced. 'I do hope you both like chili, but Gino gave me such short notice. I really –'

'Why can't you tell me now?' demanded Gino, following Lucky's lead and ignoring Susan.

'Because,' she replied, 'it's a long story.'

'I got all night.'

Her black eyes gleamed. 'Why are you so anxious to know? You want to come in with me?'

'Hey' – he laughed. 'I know what your game is. You don't have all the money, and you want me in for a slice of the action. Right?'

'Wrong.'

'Yeh?'

'Yeh. *I* am finally building *my* hotel. I don't need any partners.'

'And how have you managed that?'

'Wouldn't *you* like to know.'

'I'll know 'cos you're gonna tell me.'

'Yeh? Don't bet on it.'

They were both smiling broadly, playing games, batting words back and forth just like they used to when things were good and togetherness was the name of the game.

'Dinner will be here in a minute,' Susan said stiffly.

'Did I hear you mention chili?' Costa asked politely.

'Yes,' Susan replied, favouring him with a glance, and not particularly liking what she saw. Why did Gino have to burden her with his dull friends as well as his difficult daughter?

'Perhaps – if it's no trouble – I could have something else,' Costa requested quietly. 'A can of soup, some eggs.' He patted his stomach. 'Chili's too spicy for me. Doctor's orders.'

'I'll see what I can do,' Susan said frigidly. Gino and Lucky had moved to the end of the bar and were deep in conversation. Gino was withdrawing from her, she had sensed it for months. Now, seeing him talking to his daughter, so animated and alive, she realized she had better be careful, it was possible she could lose him. And she wasn't ready for that. Not yet.

Quickly she moved to his side and took his arm proprietarily. 'Now, Lucky, we want to hear all about what you've been doing, dear. Everything.' Her voice was honey, her tight smile, sugar. 'You know, this household really misses you. We miss her, Gino, don't we darling?'

•

Gino insisted that dinner be served in the kitchen. 'It's chili for crissake. Whatta 'ya wanna make a big deal for?'

So dinner in the kitchen it was, much to the servants' annoyance. The kitchen was their domain, they did not appreciate being banished.

Susan kept her smile in place all night, but it wasn't easy. Gino, Lucky and Costa formed a group. All Gino wanted to talk about was the good old New York days, and Costa was the perfect foil, Lucky the perfect listener.

Susan had no desire to hear any of it. The good old days sounded sordid and disgusting.

Halfway through dinner Gemma arrived home with several friends. 'I thought you were going out,' she said rudely. 'And what the hell are you doing in the kitchen?'

Susan delicately patted her lips with a napkin. 'A change of plans, dear. Gemma, you remember Lucky, don't you?

And this is Costa . . .' she paused, trying to think of his surname. 'Zennacot.'

'Zennocotti,' Gino corrected.

'Ah yes,' Susan said quickly. 'Zennocotti.'

'Hi,' Gemma said, but her heart wasn't in it. She had hoped to have the house to herself so she and her friends could relax and do a little coke. Now they would have to go elsewhere. She had no intention of sitting around with this over-the-hill group. Sulkily she left the room.

Lucky pushed her half eaten plate of chili away. She wished that she, Gino and Costa were alone. There was something stifling about Susan. Her glassy smile, and the way she tried to join in. And the house was oppressive, not homey, more like something out of a magazine. And now Gemma, the uptight daughter. Gino seemed so like his old self, surely he didn't enjoy living with these people?

'Why don't you come by the hotel?' she said to him quietly. 'I have a surprise for you.'

'What is it?'

'Come with me and you shall see,' she teased.

He didn't need much persuading. 'Let's go.'

Susan was not pleased when they left immediately after dinner. She wanted to accompany them, but Gino said, 'No, I'll be right back. You stay here.'

They piled into Lucky's rented car and raced to the hotel, laughing all the way like kids playing truant.

As she parked the car on Crescent Drive, Lucky thought of the enormity of the surprise she was just about to spring on Gino. She hadn't even told him she was married. She took a deep breath. He had to be thrilled. What other reaction could he possibly have when he first set eyes on Roberto? *His* grandson. *His* flesh and blood. Oh God! Why did she feel so nervous?

They made their way carefully along the foliage-lined paths to her bungalow. She put the key in the door, opened up and sprung the lights.

'Where's my surprise?' Gino asked genially, looking around.

'What did you expect? A Ferrari?' she jested.

'I kinda thought you'd have my portrait waiting. I always fancied hangin' on somebody's wall.'

She laughed softly. 'Wait!' she commanded. 'Fix him a drink, Costa.'

Hurriedly she went in her bedroom, shutting the door behind her. Roberto was asleep in a cot beside her bed. CeeCee was watching television in the other bedroom.

She stared at her baby, her little boy. Sixteen months old and totally sensational.

He slept face down. Santangelo black hair, jet eyes, and long curling lashes.

She loved him so very much. Gino had to feel the same way. He had to.

Gently she picked him up. He was warm and damp and smelled of talcum powder and soap. 'Roberto,' she whispered. 'Mommy's home.' The child's eyes flickered open. 'Hey – this is a really big day,' she crooned. 'You – my fantastic little boy, are just about to meet your grandpop.' She hugged him. 'Now you *are* going to be a good boy, aren't you?' Roberto displayed a three-toothed grin. He had the greatest disposition in the world.

She hugged him even tighter. 'Let's move it, baby kid,' she said. 'Let us go and make a good impression.'

Chapter 52

Lennie felt like someone had delivered a blow to his stomach. *Pow.* Right in the solar plexis. *Take that you sonofabitch.*

For a split second his eyes met Eden's. She did not nod or indicate in any way that she knew him. She merely turned to the man seated beside her and requested a cigarette. He knew she did it purposely. It was a 'don't care' gesture. A shrug of indifference – as if to say – the rest of the audience might think you're hot stuff, but frankly, *I* don't give a damn.

Thin-faced bitch.

She looked knock-out.

While all these thoughts were churning through his head he maintained a cool exterior. Did not blow a line. Just kept right on doing what he was so good at doing, while the bitch drew on her cigarette, and sipped her wine, and pretended she didn't know who he was.

She spurred him on. Made him soar. Made him hotter than a whore on pay-day. He went beyond what he had planned and rehearsed. He ad-libbed, played with the audience, ran ten minutes over, and received a tumultuous ovation.

Lennie Golden. Star. If she hadn't known it before, she knew it now. He leapt off stage, high on adulation and applause, ready to do it all over again.

'You were senfuckingsational!' enthused Jess, bright-eyed and filled with delight.

The thunderous applause wouldn't quit. He went back three or four times to take a bow, until Vitos Felicidade's theme music cut into the noise, and it was on with the second half of the show.

'Good Golly Miss Molly,' raved Jess. 'You sure gave 'em Great Balls of Fire tonight.'

Everybody was crowding his dressing room. Isaac and Irena, Matt Traynor, Mouth, with her cameras, the ever-present reporter from *Rolling Stone*.

He wanted to be alone. Needed just a few moments of peace and quiet. Jess caught the message and emptied the room while he shut himself in the bathroom, stripped off his clothes – and stood under the icy needles of a cold shower.

Eden was here.

Maybe she had come specially. Unlikely, but a thought.

He turned off the shower, wrapped a towel around his waist, and re-entered his dressing room.

Jess sat on the couch hugging her knees and balancing a glass of champagne. She raised the glass in his direction, 'Saluté.'

'Eden's here,' he said. 'Find out who the fuck she's with.'

*

Vitos Felicidade was gazing straight at her. She knew it, but she refused to react. Since every other female in the audience was swooning with joy she was not about to join the club. She was Olympia Stanislopoulos. And she could have any man she wanted. Any time. Any place.

Unfortunately, after the rather unkempt but adventurous attentions of Flash, Vitos – with his limp-wristed delivery and sickly smile – presented no challenge. But he would do. For now.

He was warbling on about lost love and passion and starlit summer nights. Frankly, Olympia decided that the comedian, Lennie something, had far more going for him than Vitos ever would. Now *he* was sexy in the same way Flash was. Street-wise – a phrase Flash had taught her which she loved.

Street-wise. It conjured up visions of someone who knew what life was all about. Vitos appeared to exist in a vacuum of perfection. He was also lousy in bed. A limp wrist was not his only problem.

She fidgeted uncomfortably. All dressed up, and another half hour of Vitos' dreary melodies. She wasn't at all sure she could sit through it.

*

Lennie played the room. The dressing room. Easier than being on stage, but a game all the same. He was getting pretty adept at fielding questions – there were two local reporters present as well as the *Rolling Stone* regular. They all wanted to know the same things. How did he start? Where was he born? When did he decide to take up comedy?

Why the hell didn't they read the neatly typed bios Jess handed out?

Dumb questions. Boring questions. Another couple of months and he would give up interviews altogether. This, of course, would make him even hotter.

Jess came back into the room. He made his way over to her, dogged by Mouth, who must have taken at least ten thousand pictures of him by this time.

'Well?'

'Bad news.'

'What?'

'She's with a couple of Vegas hoods and a compadre of theirs from LA.'

'How do you know?'

'Straight from the Captain's mouth. We're old friends – he knows everything and everybody. Believe me, Lennie, these guys are headlines, not a tiny item on the back page – so stay away. Am I reaching you?'

He nodded.

But they both knew she wasn't.

*

Eden admired Vitos Felicidade's style. He was smooth, assured, probably a thoughtful and sensuous lover.

Making love with Santino was like being in bed with a slobbering baboon. He had no idea how to please a woman. More than likely he wasn't aware that women *could* climax. All he was interested in was getting his rocks off, and a little cruelty and violence if the urge came over him.

'Whattaya think of the Spanish pimp?' he asked, as if reading her thoughts.

'Why?' she asked guardedly.

'Quinn an' Ryder thought he might be okay for the movie.'

Eden tried not to react. She knew Santino well enough to realize that if she showed one flicker of enthusiasm, Vitos Felicidade would no longer be a contender. 'What makes you think he can act?' she asked offhandedly.

'The same reasons y'think you can.' He guffawed, and was promptly sshhed by a woman at the next table.

Eden burned. 'I went to acting classes in New York,' she hissed. 'And I've appeared in a number of TV shows. Don't compare *me* with your singing Spanish pimp.'

Excellent. Now he would think she hated Vitos. And maybe they would hire him. And if they did she would have an affair with him. A discreet affair. Not so discreet if the movie was a hit. If it was, she would leave Santino immediately.

*

Vitos was nearing the end of his act. Resplendent in black tie and tails he blew a kiss to Olympia and introduced her to the audience. Then he dedicated his latest single, 'The One Love of My Life' to her, and proceeded to sing it on one knee gazing into her eyes.

She thoroughly enjoyed the charade. Once people realized who she was, they stared at her more than they did Vitos. She was newsworthy. Rich heiress with a string of husbands and a wild headline-grabbing affair with the legendary Flash.

She pulled her shoulders back and smiled prettily.

*

Matt had a new date for the gala party taking place in the private ballroom. A party to honour Lennie Golden and Vitos Felicidade. She was a retired showgirl; forty; still beautiful, and six feet tall.

Jess took one look and backed away. Tall, haughty, *tall*, elegant, *tall*, sophisticated, *tall*.

Goddamn Matt Traynor. Back to his showgirls. He was a jerk anyway.

*

Both stars had their entourages. Vitos' larger than Lennie's. Managers, agents, photographers, gofers, reporters, hangers-on. And Vitos and Olympia. But Lennie had the current cover of *People*. So they attracted equal attention as they arrived within five minutes of each other at the party.

Santino and his group were already ensconced at one of the best tables. Santino's father, Enzio Bonnatti, had taught him at an early age – '*You go to a friggin' fancy party, get there early – take the best friggin' table, and don't move ass for nobody*.'

Santino missed the wit and wisdom of Enzio. What a man he had been. A real capo. He knew how to do business, pull people's strings, and break their fucking balls if they didn't do things his way. Sitting in the ballroom of the Magiriano Hotel brought back memories. In 1975 Enzio had taken over the Magiriano. Looked after the whole Santangelo Vegas operation as a favour for Gino Santangelo – out of the country on some tax scam – and Lucky Santangelo – who ran from town when her boyfriend, Marco, got himself killed.

Fuck the Santangelos. They had paid Enzio back with threats not gratitude. And one hot September day in 1977, Lucky Santangelo – Enzio's *goddaughter* for crissakes – had arrived at his Long Island mansion and shot him. *Shot him in the stomach, the neck, and the balls. Three fucking times.*

Self-defence she had claimed. He was attacking me, trying to rape me. And the authorities believed the cunt! The case never even came to court. She was free as a fucking 747. The final straw being forbidden retribution. The 'family' said no. Carlos had no balls but Santino still brooded about it.

Fuck Carlos.

Fuck the 'family'.

The Santangelos had not heard the last of Santino Bonnatti. No way.

Chapter 53

For a moment Gino said nothing. He stared at Lucky and the baby, then he turned to Costa for an explanation.

Costa cleared his throat and was silent.

'This is Roberto,' Lucky said, with pride in her voice. 'Your grandson.'

Another long moment of silence.

Lucky held her breath. She wanted Gino to be thrilled, delighted, ecstatic!

'Hey,' he said at last, sitting down. 'Some surprise.'

'Better than a portrait, huh?' she grinned.

'What didja do, adopt a kid?' he asked.

'No. This is Roberto,' she said indignantly. '*My* baby. *Our* flesh and blood. *Your* grandson. He's sixteen months old and he's been looking forward to meeting you.'

Once again Gino looked to Costa, but Costa felt that this was a matter he shouldn't be involved in. 'I'm going to bed,' he said. 'I'll phone you in the morning, Gino. Goodnight.' He let himself out.

'Well?' Lucky laughed nervously. 'What do you think?'

'I think,' Gino replied slowly, 'that if the kid's bin' waitin' to meet me you could have arranged somethin' before this.' He held out his arms for the baby, 'Maybe I should hold him.' She placed Roberto carefully on his lap. 'Haven't held a kid for quite a while,' he said, shifting awkwardly.

'Roberto's tough. He won't break.' God! She sounded like one of those dumb new mothers. But she felt terrific. She had finally brought the two most important people in her life together.

'So,' Gino bounced the baby a little, 'you wanna tell me about it?'

'He looks like a Santangelo, doesn't he?' she asked excitedly.

'He looks like you when you were his age.'

She was thrilled. 'Really? Honestly?'

'Spittin' image.'

'I wish I had some baby pictures of *you*.'

'Hey – I was fortunate if I got a meal a day. There was no money for pictures.'

'You know something?' She bent to kiss him. 'I love you, I really do.' The last time she had uttered those words he had been close to death, after a violent heart attack. Now she was saying them again, and their estrangement of the last two years felt like it had never happened.

'I feel the same way about you, kid. I may not always have shown it – but y'know, after your mother was murdered I –'

The phone rang, cutting into his softly spoken words. He clammed up immediately.

Lucky was furious. Just when he was about to open up for the first time. He had never discussed Maria's murder with her, or even mentioned the fateful day when she was five years old and had come upon her mother's body floating in the swimming pool. Now that he was about to, the goddamn phone had to interrupt. She could have screamed with frustration as she snatched up the receiver. 'Yes?'

'Lucky, dear,' Susan's well modulated tones. 'Is Gino still there?'

She handed him the phone. 'It's your keeper,' she said, hoping he would get rid of her quickly.

He threw her a look. She lifted Roberto from his knee and took him back to his cot. When she returned Gino had hung up. *Well?* she wanted to ask. *When the Widow Perfect calls do you still run?* Instead she said, 'I guess you've got to go.'

'There's a problem with Gemma and her friends,' he sighed.

'Only you can solve it, huh?'

'Yeh. Well I'm the only one they'll listen to when I throw 'em out.'

'I'll drive you.'

'Don't worry, kid – I called the front desk, they've got a car for me.'

She opened the door, trying to hide the letdown she felt.

'Breakfast tomorrow?' he suggested. 'We can talk then.'

She nodded. But she knew it wouldn't be the same in the morning.

'Goodnight, kiddo.'

'Goodnight, Gino.'

He hugged her, but he was already on his way home.

She sat in the darkness and brooded for a while. Then she picked up the phone and dialled his number.

Susan answered.

When he came on the line he sounded harrassed. 'What's up?'

'Just a postscript. I *am* married you know.'

'I didn't know that. I kinda thought you kept the baby quiet because you weren't.'

'How archaic!' she scoffed. 'It's 1980 for goodness sake.'

'So . . . where's your husband?'

'Travelling. He's a businessman.' She paused, then added. 'You might remember him.'

'Do I know him?'

'You sure do. Dimitri. Dimitri Stanislopoulos. Olympia's father.'

Chapter 54

There were fire-eaters at the party. And jugglers dressed as white-faced clowns. And a handsome black singer. And an excellent band. There was also a sumptuous buffet, scads of gorgeous showgirls, and many more celebrities than the two stars for whom the party was being held.

Press abounded. Pretty girls in neat dresses with notepads and pencils. Sweaty photographers with bulky flash cameras. A few network people with TV cameras balanced on their shoulders.

Vitos and Lennie formed separate camps with their various entourages.

Lennie found himself surrounded by women, and since he had spotted Eden sitting at a table with a group who looked straight out of *The Valachi Papers* he didn't mind at all.

Vitos also had women fawning all over him. He responded with charm. Olympia responded with a ferocious scowl as she found herself shoved to one side.

Jess scouted the room on the lookout for someone she might have fun with. She was fed up with always being on her own – good old Jess – Girl Friday – fixer of everything. Maybe she would have a go at fixing her love life.

Matt divided himself between the two camps. His girlfriend-for-the-night fell deeply in lust with Vitos, and settled herself at his table, refusing to budge.

No great loss, Matt decided. He observed Jess chatting to a member of Vitos' band, and wondered what she had to talk to *him* about. When the conversation had gone on for more than ten minutes he went over.

'Time for a business discussion,' he said briskly, taking her arm.

'What business?' she asked, as he steered her toward the bar.

'Lennie was such a hit tonight I thought we should start negotiations for next year.'

'Now?'

'Why not?'

'Because this is a party.'

'It doesn't suit you.'

'Huh?'

'Partying.'

'You're crazy.'

'Are you and Lennie sleeping together?'

'That's none of your business.' She stalked away. It was difficult stalking when you are only five feet tall, but Jess managed it.

*

Ryder Wheeler introduced Paige to Vitos. He bowed. Clicked his heels together. Murmured, '*Enchanté*.'

Paige thought he was full of shit.

Eden danced with the tallest of Santino's friends, the one with the small mean eyes and the greasy hair. Add BO, bad breath, and sweaty palms to his list of accomplishments.

She hoped Lennie wasn't watching her.

In spite of the fact that he was surrounded by girls, she knew he was. She could have him back any time she wanted.

One sign of encouragement from her and he'd come running.

It made her feel good, in spite of Sweaty Palms grinding his semi-hard-on into her thigh.

Lennie got up, relieved Mouth of her cameras, and whirled her around the dance floor ignoring her protestations about not being dressed for it.

'You're the best looking girl here,' he said, as soon as he was close enough for Eden to overhear.

'I've got to work,' Mouth insisted. 'Take me back to my cameras.'

He noticed Eden smirking. She had an infuriating way of curling her mouth at one corner.

Their eyes met, and they both practised mutual non-recognition.

Olympia announced she wished to meet the comedian. Matt arranged it on neutral territory between the two camps.

'You're very very funny,' Olympia said, in her most charming fashion. 'I must watch your television show, I hear it's hilarious.'

Lennie smiled his thanks, and was just about to move on when he spotted Eden watching him. This time there was no curled lip. This time she was jealous.

What does it take to make Eden Antonio jealous?

One of the richest women in the world.

He gave Olympia Stanislopoulos the benefit of his ocean green eyes, and a lopsided grin. 'Wanna dance?' he asked.

She smiled. Lovely smile. Lovely hair. Lovely boobs. It was a shame she was thirty pounds overweight.

'Yes,' she said.

And they hit the dance floor to the strains of 'Street Life'.

*

The evening progressed.

Dessert was giant bowls of ten different flavour ice creams with various toppings. The handsome black singer gave his all to interesting imitations of Stevie Wonder and Smokey Robinson.

Vitos Felicidade enjoyed the attentions of every woman in the place. He failed to notice that Olympia had settled in a corner with Lennie Golden, and that their conversation appeared more than casual.

Eden noticed. She danced with Santino's lousy friends and noticed a whole lot.

Jess resumed friendship with the member of Vitos' band she had been talking to earlier. He played guitar, spoke passable English, and had very expressive eyes and hands.

Matt watched from afar. He wasn't pleased. It was obvious Jess was coming on to the guitar player because Lennie was making out with the rich broad.

Santino decided he wanted his picture taken with Vitos Felicidade. He liked being photographed with celebrities – he had quite a collection. Eden was summoned from the dance floor where she was struggling with Santino's short hairy friend. He was even shorter and hairier than Santino himself, and she was delighted to be relieved of duty.

Ryder Wheeler took them over to Vitos' table and introduced them. Vitos dazzled her with his teeth, took her hand, squeezed it imperceptibly, brought it to his lips and kissed it. His eyes were pools of desire. '*Enchanté*,' he murmured.

She thought she read a definite message – A message that said, '*I want to make love to you. Soon. Very soon. You won't regret it.*'

Santino shoved her between them for the photo. Vitos' touch made her shiver.

Santino decided he didn't like that pose, so he put himself in the middle and made the house photographer take it again.

Vitos was most cooperative. His manager had filled him in on Santino Bonnatti. They had been negotiating for weeks with Ryder Wheeler about the movie he wanted Vitos to star in. Money seemed to be the only stumbling block, and Ryder had explained that Bonnatti was the chief investor, and as such made the final decision. Vitos wanted to do the movie. He oozed charm.

Lennie observed Eden. She had the hots for the Spanish singer. Her body language was eloquent. At the same time he managed to catch every word Olympia Stanislopoulos was saying. She had overdosed on champagne, and was regaling him with tales of her life. Poor little rich girl. Too much too soon. It wasn't easy being one of the richest girls in the world. People used you for who you were. They wanted your money, notoriety, or they just wanted to be seen with you.

He started to feel sorry for her. Everyone expected the image. The rich spoilt bitch. But this was a rather sad, insecure woman, who, if she lost some weight, would be very attractive.

Not his type, of course.

Spectacular boobs.

Not his type.

Of course.

Eden was watching them.

'Why don't we get out of here?' Olympia whispered forlornly. 'I need to be with someone who cares.'

Eden was watching them.

He hesitated. 'I thought you were with Vitos.'

She shrugged. 'He's not a man, he's a puppet. Pull his string and he sings. Pull again and he smiles for the cameras.'

Eden was *definitely* watching them.

What sweet revenge to exit with Olympia Stanislopoulos while Eden was stuck with her gangster boyfriend.

He stood up. 'Let's go,' he said decisively. 'I'll buy you a drink at my place.'

Chapter 55

Lucky did not linger in LA. She had told Gino about his grandchild and her marriage before he read about it in the newspapers, and that fulfilled her obligations. Fortunately Dimitri had the power to keep the news from breaking in the press until he was ready to make the announcement.

The morning after dining at his house, she ordered a limo, booked a flight, and set off early for New York with Roberto and CeeCee.

She wasn't angry at Gino. Their evening together had been wonderful until Susan broke the spell. But she had to be realistic. Things were different now. It wasn't father and daughter against the world. It was father, with a wife, step-children, and a new kind of lifestyle. And it was daughter, with a husband and son. She had other priorities too.

She left a message at the desk for Costa. To Gino, she

wrote a short note, explaining that Dimitri had returned early from Europe and she had to get back to New York immediately.

Dimitri . . . When she had told Gino who she was married to there had been an ominous silence. He was too smart to criticize, and a muttered, 'We'll talk tomorrow morning over breakfast,' was all that he'd said.

Well, *she* was having breakfast aboard a 747. She wondered what *he* was doing.

•

'More toast?' Susan asked.

Gino shook his head.

'Tea?'

Again negative.

'How about a Danish? Prune. Your favourite.'

He got up from the table and paced the breakfast room. Lucky's note had arrived while he was dressing. It had upset him. Why was she running off?

It was Susan's fault. Susan and her goddamn phone call. Interrupting him just when he felt the time was right to speak to Lucky about her mother's murder. He had wanted to talk to her for so long . . . And then there was the subject of her marriage to Dimitri Stanislopoulos. Was she crazy? The man was old enough to be her *grandfather*. And he had a lousy reputation. The world knew he had been sleeping with Francesca Fern for years, and *she* was a barracuda.

Jeez! What Lucky needed was a little fatherly advice. Not that she'd appreciate it. She'd probably tell him where he could shove it.

But he was her father. He had to try, didn't he?

'How about some fresh grapefruit?' Susan asked cheerily.

He wanted to scream at her. Tell her to shut the fuck up.

But then he reasoned it wasn't her fault she had started to bore the shit out of him. *She* hadn't changed. *He* had. Not for Gino Santangelo the sedentary life of luxury Beverly Hills offered. Not for Gino Santangelo the openings and events, the small talk and the gossip. He was a street kid, used to a fast life. Right now he was seventy-four and feeling it.

Back in Vegas, where he belonged, he knew he'd regain his energy and drive.

*

Dimitri's New York apartment was old-fashioned, pristine, and filled with priceless antiques. Two servants and a butler lived in, and two more came in daily to attend to the more menial tasks.

Lucky arrived the day before Dimitri, and hated it. She had been to the apartment before, but living there was another thing.

Total redecoration had to take place, or she was returning to her house in the Hamptons, which she loved. It was so white and airy, and peaceful. The only thing she had changed about it was the swimming pool. The ground had been filled in, and a rose garden planted.

Sometimes, in recurring nightmares, she could still see the floating raft . . . her mother's body . . . spread-eagled . . . dead . . .

Dimitri phoned from Paris. 'How is Roberto?' were the first words he uttered.

'Fine. He wants a new room.'

'I beg your pardon?'

'Your apartment is *depressing*. Can I do something with it?'

'Do you object to my furnishings? The finest interior designer in New York worked with me on it.'

He hardly thought he should reveal that when he decorated the apartment five years before, Francesca Fern had been threatening to leave her husband. It was she who had worked with the designer with a view to moving in, but by the time it was completed she had changed her mind, and reconciled with Horace.

Dimitri had been furious. However, he loved the way she had decorated the apartment. He had no wish to change it.

'It's so old-fashioned and stuffy,' Lucky complained.

'We'll discuss it,' Dimitri replied.

'You've *got* to be kidding. No discussions. It's dull and I'm changing it.'

They talked a while longer, and when Dimitri replaced the receiver he was thoughtful. Lucky Santangelo was young, and strong-willed. Her language was sometimes startling, and she did what she wanted. He was used to a different kind of woman. Expensive jet-set beauties, with a knowledge of all the finer things in life. Lucky was a gypsy. Had he done the right thing marrying her?

Yes. She was the mother of his son and heir. And as such, she deserved his name.

In Paris, Francesca Fern had re-entered his life with a vengeance. Francesca with her red hair, wide crimson lips, and husky dramatic voice. She had been cool to him for two years, ever since their confrontation in Las Vegas at the gala honouring her. But Francesca had uncanny timing. She knew he was no longer available, so she wanted him again. She called him in Paris. 'I had a feeling you'd be here,' she murmured, her tone warmer than it had been for years. 'I'm alone. When shall we see each other? Tonight?'

Francesca was not a woman to turn down. She throbbed with sexual passion. She had been his mistress for many years, and Dimitri saw nothing wrong in continuing the affair. It certainly would not affect his relationship with Lucky. 'Tonight,' he promised.

'I've missed you,' she purred.

And so she was back in his life.

Chapter 56

Fred Lester, the publisher, called Carrie several times. He wanted to take her to lunch and discuss the book she was supposed to be thinking about. After the third call she decided that maybe it wasn't such a bad idea. Fate had brought her into the office of Fred Lester, why didn't she take advantage of it?

She agreed to lunch with him. They went to The Four Seasons and talked about her non-existent book.

'I've found the ideal ghost writer for you,' he said enthusiastically. 'Her name is Anna Robb. She works fast, and I think you'll approve of her style.'

He named two well-known television stars whose beauty and exercise books she had worked on.

'Didn't they write the books themselves?' Carrie asked naively.

Fred laughed and said briskly, 'They had neither the time nor the talent. Not that I'm casting any aspersions on *your* talent,' he added quickly. 'Maybe you don't want or need help. But believe me, if you've never done it before it's easier this way. No worries about grammar or punctuation or putting sentences together. Just a free thought flow, which Anna will capture on a tape recorder. How does that sound to you?'

Carrie had to admit it sounded pretty easy.

'Do you have an agent?' he asked.

'Do I need one?' she countered.

'If I was to lie, I'd say no. But an agent does look after your best interests. Although I'm prepared to offer you a very fair deal, and you can trust me. You do know that, don't you?'

She nodded. It was ridiculous really. She had been in his company only once before, but he seemed honest, and she liked him.

'I don't think I need an agent,' she decided.

'Let's barter,' he replied, a spark of amusement in his kindly brown eyes.

•

'You're doing *what*?' Steven snapped.

'Writing a book,' Carrie replied calmly.

He gave her a withering look. '*You're* writing a book.'

'Why shouldn't I? It's not as difficult as it seems. You sent me to the publisher in the first place. They're supplying me with a ghost writer, and paying me excellent money.' She paused, hoping his reaction would be a little more positive. It wasn't. 'I *do* know a lot about fashion and beauty and entertaining,' she continued. 'It will be a book on style.'

Steven snorted his disapproval and moved right along. 'I came to tell you we're flying to California next week,' he said flatly.

She was almost afraid to ask. 'Why?' she managed.

'Because I've hit a dead end on Freddy Lesters. Maybe that wasn't even his name.'

'It was.'

'He could have lied to you.'

She gestured hopelessly. How could she convince him it didn't matter? 'I just don't know any more.'

'I guess it doesn't affect you at all, does it?' he observed coldly. 'Why should it? You made a new life for yourself. You lived the charade pretty good.'

'I wanted to protect you,' she said in a low voice.

'Then why did you ever tell me the truth?' he blazed.

'You know why,' she whispered. 'You were working on the Bonnatti case . . . Enzio Bonnatti was once my boss . . . I sold drugs for him . . . supplied girls . . . ran his brothel . . .' She choked back sobs. 'Steven, I was warned by an old friend, *Enzio knew who you were.* He followed my life after I escaped and *he knew who you were*. Can you imagine what he would have done to you if you'd ever got him in court? He would have exposed both of us.'

'But I never brought him into court, did I?' Steven said harshly. 'Lucky Santangelo got to him first. I'd been on his case for over a year, and she just walked in and blew his balls off.'

Nervously Carrie reached for a cigarette. 'He deserved it,' she said in a shaky voice. 'Enzio Bonnatti was a monster.' She had never told Steven about that day in 1977. The real truth. Early in the morning she had rented a car, taken a gun from Elliott's collection, and driven to Bonnatti's Long Island mansion. Once there, she had sat outside his gates all day, waiting . . . trying to summon her courage. But then she had seen reason, driven back to the city, and rushed to

Steven's office. He was just leaving, and had no time to talk. She did not know he was on his way to arrest Bonnatti. She did not know that by the time he reached his house, Bonnatti would have been shot to death by Lucky Santangelo.

When Steven returned home in the evening, she revealed everything about her past and his low beginnings. If she had known Bonnatti was dead, she might not have done so. But it was too late to think that way . . . She had told Steven, and it seemed to have destroyed him.

Now, three years later, how could she give him back his pride?

'Why are we going back to California?' she asked quietly, although she knew only too well.

'We're going to pay a visit to Gino Santangelo,' Steven said evenly. 'We're going to find out if we have to continue the search for the real Freddy Lester.'

Chapter 57

They fell into bed together for all the wrong reasons, Olympia Stanislopoulos and Lennie Golden.

Ensconced in his penthouse suite they demolished two more bottles of champagne, smoked a little grass and threw off their clothes with stoned abandon. Then they got down to some serious fucking.

Olympia closed her eyes and thought of Flash.

Lennie closed his eyes and thought of Eden.

The result was a fantastic orgasm for both of them.

They took a shower together, did a large amount of coke Olympia just happened to have in her possession, and discussed what a great time they were having.

Lennie was not into drugs, but tonight he felt like it. The hell with everything.

What would Alice the Swizzle say if she could see him now? Here he was, Lennie Golden, back in his hometown. Only now he was King of the whole fucking heap.

He was a star.

He was in bed with one of the richest women in the world.

And he was loving every minute.

'We should do something wild,' Olympia decided. Her blue eyes shone brighter than diamonds. 'Something *really* wild.'

'I thought we just did!' he joked.

Olympia jumped from the bed. She looked very Rubenesque with her ripe curves and huge breasts. 'Let's get married,' she said. It came out easily, she was becoming used to saying it.

'Let's get *what*?' He was stoned, but not *that* stoned.

'That'd give 'em *all* something to think about,' she giggled. 'Can you imagine? We'd make every front page.'

'Hey . . . slow down. *I* am not even remotely interested in getting married.'

She was genuinely surprised. 'Why not?'

'Because . . . uh . . . well it's just not something I've ever thought about.'

'I've done it three times,' she observed solemnly. 'With three losers.' She moved back to the bed and sat beside him, stroking his chest. Her eyes were wide and serious and cobalt blue. 'What have you got to lose? It would be an adventure, and who knows, you might even like it.'

He began to laugh. It was such a crazy idea. 'C'mon . . .' he started to say.

She put her arms around his neck and nuzzled her luscious breasts against his naked chest. 'I'm not little Miss Nobody, Lennie. You know who I am. You know the kind of life we could have. And if it doesn't work out . . . no strings, no alimony, none of the usual crap. Who else could offer you a sweet deal like that?'

He thought about it.

Seriously.

Well, as seriously as he could after overdosing on champagne, grass and coke. Not to mention half a bottle of vodka earlier in the evening.

If Lennie Golden married Olympia Stanislopoulos, Eden would freak. The ultimate revenge! Christ! He could do it if he wanted to. She was right, what *did* he have to lose?

One night stands. A mother who never cared. Star-fuck groupies. An apartment in LA with a senile maid. Lonely nights thinking of Eden.

'Look,' he said, trying to get his thoughts straight. 'We don't know each other. We're a couple of strangers who just had a good time in bed.'

'That makes it particularly exciting doesn't it?' she sighed dreamily. 'A real magical mystery trip. What more could one ask?'

*

'I'm not going to do it, you bastard,' Eden hissed. 'You can't make me.'

Santino picked at his teeth with a fingernail, and regarded her stonily. They faced each other in the bedroom of their hotel room. Outside in the living room sat his two greasy Vegas friends.

'Y'would think I was askin' ya to run naked down the friggin' Strip,' complained Santino, his left eye twitching. A signal Eden knew meant trouble. 'All I wancha t'do is take off your clothes an' parade through the other room in ya high heels. Is that such a big friggin' deal?'

'You want me to put on a show for your lousy cheap friends,' she said tightly. 'And I *will not* do it.'

'Like hell ya won't,' snapped Santino. 'If ya wanna be in the friggin' movie, ya better.' In one swift movement his pudgy hand reached into the bodice of her new gown and tore downward. The silver material ripped.

'You bastard!' Her voice was low.

He slapped her lightly across the face. 'For openers,' he said calmly. 'You want more – then just keep up the dumb cunt act.' He walked to the door, and turned to stare at her. His eyes were the smallest meanest eyes she had ever seen. 'I wancha to parade through the other room, ass naked, like ya' don't know nothin's goin' on. Fix yerself a drink, an' walk back in here. Ya got it?'

'*Then* what do you want me to do. Sleep with them?' she blazed.

'Honey. You fuck anyone else an' I'll kill you.' He left the room.

She bit down on her lower lip trying to control a surge of anger. Who did he think he was?

She swept into the bathroom and stepped out of her ruined dress. The mirror showed her Santino's hand had left only a slight imprint on her pale skin. She added more powder, covering the redness. Then she applied blusher and lip gloss, and smoothed down her fine blonde hair.

Santino Bonnatti wanted a show.

She would *give* the bastard a show.

With great care she rouged the nipples of her small breasts so that they stood out bright red and erect. Then she removed her panty hose and fluffed out the golden triangle between her legs. Next she took an atomizer of baby oil and sprayed herself all over until her body gleamed. Several spritzes of 'Shalimar' completed the effect. All she had to add were stiletto silver sandals, and a thin silver chain around her waist.

When she considered herself ready she stood back and surveyed the result. *You're playing a role*, she told herself. *Go for it. Make it work. Don't let the sonofabitch get to you.* With haughty dignity she threw open the door to the living room and sauntered in.

Santino and his two cronies were talking. They all stopped and stared.

She ignored them and strolled to the bar.

Santino started speaking again, as if nothing was going on, but he had completely lost his companions' attention.

Coolly Eden fixed herself a glass of white wine with ice. Then just as coolly she walked back to the bedroom door, where she paused for a moment. 'Goodnight, guys,' she murmured huskily.

What an exit! In a funny way the whole thing was a turn

on. She had *enjoyed* giving them a free show . . . God, talk about drooling!

She wished she was with Lennie now. She was hot and ready and . . .

Santino flung open the door. He was in a hurry, dropping his pants as he came toward her. He didn't say a word as he forced her to her knees in front of him.

*

His manager informed Vitos that Olympia Stanislopoulos had retired to her suite. Vitos was hardly sorry, it had been a long day and he was not up to Olympia's aggressive demands in bed. He left the party smiling all the way. Several women tried to leave with him – one of the hazards of being an international sex symbol. But he managed to extract himself with charm and good grace and lousy English which seemed only to enhance his appeal.

Alone at last he let the smile drop. Thankfully. Without it he was a dour looking man in his thirties with melancholy eyes and a weak mouth. Alone at last he was able to unglue the small hair-piece which covered the tiny but alarming bald spot on the back of his scalp.

Alone at last he removed the bridge which held three of his gleaming white teeth in place.

Alone at last he undressed, and happily he did not have to hold his stomach in and shoulders erect.

Alone at last he was not obliged to create a hard-on and prove his manhood.

For once the sex symbol could relax. And he did.

And he did.

*

'Breakfast?' Matt suggested.

'Why not?' Jess shrugged. Vitos' guitar player had turned out to be a crazy gambler, and after trailing him around the tables for a while she had given up and returned to the party to find it breaking up. Matt caught her at the door. There was no sign of his girlfriend.

'Nice evening,' Jess said.

'Not bad,' Matt agreed.

They both wanted to say more, but the moment wasn't right.

*

'I do,' said Olympia. She was still stoned, but knew exactly what she was doing.

'I do,' said Lennie, slipping a cheap plastic ring on the third finger of her left hand. He had bought it at the door of THE WEE WEDDING CHAPEL OF LOVE AND HONOUR. WE WILL SERVE YOUR NEEDS 24 HOURS. He was still *very* stoned, and feeling no pain.

'I pronounce you man and wife,' said the female preacher – a vision in hair curlers and a thick velour robe. 'You may kiss the bride.'

Lennie grabbed Olympia, bent her backward in an exaggerated tango stance, and laid one on her.

Both collapsed in gales of laughter. The female preacher was unamused. It was five o'clock in the morning and she wanted to get back to bed.

Chapter 58

Dinner was being served in the Stanislopoulos' New York apartment. Three servants attended to Lucky and Dimitri's every need.

'I can't find Olympia,' Dimitri said with a grunt of disapproval. 'She's departed from New York with Brigette and left no word where she is.'

'Olympia's a big girl,' Lucky commented, picking at her salad. 'You don't want her to check in every time she makes a move, do you?'

'I expect to be able to reach her if I need to,' he grumbled indignantly.

'She'll be in touch. You said she always comes on your summer cruise, and that's only a couple of weeks off.'

'Yes.' Dimitri reached for a glass of red wine. He had arrived from Paris the day before, and had yet to inform Lucky that Francesca and Horace Fern would be joining them on the cruise. This was the perfect opportunity. He cleared his throat and presented her with a list of guests. These included Francesca and Horace, Olympia and Flash, with Brigette and her nanny. A Texas oil tycoon and his wife. And a billionaire Arab fixer with his well known socialite girlfriend.

Lucky grimaced. 'Sounds like a fun group,' she said, with more than a hit of sarcasm.

'My summer cruise is a social highlight,' Dimitri said pompously. 'An invitation is a coveted prize.'

Lucky burst out laughing. 'Sometimes you're so full of crap!'

'Why don't *you* invite some friends?' he asked, anxious to keep her happy.

'Do I have to come?' she inquired earnestly. 'Social highlights are not exactly my scene, and I have so much to do. I'm viewing sites in Atlantic City tomorrow, and if I see the right space I need to get right on it. You know, meet with builders, architects. Start things moving.'

'Naturally you must come. You are my wife now, and I want to introduce you to my friends. Even if you found the right site tomorrow, negotiations take time. My lawyers can handle everything.' He paused. 'Olympia will be on the cruise. We must tell her our news together.'

'I wonder how she's going to take it.' Lucky sighed reflectively, as two servants cleared the salad dishes and refilled the wine glasses.

'You were close once. You can be so again,' he stated. 'Perhaps you can be a positive influence on her. This ridiculous affair with Flash is headed for disaster. You can advise her.'

'Oh great. Old friend Lucky reappears and immediately tells her how to run her life. That'll go down big.'

'Olympia needs guidance.'

'Well she's not getting it from me.'

A uniformed maid appeared with a platter of thinly sliced roast beef, and Lucky helped herself. She would have to do something about these formal little dinners for two. A pizza in front of the TV was more her style.

'I have an idea,' Dimitri said. 'Why not invite your father and his charming wife on the cruise? I feel this should be a family affair.'

Lucky almost choked. Gino. On a boat. No way. Mind you, the charming wife would probably love it. Lucky could just imagine Susan frolicking with a clutch of fun-loving elderly billionaires. 'I don't think so,' she said.

'Why not?' Dimitri persevered. 'Shall I have my secretary telephone and issue an invitation?'

She shrugged. 'Okay,' she said, knowing full well Gino would never come.

*

'Yes,' gushed Susan. 'Tell Mr Stanislopoulos we would be delighted to join him on his yacht.'

She hung up the phone and immediately thought of clothes. What did she need? What should she take? A full shopping trip had to take place at once. How fortunate that Lucky Santangelo had done *one* intelligent thing in her life and married Dimitri Stanislopoulos. Although how she had landed *him* Susan would never know. What could a man like Dimitri possibly see in an uncouth girl like Lucky? She must have tricked him with the baby.

Susan remembered meeting Dimitri in Las Vegas. For one brief moment she had considered him as a prospective husband – at the time she was shopping. But it soon became obvious that all the stories about Francesca Fern were true – he talked of the woman all night. How had Lucky removed the formidable Francesca from his life? Maybe she would find out on the boat trip.

Why was she wasting time? Neiman-Marcus was waiting. Saks, Magnins, Bonwits . . . Hurriedly she left the house.

Chapter 59

'I can't believe you did this!' screamed Jess. 'Are you crazy? Insane? What?'

'A simple congratulations would be enough,' Lennie groaned.

'You –' Jess yelled, 'are positioned to be the next big star – and I mean we're talking fucking stupendous, man.'

He was lying on a couch in his suite – watching Jess bounce angrily up and down the thick carpeted length of his room. His head ached. His eyes ached. His body ached. Even his teeth were giving him trouble.

'And what do you do?' Jess yelled. '*What do you do?* You marry some nympho moneybags who'll use you to carry her *luggage*. You are certifiably *insane*.'

Lennie moved the cold washcloth from his forehead and requested – ever so politely – that she lower her voice.

Jess responded with a malevolent glare. 'Asshole!' she muttered.

'Rich asshole,' he responded wearily.

'*Dumb* rich asshole,' she shot back. 'Marrying Olympia Staniswhateverhername is just a bad joke. How many husbands has she had? How many famous boyfriends? Join the list, Lennie. You are now one of a *very* big crowd. She's the female Warren Beatty of the jet set *without* the talent. How does it feel to be one of many?'

'Jess,' he said quietly. 'Do me a favour and piss off.'

'I only wish I could.'

'Force yourself. There's an army of gorillas stamping through my head and I think we need to be alone together.'

'Oh, Lennie.' She sat down beside him and took his hand. 'I suppose you were stoned and in heat. Why didn't you just *fuck* her instead of *marrying* her?'

'I think we did that too.'

Jess shook her head despairingly. Lennie. Best friend.

Always capable of falling in the mire when it came to women.

She had arrived in his suite an hour earlier to find him sprawled on the couch, asleep, fully dressed, with the wash-cloth dripping on his forehead. It was eleven o'clock in the morning and she had attempted to move him into the bedroom. He had prised open his bloodshot eyes, and said, 'I think I've done something I'm not going to like.' Then he confessed, and there was the marriage certificate on the floor to prove it.

Now the screaming was over she tried to collect her thoughts and look at the situation logically. 'Where is Olympia?' she asked, sounding far calmer than she felt.

'I dunno,' he moaned, getting up and staggering into the bathroom. He peed, took one look at himself in the mirror, and lurched into the bedroom where he threw himself face down on the bed. No more drugs. Never again.

Jess followed him in. 'I've ordered breakfast,' she said. 'You'll feel better when you eat.'

'Don't *mention* food.'

'Get up. Take a shower. We've got to sort this mess out.'

'Piss off, Jess.'

'Don't keep on saying that. I'm here to help you.'

He scratched his head, sat up and reached for a cigarette. 'I think you've left it a little late.'

*

Olympia did not sleep. She had learned a useful secret from Flash. After an all night session of drinking and dope, the only way to face the new day was with a little help from a couple of large white pills. Quaaludes.

She took two on returning to the hotel, and by the time she had bathed and changed her clothes she was ready to set things in motion. First she called her lawyer in New York. Then the Magiriano's publicist. And – because she was not lacking in good manners – Vitos.

'Mr Felicidade is accepting no calls before twelve noon,' the operator twanged.

Tough. Mr Felicidade would just have to find out the hard way.

•

Eden awoke early and slid from bed like a conspirator. Santino slept on his back, snoring loudly.

Quietly she took some clothes from the closet, crept into the bathroom and closed the door.

Why hadn't she spoken to Lennie at the party?

Why hadn't *he* spoken to her?

She rinsed her face with cold water. The mark of Santino's slap was gone, she looked as beautiful as ever with her porcelain skin, topaz eyes and exotic cheekbones.

She applied a touch of brown shadow, blusher, and dash of lip gloss. Then she tied her fine blonde hair back in a ponytail. The young unsophisticated look. Lennie loved it.

She dressed in white cotton pants and a silky T-shirt.

Almost holding her breath she slid back into the bedroom. Santino still slept. On a table beside the bed lay a wad of bills, several items of gold jewellery, and a snub-nosed revolver. Carefully she ignored the gun and jewellery, and took several hundred dollar bills from the stack. Then, going over to the desk, she scribbled a short note. GONE SHOPPING. BACK SOON. He wouldn't like it, she knew that, but she needed to get out without being followed. And hopefully Zeko was not sleeping outside their door.

Santino was a dangerous man. Obsessive and unpredictable. She had put up with him for two years, and she was prepared to continue to do so until the movie was made. But obviously, after last night's performance, she needed insurance. And what better insurance than Lennie Golden. Especially now he was riding high.

•

'Who are *you*?' Olympia demanded imperiously as she swept past Jess into Lennie's suite.

The blonde heiress was dressed for business in a white lace dress with pink flowers festooned in her hair. She was trailed by several sales people carrying suits hidden beneath protective polythene, an array of shirts on hangers, and an assortment of boxes.

'I'm Lennie's manager,' Jess said. 'And what is –'

'Hmmm . . .' Olympia destroyed her with a sweeping look. 'I expect you've heard our news then.'

'Yes, and –'

Olympia ignored her and turned her attention to the minions with the clothes. 'Leave everything on the couch and go,' she commanded.

They did as they were bade.

When they had departed, Olympia once again directed her cool gaze at Jess. 'Now,' she said crisply, 'there are several arrangements I want you to double check. The reception is arranged for three this afternoon. The hotel is supposed to be taking care of the food and flowers – but make sure it's done properly. And *treble check* the press attendance. I want to be certain this is covered by the best. Several journalists are flying in from LA. I need a limo to meet their plane, and they must be taken care of while they're here.' She paused for breath. 'You don't *look* like a manager,' she added disparagingly. 'Anyhow, I suppose Lennie knows what he's doing. Where is he?'

Jess was almost speechless. Was *this* what Lennie had married? This shrill bossy kewpie doll, with fat legs and enormous boobs. Lennie, who had always had the cream. Class A ladies only.

She gestured helplessly toward the bedroom. 'In there,' she said. Let *him* deal with it. He was the one who had married it.

•

Vitos awoke to the sound of his own voice. It soothed him to re-enter the world listening to his soft caressing tones.

The tape/alarm clock did its duty at twelve noon precisely. He rolled over in bed and drifted in and out of sleep for a while, then he arose, exercised, showered, shaved, glued his hairpiece into place, put his bridgework in, and summoned room service and his manager. They arrived simultaneously.

While Vitos tackled fresh grapefruit, scrambled eggs, and lemon tea (he had to watch his diet at all times) his manager nervously paced the room. He had discovered Vitos when he had caught his Mexican maid drooling over the singer on a Spanish TV station.

'These wimmen in America, they lova me so much,' Vitos crooned, reflectively sipping his tea.

'Yes,' agreed his manager, wondering how to break the rumour that was buzzing all over the hotel.

'Sometimes is so difficull maka the universal language offa lova. I thinka everyones, they unnerstanda me so well.'

'Yes.'

'Ah . . .' Vitos sighed. 'Wimmen. They lova me.'

'Where is Olympia?' his manager asked quickly, seizing the opportunity.

'You hava my papers from Spain?' Vitos inquired, rising from the table and admiring himself in a nearby mirror. He practised his smile, liked what he saw, and proceeded to do a few facial exercises guaranteed to get rid of any lurking double chins. Not that he had any – but you could *never* be too careful.

'The papers haven't arrived yet.'

'Too bad.' Vitos thrust his chin forward and back. 'Maybe nota *too* bad. Thisa marriage, you really thinks I should do it? The wimmen be – how you say – broken in six.'

'Two.'

'What?'

'Forget it.'

•

'Good morning!' Olympia flung open the shower door. 'And how are *you* this morning?'

Lennie regarded his bride, who seemed to be feeling no pain. She looked fresh, bright and exceptionally pretty – if a little plump.

'I feel like camel dung,' he said dourly. 'Did we really do what I think we did?'

She selected a large towel and held it open for him to step into. 'We did.'

'Shit!'

'You're not sorry, are you?' She widened her blue eyes and managed to look hurt and vulnerable at the same time.

'Jesus! I don't know.' He knotted the towel around his waist and tried to review the situation. Here he was in the bathroom of a Las Vegas hotel with one of the richest women in the world whom he had known for less than twenty-four hours and they were married! Any moment he expected to wake up. This wasn't real life, as Jess had so eloquently pointed out – this was insane.

'We've got to talk,' he said, walking into the bedroom and searching for a cigarette. 'Uh . . . I don't know about you, but I was stoned last night. I mean *really* out of it. And . . . well . . . Jesus, in the cold light of day it's not so funny, is it?'

He fixed her with a hopeful look. He was hopeful she would agree with him, say, 'What a mistake! I came to tell you I've taken care of the whole thing – had the ceremony reversed. We are no longer legal.'

What she actually said was, 'I've planned the reception for three o'clock today. Not that we need another party, but we want to have photographs and a cake.' She laughed gaily. 'What kind of a wedding would it be without that? Oh, and my daughter, Brigette, will be *so* disappointed if we don't *do* anything. She's adorable, you'll love her. She's out with her nanny now, choosing a dress.'

'I didn't know you had a kid,' he said blankly.

'There are a lot of things we don't know about each other, aren't there?' She caressed him with an innocent smile. Olympia could play innocent – when it suited her – to the hilt. 'But that's going to be half the fun, isn't it? Finding out.' She hugged him warmly. 'I've bought you a selection of clothes. They're in the other room with your . . . er . . . manager girl. I thought you'd want a new outfit for our wedding party. Oh, Lennie, I'm so excited. In one night you've changed my life. I was really depressed. I can't begin to tell you how unhappy I was.' She lowered her lashes and her voice. 'Almost suicidal,' she whispered. 'But you've changed everything. It's as if we found each other just in time.'

He had things to say. He couldn't get them out. How could he tell her it was all a mistake? How could he back out now? *Thanks, Eden, look what you got me into this time.* He was married to a total stranger and there was nothing he could do about it.

Chapter 60

Happiness was getting back into action. And Atlantic City was exactly where Lucky wanted to be. She left Roberto in New York with CeeCee and departed for Atlantic City in high spirits.

She knew what she was looking for, and the real estate agents were eagerly awaiting her arrival. Unfortunately, the location she had been after with Gino was long gone. And prices had zoomed. Atlantic City was taking off in a way nobody had quite imagined. She had known it would be so. Damn Gino. They could have enjoyed the excitement of being in at the beginning. But the hell with it. She would build the finest hotel ever. She would create a legendary palace, a shimmering tower. And she would call it 'The Santangelo'.

•

For two days Susan and Gino argued back and forth. He refused to entertain the idea of going on the cruise unless Lucky called him personally. And Susan insisted it was an opportunity she absolutely could not miss.

Gino had yet to admit it to anyone except himself, but his marriage was over. Susan, the warm and wonderful woman he married had turned out to be an empty shell.

Wind her up and she dresses the part.

Press her button and she gives great dinner parties.

Shove her in the right direction and she spends money like it's going out of style.

Lucky had been right about her all along. Why hadn't he seen it? She'd taken him for a schmuck.

He thought about Lucky a lot. And he missed her. But there was no going back. She had married Dimitri, given birth to a baby. And not once had she consulted him.

He called Costa in Miami and complained.

'You get what you give in life,' Costa said philosophically. 'What have you ever given Lucky that makes her feel she should turn to *you* for advice?'

Gino hung up furious. Costa was getting senile.

'We'll *go* on the goddamn cruise,' he told Susan. 'I want to spend some time with my grandson, and this seems to be the only way I can do it.'

Susan smiled. 'Yes, dear,' she replied calmly. And rushed out to spend another few thousand dollars.

*

Dimitri had just put down the phone on Francesca when his secretary announced that Olympia was on the line.

'Where have you been?' he roared. 'I've been trying to reach you.'

'I'm in –'

'It's not good enough, Olympia. You *must not* vanish for days on end. For all I know you and Brigette could be in the hands of kidnappers. You are a Stanislopoulos, and you must always –'

'I got married again.'

'Christ, girl!' he thundered. 'Live with that degenerate rock person if you must. But marriage is *out of the question*.'

'I didn't marry *him*.'

She had always been impossible. Spoilt and thoughtless. 'Who then?' he demanded furiously.

'Look on the cover of *People* magazine. Lennie Golden. He's a comedian.'

'A *comedian*!'

'Stop screaming. He's better than the other three. I've got to go now, we're having a reception. Can you do me a favour and tell mommy for me?'

'Your mother doesn't know?'

'She will when you tell her.'

'Olympia –'

'Bye, poppa, we'll see you on the cruise.'

Dimitri paced his office. Olympia was the stupidest girl in the world.

He communicated with his ex-wife who did not seem unduly perturbed.

He sent his secretary out for a copy of *People* and studied the latest fortune hunter leering at him from the front page.

He phoned Francesca in Munich and she laughed.

Olympia, Olympia. He had not been blessed with a smart daughter.

*

Lucky returned full of excitement later that evening. Dimitri had just finished a solitary dinner and he was not in a happy frame of mind.

'I've found *exactly* the right site,' she enthused. 'Multi-fantastic, and no way can we lose it. You've got to put your lawyers on it *at once*.' She clasped her arms around his neck. 'I feel so great. Let's go in the bedroom and celebrate. Making deals *really* turns me on.'

'Don't talk like a cheap whore,' he said abruptly, disengaging from her grasp.

'What?' She stared at him in amazement.

'You are my *wife* now. Kindly try to remember that.'

She backed away. 'I don't think I'm hearing you right.'

'I've had an extremely tiresome day,' he said. 'And I have no need of further aggravation.'

He missed the danger in her opal eyes. The sudden storm.

'Olympia got married again,' he said shortly. 'She's irresponsible. She deserves to lose every penny of her inheritance.'

'Hey, man,' Lucky said rudely, affecting a tough New

York street accent. 'Dintja hear me? I feel hooorny. Wanna get it on?'

His face was carved in granite. 'I beg your pardon?'

'Yeh, man. An' y'can kiss my ass too.'

She slammed into the bedroom without a backward glance. No way could he talk to her like that and get away with it.

He followed her, unused to being answered back.

'Stay out of my way,' she burned.

'What's the matter with you?' he demanded.

'Think about it.'

'There is nothing to think about. I corrected you on your behaviour.'

'Corrected me? Corrected me? Who *the fuck* do you think you're talking to?'

'My wife, the mother of my child,' he hissed. 'And you *will not* use language like an alley cat.'

'Jesus H. Christ! What the fuck is going *on* here?'

He slapped her face. She sprang at him, clawing with her nails. They raked his skin, drawing blood.

He was a big man, powerful. He pinned her arms and they fell together heavily on the bed.

Lucky could not believe what was happening. She had known Dimitri for two years and he had never revealed this side of his character before. She had married an equal, not a fucking father figure who told her how to speak and behave.

He gripped her wrists and forced them backward.

She tried to bring her knee up to his balls, but he was too strong for her. She was athletic, certainly no weakling, but the strength faded from her as he concentrated on holding her down.

And then it happened. She felt his excitement and she didn't want it. Not this way. Not as the result of their violent scene.

He attempted to keep her captive while he fumbled with the zipper on his pants.

She managed to bring her arm up sharply and smash him under the chin.

He yelled in pain.

The brief moment was enough for her to roll out from under and lock herself in the bathroom. She was shaking with anger.

He did not pursue her further.

Chapter 61

There were good days and there were bad. Now that California was a definite yes, Steven felt slightly better. He was living in a one room apartment on Third Avenue, having rented out his very nice brownstone when he went to Europe.

His life was a mess and he knew it. Once he had been so full of ambition, but Carrie had ruined everything with her sordid revelations. Since returning to America he had done nothing except think about himself and his problems. He slept late, didn't eat properly, and hung around his one room dump watching television. The one friend he had contacted was Jerry Myerson. And only because he needed to borrow money.

Women, he picked up at random. Once so particular about his female companions, he now favoured any girl he didn't have to make conversation with.

What a difference to his past life. Fine upstanding Steven Berkeley. Hard working, an assistant DA with nowhere to go but up. Life was strange. He remembered with bitterness arriving at Enzio Bonnatti's Long Island mansion that fateful afternoon in 1977, set for action.

Only Lucky Santangelo got there first.

The same Lucky Santangelo he had been trapped in an elevator with only days before during the great power black out.

The same Lucky Santangelo who might – just might – be his half-sister.

Lucky.

She was difficult to forget with her smart mouth and dark gypsy looks.

Lucky.

Thank God they hadn't –

He didn't even want to think about what had nearly happened between them.

He wondered how she would feel if it turned out they *were* brother and sister. Would she even remember him?

Oh yes, she'd remember him, his pride told him that.

What pride?

He looked terrible. He had to get himself together, back to work, and put the past behind him.

Soon.

Chapter 62

All things considered, Vitos Felicidade took the news well enough. Really, there was nothing he could do but smile for the cameras (of which there were many) and pretend it was he who had encouraged the 'instant love' match.

In private, he brooded. What was wrong with him? Why had Olympia spurned him. Twice. Did she perhaps see behind the facade? Did she alone know that beneath the throbbing sex symbol hovered an insecure, plain, and ordinary man?

He did not wish to think about it. He attended the wedding reception for an hour, and then retired to his suite where he sat and sulked.

Jess did not take it so well. She sought Matt out and complained hotly. He agreed with her, and pointed out that nothing could be done.

Back at the Sands Hotel, Eden stared numbly out of the window, while Zeko played solitaire nearby. She had crept out in the morning fully intending to see Lennie, but just as she was about to enter a cab, Zeko had appeared from nowhere, and announced that the boss had said he was to accompany her everywhere she went. She had almost screamed with frustration. Instead she had smiled glassily and allowed the dumb ox to trail her around a parade of tawdry shops. Las Vegas was the pits. She couldn't wait to leave.

Paige had invited her to lunch, and she was allowed to go. But while digesting a tuna salad the news had spread about Olympia Stanislopoulos and Lennie Golden.

Hot gossip.

She had wanted to throw up. Now she was gazing out at neon and desert, wondering if she had made the right choice.

Santino Bonnatti.

Lennie Golden.

She hoped she had backed the winner.

She had a horrible suspicion she might not have.

*

'You stink,' sneered Brigette.

'You're kidding. I took a shower 'specially,' replied Lennie, deadpan.

'I said you stink,' Brigette repeated.

'You sound like a broken record.'

She gazed up at him. Huge blue (her mother's) eyes in a heart-shaped face. 'I hate you,' she uttered spitefully.

He grimaced. 'Can't win 'em all,' he said with an engaging smile.

Nanny Mabel, embarrassed, said, 'I'm so sorry, Mr Golden. She's tired, it's late, and –'

'C'*mon*,' Lennie interrupted mildly. 'It's four-thirty in the afternoon. If the kid wants to hate me – no excuses, let her do her thing.' He bent to speak to the child. 'Y'know something, Brigette is a *very* pretty name, and you are a *very* pretty young lady.'

Brigette blinked several times. Why was this one talking to her? Usually she told them they stunk, they glared at her, ignored her, and she never had to talk to them again – which was the way she liked it. Mama's boyfriends were pigs. She hated them all.

Lennie didn't wait around for a response. He was off and running. Olympia had assembled enough press to launch a hit movie, and she was loving every minute, posing for pictures like a professional. But then, in a way, she was. She had grown up with photographers on her doorstep. Olympia Stanislopoulos. Heiress. Fair game for the paparazzi and gossip columnists of the world.

Somehow she had managed to make their wedding into a special event. The cake was a fantasy, with a miniature dancing couple on top. The Magiriano ballroom was transformed into a fairyland of flowers. And the Louis Roederer Cristal champagne flowed.

He shuddered to think how much it was all going to cost. Was *he* supposed to pay? Or was this a gift from the Magiriano?

A grim-faced Jess shrugged when he asked her. 'I don't know,' she said tardily.

She wasn't happy about the whole scene. He wasn't exactly ecstatic, but what was done was done – and who knew? Maybe it would work out. Stranger things had happened.

Sure.

Chapter 63

Compromise was not Lucky's style. She had no intention of sitting around waiting for Dimitri to apologize. He had to learn, and fast, that she was nobody's doormat.

The morning after their fight she took off for the East Hampton house with Roberto and CeeCee. The truth of the matter was she was more than a little disturbed by his behaviour. She wanted an equal partnership. Not an uneven relationship with a man who felt he could call every shot. Chillingly she knew that marrying Dimitri had been a mistake. There was an age gap that could never be bridged, and no way was she ready to play the role he had in mind for her.

It did not bother her at all that he made no attempt to contact her for three days. Coolly she called his lawyers and gave them instructions to negotiate on the piece of land she wished to purchase in Atlantic City. Then she double-checked with her own lawyers to make sure everything went ahead. Dimitri had signed a legal document. The hotel would proceed whatever happened.

He arrived at the house three days later. 'Forgive me,' he said, standing on her doorstep with her favourite sterling silver roses, and a Tiffany box.

She knew apologies were difficult for him. She could have made him sweat, but she let him in, and they walked in the garden and talked it out. As much as one could talk it out with a man like Dimitri. He was of his generation and did not believe in long analytical discussions.

She opened the Tiffany box. It contained an opulent diamond choker, at its centre a huge heart. Dimitri fastened the clasp around her neck and considered everything to be alright. He kissed her chastely and informed her that Susan and Gino had accepted his invitation to join them on his yacht.

Oh, God! She had never in a million years expected Gino to say yes. She didn't know why she was so upset. Her feelings about her father were confused. Sometimes she loved him more than anyone in the world, and other times she couldn't care less if she never saw him again. It had always been that way.

'You're pleased, aren't you?' Dimitri inquired.

She swallowed her real feelings. 'Sure,' she replied casually.

She wasn't looking forward to the cruise at all. Dimitri's friends. Francesca Fern and her bumbling husband. Now Susan and Gino. And they would all be trapped on a boat together. However large and luxurious Dimitri's yacht was – it was still close quarters. An inescapable round of lunches and dinners.

Maybe Olympia and her new husband – whoever he might be, would save the day. Lucky had forgotten to ask who he was, and now Dimitri had returned to New York leaving her to prepare for the two week cruise. She did so reluctantly.

•

It seemed to Gino that the only days he got out of bed in the morning with enthusiasm were the days he was seeing Paige. She put a little zing in his life. She was bawdy and uninhibited, but most of all, she was fun.

He looked forward to her return from Las Vegas, and arrived at the Beverly Wilshire an hour early for their Friday assignation. Paige turned up half an hour late. She smelt of her usual musky scent and wore a white skirt split almost to the crotch.

'Did anyone ever tell you that you dress like a hooker?' he asked with an amused grin, sitting on the end of the bed.

'Yes.' She fluffed her frizzy hair. 'And don't you just love it.'

With one quick movement she unhooked her skirt at the waist and it fell to the floor. She wore no panties.

'Hey –' he began to laugh.

'Quick service. With a smile,' said Paige, walking toward him. 'And please leave fifty dollars on the table.'

'Cheap at the price,' Gino joked, enjoying the game.

'That's because you're a favoured client,' expressed Paige, pressing her wiry bush of pubic hair against his face.

He responded accordingly. Sex kept him young – he was sure of that. Not for Gino Santangelo the aches and pains of old age. Sex kept the vital juices flowing. As long as he could get it up he felt invincible, and Paige Wheeler gave him the best hard-on he had had in years.

What would life be like if he were married to a woman like Paige? A great deal more exciting than being with Susan day in and day out, that was for sure.

Their lovemaking took time. Paige required more than one orgasm – unlike Susan, who considered the moment she climaxed it was all over and shoved him off.

Paige enjoyed experimenting. Sometimes he wished he were younger, more athletic. But she didn't seem to mind. Anyway, he knew he pleased her.

'How was Vegas?' he asked, when Paige was finally satisfied.

She lay spread-eagled on the bed, totally nude. 'Interesting,' she replied.

'How interesting?'

'Well . . . I went to Vitos Felicidade's and Lennie Golden's opening night at your hotel.'

'How was it?'

'The service or the show?'

'Both.'

'Excellent. Lennie Golden is something special. And Vitos has a certain European charm. Naturally, everyone was talking about Olympia Stanislopoulos and Lennie Golden getting married the next day. She came there with Vitos, you know.'

'Yeh?'

'Don't you read the gossip columns?'

'Only when I'm in 'em.'

'There were parties every night. And I played a little blackjack.'

'Did you win?'

'Lost.'

'You shoulda bin with me. I'd never let you lose.'

He touched the hair on her crotch. It was damp. She stretched languorously.

'I'm gonna be away for a coupla weeks,' he said. 'Think y'can manage without me?'

'I'll try,' she said teasingly. 'Where are you going?'

'I don't know if I told you – but my daughter, Lucky – she's kinda crazy like me – married the other Stanislopoulos – the father, Dimitri. Can you believe it? He's nearly as old as me. Lucky used to go to school with Olympia.' He sighed. 'She's nuts.'

'What's nuts about marrying one of the richest men in the world?'

'Lucky doesn't need his money,' Gino said shortly, removing his hand.

'Put that back!' scolded Paige.

Gino did as she requested.

'Hmmmm . . .' Paige surrendered herself to sensual feelings.

Gino sensed her further need and bent his head to her.

Within seconds she was moaning loudly, and climaxing yet again.

In all his experience with women, Gino could not remember a woman as insatiable as Paige.

She sat up, kissed him, and said, 'Thank you. Now, tell me about your daughter.'

He shrugged. 'Nothin' to tell. She married the guy an' they've invited us on this cruise they're havin'. Susan wants to go.'

'I can imagine.'

'An' I'm goin' because it'll give me a chance to see the kid.'

'What kid?'

'I'm a grandfather.'

'Oh no!' Paige jumped from the bed, her face a mask of mock horror. 'I'm sleeping with a *grandfather*!'

'Hey –' he grinned. 'You ain't no spring chicken.'

'I'm in my forties. I am not yet ready to be bedding grandfathers.'

'Fuck you.'

'Anytime, pops.'

They both started to laugh. He got up, put his arms around her, and they rocked with mirth.

'You know somethin'?' he said. 'You're my kind of broad.'

'We're a few decades apart,' she mused, 'but we both grew up on the streets of New York.'

'You never told me that.'

'You never asked. Besides, it's not something I care to broadcast.'

He reached for a robe. 'So – tell me your life history.'

'One of these days. Right now I'm late for an appointment.'

'Jeez! I thought we'd be able to sit around an' bullshit. Don't make other appointments when you're seein' me.'

She hurried into the bathroom. 'When do you leave?' she called out.

'In a few days.'

'I'll miss you.'

'Not as much as I'm gonna miss you.'

•

Susan looked impatiently at her gold Patek Philippe watch as she sat on the outdoor terrace of the Bel Air Hotel. Paige was late. Again. She was always late, that is when she had time to see her at all. For the past few months their meetings had been impossibly brief and Susan was beginning to suspect Paige had someone else.

She frowned, and realized she wouldn't be able to stand it if Paige told her it was over between them. It wasn't fair. She couldn't take it. Paige meant everything to her.

The waiter at her elbow asked her if she would care for another drink. She ordered her third Martini, and sat back to wait.

Within minutes Paige arrived looking flustered, her hair a mess, and her outfit ridiculous.

The two women kissed.

'I am *so* busy!' Paige exclaimed. 'It seems *everyone* is into new decor. Ever since they featured the house I did for Ramo Kaliffe in *Architectural Digest* my life is not my own.'

Susan smiled politely. Paige smelt of musk and sex, she always did. Two men across the terrace were staring. Paige attracted attention wherever she went. She was not beautiful, not even pretty, but her allure spoke volumes.

'I thought you weren't coming,' Susan said reproachfully.

'You know I'm always late.'

'We're going on a cruise through the Greek Islands with Dimitri Stanislopoulos. I had to see you before we left.' Susan lowered her voice to a whisper. 'It's been two months since we've . . . been together. I can't stand it any longer.'

Paige gazed restlessly across the terrace. Her eyes met one of the men who had been staring. He raised his glass to her. She wondered if she knew him, decided it was probably a friend of Ryder's, and acknowledged him with a wave.

'Well?' Susan questioned insistently. 'Don't *you* think two months is a long time? Don't *you* miss *me* as much as I miss you?'

Paige took a deep breath. How did one tell a woman it was over? If Susan had been a man it would have been a cinch.

She picked some nuts from a dish on the table. 'Ryder has never been an easy man to live with,' she began.

'I know *that*,' Susan interrupted. 'Do you think Gino is easy? He's old and difficult and sex-crazed. I just don't know how I stand him. If it wasn't for you I –'

'Listen to me,' said Paige forcefully. She didn't want to hear about how terrible Gino was. She happened to think Gino was pretty special, and for just that reason she planned to give up all her other lovers – including Susan. 'Ryder has changed. I don't know what's come over him – but he has certainly changed, and it's for the better.'

Susan stared at her blankly. 'What?'

'I want to give our marriage a fair chance,' Paige said with false conviction.

'What?' Susan repeated numbly.

'Excuse me, ladies.' The man whose eye Paige had caught earlier was at their table. He was middle-aged and LA casual. 'I have taken the liberty of ordering champagne.'

The waiter deposited an ice bucket with a bottle of Dom Perignon next to the table.

'My friend and I decided that two beautiful women such as yourselves deserve only the best,' said the man. At which point his friend, short with a beard, joined him, and they stood there expectantly, waiting to be asked to join the party.

'Thank you,' Paige said graciously, crossing her legs.

They caught her scent and stood ramrod straight. Two hounds ready for the chase.

'I *would* ask you to join us,' she continued, 'but Mrs Santangelo has just suffered a death in the family – so I am sure you can understand this is not the right time for us to become . . . social.'

'*Sure*,' the first man said emphatically. 'Wouldn't dream of troubling you and Mrs Santer – um, maybe *you* might be free for dinner later?'

'What a tempting offer,' Paige sighed. 'But quite impossible. So nice meeting you.' She re-crossed her legs, giving them another whiff of paradise, and dismissed them by turning her back.

They got the message and walked reluctantly off.

'What do you mean – you're giving your marriage a fair chance?' Susan asked in a furious whisper.

'Exactly what it sounds like,' Paige replied calmly. 'I'm going to be faithful.'

'You!' exclaimed Susan scornfully. '*Never!*'

The waiter poured champagne.

'Please don't underestimate me,' Paige murmured. 'If I want to do something *I do it*.'

Susan's eyes filled with tears. 'What about us?' she asked mournfully.

'We'll put what we had on hold, and see what happens.'

Chapter 64

Alice Golden arrived in Las Vegas two days after her son's wedding made worldwide headlines. She was not exactly what he needed in his life at that particular moment. He had a wife, and stepdaughter and he was busy trying to get used to *them*. An instant mother was unnecessary luggage. However – to hear Alice tell it – mother and son had been inseparable. She had taught him everything he knew. And while Olympia entering their tightly knit relationship was a shock – Alice was prepared to accept her with open arms. She had given three 'exclusive' interviews to that effect before she even saw Lennie.

He greeted her warily as she was ushered into his suite by a bemused Jess.

'I found her kicking up a fuss in the lobby,' Jess whispered, 'demanding God knows what, so I thought I'd better bring her up. I don't think she remembers me.'

'My darling!' Alice exclaimed, throwing open her spidery arms. Dieting had caused her flesh to become scrawny, and her hair was bleached a 'too white' blonde. She hugged Lennie tightly.

'Alice,' he said, 'what are *you* doing here?'

'What am *I* doing here?' She gazed around the suite as if there was an attentive audience, when in fact there was only Jess and Lennie. 'What am *I* doing here? Your mother. Your flesh and blood. What am *I* doing here. Hah! A funny kind of question from a boy who just got married without a word to his caring, worrying, *lonely* mother.'

Finally she was doing Jewish mother schtick. Lennie didn't know whether to laugh or cry.

'Cut it out, Alice,' he said.

Jess hovered. She couldn't make up her mind if she should stay or go. Lennie made it up for her. 'Order tea,' he said brusquely, 'for the three of us.'

Alice was clutching a battered carpet-bag which had obviously seen better days. She placed it on the floor and looked around. 'Where's the hairness?' she asked.

'The what?' questioned Lennie.

'I think she means heiress,' said Jess, trying to stifle a giggle. 'Isn't that what you mean, Mrs Golden? Heiress?'

Alice peered at her through three sets of stiff false eyelashes. 'Who are you?' she asked crossly. 'You look familiar.'

'Lennie's old school friend, Jess Skolsky.'

Alice stared. 'The shrimp,' she said at last, bringing back every painful memory Jess had of growing up.

Alice sat down on the couch. She was wearing a cheap polyester dress, cut low to exhibit tired breasts, and short to exhibit still spectacular legs. 'I flew here,' she announced. 'The men on the plane wouldn't leave me alone. When I told everyone I was your mother, Lennie, the women wouldn't leave me alone. I have four numbers for you, but I don't expect you'll want them now you're married.'

'My wife wouldn't be thrilled,' he commented dryly.

'Where is she? I came to see for myself this . . .' she paused, determined to get the word right, 'hairess.'

'Her name's Olympia.'

'Fancy name.' She favoured him with an accusing look. 'You could have phoned me. You could have *invited* me to the wedding. You could have told me you were headlining in Vegas – my home – my town. I was a star here too, once, you know. Not *that* long ago. Alice the Swizzle. I'm *still* famous in this town. You should only know how famous. *You* should be as famous as I once was – maybe still am. Who knows if they remember . . .' she trailed off.

'Where are you staying, Mrs Golden?' Jess asked politely, thinking the time had come to ease her out. Lennie liked to be alone before the evening show.

'Here, of course,' Alice snapped waspishly. 'Arrange it for me. I *am* the star's mother you know. I deserve recognition. Without me he wouldn't be here, would he?'

'And how long will you be staying?'

'As long as my boy wants me to.'

Lennie shrugged helplessly. 'I just got married y'know.'

'That's why I'm here.'

He didn't have the heart to tell her to get lost. Who needed a mother after thirty-two years?

Whether he needed her or not she was very much present. Olympia and Alice together should be a riot. He couldn't wait.

•

The day after the reception – as soon as she was sure her wedding pictures covered the world press – Olympia phoned Flash in the south of France. A girlish voice answered.

'Get me Flash,' Olympia demanded imperiously. 'And hurry up, I'm calling from America.'

She then had an eleven minute wait before his rich Cockney tones crackled down the line. 'I s'pose it's you,' he remarked rudely. 'Fuckin' marvellous! I waited at the airport two bleedin' hours last week, an' I don't usually give airport.'

'Did you honestly expect me to come?'

'Why not? You said you was comin'.'

'I didn't come,' she said icily, 'because I don't think *your wife* would have liked it.'

'Aw shit? Is *that* what you're on about?'

'*Your wife*, Flash. *Your wife* whom you somehow neglected to mention to me. Your *pregnant teenage* wife. God, you're a prick!'

He gave a whisky-soaked laugh. 'You bin readin' those supermarket rags? Didn't think rich bints like you ever went near a bleedin' supermarket.'

'Real life does have a habit of catching up with one – rich or not. I've had all your things from the New York apartment packed up and sent to the Goodwill.'

Outrage. 'Yer *what*?'

'You heard.'

'Jesus Christ!'

'And talking of newspapers, have you read yours today?'

'You're a really stupid cow.'

'To put up with you, I must have been.'

'Get your fat arse over here an' I'll explain everything.'

'Shall I bring my husband?'

'Yer what?'

'Read the papers.'

'Aw, c'mon – yer silly bitch. You didn't go an' do it?'

'It seemed to be all the fashion.'

'Who'd you do it *with*? Not that Spanish asshole with the wig.'

'I resisted the temptation.'

'Thank Christ for that.'

'I married Lennie Golden.'

'Who's he?'

This conversation was not proceeding as Olympia had hoped. First of all she had confidently expected Flash to know all about her wedding. And she had certainly expected him to know who Lennie was.

'I really hate you,' she snapped irrationally.

'Are you comin' or not?'

'Haven't you been listening to me? I'm *married* – just like you. It's over.'

He was clearly bored. 'Suit yerself, Tubs.'

She could almost see him twitch his skinny shoulders, the way he did when he was aggravated or fed up. He didn't give a damn! Furiously she slammed the phone down. Her father had been right all along. Flash was a selfish, depraved user and she was well rid of him.

So why did she feel so blue? She was a bride again. She should be singing and laughing. At least have a smile on her face.

She visited her stash and snorted some coke. Who was Lennie Golden anyway? And *why* had she married him? To spite Flash? Kind of a dumb reason to tie oneself up.

God! What had she done? Lennie seemed nice enough, and he was attractive and great in bed – but nice guys had never been her scene. She had made another mistake. In a few weeks, after the cruise, she would instruct her lawyer to get her out of it. No big deal. Another pay off. She could afford it. There had to be *some* compensations for being rich.

Chapter 65

Lucky planned to take only sports clothes on the cruise, but Dimitri informed her – rather late in the day, that dinner each evening was a formal affair.

'You dress for dinner?' she asked, amazed.

'Tradition,' he replied.

'Whose tradition?'

'Mine.'

She searched his granite face for any sign of humour. There was none. Now that she was his wife she realized she didn't know him very well at all. In the eighteen months they had been together it had been an intermittent affair – with short blocks of time spent on his island – where they had been alone and wonderfully relaxed. Now a new Dimitri seemed to be emerging. A stuffy man with rigid tastes and a strict code of behaviour. She wasn't sure she liked the new Dimitri at all. She *was* sure she should have kept the relationship the way it was before. Why had she given in to his pressure?

The property deal in Atlantic City was almost set, and she was elated about that. But she dreaded the cruise. Hopefully she would be able to find a quiet corner and flake out.

Dimitri had decided that this year it would take place in the south of France. He didn't mention to anyone – especially Lucky – that this was to accommodate Francesca who had a gala dinner being given for her in Monte Carlo she did not wish to miss.

They flew by Concorde from New York to Paris, and from there a private Learjet transported them to Nice airport, where a chauffered Rolls waited to take them to *The Greek*, as Dimitri had modestly named his yacht.

Roberto took the journey well. He was an extremely active, happy child, nothing seemed to upset him, and Lucky felt fortunate to have found someone like CeeCee to look after him. She was a pretty black girl of twenty, with a double helping of large white teeth, a ready grin, and tightly corn-rowed hair. Lucky had discovered her working as a waitress in a hamburger joint six weeks before she gave birth.

'I'm *sooo* envious!' the smiling girl had remarked, gazing at Lucky's huge stomach while she served her forbidden french fries, a milk shake, and a large juicy burger. 'I just love babies. I've got six younger brothers and sisters back in Jamaica, and I miss the little ones so.'

They got to talking, and before she knew it, Lucky had offered her the job and CeeCee accepted immediately.

Dimitri had been disapproving. He wanted a trained English nanny for his son, not some inexperienced Jamaican waitress. But Lucky always went with her gut instinct, and CeeCee had turned out to be a gem. She loved Roberto almost as much as they did.

It was Lucky's first visit to *The Greek*, and it was huge. She had expected luxury, but the sheer opulence of it surpassed her expectations. A three hundred foot white palace with a full crew, eight magnificent staterooms each decorated by a different famous designer, an Art Deco cinema with black silk walls and state of the art equipment to show either videos or the latest movies, a gold and white mosaic swimming pool, numerous entertaining decks and areas.

The captain greeted them. An Englishman with a ruddy complexion, handle-bar moustache, and a jovial attitude. His wife stood by his side. She was in charge of the kitchen. A horse-faced woman with skin like leather. They had worked for Dimitri for fifteen years, and regarded Lucky with ill concealed suspicion. Captain and Mrs Pratt ran riot with creative financing – they did not wish the interfering presence of a wife.

'Have any of my guests arrived?' Dimitri boomed.

'Not yet, Mr Stanislopoulos,' replied Captain Pratt, welcoming them aboard. 'But we're all ready and prepared.' His flat eyes stripped the clothes from Lucky as he pumped her by the hand and said how delighted and happy they all were that the boss had found himself a wife.

I'll bet, she thought. She knew automatically they were on the take. Years running a hotel in Las Vegas had taught her many things about human nature. She had a nose for the swindlers and cheaters of the world. Automatically she smiled. How good she was getting at displaying social graces. She hoped she could keep it up throughout the cruise. And then she would be off. Atlantic City beckoned.

Dimitri took her arm and escorted her to their living quarters. A very masculine stateroom awaited her – all dark browns and earth tones. The king size bed featured a leather headboard and polished leather and brass bedside tables. The walls were padded with leather. On one wall hung a large portrait of a nude woman.

'Piccasso,' Dimitri pointed out, noticing her staring at it.

She moved through to the bathroom. Caviar marble. Cold and impersonal.

'Well?' he asked. 'Do you like it?'

'It's . . . severe,' she replied.

'I think you mean clean cut. I commissioned it three years ago from one of the finest designers in Italy.'

'It's still severe. I would have preferred something more relaxing.' She looked around again. 'Where are the books? The magazines? Even more important – where is the music?'

'What music?' he asked, frowning slightly.

He had yet to discover her passion for soul music. She felt lost without an available stereo. How could anyone design a bedroom without incorporating a great sound system?

Robert and CeeCee's quarters were certainly more cheerful. Planned originally for Brigette and her nanny, there were nursery animals climbing the walls, a mural on the ceiling depicting sky and sun, and a sunny yellow bathroom. Lucky knew she would be spending more time there than in Dimitri's austere sanctuary.

*

'God!' screamed Francesca Fern. 'Be careful with my luggage – you dolts.'

The French porters exchanged looks. They didn't understand what she said, but she was English or American – no difference – and all English speaking tourists were to be looked down upon and treated with as much insolence as they could muster on this hot and windy day. By accident on purpose one of her Vuitton suitcases (there were twelve in varying sizes) fell from the top of the cart on which they were being wheeled to a waiting car.

'Horace!' Francesca yelled. 'How dare you allow this to happen!'

Horace, who was certainly not to blame for the fall, said, 'I'm sorry, dear. It won't happen again.'

'I should think not,' snorted Francesca, as she marched regally toward the car, ignoring the gawking tourists who all recognized her, and the waiting chauffeur who knew who she was and bowed respectfully.

Horace thrust some money at the two disdainful porters. 'Please,' he begged. 'More careful. Yes?'

The men pocketed the money and ignored his plea, allowing the suitcases to slide from the cart onto the dusty sidewalk as soon as they reached the car. They had already been tipped, so they did not bother to help the elderly chauffeur load them into the trunk, but merely slouched away searching for their next victim.

Fortunately Francesca was in the limousine by that time, fanning herself and complaining about the heat. She always had something to complain about, and Horace was always around to take the blast. He loved his large volatile wife desperately, and knew – that as a great talent – she had to have *someone* to vent her frustrations on. Through eighteen years of marriage he had been the perfect target for her whiplash tongue. Mopping his brow he got into the back seat beside her.

'Hmmm,' sighed Francesca, in her famous deep mahogany voice. 'I am utterly exhausted. I could sleep for a week.'

Horace agreed with her. He always agreed with her. He thought she was the most striking woman he had ever set eyes on, and it never failed to astound him that she had chosen *him* to be her husband.

'Perhaps that's what you'll do, dearest,' he said, knowing full well it wasn't what she would do at all. When she and Dimitri Stanislopoulos were in each other's company, they were up all night, drinking, laughing, dancing. Horace did not allow his mind to wonder what else they might be doing, and he didn't venture to ask. Once he had attempted an inquiry. 'How *dare you* spy on me?' Francesca had raged. 'Dimitri is my best friend in the world, and I *will not* be questioned by you.'

After that, Horace shut up. The cruise was a yearly event, and even if Francesca did sometimes slip into bed at six in the morning, he knew it was only a temporary aberration, and soon she would be all his again.

This year, anyway, things might be different. Dimitri had taken another wife. 'A Las Vegas slut,' Francesca had exclaimed in disgust when she heard. Horace had visions of a busty blonde showgirl.

'Driver.' Francesca leaned forward and tapped sharply on

the glass partition. 'Slow down, for God's sake. You drive like a maniac.'

The chauffeur, overexerted from his bout with her suitcases (six had had to be put in a following taxi) and driving no more than forty miles an hour, said a stoic, '*Oui, madame*,' and wished he was home with his new young wife who kept him up far too late every night.

The journey toward Cannes progressed uneventfully for ten more minutes, until, for no apparent reason, the car started to weave back and forth crazily across the highway – missing other shrieking motorists by inches.

'My God!' screamed Francesca in horror. 'Horace! *Do something!*'

With a shuddering lurch the car turned inwards toward the sidewalk, smashed into a lamppost, and came to an abrupt halt. Francesca was hurled to the floor, and Horace fell on top of her. Miraculously neither of them were hurt.

'Get off me, you fool!' shrieked Francesca, removing a spiked heel shoe and hitting him randomly.

Horace raised his voice to her – the first time he had ever done so. 'Stop that,' he barked.

'Don't you tell *me* to stop *anything*,' she shouted, incensed, as she continued to hit him.

The cab driver, who had been following them, ripped open the back door, and with the help of several passers-by pulled them from the car. French curse words abounded. '*Mon dieu!*' '*Merde!*' and other such phrases were bandied about.

The driver was dragged from his seat. He had a small cut to his forehead, other than that he was quite dead.

'Horace!' screamed Francesca. 'This is all your fault! You'll do anything to ruin my holiday!'

Chapter 66

A week in Vegas was hardly the right setting to embark on married life. Especially with 'good time' Alice along for the ride. In the great tradition of mothers and daughters-in-law – Alice loathed Olympia, and Olympia returned the compliment.

'She's fat,' Alice said.

'She's a witch,' Olympia said.

'She's rude,' Alice said.

'She's embarrassing,' Olympia said.

And so it went. Lennie received a litany of complaints from both of them. And to tell the truth he didn't much care. Olympia *was* a little overweight – he made her promise to lose ten pounds. Alice *could* be a witch. He told her to behave herself or ship out. Olympia treated staff badly – Lennie noticed and called her on it. Alice was always an embarrassment. He couldn't do anything about *that*. She had been that way all her life.

The big surprise was Alice and Brigette. They loved each other! The blonde child took one look at the faded stripper and a bond was formed. Brigette had never liked a grown-up in her life. Alice had always hated kids. Together they were the odd couple – chatting about television programmes, food, and clothes – as if they were equals. Neither Olympia nor Lennie could believe it. Secretly, Lennie had always suspected his mother's mentality was in the low teenage range – but Brigette was only eleven – yet you would think she and Alice had been lifelong friends. Their relationship saved the day. Olympia accepted Alice because of it. Suddenly Brigette was behaving like a human being – a new phenomenon.

Marriage, Lennie found, had certain advantages. No more one night stands was one of them.

He certainly did not kid himself that he and Olympia were madly in love, but they had plenty of time. They'd done it, and he, for one, was prepared to give it his best shot.

He pushed Eden to the back of his mind.

Olympia, too, found that marriage (for the fourth time) was advantageous. Especially to someone like Lennie. He was not like her other three husbands, she knew that immediately. He was smarter and sexier and not obsessed with her money as the others had been. In fact, he didn't seem to even care about money. When she thrust the pre-nuptial agreement at him three days into their marriage he had signed the backdated document with hardly a glance. 'I didn't marry that part of you,' he said dismissively.

He had electric eyes, persistent lips, gentle hands, and an awe-inspiring cock.

He wasn't Flash. But he was something.

She put Flash on hold. He could wait.

*

Jess was well aware she was hardly witnessing love's young dream, but it wasn't as bad as she'd thought it would be after her initial encounter with the Greek Princess – as she had christened Olympia – even though she looked more Californian than Greek.

'Lennie,' she commented. 'I don't know what you said to her, but whatever it was – keep repeating it – she's *almost* bearable.'

He laughed. 'You've got to understand Olympia,' he stated patiently. 'Sure she's spoilt, wouldn't you be if your old man owned half the world and you grew up expecting to own the other half?'

Jess tried to put herself in that position, couldn't quite make it.

'Olympia is *very* insecure,' Lennie the analyst continued. 'That's why she treats people the way she does.'

Oh yeah? Insecure about what? Now the picture was coming clear. Lennie Golden. Champion of the underdog. He had married the richest girl in the world to save her from herself. Hah!

'When you get to know her,' he added, 'you'll really like her.'

An acquired taste, like eels on toast. 'If you say so,' Jess agreed amiably. She didn't feel like arguing. He would learn in his own sweet time.

Meanwhile, Matt was driving her nuts. Now that she had decided she really liked him – a lot – he had become 'Mister

Best Friend who will never lay a hand on you'. She wanted more than his hand, and she hinted this to him.

'You were always right about us, Jess,' he said, not getting the hint at all. 'I must have seemed like a real jerk to you when I wouldn't leave you alone.'

'No, you didn't' she replied hopefully.

'Yes. I was a jerk,' he repeated. And he had no intention of making a fool of himself again.

*

Olympia had discussed Dimitri's upcoming cruise with Lennie. He consulted Jess, and found he would be able to make it for a week, after that he had a firm commitment to do the 'Tonight Show', his first shot and he was looking forward to it. Although he was also nervous. Appearing with Carson was like receiving an audience with the Pope.

'They've promised you a seven minute spot,' Jess said eagerly. 'Freddie de Cordova said he couldn't understand why you haven't been on before. I didn't want to tell him we've been bombarding them for two years!'

Lennie decided he and Olympia would leave immediately after the last show on Saturday night, take a car to LA, the polar flight to London where they would stay overnight, and then another plane the next day to the south of France. He was enthusiastic about the trip, having never been abroad, although fortunately he had acquired a passport years before when he and Eden once planned a trip to Venice – which never came off because she ran away to LA with her actor boyfriend. Whatever happened to *him*?

Olympia enjoyed his enthusiasm. What fun it would be to show him around. She only wished they had more time.

Nanny Mabel and Brigette were due to leave two days before they did, and then Olympia came up with a brilliant idea. Why not send Alice with them? At least the child would behave herself with Alice along.

She told Lennie her plan, and he quickly said, 'Forget it.'

But somewhere along the way word leaked out, Alice got to hear, and she confronted Lennie immediately with bright red cheeks and shaking hands. 'You *can't* deny me this chance,' she stated dramatically. 'You've kept me off the Griffin Show – I know that. I'm not some *schlump* you can push in the background, I'm your mother, Lennie, your mother!'

As if she didn't tell him ten times a day. Reluctantly he agreed that she could make the trip, although he had a horrible suspicion they would all live to regret it – especially him.

The rest of the week in Vegas passed quickly. He and Vitos Felicidade were doing sell-out business, and the reviews that came out sounded as if he'd written them himself. *Variety* was particularly flattering. They described him as having a multitude of talent, with the timing of Carlin, the irreverence of Bruce, and the comic madness of Chevy Chase. Not bad. Jess clipped it out and put it with the stack of newspaper stuff she was saving for scrapbooks.

Matt threw a small dinner party the night before they left. He didn't have a date and neither did Jess. They sat sedately beside each other both thinking private thoughts that remained unsaid.

Vitos attended with a svelte brunette who licked his ear throughout dinner.

Make the most of his ear, Olympia thought, *there's not much else*.

Vitos was scrupulously charming to all and sundry, one would never have imagined Olympia had jilted him less than a week before.

Lennie got drunk, and Olympia got stoned.

In the morning he decided to give up drinking. He didn't like what it did to him, or the hangovers he endured.

Olympia was busy packing. Jess came by for lunch, she was all set to return to LA the next morning.

'Why don't you drive back with us tonight?' Lennie asked.

She shook her head. She wanted one more night in Vegas. All the better to give Matt one last chance.

*

Olympia received special treatment wherever she went, it didn't take Lennie long to discover that fact of life. In America he was starting to get VIP treatment, too – how potent fame was, not to mention the power of television. In Europe nobody had heard of him, and all of a sudden he was *Mr* Stanislopoulos. The first time he was called that he laughed. The second time wasn't so funny. And the third time he failed to see the humour in it at all.

Olympia tossed blonde curls and told him to get used to it.

'I'll *never* get used to it, lady,' he replied angrily.

London was just like he'd imagined, although it was warmer than he'd expected. A dry smokey heat rose from the asphalt streets like steam. A white Bentley met them at the airport and a matching white haired chauffeur drove them to the Connaught Hotel.

'My father always stays here,' Olympia announced. 'It has the best restaurant in town.'

Best restaurant or not they ventured out for dinner to an exclusive club, Annabels, in Berkeley Square, where Olympia met up with some English friends. They were a strange group with even stranger names like Muffy, Pinko, Nigel and Poopsie.

'The English county set,' Olympia whispered.

The men had braying accents, and the girls – although delicately pretty – looked untouchable with their perfect pink and white skin, and artfully styled Princess Di haircuts. He danced with one of them. The record playing was Sinatra's 'Come Fly With Me' and everyone seemed to be having a wonderful time. The girl smelt of stale roses as she pressed her bony body hard against his.

'Let's move on,' Olympia suggested after a delicious dinner of crab cocktail, steak Diane, and bitter chocolate ice cream.

'Aren't you tired?' he asked quizzically. Jet lag was catching up.

'Not at all,' she replied, and wondered if she should have offered him some of the great coke she had snorted before coming out. No – it was *her* supply, and she wasn't about to share it. Once they were on the boat she didn't know where she could get hold of any more – so hanging on to what she had seemed important. Besides, Lennie wasn't into drugs, he had told her, so why waste it on him?

Briefly she thought of Flash. Now with Flash there was never any problem. He was a doper supreme. Who knew – maybe they'd run into him in the South of France. He was lurking in a villa above Cannes with his teenage pregnant wife – probably both stoned out of their heads.

From Annabels they proceeded on to Tramp in Jermyn Street – another private club, but more laid back and fun than the sedate Annabels.

Tramp was run by an affable Englishman called Johnny Gold. He greeted Olympia like a long lost friend, although she had only been in the club once before, with Flash. And he was equally friendly to Lennie – in fact he even seemed to know who he was, which pleased him. Instinctively Lennie knew Tramp was his kind of hang out. He took off his tie, loosened the top buttons of his shirt, and felt instantly better.

Johnny led them into the jammed discotheque and squeezed them around an already full table. He introduced them to his wife, Jan, a striking ex-model. And some of the other people sitting along the comfortable banquette seating, including Ringo Star, Jack Nicholson, and British football star, George Best.

Lennie shifted into second gear, suddenly he wasn't tired at all.

He and Olympia staggered from the club at four in the morning, tried to dodge hovering paparazzi, collapsed into the waiting car, and slept all the way back to the Connaught.

It was a memorable evening, and by noon the next day they were on yet another plane, this time to the south of France and Dimitri's summer cruise.

Chapter 67

Lucky established attitude and position from day one. She sat back quietly and watched, feeling like a reluctant but accurate observer of life's great charade.

Actually, she was quite used to observing people and situations – having spent four long years in Washington when married to the annihilatingly boring Craven Richmond.

Now she was Mrs Dimitri Stanislopoulos, and sometimes she found herself wondering if this one would be any better. Maybe married life was not for her. Being free and single seemed a more appealing prospect every day – because every day she felt she knew Dimitri less. He had become arrogant and overbearing – a tyrant to his minions. Once he had been an exciting and skilled lover. Since they were married he seemed to have lost all interest in sex.

Francesca Fern arrived amid a blaze of hysterics. The driver bringing her to the yacht had had the bad manners to suffer a stroke and *die*, mid-journey. She was suitably outraged. She blamed her unhappy husband, Horace, for the entire incident.

Horace accepted her wrath as his due.

Dimitri consoled her with champagne and roses and a great deal of solicitous attention.

Lucky – who knew of his long time affair with Madame Fern – found herself wondering if it was indeed over as he had assured her when they were discussing the guest list. 'Francesca was once my passion,' he had openly confessed. 'But now she is merely my good friend, and I want to invite her.'

'Sure,' Lucky had said, not being of a jealous nature. And quite frankly – she hardly saw Francesca as any kind of threat – just a very famous, middle-aged woman, with a face like a horse.

After the Ferns were installed, Saud Omar, an extraordinarily wealthy Arab, and his socialite girlfriend, Contessa Tania Zebrowski – came aboard. One look and Lucky inwardly groaned. The short fat man with the 'soaked in oil' brown eyes was a definite lech, and his girlfriend – dripping diamonds and gold – was a hard, face-lifted woman, whose beauty had seen better days.

Next came Jenkins Wilder, the Texas oil tycoon, a flamboyant man in his fifties, with Fluff, his 18-year-old wife who called him 'daddy-pie' and 'bumpkins'.

That was the first day.

The next morning brought Nanny Mabel, Brigette, and an outlandishly dressed Alice, who threw her arms around a chagrined Dimitri, kissed him lasciviously, and announced, 'I feel I've known you all my life. We're family now. Let's get acquainted properly.'

Gino and Susan arrived at noon, and the yacht set sail shortly after.

The cruise had begun.

*

Friendships were formed.

The Contessa and Susan hit it off immediately.

Fluff and the Arab lech found they had snorkelling in common.

Francesca and Dimitri parried words and lingering looks.

Alice took a shine to Horace.

Jenkins Wilder spent most of his time on the phone.

Which left Lucky and Gino.

'How're you doing?' she asked.

'Why'd you run off from LA?' he asked.

'Susan looks well,' she said – for the sake of something to say.

'This guy, Dimitri, he's too old for you,' he grumbled.

What the hell are we doing here? she wanted to ask. *We don't fit in at all.*

'Hey, kid, what are we doing here?' he spoke the words aloud. Good old Gino, always ready to say what was on his mind.

She shrugged and gazed out to sea. The boat was moving smoothly through the azure blue water as they headed for St Tropez, where they were due to pick up Olympia and her latest husband. She and Gino lay on a top deck sunning themselves. Below them – on another level, Dimitri and Francesca played a boisterous game of gin rummy.

'I've no idea,' she said at last.

'You know something?' Gino reflected. 'I think we both made mistakes this last couple of years.'

She looked at him intently. It was unlike her father to make that kind of statement. What was he trying to tell her? That he, too, was having second thoughts about his marriage?

She wanted to ask him, but before she could, a servant appeared and announced that lunch was served. Whenever she and Gino were due to embark on a serious conversation, something interrupted. She hoped he would hang back, let the others go to lunch. But he didn't, he arose, pulled on a polo shirt, and offered her his hand.

'Let's go, kid,' he said. 'The more meals we eat, the sooner we can get off this floating crap shoot – and I, for one – can't wait!'

*

The Stanislopoulos yacht arrived in St Tropez harbour at seven. Dimitri made the decision that as most of his guests were probably suffering jet lag, they would remain on the boat for dinner.

Lucky was restless as she changed into a long white dress and fastened her new diamond choker around her neck, she brushed her hair vigorously and shook it into a cloud of jet curls. Next she applied a light make-up.

Dimitri changed into a dark suit, white shirt and silk tie, then preened in front of the full length mirror, dousing himself with cologne.

'This is really ridiculous,' Lucky commented. 'We're in St Tropez – on a boat – on vacation – and we're dressing up as if we're going to the first night of the opera!'

'It may seem ridiculous to you,' he replied pompously. 'However, my dear, this is the way I do things.'

'What about me?' she blazed. 'Don't *I* have a say in how things are done?'

He looked her up and down. 'That dress is excessively low cut,' he remarked. 'And you have on too much eye shadow.'

It was the first time he had ever criticized her appearance. 'Screw you!' she replied heatedly.

Dimitri stared at her, and realized with deep regret that they should never have married. Lucky was too young, too wild, and certainly too outspoken. He had hoped that when she became his wife, she would accept his authority, guidance, and superior knowledge of life. This was obviously not to be.

They were hardly on the best of terms when they sat down for dinner in the grand dining room. Dimitri was seated at one end of the table with Francesca on his left and Susan on his right. Lucky found herself at the other end with Saud Omar and Horace Fern. Gino was somewhere in the middle next to Fluff. Lucky was not pleased. Who had arranged the seating?

She picked up a silver place-card holder and discovered Dimitri's scrawl on the white card.

Damn him. She was getting good and tired of his calling every shot. As Mrs Stanislopoulos, wasn't she supposed to have some clout too?

Dinner conversation was stilted to say the least. Lucky loathed Saud, with his lecherous eyes and greasy hair; Horace was a nonentity; and the women were all boring – their conversation concerned only with clothes, designers, jewellery, gossip and servant problems.

What am I doing here? she thought. *Have I flipped out or what? Because this is just not my scene.*

Francesca had a laugh like a buzz saw. She used it often, as she and Dimitri seemed to be having a wonderful time together. Susan was all but ignored. Gino was unusually silent.

Dinner passed slowly. Caviar to begin with. Then chateaubriand with purẽed potatoes and a choice of vegetables. All this served by three Filipino maids in starched white uniforms.

This is archiac, Lucky thought, picking at her food.

By dessert she was bored out of her mind. And so was Gino – in spite of the fact that Fluff was doing her best to keep him entertained. He had given up on 18-year-olds many decades ago.

They looked at each other across the table. He shook his head as if to say *What is this crap?* She pantomimed a *How the hell would I know?* They grinned conspiratorially. God, she missed him!

Dessert was richly coated chocolate profiteroles, and as Lucky made desultory conversation with Horace, she noticed Francesca feeding the round, cream filled delicacies to Dimitri, one at a time – while their eyes exchanged heated looks, and Francesca laughed throatily and licked her darkly painted lips with a snake-tongue.

That sonofabitch is still sleeping with her.

Lucky knew it for sure, and she was furious.

Of course, she had known it from the moment Francesca arrived on board. It was glaringly obvious. The long intimate looks, the hand touching, the attention he paid her. All conclusive evidence. Lucky was no idiot. She was also not in love with him, in fact she never had been. Oh sure, for a moment she had fooled herself that maybe he was the man for her. But looking at things clearly, she had married Dimitri because it seemed the right thing to do for Roberto's sake, and also – she couldn't shirk facts – because she wanted to build her hotel more than anything in the world.

Damn! Whatever happened to love? After Marco she was certain she could never love again. Not that white hot all-consuming passion. And she was right.

Damn! Damn! Damn!

Horace was repeating some inane question. She wished he would shut up. What kind of man was he anyway? He must *know* what was going on.

She narrowed her eyes and tried to formulate a plan of

action. First of all, she decided, she was not going to humiliate herself and make a scene. That's probably what they were all waiting for, this illustrious group.

No, she would bide her time and wait for the right moment to strike.

Why couldn't Marco have lived?

Her eyes threatened to fill with tears. She blinked them away. Crying was a weakness, and above all else, Lucky Santangelo was strong.

Chapter 68

Carrie and Steven arrived in LA late in the afternoon. As usual Steven was silent, allowing his resentment and fury to bubble loudly beneath the surface. After checking into the hotel, he turned to Carrie and said, 'I'll see you at ten in the morning.' And that was it. She was on her own. He didn't care that a long, lonely evening loomed ahead of her.

'Very well, Steven,' she replied quietly, walking toward the elevator.

He went to his room – watched the phone for a while, shaved, showered, ordered a half bottle of Scotch from room service, stared at the phone.

At a quarter to seven he picked it up and dialled. A woman answered.

'This is an emergency,' he said, his voice controlled. 'I have to speak to Gino Santangelo at once.'

'Oh, dear.' The woman sounded flustered. 'What kind of emergency? Mr and Mrs Santangelo left the country yesterday. They will be in Europe for two weeks.'

'Europe?' he questioned blankly.

'France,' the woman said. 'I can try to contact –'

She was still speaking as he hung up.

Later that night he rented a car and drove past the Santangelo residence. That's when he became aware of what a protected life these people led, and realization dawned.

There was no way Gino Santangelo would listen to him even if he *was* in town. Why was he fooling himself?

Dejected, he drove around for a while, headed back to Sunset, and finally pulled into the parking lot of a bar. He had no idea it was a strip joint until he got inside, and by that time he felt like a drink and really didn't care what kind of a dump he got it in.

The place was full of men staring at a regal looking Scandinavian woman who took it off suggestively on a scuffed runway snaking between the chipped tables. Red satin stripped away to reveal smooth flesh, jutting breasts and a thick bush.

Steven ordered a double Scotch from a topless waitress in a grass skirt. She had stringy hair and perky breasts. She couldn't have been more than seventeen. He felt sorry for her, and when she returned with his drink he dropped her a big tip.

She looked at him with stoned eyes and whispered, 'I take a break at nine-thirty. I can give you a blow job in the parking lot for twenty bucks.'

Her offer offended him. Was he starting to look like a john?

'No, thanks,' he said shortly.

'Fifteen,' she whispered hopefully.

'No.'

'Ten,' she pleaded. 'I've gotta kid. He needs things.'

'What kind of things?' he asked quickly.

'Oh,' she looked around furtively. 'Food, clothes. You name it.'

'Bull.'

'I'm not shittin' you.'

'Eh – Desiree,' the barman yelled. 'What's goin' on over there? You takin' another order or what?'

She froze like a cornered rat.

'That's okay,' Steven said, 'bring me another drink.'

On stage the Scandinavian made way for an action-packed Puerto Rican with startlingly white teased hair. She was clad in a cowboy outfit which stayed on her nubile body for exactly three and a half minutes. Then she stripped, until all that remained were tassles on her nipples and crotch. She squatted down and began to twirl, while the audience of men shouted ribald encouragement.

Desiree returned with his second drink.

'How old is your kid?' he asked.

'Nearly two.'

'And you?'

'How old do you want me to be?' she replied coquettishly. 'I can play schoolgirl or whore. You wanna come back to my place later an' find out? It'll cost you fifty – but it'll be worth every dollar. If you wanna pay me sixty I can quit now, I'll tell 'em I'm sick.'

'Desiree!' screamed the bartender.

'Well?' she asked anxiously.

His curiosity was aroused. 'Quit now,' he decided.

'The parking lot in five minutes,' she mumbled, and scurried away.

He sat through a few more minutes of twirling nipples. But when the woman on stage began to pick up rolled dollar bills with her crotch, he got up and went outside.

The air was balmy and rich. He stood by his rented car and waited.

Desiree eventually appeared, wearing jeans and a T-shirt, her stringy hair tied back in a pony tail. Now she looked twelve. She walked toward an old Pontiac. 'Hand over the money and follow me in your car,' she instructed.

He did not have a large bankroll by any means, but he was caught up in the game. 'Half now, half later,' he bargained.

'You're not gonna stiff me?' she pleaded.

'You're not going to run off on me?'

'No way, man. I like you. I'll make you feel real satisfied.'

He didn't want to tell her he had no intention of having sex with her. She would consider him a weirdo and run.

Maybe that's what he was turning into. A fucked up weirdo who spent his time cruising hooker bars and searching for a father it was too late to find.

Desiree lived in a run-down apartment on a street off Santa Monica. She double-parked her car and told him it was okay to do the same. 'You'll hear 'em holler when they wanna get out,' she stated matter-of-factly.

He followed her up rickety stairs to a small room which contained her life – including a toddler asleep in a battered cot pushed into one corner, and a ragged-looking cat dozing in another.

She switched on a lamp, and said matter-of-factly, 'You're not a cop are you?' And when he shook his head she recited, 'Straight sex only for sixty. Anything else will cost you extra.'

He indicated the baby. 'What about him?'

'No kiddie porn,' she answered quickly, her blank eyes alarmed.

Steven felt helpless. And very very angry.

'I meant,' he said slowly, 'does he stay in the room? What if he wakes up?'

'He won't.'

'How do you know that?'

'Because he just won't,' she replied stubbornly.

'Who looks after him while you're out working?'

'He sleeps all the time.'

'Are you telling me you simply walk out of here and leave him *alone*?'

'He never wakes up.'

'How are you so sure?'

'Because I give him a sleeper – it knocks him out cold.' She glared at him. 'Does that satisfy you?'

He sat down on the side of the bed. 'Jesus!'

She took this as a sign, and began to pull her T-shirt over her head.

'Don't undress,' he said quickly.

She pulled her T-shirt back down. 'I gotta take off my jeans,' she complained, fiddling with the zipper.

'I just want to talk,' he said. 'Nothing else.'

Restlessly she picked up the scraggy cat, opened the door and threw it out. She was uncomfortable with talk. At least with sex she knew what she was dealing with. 'I want the rest of my money,' she whined.

He handed it over, and said, quietly, 'Do you know that giving a small child sleeping pills is very dangerous?'

'What are you – a social worker?'

'It could be fatal. And so could leaving him alone in this fire trap.'

'Don't jinx me, man.'

'Who is his father?'

She laughed aloud. '*I* don't know. I don't even care. Who gives a shit anyway?'

'Maybe *he* will when he's old enough to ask. Have you thought about that?'

'Listen, man.' Suddenly her dull eyes were alive. 'I *look after* my kid. *You* may not think it's much – but it's the best I can do. When he's old enough to ask, I'll tell him the truth. I'll tell him that I kept him with me, paid his way, and he has *nobody* to thank but me – because if it wasn't for *me* he'd be in some stupid state orphanage without anyone caring.'

Steven didn't stay around to talk or anything else. He left, her shrill words ringing in his ears . . . *If it wasn't for me he'd be in some orphanage without anyone caring* . . .

If it wasn't for Carrie that would have been his fate. And how was he repaying her? By dragging her around the country searching for a dream or a nightmare. And she was beginning to hate him for it, he knew it, and who could blame her? He was subjecting her to an ordeal that would alienate her – perhaps forever. For the first time he began to realize just how much she meant to him, and how he was making her suffer. He had shut her out. Maybe the time was right to start opening doors. This chase – this quest for the truth – was heading nowhere.

Early in the morning he called Jerry in New York. 'I need help,' he said.

'What's happened now?' sighed Jerry wearily.

'We're here in LA. Gino Santangelo's not. I called his house and found out he's away for two weeks. And you know something? I guess I finally realized you're right – if I turn up at his front door with my story, he's going to call the cops and bust my ass. Why shouldn't he?'

'You had to go all the way to California to find that out?' Jerry commented dryly.

'I drove by his house. There are gates, closed circuit TV, and armed patrol.'

'Which means you – with your black face – are not going to get near the sonofabitch.'

'Right.'

'So you're calling me for help.'

'Right.'

There was a long silence, broken finally by Jerry. 'Steven,' he said harshly. 'I'm getting sick and tired of lending you money, handing out free advice, and listening to you bitch.'

'I agree with you.'

'What?'

'I said I agree with you. If I were you, I'd have given up on me a long time ago.'

'Am I about to hear that you are abandoning this cockamamie search and regaining your senses?'

'I still need to find out who my father is,' Steven replied seriously. 'But I'm releasing Carrie from the responsibility. I'm through dragging her around the country. And – if the offer is still open – I'm coming to work for you. It's time I started paying my debts.'

'I don't believe this!' Jerry exclaimed. 'One day on the West Coast and you found God!'

'Cut it out. I need support, not wisecracks.'

'Have you told Carrie?'

'Not yet.'

'Do so. At once. And get your ass back here pronto.'

*

They were staying at the Hyatt Hotel on Sunset. The California sun was blazing and the lobby was full of tourists. Steven had arranged to meet Carrie by the front entrance at ten.

He spotted her from a distance – aloof and erect, forever stylish and ageless, she stood apart from the crowd.

She thought they were going to visit Gino Santangelo. A humiliation she was prepared to go through with for him.

He approached her from behind and hugged her. She was startled.

'We're going home,' he said. 'Back to New York.'

She searched his face, knew something had changed, and didn't ask questions.

'I've missed you, Steven' she said softly.

'I know,' he replied. 'I *do* know.'

Chapter 69

From the moment they left the Connaught and set off for London Airport, Olympia was insufferable to everyone, including Lennie. When they reached the plane he had had enough. The first thing she did was insult the stewardess.

'For Christ's sake, cut out the rich girl act,' he said in a low angry voice. 'What are you aiming for? Cunt of the year?'

'I've got a hangover,' she replied sulkily.

'So live with it, and stop taking it out on everyone else.'

She liked forceful men. It was a shame there weren't more around. 'Sorry,' she answered contritely. 'I'll behave.'

But she didn't, and by the time they arrived at Nice airport he was fuming. A helicopter was waiting to take them on to St Tropez and the yacht. Olympia climbed aboard, and promptly fell asleep.

Lennie brooded about the wisdom of what he had done. Jess – who rarely called a shot wrong – had said he was insane. If this was a taste of things to come, she was right.

The luxury and opulence of the Stanislopoulos yacht amazed Lennie. Only in movies had he seen anything like it. *The Greek* was a floating palace.

Alice ruined everything. She was the first to greet them as

they came aboard – a bizarre picture in a red striped romper suit worn with stiletto heels, fish net tights, and an abundance of make-up – including false eyelashes. 'Welcome,' she said graciously, as if it were *her* boat. 'Make yourselves at home.'

Olympia threw her a withering look. 'Alice, dear,' she said. 'This *has* been my home for most of my life. I don't need you to welcome me. Where is Brigette? And why aren't you with her? She *is* the only reason you're here. I'm sure you're aware of that.'

Olympia did not believe in holding back – she wanted Alice to get the message up front.

Lennie couldn't care less. He looked around. Servants seemed to be appearing from everywhere, taking their luggage, offering cold champagne on silver trays.

'Where is my father?' Olympia demanded of a man in a white uniform.

'He's gone ashore, Miss Olympia,' replied Captain Pratt. 'For lunch. He's due back shortly. He said you should meet him in the upstairs bar at three o'clock.'

'He's taken Brigette,' added Alice. 'I wanted to go with them, but your daddy said I should stay here.'

'Wise man,' murmured Olympia. She turned to the captain and said haughtily, 'And where are the rest of the guests?'

'Most of them are ashore, Miss Olympia.' Captain Pratt gave Lennie a quick once-over while Olympia yawned and complained about the trip. 'Will you be wanting lunch, miss?' he added.

'No,' she replied, not even consulting Lennie. 'I need to rest.'

Alice laughed gaily. 'Well, Lennie, well my *boychick*. What do *you* think of all this?'

'I think I want to take a piss and change my clothes,' he replied dourly. She had not caught him at the right moment.

*

St Tropez was at the height of the season. Tourists mixed with the natives on the cobbled harbour streets lined with fashionable boutiques and open-air restaurants. Yachts jostled for position along the small harbour, and their occupants sat out on deck sipping margueritas and watching the passing crowds. By noon there was a lunch-time parade of nubile bodies clad in the latest fashions.

Dimitri strolled with his pretty blonde granddaughter, Brigette, Saud Omar, and Jenkins Wilder. Between them the three men could buy and sell France. Easily. Several paces behind hovered various bodyguards trying to appear unobtrusive in city clothes with hidden shoulder-holsters.

All three men eyed the passing female parade with a mixture of boredom and half-hearted lust. Money had taught them most women were available – for a price. Whether the price be a new dress or a fleet of Mercedes was up for discussion. But the fact remained that the excitement of the chase was never really there, because the prize was always a foregone conclusion.

Brigette skipped happily along, holding on to her grandfather's hand. She loved being with Dimitri, he called her his little Diamond Princess and bought her anything she wanted. Anything at all. She was glad to be off the boat. Things were different this year. Dimitri had married again. and had a disgusting baby called Roberto.

Stupid name.

Stupid baby.

Brigette hated them both, and wondered why her mother hadn't told her about them. After all, the dumb baby had taken over her old room with his stupid black nanny. But that was okay really, because she had a new room, a grown-up room with blue wallpaper and a bubble jet tub. *And*, best of all, she didn't have Nanny Mabel sharing it with her – she had her new friend, Alice, and Alice was lots and lots of fun and stayed up all night long talking. Brigette didn't understand half of it, but that didn't matter. Alice was fun even if she did look a little screwy, smelled kind of odd, never stopped talking, and wore more make-up than Miss Piggy.

'We'll stop for lunch here,' Dimitri decided, pausing in front of a fashionable restaurant. Quickly a front table was cleared for them, while the bodyguards settled nearby.

Brigette had spotted an Aladdin's cave of trinkets next door. 'I want to go shopping, grandpappa,' she announced sweetly.

'Tomorrow,' Dimitri said dismissively. 'One of the women will take you.'

'I want to go *now*.' She managed to make her bottom lip quiver. 'I can go by myself. The store's right there. Look. *See?*' She pointed.

'Alright, if you're quick.'

'I don't have any money, grandpappa.'

Dimitri groped in the pocket of his sports shirt, but like most very rich people, he carried no cash.

'Here you go, honey,' boomed Jenkins Wilder, reaching into a Gucci clutch he carried everywhere and producing a stack of hundred dollar bills. 'How many will make you happy? Two? Three?'

She grabbed three hundred dollars.

'Too much,' grumbled Dimitri.

'I'm buying presents, grandpappa,' Brigette explained patiently, and skipped off.

Dimitri nodded at one of the bodyguards to follow her.

Jenkins Wilder sat back and grinned. 'C*rrr*azee lookin' broads, here,' he remarked. 'If'n I wasn't a ma*rrr*ied man I might have myself a time.'

'French women expect too much attention,' Saud said, his oily eyes watchful. 'And usually they are not worth the trouble.'

'I agree,' said Dimitri. 'English women are the most sensual.'

'God-darn – you just got yourself hitched to an American gal,' Jenkins pointed out.

This was true, Dimitri reflected, and Lucky was certainly an unusual beauty. But she was not Francesca, and he still harboured a deep passion for Madame Fern. A passion which never seemed to cool.

He was beginning to think that inviting her on the cruise was not such a good idea. Now he and Lucky were married, it was impossible to spend private time with Francesca.

Before, with only Horace to contend with, it had never been a problem. Horace never dared interfere.

Dimitri half hoped Lucky would tire of the cruise and fly back to New York. He preferred their relationship when it was not quite so permanent – but he had to marry her because of Roberto. No son of his was going to go through life without the protection of the Stanislopoulos name.

'I have also found in life,' Saud Omar contemplated, 'that English women are indeed the most erotic in the bedroom when you penetrate their natural reserve.' He lingered over the word penetrate, while his olive oil eyes surveyed the bouncing breasts of two teenage girls passing by, wearing thin knit tank tops and miniscule bikini bottoms.

'Ah never had myself a limey chick,' ruminated Jenkins Wilder. 'Ah was stationed outside of London with the army way back in fifty-one – but I was too doggawned scared of catching the clap!'

*

Lennie showered and changed into Levi cut-offs and a faded denim shirt, while Olympia lay on the bed and complained.

She complained about her father not being there to greet her.

She complained about Alice.

She complained about Captain Pratt. 'I've told poppa to get rid of him for years. He's got nasty little eyes.'

She complained about Captain Pratt's wife. 'A terrible cook. Why do you think I refused lunch?'

'C'mon,' said Lennie, trying to ignore her bad mood. 'Loosen up. We're supposed to be on vacation. Let's hit the streets and explore.'

'Explore?' she sneered derisively. 'I hate St Tropez, it's full of boring tourists and hookers.'

'I want to explore,' he said stubbornly.

'Go ahead. I'm not stopping you. But I do expect you to wait until after you've met Dimitri.'

He looked at the time, it was a quarter to three. 'That's the reason I'm here, isn't it'

She got off the bed and started to primp in front of the mirror. She wanted to snort some coke, but once again she didn't care to share it. Casually she smuggled her supply into the bathroom, locked the door, and laid down two lines.

Relief was immediate. She had been feeling lousy all day with just a few Valium to keep her going. Like a fool she had packed her supply of coke, and had only now been able to get her hands on it.

She snorted first one nostril, then the other. Clouds lifted. Her head was clear. She felt ready to take on the world.

Lennie banged on the door. 'What are you doing in there?' he yelled.

'Just fixing my hair,' she called back.

'Hurry up.' He was strangely disoriented. London had been great. But maybe agreeing to come on this cruise was a mistake. Taking on Olympia was one thing – he could handle her – even if she was turning out to be a prize pain in the ass. But the father was going to think he was after her money, and the rest of the group did not exactly sound like fun city. Plus he had Alice to put up with. And all he really wanted to do was work on his material for the Carson show.

Olympia finally emerged and took his hand. She seemed in a better humour. 'Let's go meet daddyoh!' she said brightly. 'He looks a bit forbidding, but take no notice of that, he's really easy. Just answer his questions, don't get pissed off, and I promise you we'll only have to do this once a year.'

They made their way to the upstairs deck. Greek music was playing through stereo speakers, and Dimitri was demonstrating some intricate steps to Brigette. The child was sunny-faced and laughing, while Alice stood to one side clapping her hands joyfully.

'A perfect family scene,' whispered Olympia gleefully. And then she threw herself into the whole greeting routine.

'My baby!' to a disinterested Brigette. Kiss kiss.

'Pappa!' to Dimitri, who waved her away while he finished his dance.

When he was ready, and only then, did he return her greeting.

Lennie hung back, watching from the sidelines, willing Alice to keep quiet. And for once she did.

'Poppa, I want you to meet Lennie Golden,' Olympia announced. 'My new husband.'

Christ! She made him sound like a possession! He extended his hand and wondered – for a moment – what he was doing on a huge yacht in the south of France meeting a man like Dimitri Stanislopoulos and married to his daughter. It was crazy time.

Dimitri glared at him with piercing eyes, his expression rock-hard. 'So,' he said loudly. '*You're* the latest one.'

A remark Lennie did not like, especially as his extended hand was ignored. He formulated something insulting to say. Nobody was going to get away with treating *him* like shit – Olympia's father or not.

Before he could do or say anything Dimitri suddenly enveloped him in a bear hug. 'Welcome to our family,' he boomed. 'If you are good enough for Olympia, then you are good enough for me.' A brisk wave at the barman. 'Champagne for everyone. We have much to celebrate.'

Olympia grinned and hugged Lennie's arm. 'I know,' she said. 'It's wonderful, isn't it?'

'Wonderful. Excellent,' agreed Dimitri, beaming. 'And I have a surprise for you, too.'

'What?' demanded Olympia, thinking perhaps a new diamond necklace – Dimitri was always generous when she married.

'Grandpop got married too!' chirped Brigette excitedly. 'And you have a *brother*, mama. And I'm his *aunt*. Really. Truthfully. Honestly! I'm an auntie!'

Olympia's smile stiffened. Was the limelight to be stolen from her? She looked at her father for confirmation that Brigette was lying as usual.

He nodded. 'It is true. I also am married again. And I have been blessed with a son.'

For a moment Olympia felt faint. Too much travelling and

not enough coke to ward off the effect of this latest bombshell. 'I don't believe it,' she said vaguely.

'It's true! It's true! It's true!' chanted Brigette.

'Yes it is,' said Alice, grabbing a glass of champagne from a silver tray, and joining in what she perceived as a riotous celebration.

Olympia took a deep breath. His getting married again wasn't too bad. But having a *kid* – at *his* age. She was the only Stanislopoulos heir, and that's the way it had to stay. Rich as she was, she had no intention of sharing the vast inheritance she would come into when Dimitri died. It was all hers. This just wasn't fair!

Lennie handed her a glass of champagne, and took one for himself. 'Congratulations, Mr Stanislopoulos,' he said – happy to relinquish being the centre of attention.

'I love weddings,' sighed Alice. 'Such happy times. I remember my wedding day as if it was a week ago. I wore a white cocktail dress – so smart – with a cinched waist.' She turned to Olympia who couldn't care less. 'Do you know, my dear, I had an eighteen inch waist. Eighteen inches!'

'Really?' asked Brigette.

'Yes, really. I had –'

'Alice, take Brigette for a nap,' Olympia said shortly, her tone brooking no argument.

'But mama –' Brigette began.

'Now!'

'Come along, pretty-puss,' Alice crooned, shepherding the child from the room.

'Who did you marry, poppa?' Olympia asked sweetly, knowing it couldn't possibly be Francesca, and wondering if it was that Brazilian whore who had nearly captured him a few years before. Or maybe the English socialite with the stately home and faint connections to the Royal Family. Dimitri always *had* liked culture.

'Ah . . .' he said. 'Now you'll *really* be surprised.'

Lennie felt this was between them, and a perfect time to make his escape. 'Would you excuse me if I took a walk?' he asked.

'Go ahead,' said Olympia, with hardly a glance.

He left quickly.

'Who?' Olympia persisted.

'Well,' said Dimitri, stringing it out. 'Do you remember quite a while ago I told you I had bumped into an old school friend of yours, Lucky Santangelo?'

'Yes.'

'We renewed our acquaintanceship in New York, and,' he shrugged expansively, 'things happened.'

'Things happened!' shrieked Olympia louder than she intended. 'You didn't marry *Lucky*?'

'That's *exactly* what I did.'

Chapter 70

Now that Lucky knew – was certain – that Dimitri continued his affair with the flamboyant Madame Fern, she decided to see as little of him as possible. Roberto appeared to be happy in the excellent hands of loving CeeCee, so it was easy for her to slip away in the morning and wander around the picturesque streets. She left Dimitri a note saying she had gone on a sight-seeing tour. Why should she suffer on the boat when she could be out on her own, free to sort out her feelings.

Being alone had never bothered Lucky. It was the story of her life. But now she had Roberto, which was the main reason she hadn't taken a plane back to New York and the nearest lawyer. She wanted a divorce. But she didn't want to lose the opportunity to build her hotel, and she had to make quite sure that everything was locked up before she made a move.

After wandering through the many boutiques and small shops, she took a cab to Tahiti Beach, which she had heard was the place to go. She was wearing an oversize T-shirt with a small scarlet bikini underneath and thong-toed sandals on her feet. Her jet hair hung down her back in a thick plait, and dark shades covered her eyes.

Armed with a Sony Walkman, a bottle of Ambre Solairc suntan oil, and a good book, she approached the fashionable crowded beach with confidence. She spoke a smattering of French – picked up in her youth – and she requested and paid for the hire of a striped chaise, towel, and large umbrella.

The bronzed attendant settled her in a row near the water's edge, and she lay back to relax and observe.

One of life's greatest pleasures is watching the world pass by. And on the Tahiti Beach, in St Tropez, you certainly saw some sights. Many of the women went topless, and there were breasts of all shapes and sizes and ages. Nobody seemed to object, in fact everybody was remarkably unselfconscious.

The French men favoured very small, tight bikini bottoms, and thrust their cocks out as if parading for first prize. There were some interesting contenders.

Lucky grinned. She liked their attitude. Being married to an older man she had forgotten the sheer pleasure of a perfect male body. That sweet combination of gleaming muscles and beautiful youth. She allowed her eyes – still under cover of dark shades – to sweep over their bodies, checking them out as men had always checked out women. It was an enjoyable pastime.

*

Lennie did not speak one word of French. He could say 'fuck you' in Italian, curse in German, and utter words of love in Swedish, but French eluded him. Perhaps it was because he had never slept with a French girl, and it was always his short-term lovers who taught him fragments of a language.

It didn't matter. In St Tropez everyone spoke English – sometimes fluently – most times brokenly – but they all made an attempt.

He fell in love with the place immediately. It had a laid-back ambiance that grabbed him. He was not yet rich enough nor jaded enough to see it as a dirty, overcrowded tourist-trap. He merely observed a lot of young people out to have a good time – and it appealed to him. He grabbed a seat in a sidewalk café, ordered a Cinzano on the rocks, and sat for a while. It would have been nice, he mused, to have been here with a group. Jess, Isaac, Joey, the twins, Eden . . .

How had *she* slipped into his thoughts? She had looked like a five-hundred-dollar-a-night hooker sitting at a front table on his opening night in her silver sequinned dress with her gangster friends.

Eden Antonio.

I thought you were going to become a movie star. Whatever happened?

He imagined her face when she read about his marriage to Olympia Stanislopoulos. Slanty eyes. Thin lips. Elegant nose. It must have given her a jolt. He hoped.

Or did he?

The torch was dimming. This was the first time he had thought about her since leaving America. Things were looking up.

A young couple sitting at the next table were eyeing him with more than casual interest. The girl, pretty in an outdoorsy way, caught his eye and smiled. Politely he smiled back, causing her to nudge her companion, a long-haired greaser in a studded denim vest and dirty jeans. Before Lennie could even think about moving, they were at his table.

'You *are* Lennie Golden, aren't you?' the girl asked excitedly. She had a bold suntan, with American teeth and an accent to match.

'Guilty.'

'I *told* you!' the girl exclaimed. Her companion didn't crack a smile. He had a skull and crossbones tattooed on his arm and a brooding expression. Not exactly James Dean – more the young James Coburn. He hung behind his girlfriend and scowled.

'We're Americans,' she announced, still dazzling with her teeth. 'We've been here a month.'

'What do you want – a medal?' deadpanned Lennie.

'I never expected to see *you*!' Dazzle, dazzle. 'I'm crazy for your TV show. I *love* it. Never miss it. When I'm there, of course.'

'Of course.'

'Yeah, man, it's okay,' said Mister Scowl, joining in at last.

'Glad you approve.'

They sat down uninvited, but not exactly unwelcome. Lennie felt like company, and they seemed to be okay kids.

A conversation took place. The usual. *What are you doing here? How long are you staying? Do you like it? Wanna score some great dope?*

Lennie had a feeling a few ace joints might help the trip no end. And Olympia would be delighted if he returned bearing gifts.

'Our stash is at the beach with my sister,' explained the girl. 'It's only a few minutes away. Come on, we'll take you.'

They offered him a ride in a decrepit old Renault which choked and spluttered all the way. He was hunched in the back, bent double. Nothing like getting back among the people. In a perverse way he enjoyed it. Limos, Learjets, penthouse suites, and private yachts were still a touch rich for his plebian blood. He was already working on a monologue in his head about the way the very wealthy lived. So much material! And untouched, like a virgin oil well. If he could get it together in time it would be great to use on the 'Tonight Show'.

The girl with the dazzling smile had a sister who disdained clothes and wore only a native suntan, plenty of Indian beads, and a suede G-string. Where was she hiding the famous stash? Clearly not on her person.

Her French boyfriend was clad in a black jock-strap which he patted affectionately most of the time. Between them they shared a large canvas bag filled with goodies.

'You name it. We got it,' announced the greaser, taking over, and pulling out a small package of hash which he expertly rolled into a joint. He handed it to Lennie. 'Compliments of the casa. Try it. Like it. Buy it.'

Lennie tried it, liked it, and ordered two dozen joints – 'Rolled, please.'

The greaser was only too happy to oblige, and set about his task with insouciant ease.

'I'll be back,' Lennie said, and wandered off down the beach admiring the scenery. Most of the women wore only the bottom half of scanty bikinis and acted as if they were fully clothed – jogging along the shore, running after escaping children, tonguing ice cream cones, lying back with open thighs – all the better to obtain the perfect tan.

For fifteen minutes Lennie thought he had died and gone to tit paradise. And then . . . so what? Big deal. Nipples could get boring too unless they were *really* special . . .

And then he spotted the girl with the jet hair and black eyes who had come on to him in Las Vegas. Here she was – two years later – lying on the beach in St Tropez looking as sensual and wild as ever. Naturally she was not topless. Why give a free show? She wore a dangerous red bikini, earphones, and her eyes were closed. He recognized her immediately. Somehow she had made an indelible impression.

Proceed with caution, a voice in his head warned. *Remember – she has an acid tongue.*

And one of the horniest bodies he had ever seen. Tall, slim and supple, with long legs, a small waist, great breasts, and broad shoulders.

He remembered her walk. Panther-like, graceful.

He remembered their one kiss, before he had called a halt to the proceedings. Schmuck of the year.

How was he to approach her now?

Why was he to approach her now?

You are a married man, said his conscience sternly.

So what? replied his libido.

Don't do it, said his conscience.

Go ahead, replied his prick.

She must have sensed someone staring at her. Without warning she suddenly sat up, removed the earphones, took off her shades, and returned his quizzical stare.

He was not close enough to say anything. Fortunately. Because whenever he opened his mouth she shot him down.

Did she remember him? Was she going to come over?

He stood by the seashore, waiting.

Slowly she got up. Stretched languorously, and headed toward him.

He held his breath. He might be married but he wasn't dead. This was one opportunity he wasn't going to miss. Not the second time around.

Their eyes locked. As she got closer he was mesmerized by the blackness of hers, the long lashes that surrounded them, her glowing skin, and full lush lips.

He started to say something – he wasn't sure what – 'Hello,' 'You again' – something innocuous. It didn't matter. She walked straight past him into the sea.

For a moment he was stunned, but recovery was rapid. He turned around and watched her strike out toward a floating wooden platform. Without another thought he stripped off his shirt, threw it on the sand, and plunged into the sea after her.

She was a powerful swimmer and had a good lead on him. But with his highly personal erratic crawl he set off like a piston, and caught up before she was even half way. He swam alongside her. She didn't say anything. Neither did he.

It was late in the afternoon and the raft ahead of them loomed deserted.

He noticed her ears were pierced, as her head vanished and rose beneath the surface of the sea. She wore small diamond studs.

He noticed her arms. Strong and powerful as they cleaved the water.

He sensed adventure, knew anything was possible and didn't draw back. How many times in his life was he going to come across a woman like this?

Eden.

Eden who?

*

Lucky was enjoying the game. She had watched Lennie approach through hooded eyes. Remembered him from their abortive meeting in Vegas, and immediately wondered if maybe this was what she needed – a purely physical encounter with no entanglements. If he didn't back off like the last time.

Lennie Golden. She even remembered his name. A horny looking guy. Why not put him to the test? After all, fate had placed him on the same St Tropez beach as she, and getting even had always appealed. He would be the perfect person to use to equal the score with Dimitri – who was probably still fawning all over that awful Fern woman.

She rose and strolled casually toward him. He mumbled something as she passed. She ignored him and plunged into the sea knowing he would follow. *Don't talk. Don't spoil it*, she willed.

There was a wooden raft some way from the shore and she struck off toward it.

He was behind her.

If Dimitri thought – imagined – she was the kind of woman he could screw around on and get away with it, then he lived in a dream world. Lucky Santangelo could give as good as she got. And let nobody forget it.

The raft lay ahead, empty and inviting. What must it be like to be shipwrecked, cut off, alone in the world? She often felt alone in the world – Dimitri had done nothing to change that feeling.

They reached the raft together and hauled themselves aboard. He had caught her silent message and didn't say a word. The sun was low in the sky and people on the beach were beginning to pack up and go home. A lone water-skier passed in the distance, causing the raft to rock as the waves hit. Their eyes met, and as if by unspoken agreement they moved closer. She was staring at him with those crazy gypsy eyes – black and wildly sensuous – the signal was clear.

He wanted to know who she was. What she was doing here. Everything about her intrigued him. But the timing was wrong and he knew it. Which didn't mean he couldn't go along with the game.

He reached out and pulled her to him. She moved into his embrace as naturally as if they had known each other for years. Electricity sparked as they began to kiss, long lingering kisses, tongues entwined.

Their bodies were wet. Salty flesh crushed against salty flesh. He pressed his hands into the small of her back and let her feel his hardness.

She didn't draw away, but moved her hips slowly, suggestively. He ran his hands leisurely up her spine, felt for the end of her thick plait of hair, removed the rubber band and unplaited the luxuriant mane until it tumbled damply around her shoulders.

And all the while their lips were together, tantalizingly hot.

A motor boat passed nearby causing the raft to rock again. He held her tightly, expertly flicked open the clasp on her bikini top, let it drop, and felt the excitement of her bare breasts against his chest.

She trailed her hands very very slowly down his back, tracing patterns with her fingers, and when she reached the waistband of his shorts she drew her hands to the front and caressed his hardness through the material.

He groaned involuntarily, stepped back for a moment, and struggled out of his shorts, not caring if he was seen from the beach. Not caring about anything at all except this crazy real life fantasy.

Her hands were on him, caressing, stroking, driving him nuts.

Control, a voice screamed in his head. *Don't blow it.*

He reached for her breasts. Hard nipples, soft firm contours. Beautiful. Perfect.

He peeled the bottom of her bikini down and she stepped out of it.

They sank onto the cold wet surface of the raft, neither of them noticing the discomfort. There was nothing awkward about their lovemaking. He entered her smoothly, and she wrapped her long legs tightly around his waist and moved with him as if they had been together many times before. Instinctively she knew his rhythm and he knew hers.

He was iron hard, but surfing only. The perfect wave was yet to arrive, and when it did he wanted them to ride it together.

An elderly Frenchman in a bathing cap swam toward the raft. He paused to catch his breath before climbing up, saw the entwined couple, and swam away again, thankful his disapproving wife was not with him.

Lucky closed her eyes and gave herself up to the moment. She had known, when she first set eyes on Lennie Golden, that he would be a sensational lover. And he was. And it frightened her – because this was supposed to be a mindless revenge move, just something to get her own back on Dimitri. And yet . . . it was more – much more. It was body talk at its most eloquent, and the last thing she needed in her life was another relationship.

She felt the roller-coaster ride beginning. And she knew, without a doubt, that this was not just another two dollar trip. This was the big one, the double dipper, the whirl, the cartwheel twice over.

'Oh God!' she heard herself cry out. 'Oh *Jeeeesus*!'

And she was lost in sensation. Floating in paradise. Taken over by a throbbing release which sent her into spasms of delight.

Lennie felt the same way. The intensity and depth of his orgasm took him by surprise, leaving him shaken and drained. He lay on top of her for a moment, still joined, and stared into her eyes, so deep and full of secrets.

Who was she?

He had to know.

And yet . . . maybe her way was best. She was a woman of mystery, and obviously planned to stay that way. What was he going to say anyway? *I'd like to see you again.* Sure. *And I'll bring my wife.*

He rolled off her and groped for his shorts, thankful they hadn't fallen in the sea.

She sat up, reached for her bikini, and put it on.

The sun was setting, and a chill pervaded the air. Two beachboys were stacking mattresses on the nearly deserted beach, and in the distance a blonde girl jogged by the seashore with a white police dog.

Lucky bent forward, shook out her hair, and casually knotted it on top of her head. She looked at Lennie once, briefly, and in the softest of voices murmured, '*Sayonara*, friend.' Then she dived from the side of the raft gracefully, and the last he saw of her were her strong brown arms flashing from the sea as she swam toward the shore.

He waited ten minutes before he followed. By the time he reached the beach she was gone, and he realized he would probably never see her again.

One afternoon's fantasy . . . and he didn't even know her name.

Chapter 71

'We're havin' dinner with the Spanish pimp, an' Quinn. I think we got a deal.'

'When?' Eden asked quickly.

'Tonight,' Santino replied, belching and scratching his stomach.

Eden bit back a sharp complaint. Why did he always tell her these things at the last minute? It was a quarter to six – how the hell could she look her best when they were probably meeting in an hour?

She got out of bed and hurried into her marble bathroom. 'What time and where?' she called out, turning on the shower.

'I'm takin' ya to Chasens,' Santino announced. 'Look hot – not too hot, it's a classy joint.'

She gritted her teeth. He talked to her like she was some two-bit whore off the streets.

'Be ready by seven-fifteen. Zeko will drive ya. I gotta go home now – I'll see ya there.'

She didn't bother to reply. She was already under the shower washing off his smell, shampooing her hair, feeling for the golden triangle and bringing herself to the climax he never managed to give her.

She didn't need a lot of time to get ready. As a former model she had the drill down pat. Out of the shower, towel dry, plug in the heated rollers, splurge with the Estee body cream, spray on the Estee scent. Naked, she sat in front of her dressing table mirror, cleansed her face with cotton wool and astringent, applied moisturizer, skin-tone base, shading, powder, blusher, eye shadow, eye-liner, mascara, eyebrow pencil, lip-liner, lipstick and lip gloss.

The whole routine took her fifteen minutes, and the effect was dynamite.

Next she blow-dried her fine hair and placed long coils of it in the heated rollers.

All she had left to do was decide what to wear, and that always took time. A large walk-in closet led off from the bathroom, and it was filled with clothes. She strolled up and down trying to select the perfect outfit. Something that would suit Santino, Quinn (a weirdo if she'd ever seen one), Vitos, and, of course, Chasens. Choosing the right ensemble for a restaurant was of paramount importance.

Outside her bathroom window, hidden among the dense lush foliage, Zeko finished jerking off. He had practically given up normal sex. Getting off on his boss's girlfriend was the biggest kick of all.

He zipped up and returned to the house where he picked up a copy of *Auto Mechanic* and took it in the kitchen to read.

Eden selected a narrow black dress with a wide gold cinch belt. She pulled on black patterned pantyhose, stiletto heels, and a lacy bra. Then she removed the rollers from her hair and styled it.

She was ready at five after seven, and decided to arrive at Chasens early – hopefully before Santino. Even five or ten minutes of freedom was worth *something*.

Zeko – the big ox – was in the kitchen reading. She was surprised he *could* read.

'Let's go,' she announced impatiently.

'The boss says we leave at quarter past.'

'And *I* say we go now.'

She stared coldly at the hateful man, daring him to argue.

He didn't.

*

Home for Santino Bonnatti was a gated mansion in Bel Air. Once the residence of a silent screen star, it now housed the Santino chapter of the Bonnatti family. Donatella, Santino's wife, was a plain, grossly fat woman. She was a bride imported from Sicily eighteen years before, and her heart remained in the small village she had been plucked from.

There were four Bonnatti children ranging in ages from seven to seventeen, three girls (all unfortunately fat like their mother) and one boy (a replica of his father – with the added advantage of a full head of hair). The boy, named Santino junior, was the youngest child, and the spoiled favourite of both his mother and father – who vied to give him the most attention.

'Santino!' Donatella greeted him at the door of the mansion wringing her hands, her expressive eyes full of distress. 'Santino junior – he sick. He gotta de fever. He *very* sick.' She accused him with a look. 'Where you bin, huh? I try calla your business – nothin'. Where you bin?'

Santino nearly slipped on the polished wood floor in his haste to rush upstairs and view his 'very sick' son for himself. Donatella did have a tendency to melodramatize.

'I had a meetin',' he explained. Although explanations were not really necessary. He could do as he liked and they both knew it. So long as he sent money to her relatives, kept her and the children in the style they had grown accustomed to, and fucked her every couple of months. She was not demanding, but she did expect it every once in a while, and six times a year was not too bad.

She followed him upstairs, and was right behind him as he flung open the door to his son's bedroom.

'You see!' she crowed triumphantly.

Santino junior lay in the centre of his bed, pyjamaed and

flushed. A large screen television offered a Charles Bronson movie, and the room was extremely hot.

'Son!' exclaimed Santino, rushing to his bedside and placing a clammy hand on the boy's forehead.

'You see!' repeated Donatella. 'He's gotta de fever!'

*

Eden entered Chasens like a star. She asked the maitre d' for Mr Bonnatti's table. He had no knowledge of a reservation for Mr Bonnatti. She suggested the table might be under Mr Quinn Leech's name, or maybe even Vitos Felicidade.

'Ah, Mr Felicidade,' sighed the maitre d', impressed at last. 'This way, please.'

She didn't have to follow him far, because Vitos was seated at a booth in the front room – he was with his manager – no sign yet of either Quinn or Santino.

'Good evening,' Eden said graciously, as both men struggled to stand. 'Am I early? Or is everyone else late?'

'It seems you are on time, my lady,' crooned Vitos in his best English, executing a small formal bow. 'And you are . . .?'

Didn't he remember her?

She *certainly* remembered ***him***.

'Eden Antonio,' she said smoothly, not allowing her aggravation to show. 'We met in Las Vegas.'

'Yes, of course,' sighed Vitos, not remembering at all. He took her hand and bestowed a kiss. '*Enchanté*,' he murmured.

She fluttered her eyelashes, a move she would not have dared make with Santino present. 'Thank you,' she said demurely.

Vitos' manager thrust a hand in her direction. 'You're Quinn's lady, right?'

'No. I am not Quinn's lady,' she said shortly, furious at being mistaken for Quinn Leech's dull looking girlfriend. 'I was in Vegas with Mr Bonnatti discussing my role in "My Life As A Call Girl". I'm to star in the film, you know.'

She slid into the booth next to Vitos and ordered a Martini, not noticing that he and his manager exchanged puzzled looks.

'I understand Mr Bonnatti is negotiating with you about co-starring with me,' she said, determined that this time they would remember her. And how.

'We speak 'bout movie,' saiu Vitos apologetically, 'but no call wimmen's title.'

'What?' He was not easy to understand, but his broken English sounded charming.

'Vitos means that we *are* discussing a film for him to star in. It's called "The Singer",' said his manager.

'The Singer?' she asked blankly.

They were saved from answering by the arrival of Quinn Leech, alone and reeking of garlic and whisky. 'Hiya all,' he said and slid into the booth beside Eden, imprisoning her between himself and Vitos. 'Where's Santino?'

'He hasn't arrived,' replied Eden, stating the obvious. 'And what's all this about a film called "The Singer"? I thought we were talking to Mr Felicidade about "My Life As A Call Girl".'

'Rewrite,' said Quinn blithely.

'Rewrite?' screeched Eden.

Quinn nodded. 'I take it the sonofabitch didn't tell you?'

She shook her head while anger flooded her body.

'Listen,' said Quinn, whispering confidentially into her ear. 'You think Vitos Felicidade is gonna star in a movie with call girl in the title? We changed the concept. You'll read it. You'll love it.'

'Yes, but am I still in it?' she asked bitterly.

Quinn threw up his hands. 'That's not for me to know. I'm only the director.'

'Did Santino ever tell you this was supposed to be a starring vehicle for me?' she hissed.

'Never heard that,' said Quinn honestly, ordering a double shot of Jack Daniels.

Eden slumped into silence. The bastard! The bald hairy horny bastard! No wonder he told her never to discuss the movie with anyone but him. No wonder he told her the time was not right for her to talk to Quinn or Ryder or Paige or *anyone* about the project. He was stringing her along. He was fucking her with empty promises. She felt like primal screaming in the middle of Chasens. She felt like *killing* him.

A waiter brought a phone to the table. 'There's a call for Miss Antonio,' he said.

She took the phone, held it to her ear.

'What the frig didja leave the house early for?' complained Santino.

'Where are you?' she asked, her voice constricted.

'My boy is sick,' he said. 'He's got a fever. I can't leave him. If you hadn't left the house before I told you, I coulda stopped you from goin'.'

'I'm here now,' she said.

'I friggin' *know* that. An' I want ya outta there. Pronto. Tell 'em I can't make it, an' why. Lay it on thick – I don't want 'em thinkin' I'm backin' off the deal. An' then ya split, an' get the fuck home. Ya hear me?'

'I hear you.'

'Make an excuse. Ya got the rag on, a headache, anythin'. But I wancha outta there in five minutes. Got it?'

'Yes.'

'Notheeng wrong I hope,' said Vitos, as the waiter whisked the phone away.

'Mr Bonnatti cannot be with us tonight.' Eden toyed with her Martini glass. 'His son has a temperature, and he doesn't want to leave him. He hopes you will all understand.'

Everybody assured her they understood.

'He's such a loyal family man,' she added.

'Yeah!' agreed Quinn, and under the table his hand did exploratory surgery on her thigh.

She removed it. 'Mr Bonnatti requested that someone instruct his driver, Zeko, to take the rest of the evening off. Could we send that *personal* message from Mr Bonnatti out front?'

'No problem,' said Quinn.

'You, beautiful lady, weel stays?' inquired Vitos, his liquid eyes melting with hers.

'Absolutely,' she replied briskly. 'Mr Bonnatti insisted that I should.'

Chapter 72

Lucky raced back to the yacht. Dimitri and Francesca sat on an upper deck engrossed in each other and a game of backgammon, there was no one else around. Francesca wore a green sun-dress, and a matching bandana which almost hid her flaming red hair. Dimitri was still in khaki shorts and a sports shirt.

'I thought I was late for dinner,' Lucky said, out of breath.

Francesca ignored her. Dimitri glanced up briefly, said, 'Dinner is at eight,' and returned his attention to the game. No – *where have you been all day? Why are you late?* Not even a *how are you?* Any guilt she might have felt was washed away immediately.

'Where is everybody?' she asked.

'Ah ha . . . got you!' husked Francesca, making a key move on the backgammon board.

'You think so, woman?' roared Dimitri, countering with his own cleverer move. Their laughs intermingled.

Lucky felt the sharp stab of rejection she had known all her life. Fuck 'em. If they wanted each other so badly they were welcome.

'I'm going to shower,' she said stiffly.

Dimitri waved her away – a gesture which plainly stated *don't bother me, I'm busy*. 'Dinner is at eight,' he repeated.

'Can't wait,' Lucky murmured sarcastically.

She visited Roberto, who was playing in his yellow bathtub, content and happy, watched over by the ever-smiling CeeCee.

She hugged his wet body close to her T-shirt. 'Hiya baby gorgeous,' she sang. 'How's my boy? How's my kid?'

'Mama,' he chirped happily. 'Nice nice mama.'

'He's been so good today,' beamed CeeCee. 'This is one kid who *never* cries.'

'Just like mommy,' sighed Lucky softly.

'Huh?'

'Nothing.'

Back in Dimitri's masculine stateroom she stripped off her clothes and stood under a hot shower, closing her eyes as the water beat a soothing rhythm on her skin. For a moment she allowed herself to think of Lennie and their incredibly erotic and satisfying encounter.

This time he had gone along with her game. No corny lines or bullshit. Just wonderfully uninhibited silent sex.

She shivered. Sex hadn't felt that good since Marco . . .

*

Alice wanted to complain to Olympia. She knocked on her stateroom door late in the afternoon and caught her flinging things around the room in a fury.

'What's the matter, dear?' she asked, forgetting her own problems.

'Nothing,' scowled Olympia. 'What do *you* want?'

'A nice way to talk to your mother-in-law,' clucked Alice. 'I thought we were friends.'

'What?' snapped Olympia. She was in no mood to humour Lennie's eccentric mother.

Alice came right to the point. 'I'm very insulted,' she stated, picking at her nail polish.

'Why?'

'Am I, Alice Golden, former *star* of Las Vegas – Lennie inherited everything he knows from me – not good enough to sit at the dinner table with the likes of the hoi polloi?'

'Is that a question?'

'It's a statement, my dear. A statement.' She paused dramatically. 'I have shared meals with Kings, danced for Princes. What do you think I am – a *shlub* with no feelings?'

'Please, Alice. I have a hangover and a headache. What do you want?'

'To eat dinner with my own son.'

'You're here to be with Brigette,' Olympia pointed out.

'Does that mean I can't sit with Lennie? Brigette goes to

bed at eight. Am I supposed to stay below decks with the help?'

Olympia frowned. Where *was* Lennie when she needed him? 'I don't know,' she said irritably. 'Do what you like.'

A gleam of triumph filled Alice's watery eyes. 'Thank you, dear,' she said, already thinking up stories she could entrance the dinner guests with.

*

Gino did not like France. He did not understand the language. He found the people rude. It was too hot. He hated being confined on a boat. And he missed Paige.

Susan, social as ever, insisted they spend the day with friends of hers who owned a summer villa in the hills. The man was a film star. He had a rugged profile, yellowing teeth, and badly dyed black hair. The woman – his wife – was a sharp-tongued European who, in the course of an afternoon, trashed everyone she knew – including all her dearest friends.

Gino hated every minute. He told Susan so on the way back to the yacht.

'*I* had an amusing time,' she said.

'You wouldn't be so amused if y'could hear what that bitch is sayin' about you now,' he replied.

'What you are talking about?'

'Forget it.'

He knew there was no way he was going to last two weeks on *this* trip.

*

'My game,' husked Francesca.

'You always win' laughed Dimitri.

'How true.'

'We must get ready for dinner.'

'Yes.' She snaked a white hand to his cheek, her nails blood red and inches long. 'Why did you marry her, Dimitri? Why did you humiliate me?'

'Francesca – *you're* married,' he pointed out.

'It's nothing. Horace looks after things for me. It's a marriage of convenience.'

'Divorce him.'

'I can't. It would break his heart.'

'Then what are we discussing?'

'Your disloyalty.'

'Never.'

'Yes.'

'I married Lucky to give my son his rightful name.'

Lightly Francesca scratched her nails where she knew it would have the most effect. 'Now you can divorce her,' she suggested.

*

Having got rid of Alice, Olympia threw another fit. Where the hell was Lennie? She needed someone to scream at. What good was a husband if he wasn't around when you needed him?

She had a blinding, throbbing headache. Who wouldn't when the news of a half-brother was thrust upon her? Not to mention the fact that Dimitri had married Lucky Santangelo.

Lucky and Dimitri! Unbelievable! Ridiculous! Obscene!

She marched into the bathroom, went straight to her stash, and snorted the rest of her coke supply. Then she gulped a couple of Quaaludes and tried to decide what to wear to confront her latest step-mother.

Step-mother!

What a joke!

Lucky Santangelo!

Friend.

Some friend.

Chapter 73

Dimitri was an excellent host. His summer cruises were legendary. No expense was spared to make sure all his guests had a marvellous time.

Finishing his game of backgammon he hurried to shower and change his clothes, and was ready to greet his guests as they arrived on the upper deck for pre-dinner drinks. Lucky accompanied him. She looked particularly stunning in a Saint Laurent white tuxedo, her hair loose and wild. Gino stood alone at the bar. Lucky went over to him immediately.

'I gotta get outta here,' he announced.

'So do I,' she agreed.

'Hey – maybe I can come up with some family business that takes us both to New York. Y'know somethin', kid? I really miss the city.'

'I thought you loved Beverly Hills.'

'It's too slow for me. I've had it.'

'Really?'

'I need more action.'

'What about Susan?'

'I haven't told her, but I'm thinkin' of buyin' a place in New York.'

'And dividing your time?'

'Why not?'

'Sounds good to me.'

*

'We spent such an interesting day,' said Susan to the Contessa, scooping a healthy amount of Petrossian Beluga caviar onto a cracker and disposing of it in one mouthful.

'Did you?' replied the Contessa. '*I* was frightfully bored. I like to play baccarat. I can't wait until we arrive in Monte Carlo. I am simply desperate for the tables.'

'When my late husband, Tiny Martino, was alive, we used to visit Monte all the time,' enthused Susan, trying to impress. 'Tiny was a friend of the Rainiers, you know. He and Grace were *very* close.'

The Contessa raised a pencilled eyebrow. '*You* were married to Tiny?' she questioned.

'For over twenty five years,' Susan said proudly. And then she added coyly, 'I was a child bride you know.'

The Contessa smiled and patted her hand. 'Weren't we all, darling.'

Susan waited for her to remove the pressure of her rather warm hand, each finger loaded with impressive diamonds.

She didn't.

*

Olympia was angry because Lennie appeared to have vanished. She had no intention of sitting around. If he missed dinner it was his loss. Besides, she couldn't *wait* to see Lucky. Skinny, naive, little Lucky Santangelo. Former best friend. Former confidante. Ha! It never paid to be nice to people. They always took advantage of kindness and shafted you whenever the opportunity arose.

The very thought of Dimitri and Lucky in bed together was disgusting to her. She, Olympia, had taught Lucky everything she knew. When Lucky had arrived in Switzerland fifteen years ago she had never even been *kissed*! Olympia had educated her about men and life and how to have *fun*. Just look at the thanks she received.

She dressed in an expensive gold Ungaro outfit which would have looked sensational on a tall, flat-chested model. It did not suit Olympia at all. She applied heavy duty diamonds to her ears, fingers, and throat. Then she fluffed out her long blonde curls and set off for a face-to-face confrontation.

*

'I've never been to Paris,' Alice confided to Horace, a faraway look in her eyes.

'Haven't you?' He kept glancing over to see if Francesca appeared. She had forced him to go on ahead of her, claiming that he got in her way while she was trying to dress.

'Gay Paree,' sighed Alice. 'Ohh la la!' She snatched a hot canapé from a passing waiter. 'I shall probably go there with my son. He's very proud of me. It takes talent to know talent, and he knows.' She nodded to herself. 'Ah yes, he certainly knows.'

'I'm sure,' agreed Horace.

'Shortly I will be appearing on the "Merv Griffin Show." She munched contentedly on a stuffed olive. 'I love Merv. He's such a *warm* man.'

'Good.'

She leaned intimately toward him. '*Very* good,' she said, winking slyly. 'Very, very good.'

'Excellent.'

'Yes.'

'Yes.'

*

Olympia entered the bar. Paused. Look around. Spotted Lucky immediately. Did a double take. Could not believe her skinny little nothing friend had grown into such a beauty. And not an ounce of fat on the entire package.

Lucky saw her look, and for a moment their eyes met and they were kids again, playing hookey, smuggling boys into their dorm, and indulging in 'almost' – a game they thought they had invented.

All her life Lucky had been a loner. No girlfriends, no mother, no one to giggle or chatter with. Except once there had been Olympia.

She rushed across the room, arms outstretched.

Olympia backed off.

Instinctively Lucky knew she was not thrilled about the marriage, and who could blame her? It *was* kind of a crazy coincidence. She turned her outstretched arms into a pat on the shoulder. 'Olympia! God, it's been a long time. You look great.'

Olympia was at a loss for words. Too much coke was clogging her brain. She wanted to be cool and act like she didn't care, but she *did* care very much that Lucky had dumped her, and never tried to contact her, even when they reached adulthood and could have seen anyone they pleased.

'Little Lucky Saint,' she said coolly, using the name Lucky had been known by at school. 'You certainly grew up.'

'I should hope so!'

'You were always such a dumb jerk.'

'Thanks!'

'Does the truth hurt?'

Lucky lowered her voice. 'Let's not start off being hostile, huh?'

Olympia bridled, 'Who's hostile? Certainly not *me*. Why should *I* be hostile?'

Lucky was saved from answering by Francesca's entrance. She wore a red ball gown which matched her hair. Around her neck was a magnificent ruby necklace.

Horace cringed. He had never seen the necklace before. He knew it must be a gift from Dimitri, therefore it signalled the affair was still going strong.

'Damn!' he muttered.

'Has anyone ever told you that you look like Burgess Meredith?' Alice fluttered her false eyelashes. 'I always thought he was such an *attractive* man.'

*

Lennie hitched a ride back to the port with two sun-burned German homosexuals in a convertible. They didn't speak English. He didn't speak German. But a lot of polite nodding and smiling went on.

He skipped aboard the yacht and encountered Captain Pratt. 'Did you have a pleasant look around, sir?' asked the Captain.

Lennie didn't know if it was his imagination or not, but he could have sworn the man gave him a lewd wink. 'Thanks. Yes,' he replied.

'You *are* a bit late, sir,' the Captain added. 'They're just sitting down for dinner.'

'It'll take me five minutes to change. Can you get a message to my wife?'

'Certainly, sir.'

Was that another conspiratorial wink?

'I must say, sir. Your mother is a very fine woman.'

Oh, shit. The captain wanted to *schtupp* Alice. Sorry, my friend, you're about twenty years too old for the likes of Alice the Swizzle.

'Yeah,' said Lennie vaguely, and made a dash for it.

*

Polite conversations took place as servants tended table and fine wine was poured into silver goblets. Olympia found herself seated next to Gino Santangelo. She thrust her chest forward and flirted with him outrageously. He might be an old man, but if Lucky could have Dimitri, why couldn't she give Gino a tumble?

She leaned close to him. 'Betcha don't remember the last time we met,' she whispered.

He did remember. Only too well. It was a picture fixed firmly in his mind forever. Sixteen-year-old Olympia Stanislopoulos, her bare pink ass stuck in the air, as she concentrated on giving her boyfriend of the moment a blow job.

'You know somethin' – you're right, I *don't* remember.'

She pouted. 'Come *on*. How could you ever forget?'

He knew what he *did* want to forget. This trip. These people. Tomorrow he would arrange a cable summoning him urgently to New York.

*

Olympia had said, 'We dress for dinner,' whatever that meant. Reluctantly Lennie put on a suit. What bullshit. Why was he going along with it? One night was enough. From here on he planned to take Olympia off the boat to explore. There must be so many great restaurants around, and he had no intention of spending his vacation playing stuffed shirts with the rich folk.

He checked himself out in the mirror, and wondered if he had time for a joint. Reflected beside him he imagined he saw the girl from the beach. Dark, mysterious, sexy . . . He had always gone for blondes, but she made him forget every blonde he had ever known – even Eden.

Free at last?

Yeah.

Why hadn't he found out her name at least?

He loosened his tie, ran his hands through his hair, lit up a joint, took a couple of deep drags, and set off for dinner.

•

'Business is business,' Saud Omar said. 'And women are women. And never the two shall meet.'

'What antiquated crap!' exclaimed Lucky. 'Where have *you* been for the last fifty years?'

Saud blinked, unused to women answering back. Besides, he had not been talking to Lucky, he had been making a general remark.

'I agree with *you*, Saud,' Fluff squeaked. 'I *never* want to work. Never ever! Ugh!'

'And you'll never have to, pumpkin tush,' Jenkins Wilder joined in. 'Smart girlies never have to lift a finger.'

'Only their ass,' murmured Lucky.

Alice cackled.

Francesca threw Dimitri a simmering look.

Susan said, 'I think females should all learn domestic arts in school. Cooking, sewing, and general housekeeping.'

'How about screwing?' Lucky suggested. 'I mean, shit Susan, if you go to school to learn how to take care of a guy, you may as well learn to do it properly, don't you think?'

Dimitri gave Lucky a warning glare which she ignored.

Susan blushed beet red.

Gino said, 'Hey, kid . . .'

The Contessa laughed.

Olympia scowled. Skinny little Lucky had developed a mouth.

Lennie entered the room, saw Olympia, and headed straight for her.

'Where have you been?' she demanded crossly.

'Sorry I'm late. I couldn't get a ride back from the beach,' he explained.

'The beach!' Olympia sneered, as if it were a dirty word.

'Yeah, y'know. That's the place where the peasants hang out – not everyone has a yacht to throw themselves about on.'

'Very funny. Why don't you sit down.' She addressed herself to the table. 'I'd like you all to meet my husband – Lennie Golden.'

He saw an array of jewels and old men. He also saw Alice, which filled him with dismay.

'Now, let me see,' continued Olympia, playing the perfect hostess. 'This is Contessa Zebrowski and Saud Omar. Mr and Mrs Jenkins Wilder, Susan and Gino Santangelo, Francesca and Horace Fern, and you met my father earlier.' She paused, wondering if she could get away with snubbing Lucky. Too obvious. 'Oh, yes, and this is Lucky.' She refused to give her billing.

'My wife,' Dimitri said.

'Your wife,' Lennie repeated.

He stared at her. She stared back. It was as if time stood still.

Chapter 74

Returning to the real world was just what Steven needed. He had always resisted the temptation of working in a big expensive law firm – preferring instead to do time as an assistant DA and public prosecutor, where the money was by no means great. But he was getting older and wiser by the moment, and now security and making it seemed a whole new challenge. It wasn't as if he had to grab anything that came his way – Jerry assured him he could take his pick of the many rich clients who needed help.

'Just because they've got bread doesn't mean they're all bad,' Jerry explained amenably. 'Why don't I give you the Mary-Lou Moore case? She's the cute black actress on TV with the large family image. She's suing some porn magazine who just printed naughty photos of her taken before her big success. We go into depositions this week.'

Mary-Lou Moore. Steven had watched her show a few times. A funny sit-com set in Connecticut in which Mary-Lou played the adopted daughter of a white family. She was a kid, eighteen or nineteen tops, and very pretty.

'Am I going to get all the black clients?' he asked bitingly.

'Only if you want 'em. This is a juicy case. The put-upon heroine against the bad boys. Your kind of action.'

'She signed nothing. In fact she says the pix were taken by her boyfriend when she was fifteen, as a lark. You think we've got a case?'

'I would say we can't lose.'

'Go for the big bucks. These guys can afford it.'

After getting settled at the office, Steven informed the tenants who were renting his brownstone basement apartment that he planned to move back. His luck was in. The man, an engineer, had just landed a job in the Middle East, and was prepared to vacate at once. An adjustment on the rent took place (more borrowed money from Jerry – but it would soon be pay off time) and Steven moved in.

He really was coming home after three lost years. It felt wonderful.

*

Carrie met with Anna Robb, the ghost writer Fred Lester had recommended. She was a small precise woman of forty, who wore sensible shoes and big woolly sweaters. She appeared to be physically attached to her Sony tape recorder, which she switched on the moment she entered Carrie's life.

'Just talk,' she said reassuringly, 'about anything you like. I'll be able to extract exactly what we want.'

So Carrie talked. At first about clothes, then about style, and onto the subject of entertaining. Soon she was reliving her life with her first husband, Bernard Dimes. 'We had such interesting parties,' she recalled with pleasure. 'People from the arts, ballet stars, writers. Bernard knew everyone. He was a fascinating man.'

'How did you two meet?' Anna asked, sipping the lemon tea Carrie had fixed for her.

'I don't think I want to speak about that,' Carrie replied quickly.

Anna was a skilful enough interrogator to move on to something else immediately.

They did three taped sessions within a week – each one of four hours duration. By the end of that time Carrie felt at ease in Anna's company, and had told her all she could possibly dredge up on fashion, beauty, diet, and exercise. Anna said she had everything she needed.

'But it was easy!' Carrie exclaimed.

'For you,' Anna said. 'For me the real work comes now. First I write the book, then set it into sections. We go over what I have written to make sure you approve. Then we begin to choose the pictures and decide what new ones are to be taken.'

'It's so exciting!' Carrie said.

'If the book is a best seller it's the most exciting feeling in the world.' Anna smiled. 'If it flops, it's the worst.'

'How do we make it a best seller?' Carrie asked naively.

'If I knew that, Fred Lester would be working for me.'

'Tell me about him,' Carrie said. 'He seems such a nice man. Is he married?'

'Are you interested?' Anna teased.

Carrie was taken aback. Why on earth would she be interested? She had given up on men when she divorced Elliott Berkeley and now she was too old and set in her ways to start thinking of another relationship. Besides, if she did become involved with a man again she would have to be truthful about her past. And who would want her when they heard the truth?

No. Involvements were out. She had Steven back, thank God. She had a few friends. What more could she possibly want?

'Certainly not,' she said, primly.

'He's a widower,' Anna volunteered, packing up her tape machine. 'But I think I should warn you that he's living with a woman.'

Carrie was longing to ask who the woman was, but she

didn't pursue it. How embarrassing if Anna thought she desired her boss. Quickly she began to talk about something else.

Chapter 75

Lucky had no idea how she got through dinner. She tried to avoid looking at Lennie, and she knew he was attempting to do the same with her, but it was impossible. Their eyes met constantly and when they did the electricity they generated seemed to ignite the entire room.

Over the course of dinner they both found out a few things.

Lucky – who rarely read anything other than *Newsweek*, *The Wall Street Journal*, *Blues & Soul* and books, and *never* watched television, learned – mostly from Alice – who couldn't seem to stop talking, that Lennie had hit the big time, and was now a big personality and television star.

'Didn't you read about our wedding?' Olympia asked belligerently. 'We made world-wide headlines.'

'No. I didn't see it,' Lucky replied politely, causing Olympia to pout.

'What about my Lennie on the cover of *People*. Surely you saw that?' scolded Alice.

'Sorry,' apologized Lucky.

'*He* should have been sorry,' remarked Alice darkly. 'He left me out. But they'll be writing a piece about me soon. Probably not a cover, but you can't have everything in this life, can you, darling?'

Lennie learned just exactly who Lucky was. Not only was she married to Olympia's father, but she was Lucky Santangelo – *the* Lucky Santangelo who had canned his ass two years before at the Magiriano Hotel.

Suddenly everything fell into place. Now he knew why he had been fired so abruptly and run out of town like bad eggs.

She had wanted to get laid.

He hadn't obliged.

Get rid of the sonofabitch. He could just imagine her giving Matt his orders.

With good reason he was furious.

'Are you the same Lennie Golden who just headlined at my hotel?' Gino asked.

'Yeah,' Lennie replied. What was this? Family week? Lucky with her father. Alice sitting at the table – the original proud parent. Christ! He felt like he was in the middle of a bad dream.

'You broke house records,' Gino said. 'I told Matt I want you back whenever you can make it. In fact I asked him to work out a deal with your agent – like you do a week for us every couple of months. Exclusive.'

Lucky had not realized Gino still kept an eye on things, she had thought he collected the money and that was it.

Lennie Golden headlined *her* hotel and she hadn't even known. She felt like a fool.

It's not your hotel any more, an inner voice reminded her. *You sold out, ran out. Why should you have known? Why should you even care?*

Yes, goddamn it. Why should she care? Who was Lennie Golden in her life anyway? So she had balled him – big deal. Sex was sex, and it was unfortunate that she had ever set eyes on him again.

Oh yeh?

Yeh.

•

After dinner several of the guests wished to go ashore nightclubbing.

'I want to go,' Olympia announced to Lennie. She was nicely coked up and ready to fly all night.

He, on the other hand, was beginning to feel the effects of non-stop travelling, not to mention the tension of sitting through dinner with Lucky just across the table. 'I'm gonna check out,' he said.

'Like hell you are,' Olympia replied crossly. 'You've been checked out all day while *I've* been stuck here. We are going nightclubbing, so jump to it.'

'Don't talk to me like that,' he said angrily.

'I'll talk to you any way I like,' she sneered.

He stared at the woman he had married. She had small blue eyes in a puffy pink face. Her painted lips curled derisively, and her blonde curls were drooping. Yes. Jess was definitely right. Insanity had struck.

'Listen,' he said, his voice low and even. 'Talk to who the fuck you want that way – but don't *ever* talk to me like shit. You got it?'

She refused to be intimidated. She tossed her hair back. 'I take it you don't wish to come,' she said haughtily. 'Well, *I'm* going, with or without you.'

'Have a wonderful time.'

'Don't think I won't,' she said, flouncing off.

Across the other side of the room, Lucky pleaded a headache to Dimitri, who was only too delighted.

Francesca, of course, was ready, willing and able. She did not consult Horace on his preference. 'You'll stay here,' she informed him. 'You know how you hate nightclubs.'

Since no one was inviting Alice, she put on a brave front. 'I'll look after Horace,' she volunteered.

Francesca ignored her. Francesca had a habit of ignoring most people with the exception of Dimitri.

Jenkins and Fluff Wilder elected to go. So did Saud and his Contessa. Susan said yes. Gino said no. She was tempted to take off without him, but he didn't suggest it, so she stayed – reluctantly. The Contessa was such an interesting woman, she couldn't wait to find out more about her.

As soon as the nightclubbers departed, Gino said goodnight, and he and Susan retired. Lucky felt her eyes drawn toward Lennie. He returned her gaze. Alice was regaling Horace with stories of Las Vegas. She was in her element with a captive audience of one and limitless supplies of Grand Marnier – her favourite tipple. Lennie gestured imperceptibly toward the door.

Lucky nodded her agreement. 'Goodnight, all,' she said quietly, and was gone.

Lennie waited a beat of ten, then he too rose.

'Oh, dear!' exclaimed Alice, with a girlish giggle. 'Are you leaving us alone? I'm not sure I can be responsible for my actions if I'm left alone with such an *attractive* man!'

Lennie did not know which he hated most. The cloying mother or the flirtatious ingenue.

Out on deck he looked for Lucky. She was leaning against the rail smoking a cigarette, her eyes dark and watchful as he approached.

'It's a smaller world than we think,' she said in a low voice. 'We should have left it the way it was in Vegas. Less complicated.'

He had plenty to say to her – like why did you have me fired, for starters. But words were elusive. He just wanted to hold her.

She dragged deeply on her cigarette, then flicked it over the edge. Without another word, as if by mutual agreement, they fell into each other's arms like it was the most natural thing in the world. He was ready for her at once, all thoughts of tiredness and tension gone forever.

She kissed him with her lips, her tongue, her hands caressing his face, then moving down his body with indecent haste.

He returned her kisses, slipped his hands beneath her white tuxedo, and freed her breasts from the confines of the scant silk top. 'I want you,' he muttered. 'All the time, everywhere. I want you.'

Weakly she tried to push him away. She had no desire to tell him to get lost. He awakened feelings in her long dormant. Sexually he turned her on to a degree she had forgotten existed. He was a dangerous ride, and she couldn't seem to stop herself from taking it.

Silently they kissed and caressed until it was his turn to push her away. His voice was strangled. 'What are we playing here, cocktease?'

'I never tease,' she said, unzipping his pants and sinking to her knees. 'Never.' And her mouth was on him, taking him to heaven and back and swallowing the evidence.

'Oh, Jesus!' he exclaimed. He had experienced good sex, bad sex, mediocre sex. He had *never* experienced sex as erotic and exciting as Lucky Santangelo.

'I thought about doing that to you all through dinner.' Her eyes gleamed. 'Sort of like a farewell present.'

'Hey, lady – if that was goodbye, I can't wait to see the way you say hello!'

She didn't laugh. 'It *was* goodbye. Neither of us is looking for trouble. Today was a dream . . . a fantasy . . . Now we go back to real life.'

'Are you kidding?' He gripped her by the arms. 'Do you love the old guy you're married to, or did you marry him for his money?'

'That's not your concern,' she said sharply. 'And while we're asking questions, why did *you* do the deed with Olympia? Was it her sunny personality that hooked you? Or her astronomical bank balance?'

He grabbed her urgently, bending her backwards while bringing his head down to her breasts.

'No!' she commanded.

'Yes,' he insisted. 'Oh, yes.'

She lost herself in his arms. Something was happening. A passion she hadn't felt since Marco. And Marco had been dead five years . . .

She was strangely frightened and yet exhilarated at the same time. All reason deserted her as he crushed her to him. And she wanted him again.

Captain Pratt, crouched on all fours on an upper deck, nearly fell over the edge. The rich! They were no different from anyone else. He wondered what Mr Stanislopoulos would have to say about this little lark?

What *could* he say? That very afternoon Dimitri Stanislopoulos had taken the ugly Fern woman to his study and stayed in there for over an hour with the shades pulled down and a DO NOT DISTURB sign on the door. No wonder his wife was randy, she probably never got anything from the old Greek – he was too busy giving it all to his girlfriend.

Captain Pratt stood up and brushed himself off. He wondered how much he could sell his story for. The English newspapers loved scandal and gossip – especially about the super rich. The *News of the World* or The *Sunday Mirror* would pay a fortune for some of his stories. Not to mention the *Enquirer* or the *Star*.

Yes. Captain Pratt reckoned that when *he* was ready to retire he had his nest egg waiting.

*

'We're crazy,' Lucky said, finding her abandoned clothes and struggling into them. 'Absolutely crazy. Anyone could have stumbled across us. This yacht is crawling with servants. We're *crazy*. I mean it.'

'You don't have to keep on saying it. I'm convinced.'

She turned to face Lennie defiantly. 'This is sex, just sex. You *do* know that, don't you?'

He returned her gaze. 'I don't know about you, but my marriage was over before it began. I marriéd Olympia one wild night in Vegas at the Wee Wedding Chapel of Love and Honour – can you believe it?'

She nodded. 'I know it well. It's the place chorus girls drag out of town mustangs who've scored more than a hundred grand on the crap tables.'

'You *could* say that I scored, but for all the wrong reasons. I was stoned out of my head, recovering from bitch of the century, and anxious to destroy myself. You get the picture?'

'I'm beginning to.'

'You – are probably the woman I've been looking for all my life. Only I got sidetracked by a million blondes.'

'Great sex does not a relationship make,' she observed wisely.

'But it sure beats the hell out of lousy sex.'

'True.'

'I only speak the truth.'

'When it suits you.'

'What do you mean by that?'

'C'mon, Lennie. You're a lady-killer, a hotshot lover-boy. You're not even my type.'

'And what makes you think you're mine?'

They both burst out laughing.

She touched his cheek lightly and couldn't stop herself

from saying, 'Lennie Golden, I don't know what's going on here, but I think something's happening.'

'Like a thunderbolt,' he responded.

'A flash of lightning.'

'Not just sex.'

'Nope.'

'More.'

'Right.'

'Much much more.'

'You said it.'

'And we don't even know each other.'

She stared at him. So many feelings all at once.

Before she could think of what to do or say next, Alice and Horace stumbled upon them.

'Oh!' exclaimed a startled Alice, adding a delicate hiccough. 'What are you two doing out here?'

Horace shuffled uncomfortably.

'Playing tennis,' Lennie said dryly.

Alice giggled. 'Saint Troopo is a lovely place,' she trilled, and hiccoughed again. 'So very . . . tropical.'

'St Tropez,' murmured Lucky.

'Horace is showing me the boat,' Alice offered, staggering slightly, and clutching the railing for support.

'How nice,' said Lennie sarcastically.

'Come along, Horace,' flirted Alice. 'I want to see the lifeboats. I can't swim y'know, so I must make sure everything is shipshape and ready for action.' Shrieking with laughter, she dragged a reluctant Horace off.

'My mother!' Lennie said dourly. 'The last of the all-time great swingers.'

'Does she embarrass you?'

'I'm too old to be embarrassed.'

'How old *are* you?'

'Thirty. And you?'

'I'm going to join you at that illustrious milestone in two days. It's the official beginning of being a grown up, isn't it? The end of the frivolous twenties.'

'No more outdoor fucking, huh?'

'It's not something I make a habit of.'

He gripped her by the shoulders. 'What are we going to do, Lucky?'

'About my birthday?'

'Don't be flippant.'

She shrugged impatiently. 'I don't plan to screw up anything because of you. I've told you what I think. We say goodbye and pretend nothing happened.'

'Just like that, huh?'

'I can do it if you can. Easily.'

'Oh,' he said acidly. 'Your solution to everything, right? Just blank it out. Is that why I had my ass run out of Vegas – so you could pretend our little scene never happened?'

'What was I supposed to do? Keep you around to remind me of our one night of nothing?'

'You don't can somebody just because they won't sleep with you.'

'I can do without the lecture, thank you.'

'I'm trying to teach you something.'

'Teach *me*.' She raised her voice. 'Teach *me*. Ha!'

'Don't yell.'

'Who's yelling?' she yelled.

The low throb of a motor boat announced the arrival back of the nightclubbers.

'Christ!' Lennie exclaimed in disgust. 'When am I going to see you again?'

'Tomorrow. At breakfast, lunch, *and* dinner. Unless one of us takes off there's going to be no avoiding each other.'

'You know what I mean.'

She was already moving toward the stairway. 'I gave you my goodbye present, Lennie. Let's just leave it that way.'

They both had a feeling it was impossible.

Chapter 76

Eden had every intention of ending up in the sensuous embrace of Vitos Felicidade. If she was going to stray it might as well be into the arms of the popular Spanish lover. However, sometimes the best laid plans go astray, and as the evening wore on she found herself increasingly drawn to Quinn Leech. He was a heavily bearded man in his fifties, cadaverously thin, with lecherous eyes and pawing hands. But he was a film director, and therefore he had the edge. She had seen several of his movies. Strange commercial thrillers, with more than a healthy dose of sex and violence. He liked ripping women to pieces – on screen. Feminists enjoyed ripping him to pieces – in print. His last two movies had been box office disasters. Once he had been 'a young hot director'. Now he was just marking time until his next big hit. The studios were off him, so when his old friend Ryder Wheeler had approached him about doing a movie financed by 'connected' money – he had agreed immediately. What did he care where the money came from?

Ryder had warned him up front, 'Stay away from Bonnatti's girlfriend,' he had said. 'Don't fuck with the paid help.'

But Quinn never had liked being told what to do.

They rolled out of Chasen's before midnight. Vitos climbed into his limousine with his manager, and bid Eden and Quinn a polite goodnight.

'Schmuck!' Quinn muttered as the limo slid off along Beverly Boulevard.

'Don't you like him?' Eden asked.

'What's to like or dislike? He's an empty canvas.'

She tapped her long nails against the small gold purse she was carrying and waited for him to proposition her. She had already decided to say yes.

'Where's your car?' he asked.

'Don't you remember? We sent the driver home.'

'*You* sent the driver home.'

The doorman appeared with a black Porsche.

'Can you give me a ride?' she asked quickly.

'The best you ever *had*, baby!' Quinn boasted.

He lived in the Hollywood Hills on Laurel Canyon. A black leather house in a jungle of plants.

He drank Chivas Regal from the bottle, ripped off his clothes – requested that she strip very, very slowly, and then couldn't get it up.

He suggested an alternative, a black hi-tech vibrator kept lovingly in a black leather case. And the company of his resident girlfriend who was asleep upstairs.

'Count me out,' said an offended Eden, and called a cab.

When she left he was snoring on the couch. She couldn't understand why she had chosen him over Vitos.

Zeko was waiting for her when she arrived home. 'The boss is gonna bust ya ass,' he crowed, rubbing his bald head.

'Only if you tell him,' she said shortly. 'And *if* you tell him, I shall be forced to mention how you crouch out in the bushes watching me, and jerking off when I bathe and dress.'

Her threat worked. Zeko never said a word.

When Santino appeared at the house the next day Eden told him she had stayed for dinner at Chasens.

'Why'd'ya do that?' he demanded, a muscle in his cheek twitching uncontrollably. 'When I told ya not to.'

'For you,' she replied calmly – thinking to herself that if the sonofabitch didn't come through with the movie soon, she was leaving. 'It would have looked bad if I'd left. As if we didn't care.'

Santino's eyes bulged angrily. 'When I tell ya to do somethin' – ya *do* it, get me? Whaddya think ya are, a partner?'

'Quinn Leech told me there's been a rewrite, and that the film is now called "The Singer",' she said tightly.

'He told ya that, did he?'

'Yes he did.'

'Friggin' asshole. He's got a big mouth.'

'Why didn't *you* tell me?' She glared at him accusingly.

'I gotta keep tellin' ya every little thing?'

'Rewriting the film and giving it a new title are hardly little things.'

Santino paced the room. 'Dumb cooze,' he spat. 'I need naggin' – I can get it at home. I come over here t'relax.'

Eden was not sure how far she could push it. But she had caught him off guard, so why not go all the way? 'I want to see the new script,' she said insistently. 'I want to see what's happened to my part. You promised me this was *my* film, *my* vehicle. Quinn Leech doesn't even know I'm supposed to be the star.'

His first blow struck her on the cheek.

'You bas –' she began.

His second blow knocked her to the ground. 'Doncha go givin' *me* orders,' he growled. 'I told ya to shift your ass outta there last night. But no, y'couldn't do *that*. Y'had t'stay around askin' questions – makin' me look like some stupid shithead with a ball breakin' girlfriend. Y'do that again an' ya out.'

She began to cry, more out of frustration and anger than anything else. 'Maybe that's what I want,' she sobbed. 'To get away from you.'

He glared at her with small mean eyes. 'When I'm ready,' he said slowly. 'Only when *I'm* ready.'

Chapter 77

Dimitri was planning a party. A big one. Lucky didn't know if it was out of a sense of guilt or what, but there was no deterring him from celebrating her birthday in style. She decided there was nothing to do except go along with it, and then she would leave. Gino had already arranged for a cable to summon him to New York for a business meeting.

'You'll come with me,' he told Lucky. 'You can say we have to meet with lawyers on Vegas stuff.'

She wanted to get away. It was bad enough before, but now, with the added complication of Lennie, it was impossible. Why weren't things simple anymore? Why did she look at Lennie and want to fly? Why did she look at him five minutes later and never want to set eyes on him again? She didn't understand what was going on. Lennie Golden was *not* her type. It was just sex. And yet . . .

She thought about Marco, they had spent one glorious

unforgettable night together. Then he was gunned down. She *never* wanted to experience that kind of heartbreak and loss again.

Lennie belonged to Olympia anyway. Plump, petulant Olympia, who treated her as if she was one of Dimitri's temporary girlfriends instead of his wife. She had tried to talk to her in private. Olympia brushed her aside with a caustic, 'How would you feel if I went to bed with *your* father?'

Lucky had to admit the idea was repellent.

It did not escape her attention that Olympia flirted outrageously with Gino at every given opportunity. He appeared not to notice.

The yacht sailed for Cannes, where the party was to take place. Lucky lay out by the pool watching CeeCee teach Roberto to swim. Brigette kept jumping in and splashing him in the face. CeeCee told her off, and the child yelled insults. 'Dirty black pig,' she chanted. 'Dirty! Dirty! Dirty!'

Lucky jumped up and whacked the little girl on the bottom.

Brigette looked at her for one horrified moment, and then burst into loud, phony tears.

'Cut it out, kid,' said Lucky. 'You don't have an audience.'

Brigette stopped crying abruptly. 'I hate dirty black people,' she said spitefully.

'Why?' asked Lucky calmly.

'Because, because, because . . .' She screwed up her pretty little face. '. . . because mama does!' she ended triumphantly.

'Not a good enough reason.'

The child stuck a thumb into her mouth.

'You're too old for that!' Lucky exclaimed.

'I'm not! I can do what I want.'

'Dirty baby pig!' Lucky chanted jokingly. 'Dirty! Dirty! Dirty!'

Brigette scowled. 'I hate you,' she said.

'No you don't,' replied Lucky briskly. 'You simply do not understand me.'

Brigette retreated to the other end of the pool, where Nanny Mabel sat knitting.

'Spoilt brat!' muttered CeeCee.

'Neglected brat, more like,' observed Lucky. 'I have not seen her mother pay one bit of attention to her. She just pats her occasionally like a puppy. The kid is screaming out for attention.'

'I'll give her attention,' grumbled the usually smiling CeeCee. 'I'll whip her butt!'

'I already did. It won't make any difference. She needs love.'

For a moment Lucky recalled her own childhood. She knew what it was like to be alone and unloved.

She had survived. No analysts for Lucky Santangelo – but she could see if Brigette didn't get help, the kid was in trouble.

Lennie appeared at lunchtime. They scorched each other with searing looks, but Olympia was right behind him. It was as if she sensed the electricity in the air and was not about to let it spark. She threw Lucky a vague hello, blew a kiss in Brigette's direction, and headed for the upper deck. 'Come on,' she called to Lennie.

'I'm taking a swim before lunch,' he said.

'Take it afterwards,' she ordered impatiently.

'I'm taking it now.'

'Oh, very well. Hurry up.' She vanished from sight.

He looked at Lucky. 'How are you today?'

She returned his gaze and was almost lost in his lazy green eyes. 'I'm okay.'

He quickly checked out the pool activity. Two nannies and two kids.

'I think I miss you,' he said, very quietly.

Brigette clambered from the pool and ran over to him. She flung her wet body possessively against his. 'Do you like *black* people?' she asked loudly.

CeeCee glared at her.

Lennie assessed the situation at a glance. 'I like green people, orange people, fat people, thin people. Sure I like black people. How about you?'

'I dunno.' Her mouth drooped. She had hoped he would take her side. 'Can you swim underwater? Can you teach me?' she begged.

He glanced at Lucky. She was playing with Roberto in the shallow end. 'Come on, pretty girl,' he said, swinging Brigette in the air. 'I'll teach you to be a fish. How's that?'

She squealed with excitement, wriggled free and jumped into the pool with a splash. 'Hurry up!' she commanded. 'Hurryup! Hurryup!'

He made a racing dive from the side, churned the length underwater, and surfaced next to Brigette. She climbed aboard his shoulders giggling, and he transported her around the pool.

'Me!' yelled Roberto. 'Me! Me!'

Lennie dropped Brigette off and placed Roberto on his back.

'Careful!' Lucky admonished.

'Hey, lady,' he winked. 'I'm an expert with kids.'

She met his eyes and warmth flowed between them.

For once Lucky felt unsure about what was happening. Her thing with Lennie was sex – pure sex. And yet why did she thrill to see him? Why was she shivering – ever so slightly?

He wasn't even her type. He wasn't Marco. His hair was dirty blond, his looks more Redford than Pacino. His eyes were green – killer green.

She watched him play with the kids. They screamed with laughter as he shared his attention between them. Roberto giggled uncontrollably as Lennie tossed him in the air. Dimitri, Lucky noticed, had little time to play with his son. Plenty of time for Madame Fern though.

She frowned. Of all the mistakes she had made in her life, marrying Dimitri was probably the biggest.

*

The night of the party was perfect. A clear sky filled with stars, no breeze, no humidity. The yacht, decorated with a thousand fairy lights, looked incredible. Round tables festooned with fresh flowers were set on the lower deck for a hundred guests, and on the upper deck a five piece combo played romantic ballads and soft rock.

Ceremoniously Dimitri presented Lucky with her birthday present just before the outside guests were due to arrive. A square leather box lined with plush velvet. A Van Cleef and Arpel insignia. And in the middle of the box a magnificent necklace of perfect diamonds and glittering emeralds set in white gold, with matching pendant earrings.

'Gorgeous,' purred the Contessa, who knew a thing or two about jewels.

'So lovely!' sighed Susan, thinking Gino's gifts seemed paltry by comparison.

'*Wowee!* Heavy duty!' from Fluff.

'It's beautfiul,' Lucky exclaimed, lifting the necklace from the box. 'Thank you, darling.' She kissed Dimitri chastely on the cheek. He smiled at the assorted gathering.

Francesca glared.

Olympia pouted.

Then there were other presents to open. A pair of heavy silver frames from the Contessa and Saud. A solid gold travelling clock from Jenkins and Fluff. An ugly silk shirt from the Ferns – several sizes too large. Nothing from Olympia. A cashmere sweater from Susan, and a small leather box from Gino. 'Somethin' I picked out – on my own,' he said in an embarrassed voice. 'If y'don't like it, y'don't have to wear it.'

She opened the box slowly. Gino hadn't remembered her birthday in years. Inside was a pavé diamond panther brooch studded with cabachon rubies and emeralds. It was the most exquisite piece of jewellery she had ever seen. Totally original, and absolutely her style. 'I *love* it,' she said softly, thrilled that he had chosen it himself. 'It's just great! I *really* love it!' She grabbed him in a hug.

'I love *you*, kid,' he said, very quietly. 'Happy birthday.'

Soon the outside guests began to arrive, most of them bearing gifts which were placed in a huge pile to be opened later.

Lucky was wearing a scarlet silk jersey dress which skimmed her body to the ground, and was slit at the front. She put on her new necklace and earrings, and pinned the panther brooch to the flimsy material. She looked darkly exotic with her hair piled on top of her head and a deep suntan. She circled the party. She played the role. She was Mrs Stanislopoulos to the hilt – aware it was only a temporary position.

Lennie hung back and watched. The fantasy had become a reality, and she was under his skin with a vengeance.

He caught up with her at the bar, and eased himself between a boring conversation she was having with a soignee blonde in a million dollars' worth of diamonds. 'I miss you,' he whispered.

She felt a shiver of anticipation. The blonde moved off.

'I'm horny, lonely and screwed up,' he continued. 'And this you are *not* going to believe, but I think I'm in love.'

She kept her tone light. 'Anyone I know?'

He touched her arm. 'How do *you* feel?'

'Married,' she replied flatly. 'And so are you.'

'I'm leaving Olympia,' he said quickly. 'As soon as I get back. How about you and Dimitri?'

'I don't know,' she replied honestly.

'What do you mean, you don't know? You *are* going to divorce him, aren't you?'

She resented the question. What business was it of his? 'I don't think I mentioned I was planning on doing any such thing,' she said coldly.

He touched her necklace contemptuously. 'I guess that kind of little bauble *would* make it difficult to come up with an answer.'

She was suddenly furious. 'Are you implying I'm staying with him for his *money*?'

'Give me a better reason.'

'Fuck you!' she exploded.

He wanted to defuse her anger, 'I wish you would.'

She refused to become any further involved. 'Get lost, asshole.'

Olympia walked into their conversation. Her cheeks were flushed, her breasts bulging from a low-cut yellow dress which made her look like an over-ripe banana. She was also stoned – but not mellow. And drunk – but not happy.

'You two really seem to have hit it off,' she slurred. 'What are you talking about?'

'Nothing much,' Lennie said.

'She called you an asshole,' Olympia's small eyes glinted with jealousy. 'It must have been *something*.'

'I told her a bad joke.'

'*All* your jokes are bad.'

'Thanks a lot.'

'You're a lousy comedian. You ever seen him do anything, Lucky? He stinks.' She giggled.

'As a matter of fact,' for some unknown reason Lucky found herself springing to his defence. 'I've seen Lennie on stage and I think he's brilliantly innovative.'

'*Where* have you seen him?' Olympia demanded hotly.

'I owned a hotel in Vegas once, the Magiriano. Lennie appeared in the lounge.'

'So you two met before?'

They both replied at once.

'Yes,' said Lucky.

'Not really,' said Lennie.

'What did you do, screw each other?' Olympia sneered with drunken insight.

'You're bombed,' Lennie said quickly, putting his arm around her shoulders.

She shrugged him away. 'Don't give me that solicitous husband crap just because I hit pay dirt. You probably *did* screw her. I understand if it wore pants and moved she fucked it.'

'I thought that was you,' said Lucky icily.

'*I* never had to search it out,' claimed Olympia. 'I can remember when you and I were in the South of France – on the run from school. Nobody even *looked* at you. You couldn't find a boyfriend if you stood on your head.'

'I didn't know you two were at school together,' Lennie said, trying to change the subject.

'Shut up, asshole,' Olympia said fiercely. 'I am allowed to call you asshole, aren't I?' she added sarcastically. 'Or is that a privilege reserved only for little Lucky Saint?'

He fixed her with a look which said more than words, and walked away.

'Well?' Olympia demanded belligerently of Lucky. '*Did* you fuck him?'

'Hey,' Lucky replied coolly. 'If I had, I wouldn't tell you. And if I hadn't, the same applies.' She turned her back and vanished into the heat of the party.

'Uptight bitch!' Olympia screamed after her. 'I know all about you. I know where you're coming from. Don't think you fool me with your airs and graces. You're street scum, just like your gangster father!'

'Olympia!' A harsh voice, a heavy hand. 'Do not disgrace yourself this way. Go to your stateroom until you are fit to be seen.' Dimitri's face was a thunder mask. He summoned a servant. 'Take Miss Stanislopoulos to her room. Feed her coffee until she is sober. I will not tolerate this behaviour.'

Olympia went meekly. She needed more than a joint and a few glasses of champagne – she needed cocaine and she needed it badly.

Chapter 78

It was hot in New York, the streets were awash with tourists, and the residents only survived because of air-conditioning. The offices of Myerson, Laker, and Brandon were on Park Avenue in a ritzy building. Steven was appointed a large corner office with all home comforts. A fridge, a television and video recorder, a stereo set, and a tape machine. 'Why not be able to relax?' Jerry said affably. 'I think a good working environment makes for good workers.' His own office was more like an apartment, with a small seductive bedroom leading off it in case he wished to spend the night.

'You know Jerry,' Sam Laker, one of the partners confided. 'He wants it just in case.'

'In case of what?' Steven inquired.

Sam winked knowingly. 'In case he needs to entertain a client.'

Steven reflected on how different it was to the working space he was used to as an assistant DA. Well, things were different now. He was in business to make money, just like Jerry. To hell with being a do-gooder.

His first client was Mary-Lou Moore. She was prettier than she appeared to be on television. She had waist length black hair, widely spaced brown eyes, and a devastating smile. She travelled with an entourage that consisted of her mother, her Aunt – who was also her manager, and her boyfriend, a white kid with frizzy hair and a tendency to pop bubble gum.

After an initial chat Steven got the distinct impression Mary-Lou would have nothing to say while her entourage was present.

'I'd like to speak to Mary-Lou alone,' he said formally.

The mother looked at the aunt. The aunt looked at the boyfriend. They all looked at Mary-Lou, who nodded her permission. When they had all departed, Steven said, 'Tell me about it.'

She shrugged, trying to be cool. But when she began to speak about the outrage, the humiliation and the fury the publication of the nude pictures had caused her, she seemed nothing so much as a gauche teenager. 'These scummy guys who put out these magazines shouldn't be allowed to get away with this kind of rip-off,' she said. 'Okay, so it wasn't too bright of me to pose for the pictures in the first place, but I was only fifteen – and foolin' around with my boyfriend. Did I know he was gonna *keep* them – and *sell* them?' She set her pretty chin at a determined angle. 'I want to sue.'

'It'll take time.'

'I don't care.'

'Their lawyers will defend the case. They'll try to discredit you in any way they can.'

'I'm ready.'

'You'll be involved in depositions, postponements – and finally you'll have your day in court.'

'That's what I want.'

'We're embarking on a journey. Once we get on the train, there's no getting off.'

'Go for it, man!'

After she left he picked up the offending magazine – a glossy porno rag called *Comer*. Mary-Lou was featured on six pages. The pictures were clearly not the work of a professional, but whoever had captured the fifteen year old had done a thorough job.

He had the name of the boyfriend from her past, the publishers of the magazine, and the distributors. As far as Steven could tell, she had a good case against all of them.

*

Anna Robb diligently worked at her typewriter. She had already completed four chapters of *The Carrie Berkeley Book of Beauty and Style*. It was going well.

She yawned and stretched. A break was most definitely in order, she decided, as she walked into the living room of the Manhattan apartment she shared with her lover. He was asleep on the couch, glasses on the end of his nose, pages from a manuscript scattered on the floor.

She gathered them together and woke him gently.

'I fell asleep,' he explained superfluously.

She glanced at the Cartier watch he had bought her for Christmas, and was surprised to find it was past twelve.

'It's late,' she said. 'Shall I make us some cocoa?'

He rose from the couch. 'I can't think of anything I'd like better.'

'You go to bed, I'll bring it in.'

'Don't forget the chocolate biscuits.'

'As if I would.'

He was watching the end of the 'Tonight Show' when she

entered the bedroom carrying a tray with two steaming cups of cocoa and a packet of English biscuits.

'I've been working on the Carrie Berkeley book,' she said.

He broke open the biscuits. 'How's it going?'

She perched on the end of the bed, a small birdlike woman with plain features and a warm smile. 'Very well. I think it will be a winner.'

'I certainly hope so.'

'I'll tell you something, though.'

'What?'

'There's another story under all the gloss and glitter.'

He stared at the television. 'There is?'

'Oh, yes. Definitely.' Anna nodded. 'Carrie Berkeley has a *real* story to tell. You know how I can sense these things.'

He nibbled on a chocolate biscuit. 'You're a regular Sherlock Holmes,' he commented.

'No. I just have good instincts. Plus I read between the lines and fill in the gaps.' She paused, and allowed her attention to be caught by an animal trainer showing Johnny Carson a small frisky animal. 'I'd like to discuss an autobiography with her. What do you think?'

'Let's see how the Beauty Book does first.'

'Do you think she'll go out on the road to promote it?'

'I don't know.'

Anna smiled a secret smile. '*You* could persuade her,' she said. 'She likes you.'

'What do you mean?'

'My famous instincts again. She asked me if you were married. I told her you're living with a woman.' She laughed softly. 'I didn't tell her it was me.'

'That's ridiculous. What makes you think she likes me?'

Anna raised an amused eyebrow. 'Have I stumbled on a mutual attraction?'

He was flustered. 'You can be such a stupid woman. She must be in her late sixties.'

'And so are you,' Anna pointed out.

'Such nonsense,' he grumbled.

'I'm glad you think so.' Anna finished her cocoa and went into the bathroom to prepare for bed.

Fred E. Lester gazed blankly at the television and failed to see the comic antics of Mr Carson and a playful monkey. His thoughts were drifting back in time to many many years ago.

*

Freddy was a fresh faced college boy with a smart mouth and a drunken disposition. He was on vacation and his friend, Mel Webster, fixed him up with a blind date. The girl, named Carrie, was beautiful, and black. He was shocked at being fixed up with a black girl. His family was originally from the South. 'Je-sus!' he muttered to Mel. 'She's a fucking dinge!'

'So,' Mel replied. 'Haven't you ever heard of black pudding?'

Why not? *Freddy thought.* Why not?

He didn't remember much else. A series of nightclubs and booze. The anticipation of laying a coloured girl. The champagne flowing and everyone getting high.

Next memory . . . He and Mel and Mel's date driving back to an apartment. It was a big roomy loft with a bed on each side. Mel and his girl started at it on one of the beds, and he had stumbled over to the other one and fallen asleep. It seemed only minutes later that Carrie was shaking him awake. She looked so pretty, and he felt so randy. Why weren't they doing the same as Mel and his girl?

She put up a fierce fight, but he was stronger and overpowered her until she lay helpless beneath him. He knew he was raping her but he didn't stop. Who cared? She was getting what she really wanted, what all women wanted.

After it was over she demanded money. He was angry, he threw what he had at her, took the keys to sleeping Mel's car, and staggered out of the place.

The streets were deserted, and he put his foot down, anxious to get home and shower the smell of the black bitch off him. He drove recklessly, with no thought for anyone else, and as he swerved the car around a corner, it ended up on the wrong side of the street, and smashed headlong into an oncoming truck.

The next thing he remembered was waking up from a coma in a hospital, months later, with a face that resembled a complicated road map. His scars were horrifying, but his parents could afford the finest plastic surgeons. He spent many months in and out of hospital – and all through that desolate period he kept on seeing Carrie's face. He had raped her. That's why he had been punished.

It changed his life.

Years passed. He married a good woman who bore him two fine children. He started his own small publishing firm, and over the years built it into one of the most successful houses in New York. One night, in 1960, he was at a charity ball and he saw her. Carrie. Even though she was gowned and groomed, her hair swept up and diamonds at her ears and throat, he recognized her immediately. She brought back every guilty memory. He prayed that she wouldn't remember him. She didn't.

Relief was immense. She had no idea he was the same callow youth who had treated her so badly all those years before. When he thought about it later he realized there was no way she could *have recognized him. Plastic surgery had changed his appearance considerably, and twenty years had passed. He remembered* her, *because her face was* burned *into his memory.*

He found out who she was, and couldn't help himself from following her life in Vogue *and* Harpers *and* Women's Wear Daily. *Carrie was a personality. He was glad for her.*

His wife succumbed to cancer in 1973. His children, both grown, chose suitable partners and went off to pursue their own lives. He was alone and lonely until Anna Robb came into the office for an interview one day. They had lived together for two years. It was no passionate love affair – not that he expected passion at his age. But they were compatible.

When Carrie re-entered his life he was shocked. He had never thought he would ever see her again. Over the years her name had faded from the columns, and the last mention he could remember was news of her divorce. Then nothing.

He thought back forty-two years. *'She's a fucking dinge . . .'* he had once said, that stupid, prejudiced, bigotted young man. How things had changed.

Anna had said, 'She likes you.' Was it true? Did she?

If she ever knew who he really was she would damn him to hell.

Chapter 79

Gino was the first to leave. He bid his farewells the morning after Lucky's birthday party, pleading urgent business commitments.

Susan elected to stay. 'You don't mind?' she asked in a concerned wifely voice.

'Go ahead – enjoy yourself,' he replied, looking forward to his freedom. They arranged to meet in Los Angeles in ten days' time.

He took a plane to Paris, and the Concorde to New York, where he had booked his usual suite at The Pierre. The first thing he did was call Paige in LA.

'Get on the next flight here,' he commanded.

'Don't be ridiculous.'

'I've got a present for you.'

'What?'

'Something you're gonna eat up!'

'Has anyone ever told you that you're nothing but a dirty old man?'

He chuckled. 'Be on the next flight.'

'Gino –'

'Don't give me a hard time.'

'Only if you promise to give me one!'

'You have my word.'

She called him back an hour later. 'I'll be there on Wednesday.'

'Not soon enough.'

'Don't complain. I have a business to run, not to mention a husband and family.'

He contacted Costa in Miami. 'Let's have a reunion,' he suggested.

'What's going on?' Costa inquired.

'I'm in New York. I feel good. I thought we'd look up some of the old faces.'

'Where's Susan?'

'I left her on the Stanislopoulos yacht. She's happy.'

'And Lucky?'

'She's due in tomorrow. Just a minute.' He put the phone down to let in room service who brought him a thick juicy steak, french fries, chocolate cake, and ice cream – food forbidden by Susan who was always carrying on about cholesterol and diet. He picked up the phone again and continued his conversation with Costa. 'Come on, old friend. We'll have a good time.'

Costa had a litany of complaints. 'I've got arthritis – my joints are killing me, my gums need work –'

'Fall to pieces on your own time. How often am I in New York?'

'Maybe a few days *would* be a change,' Costa mused, and then decisively, 'Yes, I'll come. Why not?'

Gino ate the steak, every one of the french fries, the ice cream and the cake. Then he belched with contentment and fell asleep on the couch.

•

Another day of long meaningful looks between Lennie and herself, and Lucky knew she had to move on. Perhaps when she wasn't facing him every day, the strong attraction would cease. God! Was this what happened when you didn't get laid for a while?

She knew, although she wasn't prepared to admit it, that it wasn't just sex. With plenty of opportunity to observe, she found him to be funny and warm and great with both Roberto and Brigette. She remembered from his original stint at the

Magiriano that he was also an extremely talented and clever comedian.

How did he and Olympia ever get together? He was too smart to put up with her shit. But even smart people get caught on occasion, and he was savvy enough to get out fast.

Lucky knew she must do the same.

'I have some family business matters to attend to with my father,' she told Dimitri. 'Papers to sign, things like that,' she added vaguely. 'I must go to New York at once.'

He nodded. His mind was elsewhere. Francesca was jealous of the diamond necklace and earrings he had gifted Lucky with, and he had to arrange for a present of equal – if not more – value to be discreetly delivered to the temperamental actress.

'Do what you have to do,' he said.

'Roberto will stay here with CeeCee,' Lucky decided. 'Perhaps I'll fly back in a few days.'

She had no intention of doing so. Cruising the Mediterranean on board a floating palace was not her idea of a good time. Especially with people like Saud Omar and Jenkins Wilder aboard. She hated that kind of man. Rich, powerful, sexist chauvinists. She could smell 'em a mile away.

So how come you married one?

Dimitri had seemed different. Unfortunately he was not.

She didn't bother with goodbyes. She doubted she would be missed by anyone other than Roberto and CeeCee. And Lennie, only he was a relationship she did not care to pursue. Dangerous territory. Olympia hated her as it was. She didn't want to make things worse.

•

'Where's Lucky?' Lennie asked at dinner.

'What do you care?' Olympia snapped. She had been bad-tempered and impossible since her outburst at the party.

He shrugged. 'Who *cares*? I just wondered.'

'She had business in New York,' Dimitri explained.

'What kind of business?' Olympia sneered sarcastically. 'Shopping for a new dress?'

Dimitri silenced her with a look.

After dinner there was the usual discussion of who wanted to do what. 'Let's go dancing,' Olympia suggested restlessly, gulping brandy and wishing she had some coke to take the edge off her nerves.

'I'd like to gamble,' the Contessa announced.

So they split into two camps. Saud, the Contessa, Jenkins Wilder, Dimitri, Francesca and Susan elected to go to the casino. And Lennie found himself saddled with Olympia and Fluff, who wished to discotheque. Alice and Horace were invited with neither group. 'You're tired,' Francesca told her timid husband. 'Get some rest.'

'We'll have a nightcap, Horace,' Alice said with a lewd wink.

'You look after my little tootsie roll,' Jenkins said to Lennie, pressing several thousand franc bills into his young wife's eager hands. 'In case you need to powder your nose, doll.'

'Thank you big daddy,' she squeaked.

A fleet of Cadillacs waited to take them wherever they wished to go.

'Regines,' said Olympia.

So Regines it was. An elegant, private club, perched next to the sea.

'Miss Stanislopoulos,' the maitre d' purred. 'Welcome back. So nice to see you again.'

They were given what Lennie presumed to be the best table.

'Let's dance,' said Olympia, bouncing toward the dance floor.

'Go ahead,' encouraged Fluff – a teenage vision in skin tight satin pants and a boob tube – more boob than tube.

They hit the floor to the strains of Stevie Wonder. Lennie made all the right moves while his mind wandered and he thought of Lucky and how much he wanted her. He had to tell Olympia that their marriage was a mistake. She must know. They had about as much in common as a Harley-Davidson and a Rolls Royce. Maybe the best way to handle it was to say nothing, simply fly to LA for the 'Tonight Show', and not come back.

Stevie Wonder was followed by a rasping Rod Stewart, after which they sat down.

Fluff was being hit upon by two leering Italians. She didn't seem to mind at all, in fact she was encouraging them with moist-lipped smiles and high pitched giggles. One of them invited her to dance, and she took off for the dance floor like a bird let loose from its cage.

'At least *somebody's* having a good time,' Olympia said pointedly, and went off to share a snort with one of her friends, an angular looking beauty in a fish-net dress. 'Where can I buy some coke?' she asked the girl, an English socialite.

'Search me, darling. I got *my* little bit of snuff from a rather peculiar type outside the casino yesterday. Ask McGuiness, he's always up on that sort of thing.'

McGuiness was an upper crust English creep with an unfortunate stutter. He led her to his source, a young English dress manufacturer with wiry hair, pin-point eyes and a thick Cockney accent. They did business in a quiet corner, and that's where she was when Flash made his entrance.

Ah . . . the aura of a rock star. Not for them the ordinary entrance. They like attention, people, and plenty of noise. Flash was no exception. He was dressed in black leather and flowing – if ragged looking – white silk scarves. His hair was long and dyed a very stern black (grey was not a colour rock stars cultivated). He wore the customary gold hoop earring – only one, and his teeth looked worse than ever.

Olympia took one peek and her heart gave a little leap.

Flash paused at the entrance to the discotheque just long enough to let the peasants know he was honouring them with his presence.

The disc-jockey – no slouch in the *I can recognize a celebrity at twenty feet* stakes, immediately abandoned the Pointer Sisters, and slyly changed over to Flash's most famous hit, 'Raunchy Lady' – written in the mid-sixties when he was living with a former nun.

'Flash!' exclaimed Olympia.

But she was not alone. Half the females in the club breathed an excited 'Flash!'

'Yeah – yeah – yeah – there's my man!' recited the Cockney dress manufacturer – who would sooner have been a full time drug dealer any day. And he pocketed Olympia's money and raced toward his hero, who he knew would spend – spend – spend!

Olympia frowned. Flash was not alone. He had a blonde on one arm, and a brunette on the other. Both jet-set groupies whom Olympia knew and loathed. No wife in sight.

She stuck out her chest (Flash was a tit man) and made her way over to his table. 'Well!' she steamed. 'We meet again.'

His eyes were bloodshot and wary as he squinted up at her.

''Ello darlin',' he mumbled at last, not sure who she was for a moment.

'How's married life?' she demanded sarcastically. 'Miserable I hope.'

'Cor blimey! It's you! Tubs!' he cackled. 'Put on a pound or two 'ave we?'

Automatically she pulled her stomach in. 'Trust you to be rude,' she spat. '*You* look like the walking dead.'

'Hello, Olympia,' said the blonde, clinging to Flash's arm as if he was a lifeboat.

Olympia favoured her with a cursory nod.

The brunette, taking care of his other arm, said nothing. She had spotted her reflection in a mirrored wall and was admiring her own sultry beauty.

'Thought you was gonna be 'ere sooner than this,' remarked Flash cheerily. 'Thought we was gonna go on yer old man's fishin' boat.'

'You missed the boat,' said Olympia grandly. 'My husband and I are on it.'

'Yer sound like the bloomin' Queen!' cackled Flash.

'Where's teenage wifey?' asked Olympia, her bosom straining the silk of a red Givenchy creation.

'Leave it out, babe,' said Flash easily. 'I don't like to be reminded.'

'You *have* got one, haven't you?' she questioned insistently.

'Yeah. An' now you've got an' old man, so we're even. Right?'

'Let's dance, Flash,' begged the blonde, tripping dainty scarlet fingernails up his leather-clad thigh.

'Not 'ere, luv,' he replied in a *don't you know Rock Stars do not put on shows in public places unless they are getting paid* voice.

'Where then?' she replied logically.

'Wanna score, Flash?' asked the Cockney dress manufacturer, overcome with joy at being close to his hero. 'It's on the house.' He tried to elbow Olympia out of the way, but she stood her ground.

Flash got up. 'If it's free, it's for me. 'Scuse us chicks, we're gonna see a man about a dog.' He put his arm expansively around his new friend who almost hyperventilated with excitement, and the two of them repaired to the men's room.

'Shit!' said Olympia.

*

Across the room Lennie watched it all. And he didn't care. Why should he? Soon he and Miss Stanislopoulos would be just a memory. The sooner the better.

Chapter 80

The first thing Lucky did when she arrived back in New York was call Gino. 'I've got a surprise for you, kid,' he told her. 'Be at The Pierre by five-thirty.'

The second thing she did was call her lawyers about the land deal in Atlantic City. It was a go situation, a few signatures and the piece of real estate she had been after was hers.

She was excited. Now the fun would start. Creating a hotel from the ground up was a challenging, exhausting but ultimately rewarding job. She should know, she had done it once with the Magiriano.

Ah . . . but the work!

She was ready. She had been idle too long. To immerse herself fully in the project was just what she needed. It would take her mind off Dimitri and his hardly subtle affair. And stop her thinking about Lennie – who was *definitely* off limits. Now she was away from the yacht and could look at things clearly, becoming involved with Lennie was sheer madness. He was married to Olympia – reason enough to stay away from him. But he was also more than a one night stand – she had a feeling he was the man who could make her forget Marco . . .

And what if he could?

No thank you. She did not want that kind of involvement ever again. It was just too painful. The best thing she could do was forget Lennie Golden. Which is exactly what she intended.

Three hours later she arrived at The Pierre. The last time she had visited Gino in his favourite suite at the New York hotel was the night her brother, Dario, was brutally gunned down in the street.

In the elevator a man in a dark grey suit asked her if she was a model. She gave him a long cool look. Raked him from head to toe. 'No,' she said slowly. 'Are you?'

This confused him. He was fifty-two years old with teenage children. Where did *she* get off asking him if he was a model? Goddamn nerve. He got out of the elevator on the fourth floor without another word.

Gino greeted her with a hug and a wink. 'Just like old times, huh?' he grinned. 'Look who I got for you.'

'Uncle Costa!' she exclaimed in delight. 'What are *you* doing here?'

While they embraced, Costa explained how persuasive Gino could be. 'A visit to the big city is not such a bad idea,' he allowed. 'And how could I resist seeing you?'

She laughed happily. 'Uncle Costa, you're a *wonderful* surprise.'

There was more to come. Gino had arranged dinner with old friends in an Italian family restaurant in Queens. Present were Aldo and Barbara Dinunzio – she, a frail little woman, and he, as fat and contented as a lazy cat. Then there were their grown children, and the children's various spouses; plus a smattering of grandchildren. Altogether sixteen people sat around the table drinking cheap red wine, enjoying delicious pasta which Barbara had personally supervised in the restaurant kitchen (the place was owned by her cousin) and finishing off with Gino's favourite ice cream.

Lucky hadn't seen these people in years, nor had Gino, but the warmth and joy at the table was contagious.

'I can't wait until you meet my son, Roberto' Lucky told Barbara proudly. 'He's gorgeous, eighteen months old and totally gorgeous! Just *wait* until you see him!'

The old woman, who had known and loved Lucky's mother many years before, clutched Lucky by the hand and squeezed tightly. 'Maria should be here today,' she said regretfully. 'She was a beauty. A gentle sweetheart. We all miss her still.'

'Hey,' interrupted Gino, as he noticed Lucky's expression. 'We'll talk about the present, not the past. When you get a peek at Roberto, you'll see a true Santangelo. He looks just like me.'

Lucky swept away the sad memories and grinned. She liked to hear her father boast about Roberto.

'He's got my eyes, my hair,' Gino continued. 'Right, Lucky? Right, kid?'

She fingered the panther pin he had given her – she had worn it ever since her birthday, while Dimitri's diamonds languished in a safe. 'Yes, daddy,' she replied softly. 'Just like you.'

*

Later, on the drive back to the hotel, Gino said, 'You wanna come up for a nightcap, kid?'

She couldn't think of anything she'd like better.

After Costa had retired to his room, they ordered Brandy

Alexanders and sat together on the comfortable couch in the living room of Gino's suite.

'This is nice,' he said. 'We gotta get around to doin' it more often.'

She nodded her agreement, and tentatively touched his arm. 'You know earlier, when Barbara was talking about Maria . . . my mother . . .' She trailed off, her voice filled with emotion.

Gino picked up the message. 'We never talked about it, huh, kid?'

She shook her head and whispered. 'Never.'

He got up and walked to the window. Then he turned and stared at her. 'Your mother was the kindest and most beautiful woman in the world,' he said gruffly. 'She loved you an' me an' your brother. She loved us all too much. When they laid a hit on Maria they cut out my heart. Y'know what I'm sayin', kid?'

This was Gino's explanation for all the years of running away from his children. Putting them in charge of nannies, and guardians and boarding schools. He had always figured if he didn't love them too much, he would never lose them.

Wrong.

But it was over now.

She arose from the couch, went to her father and hugged him tightly. 'Tell me about mommy. I want to know everything. Please. Make her a part of my life again.'

Gino needed no further urging. He had bottled up his feelings for years, and the joy of finally talking about Maria and the happy times, was wonderful.

The hours sped by and it was almost dawn when Lucky left the hotel. She felt light-headed and very very happy. Since she was five years old her mother had been missing from her life. Now she felt she really knew her. Gino had handed over priceless memories. Maria might be gone, but she was certainly not forgotten.

*

'Welcome home to the City of Angels,' Jess said formally. She met Lennie at LAX with a limousine and a travel representative who whisked him through customs as if they didn't exist.

'Nice being a star, huh?' she asked, as they settled into the back of the limo. 'Was your trip okay?'

'I think I'm in love,' he said, reaching for a sweet roll and a glass of orange juice. It was a well-stocked limo.

'Hmmm,' replied Jess briskly. 'A usual reaction when returning from one's honeymoon.'

'Not with Olympia, schmuck.'

'Oh, I see. You're *not* in love with your wife, and that makes *me* a schmuck. So what else is new, Mr Charm?'

He fumbled for a cigarette and grinned disarmingly. 'Don't get mad at me. I need comfort and advice.'

'Not that you'll take it.'

'How well you know me.' He reached forward and switched on the built-in TV. 'You're never gonna believe me, but I met the one and only lady I think I can spend the rest of my life with.'

'Don't tell me,' Jess said dramatically. 'Eden snuck onto the yacht and whisked you right out from under the Greek Princess's cute little nose.'

'Eden!' he laughed derisively. 'Who's *she*?'

Jess sighed. 'The love of your life. Remember?'

'Didn't I tell you? I'm just about to start a new life.'

'With or without the Greek Princess?' She paused meaningfully. 'Remember her? *She's* the one you just got married to.'

'Can I get it annulled?' he asked hopefully.

'Did you sleep with her?'

'Of course I did.'

'Then unless she wants to say you didn't, I don't think you have a chance in hell.'

He changed channels on the TV and reached for another sweet roll.

'True love does not seem to have diminished your appetite,' Jess remarked dryly.

'I'm nervous.'

'Of the "Tonight Show"? I can't wait to hear your new material. Isaac's coming over to the apartment later – I thought you might want to run it by us.'

'No new material.'

'*Whaaat?*'

He wolfed the roll, oblivious to her consternation. 'You don't seem to understand,' he explained gravely. 'I want *out* of my marriage – it's over – finito – kaput. How you ever let me do it I'll never know. You must have –'

'Hang *on* a moment,' she spluttered indignantly. 'How *I* ever let you do it? *I* went to bed – you were getting laid. *I* woke up – you were married. I was not exactly around to stop you.'

He leaned over and kissed her on the cheek. 'I love you, Jess. How's everything with you? Did you and Matt ever get together? What's been happenin' in LA?'

She glared at him. 'You're strange, you know that?'

'Secret of my success.'

They fell into silence. Sometimes Jess thought she knew Lennie better than anyone in the world. At others, she felt she didn't know him at all. He had asked about Matt. But did he really care? Not at all. It didn't matter. There was nothing to tell anyway. Matt treated her like a sister – she no longer cast a spell on him. Her last night in Vegas she had spent with an old boyfriend. Boring. Boring.

At least Lennie looked great, but he was unsettled and restless. Better keep him away from the booze.

'Does the bride know she's redundant?' she asked.

'I haven't told her.'

'Is she going to be pissed?'

'I don't think she's gonna light candles and shout hallelujah!' He paused. 'But on the other hand I will not be breaking her heart, just bruising her ego. She's still got a thing for Flash.'

Jess's face lit up. 'You met Flash?' she asked excitedly.

'Met him, smelled his bad breath, admired his even worse

teeth, and got stoned out of my skull just breathing the air around him.'

'Oh boy! You met Flash.'

'I'm telling you – he's no big deal.'

'Sure he's not. Like we didn't get off on his music a hundred times a day when we were at school.'

'*You* got off on him,' Lennie pointed out. 'I just liked the way he played guitar and held a tune.'

Jess began to giggle.

Lennie couldn't help joining in.

'Who'd you fall in love with this time?' she asked affectionately.

'Lucky Santangelo,' he replied, suddenly serious.

She widened her eyes in amazement. 'Are you kidding me?'

He grabbed another sweet roll. 'Never been more serious in my life.'

Chapter 81

With the departures of Gino, Lucky and Lennie, life aboard *The Greek* underwent certain subtle changes. Susan did not make a move without the Contessa's approval and consent.

Dimitri, who considered the renewal of his affair with Francesca had been conducted most discreetly, relaxed his strict code of behaviour, and spent virtually every waking hour with the volatile actress. Most of the sleeping ones too.

Horace was an embarrassing presence whom they both tried to ignore. Alice consoled him all the way to her cabin, where he had sex for the first time in four years. Francesca didn't do that sort of thing with him. Horace was just around to organize her life and handle her business affairs.

Olympia stayed on the yacht for an hour after Lennie left, then she called Flash at his villa.

'Get yer stupid knickers over 'ere,' he commanded. 'An' bring some bread, we'll 'ave a party.'

The party lasted three days, and so did Olympia. She wondered how to tell Lennie it was over between them. Perhaps she wouldn't bother. Let her lawyer do it, she paid him enough.

Fluff went on a shopping trip, then secretly ran off to Portofino with one of the Italians she had met at 'Regines'. Jenkins hired detectives to find her, and when they did, he sent his bodyguard to bring her back. She returned, a sulky pouting teenager. Shortly after, they left for Texas.

Brigette tried to drown Roberto in his bath. CeeCee caught her in the act, and spanked her until the child wept.

Two days later Brigette went to her grandfather and complained that Roberto's nasty black nanny had touched her 'down there'.

Dimitri, too caught up in his passionate affair to bother with matters domestic, instructed Nanny Mabel to deal with the situation. Nanny Mabel, drunk with power at last, spanked Brigette for thirty blissful minutes. 'And if you run to your grand-daddy and tell him,' she threatened, 'I'll spank you for another half hour.'

CeeCee thought the punishment excessive, but kept her mouth shut and an eagle eye on Roberto at all times.

Susan, one long hot afternoon, when everyone except the Contessa was ashore, went to her stateroom and lay naked on her bed. Within minutes the Contessa entered and indulged her as only Paige Wheeler had indulged her before.

Susan shut her eyes and cherished every minute. The female touch was so . . . delicate. She wondered if she could ever stand Gino near her again.

Captain and Mrs Pratt saw all, heard all, and pretended nothing was going on.

The weather in the south of France was delightful. Dimitri Stanislopoulos' summer cruise was a triumph – as usual.

Chapter 82

It was not easy for Paige to arrange a sudden and unexpected trip to New York, but she managed it. Ryder had never been a possessive husband – thank God – just a man completely caught up in his work. Putting a deal together meant everything else came second. So when Paige told him she had to go to New York to meet with an important furniture designer from Italy, and to view an apartment one of her clients was thinking of purchasing – his only concern was the dinner party they were supposed to be having for Vitos Felicidade. The Spanish singing star was causing problems with the contract he had been offered. He wanted script approval, co-star approval, billing approval. 'I think he wants to approve the way I take a crap in the morning,' Ryder announced grimly.

The movie Bonnatti was financing seemed to be taking more time to put together than a Bishop getting laid. Any producer would be getting edgy. Ryder saw the dinner party as a social occasion to soothe ruffled egos and get the goddamn show on the road.

'Postpone your trip,' he told Paige.

'I wish I could,' she lied. 'But don't you worry about a thing. I'll make sure every last detail is taken care of.'

At the office a dozen appointments had to be juggled. Business was stronger than ever. Paige had a distinct style, and right now she was hot. She called a very dear designer friend of hers, Irwin Stroll, and asked if he could possibly take over a Brazilian couple who were on their way into town with nothing but money to spend. Irwin happily agreed to help her out.

Fortunately her two teenage sons were in Europe, backpacking across France. It would do them both good. Let them find out that life was not all new convertibles and Beverly Hills glitter.

She left on Wednesday morning, and couldn't quite understand why the prospect of seeing Gino Santangelo excited her so much. On the plane she sat next to a young actor with a new TV series and one of the best bodies she had ever seen. Once he might have presented a challenge – how long would it take for her to get into *his* pants! But now it didn't seem important. All she wanted to do was be with Gino.

You're getting old, she scolded herself. And somehow she didn't mind one bit.

•

Lucky and Paige hit it off instantly. Gino brought her to dinner and said, 'Paige is an old friend of Susan's an' mine from California.'

Oh yeh? thought Lucky. *I bet.* She remembered Gino the womanizer. Susan had put a stop to all that. Now he had that look in his eyes again.

They ate at Elaine's, one of the great New York restaurants as far as seeing people and having fun. Elaine, a dark and interesting woman – who knew *everyone* – escorted them personally to a table in the back.

Paige waved at some writer friends, while Bobby Zarem – the legendary PR whiz – stopped by their table to say hello.

It turned out to be one of those evenings where helpless laughter is only a breath away, and everyone had a wonderful time.

'Who is she?' Lucky asked Gino, when Paige vanished to the ladies' room.

'Kinda Susan's best friend,' he answered sheepishly.

'Can you do a swap?'

He almost grinned. 'Don't get smart ass, kid.'

'I don't think it's smart ass, I think it's one of the best suggestions I've ever come up with! What do *you* think, Uncle Costa?'

Costa nodded, enjoying the game.

They stayed at Elaine's until 1.30 a.m. and then it was time for home and bed.

Lucky observed her father's hand on Paige's thigh before they all rose from the table. He was still going strong. She loved him for it. She loved the whole week in New York. Things were signed and sealed in Atlantic City. Meetings were arranged with architects and builders. She was back in business with a vengeance, and it was a sensational feeling.

Waiting at the apartment were three messages from Lennie, written out in the butler's spidery script. PLEASE

RETURN MR GOLDEN'S CALL, the message read, and there was a number in LA.

She crumpled the pieces of paper and dropped them in the waste basket. Olympia had found him first, she was not about to become involved.

You are involved.

I am not.

Really? What do you call it?

A transient lay.

Bullshit.

She pulled the crumpled messages from the basket and smoothed them out. Just as her hand hovered over the phone, it rang.

She knew it was him, and hesitated before picking up the receiver.

You are involved.

I am not.

'Hello.'

'Lucky?'

'Who is this?'

'Don't give me that "who is this" crap. I'm in LA. I'm doing the Carson Show tomorrow. Can you fly out?'

She reached for a cigarette, and noticed her hand was trembling ever so slightly. 'Stop living in a dream world, Lennie. What we had was . . .' she searched for the right word, couldn't find it and settled for '. . . momentarily exciting. Now it's over. Just forget it. I have.'

He ignored her speech. 'I'm contacting a lawyer. If Olympia agrees I'll go for an annulment.'

Lucky thought for a moment of Olympia . . . there was no way they could ever be friends again.

'Did you hear me?' he demanded.

She sighed. 'Do what you have to do . . .'

'I intend to. How about you?'

She took a deep breath. 'Right now I am embarking on a project. I'm building a hotel in Atlantic City. It's going to take all my time and energy.'

'You're not answering my question.'

'I didn't know you'd asked one.'

'Let me spell it out. Are you going to divorce Dimitri?'

She didn't want to be in this position. Who was he to question her?

'Why don't you leave me alone,' she said wearily. 'You're a complication I don't need in my life right now . . . just leave me alone . . .'

She put the phone down, drew deeply on her cigarette, and took no notice as it began to ring again.

*

Back at The Pierre, Gino and Paige were getting re-acquainted.

'Higher,' instructed Paige.

Gino raised his tongue a fraction.

'Softer,' she begged.

He relaxed the pressure.

'More,' she pleaded.

He buried his face in her juices and felt thoroughly at home.

*

Lennie had no new material to use on the 'Tonight Show', much to Jess's and Isaac's disgust.

'What the hell were you *doing* on that goddamn boat?' Jess complained. Then she remembered the name of his latest passion, and shut up. Lucky Santangelo. Holy shit! Lucky Santangelo. The Lady Boss. Lennie might be a star, but he was way out of his league with that one. Way way out.

'She's the girl I met in the casino that time,' he confided. 'Remember? I told you about her. She stood me up.'

'And had you fired.'

'So what?'

'Are you *kidding*?' Jess screeched. 'You went *ape-shit* about being canned.'

'It didn't do me any harm, did it?'

Jess shook her head. 'Jesus! What can I tell you. Lucky Santangelo is . . . connected. She plays games with the big boys. Her father is notorious. He's Gino Santangelo – one of the mob.'

'How many years ago?'

'Who gives a shit?'

'No, come on,' he persisted. 'You're such an expert on the Santangelos. How many years ago? 'Cos right now he's just a feisty old guy married to a movie star's widow.'

Jess was sullen. 'Believe me, Lennie. Trust me. A few years ago Lucky Santangelo was involved in a shooting.'

'What kind of shooting?'

'Oh, it was all hushed up. The rumour was she'd shot this man who was her Godfather.'

'Don't give me rumours, give me facts.'

'She shot him in the balls with his own gun, if you really want to know – something like that. The story was he tried to rape her – but the gossip around town was that it was a revenge move. He'd had her brother killed *and* her boyfriend.'

'What boyfriend?'

'Another Charmer. Marco. He looked like he walked straight out of a gangster movie.'

'What happened to him?'

'He got his head blown off in the parking lot of the Magiriano. I remember it well. I'd only been working there six months. It was frightening – like everyone was talking about some big gang war taking place, but it never happened. Lucky took off for a while, and everything quieted down. Enzio Bonnatti came in to run the hotel – he's the guy she shot.'

Lennie was silent while he digested the information. He wasn't sure whether he believed Jess or not, she had a vivid imagination.

'Matt knows the real story,' Jess added. 'Not that he's likely to tell it. The whole mob scene in Vegas is a grey area – nobody talks.'

'Thanks for the guided tour of Lucky Santangelo's life. It doesn't make any difference – I still feel the same way about her.'

'Christ! You sound like some naive jerk up from the sticks. What *is it* with you and these dumb stupid obsessions you get? I can remember the Lennie Golden who could get laid without giving a damn. What happened?'

'You know something, Jess? You're my manager, not my fucking keeper.'

They glared at each other, neither giving an inch.

The 'Tonight Show' came and went. He was good, not as good as he could have been, but Johnny seemed to like him – in fact he asked him to sit with the other guests after he'd done his bit, and they chatted, and Johnny was charming, and when it was over he got invited back.

'You were *great*. They *loved* you,' Jess enthused in the limo on the way home. 'When Johnny asks you over, you *know* you've got it made.'

He wasn't really listening, he was wondering if Lucky had watched the show, and hoped she had.

They were only hours apart, but he missed her.

*

Lucky utilized Dimitri's desk and worked on ideas for the Santangelo. She put on her Sony earphones and listened to Isaac Hayes – one of her favourite soul singers. He really let it all hang out – his deep sensuous voice expressing everything she felt.

At eleven-thirty she glanced at the television, and automatically switched it on.

'*Heeeeeres* Johnny!' said the familiar voice of Ed McMahon introducing Johnny Carson.

The most famous man on American television strolled in front of the camera and indulged in light banter with his excited audience.

Lucky fixed herself a drink and stared at the set. Halfway through Johnny's monologue she turned it off.

Five minutes later she switched it on again.

Why watch Lennie Golden?

Why not?

When he finally appeared he received a wild ovation from

the audience. Obviously, as Alice had said, he was hot.

And he was. His cutting ironic wit hit home with everyone. And he looked great too.

She lit a cigarette and blew contemplative smoke rings.

Lennie Golden.

More than just a casual encounter.

*

The day after the Carson show, Lennie cancelled a club engagement – much to Jess's fury – and flew to New York. He checked into the Regency Hotel and called Lucky. 'I'm here, and we have to talk,' he announced.

'Forget it. Nothing's going to happen,' she replied.

'Don't give me a hard time. Just have dinner with me.'

'What for? It won't do any good.'

'Because I want you to tell me nothing more can happen between us when we're face to face, and then I'll leave you alone. That's a promise.'

She hesitated.

He persisted. 'Is it a deal?'

'I don't know . . .'

'Hey, you want to get left alone, don't you? I mean I can really drive you nuts with phone calls and letters and flowers. I can hang around outside your apartment, complicate your life – you know what I mean?' He paused, then, 'If I was you, lady, I would *grab* this magnificent offer and run like crazy.' He waited a beat, giving her just enough time to make a decision. 'So – what time shall I pick you up?'

'It won't do –'

'. . . any good,' he finished the sentence for her. 'Expect me at eight-thirty.'

She started to object, but he hung up before she could argue further.

Lucky Santangelo was going to be his, and nothing was going to stop him.

Chapter 83

Francesca Fern considered Dimitri Stanislopoulos marrying again a direct insult. She brought the subject up at every opportunity, becoming progressively agitated as the cruise drew to an end.

'It is humiliating!' she complained, as they faced each other over the ever-present backgammon board. 'The *world* knows it is *me* you love. And now you have married this . . . this . . . person. How do you think I feel? You have made a public fool of me.'

He leaned over and touched her coarse red hair. Then he let his hand stray down the neckline of her low-cut dress, reaching for her prominent nipples. 'Magnificent!' he murmured. The jut of her breasts reminded him of a native African woman he had once seen pictured in *National Geographic*, and to chew on her nipples was the greatest aphrodisiac a man could know.

She slapped his hand away. 'Good God, Dimitri!' She glared at him, full of passion. 'Wasn't *my* love enough?'

Quickly he defended himself. 'I married Lucky because of the boy,' he explained, for the hundredth time.

'Yes. And now you must divorce her,' Francesca replied imperiously, her tone brooking no argument.

'I don't think so,' Dimitri said. 'She doesn't bother us. She's very independent, and quite frankly, my dear, when you are not around I need a woman by my side.'

'She's no woman!' Francesca spat viciously. 'She's a slut! I don't know how you can have touched her in the first place. She's a Romany – a Gypsy. She looks dirty to me.'

Francesca was not happy when denied her own way.

'Enough!' said Dimitri sharply. 'I never criticize that miserable dog *you're* married to.'

'Why should you? Horace has been very . . . understanding over the years.'

'Understanding indeed! He's nothing but a cuckold with no balls. A joke, my dear, hardly worth mentioning.'

She pursed her thin lips, slashed with carmine. 'Goddamn you to hell,' she hissed. 'All you want is my body. You use me. You care nothing for my feelings.'

Dimitri laughed harshly. 'Nobody uses *you*, Francesca.'

She rose from the table, tall, big-boned and sinewy. 'True,' she said haughtily. 'Nobody uses Francesca Fern – not even the big bad Greek.' Her voice began to mock. 'Dimitri Stanislopoulos, with all his money and power. Dimitri Stanislopoulos, who would *die* to be near me, but who refuses to obey my one tiny request.'

'And what about *my* request?' he bellowed loudly. 'For too many years I have been asking you to free yourself from Horace and marry me. I have begged and threatened, done everything a man can possibly do. You *dare* to talk of humiliation. *I'm* the one who has been humiliated. That you should choose to stay with such a pathetic creature when you could have been Mrs Stanislopoulos. My God, Francesca!'

'Divorce the gypsy, and we shall see,' she murmured mysteriously.

'No,' Dimitri replied, pushing the backgammon board away and getting up. '*You* divorce Horace and we shall see.'

'Don't blackmail me,' she raged. 'Don't you *dare* to blackmail Francesca Fern!'

'This is not blackmail, this is survival,' he countered sternly.

She swept her lover with a look. 'Very well,' she decided dramatically. 'The time has come.'

'For what?'

'For us to be together as you have always wished.'

'You will divorce Horace?'

'I will think about it.'

Dimitri thumped the table with his fist. 'God*damn* you, woman? Make up your mind.'

Her eyes flashed as she tossed back her mane of red hair. 'Yes,' she said. 'I will do it!'

The Contessa clasped Susan's hand. 'Goodbye, my dear,' she said. 'Or should I say *au revoir*, for surely we shall meet again.'

The Contessa smelt of Chanel. She had leathery skin and a downturned, discontented mouth. Her beauty must have been exceptional when she was young. Now she was merely chic. She made Susan feel like a naive girl, a feeling she hadn't had for thirty-five years.

'Please phone if you ever get to Beverly Hills,' Susan urged politely, and hoped she wouldn't.

'Beverly Hills,' the Contessa said with an amused smile. 'Rodeo Drive and film people.' She made both sound like dirty words.

'And Arabs,' Susan added tartly. The Contessa was a snob. And as far as Susan was concerned she was also a pervert. After their first delicious sexual encounter the Contessa had suggested that her oily Arab boyfriend join in the fun. Susan had been appalled. 'Certainly not,' she had said, and the Contessa had treated her with irritating condescension ever since.

Susan thought about Paige. She couldn't wait to see her. Paige would never dare suggest a threesome.

*

Olympia returned to the yacht, happy and coked up to the eyeballs. Dimitri was too busy to notice. Francesca had agreed to visit his lawyer in Paris and work out the details of getting rid of Horace. Then they would tell him. Together.

Olympia kissed Brigette on the cheek and counted the days before the child returned to boarding school in England. Having a daughter was such a burdensome responsibility – if it wasn't for Brigette, she would be free to do whatever she wanted. It never occurred to her that she did do *exactly* what she wanted at all times.

Flash had flown off to Germany for a recording session. They were to meet in her New York apartment in a week's time. Life would be normal again. Sex, drugs and rock and roll.

Olympia was pleased with the way things had worked out. Flash never mentioned his teenage wife except to wave his hand airily and say, 'A mistake, gel. She'll never bother us.'

Olympia felt the same way about Lennie. A mistake also. Now she had Flash back she would get rid of him. He was in California, far far away. No problem.

'Francesca's going to Paris for the day later in the week,' Dimitri announced casually over dinner. 'My plane will take her.' Horace busied himself with his cracked crab, determined to ignore the fact that his world was about to crumble. There were only the Ferns and Olympia left on the cruise, and the two children and their respective nannies.

'Wonderful!' Olympia exclaimed. 'I'll go too. I need a day's shopping.'

'Can I come, mama?' begged Brigette, who had been allowed to eat with the grown-ups as a special treat.

'Don't be so silly, darling,' trilled Olympia.

'Why not?' demanded Brigette.

'Because . . .' replied Olympia vaguely.

Brigette chewed on her thumb. 'Please, mama!' she whined.

'No,' snapped Olympia. 'Absolutely not.'

Brigette glared. 'I hate you!' she yelled suddenly, taking everyone by surprise. 'I really hate you. You're a big fat cow!'

'Brigette!' thundered Dimitri. 'How dare you talk to your mother like that. Go to your room immediately.'

Brigette weighed the chances of taking on her grandfather and decided against it. 'But grandpoppa, it's just that I never *see* mama,' she whined pathetically. 'I'm sorry, really I am. But why *can't* I go?'

Dimitri turned to his daughter.

'Ridiculous!' sniffed Olympia. 'I am not dragging a child with me.'

Brigette decided a few sobs might come in handy. She began to snivel.

'God!' huffed Olympia, and rang for Nanny Mabel, who removed the crying child immediately.

Chapter 84

A date. Lucky didn't go on dates – it had never been part of her lifestyle. 'I'll pick you up at eight-thirty,' Lennie had said. She hadn't agreed. He had merely stated what he was going to do and she had accepted it.

Now she wished she hadn't. What good would it do? Theirs was a relationship headed nowhere. She realized it. Why didn't he?

At seven o'clock she instructed the butler to say she was out of town. Then she spent the next half hour worrying what Lennie would do. Maybe it was best to see him, and sort things out once and for all.

She changed her instructions and tried to decide what to wear. Dimitri liked her to dress up, but she preferred casual, so she settled for soft black leather pants and an oversized white silk shirt which she belted tightly. Black boots, gold hoop earrings, and her panther brooch completed the outfit. She wore her hair loose.

By eight o'clock she had changed her mind again. *Why* see him? He obviously didn't understand what a delicate situation they were caught in. Like most men he probably thought he was on to a good thing – an available piece of ass presented itself and he went for it. Shit! He had suckered her. He was chasing an easy lay. That's all she was to him. Men couldn't seem to understand that women could be as sexually free as the male sex. Screw Lennie Golden. Why *should* she see him?

'I'm going out,' she informed the butler. 'When Mr Golden gets here tell him I won't be back tonight.'

'Yes, madame,' said the butler, his Englishness not betraying a flicker of interest.

Where was she going to go? Gino was with Paige, and Costa had returned to Miami.

Maybe she wouldn't go out. The hell with it. Just have the butler *tell* him she was out.

Frightened of facing him?

Absolutely not.

She fixed herself a Pernod and water and chainsmoked two cigarettes.

'I've changed my mind,' she told the imperturbable butler. 'When Mr Golden gets here, show him in.'

'Yes, madame.'

She paced the sumptuous living room. Sumptuous and perfect and expensive and boring. If Dimitri expected her to live in this apartment he had better agree to redecorate. She felt stifled, period. Why had she married him? Why had *he* married *her*? It was obvious his heart belonged to the horse-faced Madame Fern, and quite frankly she didn't care. No jealous pangs. Dimitri and she had married each other for reasons that did not include love and passion. Was this to be the story of her life? Two husbands, neither of them lovers in the true sense.

She felt lonely and restless, as if her life was one big void. *The hotel will fill it*, she thought. *My hotel . . . Mine . . . And Roberto. My wonderful little boy.*

The butler presented himself at the door. 'Mr Golden, madame,' he said with a slight bow.

She stubbed out her cigarette, took a deep breath, and turned to greet him with a falsely polite smile. 'Lennie!'

Their eyes locked and she was lost.

'Hiya, beautiful lady,' he said, walking over and taking her hands in his.

His touch made her weak. What was going on here?

'Can I get you a drink, sir?' inquired the butler, hovering solicitously.

'Vodka. On the rocks,' Lennie replied, glancing around.

'Yes, sir.'

Lennie grinned. 'I feel like I'm in a museum!'

Lucky couldn't help smiling back. 'You are,' she said softly.

Silently they waited while the butler poured, cubed, and stirred. Then he handed over the lead crystal glass and exited discreetly.

Lennie stared directly at her, raised his glass in a salute and said, 'To us. To our life together. To the way it's going to be.'

Chapter 85

Susan returned to Beverly Hills to find Gino missing and her daughter, Gemma, in residence. 'Why are you here, dear?' she asked, trying to conceal lurking resentment. Gemma was such an untidy girl. It had been quite a relief when she had set up house with her boyfriend.

'We had a fight,' Gemma explained, biting into an apple.

'Nothing serious, I hope,' fussed Susan.

'It depends on what you consider serious,' replied Gemma, discarding the apple on a polished table top. 'I caught the jerk with his hand up my best friend's skirt, *and* she wasn't wearing panties. What category would you place *that* little bit of business in?'

'Are you sure, dear?'

Gemma regarded her mother with amusement. The woman was unreal. She lived in a dream world. 'I'm sure,' she said calmly. 'How was your trip?'

Susan re-arranged a vase of flowers, carefully removing a dying rose with a tch of annoyance. 'Very nice,' she said. 'A charming group of people.'

'Who?' questioned Gemma, not really caring, but she felt she should make conversation as she had moved back home and she didn't want her mother complaining about *that*.

'Oh, Francesca Fern and her husband. Saud Omar.' An imperceptible pause. 'The Contessa Zebrowski. Lennie Golden.'

Gemma snapped to attention. 'Lennie Golden!' she exclaimed. 'Really?'

Susan finished with the flowers and began straightening ornaments. 'He's married to Dimitri's daughter,' she explained.

'He's hot,' sighed Gemma.

'Hot is a very vulgar expression,' Susan chided.

'Hot is where Lennie Golden's at,' enthused Gemma. 'Can I meet him? Can you throw one of your dinner parties or something?'

'No,' snapped Susan. 'Gino's still in New York, and I'm tired. I need to rest. It's been an arduous trip.'

Gemma reached into a silver dish for another apple and took a large bite. 'I didn't mean tomorrow,' she sniffed. 'Next week maybe.'

'Will you still be here next week?' asked Susan, hoping the answer was no.

'If the jerk doesn't come crawling to me on his knees and apologize, I could still be here next year!' Gemma smiled. She had very small, very even, very white teeth. 'I'm home, mother. To stay.'

*

Gino saw Paige off with regret. Their few days in New York together were memorable. She was his kind of woman.

He sent her off with a contented smile on her face. She enjoyed being with him as much as he enjoyed his time with her.

'I'll be back in LA in a few days,' he promised.

'Then I shall book our suite in the Beverly Wilshire,' she said warmly. 'Just let me know when.' Neither of them had any idea where their affair was going, but they were both on for the full ride.

Paige arrived home to find a depressed Ryder. 'You can shove Bonnatti, Vitos, Quinn fucking Leech, and the whole goddamn movie up your ass,' he announced.

Paige summoned wifely concern. 'Wasn't the dinner a success?' she asked.

'We haven't *had* the fucking dinner yet,' Ryder snarled. 'I had to cancel your goddamn caterers who are trying to stick me with the bill anyway. Vitos got sick, Bonnatti got called out of town, and Quinn got temperamental. I've arranged another dinner for Monday.'

'The same caterers?'

'Are you kidding? Chasen's this time.'

Paige nodded. 'Wise choice.' Then she waited for Ryder to ask about her trip. He didn't. Why should she feel guilty when he didn't even care?

Susan Martino Santangelo had left three messages. Reluctantly Paige called her back. She wasn't sure she could go along with the *I'm screwing your husband but we can still be best friends* game.

'I must see you,' Susan said.

'I'm inundated with work,' Paige replied briskly.

'It's vitally important,' Susan insisted, lowering her voice to a whisper.

Had she found out? Paige hesitated. 'Well . . .'

'Come for tea tomorrow. Four o'clock at my house.'

'You're so English!'

'Please come.'

Paige sighed, best to face up to things immediately. 'I'll be there.'

•

Gino had thought that with Paige despatched to LA he would spend a couple of days with Lucky before returning to the Coast. But Lucky informed him breathlessly on the phone when he tracked her down, that she was incredibly busy, that she would love to see him, but that right now it was impossible.

To say Gino was put out was an understatement. He was hurt and angry. He had stayed over in New York to spend time with his daughter, and she didn't seem to care.

Kids. Appreciation. What did they know? You gave up your life for them and they couldn't even be bothered to give you the time of day. Conveniently he forgot that for the past few days he had been closeted with Paige and had had no time to bother with anyone – including Lucky.

'Not even dinner tonight?' he demanded on the phone.

'I'm *really* tied up,' Lucky explained apologetically, sounding remarkably happy for someone too busy to find time to have dinner with her father.

'Sure,' said Gino. 'I understand, kid.'

But he didn't. And he decided to leave for LA early – surprise Susan *and* Paige.

Chapter 86

Falling in love is like getting hit by a large truck and yet not being mortally wounded. Just sick to your stomach, high one minute, low the next. Starving hungry but unable to eat. Hot, cold, forever horny, full of hope and enthusiasm, with momentary depressions that wipe you out.

It is also not being able to remove the smile from your face, loving life with a mad passionate intensity, and feeling ten years younger.

Love does not appear with any warning signs. You fall into it as if pushed from a high diving board. No time to think about what's happening. It's inevitable. An event you can't control. A crazy, heart-stopping, roller-coaster ride that just has to take its course.

Neither Lucky nor Lennie were expecting it. Oh sure, they were attracted to each other, the whole sexual bit was in full swing. But love?

Come *on*.

They were two strong-minded, independent, smart people who had been around the track a time or two. They were career oriented with definite goals in mind. Lucky had her hotel to build, and Lennie was set to soar as high as he wanted to go.

Theirs was an impossible relationship.

And yet . . . They were two soulmates who found each other. Two reckless, passionate people filled with a sensual zest for living.

'What are we going to do?' Lucky asked after forty-eight hours of togetherness. The most exciting, incredible forty-eight hours of her life.

'We are going to extract ourselves from the craziness we're caught up in – and then we'll do something *really* stupid – like get married, grow old, have a dozen kids. Whatever,' Lennie joked. Only he was serious.

Lucky was in a daze. No longer in control. And it didn't disturb her at all. She felt wonderful.

'We will?'

He grinned. 'Whatever.'

'Stop saying that.'

'Why? Does it turn you on?'

She leaped upon him. '*You* turn me on. You really do.'

Giggling, they rolled around the bed in her East Hampton house. The house that had once been Gino and Maria's when Lucky was just a little girl with wide eyes and an inquisitive nature.

Lennie pinned her down, and lay across her. 'Hey, lady – why are you always fighting me?' he demanded.

She put out her tongue and rolled it suggestively. 'So's you can win,' she said huskily. 'I like winners.'

He crushed her with a kiss and she revelled in his strength, the feel of his body and the smell of his skin. Her reserves had crumbled. Lennie – with his rangy good looks, light banter, admirable talent, gentleness to kids, not to mention bedroom performance – had won her over. He was the sort of man she had never known before, and he was special.

One date was all it had taken. He had collected her at the New York apartment and taken her to a Chinese restaurant where they shared spring rolls, spicy shredded beef and a bottle of vodka. Polite conversation lasted exactly ten minutes. After that they were into exploring each other's lives, trading experiences, listening, telling, revealing. When the restaurant closed at one a.m. they were still talking, so they went on to a Greenwich Village jazz joint that accommodated them until four in the morning.

'I don't want to go home,' Lucky remembered saying.

'Who's talking home?' Lennie had replied.

He took her to a place frequented by waiters and night

workers that didn't even open until dawn. There, they sat in a corner and drank endless coffee, while Billie Holiday belted blues on the old juke box, and an over-painted whore danced gaily around the tiny dance floor.

Lucky told him things she had never told anybody. Discovering the mutilated body of her mother when she was only five. The withdrawal of her father. Running away from school with Olympia when they were both teenagers. And the marriage Gino had forced her into at sixteen. 'I hated him for years,' she explained. 'But you know something, I think I always loved him.'

'I can understand the whole love/hate trip,' Lennie sympathized.

And they began to talk about Alice, and how it was to grow up with a mother who truly didn't give a damn.

At eight in the morning they stopped by the basement garage where Lucky kept her Ferrari. She threw Lennie the keys and directed him to the East Hampton house.

With Otis Redding on the tape deck and light morning traffic, it was an easy drive. At a local supermarket they bought French bread, butter, bacon and eggs.

'I can't cook,' Lucky confessed.

'I can,' Lennie assured her, adding mushrooms and tomatoes to their haul.

The East Hampton house was locked up. The housekeeper had returned to her family in Finland for a month's vacation.

'No problem,' Lucky announced, springing a downstairs bathroom window and gaining an undignified entrance.

Neither of them was sleepy, but after breakfast, cooked quite professionally by Lennie, they retired upstairs to the large white wicker master bedroom and made slow leisurely love as if it was their first time together. And then they slept – entwined in each other's arms.

Lucky awoke at dusk. Lennie sprawled asleep beside her. Quietly she went downstairs to the kitchen, opened a can, and fixed two large mugs of steaming hot potato soup. Then she switched some slow soul music on the stereo and returned upstairs.

She kissed him awake and handed him his soup. 'Sustenance,' she explained with a grin. 'You're going to need all the strength you can get.'

'Hey!' He sipped the hot soup. 'You certainly know how to open a can!'

She laughed softly. 'For you I'll learn to cook.'

'You will?'

'Not really. But it sounds good!'

He abandoned the mug and reached for her. 'C'mere.'

She didn't argue. She yearned for his touch, he made her skin electric, and every caress gave her small exquisite shocks.

They experimented with each other's bodies, teasing, holding back, testing to see who could last the longest before dissolving into orgasmic ecstasy.

'*You* are really something,' Lennie said, meaning every word.

'And you are not exactly a slouch yourself,' Lucky replied, smiling.

They talked deep into the night. She told him about Gino's tax exile and how she had taken over the family business. 'I built the Magiriano,' she said proudly. 'I was twenty-five years old and female. It wasn't easy.'

'I can imagine.'

'No you can't. Not really.'

'I'll try.'

'Try this.'

She wanted him in her mouth. She wanted to feel his hardness, the beat of his maleness. She wanted him in her power, under her spell.

He groaned his pleasure.

She smiled her triumph.

He confessed his once passionate obsession for Eden. How trivial it seemed now.

'What did she look like?' Lucky wanted to know.

'Skinny, blonde, predatory.'

'She sounds like a bird.'

'She was very beautiful.'

'Who cares?'

'I don't.'

He spread her olive thighs and buried his head between them. Her jet pubic hair felt like silk. She tasted of musky crushed flowers. Bittersweet.

She threw her arms above her head and murmured his name over and over until she came in heavy throbs of abandonment as he sucked her dry with feverish desire.

They slept through the rest of the night.

In the morning Gino called. She couldn't remember what she said to him. She didn't want real life invading her time with Lennie. Soon Dimitri would be back and things would have to be settled.

Chapter 87

Francesca dragged on a long thin black cheroot as Dimitri's plane flew her and Olympia toward Paris. 'Did you ever think about having a series of slimming injections?' she asked Olympia with harsh directness. 'There is a clinic in Switzerland . . . they specialize in weight problems.'

'Oh,' said Olympia brightly. 'Is that the place where you had your face lifted?'

Francesca frowned. 'I have never had a face lift,' she lied.

'No?' said Olympia innocently.

'No,' stated Francesca firmly.

Conversation lapsed. Olympia wished Flash had come with her. She could just imagine him with Francesca. What a collision!

She summoned the stewardess, a tall Swedish woman with tanned skin and an icy smile. When Dimitri travelled she gave him massages. Olympia imagined that was not all she gave him.

'I need a chocolate fix,' she told the Swede. 'What do we have?'

'Parfait, sundae, fresh berries.'

'Strawberries?'

'Blueberries.'

'Dip them in chocolate sauce for me, I suppose they'll have to do.'

The Swede flashed her icy smile and retreated to the galley.

'*Blueberries*, in *chocolate sauce*,' admonished Francesca, fanning her horsy countenance with a copy of French *Vogue*. 'You must be desperate.'

Olympia, secure on coke, smiled. 'Not half as desperate as *some* of the people I know,' she said, and reached for a set of headphones.

•

'How civilized,' observed Paige, gazing at the English tea Susan had set out. There were wafer thin cucumber sandwiches, light scones with a touch of cream and jam, a ginger cake, Earl Grey tea, and fine bone china plates, cups and saucers to put it all on.

'Tea was served on the Stanislopoulos yacht every afternoon at four,' Susan announced proudly.

'What a cosy little get together *that* must have been,' replied Paige, unimpressed.

'It was wonderful,' Susan sighed. She *had* enjoyed the trip. She just wished she hadn't succumbed to the Contessa's perverted advances. 'I wish you had been there,' she added, fixing Paige with an intimate look.

Paige wolfed a sandwich. Hadn't she told Susan it was all over before her trip? Surely the woman had understood her?

'I missed you,' Susan said, drawing closer on the pale beige damask couch. She put her hand on Paige's shoulder. 'Very much.'

The sound of a bee droning broke the afternoon silence. Paige shifted uncomfortably. Why were affairs so difficult to end? Male, female, there was always the final struggle.

She took a deep breath and stood up. 'Susan, dear,' she said, facing her perfectly-groomed blonde friend. 'I know we had something good together – once.' She emphasized the once. 'But time passes, and things change. I told you the last time we saw each other that Ryder and I were giving our marriage a second chance.'

Susan's clear blue eyes, beautifully tucked and stitched, filled with tears. 'I know, I know,' she said, trying to control herself. 'But I *need* you, Paige. You mean *so much* to me. We've meant so much to each other.'

Paige glanced anxiously at the door. It wouldn't do to have the housekeeper eavesdrop on this little scene.

Susan followed her glance, and rose from the couch. 'I gave the couple the rest of the day off,' she said. 'They won't be back until late. And Gemma has gone to San Francisco. We are quite alone,' she added meaningfully.

Paige nodded. One more time with Susan. A proper goodbye.

It wasn't the way she wanted it, but it would work.

Chapter 88

Reality invaded. Lennie had a career on hold. And commitments.

He called Jess in LA and listened to her yell like a deranged Indian. 'Where *are* you?' she screamed. 'You told me you'd be back in twenty-four hours for crissakes. And then you fucking vanish! You start taping the new series in two days! The network is going bananas, and so am I. Where *are* you, Lennie? Christ, don't you have *any* sense of responsibility?'

'Calm down,' he admonished. 'You'll have a heart attack.'

'I'm too young for a heart attack,' she replied dourly. 'And *you're* too young to screw up your career on account of the fact that your dick is out of control again. What happened to the stud I once knew and loved?'

'You're a princess with words.'

'And you're a major asshole.'

'Now that we both know what we are, I called to tell you I'll be back tomorrow.'

'Great. Marvellous,' she snorted her disgust. 'What'll you do? Go straight to the studio from the airport?'

'I thought you said I had two days.'

'That's right. Today and tomorrow. There's a script waiting at your hotel, read it on the plane. Your call is eight a.m. on Monday.' She paused, then said, 'Lennie.'

'Yeah?'

'I just want you to know that I hate you.'

He laughed. 'And I love you.'

'Big fuckin' deal,' she said grudgingly.

He hung up. Lucky sat cross-legged on the bed beside him clad in a huge sweat shirt, with knee socks and her hair in braids. Without make-up she looked like a glowingly beautiful sixteen.

'I guess the world is creeping up on us,' he said.

She shrugged. 'It had to happen.'

He held her with his eyes. 'I wish you could come with me.'

She nodded, seriously, wishing the same thing, but they both knew it was impossible. Dimitri was due back with Roberto, and there was much to sort out before they could be together for the rest of their lives. They had spent hours discussing their future, and a short separation was the only way to handle it. She was going to tell Dimitri it was over. And he would contact Olympia.

'I don't want to leave you,' he said, stroking her leg.

'You think I want you to go?' she replied. And she meant it.

He took her in his arms and cradled her gently.

She breathed his special smell and was content.

'You're shaking,' he said with concern.

She snuggled closer. 'I'm cold.'

'We won't be apart too long.'

'I know that.'

'I can fly back Friday after taping. I'll take the Red Eye – meet you here – we'll have all day Saturday and most of Sunday.'

She laughed softly. 'Then I shall cook you great meals.'

'Yeah. Stock up on cans. Your potato soup wins prizes!'

'Wait until you taste my wild mushroom. Mister, you ain't had nothin' yet!'

'Hey – lady – I've had the best time of my life. I want you to know that.'

She touched his cheek lightly. 'I do know.'

They made love again, and it was more tender, more caring, than either of them had ever experienced before.

Lucky slept the night wrapped in the protection of his arms, and in the morning they awoke early and drove silently back to New York.

The idyll was over.

Marco had left her once . . .

She had never seen him alive again . . .

Chapter 89

Gino did not like getting older. He didn't mind it in one way because only the fortunate were still around to tell their tale. But – on the other hand – getting older sucked. Suddenly, at seventy-four, he could see the light at the end of the tunnel, and it seemed to be coming closer every day.

Unlike Costa, he was not falling to pieces. He still had his hair – mostly grey now – but thick and strong. And his teeth – all his own. And since the heart attack, no real problems. Indigestion sometimes, a recurring ulcer, an aching shoulder now and then – but nothing to get alarmed about.

While he was in New York he went to his doctor for a full check up.

'You're in marvellous shape,' his physician assured him. 'You've got the heart and lungs of a man of fifty.'

Screw fifty. He wanted the heart and lungs of a twenty year old. One's own mortality was a frightening thing.

He flirted with the stewardess on the flight back to LA. She had copper hair – which reminded him of Paige, and a pertly pretty face – which reminded him of Cindy – his treacherous first wife all those years ago.

She responded nicely. He didn't know if it was because she found him irresistibly attractive, or because she sensed he was rich. It was not difficult to know. His suit was custom tailored, his shirts silk. His gold Rolex watch cost six thousand dollars. He knew if he invited her out she'd say yes in a minute. Women. Easy. The story of his life.

But he didn't come on to her. He felt a certain sense of loyalty to Paige. Right now she had his full attention. Every inch. And there were still plenty of inches in that department. *Plenty.*

Susan had disappointed him. Underneath all the grooming she was a cold one, and somehow he had never gotten through to her.

At the airport he took a cab into Beverly Hills. He should have phoned Susan and told her to send the car and driver, but he had left in a hurry due to Lucky's unavailability, and besides, he liked the idea of surprising Susan. She wanted every move plotted and planned – a little unexpectedness would do her good.

The cab driver was foreign. He talked non-stop in broken English about every subject that took his fancy. Gino just grunted occasionally and told him to slow down when he jumped two red lights.

The man grinned and waved stubby fingers in the air. 'I no kill you, meester!' he joked, just missing a poor old lady who was crossing the street. 'Jaywalker!' the cabbie screeched from his window.

'Prick!' the old lady yelled back, giving both Gino *and* the driver pause for thought.

Beverly Hills was manicured, peaceful and perfect. Just like my wife, Gino thought, as he paid the driver, adding a hefty tip.

'You a real gentlemans!' the cabbie said, screeching off.

Two squirrels ran across the front lawn as Gino approached the house. Susan's Rolls was parked in the front drive, and behind it was Paige's gold Porsche.

Two for the price of one. He would get to see Paige sooner than expected.

He quickened his step and reached for his keys.

*

Once rid of Francesca, whom Olympia decided was the pain of the century – even worse than Lucky if that was possible – Olympia settled down to some serious shopping. She wished to return to New York with an entire new wardrobe, and Flash on her arm. The party season began in September, and she did not plan to miss one of them.

Lennie never even entered her thoughts. He was old news. As good as divorced. The moment she returned to New York she would instruct her lawyer to terminate the marriage.

*

Susan lay naked and aquiver. Her smooth alabaster skin had not been exposed to the southern sun of France. She was pale perfection, with just a small appendix scar marring the fleshscape.

Paige had stripped to aubergine bikini panties, and a lacy matching bra from which her generous bosom bulged. She gazed down at Susan, and felt no stirring passion whatsoever. The thrill is gone, she thought.

Susan's breasts were flaccid, the nipples inverted, waiting to be brought to attention. She always *had* expected Paige to do all the work. Once the challenge had been enjoyable, now Paige didn't know where to start. A tweak here, a feel there. It did not take much to turn Susan on.

Paige gritted her teeth and bent to the task ahead.

*

Dimitri's lawyer in Paris ushered Francesca Fern into his office with great solicitousness. He had been warned, by the man himself, to handle her with great care. 'Whatever she wants – do it,' Dimitri had commanded. 'Her divorce must be expedited immediately. No hold ups. When it is done I shall decide what to do about my present wife.'

'Dimitri,' his lawyer groaned. 'If you are thinking of divorcing Lucky it will cost you a fortune.'

'Are you forgetting she signed a marriage contract?' Dimitri reminded.

'No. But you also put your signature to a paper allowing her to build a hotel in Atlantic City at your expense. It could cost you many millions.'

'She'll never do it,' Dimitri said dismissively. 'And if she doesn't handle it personally, the document becomes null and void. There is also a time limit involved. I am not a fool.'

His lawyer said, 'No, you are not.' But privately he thought any man who would prefer Francesca Fern to Lucky Santangelo had to be racing toward senility.

Francesca sat before him in a short silk dress, black stockings, and very high heeled shoes. She smelt of Calèche, smoked disgusting cheroots, and every so often indulged in a coughing fit. Her legs were heavy, and when she crossed and uncrossed them, which was often, he couldn't help noticing she wore no panties.

'If I *do* decide to divorce my husband, Horace, at Mr Stanislopoulos' request,' she said huskily, 'Horace is to be compensated handsomely, from Mr Stanislopoulos' pocket, *not* from mine. Is that clear?'

'Yes, Madame Fern,' the lawyer agreed pleasantly. 'Dimitri made that clear to me on the telephone yesterday.'

She ignored his use of Dimitri's first name, signalling a closer relationship than she wished to acknowledge. To Francesca, anyone you paid was an employee, and that's the way she treated them.

'Should I proceed with this divorce,' she mused, 'papers must be prepared for both myself and Mr Stanislopoulos to sign.'

'Naturally,' replied the lawyer. A marriage between these two without a financial contract was unthinkable.

'I have many needs,' continued Francesca, blowing smoke in his face, and crossing her heavy legs yet again.

'I'm sure that you have, Madame Fern,' soothed the lawyer, hating this horse-faced woman who talked down to him as if he was an office boy.

And then she told him of her needs, and he loathed her even more. Not only was she a bitch. She was a calculating one. Her requirements were outrageous. When he relayed them to Dimitri he hoped he would be equally affronted.

She wanted a huge cash settlement on the day of her divorce. A further fortune when she and Dimitri were married. More lump sums of money for each year they were together. A massive monthly expense allowance. An apartment in Paris, and a duplex in New York. A weekly clothes budget which would feed a family of four for a lifetime. *And*, a special clause which stipulated that over the period of a year she and Dimitri only had to spend six months in each other's company. The rest of the time they were free to travel wherever they so desired.

The lawyer tried to remain expressionless as she relayed her requests, but a nerve in his cheek began to jump uncontrollably.

'I hope you have made a full list of my requirements,' she said, standing up and smoothing down her skirt.

The lawyer rose also. 'Yes, madame,' he said politely.

'Good,' she replied haughtily. And without so much as a goodbye she stalked from his office.

Immediately he reached for the phone.

*

The Beverly Hills house was hardly a welcoming place to return to. It was less home than showplace.

Late afternoon, and the only sound was a bee buzzing.

Gino walked into the living room and found a half-eaten English tea set out on the coffee table. He helped himself to a cucumber sandwich and wandered into the kitchen which was also deserted. Then he made his way upstairs, prepared to find Susan showing Paige some new couturier creation. Women and clothes. The two went together like money and power. They spent fortunes on various expensive outfits – and then wore them only once. Who could figure it?

He smelled Paige's perfume in the air. Musk oil. She drenched herself in it. Better than the sickly sweet 'Joy' which Susan favoured.

He smiled to himself. Gino Santangelo – the scent expert. The street kid with a nose!

He threw open the bedroom door and stood quite still. A tableau greeted him. Two women frozen in shock.

The blonde, not so young but well preserved. Whiter than white skin and unexciting breasts.

The copperhead. Buxom and raunchy.

They were playing games. *You show me yours . . . I'll show you mine.*

The only sound in the entire house was the roaring in his head.

Chapter 90

Lucky tried to concentrate. It was not easy. She kept on thinking of Lennie, and when she did a stupid grin would spread itself across her face and she felt a complete fool.

'What's the joke?' one of the architects she was meeting with repeatedly asked. He was an attractive guy in his early thirties. Once she might have whiled away an evening with him – but things were different now.

'No joke,' she said, still grinning.

He flirted with his eyes. 'In that case you've got a great disposition.'

She didn't want to encourage him, obviously her permanent smile was doing so. 'Try telling that to my husband,' she said offhandedly, and turned away.

Dimitri. What was she going to do about him? Since she had left the yacht a series of pictures had cropped up in various publications taken by lurking paparazzi. All were of Dimitri with Francesca. Getting on the yacht . . . off the yacht . . . running from a nightclub . . . entering a restaurant. Arms around each other, teeth flashing. The irrepressible pair. Dimitri Stanislopoulos and Francesca Fern.

How the newspapers and magazines loved them! The aging billionaire and the prima donna actress. Both married, flamboyant, and great newspaper copy.

Lucky was thrilled his interest in Francesca seemed not to have been dimmed by their marriage. It would make it all the easier for her to tell him it was over. The perfect excuse. She wished she could drop him a short note. DEAR DIMITRI. I AM RELEASING YOU FROM OUR MARRIAGE FOR OBVIOUS REASONS. LET'S STAY FRIENDS. LUCKY.

How clean and simple it could be.

Instinctively she knew it would not turn out to be that civilized.

*

Olympia had purchased three hundred thousand dollars' worth of clothes in Paris. Plus a new sable coat, and a selection of extravagant jewellery. She had also scored an excellent supply of top grade cocaine, a substance she now needed daily if she was to function at all. How fortunate she had been born an heiress. There was no way she could imagine a man spending that kind of money on her. Men were cheap, however much they had. She had observed her father over the years, he rarely dipped into his pocket unless it was for himself or Francesca.

She glanced at the aging actress sitting across the aisle of Dimitri's private plane. What *did* he see in the old cow? And why hadn't he done something about it after all these years?

She wondered why Francesca had made the sudden trip to Paris. Maybe she would ask Dimitri upon their return. He might tell her, then again he might not.

She leaned across the aisle. 'Did you do any shopping?' she asked.

Francesca favoured her with a look. Deep-set brooding eyes decorated with sweeping fake lashes. 'Shopping bores me,' she said.

'It doesn't bore *me*,' Olympia replied, flashing a gaudy ruby and diamond bracelet. 'Beautiful things turn me on.'

Francesca smiled condescendingly. 'Perhaps if you had worked a day in your life you would realize that shopping is merely mind fodder for the idle rich,' she commented.

'What utter balls!' Olympia responded. She would have said more, but the plane was entering a summer storm, and the sudden turbulence shut her up.

*

And in the South of France Dimitri waited patiently for the return of his mistress. He watched Roberto and Brigette splash and play in the pool. He tried to ignore tentative conversation from Horace. He listened to his lawyer on the telephone from Paris, and roared with laughter when he heard Francesca's demands. 'Give her whatever she wants,' he boomed. And he meant it.

Francesca was finally going to belong to him. He didn't care *what* it cost.

*

Lennie flew back to LA, an angry Jess, and an empty apartment. The producers of 'The Springs' were not exactly wild with happiness either. Especially when he complained about the script he had been sent in New York, and read on the plane.

'It's shit,' said Lennie.

'Fuck you,' said the producers. 'We start shooting tomorrow. You want changes – you should have been here.'

Lennie sat up all night rewriting, trying to keep his concentration, thinking of Lucky.

He called her every hour until she said, 'This is ridiculous.' And still they continued talking.

'I've got to get some sleep,' she finally said. 'Dimitri's coming in tomorrow and I have to be clear-headed.'

'You'll call me,' Lennie instructed. 'I'll be back from the studio around eight, LA time.'

They had planned the scenario. Lucky wasn't going to hesitate. She was to tell Dimitri it was over as soon as possible. Then she was to move out of the New York apartment with Roberto and CeeCee, and resume residence in her East Hampton house. Lawyers would then take over.

It all sounded trouble free. With acute intuition Lucky knew it would not be.

*

Olympia sensed something was wrong immediately. She had flown long enough and far enough to observe trouble when it happened. They had been preparing to land for far too long.

The Swedish stewardess was pale beneath her tan, and it was nothing to do with the storm and the turbulence they had travelled through.

'What's the matter?' Olympia demanded, grabbing her arm as she attempted to rush past.

The woman gave a sickly smile. 'Nothing,' she said, falsely jovial.

'Don't give me that,' replied Olympia, strangely calm.

'Just a problem with the landing gear.'

'What kind of problem?'

'It's stuck.'

'Oh, wonderful!'

'Nice Airport has been alerted. But the captain feels it will right itself before we have to use emergency procedures.'

For a moment Olympia felt panic, but only for a moment. She glanced at Francesca – the prima donna slept. 'Don't wake her until you have to,' she ordered.

The stewardness nodded, visibly shaking beneath her Swedish cool.

'How long before we have to land?' Olympia asked.

'Twenty minutes.'

Twenty minutes to get the landing gear to work.

And if it didn't?

Olympia reached for her stash.

Chapter 91

Dimitri Stanislopoulos' private plane crash landed at 7.45 p.m. on Friday evening.

There were nine people aboard. Seven crew and two passengers.

Upon landing on a sea of foam, the plane careened down the runway and burst into flames. Two members of the crew managed to escape the fiery furnace and one of the passengers. All three were severely burned.

The rest of the people aboard perished.

BOOK THREE

The Summer of 1983

Chapter 92

Carrie Berkeley smiled at Bryant Gumbel as the two of them entertained America on the 'Today Show'. It was early in the morning and a steaming heat wave was searing the streets of New York. Inside the air-conditioned NBC studio in Rockefeller Centre, Carrie Berkeley, a very well preserved and stylish sixty-nine, and Bryant Gumbel, one of the best interviewers on television, exchanged words, looks, and created an easygoing banter.

Carrie was promoting the paperback of her book, written in conjunction with Anna Robb entitled, *The Carrie Berkeley Book of Style*. Already the book was climbing the best seller lists. The hard cover had hovered on the *New York Times* list for seven weeks.

Bryant Gumbel grinned – he had an irresistible grin – and concluded the interview.

He is a most attractive young man, Carrie decided, the kind of man she would like to have introduced to her daughter – if she had ever had one.

In the Green Room she rejoined the skinny publicity man assigned her by her publishers. He was admittedly gay, with carrot coloured hair and an engaging smile. 'You were dandy!' he enthused. 'You always are.'

'You'd say that, whatever I did,' she teased him.

'Naturally. I'm no fool.'

He took her arm and they left the building.

Outside there were a few autograph hunters. One of them presented a dogeared copy of her book to be signed. She did so with a flourish.

A limousine waited curbside to take her on to her next appointment. She sank back into luxurious leather, and marvelled, as she did several times a day, at what her life had become. She, Carrie Berkeley, was a published author! With a lot of help from Anna Robb. The two women had become close friends. So close in fact that Carrie had allowed Anna to pry the secrets of her life from her. And for the last year they had been collaborating on Carrie's biography, an explosive manuscript, recently completed, and now ready to show to a publisher.

'We could be looking at a half-million dollar advance,' Anna had said calmly at their last meeting. 'Your story is dynamite.'

Carrie wondered if it was worth revealing her life for half a million dollars. But then again, she had not become involved with the book for monetary gain. It was a story Anna had convinced her *should* be told. And reading the pages, at times so painful she could hardly keep going, she realized Anna was right.

So far, nobody knew about the book. Not Steven, not even Fred Lester. It was a project the two women had kept to themselves.

'We have to show the manuscript to Fred first,' Anna fretted. 'I don't think he'll pay the price, but he has the option and besides, he deserves first look.'

Carrie agreed. She knew of Anna's and Fred Lester's relationship. For months Anna had kept it to herself, but one day she had let it slip. 'You're very lucky,' Carrie said. 'He seems like a nice man.'

'He is,' Anna agreed.

'Do you think you'll marry?' Carrie asked, wondering why she felt so let down.

'No,' said Anna, and never discussed their relationship again.

Carrie was nervous about anyone reading the thousand page manuscript. It was all there in neat type-script. Her life, her shame, every innermost secret.

Ah, but the relief of letting it all out. It had been a cathartic experience.

She worried about Steven's reaction. Anna, quite rightly, pointed out that Steven was a big boy. 'You must do what you think is right,' she said. 'And Steven has to accept your decision.'

Carrie knew this was so. However, it didn't stop her from worrying.

*

'I'm ready,' Mary-Lou Moore said, her large brown eyes wide and determined. 'I'll go in fighting and I'll come out a winner!'

'You're absolutely sure?' Steven Berkeley asked. 'It won't be easy. They're really out to get you.'

'I'm *more* than sure,' Mary-Lou replied fiercely.

'Then we shall have our day in court,' Steven said evenly, satisfied she could handle it. 'The date is set. No more postponements.'

'And no more depositions either,' Mary-Lou sighed with relief. 'I *hate* those things. All those crummy lawyers digging into your past like dirty little maggots.'

Steven laughed. 'You turn an interesting phrase.'

She caught his eye. 'And so do you, counsellor.'

He glanced away and busied himself with a stack of papers on his desk. Lately Mary-Lou had been throwing some very hot looks in his direction. He didn't want to read anything into them. They were lawyer and client, that was all. Even though he did find her extremely attractive. In three years he had watched her grow from gauche teenager to a warm young woman. It had been an interesting transition. When they first met she wouldn't move without her mother, her manager, and a series of spaced-out boyfriends. Now she was on her own, with a legitimate agent and manager and no visible entanglements. She came to his office unaccompanied, and had conducted herself throughout the long and tedious steps needed to get them to court, with dignity.

'How about lunch?' Mary-Lou asked brightly. 'We should celebrate now that we're finally going to court, shouldn't we?'

He found her very appealing, but she was so young – just twenty. Besides, he never *had* believed in mixing business with pleasure. 'I have a lunch appointment with a client,' he lied apologetically.

'*I'm* a client,' she pointed out, tilting her head to one side.

'I know. And we'll be having plenty of lunches together when we're in court.'

'Can't wait!'

When she left his office he sat silently for a moment. Would it be wrong to take her out?

Yes.

Why?

Because she's still a baby.

He was forty-five, old enough to be her father. And she was an actress, a television star.

So what?

Maybe when the case was over he would take her out.

Maybe when the case was over she wouldn't want to go out with him.

He thought about her case for a moment. They had started off suing some half-assed magazine publisher. Vista Publications. But during the course of depositions and discovery, it had come to light that the publishing company was actually owned by Bonnatti Publications, and although the offending magazine had been distributed by Ravier Distribution, Inc., it turned out that Ravier was merely a subsidiary of Bonnatti. So, their case was against Bonnatti Publications and Bonnatti Distribution. And the main shareholder of both companies was a man named Santino Bonnatti. And Steven knew plenty about Santino Bonnatti. He was the son of the notorious Enzio Bonnatti, whom Steven had once almost arrested and brought before a Grand Jury. Until fate intervened, and Lucky Santangelo had killed the sonofabitch. Supposedly in self-defence.

Now he had a crack at the son. He wouldn't be able to put him away – even though he was a known dealer in prostitution, drugs, and pornography on the West Coast. But he could hit him where it hurt. In the wallet.

Mary-Lou was suing for ten million dollars. And Steven planned to collect every penny.

Jerry Myerson entered his office. 'What's happening, Steven? I just had a cancellation. Are you free for lunch?'

'If you're paying, I'm free.'

They went to The Four Seasons, because Jerry felt like it. And there they bumped into Carrie, lunching with Anna Robb and Fred Lester. She radiated style and chic.

'Your mother is something else,' Jerry said admiringly, after they were seated. 'What she's done with her life is quite remarkable.'

Steven had to agree. And he was glad that three years ago he had dropped his quest to find out who his father was and concentrated on getting his own life back on track. He was doing extremely well. So well Jerry wished to make him a full partner, and that was something to think about.

He was living in his own house again, and dating several interesting women. Things were good.

So why wasn't he happy?

Because deep down he still needed to know who his father was.

And one day he would have to find out.

One day.

Chapter 93

'Lennie!' A sharp whining command. Then louder. '*Leennie!*

He was in his study but he heard her. 'Christ! He could be at the beach and he'd still hear her.

He picked up the phone and pressed the intercom. His voice conveyed irritation. 'What is it?'

'I'm lonely.'

'I'm working.'

'I know. But I'm still lonely. Come and talk to me.'

'Give me ten minutes.'

He put down the phone and stared out the window. There was an incredible view. Lush man-made waterfalls, tropical foliage, palm trees, and greenery as far as the eye could see.

His study was leather panelled, with the latest state of the art stereo equipment, video recorders, and a TV set which could tune in all over the world.

The mansion he lived in was high up in Bel Air. It had fourteen bedrooms, fourteen matching bathrooms, and living rooms that went on forever. There were indoor and outdoor swimming pools, two tennis courts, a cosy jacuzzi which seated twelve, and a roller skating rink.

In the basement there was a large mirrored discotheque complete with flashing strobe lights and a rare collection of classic rock albums. Another room housed two pool tables. And there was also a private cinema which seated thirty people.

Not that they ever had anyone over. Olympia was paranoid about being seen – even though her burn scars were long healed, and the wonders of plastic surgery had restored her face to its former prettiness. She didn't want people over because of her weight. Once pleasantly plump, Olympia Stanislopoulos now weighed over two hundred pounds. She was a fat, blonde, bad-tempered rich heiress, who hid her blubber beneath voluminous caftans, promised Lennie she was dieting, and had one of the maids smuggle in Twinkies, chocolate cakes, and candies – in fact anything sweet she could lay her hands on.

'Lennie!' She screeched for him again.

He stood up, and reluctantly went to find her.

She was in the large kitchen gazing mournfully into a well stocked restaurant style fridge. A nervous maid hovered nearby.

'There's never anything decent to eat here,' she complained.

'We had lunch an hour ago,' he commented.

'You call carrots and celery lunch,' she sneered. 'I've heard of dieting, but this is ridiculous.'

'You should go to a clinic,' he remarked. 'It would make it a lot easier for you.'

Her blue eyes were vindictive pinpoints. 'And for you, huh? Send the wife off to a fat farm while the star gets laid.'

Here it came. The usual argument. How long could he take this shit?

'I don't know why you keep on fighting it,' he said evenly.

'The only way you'll get rid of the weight is with professional help.'

'Screw you,' she spat. 'All *you're* interested in is getting rid of me so you can turn this house into bimbette city.'

She had never caught him. But she suspected every move he made. Quite rightly so. He was hardly celibate. Getting laid was one way of killing the pain.

What was he *supposed* to do? The news of the plane crash three years ago still reverberated in his head. An urgent phone call. A distressed voice. Fragments of what had taken place. '*Your wife . . . terrible inferno . . . Francesca Fern dead . . . a tragedy . . .*'

At first he had thought Olympia had been killed too. But no. She was alive and in a coma. Severely burned. Hanging on in intensive care. A flight was arranged for him immediately. Before he knew it he was back in Europe, standing beside her hospital bed.

Olympia. Her blonde hair shaved. One side of her face and her right arm a mass of horrifying burns.

'She'll live,' one of the doctors assured him. 'But she has to be given the *desire* to live.'

Dimitri appeared at the hospital with Lucky. He was white and drawn with a strange expression on his face – a kind of pent-up madness waiting to explode.

Lucky hid behind huge black shades, preventing any glimpse of her eyes. While Dimitri stood by Olympia's bed, Lennie managed to take her to one side. 'We have to talk,' he said urgently, gripping her arm.

She did not remove her shades. In an expressionless voice she said, 'Things are different now.'

'Just a temporary setback –' he began to say.

She cut him off sharply. 'No. It's fate. We weren't meant to be together. I knew what we had was too special to last.'

'When Olympia gets out of the hospital –'

Her voice was devoid of emotion. 'She'll need you,' she said flatly. 'And you must be there for her.'

'Lucky –'

'It's not just Olympia,' she continued, calmly. 'Dimitri needs me too. In fact,' an imperceptible pause, 'he won't let me go.'

They were unable to speak any further, and shortly after, she and Dimitri departed. The concerned father obviously did not plan to hang around.

Lennie was angry. It seemed Dimitri's visit was merely a courtesy call. Didn't he care about his only daughter?

As for the situation with Lucky . . . well, it was early days . . . Once Olympia was out of the hospital . . . And Dimitri was over his shock . . . Everything would work out.

Reluctantly Lennie decided he had to stay with Olympia – at least for a while. He had married the girl, he could hardly desert her now.

He spent every day at the hospital, a witness to her unbearable agony. In America, the producers of his television show demanded his immediate return or a law suit. 'Forget it,' he told Jess long distance. 'There's no way I can leave her now.'

Jess flew in to convince him he was committing professional suicide. She was brutally frank. 'You don't love her,' she pointed out. 'And you don't need her money. So what the hell are you hanging around for?'

He looked at her long and hard. 'Because she's in a coma, and she doesn't *have* anyone else,' he explained. 'I'm not going to run out on her. Don't expect me to.'

Jess nodded. She understood. Show Lennie someone in trouble and he was there. It had always been that way.

Dimitri did not return to visit his daughter. According to one of his minions he had gone into seclusion on his island, mourning Francesca Fern.

'Where's Lucky?' Lennie had asked, trying to keep his voice casual.

'She's with him,' the man had said.

She's with him.

The words haunted Lennie.

Was she with him in every way? Were their lips touching? Their bodies entwining? Were they making love? *She's with him.*

And why not? He was with Olympia.

Oh God! Both he and Lucky were busy doing the right

thing when they should have been together. It wasn't fair.

After several weeks Olympia came out of the coma. The first thing she did was ask for a mirror. When she got it her screams could be heard throughout the hospital. Lennie attempted to reassure her. Only one side of her face was burned, the other was perfect. 'I'ved talked to the doctors,' he said confidently. 'With plastic surgery and skin grafts you're going to look as good as new.'

'You stupid fool,' she yelled, tears streaming down her face. 'What do *you* know?'

He contemplated leaving. But she was his wife, and it seemed she had nobody – only him.

'Get me some coke,' she demanded, the next day.

'Are you crazy?' he replied. 'You're on all kinds of medication. Do you want to kill yourself?'

'I don't care,' she replied blankly. 'Maybe that's what I *should* do.'

Dimitri still did not come back to visit, although he sent flowers daily, and one of his personal secretaries arrived to report on Olympia's progress to him.

'Where is Dimitri?' Lennie demanded angrily.

'Mr Stanislopoulos is not well,' the secretary replied in hushed tones. 'He's unable to leave his island.'

'What's the matter with him?'

'I'm not allowed to divulge that information,' she replied primly. But she did divulge that his wife and child were still with him.

Lucky was back with Dimitri with a vengeance.

Lennie slumped into a depression. He tried to phone the island, but Lucky was always unreachable and never returned his calls.

Another week passed. Olympia's mother, Charlotte, turned up, slightly late in the day. She arrived from New York, a tense woman, well dressed and tight-lipped. 'I would have come before,' she explained airily. 'But it was impossible.'

Why? Lennie wanted to ask. It's your daughter lying there, you cold bitch. Why was it impossible?

Charlotte stayed twenty-four hours.

'I want to see Flash,' Olympia mumbled one day. 'Has he sent flowers? Has he called?'

There were banks of flowers, too many to deal with. The cards were kept in a box, and Dimitri's secretary typed neat thank you notes. Lennie asked the woman if Flash had sent anything. He was not jealous, merely relieved that there might be a way out.

'No,' she replied, consulting a file of names in a leather book.

Lennie tracked the rock star to London and phoned him. 'Olympia wants to see you,' he said, hoping Flash would jump at the opportunity, thereby taking him off the hook.

'Listen, man,' Flash confided, 'that was over long ago – she's too effing rich for my blood. I hope she's awright an' everyfing – but it was never any big deal.'

Olympia swore that Lennie was keeping them apart.

Eventually the day came when she was ready to leave the hospital. A series of operations were planned, but they could not take place immediately, as her skin had to heal first.

'I'll take you to your father's island,' Lennie suggested, with the thought of seeing Lucky.

'No,' Olympia replied quickly, well aware of Dimitri's lack of concern. 'I want to go to California.' She had just read that Flash had bought a house there, and she was determined to see him. Without Lennie's knowledge she purchased the Bel Air mansion for ten million dollars over the phone. She didn't tell him until they arrived.

Once back in America he had no idea what to do. He had planned to stay with her only until she left the hospital, dumping her now seemed cruel. At times she was okay, it wasn't all screaming and name calling. So, much as he wanted to tell her it was over, timing was everything, and the moment was not right. Maybe after the first operation, when she began to look normal again and regain her confidence.

The producers of his TV series were suing him for millions.

Rolling Stone ran the cover story they had been working on. It made him look like egomaniac of the year.

Jess finally quit bugging him about when he was going back to work.

Alice was giving eccentric interviews to anyone who asked.

Add asshole of the year to his list of credits, for that's what she was making him look like.

Olympia and he moved into the house with an army of servants in attendance. Shortly after, Brigette and Nanny Mabel arrived for the Christmas vacation.

'Mama, you are so ugly!' Brigette crowed. 'I can't stand to look at you!'

The moment Christmas was over she was sent to stay with her grandfather, still closeted on his island.

'I hate that child,' Olympia complained bitterly. 'I plan to see as little of her as possible.'

Early one morning, a few days after Brigette left, Olympia ordered the car and chauffeur, and mysteriously went out, her face shrouded by a long scarf.

When Lennie heard he was delighted. It was the first time she had left the house. He was not so delighted when she returned an hour later, hysterical. She never told him, but he soon found out she had been to see Flash, and the rock star had taken one look at her and said, 'Cor blimey! No offence, love. But I can't take fucking disfigurement. Makes me sick to me stomach, know what I mean?'

Lennie got the news from Flash's manager, who phoned to request that she stay out of his client's life.

'Tell your shithead client to go fuck himself,' Lennie fumed, and slammed down the phone.

Shortly after that Olympia began to cling, something she had never done before. And she wanted sex. A subject which had not come up since the accident.

Lennie tried, but his desire level was zero.

Olympia was surprisingly understanding. Matter of factly she blamed it on the way she looked.

He had no excuse except the one he couldn't tell her. Lucky was in his head, his heart, his whole being. She was the only woman he ever wanted. And now, because of a tragic set of circumstances, they were apart.

Once again he tried to contact her, but to no avail. It was clear she was avoiding him. He was angry and rejected. He was also trapped. And going crazy.

The time had come to get back to work, but Jess informed him offers were sparse. Once so hot, he was now not even lukewarm. Bad publicity and a lawsuit did not help.

He had been toying with the idea of writing an original screenplay. 'Maybe we can get the financing and produce it ourselves,' he suggested to Jess.

'Why not have your wife put up the money?' she replied tartly. 'She's buying you everything else.'

It was true. Olympia sat in a chair all day and ordered things over the phone. So far she had bought him a Mercedes, a Porsche, a portable gym, legions of electronic equipment, a boat, tapes, books, clothes. She had turned into a catalogue freak. She ordered and ate, ate and ordered. And so her days passed.

The first operation on her face was a success. They flew to Brazil where she spent several weeks in a private clinic being attended to by the world's finest plastic surgeons. Lennie stayed with her all the time. He worked on his screenplay and visited her daily. She needed all the support she could get.

Dimitri sent a flower shop of roses. It was nearly a year since she'd seen him.

It was nearly a year since Lennie had seen Lucky, although he still thought of her all the time. She obviously didn't give a damn about him, otherwise she would have tried to contact him as he had her. He felt a heavy sadness, but he still refused to believe it was over.

By the time Olympia was allowed to go home her spirits had lifted considerably. She was starting to put on weight, but it didn't seem to bother her. She spent hours studying her face in the mirror and waiting for the day when it would be completely healed.

Lennie finished his screenplay and turned it over to Jess. 'This is what I want you to do,' he said. 'No more clubs or TV. And no, I am not asking my wife to put up the money.'

Jess raised a cynical eyebrow. Lennie was a comic, a TV

star. Nobody was running to finance him in a movie. After she had read the script she changed her mind. It was a hilarious comedy about crime called 'Private Dick' – with all the ingredients to become an excellent little sleeper.

She started looking into financing, and every studio turned her down. At a party she met a producer named Ryder Wheeler. He had recently scored a mild hit with a low budget movie starring the singer, Vitos Felicidade. She told him of Lennie's project and he was interested. She sent him over the script, and within three weeks a deal was set.

The rest was history. 'Private Dick' was the most financially successful film of 1981. And Lennie became an instant movie star – with a mega-bucks contract from one of the biggest studios to write, produce, and star in three more movies.

Now, professionally, he was the hottest property around.

Personally his life was a void.

For three years it had been that way.

Chapter 94

Opening nights always scared the hell out of Lucky, and this was her second one. Her first was the Magiriano Hotel, 1975, eight years before. If she closed her eyes she could still summon back the feeling. Hot and cold anticipation. Crazy excitement. It was like having a tiger by the tail and waiting for it to take off. Ah . . . the trip . . . the incredible high . . .

And now the Santangelo Hotel, in Atlantic City, was ready to be launched. She couldn't wait.

Slowly she went through the ritual of preparation. A long warm shower which she switched to icy at the end. The tingle of the cold water was almost a sexual thrill. And then the luxury of giant fluffy bath towels, towels made specially for the Santangelo Hotel in wonderful colours matching the particular bathrooms they were assigned to. Not for Lucky Santangelo boring white bathrobes. At her hotel the bath-robes were made of silk in Hong Kong, and were to be given to the guests as gifts, not added on to the bill.

After her shower, wearing a cinnamon silk chemise, she sat in front of her dressing room mirror and applied glamour. Usually she did not wear a lot of make-up, but on a night such as this she felt the need to go all the way. Dark gold eyeshadow, black Kohl pencil, burnished bronze blusher, and sensual gloss.

She looked, at 33, sensational. The years only heightened her darkly exotic beauty – made her more intriguing and mysterious. She was staggeringly beautiful in an erotic and unusual way.

She slipped off her chemise, and quite naked stepped into a long dress made of black satin, snakeskin, and lace. The dress fitted her like a second skin, skimming every curve of her supple body, and plunging daringly between her breasts.

Her hairstyle was always the same. Wild jet shoulder length curls, thick and shiny.

Satisfied with her appearance, she added her favourite jewelled panther pin, drop diamond earrings, and matching cuff diamond bracelets. On the wedding finger of her right hand she wore a huge pear-shaped diamond. Dimitri showered her with gifts. It was his way of saying thank you.

Thank you for what?

Three years previously, Francesca Fern had perished in a plane crash. He had never recovered. He was thanking Lucky for staying with him, remaining his wife, and for giving him the only reason to stay alive – his son – Roberto.

Thoughtfully Lucky stared at her reflection in the mirrored wall of her penthouse apartment atop the Santangelo. She knew that when people looked at her they saw a strong, confident, sexy woman. What they didn't see was the heart-break beneath the cool exterior. For she would never get over losing Lennie. And she must never allow herself to be caught in the lethal clutches of love again.

First Marco . . .

Then Lennie . . . Both taken from her by circumstances beyond her control.

Often she wondered how he felt. In the beginning he had

tried to reach her constantly. Phone calls, messages, even a letter insisting that they speak.

Didn't he understand? The plane crash was a warning. If she ever saw him again something terrible would happen. She knew it.

One deep breath and she was ready to go. She licked her lips, threw back her head, and strode to her private elevator.

*

'It's really something,' said Costa.

'Stupendous!' exclaimed Costa's wife.

'An achievement,' allowed Gino.

The roles were reversed as they waited in the Art Deco bar for Lucky. Costa was now married, and Gino divorced.

Costa's wife was a retired call girl of forty. Her name was Ria, and she was fond of gardening and bridge. They had met at a bridge club in Miami a year ago, and hit it off immediately – in spite of a thirty-five year age difference. Then they set up house together. Ria was truthful about her past, and Costa didn't seem to mind. They lived together for a while, and then, very unexpectedly, Ria became pregnant. Naturally Costa did the right thing and married her – even though he wasn't one hundred percent sure the baby was his. She had confessed to a short fling with an old love. Costa had experienced over thirty years of a wonderful marriage to his first wife, but it was sadly childless. He didn't care who had fathered the baby. At seventy-five he was about to become a poppa for the first time, and he was the happiest man in the world.

At first Gino had been more than cynical. Lucky also. But once they met Ria, and got to know her, they both changed their minds. She seemed to adore Costa – and besides, she had faithfully promised him she would never play around again.

Gino glanced at his watch. 'Where's Lucky?' he asked. 'I didn't fly in from Vegas to sit around waitin'.'

'Be patient,' Costa admonished. 'It's her big night.' He sighed with nostalgia. 'Ah . . . how I remember the opening of the Magiriano. What an evening!'

'Yeh. With me stuck in Israel,' Gino complained. 'Schmuck of the year!'

He was now divorced.

Susan had demanded his balls.

And everything else she could lay her hands on.

California law.

You could stick California law up the Holland Tunnel and block both ends!

He had caught *her* – and she was the one with the million dollar demands.

Ladylike cunt.

Into broads all the time.

He would *never* forget the expression on both of their faces when he caught them in the act.

Susan and Paige.

His wife and his lover.

Two dumb tramps.

He would never admit it, but he missed Paige. *She* was the real disappointment. Naturally he had never spoken to her again.

'Here she comes,' said Costa, admiringly. 'And look what she looks like!'

'Stupendous,' sighed Ria.

Yeh. Gino had to admit it. His daughter was an absolute stunner.

*

Brigette Stanislopoulos removed the heated rollers from her long blonde hair. She was fourteen years old, but she could easily pass for eighteen or nineteen. People told her that all the time. People who didn't know, came on to her like crazy, and she loved every minute of it.

Brigette attended school in Switzerland. 'L'Evier,' a strict private girl's school which both her mother – boring fat Olympia – and her grandfather's wife – Lucky, whom she had grown to adore – had been expelled from. Sometimes Brigette wondered why her mother had sent her there. And then she figured it out. It was far away and it was easy.

She also figured out – exactly like her mother before her – how to leave school after lights out. So simple. Hundreds of rich little schoolgirls had followed the path to freedom and the nearest village. The name of the game was not getting caught.

Brigette could play the game expertly. And she didn't need any help. She had no desire to pal up with any of the other girls, they were all stupid babies, whereas Brigette liked to consider herself a woman of sophistication and experience. After all, she had been around. Her grandfather was one of the richest men in the world. Her mother was a famous (unfortunately fat) heiress. And her stepfather (she liked Lennie – even though she rarely saw him. Most of her vacations were spent on her grandfather's island) was a movie star.

She had quite a pedigree, and didn't mind boasting about it. And a temper – which is why nobody went out of their way to make friends with her.

Except the boys.

In the village.

For they didn't care how bad-tempered she was as long as she allowed them liberties the other girls were not prepared to grant.

Brigette Stanislopoulos had never gone all the way.

But she planned to.

Soon. As soon as she found the right boy.

Brigette smiled to herself. She was remarkably pretty. She had all of her mother's good features, and none of her bad ones. She had great boobs. Big ones. Boys loved big ones, and she loved having them. 'Playing titty' as she called being fondled, was her favourite part of sex. Sucking the boy's 'thing' was her least favourite. Although she did it. Had to. They loved it *soooo* much. And once she had a boy in her mouth, she had him under her spell. This was a good thing to know in life.

Brigette smoothed down the bodice of the white dress Lucky had brought her specially for the opening of the

Santangelo. It was an okay dress, not spectacular, but kind of funky in a youngish way. She would have preferred something black and slinky. Black was boss. Especially with blonde hair.

Boys loved her long blonde hair. They loved to run their hands through it, and drape it over their 'things'. They loved to jerk off in her hair. Ugh! Sometimes boys were disgusting creatures.

Brigette often wondered what Lennie did to Olympia in bed.

Then she wondered what Dimitri did to Lucky.

He probably didn't do anything. He was too old. His 'thing' must have withered and fallen off by now.

Was that what happened? She decided to ask someone. Although who would know? After all, it wasn't exactly something you could look up in the reference books. What would one look under? *Prick: The decline of:*

She giggled aloud, and hoped Lucky wouldn't complain about her make-up. She did have a lot on, but she *loooved* make-up so.

*

Lucky strode regally toward her father. She moved like a leopard. Graceful, sure-footed, and dangerous.

'Kid!' He rose to greet her.

'Old man!' She grinned.

'Enough with the smart mouth.' They hugged and kissed. 'I'm proud of you, kid,' he mumbled in her ear.

'It wasn't easy,' she replied.

'Nothing worth having ever is.'

What a cliché. But true.

She flashed on to Lennie. She had seen 'Private Dick' four times, and his follow-up movie, 'Piece of Class', three.

Pure torture. Just seeing him up on the screen her body cried out for his touch. Fortunately she never had to face him. He stayed in California with Olympia. They were still married. Things must have worked out after all.

Yes and you're still married to Dimitri, an inner voice reminded. *Has your marriage worked out?*

Nooooo, he wanted to scream. She was married to a recluse. Dimitri was a poor excuse for the man he once was. He mourned Francesca. He had no intention or desire ever to leave his island again.

For a while Lucky had comforted him. Why not? He was old and alone, and he needed Roberto around just to get through the day. Eventually she announced the time had come for her to move on. The plans for her hotel were ready and she wanted to get started.

'You can go,' Dimitri stated. 'But I'll *never* allow you to take Roberto. *Never*.'

'I can take him any time I want,' she had retorted angrily.

His smile was a death mask. 'Try it and you will lose. There will be no hotel, and believe me, Lucky, one way or another you will never see Roberto again.' He paused. 'You may come and go as you please. You may build your hotel, travel, do whatever you want. But you must leave Roberto here with me. He is my son until I die. Then he is your son. Roberto will inherit everything.'

Dimitri was not a man to issue idle threats. Lucky thought about what he had said, and knew it would be a vicious battle if she decided to take the boy. And a fight for what? If she was able to come and go as she pleased, why *not* leave Roberto with Dimitri? He was safe on the island with his father – for kidnapping threats were not uncommon. And he was certainly happy. He had CeeCee to watch over him, and CeeCee loved him almost as much as she did.

After a lot of thought she decided to accept Dimitri's proposal. She would divide her life. Spend part of her time on the island, and part in Atlantic City building her hotel. There was no reason for her *not* to accept. Lennie was with Olympia. And if she couldn't have Lennie she did not want anyone. Relationships were out. Caring, needing, loving – they were all out.

Maybe an occasional one-nighter – if she so desired. No commitments. Nothing personal. Just sex.

'You have done a magnificent job, my dear,' Costa praised, also rising to greet her.

'Yes, it's unbelievably stupendous!' gushed Ria. Stupendous was her favourite word.

Lucky imagined Ria in her hooker days. She probably said things like, 'And you have a stupendous cock!'

Fancy old Uncle Costa marrying a retired call girl.

Lucky controlled mirth and said, 'I'm glad you all like it.'

She tried not to think mean thoughts about Ria, for she certainly made Uncle Costa happy. Since divorcing Susan, Gino had returned to Vegas and all his old ways. Not that Lucky saw that much of him. She had visited him in Vegas a few times, and he had come to the island on three occasions to see his grandson. Twice he arrived on his own, and once he brought a 25-year-old starlet who talked about her career and her one moment of *real* fame as Centrefold of the Year in some dumb men's magazine.

'Please,' Lucky had said. 'Find another Susan. But don't subject me to one of those again.'

Gino had grinned. What a grin! 'Hey, kid, I thought you hated Susan.'

'I did,' she agreed. 'It was Paige I liked. Whatever happened to her?'

'The broad was a fake,' Gino growled. He did not explain further.

Lucky really felt that by building the Santangelo Hotel herself, and not turning to Gino for help, she had finally come to terms with her father and their relationship. She loved him very much, but she no longer believed that his approval was the most important thing in the world.

He lived in Vegas.

She lived between Atlantic City and Dimitri's island.

It would have been easy to run back to him when his marriage failed, or when all the problems happened as she built the hotel, and there were *major* problems. She couldn't prove it, but somebody made things extremely tough for her. It was one long uphill battle with union disputes, strikes, picket lines, fights, and constant trouble.

When she investigated, the name of Santino Bonnatti kept cropping up.

Ah . . . Santino . . . A long time ago they had been uneasy friends. And then she had been forced to shoot Enzio, his father, and she knew that Santino waited – like a deadly cobra – to strike and take his revenge.

Once she found out it was Santino who was sabotaging her progress on the Santangelo, she acted.

One phone call. Without Gino to back her up.

One meeting with a very old man in New York.

A simple request.

After that the troubles had stopped.

She had been ready to take it a step further if need be. But Santino was basically a coward – she knew him of old. When he received instructions to lay off – he did so – and fast.

Gino looked around, his eyes filled with admiration and pride. 'You really did it, kid,' he said with warmth. 'The place is spectacular. Makes the Magiriano look like a toilet.'

Lucky laughed happily. 'Not quite.' She linked her arm through his. 'Hey, let's party. I feel like having fun with my old man.'

'Cut the old, kid.'

'You got it.'

Chapter 95

The sun streamed through the huge plate glass windows of the house on Blue Jay Way, but Eden Antonio did not care to remove herself from the king size bed. She lay beneath the patterned sheets and silently cursed Santino Bonnatti. He had ruined her life.

Oh God! She should never have hooked up with him in the first place. One look at the hairy-bodied, bald-headed pervert should have warned her. He was scum, the lowest. And steadily, year by year, he was dragging her down to his level. Why hadn't she realized right from the beginning what kind of evil man he was? She was no fool, she had been around. And yet Santino Bonnatti sucked her in. He let her believe she called the shots, and in the long run he would do what *she* wanted.

The truth of the matter was that Santino was in charge. He always had been.

She knew, without a doubt, that she should have got out a long time ago, for slowly and surely he was getting worse all the time. When he reneged on his promise to star her in the movie he financed for Vitos Felicidade she should have made her move then.

But no. She just sat in the house on Blue Jay Way – guarded by Zeko the baboon, and went along with everything Santino wanted. When she *did* finally get up the courage to split, he refused to let her. 'Ya'll go when *I* friggin' wancha to,' he had told her ominously. 'An' don't worry, I'll let y'know when that day is. Only don't count on it bein' too soon.'

So far the moment had not arrived. She was weak, and she knew it. The longer she left her escape the more difficult it would be. And she wasn't getting any younger . . .

She turned over beneath the sheets and lay flat on her stomach. Nobody would believe her if she told them what was going on. Nobody would believe that in Los Angeles, in 1983, a woman could be kept a sexual prisoner by someone like Santino Bonnatti.

Of course, she could go to the police if she ever got the opportunity – which she didn't – Zeko was on her case all the time. And even if she *did* go to the cops – what then? She had no proof that Santino threatened her constantly, made her do things she found repulsive and obscene, and swore he would carve her face up if she ever ran out on him.

'What about my career?' she demanded as often as possible. 'You promised me a movie. You *know* you promised me.'

He let the bait dangle, never withdrew it completely. 'Ya gotta play the right part,' he promised. 'When that comes along, it's yours, honey puss.'

The right part had not existed in the final script of the

Felicidade movie. An established actress had been cast as the love interest. Then Santino had put up the money for 'Private Dick', Lennie Golden's first film. Eden had seen the script, and *known* the girl's role was for her. 'I want to do it,' she had told Santino breathlessly. God! If she could get to Lennie and tell him what was happening to her, he would help her, she knew it.

'I got no input on this one,' Santino spat. 'I'm just puttin' up the friggin' green stuff on account of the fact I think it'll be a moneymaker.'

He was right. 'Private Dick' broke records. Lennie Golden became a star. Eden never even got to go to the opening. Santino took his fat wife, while she sat home staring at television, with Zeko lurking in a corner picking his nose.

What a horrible trap she was caught in. She lived in a beautiful house. She had gorgeous clothes – for when Santino took her out he wanted her to knock his friends' eyes out. And what else?

Nothing.

Her life was nothing.

She was nothing.

Restlessly she kicked off the sheets. A Mexican gardener working on the foliage outside nearly dropped his hose.

She reached for the phone. She knew Santino taped all her calls, but she was allowed a couple of girlfriends to have lunch with occasionally. Ulla, and Paige Wheeler – not exactly a girl, but a sympathetic friend. She was tempted to tell Paige everything in the hope that she could help.

Sure. She could really help when Eden hit the hospital with her face carved up and her looks gone forever.

*

'Faster,' ordered Santino to his driver as they sped along the freeway heading for LA after a business meeting in San Diego.

'Everything okay, boss?' asked Blackie, seated next to the driver.

'Y'know what I'm gonna put on your tombstone,' Santino

growled. 'Everythin' okay, boss? Ya sound like a fuckin' record.'

'Sorry, boss.

'Forget it.'

Santino struggled out of his jacket and folded it carefully. The slight aroma of his own sweat twitched at his nostrils. It bothered him. Goddamn deodorants. They never worked. He should go into the deodorant business – he'd own the world. Santino was not in a good mood. It had been a bad week. Lucky Santangelo had finally opened her lousy hotel in Atlantic City and it burned the shit out of him. He had done everything in his power to stop it from happening – put up road blocks everywhere – and then, just like that, his fucking brother Carlo had called him from New York. 'The word is out you're to cease bothering the lady.'

The lady! What fucking lady? Lucky Santangelo was a cunt and one of these days he was going to get her good.

'What word?' Santino screamed. 'Who from?'

'There was a meeting yesterday. A vote was taken. You are to stop harassing her.'

Santino stopped. He knew who to listen to.

That didn't mean it was over. One of these days he would get the bitch . . . one of these days . . .

Chapter 96

Like all good Californians Lennie learned to play tennis. When he wasn't filming he awoke at seven – no need to worry about disturbing Olympia – they had separate bedrooms. Then, after showering and shaving, he sometimes drove over to Ryder Wheeler's house where they played three punishing sets. Occasionally Paige was around. He enjoyed seeing Ryder's wife, she was a lot of fun and he liked hearing all the latest 'trash' – her word for gossip.

When he left there, he went home and worked. Six or seven hours locked in his study with his new toy – a word processor – was not unusual. Sometimes he would break for lunch – sometimes he wouldn't.

He had a few women dotted around the city he could call at any time – usually attractive working females, who were delighted to see him, and made no demands. They knew he was married – he could hardly hide it, and they accepted that fact. Occasionally he would visit one of them, and just end up talking the afternoon away. Sex was no big deal since Lucky exited his life. Sex was just . . . getting laid.

He knew he had to leave Olympia. Their marriage meant nothing. He had only stayed to see her through the series of operations which had restored her looks. Besides, he had no pressing reason to make the move. Lucky was not waiting. She didn't give a damn. For three years she had ignored him – not responding to any of his attempts to contact her. She was still with Dimitri – and it burned the hell out of him.

However, enough was *more* than enough, and Olympia's looks were finally regained. So was her personality. She was the same rich spoiled heiress, and when he wasn't locked away working – which was most of the time – they fought constantly.

'I think we should get a divorce,' he told her one day, as they skidded out of yet another fracas.

She stopped mid-sentence and stared at him. Pained blue eyes in a piggy face. 'I don't want a divorce,' she said quickly.

'Hey – listen.' He walked to the bar and fixed himself a bourbon. 'We were never a match made in heaven.'

'How can you say that?'

'Maybe because it's true.'

'Just because I'm slightly overweight –'

'It has nothing to do with your weight.'

'Oh yes it does,' she yelled. 'You hate me because you think I'm fat, you lousy bastard. It wasn't *my* fault I was in a plane crash. It wasn't *my* fault –'

Oh shit. Freedom was not going to be easy. Every time he brought it up it was the same old story.

'Sonofabitch,' she mumbled. 'Why don't *you* desert me too? Everyone else has. Big fucking movie star. Take off,

Lennie. You think I care? Shit. I don't care. Maybe I'll kill myself – would that be more convenient for you? Would you like that?' She began to sob theatrically.

'Cut it out, Olympia,' he said grimly. 'You know I'm not going to leave until you're ready.'

He meant what he said. After all, he had nowhere to go. And her suicide threats – which she made often – bothered him. He didn't want to feel responsible if anything happened to her.

He knew Lucky was about to open the hotel she had built in Atlantic City. Some PR had sent them an invitation to the opening. For one wild moment he had contemplated attending. But what good would it do? Screw Lucky Santangelo.

He hated her.

No he didn't.

Yes he did.

Lucky . . . Lucky . . . She was with him every day.

Once a month Dimitri telephoned and spoke dutifully to his daughter. It was always the same conversation. The 'how are you' speech, Lennie called it. The duty call.

'I can't stand him!' Olympia always shrieked when she slammed down the phone. 'I don't know why he bothers. He treated me as if I didn't exist when I was in the hospital practically dead. And I hate that bitch he's married to as well. Lucky fucking Santangelo. You know something? He wishes *I* was the one who died in the crash, not his precious Francesca.'

Although he didn't voice an opinion, Lennie was inclined to agree with her. Dimitri obviously couldn't care less if he ever saw his daughter again. She was a sorry reminder of his lost love. But his granddaughter, Brigette, was another matter. She spent most of her vacations with Dimitri, and that suited Olympia just fine. In fact, Brigette had not visited them for over a year, although she was due to arrive within days, shortly after attending the opening of Lucky's new hotel.

The last time she had been at the house was with dear old Alice, who turned up with an out of work actor of twenty, and a raving queen of fifty. The three of them got drunk and very disorderly, and Lennie had never invited her back. Alice complained at first, but he discovered that if he sent her money – lots of it – she shut up and left him alone. He hadn't seen her in over a year.

Thank Christ he had his work. It was all-consuming. He didn't think about much else. Writing and starring in movies was a twenty-five hour a day occupation. No time to worry about real life and what might have been. Just get on out there and do it.

*

Jess loved lunching with Paige Wheeler. Paige was the only person she could be seen in public with and not feel short, for Paige was only inches taller than she. And Paige talked dirty. None of the Hollywood bullshit for her. She said what was on her mind, and it was usually outrageous and funny.

'Did you ever go to bed with Lennie?' Paige asked, as soon as they were settled at a table in the Bistro Garden.

'What kind of a question is that?' Jess giggled. 'He's my friend. You don't go to bed with your best friend.'

'Oh no?' winked Paige.

'You're terrible!' laughed Jess.

The women had become friendly when Ryder started producing Lennie's movies.

'I can ask, can't I?' chided Paige. 'I think he's very hot looking. Sometimes the hot ones turn out to be duds in bed.'

'Not Lennie.'

'I thought you said –'

'His reputation goes before him. Don't forget, I've known him since we were kids.'

They consulted the menu and ordered a light lunch.

'I'm going to Atlantic City this weekend,' Jess confided over the chopped salad.

'Anything or anyone I should know about?' Paige asked. twirling her fingers around the stem of a wine glass.

Jess's eyes were sparkling. 'There's this guy – an older man –'

'The best kind,' Paige murmured.

'He sort of liked me – once,' Jess continued. 'But, you know, he was one of those guys that had it on offer all the time – so I didn't jump.'

'Good for you. Although *I'm* always wondering what I might have missed!'

'When I went back to Vegas a few years ago with Lennie, he was different. Like he didn't come on, he was very cool and –'

Paige finished the sentence for her '– naturally you wanted him at once.'

'How did you know?'

'Simple. It's always that way. They want you – you don't want *them*. You want them – they don't want you.' She leaned forward with interest. 'What's happened now?'

Jess grinned. 'He wants *me*. I think.'

'And do you –'

'Yes!'

Paige nodded with satisfaction. 'That's wonderful. Who is he? And does he deserve you?'

'His name is Matt Traynor. He used to run the Magiriano Hotel in Vegas for Gino Santangelo. Now he's running Lucky Santangelo's new hotel in Atlantic City. He's kind of fiftyish, and –'

Paige tuned out as Jess gave a full description of Matt. The sound of Gino's name evoked embarrassing memories. He never *had* allowed her to explain – and what could she have said anyway?

'– and so he called and invited me for the weekend. Says he *has* to talk to me and can't do it on the phone.'

'Sounds good to me,' said Paige encouragingly.

Jess grinned. 'I hope so. To tell you the truth, if I have to go out on *one more* date and make stupid conversation, I'll ace myself!'

*

Olympia called her drug dealer. She had several. They knew her well, and trusted her. Dealing by mail was usually out. But for Olympia Stanislopoulos, anything was possible.

She hoarded drugs. She had a formidable supply. And she

had the best place in the world to keep her stash – a secret room shown her by the realtor on the day they moved into the Bel Air mansion. While Lennie was downstairs he had led Olympia to the back of her dressing area, pressed a hidden button, and there, revealed by a sliding panel, was a small windowless room. 'To keep your dope in,' the realtor had joked.

Ha ha. Some joke.

'Don't tell my husband,' she had said quickly. 'It's a great place to hide Christmas presents.'

Never again would she be without drugs. Never. Never. Never.

Being in the plane crash was bad enough, she had ongoing nightmares about *that*. But when they deprived her of cocaine and grass and pills – all the things that kept life worth living – she was outraged.

Now she had a hoard of everything. The hidden room looked like a hospital store-room.

After she'd called her dealer and put in an order, she examined her face in the mirror and fingered her soft new skin. She was pretty again, perhaps even prettier than before the accident.

She sucked in her cheeks and imagined herself thin. Ah . . . when she was thin she would conquer the world. She would emerge from hiding and surprise everyone with her beauty.

She would surprise Flash.

That bum.

She would have him again. For sure.

Chapter 97

'You have too much make-up on,' scolded Lucky. 'But you look great anyway – so don't sweat it.'

'Too much make-up!' squealed Brigette. 'Like I usually wear twice this amount!'

'Where? In class?'

'No. Out of class. My favourite place!'

Lucky hugged her. The young girl reminded her so much of Olympia at the same age. She was very fond of the child, although Brigette was hardly a child anymore, she was almost as tall as Lucky, and looked eighteen.

'I'm glad you're here,' Lucky said warmly. 'And the dress we picked is just right.'

'Nice and virginal,' winked Brigette.

Lucky smiled. 'If you say so.' She put an arm around the girl's shoulder. 'Come along, I want you to sit with Gino and Costa.'

Brigette gazed around the crowded ballroom. She was excited to be at the opening of the Santangelo. But it wasn't cool to be excited, and above all, tonight of all nights, she wanted to radiate cool.

As they walked toward their table she thought she spotted John Travolta, and wasn't that Cheryl Tiegs? And . . . holy shit . . . it couldn't be, but it was, actor Tim Wealth. He was twenty-six and *fantastic*! Like she could *die* for him, and here she was right in the same room!

Gino greeted her with a kiss on the hand. 'Quite a young lady, now,' he said. 'And a very pretty one too.'

She liked Lucky's father. He was old, but he was more fun than Dimitri, who sat in a rocking chair all day gazing out to sea with a mournful expression on his craggy face. Brigette knew she was fortunate to be at the opening. She had been begging Lucky for months – via letter and phone from Switzerland – to allow her to come.

'Just for a couple of days,' Lucky had finally said. 'Then you have to go straight to California to see your mother. She's expecting you.'

Brigette wished she didn't have to leave at all. Spending the summer with Olympia was a depressing thought. Her mother was so weird and fat and uncool. Brigette would have been perfectly happy spending the whole vacation with Lucky. Now *she* was cool.

It was a marvellous evening, and everyone seemed to enjoy

themselves. Lucky had put together an experienced and innovative management team, headed by Matt Traynor, whom Gino had allowed her to steal.

Matt, looking dapper in a new tuxedo, his grey hair cropped close to his head, seemed to have acquired a new girlfriend. She was short with curly hair and a great body. Lucky knew she had seen her somewhere before, but she couldn't quite remember where, until Matt introduced them. Then it all fell into place. Jess. The croupier from Las Vegas whose baby had drowned. Lennie's friend. Lennie's manager.

Lucky smiled at her. 'It's good to see you, and congratulations on all your success with Lennie Golden.' *How is he? Does he ever talk about me? Is he happy?*

'Your hotel's incredible,' Jess exclaimed. 'It must have been some project to put together.'

'It was,' Lucky replied. Did Jess know about her and Lennie?

No. Nobody knew. It was their secret.

'Anyway . . .' Jess gestured around the magnificent ballroom, filled with a glittering array of first night guests. 'It's really something.'

'Thank you.' *Does Lennie miss me? I miss him.*

'Hi, Brigette.' Jess leaned across the table. 'I haven't seen you in ages. I hardly recognized you. You look so adult!'

'Oh. Hi.'

'I hear you're coming out to visit.'

'Yes.' Brigette fidgeted uncomfortably. She was fed up with being polite to everyone. Sweet little Brigette in the virginal white dress. My? Hasn't she grown up! They should only know! Across the room she watched Tim Wealth get up from his table and wander off. He was probably as bored as she was. Quickly she stood up. 'I've got to go to the bath room, she whispered to Lucky.

Without hesitation Brigette set off in the same direction as the young actor.

There were stars at the opening from every field. Lucky

moved from table to table, smiling, greeting, welcoming. It wasn't her job, but she knew how to do it better than anyone.

It was a high profile party. Vitos Felicidade entertained, the champagne flowed, there were silver bowls of caviar on every table, and the food was gourmet.

Lucky had invited Dimitri, and for one moment she had thought he would accept. But no, he decided against leaving his island. In three years she had watched him grow into an old man. It seemed that when Francesca went, his will to live went with her. All he wanted to do was stay on his island and vegetate, handing his business affairs over to minions, and taking no interest in anything or anyone except Roberto and Brigette. His son and his grandchild kept him alive.

Lucky came and went as she pleased, and while she was building the Santangelo it suited her fine. Now that the hotel was finished, and Roberto was reaching school age, she wasn't sure if she wanted to continue this arrangement. Roberto was four and a half, a sturdy, quite little boy. Was he to grow up in isolation with Dimitri looming over him? As it was now, the only friends he had were the children of servants on the island.

Brigette was another matter. She arrived for vacations. Swam, sunbathed and water-skiied. Then she returned to the real world – if you could call an expensive private girl's school in Switzerland the real world.

Lucky had enjoyed watching her change from an impossible whining brat, into a pretty young teenager. And it was especially pleasing that she treated Roberto as if he was her younger brother.

Brigette *never* wanted to visit Olympia, who appeared not to care at all. In a way Lucky felt like the child's surrogate mother. She didn't mind the responsibility, which had been hers ever since Nanny Mabel was dismissed at Brigette's insistence when she was twelve. Lucky took over willingly. She had tried to teach Brigette certain values and a sense of independence. She had also given her advice on everything from drugs to boys.

Brigette was not looking forward to spending the summer

with Olympia, but Lucky persuaded Dimitri to make sure it happened. 'Maybe now that Brigette is growing up, the two of them will get along,' she urged. 'If they don't do it now, they never will.'

As a consolation prize Lucky had allowed Brigette to attend the opening of the Santangelo, and the young girl certainly seemed to be loving every minute.

*

'I thought we might get married,' Matt said formally. 'It seems ridiculous for you to come all this way without us doing *something* to commemorate the occasion.'

Jess could not believe her ears. Several years of silence, then this.

'What do you think?' he continued matter-of-factly.

'Uh,' she stared at him dumbly. 'I . . . uh . . . *married*?'

'Yes. Unless you think it's the worst idea you've ever heard in your life.'

She shook her head. 'Why?' she asked blankly.

'Why not?'

She recovered her composure. 'Shall I give you a list?'

He backed away. 'Forget I suggested it.'

'Why?'

'Will you stop saying why.'

'Matt.'

'Yes.'

'I don't think it's such a weird idea.'

*

Brigette was outside the men's room when Tim Wealth emerged. 'Hi,' she said brightly, as if they were old friends.

He looked around to see if she was addressing someone else.

'I'm speaking to you,' she said boldly. 'We met. Remember?'

Tim Wealth was tall and gangly with a thin face, intense eyes, and longish brown hair. He wore a rented tuxedo, black shirt, and a small gold stud in one ear. He had made one movie two years before, and been hailed as the hottest newcomer of the year. Since that – nothing. Not one single script came his way.

Who can explain the vagaries of the film industry? Certainly not Tim Wealth.

After holding out for eighteen months he was finally reduced to guesting on bad TV shows. After that it was all downhill. Now he was in Atlantic City with a gay producer who promised him more than a crack at his skinny ass.

'Where did we meet?' he asked, looking her over. 'I think I've got Alzheimers, and I'm too young to die.'

Brigette blinked. 'What?'

'Forget it.'

She couldn't believe she was actually talking to him. 'I saw your movie six times,' she said excitedly. 'Why haven't you made any more?'

'Good question,' he said dourly.

'My stepfather's an actor.'

'That's exciting.'

'His name's Lennie Golden. Do you know him?'

'Do bears shit in the woods?'

'Pardon?'

'Forget it.'

Brigette soldiered on. 'My sort of aunt owns this hotel.'

'And who is your sort of aunt?'

'Lucky Santangelo. Have you seen her?'

'Could I miss her?'

'Are you with a girl?'

'Are you offering your services for the night?'

Brigette felt a tingle of excitement. Tim Wealth was even better in the flesh than on the screen. 'Yes,' she said quickly.

He stared at her quizzically. 'How old are you?'

She didn't hesitate. 'Eighteen,' she lied. 'And you?'

'I'm twenty-six pushing fifty. And if this evening goes on much longer I'll be pushing sixty.'

She giggled. 'You're bored.'

He raised an eyebrow. 'You're smart.'

'Where do you live?' she asked enthusiastically.

'LA,' he replied.

'I'm going there tomorrow,' she announced proudly.

'What d'you want, a medal?'

She giggled again and thrust her bosom to the limit in the virginal white dress Lucky had chosen.

He could not help but notice. And although Tim Wealth swung both ways, a magnificent pair of boobs always intrigued him. And his producer friend wouldn't come up to the suite for hours. 'Want to see my feet?' he questioned.

'Your *feet*?'

'My toes are famous.'

'Honestly?'

'Are you for real?'

'What?'

'Follow me, little girl.'

*

'Where's Brigette?' Lucky asked.

'Never mind about Brigette. When am I gonna see my grandson again?' Gino responded.

'Soon,' Lucky promised.

'Why don't you bring him back to America where he belongs?' Gino asked testily.

Yes. Why didn't she? The time had come.

But how? Dimitri would never agree.

'I'm going to,' she said firmly.

'Good, good.' He leaned back and looked around. The place was jumping. He couldn't have done it better himself. A lot of the party guests had already drifted out to the tables, and the satisfying whirl of roulette wheels filled the air.

'Where *is* Brigette?' Lucky asked again, but her attention was taken by Vitos Felicidade, who came by the table, trailed by his entourage, to tell her what a magnificent party it was.

She smiled. 'Thank you, Vitos.' He was costing her a fortune, but the way the audience loved the Spanish singer made him worth every cent.

He had hang-dog melancholy brown eyes. 'Would you care for a drink?' he asked, his English much improved.

'I have a drink,' she replied.

His brown eyes signalled an invitation. 'Weeth me.'

Vitos Felicidade was a heart-throb. Millions of women worldwide bought his records and desired his body. For Lucky he did nothing.

'I'm just too busy tonight,' she replied with charm. 'Maybe some other time.'

He rather liked being turned down, it was a refreshing change. 'Mebee,' he winked roguishly. 'Mebee not.'

What *was* she going to do later when the party was finished? She was on a high, the adrenalin pumping. There was no way she would want to be alone.

Sex.

Why not?

With a stranger. Someone she would never have to see again.

*

'Drink it.'

'Suck it.'

'Snort it.'

Tim Wealth issued a list of instructions, and Brigette obeyed, because she was overawed to be in his presence.

He made her drink neat vodka, and it was disgusting, like medicine. But she drank it all down anyway, because she didn't want to look like a baby.

Then he unzipped his fly, told her to kneel in front of him, and thrust his 'thing' into her mouth. Only *his* 'thing' wasn't like the boys' from the village near her school. His was limp and wobbly, like a soft rubber toy.

She did her best but nothing happened, and she didn't really mind. How she hated that moment when the warm salty liquid exploded in her mouth. *She* hated it, but boys loved it. Tim Wealth seemed different.

Pushing her away, he stuffed himself back into his trousers and walked across the room. Fumbling in a drawer he came up with a small packet of white powder which he carefully arranged in two straight lines on a marble table top. Then he handed her a rolled bank note and issued his third command. 'Snort it.'

She knew what it was. Cocaine. One of the girls at school – a rich Arab's daughter – did it all the time.

Brigette had smoked grass, but this was her first time with coke. She sniffed gingerly, spluttered and choked, and the two neat lines of white powder scattered everywhere.

'Shit!' exclaimed Tim. 'What are you, a fucking novice?'

'I'm sorry,' she gasped.

'You should be,' he complained, laying out more of his precious supply. 'Now snort it. Properly.'

Her second attempt was more successful, and suddenly she felt *soooo* good.

'Undress,' Tim Wealth commanded.

She hesitated for only a moment. Usually boys undressed *her*, and it was in a dark field or the back of someone's car. This was different. *He* was different.

She did as he requested, shedding her white dress, bra, and panties with feverish abandon. She felt funny – sort of excited and strange and expectant.

When she was fully undressed he produced his 'thing' again, and this time it was big and hard and red. And he made her kneel on the floor doggy style. He entered her from this position fast and furious.

She stifled a frantic yell. He was hurting her, but at the same time waves of feeling washed over her, and she felt a loss of control. *Wonderful* waves of feeling.

Something was happening to her and she didn't understand what.

He slapped her on the ass, hard, and began to thrust like a mad man.

The good feelings combined with the bad, and she cried out, begging him to stop.

He didn't do so until he was ready. Then he exploded with a sigh, and rolled away from her across the floor.

She shivered, and tried to get up. When she did her legs were weak and shaking and she felt the stickiness of blood.

'Get dressed, little girl, and go home,' he mumbled sleepily from his position on the floor. 'I'll see you around.'

Didn't he realize he had taken her virginity?

Obviously not.

She didn't know what else to do, so she gathered her clothes together and dressed quickly. Then she wrote her name and the phone number of Olympia and Lennie's house in LA on a message pad, which she then propped against the phone.

Tim Wealth was asleep.

His satisfied snores followed her out the door.

*

'I want to phone Lennie,' Jess said.

Matt smiled. 'You know, I used to think you were having an affair with him. I tried to like him, but I was jealous as hell.'

'Idiot!' She grinned. 'Why has it taken you all this time to tell me how you feel?'

He threw up his arms. 'Listen to you! Anyone would think that you *welcomed* me when I first came on to you. Your attitude was a killer, my dear.'

'Well you were a jerk.' Hastily she added, 'Then.'

'Thanks.'

'You're welcome.'

'I wish we were in Vegas now, we could do it tonight.'

Her grin widened, 'Oh, we'll do it tonight.'

'We will?'

'You betcha ass, Mr Traynor.'

*

'There you are!' exclaimed Lucky. 'Where have you been?'

'Exploring,' replied Brigette, innocently, her cheeks flushed, but other than that her appearance quite normal.

'I don't like you disappearing,' Lucky admonished. 'If you want to go off exploring, tell me, and I'll arrange for someone to go with you.'

'I'm not a baby,' Brigette objected, thinking to herself that at last she was fully grown up, for surely the sensations she had recently experienced with Tim Wealth made her a real woman. He had taken her virginity, and she was glad it was him and not some creepy village boy.

'I know you're not,' Lucky said patiently. 'But you *are* a very important young lady, who, one day, is going to inherit a great deal of money. And you can't just wander off without telling me where you're going. Your grandfather would throw a fit.'

'I understand,' said Brigette, although she didn't at all. Sometimes Lucky could be as dumb as all the other adults. 'Actually, I'm kind of tired. Is it okay if I go to bed now?'

'Certainly,' agreed Lucky, relieved to have the responsibility of Brigette off her hands for the night.

*

'I'm getting married,' Jess announced, long distance.

'To Matt?' Lennie replied, delighted for her.

'No! The bellman at the hotel, asshole!'

'When?'

'Soon.'

'Hey – are we having a big wedding?' he joked.

'I don't know what we're having, but whatever it is I want you to be my best man.'

'The groom has a best man – you have a maid of honour.'

'Screw tradition. I want a best man,' she said stubbornly.

'Then you shall have me.'

'*Now* you offer yourself!'

He tried to keep his voice casual. 'What's the hotel like?'

'Amazing.'

'Have you seen Lucky?'

'Sure.'

'How does she look?'

'Amazing.'

'You really are a mine of information.'

'I'll tell you all when I return.'

*

By three-thirty a.m. the last stragglers left the party. Lucky sat at a table with Matt and Jess, Gino, and a pretty showgirl he had charmed.

The indefatigable Gino. Was there no stopping him?

Obviously not. He rose to leave, the showgirl in tow. 'This

is a late night for me,' he said, putting his arm around the girl. 'I'm an old man. I'm not used to all this activity.'

'Oh yes you are,' grinned Lucky.

Gino winked and kissed his daughter. 'You're one of life's winners, kid,' he whispered affectionately. 'Don't ever forget it.'

'He's really something, my old man,' she sighed as he departed.

'We should all have such . . . uh . . . energy at his age,' admired Matt.

'Is that what they call it?' said Lucky jauntily.

Jess sipped the remnants of champagne from a glass on the table. 'When I worked at the Magiriano,' she said, '*all* the girls lusted for a night in Mr Santangelo's company.'

'Really?' Lucky smiled, although she wasn't surprised.

'And the ones who made the trip *never* returned disappointed!'

'I don't know if I should be hearing this,' Lucky laughed.

'I thought *I* was the resident stud,' interjected Matt.

'You were the resident joke!' teased Jess.

Lucky feigned a yawn. She wanted to be alone. Much as she liked Matt – *and* Jess, whom she was gradually getting to know – it had been a long night and she needed tranquillity or anonymous sex. Either would do.

'I'm going to bed,' she said. 'And may I suggest you two do the same?'

'Good suggestion,' said Matt.

'Yes,' agreed Jess, feeling shy for the first time in years.

Lucky stood up, and so did they. 'I'm very pleased for you both,' she said warmly. 'Very pleased.'

Jess gazed up at Matt – so far from the type of man she usually went for she couldn't even believe it. 'So am I,' she murmured.

As they walked from the ballroom Lucky turned casually to Jess. 'And how is Lennie?' she asked in a throwaway manner.

Jess, who of course knew everything – picked her words carefully.

'He's well,' she said slowly. 'Working hard. Sometimes I think his only pleasure in life is work.'

Lucky digested *that* piece of information while they said their goodnights at the elevator.

Once upstairs in her penthouse she couldn't sleep. She thought about what Jess had said . . . *Sometimes I think his only pleasure in life is work* . . . How true. If she didn't have Roberto she would feel the same way.

Lennie . . . *Lennie* . . . *Lennie* . . . He haunted her thoughts.

She decided to change clothes and go out. There was an all night western bar she knew of where the action never stopped. With haste she stepped from her dress, and as she reached for jeans and a shirt, her phone rang. For one wild moment she imagined it might be Lennie. Quickly she picked it up.

'Meesis Stanislopoulos.' A foreign accent, the line long distance.

She had a sudden premonition of bad news and her heart began to beat much too fast. Roberto. *Please God let nothing have happened to Roberto.*

Her voice was tremulous when she spoke. 'Yes?'

'I'm so sorry . . .'

'What?' she screamed, fearing for her son.

'Meester Stanislopoulos . . . a massive stroke . . . no time to summon you . . . he died an hour ago.'

Chapter 98

Jury selection took days. Every time Steven approved a juror, the opposing counsel would object. And vice versa. But at last a jury was settled upon, and things could begin.

Mary-Lou appeared in court from day one. She sat on the front bench and watched intently as the case unfolded.

It took a week. Moore versus Bonnatti. And at the end of that time Steven felt pretty confident they were going to win. Mary-Lou, as a witness, had conducted herself impeccably, whereas the opposition had presented nothing but men in three piece suits with weak excuses, shifty eyes and slicked back hair.

Bonnatti himself did not appear. Steven wished he had. He would have liked to have seen his face when the jury returned a verdict of sixteen million dollars in Mary-Lou's favour.

She was ecstatic. 'It's not the money! It's not the money!' she kept on repeating excitedly. 'I feel like Clint Eastwood! I stood up for something on principle and I won!'

'They'll appeal,' Steven warned. 'With an award this large it could be drastically reduced.'

'I don't care,' she shouted. 'This is my victory, and nobody can take it away from me!'

He took her out to celebrate. They celebrated all night, and he found himself in bed with a 20-year-old television star whom he had no intention of getting involved with.

She was disarmingly young, and pretty, and sweet.

'What am I doing here?' Steven groaned, after they made love.

'Didn't you enjoy it?' Mary-Lou asked, her brown eyes wide and innocent. She knew only too well he had enjoyed himself every inch of the way.

'What a question!' he exclaimed, eyeing her gorgeously compact body – the colour of milk chocolate – perhaps a shade lighter than his own skin.

'I had a perfectly fantastic time,' she grinned. 'I guess it's true what they say about lawyers.'

'And *what* do they say about lawyers?'

She giggled. 'That if you get a good one he'll be on your case forever! Steven, you sure do have stamina!'

He couldn't help laughing. God! She was pretty. But of course he must never let this happen again.

He spent the night, and in the morning he informed her sternly that it was not going to work.

She smiled happily and said, 'I absolutely agree with you.' Then she wrapped herself around him and he was lost in her sweetness.

Making love to Mary-Lou was special, and he knew it, and so did she.

When he finally left her apartment she said, 'I'll cook you dinner tonight.'

'I told you,' he replied, 'this relationship is not going to work.'

'Sure,' she grinned. 'Let's not make it work together. Be here at seven. I give great Chinese food.'

Within a week she had moved from her apartment into his house.

'God help you!' cautioned Jerry.

'Isn't she a little young for you?' ventured Carrie.

Steven agreed with both of them. But Mary-Lou took the bitterness out of him. He had never been happier in his life.

*

'We have a great offer. A firm offer,' Anna Robb said. 'I want you to guess who it's from.'

Carrie shook her head. 'I have no idea.'

'That's good,' said Anna smugly. 'Because you'd never guess.'

'Who?'

'Do you really want to know?'

It was unlike Anna to be so playful. Carrie was beginning to get aggravated. 'Yes,' she said shortly. 'Kindly tell me.'

Anna took a deep breath. 'A half a million dollars. A quarter on signing. A quarter on publication. A quarter on paperback publication. And the rest six months later.'

'Who bought it?' demanded Carrie.

'Fred!' exclaimed Anna. 'Can you believe it? Fred Lester. The original tightwad.'

'Fred,' repeated Carrie.

'Yes, my dear. And he bought it because it's the best biography he's read in years, and he thinks it will be a giant smash. He says, and I quote, "The honesty in this book made me want to cry." Now for Fred Lester to say something like that –'

Anna continued talking, but Carrie stopped listening. She

was on the road to revealing her story to the world. And it wasn't just her story, it was Steven's too, and she should have asked him.

'. . . Fred wants to see you. Tomorrow if possible.' Anna beamed, Carrie had never seen her so happy. 'He has big plans.'

Big plans. Oh God. Perhaps she had made a mistake. Sharing her life's secrets with Anna was one thing, but spreading them across the country was something else entirely.

'I don't know –' she began.

'You don't know what?' shouted Anna, quite out of character. 'Smile, for goodness sake. Smile, Carrie. You are going to be the most famous black woman in America!'

Chapter 99

'Cocksuckers!' screamed Santino Bonnatti. 'Whadda they think I am? A dummy? A mark? If they think they'll ever see two fuckin' cents of sixteen mill, they're pissin' in a high fuckin' wind. Donatella!' He yelled for his wife.

She took her time coming into the room. And then she glared at him and his henchmen. 'Your language. You gotta filthy language problem,' she hissed. 'You thinka the kids they no hear?'

Some dumb spade was hitting him for sixteen million big ones and Donatella was worried about the kids. 'Fuck the children!' he yelled.

'Fucka you!' responded Donatella. She crossed herself and gazed ceiling-ward. 'Ah God, you shoulda forgive me. I'ma married to a pig!'

'The pig who pays the bills,' growled Santino.

'Whata you want?' demanded Donatella, placing large hands on ample hips. 'You want I kissa your ass?'

He glared at her. 'I'm going out,' he said grimly. 'If any reporters call, tell them no comment.'

'Whatsa no comment?'

'Just say it. You don't have to understand it.' With that he stamped from the house. Goddamn it! He bought her everything she wanted, she lived in a fucking palace, and the fat bitch couldn't even speak proper English. Was it any wonder he ran to Eden for a little class – and a little ass.

He almost guffawed at his own wit. And then he scowled as he remembered the bad news. His lawyer in New York was a prick. He should have defended the case himself. This was America – you could goddamn well print what you liked – and if the stupid cooze had posed with no clothes on, then he was entitled to print the pictures. And anything else he wanted.

No shithead judge was going to tell Santino Bonnatti what to do.

*

Eden had just finished working out when Santino arrived. He stomped into the living room like little Caesar, sweating in his silk shirt and three piece suit. With a grunt he threw himself into an armchair, spread his legs, unzipped his fly, and commanded, 'Give me a blow job.'

Eden was outraged. Zeko was in the corner of the room playing solitaire. The maid was vacuuming out in the hall. A pool man worked outside.

'I've had it with you,' she hissed bravely. There was nothing he could do to her with all these people around.

Before she even realized it he was up from the chair and upon her, short arms flailing wildly.

Slap. Slap. Shove. Slap.

She fought back. 'You *bastard*!'

The diamond pinky ring on his little finger ripped into the smooth skin of her cheek and drew blood.

'I *hate* you!' she cried in a fury, clutching her cheek.

Zeko did not look up from his game. The maid continued to vacuum. The pool man shook solution into the pool.

Eden rushed into the bathroom and stared into the mirror in horror. Her face was ruined.

Santino followed her, a plaintive whine in his voice. 'Whydja always gotta give me a hard time?' he questioned. 'Ya ask for trouble. I got other things on my mind.'

She soaked cotton wool in witch hazel and carefully bathed her cheek.

'I gotta put up with shit at home. I come here t'get my rocks off an' relax.'

She ignored him.

He caught sight of his reflection in the mirror beside her, and straightened his tie. It pissed him off that he was practically bald, but what was it they said? Bald head, big prick.

Talking of which:

'Get down on ya knees, honey.'

Honey? He was calling her honey. He was asking her to suck him off after what he'd done.

No way.

She was through.

Somehow she had to get out.

• •

Two days later Santino informed her the perfect part had finally arrived. He threw a script at her.

She had not forgiven him for messing up her face, but she read the script anyway and cringed.

Pure pornography.

'Tits n'ass,' he argued. '*Soft* porn. There's a big difference. Ya don' wanna do it, I'll find someone else.'

She read the script again. Maybe with a few changes here and there, cut out the rape scene, work on the girl's *character*. It *was* a starring role.

'Who's the director?' she demanded.

'Ryder wants to take a shot.'

'He's a producer.'

'Reagan was a fuckin' actor. Look at him today.'

'Who's my co-star?'

'A kid by the name of Tim Wealth.'

She tried to keep her face impassive. Tim Wealth. The

young actor she had run away to LA with when she dumped Lennie in New York five years ago.

'Ya ever heard of him?' he asked.

'No,' she lied.

'Nor have I,' spat Santino. 'But they say he's good. Ya wanna do it or what?'

She sighed.

And said yes.

Tits n' ass was better than nothing.

Chapter 100

The funeral of Dimitri Stanislopoulos, held on his private island, was a sombre affair. The day was overcast and foggy in a week filled with sunshine. His friends and business associates came from all across the world to pay their respects. Lucky, dressed in black, held the hand of Roberto – who really didn't understand what was going on. Brigette, denied a trip to visit her mother, stood nearby as the coffin was lowered into the ground. Gino had insisted on accompanying Lucky to the island to lend his support. And so had Costa and his wife. Olympia had failed to show up, a sign of disrespect that would have horrified Dimitri.

'I understand that Mrs Golden is sick,' the family lawyer informed Lucky.

'What's the matter with her?'

The lawyer cleared his throat. 'I don't believe she has fully recovered from her accident.'

'That was three years ago,' Lucky pointed out.

'I know,' the lawyer replied sagely. 'But I understand that she plans to be well enough to attend the reading of Mr Stanislopoulos' will.'

Sarcasm scorched her voice. 'Naturally.'

Burying Dimitri was a strange sensation for Lucky. She did not feel like a bereaved widow. She felt as if she had lost a friend – for once she had accepted Dimitri's terms concerning Roberto, they had gotten along pretty well. Since Francesca's death he had been neither husband nor lover. But he had been a wise advisor and an excellent father to his son. She would miss him.

What now? She had her freedom *and* Roberto. She could take him wherever she wanted. The world was wide open.

Only now she had it, she didn't know what to do with it.

*

Olympia would have attended her father's funeral, she wanted to. But how could she when she looked like a baby elephant?

When she received the news, she did not believe Dimitri had died. He couldn't do such a thing to her. They were having a cold war. Eventually Dimitri would apologize for his blatant neglect, she would forgive him, and things would return to normal.

But that couldn't happen now he had died on her.

First she was frustrated, then angry, and finally she broke down and sobbed bitter tears. All her life Dimitri had been the rock in the background waiting to save her from her escapades. When she was a child he had rescued her from a cold mother and allowed her to live with him. When she was a teenager he had dealt with furious teachers who wished to expel her from every school she attended. And when she was a woman he had paid off her husbands and seen to it that her life ran smoothly. With Dimitri Stanislopoulos as a father she had never had to worry about anything.

Now he was gone.

And it was all Lucky's fault.

'That bitch killed him,' she informed Lennie. 'The hotel isn't enough for her. That bitch wants all his money.'

'What are you talking about?' She was driving him nuts. Three years of penal servitude was enough – he could not take any more.

'It all started when he married her,' Olympia ranted. '*She's* the one who prevented him from coming to see me in the hospital. She was always jealous of me.'

'He *came* to the hospital.'

'Once!' Olympia spat. 'And then somehow she got him to stay on the island.' She nodded her head. 'I don't know how she did it, but she killed him.'

'You're talking crap.'

'Am I?' Olympia fixed him with baleful blue eyes. 'What is it with you and that bitch? Why do you always defend her?' It was not the first time they had discussed Lucky, and Olympia had roared with fury and hate. 'I should know her better than you do,' she continued. 'When we were in school together I *thought* she was a friend. But believe me, she's evil, and she killed Dimitri. I know she did.'

There was no arguing with Olympia once she had made up her mind.

*

As soon as Jess arrived back in LA she called Lennie.

'Can I see you at once?' she asked.

'Meet me in the Polo Lounge,' he said. 'I feel like getting out of the house.'

They met at lunchtime, and Jess couldn't wait to flash her sapphire and diamond engagement ring at him.

He kissed and congratulated her, then said, 'I suppose this is where we go our own ways.'

She waved at an agent lunching with two blond clients. 'Are you kidding?' she exclaimed loudly. 'I'm not giving up ten percent of you. Absolutely not.' She ordered a Bloody Mary and a Neil McCarthy salad – while Lennie opted for a Screwdriver and scrambled eggs. 'Matt and I have discussed it,' she continued earnestly. 'And I'm going to commute.'

'Between here and Atlantic City?'

'No. I thought Leningrad and Paris might be more fun!'

'Ha ha. Another comedian.'

'It'll work out fine. I have the office here, and the accountant and the secretaries. Instead of putting in an every day appearance, I'll do three days a week. The rest of the time I'm only a phone call away. Does that suit you?'

He shrugged. 'Whatever you want. I thought you were going to give it all up and iron shirts.'

She giggled. 'Fuck you!

He leaned closer. 'Promises, promises!'

She took a healthy gulp of her Bloody Mary. 'Listen, star. Thank God we never did.'

A statuesque brunette in a sweeping red outfit stopped by the table. She was no juvenile, but she was remarkably striking. 'Hi, Lennie,' she rasped.

He had no idea who she was. 'Hey – how're you doin'?'

'My agent tells me you're casting. Any roles for a ballsy old broad?'

Bingo! She was a movie star from the sixties who hadn't worked in ten years. Once, in his teens, he had lusted after her body. 'Why don't I write one in?' he deadpanned.

'Why don't you?' She licked her lips and slipped him her card. 'Call any time,' she murmured as she undulated out.

'Pulling older ladies?' teased Jess.

'Anything that comes my way, pal.'

The Polo Lounge was in action. A male movie star, suffering from one face lift too many, paused in the entrance to make sure everyone got a good look at him. Two would-be starlets in tighter than tight toreador pants and second-skin sweaters giggled their way in.

'Did I tell you I saw Lucky?' Jess remarked casually.

Lennie observed the starlet duo. They swayed in the breeze, while a tall dude with a moustache whisked them to his table.

Lennie took a hefty swig of his Screwdriver. 'How is she?' he asked, just as casual as Jess.

'Not as icy as I used to think she was. In fact, she was great to me. And the hotel is a mind-blower. If you ever want to play a room again . . .'

Jess began describing the hotel while Lennie considered what might have been. Yeah. What might have been if Lucky had wanted him as much as he had wanted her.

Obviously she didn't. Staying with Dimitri and building her hotel had taken top priority.

He wondered what she would do now Dimitri was dead.

Olympia had asked him to accompany her to New York for the reading of the will. He didn't start shooting the new movie for several months, and for once he was blocked on writing, so he thought he might.

Sure.

Be casual about it.

He was going to see Lucky again after three years.

He couldn't wait.

Chapter 101

Becoming the widow of one of the richest men in the world was an awesome experience. As Dimitri Stanislopoulos' wife Lucky had been treated with a certain amount of respect by his business associates. As his widow, she was fawned over.

It occurred to her that she was now in a position of power she had never even dreamed of. Olympia and Roberto would inherit the lion's share of Dimitri's vast wealth, but that did not exactly leave her a pauper. She owned the Santangelo free and clear. She had money in the bank from the sale of her Magiriano shares. And the East Hampton house was all hers.

She did not need any of Dimitri's money, and she did not expect to get any. She had signed an agreement before their marriage relinquishing all rights to his vast estates and fortunes. The hotel was enough for her. She had realized her dream. But still, she had to attend the reading of the will. Roberto's interests must be protected. Not that she anticipated any problems, Dimitri had doted on the boy.

Gino was returning to Vegas, and Costa and Ria were accompanying him for a visit. Lucky decided it might be a good idea to send Roberto and CeeCee with them. She didn't want to leave Roberto on the island – too many sad memories. And she didn't want to take him to New York with her. She trusted CeeCee implicitly. Besides, it would be good for him to spend some time with Gino.

Arrangements were duly made. Brigette was to go with them as well and be dropped off in Los Angeles. Lucky didn't want her travelling alone. 'I really should have a bodyguard go with you,' she worried.

Brigette giggled at the very thought. 'Nobody knows who *I* am.'

'As long as we don't put Stanislopoulos on your ticket. In public you are Brigette Standing. Remember that.'

Memories drifted back. When Lucky was a girl at school Gino had insisted that she not use the notorious Santangelo name. She had been known as Lucky Saint. What a name to be stuck with! Olympia had soon uncovered her secret and they had become friends.

Once.

Long ago . . .

*

Brigette got to sit next to Gino on the plane. She was glad. Costa was so dull, and his wife, Ria, talked too much. CeeCee, she had never got along with. And Roberto – or Bobby as she called him – was just a stupid little kid.

Brigette was sorry Grandpoppa Dimitri had died. But it opened up a whole new and exciting life for her. Now she couldn't be dumped on the boring old Greek island every time she had a vacation. There was only so much swimming and sunbathing one could do. Perhaps Lucky would allow her to visit Atlantic City often. The Santangelo Hotel was a blast – oh, the times she could have there! And then maybe she could go and see Gino in Vegas – after all, they *were* sort of related, and they got along fine. Then there was Grandma Charlotte in New York. She was a pain, but an occasional weekend in New York might be fun. And there was always LA. And mommy. And Lennie.

Mommy was a big drag.

Lennie was terrific.

And Tim Wealth lived in LA.

She shivered with anticipation.

The stewardess walked along the aisle. She had on a tight skirt, too tight Brigette thought, it made her bottom look huge.

'Want a drink, kid?' Gino asked.

'Scotch on the rocks, please,' joked Brigette.

'Smack on the ass,' grinned Gino.

The stewardess smiled superciliously. She had very big white teeth. Brigette wondered if she had ever thought of doing a toothpaste commercial.

'How about a nice glass of milk, dear?' beamed Big Teeth.

Brigette scowled. Talking to her like a baby. She *hated* it when grown ups spoke down to her. Didn't they realize how dumb it made them look? She was fourteen, not four.

*

Olympia was finally spurred to go on a crash diet – not that the loss of a few pounds made any difference to her mammoth proportions, but she pretended it did. Lately she felt paranoid and unable to sleep. Somehow her never-ending supply of cocaine was not giving her the kick she needed. She had complained to one of her dealers on the phone that he was shipping her inferior stuff.

'Meet with me, pretty lady,' he had crooned. 'I gotta way to prolong that old coke high gonna see you fly!'

'I want something that'll make me feel good and stop me from eating. I need to lose a pound or two,' she said, as if conversing with a respected doctor.

'I got just what you want, pretty lady. But I have to show you how to do your thing.'

They arranged to meet in a Hollywood hotel the next day. Olympia wasn't nervous. She had never been nervous about anything in her life.

The dealer was a sallow-faced man in his forties, with peroxide hair and missing front teeth. Olympia had found him through a dealer of Flash's in New York. The man had an alarming facial tic and smelled of stale smoke. When Olympia entered the hotel room he switched on the television and locked the door.

'What have you got for me?' she asked restlessly.

The man squinted at the fat blonde heiress and saw dollar signs.

'What *haven't* I got for you, pretty lady,' he said.

An hour later she left, a spring in her step and a mellow satisfied expression on her face. She had a purse-full of goodies. Snorting heroin beat coke any day.

Lennie was working in his study when she arrived home.

'Where'd you go?' he asked, delighted that she'd ventured out.

She smiled dreamily. 'Shopping,' she said. 'The pounds are dropping from me. I have to buy new clothes for New York.'

'That's good news.'

'Oh, and Lennie,' she added imperviously, 'hire a plane. I'm not going to New York on an ordinary airline.' She swept from his study.

Only *he* would end up married to a woman who said 'hire a plane' as if she was ordering dog food.

He tried to work for another hour but it wasn't happening for him, so he went upstairs. Olympia was in her bedroom, clothes spread around everywhere.

'Brigette's arriving this evening,' he reminded her. 'And we're leaving on Monday. Shouldn't we have someone in the house with her other than the servants?'

'Who did you have in mind?' she asked, inspecting a selection of silk caftans.

He paced around the room. 'Maybe Jess.'

'Isn't she rushing back to Atlantic City and that hood she's engaged to?'

'Oh, yeah.' He had forgotten Jess was now commuting.

Olympia held blue silk in front of her. The colour complimented her eyes. If she was only a few pounds thinner – well more than a few, she had to admit – she would be the prettiest girl in the world. And pretty girls got laid. She was tired of Lennie and his feeble excuses.

'I've made a decision,' she stated dramatically.

'Yeah?' Olympia's decisions usually lasted ten minutes.

'I'm going to take a sleep cure and really lose weight.'

When they returned from New York she would cease to be his problem. He had given enough. One divorce coming up. 'That's great,' he said, hoping she meant it for her own sake.

'That's great,' she mimicked. 'I wonder if you'll think it's so great when I start taking charge of my own life again.'

'*Hey* – that's exactly what I want you to do.'

She glared. 'What?'

He smelled the beginning of a fight, and who needed it? Brigette was arriving soon. They hadn't seen her in over a year, and it would be nice if everyone was talking and not at each other's throats.

'Listen, how about Alice?' he suggested, changing the subject with a quick idea, which, if he had thought it through was madness. He was desperately trying to keep Alice *out* of the house, not bring her in.

Olympia decided she didn't feel like a fight either. 'Hmmm, they get along, Brigette likes her, and she drives. She can take her to Disneyland and Magic Mountain and all those kiddy places. Shall we have one of the secretaries phone her?'

'Yeah, good idea.' He stretched. 'I'm going over to Ryder's for a meeting.'

She frowned. 'Why do you always go to him? Why doesn't he ever come to you?'

'Because *you* never want anyone in the house.'

She narrowed her eyes. 'And it suits you fine, doesn't it? That way your freedom is assured. Yes?' She threw the blue caftan on the floor. 'Well, make the most of it husband, dear. Because things are going to be very different in the future. You've kept me shut up here long enough.'

'*I've* kept you shut up,' he snorted angrily. 'Me? Getting you out to see your plastic surgeon is a major fucking coup.'

She was too mellow to fight. 'Goodbye,' she said crisply.

'Forever,' he muttered.

'What?'

He strode from the house, threw himself behind the wheel of his Porsche and zoomed off.

*

Ryder Wheeler was on the tennis court pinging balls which bounced out at him from a machine.

Lennie settled himself in a chair next to the outside bar and watched.

Ryder managed a couple of great shots, spotted Lennie, and walked over.

'Do you always play with yourself?' Lennie asked sarcastically.

Ryder grabbed a towel from the back of the chair and swung it around his neck. 'Only when Paige is out of town.'

As if on cue, Paige emerged from the house. She wore a short scarlet dress, her legs were bare with very high heels. She looked like a Marseilles hooker.

'Hiya, sexy,' greeted Lennie.

'I didn't know you two had a meeting planned,' she said, bestowing a kiss on his forehead.

'We didn't,' Lennie replied. 'But I sure as hell needed a shot of fresh air.'

Like everyone else, Paige had often wondered about his marriage. They had all heard of Olympia Stanislopoulos, but nobody ever saw her. She never appeared in public and he offered no explanations to anyone – including the press – who speculated constantly. According to Jess the marriage endured. That was all Paige could find out.

'You'll get plenty of fresh air here. I'm off to the work dungeon.' She pecked Ryder on the cheek. 'By, bye, sweetheart.' For a moment she paused, looked from one man to the other and added mischievously, 'Tell Lennie about your new project. Talk dirty. Who knows, maybe you can get him to put in a guest appearance!'

'What new project?' Lennie asked, watching Paige out of sight.

Ryder plucked a prune danish from a plate on the table, picked up the intercom and ordered hot coffee, then leaned back in his chair. 'I'm doing a porno,' he said.

'What?' Lennie was not sure he'd heard correctly. Since making his last two pictures, Ryder Wheeler was one of the most successful producers in town.

'Soft porn, of course,' Ryder added quickly. 'Beautifully done. I'm directing.'

Lennie started to laugh. 'I don't believe what I'm hearing!'

Ryder shrugged. 'I've got everything I want. All the money

I'll ever need. So I decided to indulge myself and do something I've always hankered after.'

'You *are* kidding me?'

'No. I'm serious.'

'*You're* not a director. You're a great producer – but a director – come on!'

Ryder picked his teeth with a matchstick. 'There is no great mystique to directing a film,' he said. 'If you surround yourself with the right crew and a clever cinematographer – then you're ninety percent of the way. *And* if you can talk to actors, and pick a perfect cast – you're all the way. Besides, if anyone's going to be in the front line for pussy, it better be me.'

'You don't even *chase* pussy. You're the only guy I know who doesn't screw around.'

'I'm not doing it to get my rocks off,' Ryder explained patiently. 'If I wanted to get laid, this is climax city.' He paused. 'I am doing it, Lennie, because directing a porno is my one unfulfilled ambition. Plus one of my investors is putting up all the money, and I have a large piece of the action, which – if we want to talk video sales – is going to be tremendous.'

'What about your reputation?'

Ryder laughed heartily. 'A reputation in this town is how much money you make. Shit, Lennie, for a hip guy you sure sound like a boy scout at times.'

'Fuck you, asshole.'

Ryder beamed. 'Come by the set sometime. It beats out a game of tennis any day.'

Chapter 102

Coffee was served in fine china teacups with large ungainly spoons. Carrie decided she would buy him a set of delicate silver spoons for Christmas, but knowing Fred Lester, he probably wouldn't use them.

Fred cleared his throat for the second time, and stroked the palm of his hand across his bald pate.

Carrie crossed and uncrossed her legs. She still had beautiful legs, the wrinkles of time had not reached them – yet. Sometimes, when she looked in the mirror, she was dismayed to notice age catching up with her. But she was alive, so surely she was one of the lucky ones? She often wondered about the companions of her youth, the hookers and the strippers, the pimps and the con-men. Were they still around today? She sincerely doubted it. Life was harsh back then, and only the fittest survived.

'Your book is a gem,' Fred Lester said at last. 'A shining piece of honesty in a dishonest world.'

'Thank you,' Carrie murmured gratefully. Fred's comment was the first reaction she had received on her book. She still had not mentioned it to Steven.

Fred placed the tips of his fingers together and made a funnel. He gazed across the room, not meeting Carrie's eyes. 'There might be legal problems with some of the names you've used. It may not be possible to . . . uh . . . use all the real names.' He laughed hollowly. 'Especially Freddy Lester.'

She laughed with him. 'I never told you this, but his name brought me to you.'

He studied his fingernails. 'Did it?'

'Absolutely. You see when I finally told Steven the truth, he became obsessed with finding out who his real father was. Gino Santangelo or Freddy Lester.'

'Did you go to Gino Santangelo?'

'Almost. We flew to California, but something stopped Steven from pursuing the search. Thank God.'

It was raining on the streets of New York, and the relentless drops pounded on the office window.

'How many Freddy Lesters did you find?' Fred asked. 'And what eliminated me?'

She sipped her coffee. It was strong and hot. 'Why?' she joked. 'Are you telling me it *was* you?'

There was a moment of silence before Fred's hearty laugh filled the room. 'I wish,' he said.

'No you don't. Her tone was suddenly harsh. 'That man was an animal, with no regard for anyone except himself.' Her voice shook. 'He raped me. Even if I was once a whore I had *some* rights, didn't I?'

He calmed her. 'Of course you did, my dear. Of course you did.'

She arose and walked to the window. 'I still remember,' she said bitterly, 'the pain I had to endure.' She stared unseeingly at the stream of traffic crawling along the rain-soaked streets below. 'I was alone, with no money, no job, and a baby growing inside me. There was no other way. I *had* to go back to the only profession I knew to make a living. I had no choice. *He* gave me no choice.'

Fred rose and stood behind her. 'You have a fine son. Out of the pain came *some* good.'

She had never thought of it that way before. She nodded wearily, and was assailed by a flash of doubt. 'Steven doesn't know about the book. I don't want to upset him.'

'If your life upsets him, surely that's *his* problem.'

'I know. But –'

'Would you like *me* to tell him?'

She shook her head. 'It's my responsibility. I'll talk to him tomorrow.'

'Maybe I should be with you.'

There was something in his tone that alerted her. She moved from the window and stared at him. Slowly realization dawned. 'It's you, isn't it?' she whispered at last. '*It is you.* And that's why you're paying half a million dollars. Guilt money. It is you!'

'Yes,' he said, and a heavy weight fell from his shoulders.

Chapter 103

'Hi,' said Brigette chirpily, trying to conceal the shock she felt on seeing the size of her mother.

'You're all grown up!' Olympia exclaimed. 'Oh God! You

make me feel so *old*. Which I'm not,' she added quickly.

'Why didn't you come to grandpoppa's funeral?' Brigette asked accusingly, not wasting any time.

'I hate funerals,' Olympia said petulantly.

'Your mother was sick,' Lennie cut in.

'She looks fine to me,' said Brigette, cobalt blue eyes shining.

'So tell her,' said Lennie gently. 'She's had skin grafts and plastic surgery and God knows what. Tell your mother she looks pretty again.'

'You do look pretty, mama,' said Brigette reluctantly. 'Did anyone call me?'

'Who were you expecting?' Olympia asked, hating the fact that her daughter looked so mature and well developed for a fourteen year old.

'I have friends here,' Brigette said vaguely. 'Like from school and stuff.'

'Good,' said Olympia.

'Great,' said Lennie.

'We have to go to New York,' Olympia said quickly. 'Alice is going to come here and stay with you.'

'Who?'

'Alice. You remember her. Lennie's mother. You used to adore her.'

Brigette yawned and stretched. 'Oh, yeah.' *That old bat*, she thought. *Well, I'll certainly get as much freedom as I want with her around.* 'How long will you be gone, mama?' she asked innocently.

'Just as long as it takes,' said Olympia. And she added silently to herself – *Just as long as it takes me to make sure that bitch, Lucky, gets no more than she deserves. Which, if I have anything to do with it – is nothing.*

•

Tim Wealth moved out on his lover the day he started shooting Ryder Wheeler's movie, 'Heat'. He moved out because his lover was beginning to treat him like something less than dog shit, and who needed it? The man was only a lousy movie producer, not the second coming of Clark Gable.

Tim was working again, he could pay his own bills, and while starring in 'Heat' was hardly the lead in 'Gatsby', it was still a hot movie. In every way.

The first day on the set he came face to face with his co-star. He took one look and double-taked. Eden Antonio.

'Do you know each other?' asked Ryder, noting Tim's expression.

'No,' said Eden turning away.

Lying bitch, thought Tim. But then she had always been a liar, and a bitch.

*

Tim Wealth arrived in New York from Detroit at the age of nineteen. He quite expected theatre doors to open up for him. He was an actor, and a good one. The only doors which opened up were the doors of cars cruising Times Square looking for a fast score. He became a male hustler – not from choice – but because it paid well and enabled him to attend acting classes during the day.

One of the other students was a girl named Eden. She was the most beautiful female he had ever seen. Not only was she beautiful, but she was sophisticated and worldly – and just listening to her talk was a thrill. He hung on her every word, for Eden was classy and stylish – all the things lacking in Tim's life.

Occasionally they got to do scenes together. She wasn't a very good actress, but her exotic beauty compensated. Even though she was several years older than him, they became good friends, and even though he knew she was living with a guy, they became lovers.

One day she arrived in class with a determined look on her face. 'Listen,' she said. 'I don't know about you, but I've had it with this town. I want to head for LA and break into movies. Why don't we go together?'

'What about your boyfriend?' he asked.

'What about him?' she replied.

Once they decided to do it, she left all the arrangements to him. He had managed to save some money – the one good thing about hustling was that it paid well – cash – no taxes. And Eden expected him to pay for everything. Which he did.

Two first-class tickets. 'I want to do it properly,' Eden said.

Reservations in the Beverly Hilton.

Several new outfits for Eden to storm the casting agents with.

Four weeks into hotel life and no jobs, Tim realized he was busted out.

'Too bad,' said Eden, and moved out of his life one LA rainy morning when he was away from the room buying the trades, leaving him with a three thousand dollar hotel tab, and no way of paying it.

He was devastated. But it gave him a fast education on classy stylish women.

He skipped without settling the bill, and resumed the only sure way of making a living he knew.

Hustling Santa Monica Boulevard was not that different from Times Square.

Aged twenty-one, he was picked up one day by a well-known male super-star, whose private life was firmly in the closet. The man was married with children, but that didn't stop him from setting Tim up in an apartment with a generous clothes allowance and all expenses paid. The arrangement suited Tim fine, it kept him off the streets, allowed him to entertain girls when his benefactor wasn't around, and concentrate on his acting studies.

His diligence paid off, and in 1980 he landed the lead role in a movie, much to his boyfriend's chagrin. They parted company acrimoniously.

Smash reviews and good box office led to exactly nothing. The rejected super-star had clout, and he used it to make sure Tim Wealth's career went right down the toilet.

Which is where it stayed until the offer of the Ryder Wheeler flick came his way. 'It's kinda close to the bone,' his agent warned him. 'But it's gonna be done with class and plenty of the green stuff.'

Tim said yes. He had nothing to lose – only his modesty,

and that had never counted for much. The script read porno. But with Ryder Wheeler in charge Tim hoped it would be something more. He had once had a taste of stardom, he was desperately hungry for more.

*

Eden Antonio. She was as hot as the movie. Icy cool was how Tim would describe the lady. He had never forgotten her. But now he was older, and a hell of a lot wiser. There was no way Eden could walk all over him this time around.

She radiated style and sex, even though her figure bordered on the anorexic. Kind of a strange choice for the leading lady in a flick that promised to reveal a lot of flesh.

'It's okay,' the make-up man told him. 'The rest of the bunnies make Dolly Parton look like she got steamrolled!' Tim couldn't wait.

Tits and fags. The story of his life.

He never *had* been able to choose.

Now they were shooting the movie, and he was glad he'd said yes. Hell, if Richard Gere could show it all, why couldn't he? Although he was doing a lot more than just showing it.

Ryder Wheeler said that the kind of film they were doing was the movie of the future. 'The public wants t'see it all,' he assured his actors. 'Today it's you – tomorrow it'll be Burt Reynolds and Jessica Lange.'

Tim had his doubts. But at least – true to his agent's words – everything was being done with class and money.

The first time they found themselves alone together Eden said, 'So you didn't make it either, huh?'

'You're one ace bitch,' he replied.

'One of my main attractions,' she retorted.

They were in her dressing room. He kicked the door shut, and had her for old time's sake.

'My boyfriend will kill you for this,' she whispered. 'If he ever finds out.'

'Are you going to tell him?'

That throaty, husky laugh. 'What do *you* think?'

The second week on the set Tim met 'the money man',

Santino Bonnatti. He strutted around like he owned the world and everyone in it. He quite obviously owned Eden – whom he affectionately called 'cunt' in front of the entire crew.

'Your boyfriend?' Tim asked unnecessarily.

'Unfortunately,' she replied.

On the screen together they created sparks. Eden Antonio and Tim Wealth. And they hadn't even gotten to any of the hot stuff yet.

Ryder knew it immediately he saw the first dailies. He called Paige and told her to get right over to the screening room.

She saw Tim and Eden together and agreed with him at once.

'We've got to keep this film at a level,' Ryder said. 'I want it to be a "Last Tango" of the eighties – not a return of "Deep Throat".'

'You have no problem with that, do you?' asked Paige.

'*I* have no problem, but Bonnatti will give me a hard time. Wait and see.'

Sure enough, several weeks into shooting, Santino demanded more. 'I want more tits. I want more ass. I want more sucking and I want more fucking.'

'Don't hang back,' Ryder urged. 'Tell me what's on your mind.'

Santino glared. He was putting up money for porno, and all he was getting were long shots and clever lighting and artistic shit.

'Do it,' he warned. 'Or get your ass off my movie.'

Two days later Ryder Wheeler did exactly that.

Tim Wealth and Eden Antonio were appalled. Especially when Santino brought in a well known sleaze director who lost no time in going right for the bone – in more ways than one.

Between set-ups, when Santino wasn't hovering, and the ever-present Zeko was chasing extras, Tim consoled Eden in the privacy of one or the other's dressing rooms. They came together urgently. Eden, nervous and edgy and hungry. Tim, surprised that he could summon up feelings he thought were long dead.

It didn't take long before Santino became suspicious. He watched them in front of the camera and didn't mind what went on – because he was in control and Eden was his property. But off camera he didn't even want them to speak.

'You've got to get away from him,' Tim cautioned.

'I know,' Eden agreed.

Tim Wealth couldn't figure out why he was getting involved. Shoot the flick and run. Santino Bonnatti was bad news. The serious kind.

'If I came up with a big score we could go to Mexico and hide out,' Tim suggested.

Eden nodded. Where was Tim Wealth going to come up with enough money to assure their safe flight?

That evening he dug in his suitcase – the one he had carried to Atlantic City on his last trip with his lover. Scrunched in one corner was a slip of paper. On it was written BRIGETTE STANISLOPOULOS and a phone number.

Tim did not hesitate.

Chapter 104

Brigette was bored. Being stuck in the Bel Air mansion for weeks with an army of servants and crazy Alice for company was the pits. She had come to visit her mother and Lennie, and practically the moment she arrived they had raced off to New York with hardly a hello/goodbye. Wow – they really wanted to see her, didn't they?

She amused herself for a while by going through Olympia's closet, all of her drawers, and her desk. Then she explored Lennie's study, but he had a habit of locking things up – so she didn't get very far in there.

Alice said, 'Do you want to go to Disneyland, dear?'

Disneyland! Brigette gave her a filthy look.

Alice got the message. Disneyland was out. Instead they went to an X-rated movie on Hollywood Boulevard, and later cruised along in the back of Olympia's white Rolls Royce with a uniformed chauffeur at the wheel, watching the hookers parade Sunset.

Brigette was fascinated. 'Do they really get paid for it?' she inquired, filled with curiosity.

'*Naturelment, ma chérie*,' replied Alice. She had been picking up French phrases from a well developed foreign midget she had met in a bar. His name was Claudio, and he came from circus stock.

'What do they *do*?' demanded Brigette.

'What *don't* they do,' replied Alice mysteriously. 'Ooh la la!'

They returned to the mansion and played cards. Every day Brigette waited for the phone to ring, because she was quite sure Tim Wealth would call. While Alice wondered if she dare invite Claudio to the house. Lennie had been very specific with his instructions. 'I don't want *any* of your friends here, male, female, straight or gay. Not one of them.'

Poor little Claudio. He was gentle and quiet. And certainly very sexy for a small person. Surely Lennie would not bar Claudio from coming to the house?

'I'm bummed out,' Brigette complained constantly. 'Can't we do something funky for a change? Don't you know any *people*?'

Alice did not understand what either bummed out or funky meant – both sounded rude to her. She sighed. Youngsters today were different. Brigette seemed such an advanced teenager. Or maybe she was normal. On impulse she phoned Claudio and invited him over.

'I've got a friend coming,' she informed Brigette.

'Nice for them,' the girl muttered.

'He'll take us out.' Alice nodded to herself. She had had enough of playing baby-sitter. When Lennie had called and asked her to stay she had been thrilled. She wanted to be close to her famous son, not cut out of his life forever. But keeping an eye on a restless fourteen year old was not exactly what she'd had in mind. Claudio would definitely liven things up.

'It'll be nice to see *someone*,' grumbled Brigette. She was pissed at Tim Wealth. Weeks had passed and he hadn't even called. Soon she would have to leave LA and return to school. Who did he think he was?

'Yes,' Alice mused happily. 'We'll have ourselves some fun with Claudio.'

'Brilliant,' said Brigette.

Alice simpered coyly. 'We'll get down and get funky!'

Brigette giggled. Alice always made her laugh with her bird-like movements, dyed hair and rouged cheeks. 'Right on, grandma!'

The smile vanished from Alice's face. 'Don't call me that, dear. It makes me feel ancient.'

•

In New York the battle was on. Dimitri Stanislopoulos' will was a lengthy and complicated document. To everyone's surprise he left the bulk of his money, business interests and estates to Lucky – to be held in trust for Roberto until he reached twenty-five.

Olympia was not exactly left out. She was to receive a lifetime allowance of a million dollars a year, which she considered an out and out insult. Brigette was to get double that amount, and also a twenty-five million dollar inheritance when she reached twenty-one.

'How dare he!' Olympia screamed, as they left the lawyer's office. 'How dare that senile sonofabitch do this to me!'

Lennie was not really interested in Olympia's hysterical complaints. He had just come face to face with Lucky for the first time in three years, and he felt as if someone had kicked him in the stomach with a steel-toed boot. She was as wildly beautiful as ever in a simple black suit, her jet curls pulled severely back from her face.

She had walked toward them and offered a hug of sympathy to Olympia, who had shrugged her off with a cold glare.

He didn't know what to say. Everything seemed inappropriate. Hey – the big movie star was speechless. 'How are you?' he managed to mumble.

She barely glanced in his direction. 'Fine, thank you,' in clipped tones.

And that was it. The full extent of their conversation, followed by hours of boredom while the will was read.

He had tried to catch her eye, but she was aloof, and very remote, which destroyed him. It seemed that as far as Lucky was concerned it was over. And there was no way he could convince her otherwise while he remained married to Olympia.

'It's all that bitch's fault,' Olympia ranted on. 'She brainwashed him. She coerced him. But she needn't think for one moment that she's getting away with it, because she's not. My lawyers will fight it every inch of the way – every goddamn inch.'

•

The newspapers descended like a plague of ants, and Lucky, who had always managed to keep a fairly low profile, suddenly found herself the centre of attention. As Mrs Stanislopoulos, she had kept in the background. But as the Widow Stanislopoulos, and the inheritor of most of Dimitri's fortune, she was suddenly thrust unwillingly into the limelight. Unwanted headlines began to appear. Pictures were dug up from her days as Senator Richmond's daughter-in-law, the opening of the Magiriano, and more recent ones from the Hotel Santangelo opening night.

DAUGHTER OF FORMER MOBSTER HITS THE JACKPOT screamed one tabloid. SANTANGELO KID GETS RICH QUICK offered another.

It wasn't long before industrious digging produced the story of her attempted rape at the hands of Enzio Bonnatti, and the subsequent shooting. It had taken six years to make the headlines but now it was hot news. STANISLOPOULOS HEIRESS KILLED RAPIST.

She was outraged by the sudden loss of privacy, and when they printed a picture of Roberto, playing in the pool at the Magiriano where he was staying with Gino, she really freaked out, and called Gino immediately. 'What the hell is going on?' she demanded. 'Why are you letting them photograph Roberto?'

'I'm not,' he replied grimly. He too was upset by the unwelcome thrust of publicity. 'I got security guards throwin' the newspaper bums on their asses, but I can't control the tourists with their cameras,' he complained.

'I want Roberto out of there,' Lucky said urgently. 'At once.'

'I know,' Gino agreed. 'I was thinkin' along the same lines.'

He told her his plans. Costa and Ria had rented a house in Beverly Hills for the month. They were flying to LA that evening, and he planned to take Roberto and CeeCee and go with them. 'I can't put up with the shit goin' on here,' he said. 'This way nobody will know where we are, an' we'll get some peace.'

'Sounds good to me,' said Lucky. 'I'll join you as soon as I can.'

'No rush,' Gino assured her. 'Roberto's safe with me.'

'I know,' she replied quickly. 'But I miss him.' And she did. Desperately. A hotel was no substitute for a son.

They talked some more, and at the end of the conversation she felt better. She could finally turn to Gino in times of trouble. He understood and was always there for her. Right now she needed someone.

Lennie.

Still married to Olympia.

Why had she ever thought they had something going?

Chapter 105

If only she could get to Lennie. Eden knew he would lend her the money to free herself from the deadly clutches of Santino Bonnatti. With Ryder Wheeler off the movie, things deteriorated day by day. Her scenes with Tim presented no problem. They were steamy, but she could handle it because she was with him. However, when Santino insisted the rape scene go back in, she knew she was in trouble.

A hulking actor from hard core movies appeared on the set to play her assailant. And she sensed, without a doubt, that Santino had told the director to run the scene to its limit.

Tim slipped her some pills before he was ordered to leave the set. 'Take 'em,' he commanded. 'They'll get you through.'

She did as he said, and felt better immediately.

Santino was sitting ringside when she was called to start the scene. He sat in a director's chair behind the camera, a leer on his face, and the stub of a stinking cigar stuck between his teeth. 'Lotsa luck, honey,' he said, the concerned boyfriend.

She smiled vaguely. The pills had taken her to another place where nothing mattered.

The director, a New Yorker with dyed hair and slit eyes, said, 'Let's go with the flow, sweetie. Live it. Feel it. I'm going for one take in long shot, then we'll move in for the close ups.'

'Do I look beautiful?' she murmured.

'Hot stuff, sweet ass. You'll have every *schlong* in the theatre at full mast.'

She licked her thin lips and waited for the magic word, 'Action'.

The director called it and they were away.

She moved into the scene like the pro she was.

Eden Antonio.

Great screen beauty.

She wore a satin nightgown and not much else.

The hulking actor lurked behind a curtain waiting for his moment. At a signal from the director he moved into shot, huge and sinister. He grabbed her quickly. She was like a helpless doll in his vicious grip.

She relaxed and went limp in his arms.

'Struggle!' the director hissed.

'Yeah, struggle,' Santino repeated, leaning forward, sweat beading his brow.

Why did she have to fight? Whatever happened now was

inevitable, all the struggling in the world wouldn't stop it.

Feebly she attempted resistance.

The hulk loved that. He ripped at satin, lifted her bodily, and threw her down on the bed.

The pills had an anaesthetizing effect. She was glad. Getting raped on camera had never been a career goal.

*

'Hello, little girl.'

'Tim!'

'What a memory!'

'Why haven't you phoned me before?'

'I thought rich little girls like you wouldn't want to be bothered with broke actors.'

'Are you broke?'

'Nearly. But I think I can rustle up enough change to take you to dinner tonight.'

'Honestly?'

'Why not? You're free aren't you?'

'Oh yes.'

'I'll meet you in the bar at Trader Vic's, eight o'clock.'

Brigette replaced the receiver and squealed with joy. She had known Tim Wealth would phone, and now he had. Brilliant!

He had asked her on a date and she would go.

Except . . .

How was she going to get out of the house?

Alice was taking a nap in front of a giant TV.

She snored delicately.

Brigette shook her vigorously awake.

'Where am I?' mumbled Alice, lost for a moment.

'My girlfriend from school is here,' Brigette announced.

'Where?' panicked Alice, sitting up in a hurry and looking around.

'Not here, silly. In LA. She's visiting.'

Alice had been dreaming of John Travolta. She had read somewhere once that he preferred older women, and she knew if he ever clapped eyes on her it would be love at first sight. Mrs Alice Travolta. That would make Lennie sit up and take notice. 'How nice, dear,' she said vaguely.

'She wants me to stay overnight with her,' Brigette lied.

Alice was delighted. 'That'll be nice for you,' she said, patting her hair. Claudio was coming over and this would give them an opportunity to be alone. Looking after Brigette was one thing – but neglecting her sex life was another. Claudio was an extremely *talented* short person, and she missed his ardent attentions.

'I don't want to go to my friend's house in the Rolls,' Brigette announced. 'It's so embarrassing!'

If Alice had her way she would never go anywhere except in a Rolls Royce, ever again. What a peculiar child Brigette was.

'How will you get there?' she asked.

'I'll call a cab.'

'Lennie said –'

'Please, Ali. Pretty please! I won't tell Lennie if you won't.'

Alice failed to see the harm in allowing the girl to go by cab. 'Oh, very well. But don't talk to the driver. They're all illegals, you know.'

Brigette grinned slyly. What she planned to do was also illegal, but who cared?

She raced to Olympia's closet and scanned her clothes. Sweaters and blouses, dresses and pants, scarves and belts, jackets and pants. Browsing Olympia's closet was like being in a store. Her mother's taste was gross, and Brigette couldn't find anything worth wearing except a ragged looking leopard skin scarf hanging in the back. She could have bet it once belonged to Flash.

Excitedly she reached for it. Tight jeans, one of Lennie's jackets, and the scarf – especially if it really had once belonged to Flash – would be a cool outfit.

As she tugged at the scarf, there was a whirring noise, and part of the wall in the closet slid away revealing a hidden room.

Brigette was startled, but only for a moment. She figured

she had stumbled across the hiding place for her mother's jewels.

Inquisitively she pushed past clothes and entered the tiny room. Shelves lined the walls. And on the shelves were stacked bottles and bottles of different colour pills, glass phials, boxes of smelly brown tobacco stuff, and packets of white powder.

Brigette frowned.

Drugs?

Whose?

Lennie's? He was a movie star. Weren't all movie stars supposed to be bombed out of their minds? She had read it in *The Enquirer* or somewhere.

Curiously she picked up a packet of white powder. It looked like powdered sugar, but she guessed it was cocaine. With a rush of excitement she remembered her last meeting with Tim Wealth. He had snorted coke, and been cross with her when she sneezed and blew most of it away. What would he say if she took him a gift? He would *have* to be pleased. And she wanted to please him more than anything else in the world.

*

'Hiya, little girl,' Tim Wealth said, rising to greet her.

'I'm eighteen,' Brigette lied. 'Fade out on the little girl.'

He leaned toward her. 'I always get horny in Polynesian restaurants, how about you?'

She was weak in the knees, but she didn't want *him* to know.

'What are you drinking?' she asked, looking at his glass.

'Whisky sour.'

'I'll have the same,' she said, and hoped and prayed they wouldn't ask for her ID.

As if reading her mind he said, 'You're only eighteen – you can't be a legal drinking partner until you hit twenty-one. You want to get me arrested?'

If he only knew!

'I'll order you a Mickey Mouse drink and you can share

my whisky sour on the sly. How's that?'

She nodded happily. He was so fantastic! And understanding.

Dinner was wonderful. At least it looked wonderful. Brigette was too excited to eat. It was difficult to believe she was actually sitting in a restaurant with Tim Wealth.

'Tell me about yourself,' he encouraged over chicken chow mein. 'Are you really the granddaughter of Dimitri Stanislopoulos?'

She nodded. 'He died, you know.'

'Yeah, I read about it,' he said casually. He had read *all* about it. 'A rich old dude, huh?'

'I guess.'

She guessed. He stared at the pretty little blonde girl and wondered how best to use her. He felt no remorse that he had to do so. She was using him. Fourteen years old and pretending to be eighteen. Jail bait. Rich jail bait. *Dangerous* jail bait. She couldn't care less that because of her deception he could have got his ass slung in the can. Why should she? Everything had been handed her on a silver platter all her life, and always would be. Slightly different from *his* humble beginnings. At fourteen he was fighting off his stepfather in the outside john. Miss Stanislopoulos, with her big blue eyes and golden curls, probably didn't even know what an outside john was.

He wondered what kind of access she had to all the money that was supposedly hers. Fourteen was kind of young. No doubt she was surrounded by trustees and guardians and was watched all the time.

If she was watched all the time, how come she was out with him guzzling his whisky sour and waiting impatiently to get laid?

He asked her a few questions about who she was staying with in LA, and heard all about crazy Alice, Lennie Golden's mother.

'How'd you get here?' he asked curiously.

'Uh . . . I took a cab.' She hesitated. 'I would have driven, but my car is in the shop being fixed.'

'Oh yeah, what's wrong with it?'

'Engine trouble.' She took a quick sip of his drink and hoped he wouldn't ask any more questions.

'What do you drive?' he persisted.

She thought of Lennie's Porsche sitting in the garage. 'A Porsche,' she said quickly.

He was playing with her. 'What model?'

She struggled to get up. 'I gotta go to the bathroom.'

He stood politely. 'Be my guest.'

Chapter 106

Jerry Myerson threw the glossy magazine on Steven's desk with a resounding thud. The Bonnatti publication, titled *Comer*, featured Mary-Lou Moore in black stockings, garter belt and little else. She gazed at the camera, lips moist, expression sulky, and position precarious.

'Get a load of this,' said Jerry pointing to the writing alongside the near naked girl. MARY-LOU OPENS UP . . . SEE ALL HEAR ALL . . . FIVE GLORIOUS PAGES . . .

Steven looked. And swore. And flipped the magazine open, searching for the other photos.

'Did you know about this?' Jerry asked.

'Hell, *no*,' Steven replied through clenched teeth as he studied the rest of the pictures.

'She should have told you,' Jerry grumbled. 'This is going to blow your victory right out the window. The decision'll be reversed and she'll end up paying Bonnatti's costs.'

Steven was silent as he stared at the offensive shots. There was Mary-Lou in an empty bathtub – one leg thrown casually over the side. There was Mary-Lou lying on a chaise lounge, legs apart, with just a feather boa for company. And more of the same. Each shot portrayed – as known in the wonderful world of men's magazines – split beaver.

'Damn!' said Steven harshly.

Jerry was sympathetic. 'I know, I know. It's a shock. You thought she was a sweet kid, and all that. But believe me –

women – you never can tell what they're going to get up to next. I –'

'Spare me your half-baked philosophies,' interrupted Steven angrily, still staring at the photos. 'This is *not* Mary-Lou.'

'Steven. I know you like the girl, but –'

'This is *not* Mary-Lou,' he repeated angrily. 'These pictures are fakes.'

'What are you talking about?'

'Fakes. Composites,' Steven said excitedly. 'Her face. Somebody else's body superimposed. Jesus! I'm talking English, aren't I?'

'Are you sure they're not the real thing?'

'Jerry. Please. I'm *living* with the girl. I should know what she looks like without her clothes on.' He waved the magazine in the air. 'This is definitely *not* Mary-Lou.'

'So all we have to do is prove it,' said Jerry logically. 'And then it's back to court for a *real* pay-off. If what you say is true, my friend, this one's a piece of pie with double whipped cream. We are looking at a *massive* settlement.'

'That's three, four years down the line,' Steven pointed out. 'It's more depositions and papers and meetings and postponements. All the legal machinations.'

'Why are you telling me something I already know?'

'Because I'm not sure Mary-Lou is willing to go through it again. She's going to want these pictures never to appear.'

'Impossible. The magazine's hitting the stands any moment.'

'How would you like it if somebody did this to you?' Steven said furiously.

Jerry laughed. 'I don't think I'd sell as many magazines!'

'You asshole. Everything's a joke to you, isn't it?'

'There are certain things one cannot control. We have a legal system to take care of things – which I might point out, you are part of. So either you go with it, or you have a nervous breakdown.'

'Screw you!' Steven exploded. 'This one I'm not going to sit back on.'

Jerry shrugged. 'There's nothing you can do.'
'Just try me,' Steven said grimly.

Chapter 107

The thrill was in doing it. Now that she had achieved that feat, Lucky needed to move on to something else. She had built the Santangelo. It was everything she wanted it to be. Her hotel. Her pride. But she had no intention of sitting in Atlantic City counting the money. She wanted a new challenge, another adventure.

A business consortium wanted to buy her out. They were offering a huge profit on the two hundred million the hotel had cost to build.

Sell, she decided. Take the money and run, as Gino would say. Not that she needed the money, she was rich beyond her wildest dreams. What she *did* need was the freedom. Being tied to Atlantic City for the rest of her life was not her idea of heaven. Quietly she instructed her lawyers to proceed with the deal.

'Olympia Stanislopoulos is challenging the will,' her legal advisors informed her.

It came as no surprise.

'Tell her I'll double what her father left her,' Lucky generously decided. 'And she can have the yacht as a gift.'

Olympia's answer was swift and to the point. 'No.'

Lucky tried again. 'I'll treble what Dimitri wanted her to have, and I'll throw in the New York apartment. If she doesn't accept my offer within ten days I shall withdraw it and all previous offers.'

Olympia's reply was, 'Why wait ten days? When I get that bitch in court and prove she killed my father and forced him to change his will, *everything* will be mine.'

The lawyers rubbed their hands together gleefully. And so did the press.

•

'I'm leaving,' Lennie said.

Olympia favoured him with a glare. 'You don't mean it,' she said. 'You wouldn't walk out on me and all the things I can give you.'

They had been fighting for weeks, ever since the reading of the will. In the Bel Air house he could escape. But in their New York apartment there was no such luxury. Lennie knew he couldn't take it any more. Why was he hanging around anyway? Olympia's looks were restored – plastic surgery had taken care of every one of her scars. So she was fat. Was that his problem? Was he supposed to feel sorry for her and stay with her forever?

'I don't *want* anything from you,' he said wearily. 'You can have every single thing you've ever given me. The cars, the house, the furniture. I'm going to walk away from this marriage empty handed.'

'Empty handed, my ass,' she yelled. 'What about all the money *you've* made?'

'I made it, didn't I? It's mine, isn't it?'

'Not when I've finished with you,' she ranted. 'California law. Half of everything you have is mine.'

'And vice versa. But I don't want anything from you. So leave me alone, and I'll show you the same courtesy.'

'You fuckhead!'

'Such a lady.'

'Piss off. You're only leaving me now because I'm not as rich as you thought I was going to be.'

'Money has nothing to do with it, and you know it.'

'Sure,' she jeered. 'But you'll be sorry, just you wait. The will'll be reversed and I'll be the richest fucking woman in the world. Then you'll be *really* sorry.'

He threw clothes in a suitcase, snapped it shut, and walked to the door. 'Goodbye, Olympia.'

She followed him and hurled a lead crystal ashtray. It missed his head by inches.

He opened the door and stepped into freedom.

He should have made the move a long time ago.

Chapter 108

'How was it dear?' asked Alice gaily, as a taxi delivered Brigette to the door of the mansion just before noon. 'Was your girlfriend delighted to see you?' She didn't wait for an answer, just fluttered on with, 'Gino telephoned. He's here in Beverly Hills with Roberto – and your little uncle wants to see you.' She snickered. 'Fancy having an uncle of four and a half! Gino's sending him and CeeCee over this afternoon.'

'Why are *they* here?' Brigette mumbled truculently.

'I don't know,' trilled Alice, happy after a night with her tiny lover. '*Je ne sais pas.*'

Brigette frowned. She had been looking forward to a nice quiet day thinking about Tim. What an evening they had spent together! The most exciting night of her entire life. Tim Wealth was the biggest babe ever.

She loved him.

She would do anything for him.

He was absolute boss.

*

Tim's dressing room was their only escape. 'How did it go?' he asked Eden.

There were deep circles under her eyes and bruises on her body. 'Once for the camera, and once for Santino when he got me home,' she complained bitterly. 'If I'd had a gun I would've killed him.'

'You don't have to go that far. I'm working on a plan to get us out of here first class. How would you like to spend the winter in Acapulco?'

'I've *got* to get away from him,' she said urgently. 'I can't take any more.'

'Don't worry. It's in the works.'

She put her thin arms around his neck and kissed him with her thin lips. So different from the baby girl he had spent the night with, but much more of a turn-on. Eden Antonio pressed all the right buttons. She was one woman he knew he could spend time with and not get bored shitless.

A knock on the dressing room door made them leap apart.

'Who is it?' Tim shouted.

'You're wanted on the set.'

'Be right there.'

*

Gino, Costa, Ria, and CeeCee with Roberto, lunched in the Polo Lounge of the Beverly Hills Hotel. Gino enjoyed the scrambled eggs and smoked salmon. He also enjoyed the passing parade.

People stopped by his table. A Senator with steel grey hair and a young secretary on his arm. A large woman dripping in daytime diamonds who had once sold him a house. A stoned entrepreneur with darting nervous eyes. And finally, Paige Wheeler.

She entered, spoke with the maitre d', saw Gino, wanted to walk past his table, but good manners overcame her. Not to mention Costa, who waved and called out her name.

Paige wore one of her famous split to the crotch skirts, and a linen jacket with a polka dot blouse underneath. Her full breasts pushed aggressively against the fabric of the blouse. She wasn't wearing a bra and Gino could make out the firm swell of her nipples.

'Gino!' Warm smile. 'Long time.'

He smiled, 'Hya, Paige.'

They hadn't seen each other since he had caught her with Susan, and his subsequent divorce.

He rose, always the gentleman, and kissed her on both cheeks. She smelled the same. Musky and sexy. But she looked a little older. So did he. Big deal. Neither of them were spring lambs.

'And Costa,' she beamed. 'How nice to see you.'

Costa introduced Ria, and mentioned the fact that he was about to become a father. Paige was duly impressed.

'And this is Roberto, Gino's grandson,' Costa continued. 'Don't they look alike?'

Paige smiled at the little boy. 'Exactly,' she said.

Roberto stared at her with his huge long-lashed Santangelo eyes and nibbled on a roll. He was a shy child, and was only just getting used to being among people.

'How about joining us for a drink?' Costa asked. He knew nothing of the circumstances which had forced Gino to stop seeing her. Nobody did.

She glanced at Gino fleetingly. He didn't react.

'I can't,' she apologized. 'I'm meeting a client for lunch. Maybe some other time.'

'Call us,' urged Costa, writing their phone number on some book matches. 'We're here for a month.'

She stared straight at Gino as she murmured, 'Maybe I will.'

He still didn't react.

'Well, it was nice to see you all again,' she said cordially, and left to join her client.

'I like her. She's a very classy woman,' Costa said. 'How come you let her go, Gino?'

Gino didn't say anything. He was too busy remembering.

*

In front of the camera Eden ran her hands down Tim Wealth's chest. She kissed him passionately and felt his sharp response as he peeled the dress from her shoulders and bent her back across a table.

'Cut!' the director shouted.

Santino hunched forward in his usual ringside seat. He did not like the amount of time it took for them to separate. He mumbled curses under his breath.

They broke the clinch and Eden walked over to her hairdresser who began to fuss with her hair.

'Hey – cunt,' Santino called out loudly. 'C'mere.'

She ignored him.

'I said *come here*, movie star cunt,' Santino repeated.

The hairdresser's hand began to shake. Eden was cool.

Inside she was raging. The entire crew was on full alert. Tim had vanished into his dressing room.

Slowly she walked toward her keeper. He was a monster. A short, bald, hairy pig. And he was getting crazier every day.

'What?' she hissed.

He stood up and pulled her roughly by the arm. 'Ya got a few minutes, movie star?' he questioned.

Her voice was strained. 'Yes.'

Everyone was listening, even though they pretended they weren't.

'I feel like a blow job,' Santino announced lazily. 'Let's go to your dressin' room, movie star, I'm gonna let you suck me off.'

She froze inside. It wasn't enough she was his. He had to publicly humiliate her. He had to show the world he could treat her how he liked. If she'd had a gun she would have shot him right between his beady little balls.

Chapter 109

Lennie needed time to be alone and think things out. So he told no one he was returning to LA, not even Jess. He flew in and took a cab from the airport to his old apartment, which he had kept for sentimental reasons.

The one bedroom penthouse on Doheny smelled musty and unused. He opened up the shutters. It felt like home. More home than the multi-roomed mansion in Bel Air had ever been.

Harriet, the old crusty maid who had looked after him when he lived there, was supposed to come in and clean once a week – she was still on the payroll – but it was obvious she never did. He fingered a shelf, and thick dust ran riot.

He looked around. The bed was unmade – fond memories of a thousand little blondes. The living room was untidy. He found half a bottle of vodka, and a stack of yellow legal pads he had been working on. Once. A long time ago.

The apartment was peaceful. No servants padding around, no telephones ringing, no secretaries, and most of all – no Olympia.

He had made the move.

He was free.

Almost.

*

After the lunch break Santino left the set.

Eden held her head high, although deep down she was mortified. He had forced her to her knees like a dog, and threatened her when she tried to object. He was definitely becoming unhinged. Escape had to be soon. She was convinced that eventually he would threaten her life, not just her face.

Tim held her close in front of the camera, and then later, in his dressing room between set-ups, he held her for real; and they made love urgently. She did things to Tim Wealth willingly. Things Santino had to force from her.

'I'm working on getting us out as soon as possible,' Tim assured her. 'Maybe tomorrow. I want you to be ready for my call.'

'We can't go any place where Santino can reach me,' she worried.

'Money'll take us a long way, and I'm scoring us plenty.'

He had figured out a scam – of sorts. It involved Brigette. So what? She was a spoilt, rich brat. It was about time she learned the ways of the world.

*

The last thing Brigette felt like doing was playing with a four-and-a-half-year-old boy. And she had always loathed CeeCee.

They sat around the pool like one big happy family. Alice, in a cutaway swimsuit revealing gnarled flesh and an alarming growth of pubic hair straggling from the crotch. Alice's friend Claudio – who was perfectly formed in every way, but hardly taller than Roberto, who played happily in the pool. CeeCee, watchful as ever. And Brigette, in a white bikini, looking at least nineteen.

Brigette sunbathed enthusiastically, knowing that a tan went well with her long blonde hair. She wanted to look her best for Tim. The summer was ending, and soon it would be time to return to hateful school. She couldn't bear it. Her thoughts were all of Tim Wealth. He was unlike anyone she had ever met before. He was so moody and smart and sexy . . .

After dinner at Trader Vic's he had taken her to his apartment in Hollywood. One room. One bed. Oh! Was he sexy!

He had undressed her, made love to her, caused her to shiver and shake, and then – as a joke – he had said, 'Let's take some pictures, little girl.'

She had giggled with embarrassment when he told her how to pose in front of his polaroid camera. 'Do this. Do that. Smile. Look happy.'

At first she was shy – but after he told her the photos were for her to keep, she had relaxed and enjoyed the game. He presented her with the pictures. She presented him with the bag of white powder she had taken from Olympia's dressing room. He was really pleased.

What a brilliant adventure, spending the night with Tim Wealth. She wished she could spend every night with him.

In the morning he called her a cab, said he would phone her later, and sent her on her way.

She waited eagerly to hear from him.

*

After delivering Roberto to spend the afternoon with Brigette, Gino was at a loss. Ria had taken Costa shopping along Rodeo Drive – and the afternoon stretched emptily before him.

Since divorcing Susan he had no order to his life. He did whatever he wanted whenever he wanted. It was good, but there was something missing. He liked the companionship of a steady woman. He liked to be able to wake up in the morning and find someone there. He was too old for the quick lay – and most of the women he went to bed with now failed to hold his interest.

Finally, Gino had to admit, he was getting old.

With Paige Wheeler he had never felt old. Seeing her again had rekindled all the memories, and they were pretty good memories.

He thought he had noticed a gleam in her eye when she looked at him today. Was he mistaken, or did she miss him too?

Impulsively he drove to the Beverly Wilshire Hotel and checked into a suite.

'No luggage, Mr Santangelo?' questioned the desk clerk.

'It'll be over later. Send up a bottle of Dom Perignon and a dish of your best caviar.'

'Yes, sir.'

Once upstairs he paced the suite.

So – he had caught Paige with Susan. Well, she had never professed to be a virgin.

So – was he going to call her or what?

*

Outside 'Lina Lee', on Rodeo Drive, at four o'clock in the afternoon, Ria broke her water.

'Omigod!' she squawked. 'Get me to the hospital – quick!'

Costa, a calm man all his life, panicked completely.

A tourist from Minnesota and a concerned salesgirl took charge of the situation. If it wasn't for them, Ria might have started labour on the sidewalk.

*

'I need an estimate on a decorating job,' Gino said formally into the telephone.

Paige recognized his voice immediately. She waved an assistant from her office and leaned back in her comfortable leather chair. 'What kind of a job?' she inquired, equally formal.

'Urgent.'

'Urgent?'

'Very.'

'Hmmmm . . .' She paused as if consulting a full appointment book. 'I'm afraid I have no free time until next week.'

'Fit me in.'

She propped her legs on the desk. 'I don't know if I can . . .'

'You can.'

'Where?'

'The Beverly Wilshire. Where else?' He gave her the suite number.

'Have you any idea what you require?' she asked in a businesslike tone.

'You. And fast.'

Smiles suffused both their faces as they hung up.

*

'Have a piece of fruit cake, I made it myself,' trilled Alice, offering it around. 'All pure ingredients. Oooh la la! It's so good!'

She had covered her swimsuit with a garment which resembled a flowered tablecloth, and was trying to impress Claudio with her skill as a home-maker. Last night he had confided that he came from a titled French family. He was a secret Count. Countess Claudio! Ha! That would *really* impress everyone.

CeeCee took a bite, and promptly lost her front capped tooth on a stale walnut. Clutching the offending cap, CeeCee glared.

'I suppose we'll have to get you to a dentist,' Alice said reluctantly. 'What a nuisance!'

CeeCee nodded. She had no choice. The cold air was hitting a nerve, and she could feel the onslaught of a nagging toothache.

'I have a dentist in Marina del Rey,' Alice said with a martyred sigh. 'I'd better call him.' She huffed with the inconvenience of it all, and picked up the telephone.

*

'Hello, little girl.'

Brigette almost jumped with delight. 'I was waiting for

your call,' she said. 'I didn't think I'd hear from you this early.'

'Wanna come over to my place and play?'

'Oh *no*! I *can't*. I'm looking after my stupid uncle.'

'Your *uncle*?'

'He's four years old. And dumb.'

She missed the catch of excitement in Tim's voice as he said, 'Roberto?'

'How'd you know his name?'

'I'm not just a beautiful actor.'

Brigette giggled.

'Where is everybody?' he asked curiously. 'How come you're looking after the kid?'

'Roberto's nanny broke her tooth, and Alice and her boyfriend – he's a freak – like they all went off in the limo to get it fixed. Alice's dentist is in Marina del Rey, and Alice wanted to take her friend – you should *see* him – to look at her apartment. So . . . like I got stuck, didn't I?'

'I'm fond of kids,' Tim said quickly, his mind reorganizing the scam he had planned.

'You wouldn't like this one,' Brigette said grimly. 'He's a geek.'

'Bring him. I'll let you know.'

She giggled. 'I can't do that.'

'Sure you can. Take a cab to the corner of Fairfax and Sunset, and I'll meet you there. We'll buy the kid an ice cream and I'll drive him home. Then we can have the whole evening alone together. How's that?'

Brigette was tempted. She wanted to see Tim more than anything. But if she took Roberto anywhere CeeCee would go bananas. CeeCee was very protective. As soon as she realized she had to go to the dentist she had tried to get Gino or Costa to come and collect Roberto, but they were both unreachable. And she didn't trust the maids. Reluctantly she had left the child in Brigette's care. 'Don't let him out of your sight,' she had admonished. 'I'll be back as soon as I can.'

Brigette did not like CeeCee. She was bossy. All she cared

about was stupid Roberto. It would serve her right to come back and find him gone.

'Well?' Tim demanded. 'What's happening?'

'We're coming for ice cream,' she giggled. 'Can't wait!'

•

Things were working out better than Tim expected.

He picked up the tabloid newspaper on the table in front of him and stared at the headline above a picture of a small dark-haired child climbing out of a swimming pool. THE RICHEST BOY IN THE WORLD.

He re-read the small print underneath:

> IS ROBERTO STANISLOPOULOS
> THE RICHEST BOY IN THE WORLD?
> CLOSE FRIENDS OF THE LATE
> BILLIONAIRE, DIMITRI STANISLOPOUOS
> SAY THAT HE SOON WILL BE.
> IT WAS REPORTED IN NEW YORK
> TODAY –

Slowly Tim put the paper down. Brigette Stanislopoulos was catch enough, but now he would have both of them.

It was a piece of good fortune he could only have dreamed of.

Chapter 110

Steven didn't know whether to tell Mary-Lou or not. He agonized over what he should do, and then he realized there was only one way to go. He had to tell her. The offending magazine was just about to hit the stands. The press would be bugging her, waiting for her comments. *He* knew it wasn't Mary-Lou in the pornographic photo spread, but they were going to have to prove it to the rest of the world.

'Goddamn it!' he muttered to himself. And he wondered how slime like Santino Bonnatti could even exist.

Lucky Santangelo had eliminated Santino's father, the

notorious Enzio. She had had her reasons. According to the word on the street, Enzio had been responsible for the murder of her lover, Marco, *and* her brother, Dario. At the time Steven had been disapproving. The law was adequate. The law would have dealt with the likes of Enzio Bonnatti.

Now he wasn't so sure. The law was a long, shaky process. People could be bribed to see that justice never took place.

He cancelled an appointment and hurried home. The sooner he told Mary-Lou the better. She would have to speak to the network and the sponsors of her show. The best thing to do was to have her release a statement before the press besieged their brownstone.

He planned how to handle the situation. Dignity and denial, that was the only way.

A strong smell of gas hit him as he opened the front door. He gagged and almost choked, the air was thick with it.

Jesus Christ! Had Mary-Lou left the oven on? She hated to cook, they usually sent out for food.

He held his breath and rushed into the kitchen.

Mary-Lou was on the floor slumped by the open oven.

Next to her lay a copy of *Comer* magazine.

Chapter 111

Lucky wandered into Matt's office and perched on the edge of his desk. 'I've had it,' she told him with an exhausted sigh. 'I'm taking off for LA in the morning. I'll spend the weekend and be back on Tuesday. Can you manage without me?'

'I think we'll get by,' Matt said dryly. 'As long as calling you day or night is in order.'

The Santangelo had opened to capacity business – but there were the usual problems with chefs, managers and general staff. All controllable.

Lucky smiled ruefully. 'You know I never sleep. And you also know I like to be the first to hear everything that goes on.'

Matt said, 'So go – relax – have a rest and enjoy yourself. You deserve it.'

She picked a pencil off his desk and played with it. 'I can't wait to see Roberto. That's what I really need – a massive fix of baby love.'

'Sounds good to me.'

'Well, who knows, maybe when you and Jess do the deed you'll have one of your own.'

He laughed self-consciously. 'I don't know about *that.*'

They discussed several business matters. Matt knew of Lucky's plans to sell. She had included him in for a piece of the action. He hadn't made up his mind what he would do next. The potential buyers had offered him a firm management contract with points – but he needed to discuss it with Jess before deciding.

Business concluded, Lucky pecked him on the cheek and went off to pack. She hadn't called to tell Gino she was coming. She wanted to surprise everyone.

Chapter 112

The sound of the shower filtered through to the bedroom. Gino, clad in a bathrobe, sat on the edge of the rumpled bed and plucked a bottle of Dom Perignon from the ice bucket on the side table. Empty. Every drop gone. And he couldn't remember drinking that much.

'Hey –' he called out. 'We finished the champagne.'

'Live dangerously,' Paige called back. 'Order another bottle. There must be *some* compensations to sleeping with a rich old man!'

He chuckled as he picked up the phone. She always made him laugh. 'More champagne on the way,' he said as he walked into the bathroom, opened the shower door, and watched her soap herself. She had full, real breasts (how he hated silicone – whoever invented silicone tits should be shot), a firmly packed body, soft thighs, and an unmanageable thatch of pubic hair, copper – like the hair on her head. 'Y'know what I want,' he said.

She massaged her breasts vigorously. 'What?'

'I want you to stay the night. Just like in New York. Remember? We had some good times there, didn't we?'

She put the soap down and allowed the water to wash over her. Then she stepped from the stall and enveloped herself in a fluffy towel.

'You know I can't stay,' she said briskly.

'Why not?' he demanded.

'Because,' she replied patiently, 'I am a married woman, and I have a husband at home who will be extremely concerned if I just decide to stay out all night.'

'Will he?'

She began to towel herself dry. 'Yes, he will.'

'He doesn't mind you spending the day gettin' laid, but an all nighter is out of line, huh?'

She refused to let him get to her. 'You got it.' She dropped the towel and reached for a bathrobe.

He sat on the side of the tub. 'I missed you, kiddo,' he said. 'I tried a selection – but you're the only one can do it for me.'

She began to laugh. 'I don't believe *that*, Gino. You'll go to your grave with a hard-on!'

He grabbed her around the waist and pressed his face against her stomach.

She parted the bathrobe. 'While you're down there . . .' she murmured.

He didn't need any more encouragement.

•

Alice lingered with Claudio in Marina del Rey. She showed him her old photo albums and carefully preserved silver tasselled G-strings. He was duly impressed. Especially when she produced the set of pictures she had taken on the famous Stanislopoulos cruise.

They sipped martinis, admired the view from Alice's waterfront apartment, and made out on the couch. Alice smiled to herself. Claudio might be short, but he had the biggest *schlong* she'd ever seen.

It wasn't until an irate CeeCee phoned from the dentist's waiting room that Alice realized they were running two hours late. 'Ooh la la!' she exclaimed in mock horror. 'The *schvartze* is mad – we'd better be running.'

*

The harsh slap sent Eden reeling across the room.

'You're a cunt, that's all y'are. An' an *old* cunt at that.'

'I'm thirty-one,' Eden sobbed, out of control. 'That's not old . . .' She crouched in the corner waiting for his next move. 'THAT'S NOT OLD,' she shrieked.

'In this town it's friggin' pushin' up daisies – for a woman,' Santino spat disdainfully. He had removed his jacket and vest, and rolled up the sleeves of his striped shirt. Beating up a woman took it out of you – he was sweating more than usual.

Eden pulled herself into the foetal position – knees up to her chest – arms clutched around them. She was a mess. One eye was blackened and half-closed, her jaw was swollen and bruised purple, blood dripped from a cut lip.

Santino bore down on her. 'If ya fuck around on Santino Bonnatti, ya gotta pay the price. Understand, cunt?'

'I haven't done anything,' she whimpered.

He raised his arm to strike another blow, but thought better of it. She had learned her lesson. She wouldn't open her legs for anyone else in a hurry. She *knew* who she belonged to.

Now all he had to do was deal with Tim Wealth. Teach *him* the score.

Nobody fucked Santino Bonnatti's woman off camera.

Nobody.

Not unless he said so.

Chapter 113

'So this is the kid?' Tim Wealth asked.

'This is the geek,' Brigette agreed.

'Not a geek. Not,' Roberto asserted.

'Hold my hand, brat, and shut up.' Brigette grabbed the small boy's hand. Traffic was racing past on Sunset. All she needed was for Roberto to wander under a car. Lucky would never speak to her again.

Tim bent to talk to the child. 'Hello there,' he said.

'Ice cream?' the boy asked eagerly.

'If you're good,' replied Tim.

Brigette giggled. 'I bet people passing by think we're a family,' she said. 'I'm mommy, and you're daddy, and this is our little one.' She exploded with mirth.

Tim looked quickly around. He didn't want anyone noticing anything. Brigette was not exactly low profile in a red T-shirt with HOT STUFF emblazoned on the front, skin hugging white jeans and cascades of long blonde hair.

'Let's go to my place,' he suggested.

'Ice cream,' repeated Roberto, trying to wriggle out of Brigette's grasp.

'Shut up, Bobby,' she snapped, thinking to herself that she should have left the kid at home. What was the *point* in bringing him along? CeeCee would be furious.

So what? She was only a stupid nanny. Who cared *what* her reaction was? In fact, it would do her good to worry. Brigette would never forget the spanking she had received from her when she was eleven. The humiliation still stung.

'You promised the geek ice cream,' she pointed out. 'Let's get it over with and send him home.'

There was no way she could let Tim drive Roberto back to the house. She had already decided to put him in a cab, and then call Alice and say he was on his way. Alice would believe anything. 'Hi, Ali,' she would say. 'I'm over at my girlfriend's house and we're going to a movie. Bobby's in a cab – he should be there any minute. And I'll probably stay at my friend's tonight.' That way CeeCee couldn't say a word to her. Yeah – the brat would be okay, it was only a ten minute drive. She couldn't *wait* to get rid of him and be alone with Tim.

'I've got ice cream at my place,' Tim said.

'You have?'

'Häagen Dazs. Chocolate, Chocolate Chip.'

Brigette linked her arm happily through his. 'What are we waiting for?' She grinned, pulling Roberto along with her other hand. 'Let's go.'

Chapter 114

Information.

Carrie had the information her son required. And once Fred Lester confessed the truth it was all so simple.

Gino Santangelo was Steven's father.

Gino. A memory from so long ago . . .

He had fathered her child and had no idea he had done so.

Gino Santangelo.

Over the years she had occasionally read about him in the newspapers. Once a gangster he was a big man now, and old, as she was. And respected. Only last week she had seen a picture of him in the newspaper at a charity function in Las Vegas with an ex-President. The two men had faced the camera with their arms around each other. Good friends.

Steven's father.

She couldn't care less. But Steven needed to know.

Carrie hurried along Lexington heading toward Steven's brownstone on Fifty-Eighth Street. Her head was filled with thoughts. She was confused . . . so very confused. For forty-five years she had remembered Freddy Lester as nothing less than scum. And now he had re-entered her life. A perfectly respectable man. A good humoured man with excellent manners and a kindly face.

It was so difficult to believe he had once been the drunken pig who had raped her. The unfeeling lout who had called her '. . . *a fucking dinge* . . .'

He had told her his story while she stared at him, contempt written across her face.

He told her about his accident and his family and his life.

She had listened in stony silence.

Finally he had said, 'If I *was* Steven's father I would want to know so that I could begin to make up for all the lost years.'

Her voice was cold. 'I don't know and I don't care.'

'But I *do* know,' he had said very quietly. 'Once I was in possession of all the facts, I made it my business to find out.'

'How could you possibly do that?' she asked.

'If you are positive that Gino Santangelo and I were the only two candidates, then there is no doubt.'

'My book is the truth,' Carrie said icily. 'I don't lie.'

'Well then, Gino is Steven's father. I have an extremely rare blood type. I checked Steven's medical records – genetics prove I could not have fathered him.' He paused, then continued. 'I took the liberty of investigating Gino Santangelo's past. He was in jail between 1940 and 1947. They have a complete medical history. His blood type matches Steven's exactly.'

Fred had continued further with confirming facts. He also had full documentation of all the evidence he had collected, which he handed to her.

Eventually he stopped speaking and she gathered herself together.

'Mr Lester,' she said coldly. 'I don't wish to proceed with the plans for my book to be published.'

'But –'

She raised her hand to stop his protestations. 'Please. I need time to think. Maybe I'll feel different next week, next year. I simply don't know.'

'I hope so,' he said anxiously. 'I can't tell you how important it is to me that we publish this book. It is a –'

'Ah, as long as the names are changed,' she interrupted dryly, 'to protect the not-so-innocent.'

He gestured helplessly. 'Carrie. It all happened a long long time ago . . . .'

'Not long enough, Mr Lester. Not nearly long enough.'

She left his office and walked unseeingly down Fifth Avenue. Now it was late afternoon and she was approaching Steven's house. He had to know the truth at once.

There was an ambulance parked outside, and a small crowd had gathered to gawk.

Carrie pushed her way through. 'What's going on?' she asked a well dressed woman.

'Suicide I think,' the woman said, eyes agleam. 'Don't light a cigarette, the whole neighbourhood'll go up. Gas I think. Can't you smell it?'

For one heart-stopping moment Carrie thought the victim might be Steven. But thank God, before she could panic he came rushing out of the building, and behind him hurried two ambulance attendants carrying a stretcher.

'Steven,' she called out desperately. 'What happened?'

Chapter 115

A very pleasant nurse kept Costa sane while Ria spent hours in delivery.

He continually tried to phone Gino but a stupid machine kept on answering the phone, and Costa had no intention of speaking to a machine. Finally he called Olympia's mansion to speak with CeeCee and Roberto, but a maid informed him everyone was out.

Was there no one he could give the good news to? He, Costa Zennocotti, was, at the age of seventy-five – about to become a father.

CeeCee had bad feelings, she didn't know why, but they were powerful bad feelings. The day Dimitri Stanislopoulos died she had suffered from the same thing. Woke in the morning. Cleaned her teeth and washed. Got Roberto up and fed him his favourite hash and scrambled eggs. Then together they had gone to visit his father, as they always did.

Mr Stanislopoulos was sitting in his usual place. He looked weak and tired.

'Good morning, CeeCee. Good morning, Roberto,' he had said. Just as usual. And she had known, at once, that he wouldn't last the day through. Now she was racked with those ominous forebodings again.

She glared at Mr Golden's foolish mother and her foreign companion, for they were responsible for Roberto being left with Brigette longer than he should have been.

Brigette was irresponsible. She had no idea how to look after a four-year-old child. She was spoiled, selfish, and jealous of Roberto – she always had been.

CeeCee sighed loudly. She had not known Marina del Rey was such a long drive. If she had been aware of the distance, she would have ignored her tooth, stuck it back with chewing gum or something. On top of everything else, Alice had left her sitting in the dentist's waiting room for nearly two hours. CeeCee was silently fuming.

Finally they were on their way back to Bel Air in Olympia's white Rolls Royce.

'How long before we're there?' CeeCee asked the chauffeur.

He was a dour-faced Englishman in full uniform. 'About half an hour, madam, depending on the traffic,' he said pompously.

'Thank you.' She wished the bad feelings would go away.

Chapter 116

'Do you like me?' Tim Wealth asked.

Brigette didn't know what to say. Roberto sat at the

kitchen counter slopping chocolate ice cream all over himself, and Tim was asking her the most important question of her life. *I don't like you, I love you*, she wanted to shout out loud, but maybe it was a bit too soon. After all, he hadn't mentioned love to her.

'You know I do,' she said at last. 'I don't do the things we do with anyone else. I *more* than like you.' Hint, hint, maybe he would take it.

'I like you too,' he said, very seriously. 'But I know something about you that's bothering me.'

'What?' she asked quickly.

'More ice cream,' demanded Roberto.

Oh God! She could smack the dumb little geek!

Tim moved to the fridge and took out another carton, which he placed in front of the child.

Brigette fidgeted impatiently, and waited to find out what it was that bothered him.

He did not keep her in suspense. 'I know how old you are,' he said.

She felt herself begin to blush. 'I'm eighteen,' she bluffed.

'You're fourteen,' he countered.

'I'm not,' she lied desperately, feeling humiliated.

'You are,' he said grimly. 'And have you got any idea what that makes me guilty of?'

'What?' Her tone was sulky.

'Statutory rape.'

The only sound in the room was Roberto slurping his ice cream. Brigette wished he wasn't there. She wished the floor would open up and swallow her. Tim Wealth was just about to tell her he couldn't see her anymore and she wanted to die.

'How did you find out?' she muttered, red-faced.

'You're not exactly a state secret,' he said. 'I was reading about your grandfather and his will.'

'It's all lies.'

'What is?'

'My mother says that everything the newspapers print is lies.'

'Maybe so. But I checked, little girl, and you *are* fourteen. Your fifteenth birthday isn't until December.'

'Happy birthday to me,' she mumbled.

Roberto had spotted a television in the corner of the one-room apartment. 'Wanta watch,' he said, pointing.

Brigette flopped on the end of the couch that converted into Tim's bed.

Tim switched on the television for Roberto, and the child climbed down from the counter, took his carton of ice cream, and sat on the floor a few inches in front of it, totally absorbed.

'I don't want to be fourteen,' Brigette sulked. 'I hate it. I really hate it!' Tears filled her big blue eyes. 'And now you hate me too.'

'No I don't,' Tim said soothingly, putting his arm around her.

'Yes you do,' she whimpered.

'No I *don't*. But we've got a big problem, and you have to help me find a solution.'

She wished Roberto wasn't there. He was getting on her nerves just being in the same room.

'Don't worry,' she said truculently. 'I'm going back to school in Switzerland in a week, so I won't be such a big problem anymore.'

'Do you want to go?' he asked quickly. 'Or would you like to stay with me?'

The possibility of staying with him had never even entered her mind. But now he'd mentioned it, it was *exactly* what she'd like to do.

'How can I do that?' she asked hopefully.

'Listen to me, little girl, and listen carefully. I've got a plan.'

Chapter 117

Paige Wheeler called home at five-thirty. An urgent business trip to San Francisco had come up – she wouldn't return until the next day.

'Aren't you even going to pick up an overnight bag?' Ryder asked.

She explained about the Arab client with the private plane impatiently waiting to leave.

Ryder understood. Business was business.

Gino called the rented Beverly Hills house. There was nobody home, just the answering machine.

'This is an adventure,' Paige purred, with a wicked smile. 'I haven't had an adventure in a long time.' She lay back on the bed and stretched contentedly. 'You're so persuasive, Gino.'

'Story of my life,' he grinned. 'I've had it pretty easy when it comes to gettin' my own way.'

'I bet!'

*

Lennie worked on a new script all afternoon. He finished the half bottle of vodka, put Bruce Springsteen on the stereo, and watched the sunset from his Hollywood apartment with the unmade bed and thick layers of dust.

Christ! He felt terrific. Better than he had in a long time. And the material he had written was good, sharp-edged and full of caustic wit. He was on a roll after being blocked for months.

He was going to be free again.

No more mansions and servants.

No more Olympia.

It was as if he were starting over, and there was nobody to think about but himself.

Of course, he was rich in his own right now. He was hot A movie star.

Shit! He was just a comic who got the right breaks at the right time. No movie star, he.

There were things to be settled. Before Olympia returned to LA he had to collect his personal possessions from Bel Air. Clear out his study, take only what he had paid for. And then he would have to explain to Alice. She was up at the mansion looking after Brigette. Gently he would give the two of them the news. Brigette was basically a good kid – if she wanted to keep in contact, he'd be happy. She didn't have much of a life. Being stuck with Olympia for a mother was no smooth ride.

Tomorrow he would deal with them.

Tonight he would enjoy himself.

With that thought in mind he called Jess, and asked her if she wanted to go with him to 'Foxies'.

She was leaving on an early morning plane to spend the weekend with Matt, but she jumped at his offer, anxious to hear everything.

'Pick me up around eight,' he said. 'I'm the guy without a car.'

'You've got four cars, Lennie,' she pointed out.

'Not anymore,' he said, without one note of regret.

•

The moment the Rolls Royce pulled into the driveway of the Bel Air house, CeeCee leaped out.

'You'll break your neck, dear,' warned Alice.

CeeCee moved fast. It was past six. If Lucky ever found out she had left Roberto for this length of time she would be furious, and rightly so. CeeCee knew she was trusted implicitly, and she was very proud of that fact.

'Roberto,' she called, as she rushed into the house, trailed by Alice and Claudio – who seemed to have taken up residence. 'Roberto!'

No response.

'They're probably up in Brigette's room,' said Alice, leading Claudio into one of the vast living rooms.

CeeCee hurried up the majestic marble staircase, along a never-ending hallway. The house was ridiculously large. Six families could live in it and never bump into each other.

'Roberto,' she called out anxiously.

Brigette's room was empty. There were clothes and records and magazines scattered everywhere. But no Brigette and no Roberto.

CeeCee wished the bad feelings would leave her. They

were getting worse every moment. Without a doubt she knew something was wrong.

'Roberto!' she shouted loudly. 'Roberto. Where are you? ROBERTO!'

They searched the house, Alice complaining every inch of the way.

Two Mexican maids, who spoke very little English, professed to know nothing. Then a third maid appeared and mumbled something about a taxi.

'Did Brigette go in the taxi with Roberto?' CeeCee demanded, spacing her words to make sure the woman understood.

'*Si, si,*' the woman nodded.

'All this fuss.' Alice shook her head wisely. 'When Brigette realized we were late, she decided to take Roberto home.'

A phone call to the rented house received no reply.

'Gino's taken them out for dinner,' Alice suggested.

CeeCee nodded, hoping this was so. But the bad feelings would not leave her, and until they did, she could not be sure about anything.

Chapter 118

The paparazzi sprang into action when Olympia Stanislopoulos put in an appearance at Studio 54 in New York. She emerged from a sleek grey limousine with black tinted windows, a bountiful princess.

She wore a huge sable coat over her ample figure, and her long blonde hair flowed across her shoulders.

Accompanying her was a short snappish hairdresser – male – dressed from head to toe in studded leather; a black secretary – female – who was six feet tall; and a long-haired make-up artist – transvestite.

Olympia beamed at the paparazzi. 'Hi, guys.' Her voice was slurred, and the pupils of her blue eyes piercing pinpoints of light. She draped herself provocatively against the front of her limo. 'Wanna take my picture?'

Flashbulbs exploded as they jostled for position. Olympia Stanislopoulos looked like a pretty blonde baby elephant. These photos would front-page world wide.

'Where's Lennie?' one of the photographers shouted.

Olympia frowned. 'Lennie?' she asked, as if she honestly didn't know what they were talking about. 'Lennie who?'

A spiffy young girl, camera at the ready and shorthand going on in her head, made a good guess and said, 'Is it true you two have split?'

Olympia wrapped her sable around her bulk and headed for the entrance of the club. 'Lennie Golden,' she announced grandly, 'is a lousy husband – correction – *was* a lousy husband – *and* a lousy lay. Print that.'

She swept inside, followed closely by her adoring entourage.

*

The Santangelo casino sparkled with activity. Lucky was all packed and ready to leave. She planned to drive to New York, spend the night at The Pierre, and catch the early flight to LA.

Before leaving, she strolled through the casino. It always gave her a thrill to know she had created such excitement.

Vitos Felicidade was headlining, and the crowds were pouring out of the Diamond Room, having just sat through his first show. The women were all a-flutter, clutching programmes with Vitos' picture on the front and chattering about how gorgeous and *virile* he was.

They should only know! Lucky had spent one night in his company. He had achieved a two-minute erection and poured out all his troubles. She felt sorry for him. They had not consummated the act, merely talked the night away.

She waved to one of her pit bosses and pointed out a dealer getting too friendly with a plump brunette at a blackjack table. A stickman at the crap table called out a winner, and the crowd cheered. Two hookers careened past in low-cut clinging dresses discussing a tight-fisted john.

Lucky's dark eyes swept the room. Everything was going smoothly. She was satisfied.

•

''Ello, 'ello, 'ello. It's Tubs in full bloom, ain't it?'

Olympia peered at the skinny figure standing before her in the noisy club. Lately she was having a little trouble focusing. 'Hello,' she said vaguely.

'It's *me*, yer silly bint. Flash.'

'I *loooove* your work,' sighed the transvestite, leaning forward.

'So do I,' agreed the hairdresser, not to be left out.

'Piss off, yer two old queens,' Flash said goodnaturedly. He sat down beside Olympia, who finally realized it was him.

'Yer lookin' alright,' Flash said, peering at her face. 'Bit of added flesh, but yer really got it together, dint you?'

'I feel sensational.'

He slipped his hand beneath folds of sable and squeezed her waist. 'I always liked fat chicks. Turns me on, y'know what I mean?'

'I am not fat. Merely a few pounds overweight.'

'And some.'

'Where do you get your scarves? I *looooove* your scarves,' crooned the transvestite, stroking the stream of dirty white silk hanging around Flash's neck.

Flash grimaced. ''Ere, leave it out, will ya. What kinda bums yer travellin' with, Tubs?'

She had him fully in focus now. Flash. Rock Star. Lover. Prick.

'You treated me like nothing when I really needed you,' she steamed, staring at his pock-marked face. 'And from what I hear, things are not too good for you lately. What a *shame*,' she added sarcastically.

'I told yer,' he said slyly. 'I just wasn't inter fuckin' disfigurements. But yer lookin' good now, Tubs. Just like new.'

'What do you want?' she asked grandly.

'Whatever he wants – give it to him!' shrieked the hairdresser.

'Ooooh yes,' sighed the transvestite. 'Sooo macho!'

'Just bein' friendly,' Flash said.

'You've never been friendly in your life,' Olympia pointed out.

He stuck his tongue in her ear. 'Wanna fly?' he whispered.

His breath was tinged with garlic and tobacco. His clothes smelled of old smoke. His teeth, when he opened his mouth, were as rotten as ever.

She remembered old times. Sex, drugs, and rock 'n' roll.

Why not one more fling with a faded rock star?

Chapter 119

All her life Brigette had been waiting for something wonderful to happen. She had grown up in a world of thoughtless adults who gave her a superabundance of material possessions, but nothing much else. When she was little she could get everyone's attention by screaming, and she would carefully pick her moments. It infuriated her mother who was so pretty . . . always dressed up in furs and jewels with her blonde hair curling softly around her face. But her mother was always busy with her latest boyfriend. Forever distracted by other people.

Brigette had *loved* spoiling her mother's perfect day. It always made Olympia so mad when she screamed and yelled, but at least it forced her to notice she had a daughter.

For the last few years Brigette hadn't cared whether she noticed or not. And when her mother was in the plane crash, she had been secretly pleased. If Olympia had died, she wouldn't have to force her to notice any more.

However, Olympia didn't die. She just got fat. And Brigette grew up. And learned there was more to life than grabbing mama's attention.

Now Tim Wealth had entered her life. And Brigette knew the wonderful moment she had been waiting for had finally arrived. Forget school and lessons and everything else. Tim Wealth was her future. Tim Wealth wanted to be with her forever. He explained his plan while she listened responsively, and Roberto stuck his hand in the empty ice cream carton and edged closer and closer to the television until he was only inches away.

Tim kept on emphasizing the fact that she was only fourteen. 'If you were eighteen we'd have no problem,' he explained patiently. 'We could skip off to Nevada or somewhere, get married, and there's nothing anyone could do about it. But because you're under age, we've got to go into hiding. And to do that we need plenty of money. And to do it *successfully*, I'm talking *a lot* of bread. Multi bucks.'

'I'm *very* rich,' Brigette announced matter-of-factly. 'My grandfather just left me a fortune.'

'Sure. But it's all tied up until you're eighteen or twenty-one. Something like that, huh?'

'Yes, but it's still mine.'

'*I* know that and *you* know that, but try telling them.' He paused, and reeled her in nice and easy. 'I want to be with you all the time, little girl. You're very very special, and I don't want to risk losing you. Understand?'

She nodded, enthralled. Every dream she had ever had was coming true.

Tim roamed the room, balling his fists, talking fast, getting her involved and enthusiastic. 'Whether your mother cares about you or not she'd try to split us up,' he said. 'And so would Lennie Golden. *And* Lucky. They'd all say you're too young. We'd have no chance. They'd lock you up somewhere and we'd never see each other again.'

'I'd escape,' Brigette said fiercely.

'Yeah, well, I don't want to put you in that position,' he said quickly. 'We've got to strike before they do.'

She was completely caught up in what he was saying. 'Yes, yes,' she agreed, blue eyes shining brightly.

'This is what we have to do,' he said, keeping his voice low and moving very close to her. 'We have to get *your* money from them. It's *your* money, and you're entitled to every red cent.'

She nodded excitedly.

'But they're not going to want to give it to you,' Tim continued. 'So we've got to trick 'em.'

'How do we do that?'

'By playing a game.'

'What game?'

'Let's call it kidnap and ransom.'

She shivered. 'Is it dangerous?'

He laughed. 'Would I involve you in anything dangerous? You've got to trust me.'

'What about *him*?'

They both turned to stare at Roberto.

'He's a bonus,' Tim said. 'Kind of like insurance to make sure they pay up quickly. Like tomorrow.'

Brigette felt a twinge of conscience – only a twinge.

'After they've paid, they'll get both of you back,' Tim continued.

'*I'm* not going back!' Brigette wailed.

'Only for a couple of days while I get our escape organized,' he said hurriedly. 'Then you meet me at a pre-arranged spot, and we skip. In the meantime you describe your kidnappers as a couple of Mexicans who kept you in Santa Monica – make up whatever you like.'

'Hmmm . . . and how do I explain taking Bobby off in a cab?'

'You got an urgent phone call. A message from your mother to meet you and bring the boy.'

She giggled. 'You've thought of everything.'

'I sure have.' God! She was naive. Couldn't she see the scam he was pulling? By the time she realized he wasn't going to meet her he'd be long gone with Eden, and she'd be sent back to Switzerland in disgrace.

If they ever did track him he had two polaroid pictures of sweet little Brigette at play. She thought she'd kept all the prints, but it had been easy to slip a couple to one side. Those photos alone should be worth a million bucks to her family to suppress. Yeah. A million dollars meant nothing to those kind of people. Once he had the money it was a clear run ahead.

'How much are we going to ask for?' Brigette ventured.

'A million dollars,' Tim replied seriously. 'A million buckeroos.'

Chapter 120

By nine o'clock at night CeeCee was frantic, yet nobody else seemed to give a damn. She had been running back and forth between the rented house and the Bel Air mansion hoping for news. The rented house was empty. No Gino or Costa.

'Don't be such a worry wart,' Alice said, totally unconcerned. 'Brigette's with Roberto, so he's quite safe. They're either out, with Gino, or maybe at her girlfriend's house.'

'Who *is* her girlfriend, Mrs Golden?' CeeCee asked desperately. She was probably worrying unnecessarily – they were more than likely with Mr Santangelo as Alice said.

Alice shrugged. 'I don't know . . . a school friend. Brigette stayed with her last night.'

If they *were* with Gino, CeeCee thought, then why hasn't he left a message? 'Do you have a phone number?' she asked, still concerned.

Alice shook her head.

'How about Brigette's friend? What's her name?'

'*Je ne sais pas.*'

CeeCee was at boiling point. 'Mrs Golden!' she exploded. 'You're a disgrace. You're supposed to be in charge of Brigette and you don't even know where she spent the night.'

'Don't *speak* to me in that tone of voice,' Alice said haughtily. 'I was once a star, y'know. Everyone thinks my son is the big shot in the family, but *I* was famous before he was born. So stick that in your thinking cap and don't be so rude, young woman.'

CeeCee glared. Roberto's safety was at stake, not to mention her job, and this old crone was giving a speech about stardom. 'I just want Roberto home,' she said through clenched teeth. 'How can we find out who Brigette's friend is?'

'I don't know,' snapped Alice. 'And I wish you'd stop fussing so. They'll be back in a minute, just you wait and see.'

*

'I don't believe it!' Rainbow exclaimed. 'The man himself.'

Lennie swept her into a hug.

'Foxie!' she called. 'Come an' see what I got for you!'

Foxie came scurrying out from his office, took one look at Jess and grabbed her.

'Not her!' Rainbow laughed. She kissed Lennie jammily on the mouth. '*This* hunk.'

'A hunk, a skunk, who cares?' said Foxie, rolling his cross eyes. 'When my sweet Jess is around, nobody else counts.'

'Charming!' smiled Rainbow. 'He loves another woman!'

'And I love him, too,' Jess said firmly, cuddling the little man.

Lennie smiled and relaxed. He had neglected his friends since hitting it big. Well, Olympia would hardly have fitted in – he could just imagine her with the lecherous Foxie. Or making conversation with raunchy Rainbow.

Lucky would fit in. Lucky would fit in anywhere.

Give it a couple of months and he would call her.

Yeah.

Maybe they could start over.

Maybe.

*

Costa became a proud father at 9.40 p.m. He was ecstatic. He had a seven pound, two ounce baby daughter.

He marched along the hospital corridor handing out cigars to strangers. Then he rushed to the telephone to inform Gino of the marvellous news.

CeeCee answered the phone. 'Oh, Mr Zennocotti, where are you?' she wailed. 'Is Roberto with you?'

'Why would he be with me?' said Costa, puzzled. 'Put Gino on the line, quickly.'

'He's not here. Roberto's not here.' And she launched into a jumbled explanation.

Costa said exactly what Alice had said. 'They must be with Gino. Don't worry. I'm sure they'll be home any time now. And when they get there, have Gino call me. Pronto. I have magnificent news.'

*

At ten o'clock exactly the telephone rang in the Bel Air mansion.

'Hello,' Alice said gaily. She was quite merry on several glasses of Grand Marnier, and Claudio was feeling no pain after imbibing a half bottle of Delamain brandy.

'A million bucks,' said a muffled voice.

'What?'

'Roberto. Brigette. A million bucks for the two of them.'

'I can't *hear* you. Speak up.'

'Don't call the police, just think about getting the money together. Cash. Fifty dollar bills. Unmarked.'

'I don't understand. Who *is* this?'

'Farmer's Market. Four o'clock tomorrow afternoon. Go into the bookstore with a bag containing the money. Go over to the diet book section in the back – put the bag in the corner and leave the store by the other entrance. Don't look back. Got it?'

'Oh dear!' Alice fluttered.

'If you want to see either of them alive again you'd better follow my instructions. A million bucks. No cops. No fuck-ups. No second chances. If you do exactly as I say, the kids will be returned to the house within an hour.'

The line clicked dead.

Chapter 121

Kennedy airport was crowded with people determined to make an early start on the weekend rush.

Lucky strode straight through to the Pan Am lounge. She just had time for a cup of coffee before her flight was called.

Steven arrived at the airport fifteen minutes later. His expression was grim as he bought a ticket for the next Pan Am flight to LA. He was unshaven and unkempt, having spent an all night vigil by Mary-Lou's bedside.

Sometimes in life there are things you have to do. And sometimes staying on the right side of the law means these things never get accomplished.

Steven, for once in his life, planned to take the law into his own hands.

Steven, personally, planned to beat the shit out of Santino Bonnatti.

Chapter 122

'I'm uncomfortable,' Brigette whined. She had been whining on and off all night long. A list of complaints spewed forth from her rosebud lips.

'For crissake,' Tim said. 'Go back to sleep.'

She sat up. 'Gotta go to the bathroom,' she mumbled.

'Well, go,' he said bad-temperedly.

She climbed off the couch bed, stepped over Roberto – who was sleeping on a makeshift pile of cushions, and shut herself in the tiny bathroom. It was no fun sleeping next to Tim squashed up together like sardines in a can. It might have been fun if the stupid kid wasn't with them. She couldn't stand dumb little Bobby. Why did they have to keep him?

She imagined CeeCee freaking out. Oh, the panic she must be in!

Tim was up when she emerged from the bathroom, and so was Roberto. 'I'm hungry,' the boy said, rubbing his eyes.

Lucky would freak too. Brigette felt a bit bad about that – but it wasn't like they weren't looking after Bobby. 'I'll make breakfast,' she said cheerfully.

'There's nothing to make,' Tim replied. Now that the wheels were in motion he wanted it to be over and done with. Timing was everything.

Collect the money.

Dump Brigette and the kid.

Grab Eden.

And run.

There was an afternoon flight to Mexico City and he had booked two seats. From there, they would hire a car and drive into oblivion.

'Wanta go home,' Roberto said. 'Want CeeCee. Want mama.'

Brigette opened the fridge. There was nothing in it.

'Don't you ever eat?' she asked Tim. 'I'm starving.'

He had sent out for pizza the night before, there was some left in the box. 'Feast on that,' he said.

'Ugh!' she exclaimed. 'I'll go out to the market.'

'No you won't,' he said quickly. 'I'll do it – write down what you want.'

The last thing he needed was Brigette wandering around the neighbourhood getting seen and remembered. He thought about what must be going on at the Bel Air mansion. They were probably amassing the money and keeping quiet. Rich people didn't like publicity. His hunch was they would pay and shut up – as long as they got their kids back.

He had quizzed Brigette relentlessly about whether she had ever mentioned him to any of them.

'No way,' she had assured him. 'Like they'd freak out if they thought I was seeing someone.'

He dressed in a hurry while Brigette scribbled out a list of her requirements. Could he trust her? She seemed happy enough, but just in case, he warned her not to pick up the phone if it rang, and double lock the front door behind him when he left.

Once on the street he phoned Eden. 'Can you talk?' he questioned.

'No.' Her voice was tremulous. 'I think you have the wrong number.'

He kept his voice low and spoke fast. 'Meet me outside the front of the May Company on Wilshire just after four today. Everything's in motion. We're on our way.'

*

'Who was that?' Santino asked.

'Wrong number,' Eden replied.

'Did they talk dirty?'

'No.'

'Then why'dja hang on an' listen?'

'They repeated the number, just to see if they dialled correctly.'

'You think I'm a cunt or what?'

She was sick of his abuse – physical and mental. There was no let up. He had stayed the night to torment her. Now she had to plan her escape. It would not be easy to get out. 'I think you should leave me alone,' she said wearily.

'Yeah. I think so too. You're not gettin' any younger. *You* are an old broad – you know that? Kinda sad – but I got a heart of gold hangin' around, fuckin' ya, lettin' ya live here. Doncha think?'

'I appreciate everything you've done for me, Santino.' He had trained her to behave like a lap dog, roll over and play dead.

'I even starred ya in a movie,' he continued. 'Just what ya wanted. Right, honey?'

She nodded. 'It was very kind of you.'

The moment he left the house she was going. Zeko would be easy to lose in Beverly Hills while she supposedly shopped. There was one store she knew where the fitting rooms led on to a back alleyway. If she took a pile of clothes and left Zeko waiting in front, it would be hours before he even realized she'd gone.

'Sure, sure, sure,' Santino said expansively. He sat up in bed and stroked his hairy chest with loving care. 'I starred ya in a movie – pretty generous of me considerin' you're over the hill.'

'Thank you,' she murmured.

'Ya paid me back tho'.'

She had no idea where he was heading. Silence was safest.

'Yeah,' Santino said reflectively. 'Ya certainly paid me back. An' how.'

Her face felt terrible. She could hardly see out of her left eye and her lip was swollen and sore. What a mess she must look.

'I got a head for revenge,' he said vindictively. 'Cross Santino Bonnatti an' you'd better not walk down any one way streets on a dark night. Not even ten years later. Ya gettin' my drift?'

'I've never crossed you.'

'Whaddya call fuckin' your co-star?'

'I didn't.'

A smash across the face.

She felt her teeth rattle. 'I *didn't*, you bastard!'

'Maybe ya did an' maybe ya didn't,' he said mildly. 'I figured it might be a gag t' find out.'

He had opened the cut on her lip. Blood dripped slowly onto satin sheets.

Chapter 123

Where was Gino? A message from him turned up on the answering machine saying he would be out all night, but leaving no clue to his whereabouts.

Alice, when she received what she considered to be a garbled phone call about kidnapping and ransom, sat in shocked silence for a few moments, and then had hysterics.

Claudio sent for CeeCee. She immediately located Costa at the hospital, then collapsed in a chair shaking and muttering to herself. Shortly after, Costa arrived at the house and tried to take charge. 'No police,' he kept on saying. 'No outside help until we hear from Gino.'

'What about Lucky?' wailed CeeCee. 'She'll go crazy. She'll blame me, and it *is* my fault.'

'It's nobody's fault,' Costa said wearily. This was turning out to be the worst night of his life as well as the best. He attempted to reach Lucky at the Hotel Santangelo, and spoke to Matt, who told him she was flying into LA on the early morning flight. 'You can reach her at The Pierre if it's important,' Matt added.

Costa didn't know what to do. If she was coming in anyway why worry her? He decided to meet her at the airport. In the meantime he tried to reach Olympia and Lennie.

A maid informed him that Miss Stanislopoulos was out, and that Mr Golden no longer lived there.

'Where is he?' Costa asked.

The maid, who had been awakened from her sleep, was uncooperative and professed not to know.

Costa spent a restless night. He ordered a still hysterical Alice upstairs, with Claudio to comfort her. And he sent CeeCee back to the rented house to wait for Gino. Meanwhile, he sat up in Lennie's study all night, counting the minutes, and trying to figure out who could possibly have snatched the kids. They wanted – whoever they were – a million dollars in cash. An impossible task to get together by four o'clock in the afternoon. Although if anyone was able to do it, Gino and Lucky could.

Costa just wished he could contact one or the other of them. He had made a bad decision by not trying to reach Lucky before she left New York, but when he did finally decide to call her she was already on her way to the airport.

He checked with the hospital. His wife and baby were doing fine.

He didn't feel so fine himself. He felt like an old man.

•

'Gotta tell you – you make me feel sixteen again!' Gino beamed, in the morning. 'Well . . . maybe twenty.'

Paige stretched luxuriously. 'God, Gino. You *really* must have been something when you were young.'

'Horny, hot-headed – they used t'call me Gino the Ram.'

Paige laughed aloud. 'The Ram! I love it. Tell me more at once!'

'Well, I kinda lived between foster homes, an' there was this one woman – she had the biggest bazookas I'd ever seen – an' she expected me t'call her mom.'

Paige sat up in bed. She looked good in the morning, not

washed out like a lot of women her age. 'What *did* you call her?' she asked eagerly.

'Anything except mom. I was thirteen – an' she kinda showed me the way t'go.'

She nodded knowingly. 'Ah . . . so you received your sexual education from an older woman.'

'Yeh. An' I learned how t'fuck, too.'

'Gino!'

'Don't tell me I finally shocked you?'

'Never.'

'What are you? Unshockable?'

'Yup.'

'Tough broad.'

'Tougher than you.'

'Yeh?'

'Yes.'

He reached for her, but she evaded his move. 'It shocked you when you discovered me in bed with Susan, didn't it?' she asked quietly.

Silence hung heavy. He had been prepared to forget that little incident – now she was dragging it up.

'As a matter of fact,' she continued, determined to get it out in the open, 'Susan and I were having an affair long before she met you. We were –'

'I don't want to know about it,' he interrupted roughly.

'I think you should. When you and I got together I realized that I wanted you a great deal more than I did her. Susan was reluctant to let go – the day you found us together was my goodbye.'

'Some goodbye,' he snorted.

'Haven't *you* ever taken a lover to bed to let them down easily when it's over?'

'I'd sooner see you in the sack with a young stud than with my wife,' he said tightly.

'Next time I'll try and oblige.'

'Hey –' He pulled her down close to him. 'Has anyone ever told you that you got a big smart mouth?'

'Not lately.'

He rolled on top of her, groaned and rolled off.

'What's the matter?' she asked, concerned.

'Why should I do all the work? I'm an over-the-hill stud – you're the sex maniac. Go to it, Mrs Wheeler.'

She sighed. 'My oh my,' she said, shaking her head. 'Whoever your teacher was, she certainly did a thorough job!'

*

Lennie slept, cocooned in good feelings. He was working again – the creative juices flowing. He was back among his friends – an evening with Jess and Foxie and Rainbow was pure enjoyment. And he was free.

He got up in the morning and went straight back to work with a stack of yellow legal pads, a ballpoint pent, and just his mind for company.

Later he would call Alice and give her the news of the impending divorce. She would probably have a nervous breakdown when she realized he would no longer be married to one of the richest women in the world. She had liked having a Stanislopoulos for a daughter-in-law.

Oh well . . .

Too bad.

Poor old Alice.

Chapter 124

Tim whistled as he headed back to his apartment carrying a paper sack containing milk, orange juice, bread, jam, and ice cream to keep the kid quiet. The hustle was going to work like a dream. He had been thinking that perhaps after Mexico he and Eden might head down to Brazil.

Ah . . . Rio. Ipanema Beach. Copacabana. With a million bucks to keep them company they could do anything they wanted. Maybe he'd give up his acting career that wasn't going anywhere in a hurry and become a songwriter or a beach bum. He would soon be able to afford to do whatever he wanted. Anything at all.

He balanced the paper sack and groped for his keys as he walked up the outside stairs to his apartment, calling out, 'It's me,' as he turned the key in the lock.

And then he didn't know what hit him. Someone came up behind him and hurled him to the ground, shoving him inside the apartment with brutal force.

The paper sack of groceries went flying – milk spilt, ice cream splattered the walls, orange juice dribbled on to the floor.

'What the fu –' he began to say. But a sharp kick in the guts shut him up.

Both Brigette and Roberto started to scream in alarm.

'What we got *here*?' said Santino Bonnatti, stepping over Tim, nodding to the two hoods who had gained entry for him, and staring at Brigette and Roberto. 'Family fuckin' circle?'

'Who are you? What do you want?' Brigette gasped. And then she sprang at one of the hoods who was casually and methodically kicking Tim as he tried to curl up in a ball to protect himself.

'Leave him alone!' she yelled.

'Leave him alone,' copied Roberto, running to her side and clinging to her leg.

Santino's lip curled in disgust. Where did Tim Wealth inherit kids for crissake?

Chapter 125

A very friendly Chinese man received no conversation at all from Steven on the five hour flight to LA. Up in first class Lucky gave the same treatment to an elderly businessman with bad breath.

Neither of them ate. Neither of them watched the movie. Upon landing at LAX they hurried from the plane and managed to disembark at the same time, coming face to face at the point where first class meets tourist.

'Lucky Santangelo,' Steven said.

She hesitated for only a moment, and then remembered. 'Mister DA,' she said with a wry grin.

He grimaced. 'No more.'

'You gave it up? I felt for sure you'd end up Mayor of New York City.'

They walked together down the corridor linking the plane to the airport. He felt so strange seeing her again now that he knew there was a wild possibility they shared the same father.

'Last time we met I was just about to be arrested.' She turned to look at him. 'Remember?'

'Oh, I could never forget that,' he said. 'You shot the guy I'd been working two years to indict.'

'Self-defence.'

'Sure.'

'Really.'

She recalled their meeting six years ago. The long sticky New York blackout of 1977. And she had been trapped in an elevator with Mister Steven Berkeley for a whole night – nine long hours. They had become friends – of sorts. They had almost become lovers.

A day later she had discovered he was the DA working on a case against Enzio Bonnatti. She hadn't seen him since.

'Do you live here?' he inquired politely.

She shook her head. 'Do you?'

'Just visiting.'

'What do you do now you're not a DA anymore?' she asked curiously.

'I sold out. I'm a lawyer.'

They stepped aboard the moving runway. She remembered going to his apartment that hot and humid morning because she had lost the keys to hers. He let her take a bath and borrow some of his clothes. God, he was so straight! But he had been tempted until his girlfriend invaded the mood that was starting to take place.

'Did you ever marry that girl – Eileen, wasn't that her name?'

'Aileen. No I never married her.'

Lucky grinned. 'Good. She ruined the start of what could have been a beautiful relationship.'

He forgot his anger for a moment and took her by the arm. 'Many years ago your father, Gino, knew my mother.'

She stared at him. He was startlingly handsome with his tight black curls, chocolate cream skin, and deep green eyes. 'Really?'

'He owned a nightclub, "Clemmie's", in the thirties, I think.'

'That's right.'

'Well –'

'Lucky!' Costa was at the end of the runway waving frantically.

She waved back, wondering how he knew of her arrival.

'My uncle,' she explained to Steven. 'It was . . . nice seeing you again. Take care.'

Was it his imagination or did he see a flash of himself in her goodbye smile?

He watched her out of sight and knew, once and for all, he had to find out who his father was.

*

There were drugs everywhere in Flash's hotel room, and Olympia was floating in heaven. She and Flash had soared through the night on a trail of good times, and she never wanted to leave his side again. He was no longer a reformed heroin addict – he had been back on the stuff for a while – and seeing Olympia in Studio 54 had sent dollar signs doing neon dances in front of his eyes.

The truth was that Flash was broke, busted, and a bum. His former group refused to have anything to do with him; and his teenage wife had thrown him out.

Olympia appeared at the right moment.

Olympia was cool to get high with.

Olympia could buy him anything he damn well wanted.

They started off on coke, switched to freebasing, and ended up doing speedballs – a mixture of cocaine and heroin.

It was a long night – only interrupted by a series of drug dealers who came and went with their variety of wares whenever Flash summoned them.

Levine, a former groupie, turned addict and pusher, had serviced the happy couple at six in the morning.

'Come back in a few hours,' Flash instructed her. 'Bring me everything you got – grade A.'

Levine promised she would.

Flash promised that if she delivered what he wanted he might strum her a few notes on his guitar.

Levine said, 'Yeah!'

Olympia just smiled.

Levine returned at ten-fifteen in the morning with a whole bunch of goodies. She had stopped off at her apartment and collected a small Sony tape recorder. If Flash was going to play, she was going to get it down. Yeah!

The hotel was a dump, but it was a comfortable dump, and Flash liked the bohemian atmosphere of the place.

Levine knocked, and then opened the door with the room key Flash had given her.

She took one horrified look, turned around and ran.

Chapter 126

Santino Bonnatti strutted around Tim Wealth's one-room apartment. 'Ya got a dump here,' he remarked, picking up a framed picture of Tim and smashing it viciously to the floor.

'Wanta go home,' screamed Roberto, clinging tightly to Brigette.

Tim attempted to get up, but Santino's hood kept a heavy foot on his stomach.

'WANTA GO HOME!' yelled Roberto.

'Shut the fuck up,' Santino glared.

Brigette shivered. She wanted to go home too. She had no idea what was going on, but whatever it was she was scared.

She spoke up in a shaky voice. 'I'm taking Bobby home, Tim.' Nervously she edged toward the door.

Tim saw a million dollars taking off. He also saw a lot of trouble in store for him if he didn't do something about it.

One of Santino's hoods blocked the door.

'Let 'em out,' Santino said. 'An' don't go runnin' for help or your little brother'll be missin' an arm.'

'We won't,' said Brigette gratefully. She gripped Roberto's hand tightly. 'Come on, Bobby.'

The hood stood to one side.

Santino walked over to Tim. 'Pretty boy shithead actor,' he snarled. 'Ya really think ya gonna fuck my woman an' get away with it?'

Brigette hustled Roberto from the apartment.

'Ya really think that?' Santino continued incredulously. ''Cos if ya do, you're a bigger prick than I thought ya was.' He kicked Tim in the neck with the tip of his shiny pointed Italian shoe.

Tim began to gag.

'I'm gonna break your fuckin' arms an' your legs. An' I'm gonna smash that pretty boy face outta action for a while.'

'I can pay you not to,' Tim gasped, grabbing for survival. Better to share than to have nothing at all. 'I can split a million bucks with you if you get those kids back.'

Santino poked at Tim's throat with his shoe. 'What kinda shit ya talkin'?'

'Those kids are special,' Tim choked. 'She's a Stanislopoulos, and so is the boy. He inherits the whole goddamn fortune. His mother is Lucky Santangelo and Dimitri Stanislopoulos was his father. I've got a million dollar scam going.'

'Are you shittin' me?' Santino's beady eyes were ablaze.

'I wouldn't do that,' Tim said desperately.

'Naw, ya wouldn't do that,' Santino mused. He nodded to one of his henchmen. 'Get 'em back, Blackie. Now.'

The man raced from the apartment.

Tim rubbed his throat where a purplish lump was forming. 'Can I get up?'

Santino wasn't listening. He was remembering.

No retribution, huh? That's what *they* thought. That's what they all thought. Even that chickenshit Carlo. But now . . . with the kid in his possession . . . *her* kid . . .

Jesus Christ! It was manna from heaven.

Chapter 127

On the drive to the Bel Air house Costa told Lucky the whole story. As she listened she went white and silent. Her black eyes shone with fury.

'Where's Gino?' she demanded, when he had finished.

'I don't know, he left a message on the machine saying he wouldn't be back all night, and he hasn't called this morning.'

'Does he have a girlfriend here?'

'No one I know of.' He hesitated. 'We did bump into Paige Wheeler yesterday at lunch. You don't think –'

'Call her home and her office.'

'Good idea.'

Lucky's tone was fast and businesslike, although inside she was burning with horror and frustration. The one thing she had always dreaded was happening, and she was out of control. 'Has anyone checked the cab companies? Found out what driver picked Brigette up, and where he took her and Roberto?'

Costa shook his head. 'No,' he replied sheepishly. Why hadn't *he* thought of that?

She didn't want to look at him. He was just a tired old man who didn't know what to do. But how could she blame him?

She glanced at her watch. It was near to noon. 'God, Costa!' she couldn't help exploding. 'Why didn't you phone me the minute this happened? And how come Matt wasn't alerted? You know we can trust him. We should have started getting the money the moment Alice received the call.'

He bowed his head. 'I know. It was an error in judgment. You were on your way here anyway . . . so I thought . . .' he trailed off miserably.

Don't scream at Costa, she warned herself. *Stay calm. Work things out. Roberto's going to be fine. He's with Brigette. She'll look after him.*

How come Brigette left the house with Roberto in the first place? And why hadn't Costa checked the cab companies immediately?

Oh God! Where was Gino? He would have taken care of things by now.

Thinking aloud she said, 'I'll contact Boogie. I can arrange to raise the cash in Vegas, and I'll charter a plane for him to fly in with the money. Once we get to the house I'm going to have to call in some favours.'

Alice, with an attentive Claudio and a red-eyed CeeCee, waited at the Bel Air mansion.

'Who's he?' Lucky demanded at once, staring straight at Claudio.

'My gentleman friend,' Alice replied tremulously. 'I don't know what I would have done without him.'

Lucky immediately decided he needed investigating. It was impossible to decide who was involved in this. Alice could have engineered the whole thing with the help of her tiny friend and some outside accomplices.

'Has anyone contacted Olympia?' she asked.

'Olympia's not home,' Costa said quickly. 'I've left messages.'

'How about Lennie. Isn't he there?'

'Apparently not. According to the maid, he's moved out. They don't have a number for him.'

Lucky paced restlessly around the room. 'I need to be alone,' she said.

They left, and she sat by the phone thinking. After a few moments she made a private call to an old business associate of Gino's. 'This is Lucky Santangelo,' she said guardedly. 'I'm calling in a favour you owe my father. I need a car with an experienced driver. And two armed men. I also want a surveillance van, and a two-way tracking system. I want the best, and I want them within an hour.'

Immediately after that she put everything in motion as far as raising the cash was concerned. Thank God for Vegas, Gino's friends and Boogie. She could have gone to a bank, but most of her assets were not liquid, and although she was able to come up with the money, it would have taken time and hassles. The major problem now was whether the money would arrive in time. Boogie had to collect it, get on a plane, and arrive at Farmer's Market before the four o'clock deadline.

She was only thinking as far as four. After that her mind went blank.

What if Roberto and Brigette were not returned?

What if they were *never* returned?

She shuddered and refused to think the unthinkable.

*

'Why don't we drive to San Francisco for the weekend?' Gino suggested. 'You're supposed to be there anyway, so let's go for it.'

'Oh, you drive too,' teased Paige.

'I do things you ain't never even heard of, kiddo.'

She smiled. 'There's not much *I* haven't heard of.'

He was full of enthusiasm. 'I kinda fancy a drive. We can take the coast highway – stop off at an inn for the night – hit San Francisco Sunday mornin', an fly back Monday. What d'you say?'

She sipped her coffee. 'You sound like a travel agent.'

'C'mon, Paige, take chances.'

She laughed. 'What the hell do you *think* I'm doing?' She paused for a moment, then gazed at him meaningfully. 'I'm a married woman, Gino.'

He met her gaze head on. 'So what?'

'So I shouldn't even have spent the night, let alone take off for a dirty weekend.'

He considered her remark before answering. 'So, that's

what I am to you, huh? One dirty weekend comin' up.'

'Just keep on coming!'

'You got a mouth for a broad.'

'And don't you *looove* it!'

'We goin' or what?'

'I think you talked me into it.'

*

Lucky paced Lennie's study. It was so strange to be in his house, his room, among his things. She picked up a leather-bound script and gazed at it blankly.

She thought of her son. Roberto. He was so strong and full of curiosity and energy. So alive.

If whoever had him so much as *touched* him . . .

She would kill.

She had done it before.

CeeCee timidly entered the room and announced the arrival of the cab driver Lucky had tracked down with two phone calls.

'Show him in,' Lucky said flatly.

A bull-necked man with a dark complexion and bulbous nose entered the room. He wore ludicrous shorts and a Hawaiian shirt.

Lucky waved a hundred dollar bill at him. 'I want to know everything you can remember about the girl and the little boy you picked up here yesterday afternoon.'

The man's eyes stuck to the money like glue. 'Picked 'em up at four-thirty,' he said, licking fleshy lips. 'Took 'em to the corner of Fairfax and Sunset – right outside the Thrifty drugstore. I kinda thought it wasn't exactly the right neighbourhood for 'em to be in. Nice lookin' chick.'

'What happened after they got out of your cab?'

'Well she was kinda starin' around as though she was meetin' someone.'

'And did anyone approach them?'

'In the T-shirt *she* was wearin', every guy on the street was stoppin'.'

'What colour was it?'

'Red an' tight, an' she had some kind of writin' on it.'

'What did it say?'

He made a face. 'I got a memory – not *that* good.'

'Was the little boy okay. Or did he seem upset?'

'He was happy. Kept on talkin' about gettin' an ice cream.'

'Anything else?'

'I think they went off with some guy, but I'm not sure. The light was green an' I was turnin' the corner.'

'What did he look like?'

He shrugged. 'I don' know. Young, thin. I only got a glimpse.'

She handed him the money.

He stretched it out and held it up to the light.

'It's real,' she said.

'I know that. I'm just checkin'. Habit, y'know.'

'Would you recognize the man they went off with if you saw him again?'

'Naw.'

'Thank you.'

'Thank *you*. Easiest money I ever made.'

Not much information there. But it showed that wherever they'd gone was of their own free will. Nobody had snatched them off the street.

Lucky thought about Brigette and the cab driver's telling words. Everyone treated Brigette like a child – including her. But she looked like a woman, and a sexy one at that. Maybe some guy had gotten hold of her . . . some guy with big ideas and a dirty mind . . .

Abruptly Lucky hurried from the study. CeeCee hovered outside. 'Where's Brigette's room?'

CeeCee escorted her upstairs, and they entered Brigette's domain. It was a teenage mess.

Lucky stood for a few moments just looking and remembering when she was very young where she used to hide things.

Under the mattress. Nothing. Behind a picture frame. Nothing. Beneath a stack of magazines. Bingo! A small square book with MY DIARY printed on the front.

She opened it, and a scattering of polaroid pictures fell out. Quickly she scanned them, and knew her hunch was right. Some guy had gotten hold of Brigette . . . And how.

Chapter 128

The big man swooped down and picked Roberto up before Brigette could do anything. 'Mr Bonnatti wants to see ya,' he growled.

Roberto tried vainly to wriggle free. Nobody on Hollywood Boulevard took any notice of the blonde teenager and the hulk of a man carrying a small yelling boy. Brigette figured she could make a run for it – but how could she possibly leave Bobby?

'Who's Mr Bonnatti?' she asked, trying to sound brave.

'Don't worry about that,' said the man. 'Just tell the kid to shut up, an' let's go.'

Dragging her feet she followed him back to Tim's apartment.

By the time they got there Tim was sitting on the couch. He looked white, but at least he wasn't lying on the floor with someone's foot at his throat.

'Uh . . . Brigette,' he said in a strained voice indicating Santino. 'This man's a friend of mine. We . . . er . . . we were involved in some hassle about money I owed. Everything's okay now.'

The hood put Roberto down, and the little boy promptly kicked him on the shin.

Santino beamed. 'I'm sorry if we upset ya. Just clearin' up a few matters.'

Brigette stared at Tim. Something wasn't right and she knew it. 'I want to take Bobby home,' she said shakily.

He wouldn't look her in the eye. 'You can't,' he said. 'Not yet. You know we have it all planned.'

'I'm gonna be a partner in ya little sting operation,' Santino joined in smoothly.

She hated him. He smelled of sickly sweet aftershave and made her skin crawl.

'I don't think I want to do it any more,' she said uneasily.

Santino leered. 'No choice, chicken.'

'Wanta go home. Wanta go home,' Roberto chanted, jumping up and down.

Santino walked over to Brigette and took her chin in the palm of his hand. 'Sweet stuff. Young stuff,' he crooned. 'Howdja like to make me happy?'

Panic flooded her body. 'Don't touch me,' she warned, backing away.

'Whacha gonna do about it?' he asked, and with one fast move he pinned her arms and brought his fleshy lips down on hers, thrusting into her mouth with his thick tongue.

She gagged and began to scream as she struggled free.

Santino whacked her across the side of the face with all his strength. 'Just shut up, ya stupid little cunt!' he shouted.

She fell to the floor and started to sob. Roberto ran over and bent to comfort her.

Tim took a deep breath. Life wasn't easy. He didn't want this to happen, but there was nothing *he* could do to stop it.

*

Zeko was on her case with a vengeance.

'I'm going shopping,' Eden announced aloofly.

'Mister Bonnatti said y'ain't t'leave the house.'

'Mr Bonnatti can go fuck himself.'

Zeko shrugged. 'He gives the orders. I just listens to 'em.'

Eden tried another tactic. Maybe she could get the big goon to feel sorry for her. 'Look at my face, Zeko,' she said mournfully. 'I'm all beaten up. I need special creams and lotions to put it right. Please take me out. I won't tell him.'

Zeko considered her request and nixed it. He knew better than to cross his boss when it came to a definite order.

'You jerkoff asslicker!' Eden screeched, realizing she was not winning him over. 'No wonder you're nothing but a dumb watchdog.'

She slammed into her bedroom and tried to think of a way

to escape. Santino had her locked up, a prisoner. Who knew *what* he was planning to do with her next? She had heard stories of mobster's girlfriends being shipped over the border when they were finished with. Sent away to do time in some foreign brothel. Santino had told her of one girl who ended up hanging herself in a Mexican whorehouse.

She shuddered. The house was rigged with alarms. She couldn't even walk out the front door without bells signalling her departure. And even if she did, Blue Jay Way was high in the Hollywood Hills, and Zeko kept the car keys on a string around his neck.

She picked up a lamp and hurled it across the room, sick with frustration.

Then an idea came to her. A brilliant idea.

There *was* somebody who could save her. One person.

Chapter 129

'Paige Wheeler is in San Francisco. Nobody seems to know where she's staying,' said Costa wearily. 'I, personally, have checked six of the best hotels. She's not registered. Neither is Gino.'

Lucky glanced up. She had just started reading Brigette's diary. 'Maybe she never went to San Francisco. Could be she and Gino are shacked up somewhere here. Have Alice and CeeCee start checking. Begin with the Beverly Hills Hotel, and then the Beverly Wilshire.'

Costa nodded. 'Have you found out anything?'

'I'll let you know.'

Brigette's writing was almost illegible, and her entries erratic. Lucky started with the most recent. It must have been written on the day before her disappearance.

DINNER WITH YOU KNOW WHO!!! TRADER VICS. GOT BOMBED. THEN WENT BACK TO HIS PLACE IN HOLLYWOOD. DID EVERYTHING!! EVERYTHING!!!!! GAVE HIM COKE FOR PRESENT. HE WAS PLEASED. TOOK RUDE PICTURES FOR FUN! WISH I HAD PIX OF HIM. NEXT

TIME I'LL ASK HIM. HE'S SO AMAZING! I CAN'T BELIEVE IT! DREAD LEAVING. STAYED ALL NIGHT. TOLD ALICE I WAS WITH A GIRLFRIEND. SHE'S SO EASY. I LOVE TIM. I THINK HE LOVES ME!!!!

So, his name was Tim. It was a start. Quickly Lucky flicked back over the pages. It was mostly all the same stuff. BORED! BORING! ALICE IS SO DUMB! And an occasional YOU KNOW WHO HASN'T CALLED YET.

And then she hit pay dirt. The opening night of the Santangelo.

FANTASTIC AWESOME EVENING!!! MET TIM WEALTH! THE ONLY TIM WEALTH! AND HE'S EVEN BETTER IN THE FLESH, AND I MEAN FLESH! FINALLY DID IT, WITH HIM!!!! CAN'T BELIEVE I DID IT. BUT HE'S SO FULLY COOL AND BRILLIANT. TOTALLY. I LOVE HIM OF COURSE. TOLD HIM I WAS 18!!!

Lucky dropped the diary and jumped up. Who the hell was Tim Wealth?

She picked up the phone and reached Matt in Atlantic City. 'Get hold of the guest list for opening night, and tell me who Tim Wealth is.'

One thing about Matt, he was completely organized. Within minutes he had the list in front of him. 'No Tim Wealth listed.'

'Damn! Do you know who he is?'

'No idea. Why? What's up?'

'Nothing I can go into now.'

'Maybe Jess knows, hang on, I'll get her.'

Lucky glanced at her watch. It was coming up to one-thirty. Soon she would have to leave for the airport to meet Boogie and the money.

Jess came on the line. 'Tim Wealth starred in one movie about four years ago. He's a good actor, I don't know why he hasn't done anything since. He just sort of faded into obscurity.'

'He was at our opening. Right?'

'I didn't see him.'

'Jess. Please tell Matt to find out his current address immediately, and to call me at once at Lennie's house. It's urgent.'

'I don't believe this! I was with Lennie in LA last night. He didn't tell me you two were –'

'Is Lennie in LA?' Lucky asked, surprised.

'Aren't you with him?'

'No. I'm at his house because – look – I can't go into it now. Where can I reach him?'

Jess was perplexed. She couldn't figure out *what* was going on. 'He's staying at his old apartment.' She gave Lucky the number.

Costa entered the room. 'Gino was registered at the Beverly Wilshire. He checked out an hour ago.'

'Shit!' exclaimed Lucky angrily.

'What?' questioned Jess.

'Nothing. Get me that address.'

She hung up. Costa looked worn out. 'Why don't you go to the hospital and visit Ria and the baby,' she suggested. 'There's nothing else you can do around here.'

'I'm coming to the airport with you,' he said.

'No you're not.'

'Yes I am.'

'Go visit your baby, Costa. It's just a question of timing now. I think I know who has the kids.'

'Calmly you tell me! Who? What?'

'I'll have an address in a minute.'

She closed her eyes. Her head was pounding. This was the nightmare of her life. She thought of Lennie, and wanted to call him. But what could he do except interfere? She had to do this her way. No outside help. Not even Lennie.

The phone rang. She grabbed it.

'I don't know how I do it, but I always do,' Matt said smugly, and he gave her an address for Tim Wealth.

Chapter 130

A stretch. A yawn. Lennie had worked enough for one day. His scribble filled thirty pages. Not bad. He was on a roll, the script was coming nicely.

Maybe he should call Alice, couldn't put off giving her the good news forever. Lazily he reached for the phone, and it rang as his hand hovered over it. It could only be Jess, reporting on her trip. She had taken a ride into New York on a Learjet owned by a dissolute record producer who swapped boyfriends the way some people swap Christmas presents.

'Hiya. Good flight? How many attendants did little Mary Sunshine have?' he asked cheerily.

'How'd you know it was me?'

'Because,' he explained patiently, 'you are the only person who knows where I am.'

'Not any more.'

He groaned. 'Who have you told?'

There was a smile in her voice. 'Lucky.'

He tried to sound disinterested. 'Oh yeah?'

'I thought you wouldn't mind.'

He didn't know whether he minded or not. He wanted to see her – desperately. On the other hand he wasn't so sure if it was too soon. They both needed time to adjust.

'Why'd you do that?'

'Actually,' Jess said, 'she's over at your house now.'

'Olympia's house,' he corrected.

'I don't care who the house belongs to, she's there.'

'Doing what?'

'Sounding fraught.'

'Can you be more explicit?'

'Call her.'

'You're a big help.'

'Do it.'

'Piss off.'

He hung up and made a decision. He wouldn't call, he would go there. He needed to see her more than anything else in the world.

*

Brigette knew something was terribly wrong. Roberto and she were caught in an evil trap, and it was all her fault. Fright racked her body as they huddled together in the back of a car with rough thugs on either side. Santino sat in the front, next to a stony-faced driver. He leaned over the seats and chatted pleasantly.

'I got plans for y'two kids,' he said. 'We're gonna do things together ya thought only the big boys an' girls could do.' He leered at Brigette. 'Ya think that crap actor was somethin', wait 'til *we* get it on, chicken.'

She shuddered, and held tightly on to Roberto. For the first time in her life she was truly afraid, and not just for herself. For Bobby, who was only a baby. And for Tim: What had they done with him? She'd been hustled from the apartment and made to wait in the car for fifteen minutes. When Santino appeared, Tim was not with him.

'Stop snivellin',' Santino growled at Roberto.

'Where's Tim?' she asked fearfully.

'How was he in the sack?' Santino leered. 'Hot stuff, honey? I'll show ya hot stuff. I'll show *both* of ya.'

Chapter 131

There was just time to stop by the address Matt had given her for Tim Wealth before heading full speed to the airport. It turned out to be a house on Laurel Canyon.

The two men 'lent' her by Gino's old business associate were low key and youngish. Both seemed sharp-witted and competent. They called themselves Caveman and The Guardian. A third man drove the car, a 1980 Lincoln with a telephone.

She filled them in on the action, and they nodded as if they had been involved in this sort of scam all their lives.

The house on Laurel Canyon had gates and an electric entry system. The servant who answered was willing to buzz them through after three simple words. 'Sparkletts water delivery.'

They drove to the back entrance and waited for the door to open. Then Caveman and The Guardian stepped by the startled houseman, flashing phoney FBI cards and guns.

Lucky followed. She liked their style.

They checked the house quickly and methodically. The ground floor was deserted. Upstairs, the owner of the house sat in the centre of a purple circular water bed watching a soap opera and blowing his nose. 'God save me!' he twittered, as they invaded his bedroom.

Lucky took command. 'Drug squad.' She stepped forward. 'We have a warrant for Tim Wealth.'

The man fluttered well manicured fingernails. 'A scene from one of my own movies! Don't hurt me, I'll do anything you ask.'

'Tim Wealth,' she said menacingly.

'I haven't seen *him* in weeks. He moved out with two of my favourite Guccis, eight hundred dollars, three cameras, and a clutch of cashmere. Actors! Never again!'

'Do you have an address for him?' she asked authoritively.

'I don't have one and I don't want one.' He fidgeted uncomfortably. 'Are you *sure* you're from the drug squad? You look awfully familiar.' He squinted. 'I think I must see your search warrant.'

'Look – we have to find him,' she said sharply. 'And if you don't tell me where we can locate him, then you'll be booked as an accessory. Am I making myself clear?'

'Try his agent, Zack Schaeffer.' He peered at her, searching his memory, and then it came to him. 'Is this some sort of ridiculous joke?' he asked peevishly. 'You're that woman from the Santangelo Hotel in Atlantic City. I was at the opening . . .' He struggled clumsily from the bed, resplendent in purple pyjamas. 'My God! This is one of those TV shows isn't it? Where are the cameras? Oh God! I'll be a laughing stock. I refuse permission, you'll never be able to use it. I'll sue. I'll . . .'

His words floated after them as they hurried from the house.

*

On his way to Bel Air, Lennie rehearsed his lines. Nothing intense, yet not too casual. *Hey, I left Olympia.* No. Too impersonal. How about – *Yeah. I finally made the move.* Or even better – *Lucky, what are you doing here? Did you know Olympia and I separated?*

Christ! He felt sixteen. Why couldn't he just tell her his feelings?

He entered the house and sensed something was wrong immediately. Alice lay on a couch in the living room, pale and wan. She clutched a glass of amber liquid, while a middle-aged man of Lilliputian size sat beside her, eyes glued to a flickering television.

'What's going on?' Lennie looked around and didn't like the whole scene. He had clearly told his mother not to bring any of her friends to the house.

'Lennie! My son,' Alice fluttered, sitting up and gesturing dramatically. 'They've kidnapped Bobby and Brigette. They've taken the babies.'

Chapter 132

There were three cars parked in the driveway of the Bonnatti residence. Steven pulled up behind a sickly yellow Toyota in the Hertz Ford he had rented at the airport. A call to the hospital in New York on arrival had given him the news that Mary-Lou was hanging in there. Carrie had elected to stay with Mary-Lou's family at the hospital when he informed her that he had to go immediately to Los Angeles.

'Why?' she had asked, with concern.

'Because sometimes,' he had replied calmly, 'the law does not cover getting through the day.'

'I don't understand . . .'

It didn't matter whether she understood or not. He knew what he had to do.

He got out of his rented car and rang the doorbell.

Donatella Bonnatti herself answered the door. For years Santino had tried to train her to use servants, but Donatella had no use for people waiting on her, she preferred to be a martyr and do everything herself. 'You thinka they clean? No! They cleana like shit!' she would complain hotly. 'You thinka they cook? Pasta shit they cook!' So while Santino surrounded himself with bodyguards, Donatella preferred the company of two elderly Italian aunts who did things the old way and came by the house three times a week.

Today she was on her own. And even though it was Saturday, she had decided to scrub down the vast kitchen floor while Santino and the children were out.

She came to the front door, hair awry, plain features shining with the sweat of hard work, a flowered cotton housedress covering her considerable bulk.

'Whata ya want?' she asked, looking Steven up and down.

Naturally he assumed she was the maid. In one hand she held an old-fashioned broom which she leaned on as she surveyed him with sharp Sicilian eyes.

He spoke slowly, measuredly. 'I need to speak to Santino Bonnatti. It's a matter of urgency.'

She sucked on a hard candy. 'You gotta the appointment?'

'I flew in from New York. I came straight from the airport. Is Mr Bonnatti home?'

Donatella was not aware Santino was doing business with blacks. He told her nothing. She only knew his secretiveness sometimes drove her mad. As her husband, he should share things with her, but he confided nothing.

'Whatsa this about?' she asked.

'Who are you?' Steven replied.

She laughed hoarsely. 'You think I'ma the maid, huh? I

know, I know.' She smoothed down her housedress. 'Nobody worka their ass in Beverly Hills. I'ma Mrs Bonnatti.'

*

Gino and Paige stopped for a leisurely lunch somewhere along the Pacific Coast Highway. They enjoyed fresh lobster and a bottle of wine. They enjoyed each other's company.

In all his years Gino had never been really involved with a married woman. Oh sure, he had experienced one night stands, afternoon matinees and the like. Once, long ago in his youth, he had indulged in a steamy affair with the super-sophisticated Clementine Duke – wife of a Senator. But this thing with Paige was different. He was an old man and she allowed him to feel alive. She made him laugh, and he knew he wanted her in his life on a permanent basis.

After lunch he broached the subject casually. 'You ever thought of leavin' Ryder?'

They were seated at a table by the window overlooking a magnificent ocean view. She gazed out to sea. 'Ryder needs me,' she said quietly. 'So do my children.'

'Bull*shit!*'

'True.'

'Your old man wouldn't give a camel's crap if you walked out tomorrow. An' your kids are all grown up.'

She looked at him levelly. 'Thanks a lot. You certainly know how to make a person feel wanted.'

'C'mon, kiddo. *I* want you. That's what I'm sayin'.'

'You've got me.'

'For a lousy weekend.'

'Maybe more might be too much for both of us.'

He couldn't figure her out. Why wasn't she jumping? All his life women had jumped.

Maybe that's why he liked her. Paige did what she wanted, *when* she wanted.

'I'd better call the house,' he said, getting up from the table. 'Otherwise they'll be summonin' the FBI.'

She watched him walk from the restaurant. He had style, Gino Santangelo, real style.

Chapter 133

Seeing Boogie made Lucky feel safe. He was always at her side in times of trouble, and she knew she could depend on him.

He was his usual understated self in faded army fatigues and scuffed sneakers. Under his arm he carried a leather bag stuffed with the ransom money. His pale blue eyes darted this way and that as they hurried toward the car.

She told him once again everything she knew. 'Do you think we should bring the police in?' she asked anxiously, not quite sure of her own decision.

'No way,' he said. 'No outside interference.'

She was glad he was with her. Since Gino was on the missing list, Boogie was her only security.

'This is what we're going to do,' she explained. 'We'll make the ransom drop at Farmer's Market, and hope and pray the children are returned. Caveman will follow the money pick up –'

'No. I'll do that,' Boogie interrupted quickly. 'There's nobody better at shadowing than me.'

'Good. We'll have a surveillance truck with full telephone contact and radio communication. Everything's being set up.' She waved a slip of paper at him. 'This is the latest address of the guy I think's involved. Tim Wealth – an out-of-work actor. The Guardian is checking the address now – he'll phone as soon as he comes up with information.'

Boogie looked at her penetratingly. 'And how are you coping?'

She was silent for a moment. When she finally spoke her voice was tense yet laced with steel. 'I'll be all right, I just want the children back safely. And when I get them . . .' Her black eyes hardened. '. . . the sonofabitch who took them will wish he never lived.'

Chapter 134

The Bonnatti living room was immaculate, every piece of furniture polished to a dazzling shine. The damask couch featured plastic coverings on each arm, and there was a black grand piano in one corner with an old lace shawl thrown over it, and lots of fake antique frames filled with family photographs on the top.

Steven didn't care to sit down. He was not there for social niceties. 'Mrs Bonnatti,' he said. 'Your husband is the lowest form of human life.' He threw the copy of *Comer* magazine he had brought with him onto a table. 'The lady on the front is my fiancée,' he said angrily. 'Or rather, the face is hers, the body is not.'

'Eh! Why you showa me this?' Donatella shrieked. 'I no lika these filthy magazines inna my house.'

'I'm glad to hear that,' Steven said harshly. 'But your husband has no such objections. He *publishes* them.'

He picked up the magazine and flicked through it until he reached the pictorial spread that purported to be Mary-Lou. 'Take a look at these pictures, Mrs Bonnatti.' He thrust the magazine toward her. 'These are *fake* pictures. You understand me? Fake! Mary-Lou Moore's face and somebody's else's body.'

'I no looka this dirt,' Donatella insisted, sorry now she had invited this stranger in. She had hoped to find out something about her husband, but not this sort of something.

'Mary-Lou Moore tried to kill herself because of these pictures,' he said roughly. 'She tried to kill herself because of your *sick, sadistic* husband.'

'I donta know nothing,' Donatella said sulkily.

'No? Well isn't it about time you started finding out? If I were you I –'

The phone rang and he stopped abruptly. Glad of the diversion, Donatella rushed to answer it. If it was Santino she would order him home at once. He would be angry she had allowed a stranger into the house, especially a *black* stranger. Santino was always warning her about crime and robberies, and the very risk of stepping out onto the street.

Goddamn Santino. If he was involved with filthy magazines she would never forgive him. He had a publishing company, but they published computer and technical things, Santino had told her so himself.

Ah . . . but could she trust him? He never confided much of anything. She knew he was involved in certain bad things, but over the years she had grown used to his secretive ways concerning business. 'Never you bringa anything home,' she had once warned him. And he never had.

Now she had pornography in her own house, and the black man claimed Santino was responsible.

She picked up the phone. 'Whosa this?' she shouted.

A husky female voice. 'Mrs Bonnatti? Donatella?'

Impatient. 'Yes, yes. Whosa this?'

'There is a house on Blue Jay Way in the Hollywood Hills where your husband keeps his mistress,' the voice whispered.

'What? Whata you talking?'

'Mistress. Girlfriend. Sexual playmate.' The voice murmured the full address, then added, 'Why don't you come over and see for yourself?'

Click.

Chapter 135

The Irish maid in the New York hotel complained to the night manager when she got off duty at 6 45 p.m. 'Goddammit, Albert, I can't be gettin' inta room four twenty-five all day long.'

'Don't worry about it,' the long-haired manager replied.

'I ain't *worried*,' she replied scornfully. 'But I got half me supplies locked up in that big storage cupboard in the bathroom.'

'You'll get 'em out tomorrow.'

'If he's not lyin' dead in his bed,' she sniffed.

'Who?'

'That musician person – Flash.'

The night manager twitched his nostrils. He had just returned from vacation and didn't know the legendary Flash was staying with them. 'Why do you say a thing like that?' he asked, thinking the woman was a flake, but he'd humour her anyway.

'It wouldn't be the first time in this hotel,' sniffed the maid. 'And that room is too quiet today. He's usually got music playin' and people comin' and goin'.'

'Let's go see,' suggested the manager, eager to meet the rock star.

The maid laughed derisively. 'Look at you! Can't wait to view a body! Shame on you.'

'Come on,' he encouraged, walking out from behind the desk.

'Go yourself,' she said rudely. 'I'm off to cook me husband's dinner, and he doesn't take kindly to its bein' late.'

She hurried off, and the busy switchboard caught the manager's attention. He fielded a few calls, then decided that maybe he should take the opportunity of meeting the great Flash in person. He removed the pass key from a drawer, and left the desk in charge of a stoned Puerto Rican porter. Not that he was exactly straight himself. Nothing serious. A couple of Quaaludes just to get him through the night shift. Maybe Flash would have something better to offer him.

Puffed with anticipation he rang for the rusty elevator.

Chapter 136

They made it to Farmer's Market on Fairfax with twenty minutes to spare. Parked next door in the CBS parking lot was the surveillance van Lucky had requested. It's driver was an ex-detective named Dave.

'Wire both me and Boogie,' Lucky instructed, 'I'll do the drop and Boogie's going to handle the tail. You'll stick with him, and keep in full contact with me.'

'No problem,' Dave said. He was tall and agile, and would be well compensated for his trouble.

Lucky hoped he was smart. She needed smart more than anything.

*

Santino had a naturally suspicious nature. And even though the people who worked for him professed to-the-death loyalty he didn't trust them one inch. Certainly picking up a million bucks cash was too much temptation to put in anyone's path. So he decided to stay along for the ride, and see that a couple of hundred thousand didn't vanish along the way. If what Tim Wealth promised was true, the entire operation was a cinch.

Lucky Santangelo must be going through the fucking ceiling, and he was glad. She would go through a whole lot more before she ever saw her kid again – *if* she ever saw her kid again.

Santino smiled to himself. What a day this had turned out to be – there was no revenge sweeter than a revenge long awaited.

*

Farmer's Market was a tourist's paradise, a large complex of open air souvenir shops, trinket emporiums, and a covered food market selling everything from mangos to Italian salami.

Lucky found the B. Dalton bookstore right in the middle. Slowly she walked toward it, carrying the leather carry-all containing the ransom money. Outwardly she was calm, but a cold anger beat inside her head, and she wanted to scream aloud with fury and frustration.

The bookstore was busy, business was brisk. Eyes watchful, she looked around for the diet book section. A fat woman in white polyester pants perused Jane Fonda's exercise book, but apart from her the area was quiet.

Lucky consulted her watch. Two minutes to four o'clock.

The fat woman put the Fonda book down and ambled off.

Lucky looked at her watch again. One minute to go.

She wondered where Boogie was, but it didn't worry her when she couldn't see him. Boogie blended into a crowd and vanished.

Four o'clock exactly.

Carefully she placed the leather bag in a corner and left the store by the other entrance. Once outside her immediate instinct was to go back in and grab the person who made the collection. But she couldn't do that. She had to wait. See if the children were returned. Just wait.

Boogie would take care of that end of it. There was a hidden tracking device in with the money. It wouldn't get far without Boogie.

*

Santino elected Blackie to make the pick-up, while he waited in the car with Roberto and Brigette and his other two henchmen. They parked on the street outside K-Mart, a block away. Blackie was large and lantern-jawed with lank hair and a permanent scowl.

'Don'tcha take long gettin' back here,' Santino commanded. He leaned over and patted Brigette on the thigh.

She shrank away from him.

'Teenager an' I can't wait to get it on,' Santino leered. 'That right, chicken? That right?'

Chapter 137

'Slow down,' Paige said. 'You're going to kill us, then you'll be no use to anyone.'

'You wanna drive?'

'Frankly, yes.'

Gino swerved her Porsche into the side of the road, and they changed places. She buckled her seat belt and instructed him to do the same. He did so reluctantly – taking chances had always been more his style.

Expertly she steered the car back into the flow of traffic on the Pacific Coast Highway. They still had a good two hour drive to go before hitting LA.

'I never felt so helpless in my life,' Gino groaned. 'When I get my hands on the motherfucker who's responsible he'll wish he never lived.'

'Don't talk,' Paige responded, driving even faster than Gino, but less erratically. 'Save your energies. Lucky must be frantic, she'll need you when we get there.'

'I should've been with her,' Gino lamented. 'Jeez! Who would do a thing like this? Who would *dare*?'

*

Lennie wanted to call the police.

'You can't do that,' Alice said, with a firmness unlike her usual self. 'Lucky says everything is under control.'

'Under *whose* control?' he shouted angrily. 'And why hasn't anyone reached Olympia?'

'We've tried,' Alice said, 'and she's unreachable.'

'Jesus Christ!' he exploded. 'Brigette *is* her daughter. She should be here. Or at least know what's going on.'

'I keep on trying.'

'Where's Lucky now?'

Costa entered the room. 'I just heard from her. The money has been dropped off. Boogie's tailing it. All we can do now is wait and see if the children turn up.'

'Well I can't sit around waiting,' Lennie yelled. 'Where is she? Give me the phone number of the car.'

Reluctantly Costa did so. 'She won't like being bothered,' he warned. 'She wants the line kept clear.'

'I don't give a fuck *what* she wants,' Lennie shouted. 'I'm involved. Too bad if she doesn't like it.'

*

Donatella Bonnatti stared at Steven. 'Eh – Mister Berkeley. You coma see my husband. He no here. So now you go, huh?'

Steven studied her carefully. She was agitated and impatient. Whoever was on the phone had upset her. His hunch told him it wasn't Bonnatti, but it was something to do with Bonnatti.

Donatella stalked to the door. The buttons of her housedress strained, revealing a large bosom and sensible underwear. 'You leava now. I have to go out.'

Steven nodded. 'I'll be back to see Santino.'

She was distracted, dying to get rid of him. The pornographic magazine and Santino's involvement didn't seem to matter to her anymore. Something else was on her mind.

'You do whata you wanta do. Okay. Okay.'

She hustled him out of the front door and slammed it firmly.

He sat behind the wheel of his rented car, drove down the driveway to the street, parked and waited. Fifteen minutes later the Toyota appeared, Donatella at the wheel.

She set off toward Hollywood.

Steven followed.

Chapter 138

Eden paced the house restlessly. She attempted to put make-up on her face, but her image was distorted by the marks of Santino's vile fists. Not forever. Thank God. Bruises and black eyes healed. A week, two weeks, and she would be back to normal.

Zeko sat out by the pool facing the house, tossing nuts into his ugly open mouth. He was a cretin. She hated him almost as much as she hated Santino. They were both pigs who thought all women were less than human.

She stared at the kitchen clock. It was past four. Tim was waiting for her, and there was no way she could show up. Screw Bonnatti. She would get away from him eventually – one way or the other.

Outside in the driveway she heard a car pull up. Hopefully she ran to the front window and peered out, only to see Santino emerge. He was accompanied by the two goons he always travelled with, and there was a young teenage blonde and a little boy with them.

Was he bringing his children to see her? She could not believe even Santino would stoop that low.

Quickly she rushed into her bedroom and closed the door. It was cool in there, with just the slight hum of air-conditioning to keep her company.

She heard people enter. There was no way she was coming out to meet them. He couldn't make her. What could he do? Kill her?

*

'C'mon, chicken,' Santino leered, pulling Brigette inside the house.

Her heart was beating so fast she could almost here it. Alice had told her stories about girls who disappeared from home. 'White slavers,' Alice had clucked knowingly, 'sit next to unsuspecting girls in movie theatres and stick needles in their arms. Then they spirit them away to God knows where.'

Brigette had laughed at Alice when she told her lurid tales like that. She had sneered at Lucky when she spoke of possible kidnappers. But now that she realized the seriousness of her situation, she knew how right they both were with their warnings and admonishments.

She wondered what was going on up at the house in Bel Air. Was Lucky there? Olympia? Gino? Lennie? Had they called the police? Were they searching for her and Roberto?

She felt like a little girl again, lost and lonely. And yet she had to be strong for Roberto. He trusted her. He clutched her hand as if his life depended on it. Maybe it did.

She spoke up bravely. 'You've got the money,' she said, desperately trying to keep the tremor out of her voice. 'Now you're supposed to let us go like Tim promised.'

Santino cackled. 'Tim. Who's Tim?' He threw a glance at

one of his hoods. 'Any of ya guys know who Tim is?'

'Never heard of him, boss,' said Blackie.

'Naw, don't know,' agreed the other yes-man.

'C'mon, chicken,' Santino urged, pulling Brigette toward the bedroom. 'Bring the boy too. He can watch – get an early education.' He roared at his own humour. 'The three of us gonna make a pretty picture – a pretty picture ta send t'his mommy.'

He kicked open the bedroom door.

Eden faced him.

'Out, cunt,' he ordered.

'W . . . w . . . what's going on?' she stammered.

'Wait outside an' don't disturb me. Ya unnerstand English?'

Brigette looked at her pleadingly, relieved to see another female. 'This man has kidnapped us,' she began to say. 'He's –'

The back of his hand caught her across the cheek.

Roberto screamed.

Eden backed from the room as he hit the boy too. She couldn't help them. She couldn't even help herself.

Chapter 139

The die was cast. Whatever happened now was out of her hands.

A phone call from The Guardian summoned Lucky to an apartment house off Hollywood Boulevard. Tim Wealth's apartment.

Caveman accompanied her from the car. Contrary to his nickname he wore a sports jacket and neatly pressed pants – he looked like a college graduate, but she knew he carried a solid piece, and hoped he was reliable in times of trouble.

They walked up the outside staircase dodging homecoming school students, and an irrascible old drunk blocking everyone's way.

The Guardian let them in. He had edgy grey eyes that scanned the landscape.

Lucky entered the small apartment and stood stock still. A body was slumped on the floor. A body which not only had been roughed up, but shot in the head.

'Tim Wealth,' The Guardian said tersely. 'I got here before he left us.'

Lucky held her breath. 'And?'

'We got more grief,' The Guardian offered grimly. 'Have you ever heard of a man named Santino Bonnatti?'

Her heart stopped. 'Bonnatti?' she whispered.

The Guardian nodded. 'Santino has the children.'

Chapter 140

Blue Jay Way was a quiet winding street high in the hills above Hollywood. There was not much passing traffic, just the occasional resident running an errand.

Boogie, in the back of the surveillance truck, figured it was the perfect hideaway to keep Roberto and Brigette. He was sure they had hit pay dirt when the Mercedes they were following slowed down. He was more than sure when he observed three men get out of the car, and with them were the children. One of the men looked vaguely familiar – but he couldn't put a name to the face.

For a moment he had to decide whether to take them there and then. But the odds were stacked against him. Three guys – probably carrying – and anxious to hang on to a million buckeroos. There would be crossfire. Someone could get hurt, and there was no way he planned to risk endangering Roberto or Brigette. Besides, Lucky would never want them involved in any kind of shoot out.

He waited until they were all in the house, then he tried to contact Lucky on the car phone. Her driver took the call and told him to wait.

Minutes ticked by slowly. He was patient, thoughtful. The decision was ultimately hers.

When she came on the line he could hear the icy anger in her voice. 'Where are you?' she asked urgently.

He gave her the address and the news.

She relayed the information to her driver and told him to get there fast. Then she said as calmly as she could manage, 'Was one of the men Santino Bonnatti?'

With dull realization he knew the familiar face was indeed Bonnatti, and the implications became clear.

'How do you want to proceed?' he asked. 'Maybe now we should bring the police in.'

'It'll take too much time,' she replied, mind racing. 'Caveman and The Guardian are with me. And you have Dave. We're going to deal with it ourselves – it's the only way.'

'I don't know who else is in the house,' Boogie said. He had learned a long time ago never to argue with Lucky Santangelo.

'Find out what you can,' she replied tensely. 'We're on our way.'

Boogie left the van and went to the front to alert Dave. 'She wants to go with it,' he said. 'Her kid's in there. Are you with us?'

Dave nodded, and patted the concealed .38 he kept strapped to his waist.

'She'll be more than generous,' Boogie promised.

'The money doesn't matter,' Dave said. 'I don't like people who fuck around with children. They need a lesson.'

'Amen,' said Boogie. 'I'm gonna check out the action.'

The two years he had spent in the jungles of Vietnam made him light on his feet and a mover of stealth and lightning. He vanished into the deep undergrowth around the side and made his way up a hilly incline of bushes and scrub.

Before long he had a perfect downward view of the house.

•

Lennie sat in his study and kept on trying the number Costa had given him for the car.

It was continually busy.

He swore to himself and thought of how Lucky must be feeling. She needed him. And if only he could get through to her and find out where she was, he would be there. There was nothing he wouldn't do for her.

Alice came into the room and placed a cup of coffee on the desk. It was the single most thoughtful thing she had ever done for him, but who could sit around drinking coffee at a time like this?

Bingo! Finally he was connecting. The line rang, and a man answered.

'Yeah?'

'Put me on to Lucky.'

The sound was muffled, then her voice.

'Where are you?' he demanded.

She knew it was him immediately, but this was not the time for a reunion.

'I'm taking care of it, Lennie,' she said breathlessly.

He exploded with fury. '*You're* taking care of it. What about the police?'

'No police,' she said calmly. 'Trust me.'

'Where are you?' he repeated urgently.

'I can't tell you.'

'Like hell you can't!' He had never felt so helpless in his life.

'We're approaching Blue Jay Way,' The Guardian said.

'I've got to go,' Lucky breathed into the phone. 'I'll have the children any minute.'

'Where the fuck *are* you?' Lennie screamed.

There was no harm in telling him now. By the time he got there it would be all over.

'No police,' she insisted.

'You got it.'

Quickly she told him where they were. He threw the phone down and raced from the house.

Chapter 141

The night manager of the New York hotel stood outside the door of room 425, and knocked several times.

When there was no reply he slipped his pass key in the lock, and entered.

At first he thought they were asleep – the legendary rock star and the fat blonde. They were sprawled grotesquely naked across the bed.

The night manager stood very still and listened for the sound of breathing. He drew closer, observing the signs of an all night dope party. There were bottles of pills spilled on a bedside table, an empty syringe, a half filled glassine bag of white powder, and other drug paraphernalia.

The night manager sniffed, smelled death, and shuddered. It wasn't the first time he had witnessed such a sight, and it probably wouldn't be the last. But he had never seen a famous person dead before.

The room was horribly silent, only the street sounds outside broke the oppressive hush.

Gingerly he moved even nearer and peered at Flash, who was open-mouthed, his rotting teeth on show.

With a stealthy movement he tasted a touch of the white powder lying in the half empty bag next to the bed.

Cocaine.

He pocketed the bag quickly.

Then he looked at the blonde. She was puffy-faced, her skin a mottled purple – there was something vaguely familiar about her.

Police sirens screamed outside and he jumped, wondering if they were going to stop. They didn't. They faded into the distance, a regular New York sound.

He supposed he had to do something about this mess. Jesus. It would be an all night gig what with the news interest and everything. The press were probably going to go crazy.

In fact, the press were going to want to interview him. For sure.

He looked at the unhappy couple one last time, and picked up the phone.

*

The news hit the wire services just in time for the ten o'clock evening news in New York. In Los Angeles it was seven o'clock.

How the media loved a famous death. Even better, a *double* famous death.

And this one had all the ingredients.

Money.

Sex.

Drugs.

And rock 'n' roll.

What more could they ask for?

Chapter 142

'Take your clothes off, chicken,' Santino ordered.

'You'd better leave me alone,' Brigette warned, her eyes dilated with fear.

Santino laughed. He had locked the door and pocketed the key. The real world was shut out and he was alone with this little blonde piece of ass whom he couldn't wait to stick it to.

Ah . . . but he was not quite alone. Also in the room was the boy. Lucky Santangelo's son.

If he'd planned it in his most imaginative of dreams he couldn't have arranged it better.

He took off his jacket and snorted with mirth.

Brigette's eyes were drawn to the snub-nosed revolver he kept in a shoulder holster strapped to his arm. Her skin crawled and she felt faint as she watched him swagger over to a video camera set on a tripod overlooking the bed and switch it on.

'Okay, quit stallin'. Get your clothes off,' he snarled, removing the gun from its holster and pointing it at Roberto, who crouched petrified in a corner. '*Now*, chicken flesh, or the boy's gonna get it.'

She was weak with terror. This wasn't happening to her. It was all a horrifying dream.

She began to cry.

'Move your ass in front of the camera,' Santino commanded.

Slowly she did as he ordered.

Suddenly Roberto jumped up and ran over to him, pummelling his leg with tiny fists. 'Stop it! Stop it! Stop it!' the boy yelled.

Santino shoved the child away with a brutal thrust, sending him skittering across the room.

Brigette's sobs increased, but that didn't bother Santino. He fixed her with a lascivious expression. 'Get 'em off, chicken. Now. Or I'll shoot this noisy little fucker right in front of your big blue eyes.'

*

Donatella drove past the house on Blue Jay Way and recognized Santino's car at once. She uttered a long stream of Italian curse words and some English ones as well.

Lying, cheating, whore-mongering Casanova *basta*!

How dare he. HOW DARE HE!

Father of her children, faithful husband – or so he had always sworn. She had given him the best years of her life and he was nothing but a rutting gutter dog.

She parked and squeezed her angry bulk from behind the wheel.

*

As Donatella left her Toyota, so the Lincoln pulled up in front of the surveillance truck further up the hill.

Boogie was there to greet Lucky as she jumped from the car. 'Santino's in the house with three other men,' he stated quickly. 'And there's a woman inside too. This is how I see it; Caveman and The Guardian cause a diversion at the front, while I enter through the back.'

'And what will I be doing? Knitting?' she asked acidly.

'You should stay in the car. I'll bring the children safely out. Trust me.'

'Your scenario stinks,' she said coolly. 'I'm coming with you.'

'You'll slow me down,' he pointed out.

'Bull. I'll follow. If I get left behind, that's my fault.'

'It could get dangerous.'

She stared at him. 'Do you know me, Boogie? Do you know me at all?'

There was no point in continuing the argument. Nobody told Lucky Santangelo what to do.

'I'll brief the guys,' he said. 'And then we'll move.'

*

Muttering to herself, Donatella crunched along the short gravel driveway. Before leaving her house she had changed from her housedress into a sombre brown suit, and sturdy high pumps. She had combed her hair and put on scarlet lipstick and blue eyeshadow. Donatella had never mastered the art of applying make-up, and she looked a sight.

Still muttering, she rang the doorbell of the house on Blue Jay Way, where she confidently expected to find her husband in the arms of some filthy cheap prostitute.

*

'Who's the woman?' Cavemen questioned, watching Donatella approach the front door.

'It doesn't matter,' Lucky replied. 'She'll be helpful as far as a diversion goes. You'll enter behind her – stall a confrontation – think of something to keep a dialogue going at the front – while we hit the back.'

'Does the FBI scam work for you?' The Guardian asked, flashing his phony ID card.

'Perfect,' Lucky said. 'Go for it, fellas.'

She followed Boogie on his trip into the surrounding underbrush.

•

The Hollywood Hills were confusing. So many winding streets, and all with cul-de-sacs and turnings and more winding streets.

Steven had lost Donatella Bonnatti in her yellow Toyota when she turned off Sunset onto Doheny Drive, and now he couldn't find her.

It didn't really matter. He would go back to the Bonnatti residence and wait, for he knew what he was going to do to the scum when they finally came face to face.

•

'What the hell is he doing with those kids?' Eden asked Blackie, who was in her kitchen searching for something to stuff in his slobbering mouth.

Blackie made a non-committal gesture. Today – if only for a few moments – he had possessed a million bucks. What a moment!

He conveniently forgot that today he had also murdered a man. Cold-bloodedly and with malice shot him in the head.

'You make me sick,' Eden said, her voice full of disgust. 'You work for and ass-kiss a man who is lower than dirt.' She pushed her face toward him. 'Look what he's done to me. What do you think of a man who can do this?'

Blackie threw her a cursory glance. 'Who cares?' he said, gnawing on a large piece of cheese.

Eden heard the doorbell ring and held her breath . . .

•

'Yeah?' Zeko said suspiciously, opening up a crack.

Donatella gave the front door a hefty kick, hurting her foot in the process. 'Whata *you* do here?' she demanded. 'Where you putta my husband?'

Zeko's mouth hung slackly open. 'Mrs Bonnatti!' he

stuttered.

'Yeah. I'ma Mrs Bonnatti. So what? So now I coma inside. Outta my way, you biga oaf.'

Zeko was stumped. What was the boss going to say about *this*?

He loosened his hold on the door, and failed to notice the two men coming up behind her.

'FBI,' one of them said, holding up identification. 'We're investigating one of your neighbours. We'd like you to answer a few questions.'

Chapter 143

Brigette cowed, naked, in the middle of the big bed. Tears streaked her cheeks. The sick revolting man had touched her, forced her to pose for the camera. And now he was undressing Bobby and cackling with amusement as the little boy kicked and struggled.

She shuddered at the things he threatened next. He had told her in explicit detail what he was going to do to Bobby, as frenziedly he stripped down to his underwear. He wore boxer shorts with hearts on, and his erection poked obscenely at the material.

Bobby was screaming, and the very sound of his anguished cries wrenched at her heart. It was her fault Bobby was here. *Her fault*.

Santino's concentration was on the child. He was preparing to commit an act so vile . . . so indecent . . .

•

Boogie moved swiftly, silently, down through the cactus, weeds and hillside brush.

Lucky managed to stay close behind him, oblivious to the overhanging bushes and branches that scratched and tore at her face and hands.

They were nearing the back of the house. A large swimming pool spread out before them, and around it were glass doors leading into the house.

'We'll bust right through,' Boogie muttered, drawing his gun. 'You'll have the kids back any minute. I promise you Lucky, any minute.'

*

'Mrs Bonnatti?' Eden questioned, shoving past Zeko and confronting the big woman at the front door.

Donatella peered at her. 'You gotta my husband here?' she said loudly. 'My Santino?'

'Yes. He's here,' replied Eden. 'But before you see him I think you and I should talk.'

'He sleepa with you?' Donatella demanded. 'You tell me truth.'

The Guardian seized the opportunity to push past Donatella into the house.

'Wait a min –' began a confused Zeko. But Caveman, close behind The Guardian, pulled a gun and said, 'Save your words, shithead. Where are the kids?'

'Whosa these people?' shouted Donatella. 'Whatsa happening?'

'Just get against the wall and shut up,' Caveman commanded. He gestured to Eden. 'You too, sweetheart.'

Blackie came lumbering out of the kitchen. Caveman waved him to join the crowd. Blackie tried to duck back, but Caveman said, 'One more move and you're dead, fucker.' Blackie froze.

An almighty crash came from the back of the house. And then a gunshot.

One.

Two.

Three.

Eight Months Later

May 1984

Chapter 144

The air in the courtroom was heavy with silence.

Lucky stared into the distance, her black opal eyes mirroring no emotion, although inside she was churning with unbridled anxiety and tension.

The court clerk began to read the form aloud, his voice a nasal whine.

'On this day of May the Fourth, Nineteen Eighty-Four. In the State of California . . .'

Words. So many words. And where were they leading to?

She glanced quickly around the courtroom and fixed on Brigette sitting in the front row. The young teenager was solemn, her pale face expressionless, her blonde hair tightly drawn back in a sedate braid.

Lucky was angry that she had been allowed to come. The nightmare was behind Brigette now, there was no reason why she should be reminded.

The Court Clerk droned on.

Lucky held her breath and hoped . . . prayed . . .

It was a foregone conclusion that she would be found guilty. The newspapers had crucified her long ago. *Lucky Santangelo. The mobster's daughter*. Gino had not been involved in organized crime for over twenty years – and yet the stench remained.

Lucky lifted her chin proudly, she refused to crumble. She was prepared to take whatever they handed out.

'And we, the jury,' the clerk continued sonorously, 'do find the defendant, Lucky Santangelo,' a pause, 'guilty of murder in the second degree.'

The verdict jolted through her like an electric shock as the courtroom erupted.

Voices.

Noise.

A hundred stampeding feet.

The buzz filling her ears, her eyes, her nose, her throat.

The buzz was suffocating her.

She gazed at the movement in the courtroom, her black eyes glassy. The scurrying figures . . . rats running for . . . God, what *were* they running for?

Telephones. Deadlines. The business of getting the news out first. Supplying the greedy masses with their fix of junk-news.

Suddenly a piercing anguished scream shuddered through the courtroom as Brigette leaped to her feet.

'NOOO!' the young girl yelled. 'NO! NO! NO! LUCKY SANTANGELO IS NOT GUILTY. *I* DID IT. *I* SHOT SANTINO BONNATTI. I'M THE GUILTY ONE!'

Epilogue

September the first, 1984, was a beautiful day for a wedding. The sky was blue and cloudless, the sun bright, but not unbearably hot. The white house, standing in the middle of lush gardens filled with flowers, seemed peaceful and welcoming.

Roberto, now five and a half, strode around greeting guests in his dark suit. He was a sturdy lad, undeniably goodlooking with his long lashed jet eyes and black curly hair. CeeCee hovered watchfully in the background, ever alert, as were the security guards who ringed the perimeter of the house, and the plain-clothes detectives who mingled unobtrusively and checked out the arriving guests.

Costa, Ria, and their baby, were among the first to get there. Alice rushed to meet them. She wore ribbons in her dyed red hair, and a bright green, swirling chiffon dress. *People* magazine had just photographed her, and she was dizzy with success. Claudio had been replaced with German Rolf, an aging pop singer with pointed teeth and a tendency to whistle non-stop.

•

Jess and Matt arrived shortly after. Matt was dressed conservatively in a grey suit, while Jess positively bounced in a polka dot maternity dress. She was expecting twins any moment, and as Lennie so rudely joked – she looked like a ripe watermelon just about ready to burst.

•

Steven Berkeley drove up in a bronze Rolls Royce, a wedding present from his bride, Mary-Lou, who sat beside him. They had done the deed a week after she was released from the hospital.

Carrie accompanied them. As usual she was her usual

soignée self. *Women's Wear Daily* had just elected her to their Best Dressed Hall of Fame.

As a wedding present Carrie had handed Steven a copy of her manuscript. 'It's up to you whether I publish or not,' she had said. And then she finally revealed who his true father was, because he had every right to know.

Steven had taken Mary-Lou to Europe for their honeymoon, and while there he read his mother's story. When they returned he told Carrie he thought it would be a crime if she *didn't* allow it to be published. Then he took a copy of it, and the relevant documents concerning his parentage, out to California, where he visited Lucky Santangelo in jail.

The newspapers were making Lucky an example. After all, she was a woman who had gotten away with murder once, and they were determined that all the money and influence in the world could not buy her freedom twice. Especially since the man she was accused of shooting was the son of her original victim.

GANGLAND VENDETTA the headlines had screamed. NO BAIL FOR LUCKY SANTANGELO.

He told her everything. 'Our lives seem intertwined in every way,' he said before leaving. 'I don't know if you ever want to accept it or not, but I'm proud to have you as a sister. And I'll do everything I can to help you.'

Not only did Lucky accept him, she convinced Gino he had a son. And although it took him months to believe her story, he finally agreed to meet with Steven – and maybe – only maybe – forge some sort of relationship.

•

Brigette wore a white dress. A virginal dress. A maid of honour dress. She looked devastatingly pretty with her pale skin, huge blue eyes, and lush body.

Brigette was now one of the richest girls in the world. She had inherited all of her mother's fortune, plus she had her own trust funds, which were enormous, and also the allowances from her late grandfather.

Brigette attended a private girl's school in Connecticut,

and spent the weekends with Lucky – who had willingly taken on the role of legal guardian.

Once a month she had to visit a probation officer – purely a formality to avoid the press screaming she had gotten off scot-free because she was Dimitri Stanislopoulos' granddaughter, had money, and powerful contacts in the right places.

Brigette sometimes suffered from nightmares. They were always the same:

Tim Wealth

Smiling

Happy

Saying

'*How y'doin', little girl?*'

And a picture of his dead body while Santino Bonnatti stripped off her clothes and did his degrading deeds.

She remembered that fateful day in terrifying detail.

The gun.

Santino's gun.

Lying on the table.

Santino. So intent on trying to molest Bobby. His filthy face a smirking mask. She had to stop him . . .

She crawled, sobbing across the bed. Reached for the weapon.

Bobby's stubborn baby voice one long scream of terror.

With shaking hands she picked up the gun.

His gun.

Instinctively she pointed and squeezed the trigger.

The explosion threw Santino back, and blood spattered from a gaping hole in his shoulder. He looked at her with surprise and fury spilling from every pore. 'Ya little cunt –' he started to say.

She pulled the trigger again, and a third time.

Thick blood splashed everywhere as he fell to the floor without another word.

And that's what Lucky found when she dashed into the room.

From then on it was all a blur. Lucky prising the gun from

her shaking hands, wiping the handle clean, grabbing the tape from the video machine and ordering Boogie to get the children out.

And then a large woman appeared in the doorway and started to scream hysterically and point an accusing finger at Lucky. 'You did it!' she wailed. 'You whore! You shota my husband. You killed him. I saw you!'

In the ensuing confusion she and Roberto were hustled away by Boogie, who wrapped them in blankets and spirited them out the back to a waiting car. They were rushed to the house in Bel Air, given sedatives and warned never to mention what had taken place.

The next thing she knew, Lucky was arrested for murder, and Brigette stayed silent, until she could hold her guilty secret no longer. She confessed at the trial. She would have done it before but she was too frightened. After her confession there was complete confusion. Eventually the true facts were revealed, and the incriminating video tape produced. Lucky was released, and Brigette – being a minor – was put on probation for a year only. After all, it was a clear case of self defence.

She was glad she had confessed. At first Lucky was angry at her, but one day she had taken her by the hand, looked her in the eye, and said, 'Thank you. What you did took a great deal of courage. And I'm grateful.'

Now life was okay. Although it wasn't perfect. She missed her mother. Olympia. She really missed her a lot.

•

'Hey,' Gino said, 'you're lookin' good.' He clapped Costa on the shoulder.

'I'm not feeling good,' Costa complained mournfully.

'Always bitchin',' Gino laughed. 'Always carryin' on.'

'My arthritis is bad,' Costa groaned. 'I've got pains in my shoulder. My –'

'Cut it out!' Gino exclaimed. 'Who needs a list of your problems? Think healthy. Stay healthy. It's the only way, pal.'

Gino was a wonderful advertisement for his own words. He still looked years younger than his age – although his hair was finally grey, and a slight twinge of bursitis reminded him he was human. But he enjoyed life. He had a beautiful daughter. A grandson to carry on the family tradition, and excellent health. Oh yeah – and he also had a newfound son. Bizarre, but apparently true. Steven was a complex and interesting man, he was just starting to get used to him.

He did not have Paige Wheeler. Of all the women in his life, she was the one he had never been able to possess.

They still saw each other. Afternoons in the Beverly Wilshire, an occasional weekend, but she simply refused to leave Ryder.

Gino kept trying, it gave him a challenge. It kept the juice in his life.

*

Lennie checked himself out in the mirror. He was nervous as a tiger in the circus. And yet he was also incredibly elated. High. Charged.

For the second time he was taking the step. And this time he was in control of his senses. And this time he knew it was forever.

Lucky Santangelo.

Dangerous.

Stubborn.

Strong.

Crazy.

Sensual.

Everything.

He had thought – once – that Eden was the woman for him. Poor pathetic Eden, who stood up in court and gave evidence about what had taken place in the bedroom of the house on Blue Jay Way – when she knew nothing. He, of course, had arrived too late. It was all over by the time he got there. Lucky had handled it her way.

Eden and he came face to face one day outside the courtoom. 'Lennie.' She placed her hand on his arm and stared piercingly into his eyes. 'I missed you so much, but Santino kept me a prisoner. Can you understand how difficult it has been for me?'

He felt nothing. It was as if their years together had never been.

'I want to see you, Lennie,' she murmured seductively. 'I think I could be just about ready to make a commitment.'

He tried to let her down gently. But there was no such thing as gently with Eden. 'Big star now, huh?' she hissed. 'I knew it would go to your head.'

Eden was past history.

He adjusted his tie. Silk tie. White silk shirt. Black Armani suit. And black tennis shoes.

Well – nobody had ever accused him of being conventional.

*

'Hey – daughter.' Gino put his head around the door. 'We about ready?'

Lucky turned to look at her father. 'You've never called me that before,' she said softly.

'Called you what?'

She smiled. 'Daughter.'

He came into the room. 'Y'know somethin'?'

'What?'

'I kinda always forgot t'tell you this – an' I guess it's not important – 'cos you know anyway.'

'Yes?'

'I love you, kid. I *really* love you. And I'm proud of you. Real proud.'

She blinked away tears – because it wouldn't do to cry on her wedding day, and fell into his arms. 'I love you too, daddy.'

'Hey –' He gave her a gentle shove. 'You're wrinklin' the suit.'

Gino. So sartorially splendid. So great looking. She didn't care about his past – so what that because of him and his public reputation she had been allowed no bail. And seven months spent in jail for a crime she did not commit was tough, but she rode it out – took it like a Santangelo. What she *did* care about was Gino the man. Her father. She loved him, and now she could freely admit it.

'Whyn't we move on out?' Gino suggested. 'The guests are ready, an' so is my arm.'

He extended it in a courtly fashion, and happily she attached herself.

Lennie was waiting.

*

They were married in the garden of the East Hampton house. Lucky Santangelo and Lennie Golden.

Lucky stared at her bridegroom to be as she walked toward him. He turned and met her gaze.

Electricity sparked. They were destined to be a lethal combination.

Gino gave his daughter away.

Roberto was a page.

Brigette the maid of honour.

And Jess, Lennie's best man.

It was a perfect wedding.

[illegible] enough, and [illegible] [illegible] [illegible] father. She loved him, and [illegible] she [illegible].

[illegible]

[illegible]

Louise was waiting.

Lucy [illegible] Hampstead [illegible]

Lucy [illegible]

Lucy [illegible] walked toward him. He turned and [illegible]

[illegible] to be a [illegible] combination.

O ye gentle [illegible] away,
To heaven [illegible]
[illegible] of [illegible]
And [illegible] best [illegible]
It was a perfect wedding.

The World is full of Married Men

For Elsa with all my love

1

'When I was fifteen, I was amazing, absolutely amazing! Dear Mummy was terrified to let me out on my own, she felt I was bound to come home pregnant, or something silly like that.'

The speaker was Claudia Parker. The listener was David Cooper. Claudia was in bed. She was a very beautiful girl, and she knew it, and David knew it, so everyone was happy. She had long, shiny ash-blond hair, which fell thickly around her face, and a deep fringe down to her eyebrows, which accentuated her enormous, slanty green eyes. The face was perfect, with a small, straight nose and luscious, full lips. She wore no makeup and no clothes, and was covered by only a thin silk sheet.

David sat at the end of the bed. He was forty and looked it. He had black, slightly curly hair, and a well-lined strong face. His nose was rather prominent, and he wore thick, hornrimmed glasses. He was a masculine-looking man and enjoyed a great deal of success with the opposite sex.

'So eventually I left home,' continued Claudia. 'I mean it was just all too impossible and dreary. One night I sneaked out, never to return. Actually, I met this marvellous boy, an actor, and he brought me to London with him, where I've been ever since.' She sighed and wriggled around under the sheet. 'Got a cigarette, darling?'

David produced a packet of filter-tips from his dressing-gown pocket and handed one to her. She took a long drag. 'Want to hear more of my lurid background?'

'I want to hear everything about you.'

She smiled. 'You're so sweet. Not at all dull. I thought when I first saw you, you would turn out to be an absolute bore. But how wrong I was. I'm mad about you!' She leaned over to where he was sitting. The sheet was left behind as she wound her arms around his neck and started to nibble at his ear. She had a quite fabulous body.

He pushed her back on the bed.

'Want me, baby?' she whispered. 'Want me badly?'

He grunted his assent.

Suddenly she twisted herself free, jumped off the bed, and ran to the door. 'You're too much,' she said, 'but not now, darling. Maybe you can do it again so soon, but I need a little rest.' She giggled. 'I'm going to have a shower, then maybe we can get some lunch out; and then, baby, then we can come back and make it all night long!'

She vanished through the door, and David heard water running in the bathroom.

He thought about Claudia, and the way they had first met. Was it really only three weeks ago? He had had a particularly hard day at the office, and Linda his wife had been nagging him about all the extra work he seemed to be doing, and how she never saw him any more. It was nearly six, and he was just getting ready to leave, when Phillip Abbotson darted into his office. 'Listen, Dave,' Phillip said, 'do you have a spare moment to come down to the studio and make a decision for us? We've got two girls testing for the Beauty Maid soap product, and it's a dead heat. We just can't decide.'

Reluctantly David went with Phillip to the ground-floor studio in the enormous Cooper-Taylor advertising building. It was owned by his uncle, R. P. Cooper, who had two sons, and Sanford Taylor, with no sons but a son-in-law. Therefore, David came sixth in the line of importance, which in a business of such a size was quite important, but not important enough as far as David was concerned. He was in charge of the TV section, and since Beauty Maid soap was to be featured quite heavily on Channel 9, it was necessary to pick the right girl.

They entered the studio, and David immediately spotted her. She was sprawled in a canvas chair, wearing a white terry-cloth robe. Her hair was piled high on her head, and she was eating an apple. The other girl came into focus next. She was chocolate-box pretty, prim, and virginal-looking. However, her figure belied her face. She had a huge bosom. the largeness of which was emphasized by the flesh-coloured swimsuit she was wearing.

'What tits!' muttered Phillip.

'Is that all you ever think about?' said David.

Phillip called for silence in the small studio and gestured to the Chocolate Box girl. She made her way onto the small set, where a fake bathroom was located. She climbed daintily into a large. round marble bath. flesh-color swimsuit and all. and a prop man rushed eagerly over and sprayed her ample proportions with bubbles. Someone else thrust a large bar of soap into her hand. and then Phillip shouted. 'O.K.. let's do it.'

The cameras started to turn. and David watched the scene on a small closed-circuit screen.

The girl flashed a toothy smile at the camera. 'I'm a Beauty Maid.' she cooed. She lathered the soap in her hands and spread it luxuriously up her arms. first one. and then the other. 'Beauty Maid was made for me. It's so creamy. so smooth. so datable.' She drew one long leg out of the bubbles and lathered that too. 'Why don't you try Beauty Maid. and then you can be a Beauty Maid too!' She smiled at the camera again and shifted slightly, so that her ample bosom was well in focus.

'Cut.' shouted Phillip. 'Miss Parker now. please.'

David turned to watch as Claudia changed places with the other girl. She had a pantherlike grace all her own. Her voice was low and sexy as she read her lines. When she was finished she casually shrugged her way back into her robe and went and sat down. Chocolate Box still bounced around the set.

'The Parker girl.' David said to Phillip. 'No contest.'

As he left the set. Claudia caught his eye. She smiled. and he felt a hint of promise in her smile. He returned to his office, packed up a few papers. called Linda to say he would be home for dinner. and then left.

Claudia was standing outside the building.

'Hello.' she said. 'Small world.'

They talked for a few minutes about the tests. and Beauty Maid soap. and the weather. and then David suggested dinner. Claudia said she thought that was a divine idea.

They went to an intimate Italian restaurant in Chelsea. where

David knew he was unlikely to be spotted by any of his or Linda's friends. He called Linda on the phone and made his excuses. She sounded upset but understanding. Claudia called a boyfriend and cancelled him out. They ate cannelloni and talked and held hands. and there it all began.

Suddenly Claudia returned from the bathroom. 'Darling, what have you been doing?' she questioned.

David pulled her down on the bed. 'Thinking about you, and how you picked me up.'

'It's not true!' she protested. 'You're just a dirty old man who fancied me as soon as you saw me in that bath!' She was wearing her white terry-cloth robe again. David ran his hands underneath it. She shivered. The phone rang. 'Saved by the bell,' she giggled. and rolled over to answer it. It was her agent.

David dressed slowly. watching her all the time. She spoke animatedly on the phone. occasionally pausing to stick out a small pink tongue at him. Finally she hung up. 'Oh, you're dressed,' she said accusingly. 'I've got simply marvellous news. I have an interview with Conrad Lee tomorrow. He's over here looking for a completely new face to star in his latest film; it's all about the Virgin Mary or something. Anyway. I'm to see him tomorrow night at six, in his suite at the Plaza Carlton. Isn't that exciting?'

David wasn't pleased. 'Why do you have to see him at night? What's wrong with during the day?'

'Baby, don't be so silly. My God. if he wants to get laid. he can get it just as well in the morning as any other time.' She marched crossly over to the dressing table and meticulously started to apply her makeup.

'All right. I'm sorry I spoke. I just don't know why you want this stupid career of yours. Why don't you—'

'Why don't I what?' she interrupted coldly. 'Give it all up and marry you? And what do you suggest we do with your wife and kids. and all your other various family entanglements?'

He was silent.

'Look, baby.' Her voice softened. 'I don't bug you about things. so just forget it. You don't own me, and I don't own you, and that's the way it should be.' She applied lip gloss with a flourish. 'I'm starving. What about lunch?'

They went to their little Italian restaurant, and good humour was restored.

'Sunday's such a dreary day,' said Claudia. 'It just sort of sags along.' She drank her red wine with relish and smiled at the short, fat proprietor, who grinned happily back. 'Do you know everyone believes they are beautiful: I'm sure of it. They look in the mirror, and they see two eyes, a nose, and a mouth, and that's it, they think—what a gas!'

Her laughter lit up the restaurant, and David laughed with her. She was such a beautiful, vital girl. He had had affairs outside marriage before, but this was different; this time, for the first time, he wished he was free.

'I met this man once,' said Claudia. 'He promised me a yacht in the south of France, a villa in Cuba, lots of jewels and all that jazz, and then he just disappeared. I heard later he was a spy and got shot. Isn't life funny?'

After lunch they drove through the West End looking for a film they would like to see.

'Look at all those nuts,' exclaimed Claudia, watching a large procession heading toward Trafalgar Square. 'Can you imagine spending all your spare time rushing around tying yourself to embassies, and sitting down all over the place? And all the fellas have beards. I wonder why.' She snuggled up closer to David. 'Let's forget about the movie, let's go back to my place and screw. I feel like getting laid again, don't you?'

Who was he to argue?

2

BAN THE BOMB, the banner attached to the stout lady's back announced quite clearly.

PEACE EVERYWHERE, declared a large notice held aloft by a bearded young man.

END NUCLEAR WARFARE, stated a ragged piece of cardboard clutched gamely by a harassed woman, also clutching two scruffy-looking children by the hand.

This group, along with several hundred others, marched slowly into Trafalgar Square. Many had arrived before them, and there was a milling crowd around Nelson's Column and the fountains.

Linda Cooper was already there. She was squashed between an earnest-looking group of young girls with long, untidy hair and grubby-looking outfits, and a bespectacled gentleman who kept up a constant muttering to himself.

Linda was an attractive woman in her early thirties, with short auburn hair partly concealed beneath a chiffon scarf. She wore a cream Chanel suit which looked out of place in the company she was with. One would imagine that ten years earlier she had been very pretty indeed, but the prettiness had been replaced with an expression of resignation. There were little lines, a certain amount of tiredness, and slightly too much makeup, but the overall effect was attractive.

She glanced around. It seemed funny to be standing there, part of the crowd, without David. It was so seldom that she did anything or went anywhere without him, but more and more lately there had been long business trips and late meetings, and he seemed to have become so completely involved in his work, almost to the exclusion of all else. She sighed. It was only by chance really that she was at the meeting today. David was away, and suddenly she felt she must get out of the house and do something different for a change. The children were in the country with her parents for the weekend; she had declined to go, thinking that David would be home, but at the last moment he had had to rush off as usual. She had found herself alone, and eventually decided she couldn't bear to sit around the house all day, so she had phoned Monica and Jack and they had asked her over to lunch. But it was a mistake; they were really David's friends from his bachelor days, and she always sensed a certain forced gaiety about them, a sort of 'so David finally married you' attitude, 'well, he could have done worse.' After an hour and a half she excused herself on the pretext that she had to get home, there was so much to be done before the children arrived. What, she could not imagine, but Monica and Jack didn't argue, so she left.

It was while she was driving home that she noticed the marchers and the banners and the crowds, and on impulse she parked her Mini in a side street and made her way into Trafalgar Square, which appeared to be the general gathering point.

It was a subject she had often thought about and secretly wished that she could be part of. To protest seemed the very least one could do, if not for oneself, for one's children.

The end of an era was taking place. Nineteen sixty-nine and people were speaking out. She wanted to be one of them.

The bespectacled man standing beside her suddenly looked at his watch. 'It's three o'clock,' he announced excitedly.

There was a sudden surge forward of the crowd, and a general shouting and yelling. Small groups of people seemed to disintegrate from the mass and rush toward the road, where they promptly sat down in front of the traffic. Linda was carried forward with the crush and found herself near the edge of the pavement. There were a lot of policemen pushing and dragging and lifting the squatters from the road. As soon as one person was removed another immediately took his place. The mob was delighted. They chanted various slogans and cheered and booed the police. The large blue police vans gradually began to fill up, but undaunted, new squatters appeared.

Linda felt marvellous. 'Ban the Bomb,' she shouted. *She* was protesting about the bomb. *She* was actually involved in a meeting of worldwide interest. *She* was, in a minute way, helping to protect the future of her children. It was an exciting experience.

'Ban the Bomb,' joined in the people near her.

'Come on, darlin'.' A dark-haired young man grabbed her by the arm, and together they rushed onto the road. They sat in the face of an oncoming taxi, and the irate taxi driver growled, 'Bloody barmy, the lot of 'em.'

Linda had a feeling of complete exhilaration, and then a pink-faced constable was grabbing her under the arms and pulling her to the side of the road. She started to struggle and another policeman joined them and took hold of her legs. There was a moment of immodesty as she felt her skirt hike up above her knees and then they unceremoniously dumped her back on the pavement.

Helping hands got her to her feet, where she discovered she had lost her shoes and somehow or other cut her arm. Her scarf had vanished and her hair fell around her face.

'You look a right mess don't you?' It was the dark-haired young man again. 'Want to give it another try?'

A girl grabbed him by the arm. 'Oh, come on, Paul,' she said. 'Let's go. We don't want to get lumbered down to Bow Street again.' She was small, with long, pale-yellow hair, and she was very young.

Paul ignored her. 'Look,' he said to Linda, 'you had better come with us. I've got a mate lives near here and we can maybe get you some shoes.'

'Well . . .' started Linda.

'Let's not hang about, Paul,' said the girl crossly.

'All right,' decided Linda, and the three of them started to push their way to the edge of the crowd.

Paul took hold of her arm and guided her through the mass of people. His lank-haired girl friend trailed miserably behind.

'My name's Paul Bedford, what's yours?'

Linda glanced at him. He was tall, with slate-grey eyes. She guessed he must be about twenty-two. She found him uncomfortably attractive.

'Mrs. Cooper,' she said firmly.

He gave her an odd look, half-amused, half-puzzled. 'Mrs. Cooper, huh?'

The pavement was cold and hard on her stockinged feet, and she found herself wishing she was safely home and not rushing around Trafalgar Square with some strange young man whom she had only met ten minutes before.

'I have a car parked close by,' she said. 'I think it would be better if I got back to it. I'm sure I have some old shoes in the trunk.'

But Paul was already leading her across the road into Newport Street. 'We're here,' he said, banging on a battered yellow door. 'At least come up, we'll bandage your arm, and then I'll take you back to your car.'

The girl friend looked sulky.

'All right,' said Linda.

A makeupless, white-faced, black-haired girl finally came to the door. She wore a tattered blue-and-gold brocade Chinese housecoat and once-white fur slippers. 'Hi, baby,' she greeted Paul brightly, 'and how's little Mel?' She nodded at the girl friend. 'Come on up.'

They followed her up a narrow staircase into an enormous room painted completely black. There was a large bed in one corner, a lot of books and cushions scattered around, and a record player with Miles Davis turned up full volume. This appeared to be the full extent of furnishings.

'Where's your old man?' asked Paul.

'He went down to join the crowd,' said the girl.

'We need a drink,' said Paul. 'Got hung up in the middle of it. This is Mrs. Cooper; she cut her arm and lost her shoes. Had a right punch up.'

The girl smiled. 'You always manage to involve people. Sit down and I'll get you a beer, it's all we've got.'

'Come on,' said Paul to Linda, 'we'll fix your arm up.' He took her into the bathroom, which was surprisingly white and antiseptic-looking. 'So where's Mr. Cooper then?' he asked.

She looked at him coolly. 'He's away on business.'

'What's your name when it's not Mrs. Cooper?'

She hesitated, then said, 'Linda. Why?'

'I just wanted to know.'

They looked at each other for a long moment before she glanced nervously at the floor. This is ridiculous, she thought. What am I doing here with this boy? What would David think? I must get out.

They discovered a box of Band-aids and Paul put one over the cut on her arm. 'Was this your first meeting?'

'Yes,' she replied. 'Look, I simply must get back to my car now. It's really awfully nice of you to have taken all this trouble, but I have people expecting me at home, and they will be worried if I'm late.'

'Fine,' he said. 'I'll take you. Can't have you wandering about London with no shoes on.'

They went back into the large black room. Lank-haired Melanie was sitting clutching a can of beer. She jumped up when Paul came in and rushed over to him. Linda decided she wasn't very pretty, much too thin, and that awful hair!

'Have some beer,' Melanie offered. She had a whiny voice.

'No, we're splitting,' said Paul. 'I'll be back soon. You wait here.'

The girl obviously wanted to argue but didn't quite dare.

Paul kissed the owner of the room. 'I'll be back,' he said.

Linda said good-bye, and they left.

In the street he took her arm again, but she shook it free saying, 'I don't like my arm held.'

'What *do* you like?'

She didn't reply.

They walked in silence to where her car was parked. She felt embarrassed and inelegant in her stockinged feet. Besides, the pavement was cold and hard and she wished she was safely home.

When they reached her car he helped her in. 'Where do you live?' he inquired politely.

'Finchley. We have a house there.'

'Hey, we're neighbours. I live in Hampstead.' He stood on the pavement leaning against the car door. 'You can drop me there. Do you mind?'

'I thought you had to go back for your girl girl friend,' she said nervously. She just wanted to drive off and leave him standing there. She knew how attracted she was to him, and somehow she felt very vulnerable.

'That's all right. Mel will find her own way home. She usually does anyway.' He walked around to the passenger seat and got in.

It's now or never. she thought. Either I tell him to get out or I'm accepting the fact that he's interested and letting him know that I'm interested too. She felt him staring. She started the car.

Linda drove expertly through the traffic. Paul sat silently beside her, his silence making her even more aware of his presence. Eventually she spoke. 'Your girl friend isn't going to be too pleased with you, saying you would be back and then just disappearing.'

'It doesn't matter.'

They lapsed into silence again. She decided that when they reached Hampstead she would stop the car, wait for him to get out, and then wave good-bye and drive quickly away. She would give him no chance to talk about seeing her again. Instinctively she knew he would want to.

'I noticed you immediately,' he said.

'What?' she replied, startled.

'I said I noticed you immediately,' he repeated, 'in the crowd. You looked out of it, sort of lost. You wanted to be part of it and yet couldn't quite make it. So I grabbed your arm and pulled you into the road and then you were all right, you forgot yourself, y'know?'

'I don't know what you mean,' she said defensively.

'Oh, come off it, you know exactly what I mean.' He yawned rudely. 'Where's your old man then? Where's your kids? You *have* got kids, haven't you?'

'Yes, how do you know?' she said defensively.

'Easy. I can sum you up in a minute. Married maybe ten years, nice little house, husband away a lot, kids growing up and leaving you behind. It's true, isn't it?'

Her first reaction was one of anger, stop the car and tell this rude little boy to get out. But wait a moment, what he was saying was very near the truth. Wait, hear him out, what harm could it do? She was curious too. How did he know? Did she look the part so completely?

She forced a smile. 'You're very sure of yourself, aren't you?'

'Yes. I am. I can see it in your face. The way you look. Everything about you.'

'We've reached Hampstead,' she said quickly, and swerved the little car abruptly into the kerb. 'Thanks for the summing up. It was great fun for you, I'm sure. David would have been amused. Good-bye.' She stared straight ahead and waited for him to get out.

He didn't move. Just said quietly, 'Can I see you again?'

She turned to look at him. His eyes penetrated deep into her own.

'I don't understand you. First you dissect my life, pull me to pieces, and then you ask to see me again. No, you can't. I'm in love with my husband. I have two wonderful children and I live a very nice life, thank you. I think you are pushy and rude, please get out of my car and go away.'

'I would like to see you again. I think you need someone like me.' He opened the door and got out. 'Anyway, if you change your mind, I'm in the phone book.' He turned and walked away.

She watched him go. He's a creep, she thought angrily. He's very thin, probably never eats. So young, but so knowing. *I would like to sleep with him.*

She halted her train of thought abruptly. I would like to *what*? she asked herself incredulously. Sex had always been synonymous with David. She had never had an affair, she had gone to her marriage bed a virgin, and now this thought was in her head. Oh, there had been many boys she had dated, necked with, before getting married, but never anything more serious than that. David is a wonderful husband, she thought, a wonderful lover. But when did he ever make love to her these days? Maybe once a fortnight, and then it was a quick ten-minute affair out of which she derived no particular pleasure, and afterward he would turn over go straight to sleep and snore, and she would lie awake for a long time thinking how it used to be before the children, when they were first married.

She sighed and started the car. It was impossible to turn the clock back.

The house was empty: even the dogs were away with the children. and their live-in Spanish maid. Ana. was out for the day. It was depressing. Linda switched the television on in the bedroom and noticed that it was nearly six. David had said he would be home around nine. so there were three hours to kill. She had no intention of watching television. but it was nice to have human voices around her. She decided to phone her mother and see how Jane and Stephen were behaving themselves.

Her mother's voice was placid and comfortable, 'Hello, Linda, dear.'

'Hello, Mother. How's everything?'

'Oh, fine, dear, fine. Jane's having her bath now and Stephen's right here. Wait a minute, hang on, he wants to speak to you.'

There was a pause, and then Stephen's thin excitable voice came on the line. He was eight. 'Hello. Mummy. We're having a smashing time. Grandma made lots of gooey cakes for tea, and that pig Jane tried to eat them all, so I pushed her off the chair and she started to cry and . . .' He carried on at great length about the cakes, and then her mother's voice came back on the line.

'Daddy will be driving the children back after lunch tomorrow, so you should expect them around four. How is David? Did you have a nice peaceful weekend together?'

'Yes, Mother. very peaceful.' replied Linda ruefully. 'All right, then. I'll speak to you later in the week. Thanks for having the children. kiss Janey for me. Bye.'

What now? Feeling slightly hungry, she went to the kitchen, but she hated cooking just for herself, so she finally settled for a cheese sandwich. There seemed nothing else left to do except to go to bed and wait for David.

Bed. David. the two thoughts connected in her head. and an idea formed. She rushed to her closet and hunted around until she found what she was looking for. A slinky black negligee she had bought in Paris several years ago and never really got around to wearing. It had always seemed too frivolous. She held it up against her and then returned to the kitchen to iron it. Well, this is what they say in all the women's magazines, she thought, smiling. Shock your husband into realizing how utterly sexy and devastating you really are!

After the negligee was ironed, she ran a long, hot bath and borrowed some of Janey's Baby Bubbles to throw in. For good measure she added some Chanel No. 5 cologne; until it all looked very luxurious and inviting. Next she creamed her face, set her hair, and then climbed into the bath and relaxed.

The phone rang. Wrapped in a bath towel, trailing bubbles, she hurried into the bedroom to answer it.

'Hello.'

'Hello, Linda?'

'Yes.'

'This is Paul Bedford.' A long silence, and then his voice again. 'You mentioned David and Finchley, so it was easy to trace you in the phone book. Look, I'm sorry, I wanted to apologize for earlier. I didn't mean to upset you. Will you forgive me?'

'There's nothing to forgive,' she said coolly. 'It certainly didn't bother me one way or the other.' She was tempted to say good-bye and hang up, but she waited to see what he would say next.

'That's all right then.' He sounded relieved. 'You know, when I like people, I mean really like them, I always seem to come on too strong. I don't intend to, but it just happens. Sort of reverse action.' He paused, then continued. 'A friend of mine is having a party tonight; he lives near you, and I thought you might like to come.'

'I'm sorry, I can't,' she answered quickly.

'No harm in trying. Maybe some other time.'

'You'll have to excuse me, I'm in the middle of taking a bath.' Then she added, 'Thanks for the thought, anyway. Good-bye, Paul.'

'Good-bye, Linda. Sorry about dragging you out of the bath. The party doesn't start until ten, so if you should decide you want to go, my number is Hampstead 09911. Bye.' He hung up.

0–double-nine-double-one. So easy to remember. She shivered and made her way quickly back to the bathroom. The bubbles in the bath had gone flat, and the water when she got back in was lukewarm. She was secretly pleased that Paul had phoned; it made her feel desirable and wanted, a feeling she couldn't remember having had for a long time. Tonight things would be different. She would make David realize that everything could and should be as romantic as it was when they first knew each other. After all, just because two people were married didn't mean that romance had to go by the board. I'm only thirty-three, she thought; that's still very young. Well, certainly not old. She climbed out of the bath and studied her body in the bathroom mirror. I could do with going on a diet, she mused. Her legs were shapely but a little heavy around the thighs, her waist was quite slim, and her breasts, although large and full, were still firm.

She slipped into the negligee. It clung flatteringly, and she was pleased with the effect. She applied a light makeup and combed out her hair. Then she turned off the television and put on the stereo. Sinatra was much more acceptable than some stupid sit-com.

The stage was set, the player was ready, it was nearly nine. A glass of wine would be nice, she thought. There was a bottle of rosé in the fridge, so she went and got it.

An hour passed. The wine was drunk, Sinatra was silent. The black negligee had been replaced with something a little warmer. The television was back on and Linda huddled morosely in front of it watching an old movie.

She was a little loaded. The emptiness of the house seemed to press around her. Where was David? He had said nine o'clock. If he was going to be late, he could at least phone. Perhaps he had had a car accident. Perhaps he was lying badly injured or even . . .

The phone rang. First, the operator's cool efficient voice, and then David, obviously in a hurry. 'Look, I'm held up with these people here. I had to drive over from Leeds to Manchester, and I'm bushed. Not going to risk driving back tonight; it's a filthy night. I'll leave early in the morning and be home at eight.'

'But David, I'm expecting you.' She tried to keep her voice pleasant. 'Why couldn't you have let me know earlier? It's nearly ten, and you promised you'd be home by nine.'

'I can't talk now, I'll explain tomorrow.'

Her temper suddenly snapped. 'I don't care about tomorrow. What about *me?* I've had a bloody miserable weekend, and tonight I've just sat around waiting for you, and *you* couldn't even bother to phone. At least if I'd known I could have gone to the films or something. You're just selfish, and I can't—'

His voice was cold and unemotional. 'I'm with people now. I'll see you tomorrow. Good-bye.'

The line went dead. For a moment she sat very still trying to control a choking feeling of complete frustration. He had hung up on her, he hadn't even bothered to wait for her to say good-bye.

At last she replaced the receiver, only to pick it up again and dial. The ringing tone seemed very loud in her ear. I've had too much to drink, she thought vaguely. Then a voice was saying hello and she found herself replying with, 'Hello, Paul, this is Linda Cooper. About that party . . .'

3

It was four o'clock when David and Claudia arrived back at her apartment. She lived in a converted house at the back of Knightsbridge, all very new and modern. She occupied the top apartment which had the advantage of a small roof garden.

David had often found himself wondering how she could afford it. All her furniture was new and obviously expensive, and she had an enormous wardrobe of clothes. She was an actress and model, and from what he knew of both professions, unless you were extremely successful you didn't earn a lot of money. Certainly not enough to keep Claudia in the style she obviously liked. He had mulled this problem over and come to no satisfactory conclusion. Eventually he had decided that she must have a rich father, although this didn't really tie in with the bits and pieces he knew of her background.

According to Claudia she had left home at fifteen, and arrived in London five years ago all set to be a movie star. Now she was twenty, very beautiful and sparkled like champagne. But no movie star.

He had known her only three weeks and in that time seen her as much as twelve times. She was always available, there didn't appear to be any other man in the picture. She accepted the fact that he was married, and didn't nag about it as a lot of women might. She never mentioned money to him. He had seen that she did the Beauty Maid commercial, but apart from that she hadn't worked at all.

He decided that he had to find out more about her. Maybe she needed money and was embarrassed to mention it. He resolved to bring the subject up.

When they entered, Claudia rushed about making a great show of fixing the bed and generally tidying up. She was most undomesticated. A cleaning woman came in every day except for weekends. She made a disgusted 'ugh' when she came to the dirty dishes in the kitchen.

David followed her in. 'I'll buy you a dishwashing machine,' he said, slipping his arms around her waist.

She turned, laughing. 'You're joking, of course. A dishwasher! What a *terrible* present. I'll have something more romantic than that, thank you!'

'What do you want? We'll go shopping tomorrow.'

'I want, let me see now. I want a Ferrari, two mink coats, lots of diamonds, a beautiful penthouse in New York, and a villa on the Riviera!' She started to laugh. 'Can you afford me?'

'I'm serious. Will you settle for a mink jacket? Go and order it tomorrow.'

She stared at him and licked her lips. 'I'd adore that. But if you want me to have it, surprise me, none of this ordering jazz. I like surprises.'

He grinned. 'A surprise it will be.' He wondered if now was the time to bring up her financial situation, and decided against it. Later, when they were in bed.

'When do you turn into Cinderella tonight?' she asked suddenly.

'I should leave about eight-thirty.' He stroked her hair. 'But I can always stretch a point, depending on what the main attraction is.'

She giggled and pulled off her sweater. 'The second feature is starting now. The main attraction should prove to be very interesting indeed!'

Sometime later, when David looked at his watch, he was surprised to find it was well after nine. Claudia lay asleep beside him, her long hair in disarray around her face, her makeup smudged and faded. She looked very young. Her clothes were scattered around the bedroom, leading in a trail from the kitchen. As if she sensed him looking at her, she opened her eyes, yawned, stretched, and made contented noises.

'You're like a cat,' he said, 'sometimes an innocent little kitten and sometimes the wildest, dirtiest alley cat around.'

'I like that. I can see myself telling it to someone in the years to come. There was this guy, and he said to me, you're like a cat, sometimes—'

He put his hand over her mouth. 'Don't say that. There will be no other guys, only me. I love you and I want to marry you.' He surprised himself with the words, but there they were, spoken aloud for all to hear.

'You know, it's amazing,' she said, 'how very simple it is for married men to propose. I guess it's an easy thing for them to say, because really they are all safe and secure, and they know they can lay out this tasty bit of bait without a hope in hell of getting trapped themselves. Marry me, my darling, only don't let my wife find out!'

He was furious. So, all right, he hadn't really meant it. Correction, he *had* meant it, but, as she had said, he was secure in the knowledge that it was not possible. However, the fact that she realized this infuriated him. Why did women always seem to have so much insight into the things men said?

'I could get a divorce,' he offered.

'Are you going to?' she replied coolly.

'I don't know.' He pulled her to him. 'It's not just me and Linda; there's the children to consider. But I do love you, and one day, when my kids are a little bit older, well then, everything will be okay. In the meantime I can look after you. I don't want you to work. No more interviews. I'll give you money.'

She stared up at him with her large, slanty green eyes. 'I'm glad you have it all figured out.' She caressed his back, and he felt desire rise up in him again. She had only to touch him and he wanted her. 'There's only one little problem. I don't want to marry you. Not even if you were free, and we could rush off and do it now.' She wriggled away from him and got off the bed. She stood looking at him, completely naked, and continued, 'I want to do what I want to do, whenever I want. No ties, no strings. I don't want marriage, it means nothing to me, so don't offer it like it's a golden hoop, because I'm just not going to jump. So I love you now, today. But tomorrow, who knows? That's me. I don't pretend to be someone I'm not, so why don't you do the same?'

He couldn't control the choking excitement he felt. Her words didn't matter. He dragged her back on the bed and let loose his fury and frustrations. She tried to struggle but he crushed her beneath him until her struggling stopped and became part of him.

For David it was devastating; when he was with Claudia it always was. Each time it was more, emotionally *and* physically.

'You'd better get up. It's past the witching hour, and wifey will be waiting.' She stretched languidly.

'Don't be a bitch. Anyway, I think I'll stay.'

She kissed him. They phoned Linda, and Claudia pretended to be the operator so that the call appeared to be long distance.

Afterward she said, 'No bastard would talk to me that way and get away with it. I feel sorry for your wife.'

'Do you?' he said shortly. It annoyed him when she discussed Linda.

'Yes, I do, although it's her own fault.'

'What do you mean by that?'

'What made me more exciting to you than her? Because I'm newer and younger and prettier. Am I prettier?'

'Yes, you're prettier.'

'But you shouldn't *have* to look around. She should make bloody sure that she's always new to you. Most women seem to get married and then stop trying. We've caught the fish, now we can put away the bait and only bring it out on special occasions. I'm not saying that you wouldn't screw around once in a while. All men do, even the happiest of married men. But that's all it would be, there would be no affairs like me, you wouldn't need them.'

'Thank you, marriage counsellor Parker, but I have a feeling that you are addressing the wrong party.'

'Shall I speak to your wife? What shall I say? Darling, in strict confidence, I'm banging your husband. This isn't really necessary. If only you weren't so dullsville he might fancy you again. Liven up a bit, and back he will come.'

They both started to laugh. 'You *are* a bitch. Is that why I love you?'

'No,' she giggled. 'You *know* why you love me.'

They got up and she busied herself in the kitchen making sandwiches while David prowled around the flat thinking how he could bring up the subject of her finances again. She had annoyed him with her little speech about not wanting to marry. But really he wasn't too annoyed, because on thinking it over he decided she had only said it as a defence mechanism. She knew they couldn't get married, so to save face she had probably convinced herself that she didn't want marriage anyway. On thinking it over even further he was almost pleased, because it put him in the enviable position of being able to have his cake and eat it too. He didn't really want to leave Linda. In his own way he loved her, although she had ceased to attract him sexually shortly after they were married. He had compensated for this by different affairs throughout the years, and to Linda he had been more than generous materially. She was the perfect wife figure. A lovely hostess and mother.

No, he certainly didn't want to leave Linda. He felt no particular guilt about being unfaithful to her. Although if *she* was to him . . . But no, that was unthinkable. The very idea of Linda being unfaithful was ridiculous.

Claudia was licking mayonnaise off her fingers in the kitchen. She wore a pink kimono and had tied her hair away from her face.

'You look about fifteen,' he said.

'And you look about fifty. What *is* on your mind? Are you brooding because I turned down your gallant proposal?'

'I want to talk to you seriously. Bring the sandwiches and come and sit down.'

She followed him into the living room, and munching a sandwich, sat down on the floor near his feet. 'What seems to be bothering you, David?'

'Look, darling, I've been thinking a lot about you.'

She laughed. 'I should hope so.'

'This is serious,' he continued. 'I've been worried about how you manage financially. This apartment can't be cheap, and I want to help you out. I mean, frankly, where *do* you get your money?'

She sat very still. Her eyes glinted dangerously. However, she managed to keep her voice pleasant. 'Well, baby,' she said sweetly, 'what makes you want to know?'

He didn't observe the danger signals. 'Of course I want to know. Do you get an allowance from your father, or what?'

'Come *on*. I haven't seen my family in five years, and I don't care if I ever see them again. My old man wouldn't give me a penny to go to the bathroom with.' She sat silently then, and David realized that she had no intention of answering him.

'Claudia, I want to know,' he said sharply.

She arose. 'I don't like being questioned. I'm not asking you for anything. I don't *want* anything from *you*.' She started to shout. 'Leave me alone with your questions. What's on your mind? Where do you think I get my money from? Do you think I'm a whore? Well, if I was, wouldn't I be asking you for money?' She was crying now, and he was shocked that he had provoked such anger. 'It's *my* business where I get my money from, and if you don't like the idea of that, then let's just forget it,' she yelled.

He caught her mood of fury. 'All right,' he said coldly, 'we'll forget it.' He marched into the bedroom and dressed. She didn't follow him.

When he came out she was sitting on the sofa reading a magazine and didn't look up.

He stood there, undecided about whether to walk out or not. 'Are you going to tell me?' he demanded.

She continued reading and didn't answer him.

'Good-bye,' he said, and left.

In the hall outside her front door he immediately regretted this move. He couldn't go home, and he debated making it up with Claudia, but that was impossible. If he gave way to her now, he would be admitting defeat, and he never admitted defeat to any woman. No, he decided, let her burn a little, and she would soon come running back. They always did.

He went downstairs to his car, having decided to spend the night in a Turkish bath. He was puzzled about why Claudia was so secretive about the source of her income; it could only mean that there was something he wouldn't like. Well, in that case, when she told him, he would stop it, whatever it was, and then she would be dependent on him, which was exactly the way he wanted it.

He drove to the Turkish baths in Jermyn Street, and after going through the hot and cold steam baths and having a massage, he was quite happy to settle down in his small white cubicle, where he promptly fell asleep. Tomorrow he would settle everything.

4

Paul looked younger than Linda remembered him. He was wearing a black sweater and tight black trousers. She had decided to wear a plain dark-blue dress after discarding several other outfits. They met at a prearranged spot. Paul helped her out of her car and said he would drive, as he knew the way.

'I'm glad you changed your mind. What did it? My unbelievable charm?' he grinned.

'I don't know.' All the wine she had drunk and the rushing to get ready had finally made her tired. 'Maybe I shouldn't have come. I don't know why I'm here, really.'

He looked at her. 'I'm glad you're here. I don't think you'll be sorry you came. In fact, I promise you that.'

They drove a short way along the Heath until Paul pulled into the drive of an old rambling house. Its windows were ablaze with lights, and the belting voice of Solomon Burke screamed out from the stereo. A couple were arguing in the open doorway, and as they arrived, several more people came pushing through the door with much laughter and yelling. Paul parked the car and they went in.

The scene that greeted their eyes was wild to say the least. The front door led into a small hall with big rooms off either side of it and a large staircase in the centre. The staircase was littered with various people, a lot of men with beards, girls sitting and standing, and everyone steadily drinking. The room on the right was filled with couples, dancing or just standing and necking. There appeared to be no furniture, only a rather battered stereo set balanced precariously on the windowsill. The room on the left featured a thin girl with stringy red hair taking off her clothes to the beat of some bongos being hammered on by a West Indian clad only in white shorts. No one was taking much notice of them. Mostly people were watching a blond boy at the other end of the room, who was standing on a chair, quite naked, reciting an obscene poem.

Paul squeezed Linda's arm. 'Come on,' he said, leading her up the stairs, greeting people as he went. 'Let's get rid of your coat, then we can get a drink.'

Upstairs there were more rooms equally devoid of furniture. Paul steered her into a room with a bed creaking under the weight of many coats. Two girls were staring deep into each other's eyes in a corner, and another girl was either asleep or had passed out at the bottom of the bed.

Linda took off her coat and felt too dressed up in her neat blue dress. Paul said that she looked great, and took her to find a drink. They went downstairs to the room on the left. The redhead had abandoned her strip and was sitting on the floor, someone's sweater covering her. She grabbed hold of Paul's leg as he went by. 'Hello sexy, wanna make it?' Her voice was slurred. 'I've got a great body. How 'bout you?'

Linda found herself separated from Paul, so she headed toward a table where the drinks appeared to be coming from.

A fat man pounced up behind her. 'You look very smart,' he said. 'Who *are* you?' His face was beaded with sweat, and his breath a combination of onions and stale beer. 'You want a drink?'

'Yes, please,' she said, trying to edge away from the full blast of his breath.

He poured her a very large Scotch in a cracked glass. She drank it down hastily.

'Let us go and dance,' he said, and put his arm around her waist. She could feel the hotness of his hand penetrate her dress through to her skin.

'Not just now,' she said, trying to disentangle herself.

He licked his pudgy lips, and then Paul arrived. 'Hello, Bruno. I see you've met Linda.'

The fat man removed his arm. 'Oh, she's yours, is she?' he said hastily. 'I don't know what they see in you.' He wiped his mouth with a plump pink hand and ambled away.

Paul laughed. 'Don't take any notice of him,' he said, and

then was suddenly serious. 'You're great, you know that?' He took her hand.

'Thank you,' she said. She had never been able to accept compliments easily. Quickly she drained her glass. 'I'd like another drink.'

He poured her a large Scotch which she drank down fast, feeling its burning effect almost immediately. 'I think I should go home,' she said weakly: 'I'm almost drunk, you know.'

'I know.' He pushed her toward the wall, and then leaned forward and kissed her.

She closed her eyes as she felt the intimacy of his tongue penetrate her lips. His mouth was persistent and demanding. She felt she should push him away but didn't have the strength, and anyway, she didn't want to. It was a long time since she had been kissed like this. David never kissed her anymore, and she had forgotten how exciting it could be.

'Oh, so here you are.' The whiny voice was familiar, the note of anger unmistakable. Paul straightened up. Melanie was standing there, her yellow hair hanging in a straight curtain around her thin, flushed face. 'I thought you were coming back for me.' She glared at Linda. 'Or have you been so busy that you couldn't find time?'

'I'm sorry, Mel, thought I said I'd see you here.'

'Well, you didn't.' Her voice was becoming shrill. 'And how's Mrs. Cooper? Recovered, I see.'

'Can it, Mel,' said Paul abruptly. He steered her away from Linda and into the hall. 'Look, I'm sorry, but that's the way it is.'

'That's the way what is?' Her dull eyes filled with tears.

'It's been great, but we've been heading this way a long time now, and it's best to forget it. I still like you and all that bit, but, well, you know . . .'

'No, I don't know. And anyway, what can you see in that old bag in there?' She started to cry. 'I hate you, Paul.'

'Look, kid, you're seventeen, there'll be lots of other guys. You'll soon forget me. We're just not—'

'We're not what?' she interrupted angrily. 'God, I hate you!'

He shrugged and walked away. Linda was deep in conversation with the fat man again. 'Do you want to go?' he asked.

'No.' Her eyes were bright. She was now very drunk. 'Bruno's going to teach me a new dance.'

'Bruno can find a girl friend of his own. I'll teach you anything you want to know.' He warned Bruno off with a look, took her into the other room where the dancing was going on, and held her very tight. 'I want to sleep with you,' he whispered.

'I want to sleep with you too,' she whispered back. 'I mean, I don't want to, but it would be nice, but I . . . Oh, God, I think I had better get some air.'

He kissed her again. This time she kissed him back, and their mouths met in mutual enjoyment. They stood still among the dancers, lost in their own little world. His tongue explored her mouth, and she felt a sudden urgent desire for him. He pressed her very close and then released her.

'You wait here,' he said. 'I'll get your coat.'

She stood patiently waiting, the liquor she had drunk falling over her in waves. She couldn't think clearly at all, her head buzzed, and she wanted to be back again in the safety of Paul's arms. There was a lot of noise coming from the hall, and she wandered out there. Two men were fighting. It was the fat man, Bruno, and the West Indian who had been playing the bongos earlier. They screamed obscenities at each other and rolled about on the floor. No one tried to stop them.

'Why are they fighting?' she asked a girl standing near her.

'Oh, darling, Bruno always has to fight with someone,' the girl said. 'It wouldn't be Bruno if he didn't.'

The West Indian's nose began to bleed, and there was a lot of blood. Linda suddenly felt sick. She edged her way to the front door and out. The cold air had a slightly sobering effect. She went over to her car and sat in it.

Eventually Paul arrived. 'I was worried. I thought you'd walked out on me.' He got in the car and put his arm around her. She pulled away. 'What's the matter?' he continued.

'I feel terrible. I think I'm going to be sick.'

'Oh, great, let's go back inside and I'll get you upstairs to the bathroom.'

'No, I don't want to go back in there.'

'You'll feel better in a minute.' He put his arm around her again, and this time she didn't pull away. He kissed her, while his hands explored her body.

She felt weak and her head spun, and when she shut her eyes everything whirled round and round. She could feel Paul touching her, and his mouth on hers, but it all seemed like it was happening to someone else.

Abruptly he let go of her and started the car. They seemed to be driving for ages, but really it was no time at all. Then he was helping her out of the car, and they were climbing a lot of stairs, and then they were in a room, and he was pushing her onto a bed.

She didn't struggle when he unzipped her dress and pulled it off, because, after all, this wasn't really happening.

He kissed her slowly. The bed was soft, and she felt very comfortable. His arms were strong and warm, and his hands created a fantastic excitement in her. He rolled her over on her stomach and she felt him undoing her bra.

'I'm not here,' she whispered. 'I'm on another planet. I'm very drunk, you shouldn't take disadvantage of me, I'm at an advantage . . .' She started to giggle.

He began to kiss her back, and then she was suddenly lost in a raging passion which seemed to go on forever and ever.

'I love you,' one of them said.

'I love you,' the other said.

It was good to be wanted.

Linda awoke at five in the morning. She opened her eyes in disbelief, and was parched with an awful thirst. Her eyes felt heavy and her face like sandpaper. She looked around and discovered she was in a small untidy room. Paul was sprawled across the end of the bed asleep.

She sat up slowly and looked for something to cover herself with. Her head felt it would split open if she moved too rapidly. She pulled a cover off the bed, and wrapping it round her, she got up.

Paul didn't stir. She groped her way to the door and found herself in a tiny hallway piled high with clutter. She made her way through to the bathroom. which was small. rusting and old. She switched on the light. It was a naked bulb. and when she turned on the cold-water tap a large black spider ran disdainfully across the basin. She almost screamed.

Quickly she drank four mugfuls of water. It tasted faintly of toothpaste but made her feel a little better in spite of that.

She stared in the mirror above the basin. Her makeup was smeared and etched into deep lines about her face. Her hair was untidy and matted. I look like I belong here. she thought vaguely.

She padded back into the bedroom and searched for her clothes. When she found them she dressed quickly. She looked at Paul. He slept deeply. She stared at him for a long time and then. finding her coat. she left.

It was cold and silent in the street. Her car coughed and spluttered. and she thought that it would never start. At last it did. and she drove home through the deserted streets.

She let herself quietly into the house and went straight to her bedroom. Everything looked clean and new. She took a hot bath and then collapsed into bed. where she lay and thought. She felt tremendously guilty. and angry at herself for having allowed it to happen. Yes. she had been drunk. but was that any real excuse? She had never imagined herself in the role of the unfaithful wife and it was not something she accepted easily.

What would David say?

Why was her first thought always of David?

At last she fell asleep knowing that in the morning she would have to face him. and that wasn't going to be easy.

She tossed and turned. It was a long and restless night.

5

David left the Turkish baths at eight in the morning feeling refreshed and invigorated. He contemplated phoning Claudia but then decided to wait the day out and see if *she* called him.

He parked his car. bought the morning papers. and then made his way along Park Lane to the Grosvenor House Hotel where he planned to breakfast before going home.

He ordered bacon. eggs. toast. and coffee. and sat back to scan the papers. His eye was immediately caught by a half-page picture on the front page of the *Daily Mirror*. It was captioned MORE NEAR-RIOTS IN TRAFALGAR SQUARE. and the picture was of an angry mob of people surrounding two policemen who were in the process of carrying a woman away from the road. The woman's skirt was high above her knees. so high that you could glimpse her panties. Her hair was flopping over her face. and one shoe was about to fall from her struggling foot. It was an effective picture.

The waitress arrived with his breakfast order. She was plump and cockney. She peered over his shoulder at the paper. ''Ere what does she think she looks like.' she muttered. 'About time all this rubbish was stopped. A load of showoffs. that's what they are. They should lock the lot of 'em up!' She wandered away. cluck-clucking about nothing in particular. David stared at the photo. horrified. The woman was unmistakably Linda. His Linda! He shook his head in disbelief. What was she doing? What was she thinking of?

He gulped his coffee. scalded his tongue. swore. found himself unable to eat anything. and called for the check.

The waitress padded slowly back. 'What's the matter. dear? Everything all right?'

He thrust money at her. 'Everything's fine,' he said and

stormed out.

A parking warden was in attendance beside his car. David brushed impatiently past him.

'I'm afraid you'll have to wait while I finish writing out this ticket, sir,' said the warden. 'I suppose you are aware that this is a restricted zone for parking?'

'Just give me the ticket and get on with it,' said David brusquely.

The warden glared at him and then proceeded to take his time.

David drove away, his face grim. He envisaged what he would say to Linda. The whole thing was so utterly ridiculous. His wife at a protest meeting! It was ludicrous. She didn't know anything about politics or bombs. The kitchen, the children, and social activities such as tea with the girls and dinner out twice a week were her province. Ban the Bomb indeed! Who did she think she was?

Claudia was forgotten. He put his foot hard down on the accelerator and raced home.

Ana let him in. 'Mrs. Cooper, she sleep late,' she announced. 'You like tea?'

'No,' he grunted, already halfway up the stairs to the bedroom.

Linda was asleep, curled up and buried beneath the covers. He drew the curtains, throwing glaring daylight into the room. She didn't stir. He paced the floor, coughed loudly, and when she still didn't appear to show any signs of waking, he went over and shook her roughly, thrusting a copy of the *Daily Mirror* in front of her face as she sleepily opened her eyes.

'What's all this about?' he demanded angrily.

Oh, God, he had found out about her and Paul! How? So soon. She sat up quickly.

David stood there glowering at her as he continued talking. 'What is this? Some secret ambition to make yourself look a complete fool?' He brandished the paper at her again, and she took it from him.

A feeling of relief swept over her when she realized that this was what he was so furious about. 'What an awful photo!' she exclaimed 'I didn't know they were taking pictures.'

'Is that all you have to say?' He mimicked her. 'I didn't know they were taking pictures!' He snatched the paper away and in a loud and angry voice said, 'What were you doing there anyway? What were you thinking of?'

'I had nothing else to do. I just found myself there. I'm sorry that you're so angry about it.'

'I'm not angry,' he screamed. 'I like to see photos of my wife smeared all over the papers, with her skirt around her waist, accompanied by a load of layabouts.'

She got out of bed. 'I'm not going to sit here while you yell at me. Perhaps if you spent a weekend at home for a change this might not have happened.'

Just then the telephone rang. Linda suddenly felt very hot and flushed. Supposing it was Paul? Should she answer it, or would it be best to let David pick it up, and then maybe Paul would hang up. She was convinced it was he.

David swooped down on it and barked into the receiver, 'Yes?'

Linda held her breath, while David launched into a long conversation with someone from his office. She took advantage of his preoccupation on the phone and dressed.

When he had finished talking, he seemed a little calmer.

'Do you want some breakfast?' she asked.

'No. I have to make some calls. There's this party tonight to launch the Beauty Maid soap product; I had forgotten all about it. You had better meet me at the office at seven, and we'll go from there. I hope to Christ nobody saw your publicity.'

She groaned inwardly at the thought of another party, and then mentally planned her day, which included being at home to greet the children and a visit to the hairdresser's.

David meanwhile had his own thoughts. Claudia would most certainly be at the party, she was being paid to be there. He wondered if it would be possible for him to effect a quiet reconciliation without everyone in the room noticing. Had to be sure that Linda didn't become suspicious, she seemed to be getting a little too concerned about him being away so much. Maybe she was beginning to suspect him, although this seemed unlikely, as he had managed to get away with various affairs throughout the years and she had never found him out yet. At least he would be able to see Claudia. He started to make his business calls.

The children burst back into the house at exactly four o'clock. Linda's father was always prompt. She had just returned from the hairdresser's. and Stephen flung his small. wiry body at her, practically knocking her down.

'We've had a smashing time. Mummy.' he exclaimed. 'I'm starving. What's for tea? Grandma makes lovely cakes!'

His sister, Jane, gave Linda a small kiss. She was six and rather shy. 'I'm glad we're home. Mummy. Your hair looks all pretty. Are you and Daddy going out?'

Linda greeted her father and they sat and chatted while Ana served tea and the children rushed around rediscovering their various toys.

She was only half listening as her father droned on about Stephen and Jane's activities during the weekend. She thought about Paul. What did he think of her? Why *hadn't* he telephoned? What would she say if he phoned and David was there?

Finally her father left. and when the children were settled with Ana. having their dinner. she began to get ready. Just as she was about to leave the house. the telephone rang. She so expected it to be Paul that she felt herself break out in a sweat and her hand started to shake as she picked up the receiver. 'Hello.'

'Hello. darling, it's Monica. How about *you*, then! Aren't *you* the dark horse! Fancy leaving us yesterday and not saying a word about where you were going. What does David think about it all?'

'Oh,' replied Linda. 'he's not too pleased.'

Monica laughed. 'Not to worry. Jack and I think it's marvellous. Anyway. sweetie. we're having a few people over after dinner tonight. and we would *love* you and David to come.'

'I don't know. Monica. We have to go to a press party launching the new soap product. I can't say what time we'll be able to get away.'

'Never mind. Just come along when you're finished. You know us, we're *always* late.' She gave no chance to protest. 'See you later, then. Bye.'

Linda replaced the receiver. She really wasn't too fond of Monica and Jack, and certainly didn't feel like seeing them later. However, she would have to tell David, and he would probably want to go.

She left the house in a bad mood with a headache, half-angry and half-relieved that Paul hadn't phoned. She desperately wanted him to, otherwise, what had it all been? A quick one-night affair? A meeting of two people with no more in common than a few hours in bed? However, if he *did* phone, she wanted to tell him that she couldn't possibly see him again, that it had all been a big mistake.

She sighed. At least that way she would be regaining a small amount of self-respect by denying herself something she really wanted. It was all so unexpected. She had really never thought of herself as the sort of woman who could have an affair. And Paul was so much younger than she, and so different from the type of people she knew and mixed with. How had it happened?

She searched her mind and finally concluded that it must be her fault. She resolved to try and put the episode out of her mind and to work desperately to make things more satisfactory between herself and David.

That decision made, she felt better.

It was nine o'clock before Claudia appeared at the Beauty Maid party. David had been watching for her all evening, and suddenly there she was. She materialized beside him, looking exceptionally beautiful, and murmured, 'Good evening, Mr. Cooper.'

He was taken off guard. He was standing talking to a group which included several press and Linda. He became flustered.

Claudia noticed and smiled faintly. People were looking expectantly at him, waiting to be introduced. At last he said, 'Oh, this is Claudia Parker, our Beauty Maid girl.'

Claudia smiled at the group. She was flushed and her eyes shone. David knew at once that she was a little drunk. She wore an orange dress, dangerously low cut, and the women in the gathering found themselves standing up straighter and throwing out their bosoms, as if in answer to this sudden challenge. The men were all obviously impressed.

'Miss Parker?' Ned Rice, a small beady-eyed reporter, pressed toward her. 'What do you *really* think of Beauty Maid soap?' His eyes darted toward her bosom.

Claudia played up to him. She fluttered her very long eyelashes and gave him one of her deep, sexy looks. 'Well,' she said at last, 'actually, I'm an actress, therefore I don't feel I can give you a serious opinion on soap. As a matter of fact, I've just come from seeing Conrad Lee, and he's very interested in having me in his new movie.' She shot David a triumphant look.

Ned Rice was most interested. 'Sounds wonderful. Perhaps we could do a piece about you on our film page.'

'Yes, I'd like that,' she smiled. 'I'll give you my phone number.'

David could stand it no more. He gripped her by the arm, smiled tightly, and said, 'I hope you will excuse us, Miss Parker is here for a purpose. She will be demonstrating our product, and I think she's due to begin pretty soon, so I had better get her over to Phillip Abbottson.'

'Oh, well, Miss Parker,' said Ned Rice, 'I'll see you later and we'll get together on this.'

'Fine.' She gave one last radiant smile around the group and followed David.

As soon as they were out of earshot he exploded. 'You're drunk,' he accused. 'Where have you been? You were supposed to be here by eight.'

She gave him a cool look. 'David, baby, you're nothing in my life, so why don't you just leave me alone.'

'You fucking bitch,' he said in a low voice. His grip tightened on her arm.

'I'm going to make a scene if you don't let go of me,' she said quietly. 'I'm tired of you telling me what I should do. I'm not someone's wife who has to answer questions and account for every second of her life.'

At that moment Phillip Abbottson rushed up to them.

'What *is* going on?' he asked. 'Claudia, you were supposed to be here an hour ago. We're waiting to unveil the display. Get changed, for Christ's sake. You think we want to be here all night?' He gave David an odd look and then with Claudia in tow rushed off again.

Ned Rice sidled up to David. His plump, pasty wife was talking to Linda across the other side of the room. 'Quite a bit, your Miss Parker,' he said with a leer. 'I bet she's a hot little number, a real tiger.'

David endeavoured to remain calm. 'I wouldn't know.'

'In that case I expect it's all right for me to have a bash.' He nudged David. 'These starlets are all the same, y'know. You've just got to tell them you can get their name in print and they open their legs without you even asking.'

David was saved from answering by the arrival of Mrs. Rice and Linda from across the room.

Ned affectionately patted his wife's plump shoulder. 'Enjoying yourself, love?' he asked. Then he waggled an accusing finger at Linda. 'And what were you up to, making front-page news this morning?'

David was beginning to dislike Ned Rice more and more.

Just then the lights in the room were dimmed and a spotlight was focused on a mock stage, set at one end of the room. Phillip Abbottson was standing poised at a microphone. As soon as the chatter died down he launched into a long speech about Beauty Maid soap. He was a good promoter and made a simple bar of soap sound like a solid block of gold. At the end of his speech there was polite scattered applause, and then he stood to one side and said, 'And now I would like to introduce you to Miss Beauty Maid herself!'

The curtains were drawn back, and there sat Claudia, in a marble bath surrounded by bubbles, in fact, an exact replica of the set that was used in the television commercial. She was wearing a flesh-coloured swimsuit, but of course no one could see it, so the general assumption was that she had nothing on beneath the bubbles.

David felt a surge of excitement.

Claudia smiled at her audience and started to recite her

Beauty Maid speech.

Ned Rice whispered something obscene in David's ear.

Mrs. Rice said to Linda, 'Isn't she a pretty little thing?'

Linda stared blankly into space, her thoughts on the night before.

When Claudia finished speaking there was hearty applause from the men and a few jealous titters from the women. Then the curtains were drawn and Phillip appeared back at the microphone with more to say.

David excused himself and made his way behind the stage. The marble bath was now empty, and he noticed a small door at the back of the dais. He hesitated and then went through it.

Claudia was patting herself dry with a towel. She was in a very small office, and her clothes were scattered around in her usual untidy style. She was wearing the flesh-coloured swimsuit, which clung to her like a second skin.

She looked at him wearily. 'What now?'

He walked over to her and put his hands on her shoulders. 'I'm sorry,' he said. 'No more questions.'

She threw him her wide-eyed look. 'Promise?'

'I promise.'

She smiled and snaked her arms around his neck. 'All right, you're forgiven.'

He bent down and kissed her warm, soft lips. Her body was still wet as he put his hands in the top of her swimsuit and slowly peeled it down.

'Not here, you idiot,' she whispered. 'Someone might come in. Anyway, you'll be missed.'

He let go of her and went and turned the key in the lock.

She was giggling softly. 'Oh, David, you really like to take chances.'

He cupped her breasts in his hands and bent to kiss them. She moaned, 'Go on then, you son of a bitch. Do whatever you want, I don't give a damn!'

6

The gathering at Monica's and Jack's was in full swing when Linda and David arrived. It was a mixed crowd, for Monica liked 'group variety,' as she put it. Monica herself was a largish woman heading rapidly toward forty and desperately trying to pull back the other way. She had a lot of very-bright-red hair, which was inclined to be frizzy, and her face, although heavily laden with Elizabeth Arden, was somewhat outdoorsy and even a little horsey. She used a heavy, overpowering, musky perfume which enveloped you like her personality, and was given to talking in a shrieky sort of a voice, her conversation always well peppered with 'dahling' and 'sweetie' and 'oh, my God!'

Jack, in contrast, was rather reserved. He was a little older than David, but they had been close friends for a number of years. He smoked a pipe and had a twirly grey moustache. He always wore suede jerkins or some sort of similar sporty attire. One could imagine him with an enormous mansion tucked away in some rural part of England, walking a large dog through his spacious grounds. He owned a chain of garages and in his younger days had fancied himself as a racing driver. Even now he would often take a test spin on the track to keep his hand in.

Monica grabbed Linda when she arrived, and proudly, with her arm around her, she marched her into the living room and announced dramatically, 'And this is our famous ban the bomber!'

Linda was terribly embarrassed. Monica made her sound like some new type of aeroplane! She knew most of the people there, and they all made some sign of greeting. There was one couple she hadn't met before, a thickset, very dark man, and a silver-blond haughty-looking girl. Monica, as soon as she had finished with her dramatic announcement. introduced her.

'I'd like you to meet Jay and Lori Grossman. friends of mine from America. Jay's here to direct the new Conrad Lee picture.'

'Really.' said Linda. 'How interesting. I met a girl earlier this evening who's going to be in it.'

Jay raised a quizzical eyebrow. 'That *is* interesting.' He spoke with a short. sharp. New York accent. 'We haven't cast at all yet. apart from the male star.'

Linda smiled. 'I expect she's suffering from delusions.'

'What's her name. anyway?' Jay asked.

Linda frowned. 'I can't really remember. My husband will know. she just did a commercial for his company.'

Just then Monica arrived with David and made the introductions again. He had been in a very good mood since leaving the other party. He put his arm around Linda and started to chat easily to the Grossmans.

'Darling.' Linda interrupted him. 'what was the name of that little girl who was doing the Beauty Maid thing?'

'What?' he asked. feeling immediately guilty. 'Why do you want to know?'

Linda looked at him strangely. or anyway he thought she did. 'Do I have to have a reason?' she asked.

He felt the tension build in the short silence that followed, and then he laughed weakly and said, 'Of course not. It's Claudia Parker. Why?'

Jay shook his head. 'Never heard of her.'

'What is this?' questioned David.

'Well.' said Linda. 'you remember she said she was going to be in the new Conrad Lee picture. Jay's directing it. I thought he would know about her. Anyway. apparently she isn't in it or going to be.'

'She didn't say she was in it at all.' said David coldly. 'She said she had been to see Conrad Lee and he liked her. that's all.'

Jay laughed. 'That accounts for the confusion. Conrad is always seeing these poor little broads and stringing them along. Confidentially. the girl is already cast. An unknown Italian kid of sixteen. It builds up the publicity for the film. If we put on a big search for the right girl, and Conrad enjoys seeing them, it makes everyone happy.'

David scowled at him. 'Everyone is happy except the girls whose hopes he builds up.'

Jay shrugged. 'That's show biz. Most of them know the score, and the ones that don't soon learn.' He turned to his wife, who so far hadn't opened her mouth. 'Isn't that so, sweetheart?'

Lori Grossman nodded. Her face never seemed to register any expression. It was like that of a beautiful, but quite blank, painted doll.

'That's how Lori and I met,' Jay continued. 'She was an actress, came for a part, and instead got me. She's my third wife. The other two were actresses as well. I probably met them the same way. Don't even remember now.'

At last Lori spoke. Her voice was a thick Southern drawl. 'I sure would like another drink, honey.'

'Certainly, baby.' Jay stood up. 'How about you, Mrs. Cooper?'

'Please call me Linda. I'd love a gin and tonic.'

Jay went off to fetch the drinks, and Monica arrived back and claimed Linda, dragging her over to some other people to show them the famous newspaper clipping.

Lori crossed long shapely legs.

David's eyes wandered. 'What part of America are you from?' he asked pleasantly.

'I come from Georgia, honey.' She blinked lazily at him. 'But I've lived in Hollywood for the last five years.'

He studied her. She was older than Claudia, about twenty-seven, he reckoned. She looked like one of those thin models out of *Vogue* magazine, everything carefully perfect. He found himself attracted to her. The very perfection made him wonder what she was like in bed. He wondered if that beautiful chignon of silver-blond hair stayed in place; one somehow couldn't imagine her with it out of place. 'How long are you here for?' he asked.

'Several months, I guess,' she drawled. She apparently had no conversation except to answer questions.

There was a silence until David said, 'You and your husband

must come over to our house for dinner one night.'

'That would be fun.' She smiled, displaying two rows of even, white, obviously capped teeth.

Jay returned with the drinks. 'Where's that lovely wife of yours?' he asked.

'Honey, there's no ice in this drink,' said Lori petulantly.

'Screw the ice,' said Jay. 'This is England, baby, they don't go so big on the ice bit.' He turned to David. 'Listen, we have to meet some friends soon at the Candy Club. How about you and Linda coming along with us?'

'This is our second party tonight, and I don't know how tired Linda is, but it sounds like a good idea to me,' David said. 'I'll ask her.'

'Hell, you must come,' said Jay. 'Lori does the craziest dancing you've ever seen. I'll go ask Linda myself.' He went off.

Lori said, 'Gee, honey, what do you do without ice!'

David laughed. 'We usually have ice, we're not that uncivilized. I suppose they've run out.'

She screwed up her nose. 'I like ice,' she stated, and then stared blankly off into space.

He looked at his watch. It was past twelve. Claudia would be safely in bed. She had promised that she was going straight home. 'You've left me fit for nothing else!' she had joked. He wondered if he could telephone her, but then decided it was too late. He didn't want to wake her, and anyway there was nowhere really private that he could phone from. The Candy Club sounded like a good idea, and Lori Grossman's dancing even better.

Jay returned with Linda, smiling broadly. 'I never get no for an answer,' he said with a wink. 'We're all set. Shall we make a move?'

Monica was quite frosty when she found David and Linda departing with the Grossmans. 'Honestly, darlings,' she complained, 'you've only been here two seconds!'

However, they left, and piled into David's Jaguar.

Lori was wrapped in a full-length black-diamond mink coat. It reminded David that he had promised Claudia a jacket. He would get it the next day. she had been so sweet earlier. Or was sweet the right word?

Linda and Jay hit it off very well. They chatted about the differences between England and America. and schools. and where it was best to bring up children. It seemed Jay had three children. all from his previous marriages. Eventually he said to David. 'Hey. your wife is beautiful *and* intelligent. quite a combination.'

Linda was beginning to feel much better. her headache had gone. and she had had just enough to drink to take away any tiredness. She pushed Paul to the back of her mind and was enjoying talking to Jay.

They arrived at the nightclub. Jay asked to be taken straight to Conrad Lee's table.

The great Conrad Lee was a tall. voluble. half-French. half-White Russian man in his late fifties. He was totally bald. very suntanned. with piercing eyes which seemed to glare right through you. even in the dimness of the night-club.

He was at a table with six other people. and he leaped up and embraced Lori. When Linda was introduced he kissed her hand. He smelled strongly of garlic.

The waiters busied themselves trying to squeeze more chairs around the already crowded table while Jay attempted introductions. but it was more or less hopeless as the noise of the band was so loud that you couldn't hear yourself speak.

David stared in amazement and fury at Claudia. She sat beside Conrad. her hair tousled. one strap of her dress falling off her shoulder. much cleavage. She was very drunk. When Conrad sat down his hand caressed her shoulder. pushing the other strap of her dress down. There was another girl on the other side of Conrad. a plump brunette. He had his arm around her too, pinching chunks of her fleshy back between his fingers.

'Got two lovely little girls here.' Conrad said to Jay. and then with a wink. 'Maybe we can use them in the picture.'

Jay raised an eyebrow at Linda. 'See what I mean,' he said with a smile.

'That's the girl I was talking about.' Linda whispered.

'Sure,' said Jay. 'She's got as much chance of getting in the picture as a fly!'

Claudia noticed David then. She was too drunk to be surprised or shocked. She just waved gaily and said. 'What a small world!'

David remembered her saying those exact words to him the first time they met. He scowled at her.

Conrad took Lori off to dance, then Jay claimed Linda, and they went off to dance too.

David sat down in the empty chair beside Claudia.

'You lousy bitch!' he said in a low voice. 'Going straight home to bed; well, I suppose you'll be doing that eventually.'

She looked surprised. 'Baby, what's the matter? I *did* go home, and then Conrad called and said he would like to see me again, so he could come to some decision about the part. I have to think about my career, don't I?'

'You're drunk,' he said in disgust. 'You're acting like a cheap whore. Do you honestly believe all this shit Conrad is feeding you about putting you in his stinking film? I credited you with more brains than that.'

She looked at him coldly. 'Shut up, you make me sick. You're just jealous, that's all. The only time you act sweet is when you've got a hard-on!'

He wanted to slap her. She sat there, glaring at him, and for one lucid moment he saw not his beautiful Claudia, but a hard calculating face over a well-developed, highly exhibited body.

'Your tits are hanging out!' he said.

'So?' she replied. 'Why not? Are you the only one that's supposed to see them?'

The plump brunette the other side of David suddenly tugged his arm. 'Are you a film producer too?' she asked. Her eyes were large and round and somewhat bloodshot.

'No,' he said curtly.

Conrad and Lori returned to the table. David stood up. Lori was very tall. She stood there remote and cool. David could see that Claudia was watching her jealously. He took hold of Lori's arm quickly. 'What about another dance?' he said. 'I want to see this wild dancing of yours.'

Claudia shot him a dirty look and then focused her charm on Conrad again.

'That would be fun. honey,' drawled Lori, and they headed for the dance floor.

She danced beautifully. 'I used to be a showgirl in Vegas,' she confided.

The evening dragged on. Claudia got drunker and drunker, and she and Conrad closer and closer. The plump brunette was obviously forgotten. Linda and Jay chatted on. Lori sat silently, only speaking when someone spoke to her. David lounged morosely. watching Claudia and Conrad and occasionally attempting to flirt with Lori in case Claudia might be watching *him*.

At two in the morning Linda said with a yawn. 'I think we had better be going. I'm absolutely exhausted.'

No one else in the party seemed interested in leaving, so they said their good-byes. Claudia said good-bye with a drunken smile and then turned to concentrate on Conrad, who by this time was as drunk as she was.

Jay insisted on coming with them to the car where they exchanged phone numbers and promised to all get together again soon.

At last they were alone. Linda leaned back in the car and closed her eyes.

David said. not really meaning it, but wanting to take his bad temper out on someone. 'You and that phony director were getting very friendly.'

She opened her eyes. 'No more friendly than you and that trampy soap model.'

He shot her a dark look. 'I didn't even talk to her. I don't know what you mean.'

'Oh David. really.' She sighed. 'You didn't even talk to *anyone*, you were so annoyed she was with Conrad Lee. Any fool could see that.' She paused, then added curiously, 'Have you ever taken her out?'

He stared furiously at the road ahead. 'What a ridiculous question.'

'I just wondered. You seemed so interested in her. Even at the first party you kept on getting in little huddles with her.'

'She works for us. Linda I was trying to see that the display thing went off smoothly. that's all.'

They lapsed into silence. He switched the car radio on.

'Darling,' Linda said quickly, tentatively, 'what's wrong?'

'What do you mean, what's wrong?'

'I mean, what's wrong with us? What's happening to us? Why are we so far apart all of a sudden?'

He turned off the radio. 'I didn't know we were so far apart.'

She looked out of the car window—they were driving through the park, and the trees looked dark and ominous as they sped past them. 'It's funny, David, this must have been starting to happen to us for years, and yet neither of us realized it, neither of us tried to stop it. We're almost like strangers now, and the only thing we have in common are the children.'

'I think you're overtired, you're talking a lot of nonsense.'

'A lot of nonsense,' she repeated. 'Is that what you really think?' Tears started to roll silently down her cheeks. 'When did you last make love to me? When did you last *want* to?'

'Oh, so that's what this is about.'

She fought to keep her tears under control. 'No, that's not what this is about, but it's part of it.'

He pulled the car into the side of the road and stopped.

Then he turned to face her. What could he say? That he didn't find her exciting anymore? That Claudia was a better lay? She was right, really, they were far apart.

'Do you remember our honeymoon?' she questioned.

Yes, he remembered their honeymoon. Spain, hot and sticky, and long pleasurable nights with Linda, an innocent young Linda, who awoke all sorts of desires and ambitions in him. 'Yes, I remember our honeymoon,' he said quietly.

'Why can't things be like they were then?' She looked at him plaintively.

'Linda, we're both ten years older. Things don't stand still, you know.'

'Yes, I know.' She thought—Paul makes me feel ten years younger. He makes me feel attractive and desirable. He makes me feel wanted.

David said, 'We'd better be getting home. I need to get to the office early in the morning.'

'Yes, all right.' She thought, why don't you take me in your arms? Why don't you throw me down on the back seat and make love to me here? Why don't you worry about what *I* need?

They drove home in an uneasy silence, both realizing that there was more unsaid than said.

The house seemed cold and dark. Linda went in to look at the children. Jane slept curled up in a ball, her thumb stuck firmly in her mouth. Stephen had kicked all his covers off and nearly fallen out of bed. She covered him and kissed him lightly on the forehead. They were so innocent, her two precious children. So young and pure.

David was taking a shower. Linda undressed and settled into bed. She wondered if because of what she had said he would want to make love tonight.

He didn't He returned from the bathroom, got into bed, switched the light off, muttered, 'Good night,' and appeared to go straight off to sleep.

She lay there angry and frustrated. I tried, she thought, I really tried to talk to him. But he doesn't seem to care what's happening to us, he doesn't seem to *mind*.

The morning dawned bleak and raining.

David was up at seven. He shaved, showered, and dressed without disturbing Linda. He was out of the house by eight.

She awoke shortly after. Jane was standing beside the bed. 'Mummy, can I come in for a cuddle, please?' the little girl requested.

'Yes, of course, darling.'

'I hate Stevie,' Jane confided. 'He's a nasty, rough boy. I wish boys were girls!'

'Yes, that's a very good idea,' replied Linda, smiling.

The morning passed in a flurry of domesticity. The children started school the following day, and there was a lot to be done. School uniforms to be assembled, books to be found, everything washed and clean.

Linda had no time to think, and in the afternoon she had promised to take them to a movie.

There was no message from Paul. She was both hurt and yet relieved.

When they returned from the theatre she phoned David. He wasn't in the office so she left a message for him to call her as soon as he returned. Jay Grossman had phoned and left a number. She rang him back.

'We were wondering if you and David would care to join us for dinner tomorrow night?' he said. 'Lori just can't wait to go to the Savoy Grill—she's heard Princess Margaret goes there and figures we're bound to be at the next table!'

Linda laughed. 'I'll have to check with David. Can you call back later?'

David didn't phone until past seven. 'I'll be late,' he said shortly.

'How late?'

'I don't know, probably around twelve.'

'Where do you have to go?'

His voice was angry. 'What is this, a cross-examination?'

She replied coldly, 'No, it's not a cross-examination, but I think I'm entitled to know why you're going to be late.'

There was a silence, then, 'I'm sorry, of course you are. I'm tired, I suppose. Actually, I've got a late meeting with Phillip.'

'Why don't you bring him back here and I'll give you both dinner.'

'No, it's all right, we'll grab a sandwich next door and get on with things.'

'I'll see you later, then.'

'Yes, don't wait up.' He hesitated, then asked, 'How are the children?'

'They're fine. In a state of excitement about school tomorrow.'

'Give them a kiss for me. Bye.'

'Bye.' She hung up and yawned. It's an early night for me, she thought, then she remembered that Jay would be phoning back about dinner the following evening. Quickly she picked up the phone and dialled David's private number at the office. It rang and rang, but there was no reply.

She hung up and went and looked in the phone book for Phillip's number. David was probably in *his* office. She couldn't find Phillip's number, but his home number was there, so she dialled that. His wife, Mary, answered.

'I'm sorry to bother you,' said Linda, 'but can you give me Phillip's private number at the office?'

'Yes, of course,' said Mary, sounding slightly surprised. 'I'm expecting him home any minute, so I don't think there will be any reply.'

Now it was Linda's turn to sound surprised. 'But isn't he working late with David?'

'No, he's definitely on his way home. We've got his mother for dinner. He'll be here any minute.'

'Oh,' said Linda quietly. 'I must have made a mistake.'

'Hang on a sec,' said Mary. 'I think I hear him at the door now.'

Linda was left hanging numbly onto the receiver. She felt stunned. So David was lying. Why was he lying? How long had he been lying? And why was it only now, when she herself had been unfaithful, that she had to find out? It was obviously another woman. She felt sick.

Phillip's harsh voice boomed down the phone. 'Hello, Linda. What's your problem?'

She forced her voice to be light. 'No problem, Phillip, I'm just trying to track David down. I thought he said he was working with you, but I must have got it wrong.'

Phillip sounded embarrassed. 'I can't help you. David left the office early today.' He added as an afterthought, 'He's probably out with Mr Smythson or someone from up north. We seem to have a whole group of people visiting this week.'

'Thank you, Phillip,' said Linda. She wanted to say, 'You don't have to try and make excuses for him.' Instead she said, 'I'm sure you're right. Good-bye.'

So this was the answer to her questions. It all tied in. Late nights home, weekends away on business, no real physical interest in her. This must have been subconsciously why she found herself in bed with Paul. They say there is a certain point in every marriage where a woman is at the crossroads as to whether to go to bed with someone else or not, and depending on the state of her marriage at the time, she makes her decision.

It's true, thought Linda; if things had been all right with David and me, then I would never have looked twice at Paul.

It all seemed so wrong. and to add insult to injury. Paul hadn't even rung her. She felt used. By both of them. And she didn't even know what move to make next. Tears seemed threateningly and uselessly close.

7

David awoke on Tuesday morning early. with one thought uppermost in his mind. and that was to get out of the house, reach a telephone. and phone Claudia.

It was seven o'clock. and Linda lay sleeping quietly. so quietly in fact that for a moment he contemplated using the phone in the house. but realizing the probable folly of this. decided against it.

He shaved. showered. dressed hurriedly. and left. He drove as far as Baker Street before stopping at a pay phone. He dialled the number and listened to it ring. but no one answered. so he redialled. but still no reply. He let it ring for a long time. but to no avail. At last he reached the obvious conclusion that she was either out or too deeply asleep to be disturbed.

He jumped back into his car. and with a sudden flash of decision drove to where she lived.

This time it was the doorbell he rang to no avail.

'Bitch!' he muttered to himself. 'Dirty little bitch!'

He hung around outside for a while. but eventually realizing the futility of this. he drove sourly to his office.

Every half-hour he rang her number. getting more and more angry each time it wasn't answered. At eleven it was finally picked up by her cleaning woman.

'Miss Parker,' he snapped.

The daily's voice was full of cockney richness. 'I fink she's asleep. 'Old on a tick. I'll go 'ave a look.' She returned after a short pause. 'She ain't in,' she stated. 'Any message?'

He said. 'You don't happen to know what time she went out?'

'Can't say that I do. Don't fink she's bin 'ere since yesterday, 'cos 'er bed ain't bin slept in.'

'Thank you,' he said. 'There's no message.'

He imagined her with Conrad. Her smooth, beautiful body

crushed to his. going through the motions of love-making which she practised so expertly. He could almost hear her small exquisite cries of excitement. her little moans. and the way she muttered crude words in a low. throaty voice. He swore.

After that he rang her apartment every hour. putting the phone down when the cleaning woman answered. He was furious with himself for being so hung up about her. He had always prided himself on never getting too deeply involved emotionally. always being able to shut other people out of his life when he had had enough of them. But this time it was different. Whatever she did. he couldn't seem to get Claudia out of his mind.

At four o'clock she finally picked up her phone. The record player was very loud in the background. and she sounded in good spirits. He listened to her voice saying 'Hello.' then a pause. then—'Hello. is anyone there?' Then another longer pause. and then—'Oh. screw you. whoever it is!' And the phone was slammed down.

He left the office at once and drove straight over to where she lived. He didn't want to fight with her on the phone. he wanted to see her. hear the excuses. watch her lie.

She answered her front door and looked surprised and a little guilty to see him. She was wearing very tight white slacks and a mansized black sweater. Her face was devoid of any make-up. and although she looked tired. her brilliant green eyes shone with an alert. triumphant expression.

'Surprise. surprise!' she said. 'Come on in.'

He followed her into the flat. A very loud Rolling Stones 'Satisfaction' was turned up full volume. A half-bottle of Scotch and a giant pink fluffy toy poodle stood on the table.

'Want a drink?' she asked.

'It's four o'clock in the afternoon.' he said coldly.

'Oh. dear!' she muttered. like a naughty child caught doing something wrong. She poured herself a stiff Scotch. lit a cigarette. and flopped down on the floor. 'Well. David. what is there to say?'

'There's plenty to say.' He paced the room angrily and added menacingly. 'Plenty.'

She giggled. 'Do stop it with the wronged-husband bit. I *told* you I wasn't tied to anyone. I warned you that no man tells me what to do.'

He shook his head at her. 'I don't understand you. Sometimes you act like a cheap whore.'

She rolled over on her stomach, taking a long drag of her cigarette, and blowing the smoke toward him. Then she said calmly, 'I'm in a very good mood today, nothing can spoil it, not even you.'

She rolled onto her back and stretched, the taut outline of her breasts appearing through her sweater. He felt the familiar hot desire creep up on him.

'Conrad Lee is a very important man, and he's going to do a lot for me.'

'Sure, he'll do a lot for you,' said David bitterly. 'He'll do a lot for you in bed.'

'I'm testing this week for his new film. How about that?'

'Balls!'

'You're just jealous, that's all. You'll see, he's going to make a star out of me.'

'You're making a fool of yourself. The *director* of the film said that this is Conrad's hobby, stringing along little girls like you.'

'Come on, David dear. The last thing I am is a little girl. I'm nobody's fool. I know the score. *You* should know that.'

'How was he in the sack?'

Her eyes met his. They were big and green and bright. 'He wasn't anything like you.' She stood up and wrapped her arms around him. 'No one's like you,' she whispered, 'no one's ever been like you.' The fight was over.

It was slow, and warm, and tender. Afterward they lay on the floor where he had taken her, locked in each other's arms.

She kissed him softly. 'You must understand,' she whispered, 'it doesn't mean I don't love you. When I sleep with him, it's nothing. He's a pig, an old pig. But, baby, I want to be in his movie. I want to be in it *so much*. And I'm going to, I promise you that.'

He flicked his hands over her soft breasts. 'You're so beautiful, when I'm with you I don't care what you've been doing. So get in his lousy movie if you must. But don't sleep with him or anyone else again, or I'll beat the shit out of you!'

She pressed closer to him. 'I love it when you play tough.'

It's impossible, he thought, impossible that it can happen again so soon, and be that much better. She's like a tigress. They should cage her naked in the zoo for all to see, for only seeing is believing. And they should pin a notice to her cage—'Do not feed. Only eats men.'

Out of the blue Claudia said, 'Your wife's very attractive, isn't she?'

'She used to be. I suppose she still is, really.'

'How old is she?' asked Claudia, a typical woman's question.

He wasn't interested in discussing Linda. 'Thirty something. I don't know.'

'I wonder what *I'll* look like when I'm thirty.'

He was saved from answering by the phone.

Claudia reluctantly lifted the receiver.

'Oh, hello,' she said softly. She glanced quickly over at David. He immediately wondered who it was. 'I'd like that,' she was saying. 'About what time?' She balanced the receiver under her chin and fumbled for a cigarette from the table. 'All right, see you tomorrow. Look forward to it.' She hung up. 'I'm starving!' she exclaimed. 'I feel like going out for a fabulous exciting dinner.'

'Who was that?' he asked, trying to keep his voice casual.

'Who was what?' she asked, knowing perfectly well what he meant.

'On the phone.'

She hesitated for just a second too long before saying, 'It was my agent. He wants me to have dinner with him and his wife tomorrow night.'

'Friendly of him, just like that he starts asking you to dinner.'

'Yes, just like that,' she said patiently. 'As a matter of fact, I called him earlier and told him I wanted to see him about this Conrad thing. I'm going to take a long bath. Can we go out later? Or have you got to rush home?'

He thought she was lying, but what was the point in arguing.

'Do you *want* me to be free?'

'Of course I do. otherwise I wouldn't have asked you.'

'I'll phone home. Where do you want to go? I'll book a table.'

'Let's go somewhere great for a change. We always have to hide out in some old dive. What does it matter if we're seen. After all. I *am* Miss Beauty Maid. so I'm business. really. Let's go to Carlo's.'

Carlo's was a very expensive. very fashionable Italian restaurant. It was *the* place to go. *the* place to be seen. David knew he was taking a ridiculous risk going there with Claudia. He was sure to see people he knew. However. on the other hand. he *wanted* to be seen with Claudia. He *wanted* people to know that she was his.

'O.K., you go and make yourself pretty. and I'll book a table for eight o'clock.'

She kissed him lightly. 'Divine. darling.'

He gave her a playful tap on the bottom. 'Put some clothes on. or we'll never get out!'

Giggling. she retired to the bathroom.

He read the evening papers. booked a table at the restaurant. He felt guilty about phoning Linda. but eventually he did. and then snapped at her when she asked what he had to do. He produced some suitable lies. felt badly about the whole thing, inquired after the children in a fit of conscience. and then hung up.

Claudia reappeared after a time. transformed. Her glossy ash-blond hair was piled on top of her head in studied confusion, her makeup was smooth and perfect. She wore a slinky black dress and rows and rows of jet beads. She looked stunning.

David told her so. and she smiled and preened and showed off her dress to him. flitting around the room like some beautiful exotic bird. 'Isn't it *exciting* going out somewhere *decent* together!' she exclaimed. 'I do wish we could do it more often.'

In the car on the way to the restaurant he had second thoughts. It was a stupid thing to do. Linda was bound to find out. and then what? Especially as she seemed to be so sensitive about their marriage lately. He glanced quickly over at Claudia. She was fiddling with the radio. trying to find music.

'Why don't we drive out somewhere nice in the country instead?'

She stared at him, her big eyes frosty. 'I knew you'd get cold feet. *You* go to the country. Let me out. I'm sick of hiding all over the place.'

'All right, we'll go to Carlo's.' To hell with it. Linda probably wouldn't find out. They said wives were always the last to know.

The restaurant was very crowded. The headwaiter said their table would be a few minutes, so they sat at the bar. Claudia greeted several people. David was relieved to see no one he knew.

A girl came up to them, dragging a weedy-looking young man behind her. She was thin and suntanned, and quite pretty. 'Gorgeous!' she said to Claudia. 'You look fabulous! Where *have* you been, haven't seen you for ages!' She dragged the young man alongside her. '*You* remember Jeremy.'

Jeremy blushed and stuttered, 'Hello.'

'We're engaged! Can you imagine!' She giggled and gave Jeremy a playful poke in the ribs. He looked acutely embarrassed.

'Shirley!' exclaimed Claudia. 'How marvellous!' She turned to David. 'Shirl, darling, this is David Cooper, a very old friend of mine.'

Shirley extended a small suntanned hand, and David shook it briefly.

Claudia continued, 'And, David, I'd like you to meet Shirley's fiancé, the Honourable Jeremy Francis.'

Jeremy edged forward. 'Jolly glad to meet you, old boy.' He had sandy-coloured skin, liberally dotted with angry red acne.

'Sit down and have a drink,' said Claudia. 'We must celebrate!'

They found extra chairs and sat down. The girls immediately went into a huddle about the dresses they were wearing. The Honourable Jeremy sat uncomfortably on the edge of his chair. He was extremely tall, and his knees bumped David's under the table.

'We're going to have an *enormous* wedding,' Shirley was now saying. 'It will be simply marvellous. Jeremy's parents know absolutely everyone!' She flashed a large emerald-and-diamond ring at Claudia. 'Look!' she said dramatically. 'Asprey's!'

Claudia said. 'It's divine. I love it. I'm so happy for you both.'

'And now, what about *you?*' questioned Shirley, shooting a meaningful look at David.

Claudia laughed. 'You know how *I* feel about marriage. It's not for me, Shirl baby. *I* like being single. Anyway, *you* met Jeremy first!'

Jeremy blushed and looked suitably flattered.

David stood up. 'I think our table's ready.'

'Did you *book?*' said Shirley wistfully. 'We forgot, and now we've got to wait simply ages for a table, and I'm *starving.*' She hesitated for a second or two and then continued. 'I say, why don't we all have dinner together? I haven't seen you in *such* ages, Claudia, and it would be great fun!'

'We have a table for two,' said David grimly.

'We don't mind being a bit cramped, do we, Jeremy?'

Jeremy nodded blankly.

'What do you say?' Shirley turned to Claudia.

Claudia looked hopelessly at David. 'Fine, we'd love it.'

They followed the waiter to their table, Shirley waving and smiling to several people on the way.

'I think this is a simply marvellous place,' she said to Claudia as they reached their table. 'I'm sure if one sat here for a week one would see absolutely everyone one ever knew pass by, sort of like London airport!' She giggled loudly.

David sat through the dinner in sullen silence, and Jeremy didn't have much to say, so it was Shirley who did all the talking, with Claudia occasionally joining in. Shirley was an avid reader of *Queen* magazine, especially the society pages, and her main topics of conversation were who had been seen with whom, and what good parties were going on. Jeremy apparently was asked to most of them, and Shirley went into minute details about the most boring items. For example, Lady Clarissa Colt wearing the same dress to two different parties, and the Honourable Amanda Lawrence having a coming-out party where they ran out of champagne. 'It was too awful,' wailed Shirley. 'One just *never* should run short of champers! Too embarrassing!'

Eventually. when they reached dessert. Jeremy took her off to the small dance floor where they clung limply together.

'Let's get out of here,' said David. 'I've heard just as much as I can take from the stupid, snotty cow.'

'I'm sorry, baby,' replied Claudia soothingly. 'She is a bit much.'

'A bit much! That's an understatement if ever I heard one. Who is she. anyway?'

A smile played softly around Claudia's mouth. 'When I first came to London, I worked in a club. Miss Fancy Pants worked there too.'

'What were you doing in a club?' asked David. surprised.

'I had to earn some money. and this actor I arrived with never seemed to work, so I took a job in a club.'

'Doing what?'

'The dance of the seven veils!' she laughed.

'What! You must be joking.'

Her smile faded slightly. 'I'm not joking. Look, I had no talent for doing anything else: It was either that or being a hostess and getting pawed about by a lot of dirty old men. I would sooner take my clothes off any day. They could look. but they couldn't touch.'

'I don't know anything about you. really. do I?'

Her large eyes turned suddenly remote. 'You've never bothered to listen. Like all men. your prime concern is to get me in the sack as fast as possible.'

There was a short silence. then she gave a quick. brittle laugh. 'I'm sorry. my past is a big drag anyway. why *would* you want to hear about it.'

David was about to reply when Shirley and Jeremy returned.

'Jeremy's made the most divine suggestion,' said Shirley. 'There is a simply dinky little nightclub opened down at Windsor. and he says why don't we all pop down there.'

David looked at her sourly. 'At the Castle. naturally.'

For a moment Shirley's pale blue eyes glinted angrily. then she grimaced and laughed quickly. replying. '*No* sweetie, *not* at the Castle.'

'Count us out, then,' snapped David.

'I say, old chap, are you sure?' stammered Jeremy.

Claudia broke hurriedly into the conversation. 'David's tired: You two run along, and if we change our minds we'll join you later.'

'All right,' said Shirley. 'But *do* try and make it.' She grabbed Jeremy by the arm. 'Come along, sweetie, we'll leave these two lovebirds on their own.'

She shot a dark glance at David, waved gaily at Claudia, and towing Jeremy along behind her, they made their exit.

Claudia started to laugh.

'I don't happen to think it's so funny,' said David grimly. 'I suppose I'm stuck with the check as well. Many thanks for a delightful evening.'

Her laughter increased. 'I'm sorry. But honestly, it *is* funny. If you had known Shirley a few years ago, well, I mean, you just wouldn't believe it. She was anybody's and everybody's!'

His tone was cold: 'And you?'

Abruptly she stopped laughing. She stared at him for a few seconds and then said slowly and deliberately, 'I think we have just about reached the end of our relationship, if you could ever call it that.' Before he had a chance to reply, she got up from the table, and threading her way through the restaurant, vanished out of sight. Quickly he called for the check.

'It's David Cooper, isn't it?' The voice was loud and American.

David looked startled. There stood Jay Grossman. 'Well, hello,' he said uneasily.

'Where's Linda?' Jay stared pointedly at the recently occupied place across the table.

David wondered if he had seen Claudia leave, then decided he hadn't. Otherwise, as he was only a casual acquaintance, he would never have made such an obvious remark. 'She's at home,' said David, then indicating the rest of the table he continued, 'I had a business meeting and they all had to rush off.'

At that moment the waiter presented the check.

David threw down some money and quickly got up.

'Nice seeing you, Jay.'

Jay was not to be dismissed. 'Come and say hello to Lori. She'd be most upset if I told her I'd seen you and hadn't brought you over for a drink.'

'Only for a minute,' said David reluctantly. 'Linda's expecting me home.'

The Grossmans were sitting at a table across the other side of the room. David was pleased to note that they couldn't see his table from where they sat. Jay had only spotted him by chance on his way back from the men's room.

Lori looked as aloof and perfectly groomed as before, every shining blond strand of hair arranged carefully in place, her face a mask of flawless makeup. She wore a pale-brown chiffon dress, which dipped revealingly between her breasts.

'Nice to see you again,' said David, unable to keep his eyes from straying down her neckline.

'Likewise,' she replied in her faintly suggestive, empty drawl.

'Come on—sit down and have a drink,' said Jay.

'Well—' He sought wildly for an excuse, couldn't find one, and anyway, what the hell—Eyes fixed firmly on Lori's neckline, he sat down.

'What'll you have?' asked Jay.

'A Scotch on the rocks.'

Jay summoned the waiter while Lori produced a small gold compact and proceeded to touch up an already perfect makeup.

'I spoke to Linda earlier,' Jay said. 'She mentioned she was going to talk to you about joining us for dinner tomorrow night.'

'Oh,' said David blankly—his mind was half on the fact that Claudia had walked out on him—what a bitch! and half on the fact that he had a strong fancy for Mrs. Cool. Dumb Grossman. What a revelation to get her into bed and penetrate beneath the layers of makeup, eyelashes, and hair pieces. 'Good idea. Where do you want to go?'

'Lori rather likes the idea of the Savoy Grill.'

'Yeah.' Lori put down her compact for one brief moment. 'I've heard it's fantastic. You get to see Princess Margaret and that cute guy she's married to.'

'They don't exactly do a cabaret there,' said David, smiling. 'But they have been known to go there.'

Jay said. 'Shall we meet at our hotel?'

They chatted a short while longer, and then David made his excuses and left. He tipped the attendant who brought his car around and sat morosely in it. Screw little Miss Hot Pants Parker. She was becoming too much. First of all she talked him into going to a restaurant he didn't even want to go to. Then she lumbered him with her dreary friends. Then she admitted to working in a strip joint, and got insulted when he commented on it. And then she had the utter nerve to walk out on him!

On top of all this, she had been to bed with that fat slob of a producer the previous evening. She was nothing but a slut, an easy lay. If he wasn't careful he might even *catch* something from her.

She could get lost. He was going home.

He headed his car toward Hampstead. It was ten o'clock.

8

After a while Linda stopped crying. Where was *that* going to get her? She went into the bathroom and washed her face. then stared at her reflection in the mirror. She didn't know what to do. She knew she couldn't face the prospect of sitting around waiting for David to finally arrive home. fresh from the arms of some tramp. She had no one to telephone. Since marrying. she had gradually lost touch with all her girl friends—they had all drifted apart. got married. and gone off to live in different parts of the country. She thought of phoning her mother. but to confide in her would be ridiculous. Her mother had never really approved of David and would be only too pleased. In desperation she phoned Monica.

Monica was cool. 'Absolutely charming the way you stayed five minutes and then dragged off my most important guests. I mean. really, darling—a bit off.'

Their conversation was brief. and when Linda hung up. she thought, the hell with it. I'm not a child. and she picked up the phone again and dialled Paul's number.

He answered immediately. 'Hello.'

She got cold feet and froze, not saying anything. Then she hung up in a panic.

He phoned back at once. 'Linda, this is Paul; I know you just called me.'

She was taken aback.

'Look—I've been *waiting* for you to phone. I knew you would. Can I see you? Can you come over?'

'When?' she muttered weakly.

'How about now?'

'I don't know . . .'

'Please, I must talk to you '

'Well, all right. I'll be there in half an hour.'

'Great.' He gave her the address in case she had forgotten it.

She was surprised. Ego had told her that he would remember her, but she hadn't expected him to be *waiting* to see her, *expecting* her to phone.

She got ready swiftly before she changed her mind, and drove the five-minute distance to where he lived. It was an old house converted into apartments, squashed between a butcher's shop and a vet on the main High Street. She climbed five flights of stairs before reaching number 8.

He answered her knock immediately.

'I don't really know what I'm doing here,' she blurted.

He took her by the hand and led her inside. 'You look lovely. I've been going mad waiting for you to phone.'

'Why didn't *you* phone me?'

'Look, Linda—I understand your scene. I don't want to put you in a bad position. It was up to you to make the next move.'

He made her feel very young, although she could give him at least ten years. 'I know nothing about you,' she murmured.

'You're always saying that,' he replied. He was wearing paint-stained faded Levi's and a white sweater. He looked very attractive.

They were standing in a small, dark room with black walls hung with lots of paintings, some framed, some unframed, mostly nudes with exotic thin faces, masses of hair, and voluptuous bodies. The only furniture was a teak Danish dining table—piled high with papers—and a battered old scarlet couch. She sat on the couch, and he offered her beer or vodka. She elected to have vodka.

He fixed her drink, then put a Billie Holliday record on and sat beside her.

'About the other night,' she began nervously, 'it should never have happened—I'd had a fight with my husband, and I had too much to drink. . . .'

He took her hand. 'You don't have to make excuses. It did happen, and it was great. If you're embarrassed about it, well, you didn't *have* to see me again. I didn't call you back for that reason.'

She took another gulp of vodka. 'I just wanted to explain.' She hesitated and then rushed on. 'I just didn't want to leave you with the wrong impression of me.'

'You left me with a beautiful impression. your perfume was all over my bed. and the smell of your body. and the way you cried out when you came.' He reached over for her and she halfheartedly tried to pull away. But their mouths met and she was lost. He was young and full of strength. and this time she was almost sober. His whole feeling seemed to be to try to please her. and in return she found herself twice as adept at thrilling him. They made love for a long time. and it was very very good. Afterward they lay and talked.

She felt so peaceful and protected by him. He listened quietly while she told him about David and his indifference toward her. She told him everything about herself. about the children, about her life. They smoked cigarettes and drank more vodka.

She found out about him too. He was an artist. He had left art school a year before and was now working as assistant to the art editor of a glossy woman's magazine. The paintings on the wall were all his. She found out they were of an ex girl friend called Margarethe.

It was a sad story. They met at art school and fell in love. After living together for six months they decided to get married. Paul's mother was dead and his father. a retired businessman, lived in Cheltenham. He took Margarethe to meet father. She met father, and three days later she married him.

Paul was stunned: he couldn't believe it. He had a terrible fight with both of them and hadn't seen or heard from them since.

'I couldn't accept it.' he said. 'I don't believe she could have loved him: I suppose she wanted his money. *I* couldn't offer her any security.'

'How do you feel about her now?' questioned Linda.

'I don't know.' he said moodily. 'She's a bitch. They just went off one afternoon and came back married.'

'Why do you still keep your paintings of her around?'

He shrugged. 'Just to remind me not to be such a jerk again. I can't make it with girls anymore. y'know. Maybe once or twice, then I just don't want to know.'

She remembered whiny-voiced, pretty little Melanie.

'I imagine I'm all right because I'm married?' she guessed.

'I think you're great.'

They lay in silence for a while, both mulling over their problems.

'The thing that really gets me,' he said, 'is imagining Margarethe living in Cheltenham with my old man. She was such a swinger. She liked to ball more than anyone I ever knew. I just can't see her fancying him. He's so old.'

'What was your mother like?'

'It's a long story.'

She leaned over and kissed him lightly on the forehead.

'Tell me about it,' she said gently.

'You sound like a psychiatrist,' he laughed. 'Actually, it's a *lousy* story. She killed herself when I was fifteen.'

Linda was shocked. She wanted to ask why—but Paul had turned over on his side and closed his eyes. 'It's a drag,' he muttered. 'I'll tell you about it some other time.'

After a while she looked at her watch, and seeing that it was past eleven said, 'Look, I had better be leaving. David's going to be home at twelve.'

'Why don't you stay the night?' he mumbled, his back still to her.

'I'd like to, but I just can't not be there when he gets home—he knows I never stay out—he'd probably call the police.'

'It's funny, isn't it,' Paul said. 'All the little birds I bang and can't get rid of.' He put on a high thin voice. 'Oh, darling, let me stay the night—Mummy and Daddy never expect me before morning.' They both laughed. 'I tell you, it's horrible, they just will not go. And you know what it's like to screw someone and then not be able to stand them near you after. Y'know, Linda, you're the first female since Margarethe I've asked to stay the night—and you say no.'

She dressed slowly as Paul lay lazily back in bed watching her.

'Y'know, you're very sexy. I wouldn't mind seeing you in long black nylons and a black garter belt.'

'What would you do. take pictures?'

'No—I'd paint you—sort of lying on a sofa. *Very sexy*. Can I?'

'I'll think about it.' She laughed. slightly embarrassed. Eventually she was ready to go.

'When am I going to see you?' he asked.

'I don't know.'

'Tomorrow?'

'I don't know. Paul. It's very difficult for me to make plans.'

'You can't leave without telling me when.'

'I'l phone you in the morning.'

He gave her his phone number at work. kissed her long and hard. and she set off on her journey home. It was eleven-thirty.

9

Claudia left the restaurant in a fury. She hailed a taxi and directed it to Conrad Lee's hotel She was fed up with David Cooper. Stupid bastard—just who did he think he was? At first their affair had been fun. She enjoyed affairs with married men, they were a race apart, and always a challenge. Also, she had misguidedly thought he might be able to help her career.

Nothing. He had done absolutely nothing. Being Miss Beauty Maid appeared to lead to a dead end. He hadn't even given her a decent present, just a lot of unkept promises. So where was the famous mink jacket she was supposed to get? She didn't want money from him. How dare he offer her money like some cheap whore. But presents were a different matter.

'Cheapskate,' she muttered under her breath. He had even complained about picking up the check in the restaurant.

The taxi pulled up at the hotel, and a doorman leaped forward to escort her in.

She strolled coolly over to reception. 'I'd like to speak to Mr. Conrad Lee.'

They put her through on the house phone. After a while the operator said there was no reply.

'Would you try the phone in the bedroom please,' she said.

The phone rang several times before it was picked up. 'Yeah?' His voice was thick and unfriendly.

'Conrad, this is Claudia Parker.'

'Who?'

'Claudia Parker,' she repeated patiently. 'You can't have forgotten last night already.'

There was a short pause: then, 'Oh, yeah, of course. How are you, baby? What can I do for you?'

'Your secretary called me earlier about seeing you tomorrow

night—I was out with this dreary guy, and I suddenly thought the hell with it, what about tonight.'

He laughed, coughed unattractively, and said, 'Listen, baby, I'm all tied up tonight.'

'Oh.' She sounded disappointed. 'Look, I'm very adaptable. I never find three a crowd.'

'Do you mean what I think you mean?' he questioned.

'Of course I do,' she purred. 'You were so fantastic last night, I don't mind sharing.'

'Hang on a minute,' Conrad said, and the phone was muffled. She waited patiently, and soon his voice came back full of interest. 'Come right on up. We'll be waiting.'

She hung up, smiling, and made her way leisurely to the powder room, where for the next twenty minutes she touched up her makeup and rearranged her hair so that it fell around her shoulders thick and shiny. She looked very gorgeous, young, sexy and pretty. Her figure was shown off to its best advantage in the low-cut black dress she was wearing.

A half-hour had passed by the time she finally knocked on the door of his suite.

He answered it immediately—wearing a green-and-orange-striped bathrobe. 'Where the fuck have you been?' he demanded.

She smiled apologetically, walked into the living room and sat down, crossing her legs carefully to be sure there was the maximum amount of thigh showing. She knew she looked great.

'I'm so sorry,' she said. 'I know you're going to think I'm terrible. But what I said on the phone about a threesome and everything. Well, I am sorry, but I just can't.'

He stared at her disbelievingly. 'You can't?' he said thickly.

She shook her head slowly, fluttering long black eyelashes. 'I guess I wanted to see you again so much, that I said it—but really, it's not my scene.'

'It's not your scene,' he repeated blankly.

'No.' She licked her lips, crossed her legs the other way, and waited.

'Look, baby,' he said at last. 'You called me while I was balling this chick'—he indicated the bedroom—'you called *me*, right in the middle. Nobody asked you to—but there you were on the phone—asking. and I mean asking. to join us. So what happens—you get me all hot over the idea of a scene—I stop halfway with this other broad—wait a goddam half-hour. and then you mince in here saying you can't make it.' His voice had been rising excitedly. and now he was almost screaming.

She stood up. 'What can I say?' She walked over to him and put her hand on his arm. 'I was drunk last night. but in spite of that I remembered it as something special. Now I'm sober, and can I help it if I don't want to share you?'

He looked at her admiringly. 'You're a smart little cookie. I suppose you want me to get rid of—' He gestured toward the bedroom.

She kissed him. pressing herself up against him. 'That's the general idea.'

He pushed her away. 'All right. baby—but don't think you're fooling me, because I know exactly what you're doing. You happen to be a lot sexier than her, so I'll pay her off. Is that what you want?'

She looked at him wide-eyed. 'I don't know what you're talking about,' she said. 'Do whatever you like. I'll still be available tomorrow night. I can always go now.'

His eyes swept over her body. 'No, you stay. Wait in the john.'

She smiled and walked obediently into the guest bathroom, in the hall. He kept her waiting about five minutes. Soon she heard a shrieky female voice. and then a door slammed.

Eventually he threw open the bathroom door—he had discarded his vibrant bathrobe and stood there with nothing but his suntan and a hard-on. 'Let's go. baby,' he said. 'I just had to give that broad fifty bucks, so you'd better make it worth my while!'

David parked his car in the garage and let himself into the house. It was strangely quiet. He supposed Linda had gone to bed early. so he made his way upstairs and looked in on the children, who both slept peacefully. Jane woke up and sleepily requested a glass of water. He got it for her. and she threw her arms around his neck and said, 'I love you, Daddy.' He settled her down and went into the main bedroom. It was empty. He was mildly surprised. Where was Linda? He knew the rest of the house was deserted. She must have gone to a movie or something, but it was most unlike her.

He checked through the window and saw her car was not in the drive, and then he looked around for a note—no note.

He went along to Ana's room and knocked. The maid came to the door clutching her transparent nylon nightdress around her. She had an unfortunate shadow of a moustache.

'Where's Mrs. Cooper?' he questioned.

'She went out maybe eight o'clock,' said Ana. Her English was not too good, and she didn't volunteer any further information.

'Did she say where she was going?'

'No.'

'What time she would be back?'

'No.'

The conversation was finished.

He went back to the bedroom, showered, and fell asleep reading the papers on the bed.

That was how Linda found him when she came in. She was agitated, he had said twelve o'clock, and he was always later than he said he would be. Fortunately he was asleep, as her makeup was smudged and her hair a mess. She knew if he saw her he would know. She made it into the bathroom quickly, got out of her clothes and into a robe. Then she ran a bath. At least if he woke up now it wouldn't matter.

David awoke. 'Where the hell have you been?' he demanded.

'I went to a movie. Where were you?'

'You know where *I* was. The movies get out a quarter to eleven—where have *you* been for the last hour?'

'I suppose you were with Phillip,' she said, ignoring his question.

'Yes—you know I was.'

'I was with him too.'

He stared at her blankly. 'What are you talking about?'

'I was with Phillip as much as you were.'

'Have you been drinking?'

'No, David, I haven't been drinking. I called the Abbottson house after speaking to you earlier, and while I was talking to Mary, Phillip came in and he knew nothing about a meeting with you.'

David thought quickly. 'Yes, things were a bit of a mess. I thought he was coming back later, but then I realized he said he couldn't, so I had to take those people from out of town to dinner.'

She raised an eyebrow. 'But you just *said* you were with Phillip.'

'Yes—well, that was because I knew you wouldn't understand.'

'You were right, I *don't* understand. Now, please, can I take a bath?'

'You're so ridiculous, Linda.' His voice was becoming louder. 'Look, I've been home for hours. I took these three men to Carlo's, and I ran into Jay and Lori Grossman. *Now* do you believe me? They want us to have dinner with them tomorrow, and I said it was all right. You can ask *them* who I was with. O.K.?'

Maybe he was telling the truth. 'Oh, all right,' she said wearily. She was too tired to fight.

He stalked back into the bedroom. She took her bath. Their thoughts were on separate planes. Neither of them really wanted to get involved in long discussions about who had been where, as it was dangerous ground and they could both end up getting found out.

When she came to bed he thought how good she looked in a long silk nightdress which clung seductively.

He broke the silence. 'Where would you like to eat tomorrow?'

She was noncommittal. 'I don't mind.'

'Jay says Lori wants to go to the Savoy Grill—a bit conventional, but I suppose as they are visitors here we should oblige.'

'I suppose so.' She turned out the light on her side of the bed and lay with her back toward him.

'What's new with the children?'

'Oh, nothing much.'

He lit a cigarette. 'I'm not tired,' he remarked.

'Why don't you read? There's a book on the table you started three months ago.'

'I don't feel like reading.'

'Then turn your light off and go to sleep.'

'That's a pretty nightdress, is it new?'

'No, I've been wearing it for the past two years,' she sighed patiently, wishing he would just shut up.

He leaned over and cupped her left breast with his hand. She shrank away immediately. Oh, God, no, she thought, not tonight—please God, not tonight. After all those nights I've lain here and ached for him, he couldn't possibly pick tonight.

He lounged across the bed after her. 'What's the matter?'

'Nothing.' She forced herself to turn around and face him.

Fortunately he took her quickly. He had long ago given up on preliminaries with her. The sexual act with David gave her absolutely no pleasure. She felt vacant and used. Vaguely she wondered if all men became like this after you married them. At first anxious to please, thrilled to bits if they got to fondle you for half an hour. But after the marriage—a quick lay and that was all.

'That was marvellous,' he said. 'How was it for you?'

She simulated pleasure. 'Marvellous.' She repeated his adjective, unable to think of anything else to say.

He turned the light out. 'Good night.'

She squeezed her eyes shut to keep in the tears. 'Good night.'

He lay there and thought about what a bitch Claudia was.

She lay there and thought about how virile and sensitive Paul was.

Finally they both fell asleep.

10

'I want to stay the night.' Claudia said. stretching languorously.

Conrad was on the phone to room service. He sat on the side of the bed. rolls of suntanned flesh around his middle. his bald head shining with sweat.

'This is Mr. Lee. suite 206—send me up six pieces of lightly buttered toast spread with caviar—the best stuff. Also a bucket of ice. a glass of milk. and a dish of chocolate ice cream.' He glanced over at Claudia—'You want anything. baby?'

She shook her head.

He spoke into the phone again. 'Add on some chocolate cake and cream—a jug of cream. O.K.. that's all. Make it fast!'

'I'm going to stay the night.' Claudia announced.

'What do you want to do that for?'

''Cos I want to go to the studio with you tomorrow like you promised. I'm not letting you out of my sight!'

He laughed. 'Baby. you're too much! I've been married three times. and I thought I knew broads pretty well. but you're something else!'

She laughed too. throwing her head back so that her hair spread out around her. 'Wouldn't you sooner I was honest?' she asked. 'I'm not some naïve little piece. you know. I like you. But I don't see why you shouldn't help me.'

'I haven't promised you anything.'

'Yes you have. you promised me a test.'

'So I promised you a test. So what if you're lousy?'

'I won't be lousy.' She smiled. 'I may not be able to act. but I photograph like a dream! And in the sort of movie you're making. I'm sure you can find something for me.'

There was a discreet knock on the bedroom door. 'Your order is here. sir.' a voice said.

Conrad lumbered off the bed and reached for a paisley silk dressing gown.

God—you're old and fat. Claudia thought. 'I love your dressing gown, darling.' she purred.

'Simpson's,' he said, pleased. He grabbed some change off the dressing table and disappeared into the other room.

Claudia rolled across the bed, twining herself around in the sheet. 'I'm going to get in his damn movie if it kills me,' she muttered to herself. 'I haven't screwed *that* for nothing!'

He came back into the bedroom munching on a piece of toast. 'This is lousy caviar—you want to go out somewhere?'

'What time is it?' she asked, surprised.

He consulted a large gold watch. 'One-thirty—what's open?'

She thought quickly. If they went out she wanted to be sure that she came back to the hotel with him after. She was determined to stick with him until he got her a test.

'All the clubs stay open till around four,' she said. 'And we can stop by my apartment so I can get some clothes to wear to the studio tomorrow. Great idea.' She jumped out of bed.

He studied her figure. 'You know, you've got a gorgeous body. How would you feel about appearing on the screen nude?'

'I hadn't really thought about it.'

'Think about it. There's a part you might be right for. I can test you.'

'When?' her green eyes gleamed.

They went to a new discothèque—Charlie Brown's. It was jammed, but they were squeezed onto an already full table due to the fact that Conrad slipped the headwaiter money. The records were so loud you couldn't hear yourself speak. On the tiny dance floor couples were jammed frantically together. There was a scattering of well-known people, a lot of girls with long straight hair covering half their faces, and a few representatives of the latest rock groups sporting hair as long as the girls'. It was very dark.

At their table was a photographer Claudia knew. She greeted him with a kiss and introduced him to Conrad. He was with one of the top models of the moment, a tall slim girl who photographed out of this world.

Claudia couldn't sit still; the music swept over her in great waves.

'Want to dance?' she asked Conrad.

He nodded and they struggled to the dance floor, where she broke loose in wild sinuous gyrations while Conrad just sort of stood there jiggling about. It was hot and the sweat started to trickle down his face.

You think you're a real swinger, Claudia thought. Don't you know you're too old to do this?

She said, 'Darling, you're a peachy dancer!'

'Sweetie pie!' The voice was unmistakable. Right beside them on the dance floor was Shirley, complete with the Honourable Jeremy. 'Where's your divine boy friend?'

Claudia smiled. 'Thought you were going to Windsor,' she yelled.

'We did, but it was absolutely *too* dreadful. I mean, it was almost empty. Can you imagine anything more ghastly?'

The Honourable Jeremy nodded vehement agreement.

By this time Conrad was sweating profusely. 'Let's sit down,' he said weakly.

'Sweetie, we will come over in a minute. Where are you sitting?'

Claudia smiled and waved, pretending she hadn't heard. She didn't relish the thought of being stuck with Shirley and Jeremy again.

When they got back to their table it was even more crowded, and there was a great squeezing up of people to make room for them.

The model said to Conrad, 'I adored your last film. Will you be making your new one in this country?'

The photographer asked Claudia to dance. She accepted, not too eager to leave the skinny model chatting up Conrad, but anxious to dance again, and Giles, the photographer, was a wild dancer. She had indulged in a short affair with him at one time, but then they decided it was more fun to be mates. They were too much of a kind to be lovers. Occasionally, if one of them was at a loose end, they would call each other and spend an evening together, and if they felt like it, end up in bed. But it was purely a brother-and-sister relationship with a little sex thrown in. Giles was very good-looking in a dark Spanish way. Women were mad for him. and his services as a fashion and society photographer were in demand.

'Who's the father figure?' he asked cynically. 'Cindy says he's a big Hollywood mogul. and I think she fancies big Hollywood moguls.'

'You can tell her to keep her false nails off this one. he's already been bagged!'

They did a ritual dance together—him standing very still and giving rhythmic sexy twitches and she almost bumping and grinding before him.

'Fancy a bit of pot?' he asked conversationally.

She glanced over at their table. More people had joined it. and Conrad seemed quite happy ordering drinks and talking loudly with a lot of arm-waving.

'Yeah. great idea.' she said.

They slipped off the dance floor and out onto a balcony that extended along one-half of the club. It was windy and surprisingly quiet. as the windows and doors from the club were all soundproofed.

Giles lit a joint and they took it in turns to drag deeply on it.

'I've got to get in the right frame of mind to screw that bag of bones.' he said. 'We're doing a big layout for *Vogue*. and I want to have the right atmosphere between us. Christ. I tell you. it's like banging a skeleton!'

They both giggled. 'Lots of luck.' laughed Claudia. 'How would you like mine? Attractive. isn't he?'

'I'd suggest a foursome.' said Giles. 'But I know we'd only end up doing it to each other. so what's the use?'

They both collapsed in gales of laughter. then Claudia said, 'C'mon. we'd better get back inside.'

'What's the scene?' Giles asked. 'You going to become a big movie starlet?'

'Star—baby—star.'

They walked back into the noise and heat and rejoined their table. Cindy was listening attentively as Conrad told a long boring story about how he first arrived in America at the age of fourteen. Shirley and the Honourable Jeremy had also squeezed around the table.

'Sweetie—what a fascinating man!' gasped Shirley. 'Such a history!' She simpered at Giles. 'Hello, poppet.'

'Hello, Shirley—how's business?'

'Business?'

He laughed. 'Forget it, baby.'

'I say, old man,' stammered Jeremy, 'liked those photos you did of Shirley—jolly fine set.'

'I'm a jolly fine photographer,' mocked Giles.

Claudia decided it was about time she came between Cindy's adoring gaze and Conrad. She snaked her arm around his neck and whispered something in his ear.

He looked surprised. 'Here?' he said. 'Now?'

She giggled. 'No one will see. Want me to?'

He laughed hoarsely. 'You're a wild broad. Save it for later, huh?'

Conrad ordered champagne for the whole table, and everyone proceeded to get well and truly loaded. 'I'm going to throw a big party tomorrow night,' he said.

Claudia was delighted. 'For me, darling?'

'Yeah, for you—anyone—you're all invited.'

'Oh, goodie—how super,' trilled Shirley. 'Where and what time, sweetie?'

'Make it at my hotel—Plaza Carlton—I'll take over a big room there—about ten o'clock.'

'Crazy,' said Claudia. 'Did everybody hear that—tomorrow at ten.' She kissed Conrad's ear. 'I'm just going to the loo—be right back.' She threaded her way through the crowded tables to reception. 'I want to make a quick phone call,' she said to the girl behind the desk.

'Go ahead,' said the girl passing over the house phone.

It was after three o'clock. She dialled the number slowly, a strange smile playing around her lips.

A sleepy voice answered the phone.

'Hello, David darling,' she whispered. 'I'm having a great time: how about you?' She hung up immediately. 'Just letting my husband know everything's cool,' she said to the surprised girl and swept back inside.

Waking up the next morning was not too much fun. Seeing Conrad asleep beside her like a discontented slug made her stomach turn. Her head felt heavy and her skin like much-used parchment. She made it to the bathroom and took an icy-cold shower. It was absolutely freezing agony. but the after-effects were worth it.

They had not returned to Conrad's hotel earlier that morning but instead had ended up in her apartment.

After the shower she dressed carefully and did a meticulous makeup. all ready to accompany Conrad to the studio. Then she made some coffee and finally shook him.

He awoke badly. Much coughing and foul sounds in his throat, bloodshot eyes. bad breath and B.O. 'Christ. what time is it?' he muttered. the universal cry of people waking up in other people's apartments.

'It's just ten o'clock.' She handed him some coffee.

'Where's the phone?'

She groped around under the bed, where she had placed the phone off the hook.

He called his secretary and issued a list of instructions. 'I've got to go back to the hotel and get changed,' he said. struggling into his clothes.

'I'm coming with you.'

'What for?'

'For my test you promised me.'

He stared at her. 'I'm not going to forget your goddamn test—but it can't be done just like that. today: it's got to be set up.'

'I'll come with you while you set it up.'

He shook his head. 'You don't give up. do you.' He picked up the phone and called his secretary again. 'Listen. I want a test fixed for a Miss Claudia—' He looked at her blankly.

'Parker,' she said quickly.

'Parker. Fix it up as soon as possible. Her agent will call you later today to get the details.' He hung up. 'O.K.. baby?'

She kissed him. 'You bet! Listen. you haven't forgotten the

party tonight?'

'Party?'

'Yes. Don't you remember? You asked a whole group of people to a party tonight at your hotèl.'

'Oh, yeah—that's right. I'll get it in hand, and I'll see you later.'

'I'll come by a couple of hours early in case you need anything.'

'The way I feel right now, I won't need anything—but you never know.' He gave a ribald laugh and left.

11

Linda phoned Paul at work as soon as the children had gone to school and David to the office. He was anxious to see her.

'I can't manage it,' she said.

He was most persuasive and eventually she agreed to meet him during his lunch hour.

It was a crisp sunny day, and they met in Green Park. She had never seen him in a suit before, and it didn't look quite right somehow. She decided it was because it was off the rack and store bought suits always managed to look just that little bit wrong.

They strolled along hand in hand, but Linda didn't feel easy. She felt overdressed in her smart outfit with matching crocodile shoes and bag. She knew she looked all wrong strolling hand in hand with Paul Bedford in Green Park. It wasn't that she felt old, or at least older than him—but she felt, in spite of the fact that she didn't want to feel that way—she felt as if she was slumming.

'What's on your mind?' he asked. 'Something bothering you?'

'I don't know, Paul. This is all wrong. I'm not the sort of woman that can get involved in an affair. I have my children and my home, and I feel I have to keep trying with my husband. I can't just give up and become involved with you. That's no answer at all.'

He was irritated. 'What's the matter, Linda? Frightened of losing your security if David finds out?'

'No. I'm frightened of losing my self-respect.'

They walked in silence for a while and then he said, 'What are you trying to say?'

'I'm trying to say that I can't lead two lives. I want to stop it now before it goes any further.'

His voice sounded bleak. 'I don't want you to leave me. I've been waiting to meet someone like you. You're a warm person. I *need* a warm person. I won't make any demands on you, just to see you when you're free.'

'It's not enough for either of us. I don't think we should see each other again.' She withdrew her hand.

His mood changed. 'You're like all the others. I should have known you're just a hard bitch at heart frightened of losing all your home comforts. Women have hearts like bloody adding machines. Look at Margarethe—dropped me for my father just because he had a few bob. My bloody mother killed herself to get away from him. Fuck the lot of you.'

'I'm sorry, Paul—but I'm not going to be a substitute for your mother, *or* Margarethe. I'm too old for that. Forget the past and go and find someone you can be happy with.'

'Is that what you want?'

'Yes. It is.'

He sneered at her. 'Well, you were a bloody easy lay—and not bad for an old bird.'

She turned and started to walk quickly away.

'Who's going to screw you now you randy bitch!' he yelled after her.

She felt the colour rise in her face, and started to run, not stopping until she reached her car.

She drove home, cold tears running down her face all the way.

The Grossmans were sitting in the bar of their hotel, Lori cool in pale-lilac chiffon, silver hair swept back in elaborate curls, neckline plunging to show off two satin-smooth white breasts.

The Coopers arrived to meet them on time. Linda was wearing a black silk dress and pale-beige mink wrap. David, conventional in a midnight-blue suit, white shirt, blue tie, and big sapphire cufflinks.

They all had a drink and then moved on to the Savoy Grill.

Jay enlivened the evening with amusing tales about Hollywood, David chatted amicably about business and politics. The two women were mostly silent. Lori was obviously disappointed that Princess Margaret wasn't there. She complained about the lack of ice and checked her makeup a lot.

Jay finally said, 'For Christ's sake, stop looking in the mirror, we all know you're beautiful, it's the reason I married you, isn't it?'

She pouted a lot after that.

When they were at the coffee stage, Jay said, 'Hey—how about dropping by the party Conrad's giving tonight. We promised we would.'

'I'm really tired,' Linda said apologetically. 'It was the children's first day at school and what with all the preparation I'm rather exhausted.'

'Come on, Linda,' said David jovially. 'We'll go for an hour.' He was feeling rather pleased with himself due to the fact that he had avoided getting in touch with Claudia all day. Little tramp, teach her a lesson. And how about that phoning him up in the middle of the night to make him jealous? He would show *her*. She would have to come begging to be forgiven.

'Yes, Linda, you must come,' said Jay. 'It will be a laugh, I can promise you that.'

'Just for an hour then,' she said reluctantly.

She accompanied Lori to the ladies' room, where between applying powder and blusher Lori drawled, 'That son of a bitch thinks I'm a damn idiot. He'll find out who's the idiot when I get half of everything he's got.'

'I beg your pardon?' said Linda politely.

'It's California law—I *know* it's California law.' At that Lori sank into silence, carefully applying another coat of lip gloss.

The party was in full swing when they arrived. There were sixty or seventy people there already, and more arriving all the time. Huge buffets of food covered one side of the room, and there were three bars strategically placed, and a six-piece live group to which people were dancing.

They pushed their way through to the nearest bar and ordered drinks. Jay appeared to know quite a few people. He introduced everybody, and soon David was chatting away.

'Come with me to find Conrad,' Jay said to Linda. 'I've got to let him know I put in an appearance.'

They found Conrad sitting at a table eating chocolate ice cream and drinking straight bourbon. Claudia was by his side—wearing a bright-red ruffled dress and a lot of fake diamonds.

Conrad issued genial greetings and invited them to sit down, moving two other people to do so.

'You remember Mrs. Cooper—Linda,' Jay said.

'Sure, sure, what do you think of the party? I know how to do these things right, huh?'

'You certainly do,' Jay said admiringly.

'Hallo, Mrs. Cooper,' Claudia said, slurring her words. She had been drinking steadily for several hours. 'Is *Mr.* Cooper about?'

'Why, yes,' said Linda. 'Did you want to see him about something?'

'Yes, as a matter of fact I do.' She knocked a glass down on the table accidentally, the dark alcohol making a splashy stain on the tablecloth. 'I want to tell him what he can do with his bloody Beauty Maid campaign. Stuff it up his ass—that's what he can do with it.' She hiccuped.

Linda stared at her coolly. 'I'll see he gets the message, dear,' she turned to talk to Jay.

Claudia stood up. 'Think I'll give him the bloody message myself,' she said and weaved unsteadily off.

'What's the matter with her?' Linda said.

Jay shrugged. 'I don't know. What's with your girl friend, Con?'

Conrad laughed. 'The broad's nutty. I've promised her a bit in the movie. It's gone to her head.'

'What bit?'

'How about a semi-naked broad standing beside the credits, sort of torn-slave-dress jazz. This kid's got a great body—and if she photographs O.K., we'll use her. Whattayasay?'

'Fine,' said Jay with a smile. 'Sounds like it has a lot of class.'

Linda rose from the table. 'Excuse me a minute,' she said. She walked around the room looking for David, but she couldn't find him or the girl. She sighed. It was probably nothing—the girl was drunk.

She spotted Lori surrounded by a group of admiring males and went over.

Lori was saying. 'Well, where I come from women are treated like ladies. You see—'

'Have you seen David?' Linda interrupted.

'Yeah.' She hardly glanced at Linda. 'He went out on the terrace.'

It's stupid, Linda thought. I shouldn't be tracking him down like this, it's childish. She made her way onto the terrace and found it deserted.

Just as she was leaving, she heard a low, throaty chuckle. She looked again and saw over in the corner a couple in a close embrace.

She backed into the shadows and edged nearer. The girl was pulling his head down to her breast, which was popping out of the top of her dress. She was fondling him intimately.

'You're the craziest, Claudia,' he muttered. 'The best ever.' Now he was pulling her dress right down so it hung around her waist. 'I missed you so much. One night without having you was murder.'

Shocked and sickened, Linda backed away. They hadn't seen her. Dazed, she wandered back into the main room.

She was heading for the door when Jay appeared and grabbed her arm. 'What's the matter? You look terrible, what happened?'

She looked at him with unseeing eyes. 'I've got to get out of here,' she mumbled, pushing his arm away and making for the door.

He caught hold of her arm again firmly and steered her to the nearest bar.

'The lady wants a large brandy, and fast,' he said. 'Now, tell me what happened.' He took her hand and held it tight. 'Tell me,' he repeated in a softer voice.

She looked at him with eyes full of shock. 'I suspected he played around—maybe—once in a while up in Manchester or somewhere—but this . . . With me right here. It's horrible.'

The waiter brought the brandy, and she took large gulps.

'I—I was looking for David. I wanted to warn him about that

drunk tramp. Lori said he was on the terrace. I went out and he was there with her. They were necking—she had half her dress off. They were saying these things to each other . . .'

'Oh, God!' said Jay. 'That stupid son of a bitch. Look—the girl was drunk. Maybe he was trying to get rid of her.'

Linda's eyes were scornful. 'With words like—one night without having you was murder.'

'What do you want to do?' asked Jay. 'Shall I take you home?'

She shook her head. 'What *can* I do? This is it for me. I'm finished with him. I want a divorce. I hate him.' Her voice shook. 'I don't ever want to speak to him again.'

'Look—it's no good making decisions while you're upset. Let me take you home. I'll come straight back and talk to David, tell him not to go home tonight.'

She laughed bitterly. 'Tell him not to ever come home again. Tell him to go off with his "best-ever" little slut. Tell him he can do what he wants—'cos I don't care anymore. I'm through.' She took another large gulp of brandy. 'I'm going to start crying in a minute—please get me out of here.'

They got a taxi outside the hotel. Linda was worried that either Lori or David would miss them and that maybe David would race her home, but Jay reassured her. 'I'll be back within an hour, and if he does miss you he'll just be looking around. As for Lori, she won't even know I'm gone.'

Linda sighed. 'I'm so embarrassed, dragging you away from the party and everything. The whole situation is so awful.'

'Don't be embarrassed.' He took her hand comfortingly. 'If it's any solace I was involved in exactly the same situation myself. In Hollywood at a real swinging party, my first wife, Jenny, vanished. I searched all over and eventually found her in bed with the host. So you see, I *do* understand.'

'What did *you* do?'

'I was a schmuck. I gave her another chance, came home early one day and found her banging the delivery boy.'

They sat in silence for a while, then Jay said, 'I suppose for some people one woman or one man is enough—but not for any of the people *I* know. I guess one gets what one deserves out of life. I've been married three times—each time to a beautiful girl with about as much thinking power as a rabbit. It must be a sickness with me—I marry stupid, dumb, beautiful broads.'

Linda hesitated. 'I—I was unfaithful to David this week. The first time in eleven years of marriage. I'm so ashamed about it now. It was with a boy—a twenty-two-year-old-boy—I don't know why . . .' She trailed off. 'David hadn't touched me in months, we were so far apart, he was never home. It just happened. I suppose I'm as guilty as he is.'

'Never feel guilty. What good can that do? Sleep on things, and see how you feel in the morning. You've got young children; don't make any hasty decisions.'

'Good night, Jay—thank you for everything.'

'Linda, I'll call you tomorrow. Rest easy—it will be all right.'

Claudia found David in a group with Lori. She edged quietly up behind him, and pressing her body against his back, she covered his eyes with her hands and said in a Marilyn Monroe-type voice, 'Guess who, baby!'

There was no mistaking that body. He was surprised, and sharply excited. She had the most incredible effect on him: he just had to know she was there to want her. He turned slowly, eyes looking around to see if Linda was anywhere about. She wasn't.

'Hello, Claudia.'

'Hello, Claudia.' She mimicked his voice. 'Don't I get a better greeting than that? By the way, you can stuff your Beauty Maid campaign up your ass, cha-cha-cha!'

The group he had been standing with were all listening, including Lori.

He took Claudia firmly by the arm, bruising her flesh. 'Let's go and find Linda,' he said, walking off and pulling her with him.

'Let's go find Linda!' she said incredulously. 'You've got to be joking!'

He marched her onto the terrace, finding a deserted dark corner. As soon as he let go of her she wound her arms around his neck and kissed him. 'Did you miss me?' she whispered. 'I was going to be so mad at you, but I couldn't.' She giggled. 'I'm smashed. you know.'

'You're a bitch. leaving me sitting in that restaurant. phoning up in the middle of the night. *You* were going to be mad. What about *me?*'

She nibbled his ear. rubbing her body against him.

Her dress was held up by two thin shoulder straps. He peeled them off. pulling her dress down to her waist. She wore nothing underneath. Hungrily she guided his mouth to her breasts.

All sense of reason was gone. He was with Claudia and he had to have her. It didn't matter that they were in a public place. That his wife was somewhere around. That anybody could appear.

It was dark. He pushed her down onto the cold concrete ground and lifted her skirt. She wore no panties. and she was giggling.

He took her quickly. It was all over in a minute. 'Christ!' he muttered. 'Christ!'

She lay there still giggling. her dress bunched around her waist. He pulled her up and looked around. relieved to see that no one had come out. She was unconcerned.

'We've got to go back inside separately.' he said.

'Screw you!' she replied.

'You just did.' He straightened his tie and wiped a handkerchief around his face to remove all traces of lipstick. 'I'll phone you tomorrow. I'll get away early from the office and come over. I've got a surprise for you.'

'You've always got a surprise for me. You're the man with the permanent hard-on!' She laughed. 'What a titl for a television series—I can see it now—The Man with the Permanent Hard-on—starring Dick Hampton!'

He kissed her. 'You go in first—go straight to the ladies' room. you look a mess.'

'Thank you. kind sir. Are you sure you're finished with me?'

'Go on. be a good girl. I'll try to phone you later.'

She stuck out her tongue at him—waggling it obscenely—and then sauntered off through the French windows completely at ease.

He took a deep breath—what a girl. After a safe five minutes he followed her in. The party was still in full swing. He grabbed a drink from a passing waiter and started to look for Linda. This was becoming a dangerous habit. bumping into Claudia at parties.

He observed Lori dancing with a seedy actor. She was moving her hips in steady bumps and grinds. and smiled coolly at him. She certainly knew how to move.

He edged closer. 'Seen Linda?' he asked.

She looked deadpan. 'Last I saw of her she was heading toward the terrace looking for you.'

'The terrace?' he said. stunned.

'The terrace. honey.' She swayed away from him.

He started to look for Linda seriously. He ploughed his way across the room. through groups of people laughing and chatting. A girl grabbed his arm: she was thin and pretty. and he remembered her as a friend of Claudia's from the restaurant.

'Hello. ducky.' she cooed. 'Fancy seeing you here.'

'Hello.' He looked around for her chinless boyfriend.

'Oh. Jeremy's gone to fetch me another drink.' She didn't leave go of his arm. 'Super party—but I didn't expect you to be here.'

'Why not?' he said patiently. She was far too thin for him to find attractive.

'I know we're all very modern and everything. but you struck me as the jealous type.'

'What are you talking about?' He shook his arm free.

'After all—this party is being given by Conrad Lee for Claudia. and I shouldn't have thought you would come. I mean. one shouldn't mix business with pleasure. should one? And you're obviously pleasure. and he's obviously business.' She smiled blandly. 'Here comes Jeremy with my drink. see you again.' and she walked off.

He stood there furious.

Claudia hadn't mentioned Conrad Lee, or the fact that the party was for her. Bitch! Bitch! Bitch!

The quest for Linda was forgotten. and a new one for Claudia began. He wanted to get a few facts straight.

*

Jay arrived back at the party. He was thoughtful. It was a tricky situation telling another man he couldn't go home to his own wife. It could easily end in a punch on the nose. He saw David across the room talking to a girl. David Cooper. An attractive man, big and dark, and the ladies all fell for him. Lori had said she thought he was probably fantastic in bed, but from talking to Linda it didn't sound that way. Lori had a habit of thinking most men were fantastic in bed, her way of letting him know that she didn't think *he* was.

He approached David quickly, best to get it over with fast, and told him the situation.

David was suitably flattened. He tried to deny it, but when Jay told him word for word what Linda had said, he was forced to admit it.

'You're an idiot,' Jay said. 'You've got a great wife. If you want to fuck around, why do it under her nose?'

'What is she going to do?'

'She mentioned divorce.'

'That's ridiculous. She's got no proof. So I kissed a girl at a party—what does that prove? I'm going home. I'm not going to be shut out of my own house.'

Jay shrugged. 'I can't stop you. I can only offer advice. She's in a state of shock, going home tonight will only make things worse. If you wait until morning I'm sure you'll both see things a lot clearer.'

'I know Linda. She's upset, but I can explain things to her.'

Jay glared at him. 'I promised her you'd stay away tonight.'

David glared back. 'Tough, my friend, because I'm going home now.'

They held the glare a few moments and then Jay said, 'Good night, schmuck. Don't forget to say good night to your girl friend. You'll probably find her kissing Conrad's ass.'

12

When David arrived at his house and put the key in the front door it wouldn't open. He lit a match to make sure he was using the right key, but although it turned smoothly, the door remained tightly shut. Realization dawned. Linda had bolted it from the inside.

He went around to the back door, but that was also tightly barred. A strong, choked anger rose in him. He returned to the front and pressed his finger firmly down on the bell push. The jangly sound of the buzzer was loud and insistent. There was no response. He tried it again, this time leaving his finger there for several minutes. A light went on in the upstairs window. It was the maid's room. He waited impatiently for her to come down and let him in, but nothing happened, and after a while her light went out again.

He was furious—Linda was obviously up, and had told Ana to ignore the bell. He kicked savagely at the door but only succeeded in hurting his foot.

This is incredible, he thought: who the fuck does she think the bloody house belongs to?

'Listen, Linda,' he shouted, 'don't do this to me—open the door or I'm going for the police.'

The house loomed still and dark before him. He banged on the door with his fists—nothing. He leaned on the bell push again—nothing. Then, faintly, from upstairs, there floated down the sound of a child crying. He stood there, undecided about what to do. He felt guilty about waking the children, but after all, it was Linda's fault for not letting him in. He pushed the bell firmly and insistently for one final time, and to his surprise the bolts were pushed back and the door opened a few inches. He went to push it farther open, but it clanged to a shuddering stop—held by the safety chain.

Linda peered out at him, white-faced and angry. 'Go away, you make me sick.' Her voice sounded flat and tired.

'Come *on*, let me in, we'll talk about it. It was nothing—I was drunk.'

'I don't want to talk to you. I don't want to see you. Go back to your little tramp and leave me alone.'

She slammed the door in his face.

He swore, hammered on the door, and shouted, 'You'll be sorry, Linda. I'll bloody go away and I won't come back!'

She didn't return. Furious, he strode back to his car, got in, and started it viciously.

When David left the party, Jay phoned Linda and warned her. He then got hold of Lori, who was dancing closely with a swarthy-faced ambassador, and sat her down in a corner.

'You saw David take that broad out on to the terrace. What's with you, big mouth? Why did you tell Linda?'

She looked uninterested. 'I don't know what you're talking about, honey,' she drawled. 'Is something going on?'

'Yeah, something's going on.' He shrugged disgustedly. 'Are you really as dumb as you pretend to be?'

She looked sulky. 'You're so nasty to me, Jay. I don't know why I married you.'

'Would two mink coats, a sable, a mansion and several cars jog your memory?'

She stood up, smoothing her hands down her body, ironing imaginary wrinkles from her dress. 'I'm going to dance again; you interrupted me before—that was a very sweet, important guy I was dancing with.' She walked off, beautiful, cool.

Jay shook his head in despair. She was an idiot or a bitch or a clever combination of both.

The noise at the table where Conrad and his group were sitting was becoming progressively louder. Shrieks of drunken laughter, spilt drinks, Claudia climbing on the table and dancing, with the men all peering up her skirt, becoming aware of the fact that she had no panties on. Egged on with screams of drunken encouragement, she started to peel her dress off.

Jay viewed the scene. He was horribly sober. They all seemed to be behaving like a bunch of wild monkeys. He felt disgusted.

A large crowd was gathering around the table goggle-eyed at Claudia's free show. The foreign ambassador rushed over with Lori. It was a fast strip-tease as Claudia only had her dress to take off. She kicked it from the table. and then proceeded to dance to the music. Bumping. grinding. Her body glistened proudly, and the men in the crowd pressed closer and closer, while the women. suddenly jealous at such perfection, started to try and move them away.

A very harassed-looking man in pinstripe trousers and black jacket pushed his way toward the table. He represented the management. Shocked and horrified he approached Conrad, who waved him drunkenly away. 'We shall have to call the police unless this—this—woman gets dressed at once.'

Claudia stuck her tongue out at him. the only part of her that hadn't been exposed to public view.

Eventually, of course. the police arrived. They wrapped Claudia in a blanket. hauled her off to the police station. and booked her for indecent exposure.

The next morning it was headlines. Claudia was a star—for the day, that is. She was photographed and quoted while Conrad immediately cashed in on her wave of publicity by announcing that she would be appearing in his new film. He contacted her agent and signed her for two days' work.

She was delighted. She returned from the police station at lunchtime, triumphant. She gave a press reception. posed for countless more pictures. and then was taken off to the studio in a chauffeured car for makeup and hair tests. She didn't see Conrad, efficient professionals took over. She was pleased. he had served his immediate purpose.

When she returned from the studio in the evening. David was propped outside her front door.

Sober and giddy with her sudden success, he didn't look so good to her. 'What do you want?' she said coldly, and then added with a burst of enthusiasm. 'Hey—did you see me in the papers today?'

He trailed her into the apartment and immediately fixed a drink.

She flitted around talking excitedly, forgetting her coldness of a moment before. After all, David did belong to someone else, and it was she he was coming to.

'I'm going to take you out to dinner tonight, where do you want to go?' he asked.

She laughed. 'Oh. I see. All of a sudden I'm a star, and you want to be seen with me. What about wifey tonight? Aren't you frightened one of her spies will see us?'

'You don't have to worry about Linda. I've left her.'

Silence hung heavy in the room until slowly Claudia walked over and kissed him hard. 'You've left her for me?'

'For you.' He ran his hands down her back, enclosing them around her buttocks. 'When I saw you in the paper this morning and read what happened, I knew we couldn't go on any longer unless it was together. So I told Linda. I said I want a divorce, and here I am.'

She shook her head in disbelief. 'You really left her for me. Isn't that wild!'

'I'm going to divorce her and marry you,' he said firmly.

She wandered around the room. 'I don't want to get married, but thanks for the thought anyway. Hey—baby, we can do what we want, go where we want. It's too much!'

He followed her around the room. 'Don't you understand. I said I'd marry you.'

She laughed. 'But I don't want you to.'

'But I want to.' He grabbed hold of her. She was wearing a clingy orange sweater, matching slacks, and shiny white boots.

She slipped away from him. 'Listen, baby—let's get clear on the subject. I don't—do not have, I repeat, any desire to make the wedding-bells scene—so don't keep on making the offer like it's such a damn big deal. I don't want to marry you.' She was almost shouting, and sensing her mood, he dropped the subject.

'Where shall we go?' he said. 'We can go anywhere you like.'

She stretched, catlike in her orange outfit. 'I'm tired. I don't feel like getting dressed and going out.'

He looked surprised. 'You're always complaining we never

go anywhere—and now that we can go wherever you like—you don't want to go.'

She flopped in a chair. her legs thrown casually over the side. 'Ever heard the story of the kid that wanted some candy—moaned and cried and carried on till eventually it got candy—then ate so much it was sick?' She giggled. 'Get the message?'

'What the hell's the matter with you? Don't you understand what I've done for you today?'

She shrugged. 'For me? I should have thought it would have been for yourself. Where are you going to live?'

'I'm taking an apartment. I thought in the meantime I'd stay here with you. then we can move into the new place together.'

She studied her fingernails. admiring the pearly glow. 'Is it a penthouse?'

'Is *what* a penthouse?'

'The apartment you're taking.' There was a pause. 'Well. *is* it?'

'I don't know. What the hell does it matter? We'll find a penthouse if that's what you want.'

She smiled at last. pleased and purry. 'Yes. that s what I want. Can I start looking tomorrow? It's going to be too crowded for the two of us here.' She held out her arms to him. 'I'm sorry I've been bitchy. but it's been a busy day.'

He fell into her arms and kissed her. feeling the familiar immediate desire rise in him. She kissed him hard. running her tongue across his teeth and scratching the back of his neck with sharp nails. He started to reach for her body. but she pushed him away and leaped up. 'Not now. baby. Let's go to dinner. and then—think of it—we can come back home together. It will be a whole different scene.'

She switched on the stereo. and the sound of the Stones filled the room. She danced around. throwing off her sweater and wriggling out of her slacks in time to the music. She wore a brief white bra and the shiny white boots.

He watched her. mesmerized: 'Don't you ever wear panties?'

'Why spoil the line?' She laughed. 'Does it bother you? I've never had any complaints before!'

She vanished into the bathroom, and he heard the sound of a bath running. He followed her in. She was bending over the bath, filling it with bubbles. She had discarded the bra, but the boots remained.

He grabbed her from behind. She struggled weakly, half laughing. He tried to hold onto her and get out of his clothes at the same time, but she slipped and fell into the bath. By this time she was helpless with laughter, very wet, and covered in bubbles. She stuck her legs over the side of the bath with her boots still on.

He undressed hurriedly and followed her into the bath. The water cascaded over the side.

'I think I'm going to like living here," he said.

13

The sun was streaming into the bedroom and David couldn't sleep any longer. Claudia lay sprawled beside him, taking up more than her share of the bed. She claimed she couldn't sleep with the curtains closed, which accounted for the fact that every morning the light woke him too early. He glanced at his watch. It was only half-past six, and they hadn't got to bed until four. He felt tired and dreadful and hung over. It was no use getting up and pulling the curtains now, as he couldn't go back to sleep once he was awake.

The spacious bedroom was a mess. Claudia had a habit of stepping out of her clothes all over the place and just leaving them. One had to pick one's way through the debris in the mornings.

It's amazing, he thought, how my life has changed in six short months.

The new dress he had bought her lay in a crumpled ball at the bottom of the bed. It was red pleated chiffon, and she had seen it in a window in Bond Street, and he had surprised her with it the next day. The surprise had cost him a bomb.

He picked it up. She had spilled a glass of wine on it, and there was a crumpled stain.

In the green-marble bathroom leading off the bedroom, the mess continued. She had not emptied the bath, and it was filled with cold, dirty water. Bottles of makeup and hairbrushes and perfumes were scattered everywhere. The sink was clogged with soap and hair left to congeal beneath a dripping gold tap.

Beneath the mess it was a beautiful apartment. A penthouse, as she had wanted, in a new apartment building in Kensington. It cost far too much money a week, a fortune, in fact. But Claudia loved it and did not care to move.

He emptied the old water and picked up the bath towels. He really wished she would learn to be tidy, but it seemed impossible for her. With Linda, there had never been a thing out of place.

He went through a mirrored hallway to the kitchen. Here there were stale cups of half-drunk coffee, dirty dishes piled high, full ashtrays creating a bad odour.

Fortunately it was Friday, which meant that they had a new cleaning woman starting. The last one had left in disgust when she found out they weren't married, leaving a cryptic note saying, 'I'm not used to such filth.' At first he had thought she was referring to the state Claudia left things in, but the porter had told him what she really meant.

He made a cup of strong tea and managed to burn a couple of pieces of toast. Claudia had acquired a small, yappy Yorkshire terrier, which suddenly came bounding in, anxious for a walk, no doubt. It usually slept on the bed with them and would burrow beneath the covers at night. David hated it. He couldn't stand small dogs.

He left it sniffing around the kitchen and went into the huge, open-plan, living-dining room. This was the *pièce de résistance* of the apartment, a beautiful spacious room, one wall completely glass, leading onto a landscaped patio. Another wall marble, and the rest of the wall space mirrored. The room was chaotic. They had had people in for drinks before going out the previous evening, and half-empty glasses seemed to be all over the place. Overflowing ashtrays, spilled nuts, magazines, photographs of Claudia, cushions on the floor. Thank God it would all be cleared up today. David liked order.

He went to the front door and collected his papers, extracting the *Times* and *Guardian* from among the various film and fashion magazines Claudia seemed to have delivered daily.

He drank his tea—it was too strong. Ate his toast—it was burnt. Read the papers through bleary eyes. Soon it would be time to get dressed and go off to work.

Linda woke early. The sun was shining and it was a lovely day. She felt good. At last she was starting to enjoy the selfish pleasures of sleeping alone. Taking up the whole of the bed, waking and sleeping when she pleased, always being able to get into the bathroom.

It had been hard at first, the decision to get a divorce. She kept thinking of the children without a father. But the fact that David had moved out and set up home with Claudia had helped her to be strong.

She had found a good lawyer and put herself in his hands. It was quite simple, really.

Today was the day she was going to appear in court, stand calmly before a judge, and state the facts. Her lawyer, a short, stocky, grey-haired man, would be by her side. An inquiry agent would be there to offer relevant information. Her counsel was tall, attractive, and sympathetic. They had all assured her it would go quite smoothly. It was undefended and clear-cut.

She dressed, choosing her clothes carefully. A dark-brown neat suit, low-heeled shoes, not too much makeup. Surveying herself in the mirror, she thought she looked the part. An abandoned wife, sad, courageous, alone.

The children were staying with her mother. She ate a solitary breakfast of boiled eggs and coffee, wishing that she hadn't sent them away, wishing that their noisy laughter filled the house.

When she finished in court, she was going by train to join them for the weekend, and they would all return to the house together on Monday.

The house belonged to her now. Financial arrangements had been amicable. She had the house and a fairly generous support settlement for herself and the two children.

David visited the children every weekend, either on Saturday or Sunday. Linda always managed to avoid seeing him. In fact, she hadn't seen him for three months, and then it had been in her lawyer's office to make the financial settlement final.

She made only one stipulation about his seeing the children, and that was that she didn't want them in Claudia's company at all. He didn't argue on that point.

She finished her coffee. Soon it would be time to go to her lawyer's office and accompany him to court.

*

Claudia woke at eleven. There was someone ringing the doorbell. She groped her way to the front door, struggling into a flimsy pink negligee covered with makeup stains.

A short squat woman stood facing her. 'I'm Mrs. Cobb,' she announced. 'The agency sent me.' She had heavy red hands and a scrubbed old face.

'Come in, Mrs. Cobb,' Claudia said, stifling a yawn. 'I'm afraid it's an awful mess, but I'm sure you'll cope.' She took her into the kitchen and gestured under the sink. 'You'll find everything you need there. Excuse me if I leave you to it, I had a very late night.'

Mrs. Cobb looked grimly around and didn't say anything.

Claudia took an open can of peaches from the fridge and tipped them into a dish. 'My breakfast,' she said with a bright smile, and stopping to collect the magazines and papers from the living room, she went into the bedroom.

Propped comfortably back in bed, she leafed idly through the papers, the *Daily Mail* being her favourite. It was the show page that interested her. She scanned it eagerly, looking as usual, for any mention of Conrad Lee. She was delighted, today there was a whole article on the location of his film in Israel. It stated that the company would be returning to England at the end of the week for studio work.

She made a big pencil ring around the piece and phoned her agent on the shell-pink bedside telephone. She still had two days' work to do on Conrad's film. Things had become rather complicated, and the unit had gone on location before reaching her scenes. However, the film company had given her agent constant promises that as soon as they returned she would be needed for her two days' work.

She gave her agent the good news, and he promised to look into it immediately.

She stretched languidly. The past few months since moving to the penthouse had been fun, although David was becoming a bit of a bore. The penthouse was the most beautiful apartment. All her friends were very impressed. She had done lots of photo-sessions there, and she was always pleased when they appeared in various magazines—saying lovely young actress and model,

Claudia Parker, relaxing in her luxurious penthouse.

Giles was coming over at two o'clock to do a nude layout for a prominent American men's magazine. She hoped David would be working late as he disliked Giles intensely, in spite of the fact that he didn't even know she had had an affair with him. Anyway, if he knew she was doing a nude layout he would be furious. He was very old fashioned that way.

The magazine was paying her and Giles a lot of money to do the spread. And anyway, she didn't mind showing off her body. After all, it was certainly worth showing.

She lounged back in bed, yawning. Soon it would be time to start preparing herself: until then she could relax.

David arrived at his office tired and bad-tempered.

His secretary greeted him with a worried face. 'Mr. Cooper, your uncle wants to see you at once. His assistant said you should go straight to his office.'

What now? Being summoned by Uncle Ralph was never good news. His uncle had been most disapproving about his split-up with Linda. Divorce was a frowned-upon sin, and Uncle Ralph could be very religious when it suited him.

Uncle Ralph was sitting like a small, bald buzzard behind his desk in his early-Victorian-style office. His secretary, Penny, a wide-eyed blond, ushered David in.

He appraised her sexy long legs in her ultrashort skirt. Trust Uncle Ralph to have the only good-looking secretary in the building.

'Good morning, David.' Uncle Ralph grunted. 'Sit down—sit down. Wanted to have a word with you about the Fulla Health Beans account.'

'We don't have it anymore.'

'Exactly—exactly. That's what I want to talk to you about.'

His uncle launched into a long lecture about why they had lost the account, which to his way of thinking was because of David's unenthusiastic attitude, and the fact that he always seemed tired. He hinted that perhaps the job was too much for him.

David listened carefully, dissecting every word Uncle Ralph

said. because every word Uncle Ralph said always meant something else. What he was actually saying was. 'Don't come in here dragging your arse because you've been up with a hot piece all night. Either work or get the hell out.' He concluded the lecture with the information that Mr. Taylor of the Fulla Beans account was in town for one more night. and that he was prepared to reconsider his decision about withdrawing the account.

'Now. you take him out to dinner.' Uncle Ralph said. 'Tell him our plans. lay it on thick. Get him drunk. entertain him. Take him to a nightclub and fix him up with a hostess. Keep him happy. Whatever happens. I want that account back.'

'Yes. sir.' David got up.

Penny was sitting behind her desk in the outer office. legs crossed neatly beneath her desk. She smiled at him, an open invitation in her innocent wide eyes. He wondered vaguely if she was sleeping with the ugly old buzzard: the rumour around the building said she was. He wouldn't mind knocking a piece of that off. get one over on Uncle.

He leaned over her desk. 'How come I only ever see you here?'

Her smile widened and she started to reply. but the buzzer rang on her desk and she jumped up quickly. Uncle Ralph had anticipated the pass and was summoning her to the safety of his office.

She scampered off. sexy legs seductive beneath a short skirt.

David returned morosely to his own office and his own secretary. who was pale and mousy and flat-chested. She had an intense crush on him. which she tried to conceal. making it all the more obvious.

'Mr. Cooper.' she said anxiously. 'is everything all right?'

'Everything's fine.' He sat glumly at his desk. The thought of entertaining Mr. Taylor of Fulla Beans to an evening on the town was depressing.

'Oh. dear. Mr. Cooper.' His secretary was almost wringing her hands. 'Oh. dear. it had to happen today too.'

'What's so special about today?'

'It's your divorce today.' She lowered her eyes. 'Well. I

mean—'

So it was—he had forgotten all about it. It seemed strange that Linda could go into a court somewhere and divorce him and he didn't even have to be there. It didn't seem right.

His lawyer had written informing him of the date a while ago. He had said that they would send someone along purely as a formality.

His secretary stood nervously by the desk.

'Thanks for the cheerful reminder, Miss Field,' he said.

She flushed. 'I'm so sorry—I thought you knew. . . .' Her words trailed off. 'Would you like some coffee, Mr. Cooper?'

'That would be nice, Miss Field.'

She fled gratefully almost tearfully from his office.

'Sonofabitch!' he muttered. 'Sonofa*bitch!*'

The entrance hallway into the courts exuded an atmosphere of gloom. There were people scurrying in all directions, and long passages and stairs everywhere. The overall atmosphere was most depressing.

Linda's lawyer gripped her firmly by the arm and manoeuvered her up various flights of stairs and into a series of old elevators. It seemed to take ages to get to wherever they were going.

'I hope your case will be heard before the luncheon recess,' he said. 'Chances are that it will be.'

'How long will it all take?' she asked nervously.

'Not too long. It's all very straightforward. Shouldn't require a lot of time.'

They had arrived in a long hallway with benches along the walls, and this, Linda presumed, was where they would wait. It was crowded with people, and there was a scattering of men in long white curled wigs and black gowns.

Her lawyer called one of them over. 'This is your counsel, Mr. Brown.'

Mr. Brown was tall and distinguished-looking, with a tanned, crinkly face. He had a soothing, hypnotic voice, and he discussed the questions he would ask Linda briefly.

She felt sick. The whole thing was so awful. Her stomach was fluttering. She wondered if there was a ladies' room close at hand where she could go and collapse.

Her lawyer said. 'I think it might be a good idea if we go in and sit through a couple of cases before yours. It will give you a chance to see how things are done.'

She nodded bleakly. He led her through an ordinary door into an ordinary room. and she got a jolting shock. Instead of a huge. stately-looking courtroom as she had imagined. it was a small plain room with about six rows of benches where onlookers sat. There was a small. slightly raised desk where the judge presided. and a raised wooden dais where the witness stood. It was awful. Everyone was so close to everyone else. It was like someone's living room converted into a court for a day.

She sat on a hard wooden bench. A slightly built man was standing on the witness dais being questioned.

'And did you know at that time that your wife had had intercourse with Mr. Jackson?'

'Yes. sir.'

'And it was the same day that she packed her bags and left?'

'Yes. sir.'

'Leaving you in the matrimonial home with the children of your marriage. Jennifer and Susan?'

'Yes. sir.'

The case droned on. the slightly built man expressionless as he was asked question after question.

The judge sat wisely on his bench. nodding occasionally and looking for all the world like a senile old owl. At the conclusion of evidence he said. in hardly more than a mumble. 'Divorce granted. Custody of the children. Maintenance referred to chambers. Next case. please.'

The expressionless slight man suddenly broke into smiles. his shoulders straightened. and he left the room happily.

The next case was a mousy-looking blond with a heavy cockney accent who was out to divorce Joe—from the sound of it a wildly attractive sex maniac.

It's so unfair. Linda thought. we're the innocent ones. and we're the ones who have to stand up in this stupid little room and reveal the most personal aspects of our lives.

'Were your marital relationships satisfactory at first?' counsel asked.

'I should say so!' the mousy blond replied, drawing a muffled, ribald laugh from somewhere in the courtroom.

At last it was Linda's turn. She stood shakily in the witness stand, horribly aware of how close everyone was to her. She resented the rows of spectators. Why *should* they be allowed to sit there and stare and listen? It wasn't fair. After she was sworn in her counsel began the questions. She answered in a muffled, quiet voice, eyes staring straight ahead.

A document was produced from an inquiry agent, and the judge inspected it briefly. Her counsel continued with the questions, which were really statements of fact which she had only to confirm. Eventually he indicated to the judge that he was finished.

The judge adjusted his glasses, peered for a few brief seconds at Linda, and then said, 'Divorce granted, custody of the two children, and costs to be paid by the husband. Maintenance and access referred to chambers.'

It was all over. She left the stand in a daze. Her lawyer rushed over and took her arm. 'Congratulations,' he whispered.

Giles was late, of course. He was always late. When he arrived he was laden with cameras and looked tired. 'Give me some strong black coffee, darling,' he said. 'I've had a terrible morning shooting bras in the middle of the New Forest.' He collapsed in a chair, stretching his legs out and yawning. 'Y'know, this is a great pad, almost worth putting up with your boyfriend for.'

'Almost?' questioned Claudia. She had done a skillful makeup. Pale, creamy base, cleverly blended blusher, pale lipstick and huge fluttery eyes. She looked fabulous.

'Yeah, almost. I mean, darling, he's such a pain. Hey, you look great: wish we were shooting this at night. How late can I stay?'

'Until David gets home. You know how jealous he is. I'll give him a buzz around five and see what time he'll be here.'

'I want to shoot some wild stuff on the terrace—sort of get

you silhouetted against the view of London jazz. Lots of hair flowing about and all that shit.'

'Sounds good to me.' She was wearing a pink denim shirt tucked into matching pants with a huge gold-buckled belt and white boots.

'Nice outfit,' he said. 'We can start off with that, discarding it bit by bit.'

'So how's your love life?' she asked. 'Still with that skinny model?'

'Yeah, we break up about every two weeks regularly, but then it's back-together-again time.'

'I see her on the cover of every magazine I pick up. It's amazing, 'cos she's not really that great-looking, but she photographs beautifully.'

'She's got a camera face, y'know. She sees a camera and the face switches on, comes to life. Otherwise, it's just static. I guess our affair keeps going because she's really screwing my camera and I love the results. She's making me a bomb. I can't miss with anything I shoot of her.'

The phone rang. It was Claudia's agent with good news. It was true, the unit was returning in a few days, and she would probably be needed the following week.

'The director is flying in today,' her agent said. 'And the company is going to try and pin him down to a definite date.'

'Fabulous.' She was delighted. She had waited six months for this.

'Let's get started,' Giles said when she hung up, 'before I go to sleep.'

He worked fast, using three different cameras. He threw himself completely into it, becoming utterly absorbed in what he was doing.

Claudia of course blossomed before a camera, pouting, smiling, giving a tiger snarl, big, big sexy eyes always innocently staring, lips open and glossy. She undid the pink shirt, letting it fall casually open. There was nothing underneath.

After a while Giles said, 'Take your shirt off and fold your arms across your boobies. That's it—great! Give me a snarl. That's beautiful, baby. One leg slightly bent—a surprised look, marvellous! Now cover your boobies with your hands, give me the big-eyed-baby look—beautiful!' He kept shooting picture after picture. 'You look terrific. Turn your back to me and swing your head around quickly, let your hair fall—great! Hey, listen, I've got an idea if you don't mind getting wet. Put the shirt back on and I'll hose you down with water, it'll look dynamite!' He picked up the water hose used to water the plants and turned it on her.

She screamed and laughed. 'It's cold!'

He dropped the hose and picked up his camera.

He was right, it was effective. Her clothes had moulded themselves to her body, and her nipples stood out firm and strong through the shirt.

After an hour on the terrace Giles said, 'Let's go inside, baby. I've got some beautiful stuff of you out here.'

She was shivering.

'Lead the way to the shower,' he said. 'I don't want you catching cold. Strip off slowly. I want to capture it all.'

He followed her into the bathroom with his cameras, catching every moment as she wriggled out of her wet clothes and secured her hair with a couple of pins. Next she stood under the shower, her body gleaming as the rivulets of water hit her.

He said, 'Lean back, close your eyes, just let the water fall over you. Great! Bring your arms up behind your head, lovely, darling, that's lovely.'

They finished in the bathroom and Giles said, 'Now for some stuff in the bedroom, and then we should have it made.'

She put on a filmy black chiffon robe trimmed with feathers and let her hair down. The robe was transparent, casting a black haze over her body.

'Lie right in the middle of the bed, bring your head up, bend one knee ever so slightly, no, your left knee, darling—that's it. Wet your lips and give me the look. No, that's too hard, a soft look like you just made it.' He took a few shots and then put his camera down. 'Listen, you want these pictures to look really good?'

'Of course I do—what's the matter?' She sat up, her perfect breasts falling free of the robe.

'You just haven't got the right look, you're trying too hard. You gotta relax, kid.'

She stretched. 'I'm relaxed.'

'Yeah. I know. but you know what I want, I want the cat-that-just-got-the-cream look.'

'So give me the cream . . .' She reached for him.

'Just what I had in mind.'

They made love easily, slowly, almost offhandedly, and afterward he got quickly up and picked up his camera. 'Stay just as you are. That's perfect. *Now* you look authentic!'

David phoned Claudia at five o'clock. He had been trying to make up his mind whether to take her along with Mr. Taylor of Fulla Beans or not. Eventually he had decided it would be better not to, as he would pay more attention to her than to Mr. Taylor, and that would defeat the purpose of the whole outing.

'What are you doing?' he asked.

She giggled. 'Just lying around.'

He told her about the evening ahead and she said, 'That's all right, I'll find something to do.'

'Why don't you get an early night? I'll wake you when I get in.'

She suddenly laughed. 'Hey. David. I feel like a wife. Are you sure you haven't got some hot little number standing by your side?'

'Honestly. Claudia. don't be so stupid.'

She laughed. 'Don't worry about it, I wouldn't mind. Anything *you* can do *I* can do too.'

'It's a business dinner. Now. what *are* you going to do?'

She paused, then said, 'The President of America.'

'What?'

She laughed again. 'I'm only joking. Go on, I believe you. Have a nice dinner. I shall probably ask a few people over, and we'll sit around and wait for your esteemed return.'

'All right,' he said reluctantly. 'An early night would do you much more good.'

'You're beginning to sound *so* uptight.' She mimicked his

voice. 'An early night would do you much more good!'

He ignored her comment. 'I'll phone you later. Be good.'

'Yes, sir. Anything else, sir?'

'Good-bye.' He put the phone down, annoyed at the way she spoke to him. Annoyed by the fact that he was still so jealous of her. Annoyed by the fact she was going to ask people over. He would have to try and find Mr. Taylor a randy hostess and get rid of him early. He went into his private bathroom to change his shirt and shave.

Miss Field knocked nervously to say good night, and he rewarded her with a glimpse of his naked chest. She blushed deeply, and he wondered idly if she had ever been laid. He really couldn't imagine it. She wore long knee-length pink bloomers which he had noticed when she sat opposite him taking dictation. Also she was flat-chested, and who would want to lay a flat-chested, ugly girl? Once he had screwed the most horrifying-looking girl, cross-eyed, bad teeth, acne, but she had had the best and biggest knockers he'd ever seen, and wild legs. She had been a great lay, too, but he hadn't bothered to see her again, that face was too much.

David had met Mr. Taylor once before briefly. He was fat and middle-aged with thinning brown hair plastered neatly to his scalp to give the impression that it wasn't thinning at all, but just grew that way. He had a thick Lancashire accent and a thick Lancashire wife with two matching sons. He was a bore.

David met him in the bar of his hotel. He had been drinking lager beer but switched to Scotch as soon as David arrived. David tried to be charming—but Burt Taylor's idea of charming was a person who drank fast and told an everlasting run of dirty stories. David tried to please, and Burt rewarded him with hearty guffaws and conspiratorial winks. By the time they arrived at the restaurant, David was well on the way and Burt already there—drunk, that is.

David tried to insert a little business into the conversation, but Burt switched it neatly back to the subject of sex by remarking how he bet David had a lot of hot ones passing through his job.

'All those little model girls,' Burt said, 'that's how they get the job, by sleeping with you, isn't it?' David didn't argue.

Eventually they left the restaurant with Burt singing snatches of old Rugby songs.

David patted him on the back. 'Let's go and have some fun.'

They went to a plush nightclub filled with tired painted hostesses, and jocular, lecherous, out-of-town businessmen on expense accounts. The maître d', a smooth, suave Cypriot, asked if they would care to meet two nice young ladies.

'Yes,' Burt boomed. 'Only make sure they're not all that nice.' He roared with laughter.

A few minutes later two girls arrived at their table. One was tall and buxom, with red hair and a strapless green velvet dress, she was about thirty. The other was smaller and slightly timid-looking—in spite of a dress cut low enough to reveal almost all of her scrawny bosom. She was very young.

They both tried to attach themselves to David, but he excused himself from the table, realizing he hadn't phoned Claudia.

A man answered the phone, and he was told to hang on while the mystery voice located Claudia. 'Shit!' David mumbled. There was so much noise and music coming through the receiver. What was going on? He hung on grimly, feeling the alcohol pounded out of his body by a sudden mad anger. By the time Claudia spoke he felt almost sober.

'Hi, darling,' she cooed. 'Where are you? I'm having a marvellous time. It turned into a party.'

'Who answered the phone? Who's there?'

'I don't know, heaps of people. Hurry home, baby.' And she hung up.

He stood in the booth for a few minutes, then, intent on getting rid of Burt Taylor, he hurried back to the table.

Burt had ordered champagne, naturally, since David would be paying the check. The two hostesses were flanking him on either side, and he looked blissfully happy.

David thought the best thing to do was to get hold of the big brassy redhead and proposition her to take Mr. Burt Taylor off somewhere. He obviously preferred her to the younger one.

There was a corny Latin-American band playing. 'How about a dance?' he said to the redhead.

She smelled heavily of cheap perfume and pressed herself groin to groin with him. 'I like you.' she lisped.

He managed to push her away a little. 'Hey. listen. you want to make yourself some money?'

She looked interested while he explained the proposition. They bargained. reached an agreement. and sat down. David carefully slipping her the money beforehand.

Burt Taylor seemed put out. He took David to one side.

'I saw her first. boyo. I don't want the skinny bit.'

David smiled. this was going to be easy. 'It's all right, She can't stop talking about you. you've got it made.'

'In that case . . .' Burt leered. 'we won't be wasting much more time here.'

David reckoned another half an hour and he would be home. He patted Burt on the shoulder. 'I'll get the check,' he said.

There were photographers outside the court waiting for Linda. The fact that Claudia Parker had been named as the other woman made the case newsworthy.

'Over here,' one of them called.

Linda rushed straight ahead. her lawyer gripping her arm. The cameras clicked.

'What do they want?' she questioned. 'Can't they leave people alone. I'm nobody.'

Her lawyer hailed a passing taxi and pushed her in. 'It's best for you to get away from here. Congratulations again. We'll be in touch with you.'

'Don't you want a lift?' she said. trying to delay being left on her own.

'No. My office is just around the corner. Thank you all the same. Good-bye. Mrs Cooper.' He was gone. and the taxi was moving off down the street.

'Where to. lady?' asked the cabdriver.

She sat there in a daze. It had all happened so quickly, it was like a dream.

'Where to. lady?' the cabdriver repeated impatiently.

She didn't feel like rushing straight to the station. She felt like a drink and a cigarette and a half-hour of quiet relaxation.

'The Dorchester.' she said. It was the first place that came to mind.

The bar was fairly crowded. mostly with businessmen. but she found a secluded table. ordered a sherry. and sat back to enjoy it. She decided she would have lunch there. It was good to be on her own. She would order smoked salmon, fresh strawberries with cream. maybe even drink champagne.

'It is Linda Cooper. isn't it?'

She looked up. hesitated. and then said. 'Jay—Jay Grossman. Why, I would hardly have recognized you. What a wonderful tan.'

He sat down. smiling. 'I just got in from Israel. How are you? It's been months and months.'

'I'm fine.' She smiled back at him.

'And David?'

'David? I don't really know. I just divorced him about half an hour ago.'

Jay looked surprised. 'You really did it. then. Was it about that night?'

She nodded. 'Yes. it was about that night. He's living with her now.'

'Wow, you certainly mean what you say.'

'How is Lori?'

'Lori is very happy. Lori is married to a Texas oil tycoon who buys her two mink coats a week. so she's very happy.'

'You mean you've divorced too?

'Yes, I'm divorced yet again. We do these things quickly in the States. She went to Nevada and shed me in six weeks. Extreme mental cruelty. I think she said. Then she married this other man the very next day. The only good thing is she didn't knock me for any alimony or settlements so I was lucky. Supporting the other two ex's costs me enough.' He laughed. 'Are you meeting anyone?'

She shook her head.

'What about having lunch with me?'

She smiled. She liked Jay. 'I'd love to.'

'Good.' He stood up. 'I've just got to rearrange a few things. I'll be right back.'

After he left. Linda quickly took out her compact. She studied her face and added more lipstick. She wished she looked a bit more glamorous. but she had deliberately dressed-down to appear in court Jay was a very attractive man. Since separating from David. Linda had only been out on one date. partly because her lawyer had warned her not to. and partly because she didn't want to. The episode with Paul had left its mark. and she preferred to stay at home or visit married friends. The one evening she had gone out had been a bore. And to add insult to injury. her date had expected her to go to bed with him. Divorcees. she gathered from him. were supposed to include sex in the evening's activities.

Jay returned to the table. 'Everything's under control. Where would you like to eat?'

They decided to stay where they were. They moved into the restaurant. and Jay entertained her with amusing anecdotes about the location and idle gossip about the people involved. He took her hand over coffee and said. 'My God. it's nice to be with someone who has a brain and not just a body. You know. I really like you. Linda. you're a nice person.'

She smiled a little stiffly. She didn't want Jay to think of her as such a nice person. Nice was such a dull word. it conjured up twinsets and sensible shoes.

He looked at his watch. 'Wow—it's nearly three o'clock; I've got to rush.' He called for the check. 'Let me drop you at the station. I've got a studio car.'

'No. it's out of your way. I can easily get a cab.'

'If you insist. I'll put you in the cab. though.'

They left the restaurant and walked through the lobby. where Jay was hailed by a couple standing there. The woman was tall. blond. and pretty. The man short. stocky. and red-faced.

The man said. 'Oh. Mr. Grossman. sorry you couldn't make lunch. This is my client. Miss Susan Standish.'

Miss Susan Standish smiled a direct smile at Jay. She had very small white teeth and looked even prettier when smiling.

Jay smiled back. Linda saw his eyes flicker with interest as they swept over Miss Susan Standish. Tall. pretty blonds were obviously his type.

'I'll be right back,' he said, and took Linda to the entrance. He made no comment about the couple he had obviously stood up for lunch. He kissed her on the cheek. 'Linda, let's do this again sometime. When will you be back?'

'Thank you for a lovely lunch, Jay. I'll be home on Monday.'

He saw her into a cab. 'I'll talk to you then,' he said.

The phone rang and Claudia stretched languorously across the bed and picked it up. She spoke briefly, and with a grin she hung up.

'Baby,' she said to Giles, 'tonight we can have good times. David won't be home till late!'

Giles said, 'What are we waiting for. Let's have a party. Get on the phone. Call the liquor store first.'

They picked out names at random. Giles would say, 'Remember that kooky little girl who always wore those terrible thigh-length black boots . . .' and they would track her down, inviting another half-dozen people en route. Claudia changed into a startling silver-lamé cat suit. Giles snatched a nap, sprawled across her bed, and eventually people began to appear.

By the time David phoned again the party was in full swing. Claudia was completely stoned. She didn't even know who half the people were. The music was so loud that the tenants in the apartment below had complained three times. They had stopped phoning, as the last time a beautifully spoken debutante had told them exactly what to do in explicit detail. She was now accommodating an out-of-work window cleaner on the couch in full view of everyone.

'Great party!' Giles said. 'What happens when big daddy comes walking in?'

'Big daddy's going to have to join in the fun, or big daddy can walk right on out again.'

'Darling, sweetie pie—how divine of you to invite me.'

Claudia blinked, focusing slowly. 'Shirley, baby, how are you?'

'I'm fine, simply fine. Just got back from the most divine holiday.'

'You look wonderful, all that crazy suntan. Where's the Honourable whatnot?'

'Ditched him. darling. I've got the most divine man now, simply a poppet. You'll be amazed.'

'Grab a drink. and join in the fun. It's all happening here . . .' She trailed off as an Italian waiter type grabbed her from behind. 'You is beautiful.' he said. 'I eat you up.'

'Really.' Shirley said. 'it looks like you're in good hands. I'll see you later. sweetie.' She left Claudia struggling with the Italian.

Claudia had never seen him before. 'Leave me alone. you oaf.' she said.

He was very strong. 'You beautiful.' he said proudly. Obviously his English vocabulary was limited. He twisted her around in his arms and kissed her.

'Your breath stinks!' she exclaimed. still struggling.

He held her even tighter and kissed her again.

It was at this moment that David appeared. He stood furiously in the doorway of the apartment. Spotted Claudia immediately, and striding across the room he hauled the Italian away from her—smashing his fist into his face.

The man slumped to the floor. blood seeping from his nose.

David then turned his attention to Claudia. 'You fucking tramp.' he said. and brought his arm back-handedly across her face.

Nobody really noticed what was going on. The music was too loud and they were all too stoned.

'Get these dregs out of here.' David snarled.

She rubbed her cheek. her eyes huge and filled with tears—more from pain than from anything else. 'You *sonofa-bitch*,' she screamed. 'How dare you hit me—*how dare you*?'

'I'll do what I want to you. I bought you. didn't I? Now get this damned place clear.'

'You can go to hell and back. you bastard.' She bent to the Italian and cradled his head in her arms.

'I'm warning you. Claudia. you're pushing me too far.'

She ignored him.

He stood for a few seconds, then said, 'Right.' He marched into the bedroom.

It was at this particular moment that Giles was reaching a

hard-fought-for climax with a skinny redhead. It was unfortunate that it happened to be right in the middle of David's bed.

David swore loudly, but nothing bothered Giles. He kept on going, although the girl squeaked and attempted to object.

David grimly took a suitcase from the top of a cupboard. He methodically sorted his clothes from Claudia's, packing as much as he could.

Giles and the girl got up. She glared at David as she rearranged her clothes. 'Some people just don't care,' she muttered. 'They barge in anywhere.'

Giles made a mock bow. 'Performance over, next show at four o'clock.'

They walked out of the bedroom.

David locked the door behind them and continued packing. He finally filled three suitcases. His mind was cold with anger.

He unlocked the bedroom and strode to the front door with two of the cases. The party was still in full swing. He returned for the third suitcase.

'Bye-bye, darling,' Claudia yelled above the noise. She reeled across the room toward him. The front zipper on her cat suit was undone to her waist, and her breasts pushed forward to escape. Her hair was wild, and blood smeared her face.

'You look lovely,' he said. 'Just like the drunken little slut you are.'

She laughed. 'Get stuffed,' she shouted. 'Get lost asshole—don't come back. You're a bloody bore.'

Giles joined her. 'You tell him, kid,' he said, slipping his hand inside her open zipper.

She made an obscene gesture and turned her back.

David left.

14

'Well, look, darling, what *is* happening?' Claudia's voice was edgy and cold on the phone. 'I mean, they've been back ten days now, and they should be able to tell us *something*.'

Her agent was noncommittal. 'I can't get any definite date out of them.'

'But I signed a contract for two days' work—a contract, remember?'

'Yes, I know. But they've paid you for the work you were supposed to do. They don't have to use you.'

She snorted angrily. 'What kind of an agent *are* you? I'm supposed to be in that film. It's a big film, and it will do me a lot of good—a lot more good than these walk-on bits you keep offering me. If you can't do it, tell me, and I'll get someone who can!'

Her agent's voice was resigned. 'I'm doing my best.'

'Your best's not good enough. Forget it, I'll do it myself. *I'll* call Conrad Lee.' She slammed the phone down.

The apartment was in a terrible mess. The new cleaner had walked out the day after the party. Actually, the party had still been going on the next morning when she arrived, and she had taken one horrified look at the red-headed boy wearing Claudia's cat suit who answered the front door, and left.

It had been a good party, lasted three days in all. Claudia didn't remember much about it, really—but Giles assured her it had been a mind blower.

David hadn't returned. He hadn't phoned and he hadn't communicated in any way, although a mousy secretary had arrived one day about a week later to collect his mail and request that in future it be forwarded to his office.

Claudia didn't miss him. She was rather glad he had gone.

Life was too confining with someone watching every move you made. She had fallen in with David because it was easy, and he had left his wife, and it just sort of happened. It was rather nice having all the bills paid and lots of new clothes and no problems.

Now she would have to think about going back to work, a secret job she had which had always given her enough money to lead a comfortable, independent life. It would be better to be in Conrad's movie and become a star and make lots more money that way.

The other way gave her a vicarious thrill, though, and none of her friends—no one—knew about it. She had always kept it a closely guarded secret. Before she was living with David all her friends had wondered but never found out how she managed to be so financially secure and independent. The job excited her. She wore wigs and did special creative makeup jobs, completely disguising her own features. She starred in glorious Technicolor in porno movies! In four years she had been in thirty of them, making a lot of money along the way. So successful was she at the disguise jobs that she was known as three completely different girls, all in constant demand by the voyeurs who got to see the finished products. If she wanted to work again all it would take was a phone call. This is Evette—or Carmen—or Maria—and arrangements would be made. She was paid cash, and she contacted *them*—they had no way of reaching her. It was a satisfactory arrangement.

However, she wasn't sure that she wanted to go back to doing that. Sometimes her co-stars left a lot to be desired, and of course, if you weren't in the right mood, it could be pretty grim.

No—to appear in Conrad's movie was the best thing, and if her agent couldn't fix it, she certainly could. Conrad would probably be delighted to hear from her again.

She phoned the hotel he had stayed at on his previous visit, but he wasn't registered there. She phoned the studio and spoke to a secretary who took her name and said she would pass Mr. Lee her message. She tried to find out where he was living, but the girl was polite but firm—'We're not allowed to disclose Mr. Lee's address,' she said. 'I'll certainly see he gets your message.' It wasn't very satisfactory. Claudia wanted to get to him personally.

Giles would be able to find out. Giles was able to get hold of anyone. She called him at his studio, but there was no reply.

'Dammit!' she muttered, finally getting up.

There was a stack of bills by the front door. David had stopped paying for everything since he had left, and the bills were steadily mounting. She couldn't stick him with any of them, as the apartment and everything was in her name. It was a question of getting hold of Conrad and becoming a star.

Linda stayed in the country with her parents and the children much longer than she expected to. It was so peaceful, the children were out playing all day, while she sat in the house with her mother fussing around her. It was very relaxing, and knowing that to return to London was to be the beginning of a new life, she clung onto the limbo period of being with her parents.

Her mother wanted her to stay there permanently. 'Sell your house,' she urged. 'There's plenty of room for you here.'

Linda rejected the offer. Her parents' home was just a temporary retreat, and tempting as the thought was, it would be a mistake to stay. She would be buried there, stifled. Her mother would take care of everything, even to bringing up the children. Linda would become the elder daughter of the family.

One Saturday afternoon David turned up. It was the first time she had seen him since the divorce.

'I tried phoning the house, I was worried,' he said. 'I thought you'd be here.'

Her voice was stilted, cold. 'Why didn't you phone first? Why did you just come?'

He was ill at ease. It was strange to see David groping for words—he who was usually so sure of himself.

'I wanted to see the children.' A note of indignation crept into his voice. 'I'm supposed to see the children, you know.' He looked thin and tired. 'I've left Claudia,' he blurted out.

She looked at him dispassionately. 'Really.'

'You look marvellous,' he said.

She did look well. Her skin was glowing from long walks in

the country, and her hair was shining and unset, tied casually back with a ribbon. She looked slim in a pair of slacks and a loose shirt.

She gestured outside, 'The children are in the garden. I'll call them in.'

He put a hand on her arm. 'I said I've left Claudia.'

She brushed his hand impatiently away. 'I heard you the first time, David. I'll get the children.' She walked quickly from the room.

He stayed the whole afternoon, chatting amicably to her parents, entertaining Jane and Stephen with all sorts of games.

David is turning on his well-known charm, Linda thought miserably. I wish he'd go away.

He finally left at six. Her mother wanted to ask him to stay for dinner, but Linda hissed at her, 'Don't you dare.' His charm had worked. 'He really wants you back,' her mother said after he had gone.

She was really saying you should go back to him. Linda knew the signs.

Her father was less direct. 'That boy needs a father,' he said, when Stephen played up before going to bed.

Her mother said later in the evening, 'Poor David looks so unhappy.'

It was too much for Linda. They just didn't understand. They meant well, but she had had enough.

The next morning she told them she was going back to London, and on Monday morning she packed, and amidst tears from her mother and gruff words of wisdom from her father, she and the children were put safely on a train.

She was glad to be back in her own house. The children were pleased and excited to be reunited with all their books and toys, and cries of 'super' and 'that's mine' rang through the house.

Ana gave her a list of phone messages, and among them were two calls from Jay Grossman. He had left his number. She didn't call back. She thought about it, but somehow she felt if he really wanted to see her he would try again.

Monica had phoned. They hadn't spoken since the separation, they were David's friends. She phoned her.

Monica was delighted. 'Darling,' she exclaimed, 'I'm having a little dinner party—I'd love you to come.'

Linda was hesitant. 'When?'

'Tomorrow night. I must see you, it's been such ages. Will you come?'

She hesitated. 'I don't know. Have you invited David?'

'What do you take me for? Of course not. I don't want any other excuses. I'll see you tomorrow, eight o'clock. Don't be late.'

It was settled. It might be fun. Monica always invited interesting people. She would go to the hairdresser's and then buy a new dress. It was about time she started going out again.

Claudia sprawled untidily on a sofa at the back of Giles's studio. He was hard at work photographing a languid brunette clad only in a silver body stocking.

Claudia yawned. 'Why the hell don't you answer your bloody phone? You could have saved me a trip.'

Giles didn't look around: his concentration was completely on the model. After a few minutes he stopped, told the girl to take a break and wandered over to Claudia. He lit a cigarette, and stuck it in her mouth.

She took a long drag, spluttered and choked. 'Jesus Christ! Smoking pot at this time of the day! You're too much!'

He laughed, took it back and said, 'What do *you* want?'

'I came to see you,' she replied coyly. ''Cos I love you.'

'Cut the crap. I'm busy. What do you want?'

'Actually'—she stretched—'I need Conrad Lee's number—I thought you could get it for me.'

'Things must be tough if you're chasing him again.'

Her voice was irritable, sometimes she couldn't stand him. 'Things are not tough—and I'm not chasing anyone.'

He laughed. 'Don't forget it's me you're talking to, baby.'

'How could I possibly forget?'

They exchanged stares. 'All right,' he said, 'keep cool, I'll get it for you.' He made a few calls and got her the number.

She wrote it down and smiled. 'Thank you, darling,' she purred.

'That's all right, sweetheart—now get the hell out of here. I've got work to do.'

Claudia went shopping. She bought a white-and-gold-silk-jersey dress and gold spiky-heeled shoes, unfashionable but sexy. She went to the hairdresser's and had her hair elaborately piled on top of her head. Back home, she bathed, splashing half a bottle of musky oil into the water. She took two hours with her makeup—worrying until it was perfect.

By the time she was dressed it was seven o'clock. She dialled the number Giles had given her. Conrad's unmistakably accented voice answered.

She smiled. It was all going to work perfectly. She sounded cool and efficient. 'Mr. Lee?'

'Yes.' His voice was gruff.

'I am calling for *Star* magazine. You may know we are featuring your photograph on our cover this week, and I wondered if you might answer a few short questions about yourself.'

He became friendly. 'My picture, huh? Sure, I'll answer a few questions.'

Conceited pig! 'Thank you so much, Mr. Lee, if you will just give me your address I'll be right over. It will only take a short while.'

He was surprised. 'Can't I answer them now?'

'No, Mr. Lee, it's important to get your comments in person. I'm such a fan!'

'All right, all right.' He gave her his address.

Controlling her laughter she hung up, admired her reflection in the mirror and buzzed the doorman for a cab.

Conrad lived in an imposing house in Belgravia. The door was opened by a manservant in a white jacket who ushered her into the library. She waited patiently for fifteen minutes, until at last Conrad lumbered in. He hadn't changed. A fat cigar was stuck between his fleshy lips, and he wore the same green silk smoking jacket.

She arose, deliberately posing her body so that the thin silk dress clung even tighter. She knew she had never looked better. 'Hi.' She smiled provocatively.

He came to an abrupt standstill. She could see he didn't

recognize her. He plucked the cigar from his mouth. 'Are you the broad from *Star*?'

'Do I *look* like a lady journalist?'

His piercing eyes roved over her body. His memory stirred. 'Hey—you're the broad from the party I gave.' His voice changed. 'Hey—what's going on here—what is this?'

'You're a difficult man to get hold of. I've left lots of messages for you.'

'So?'

'I thought it was about time we got together again. Don't tell me you've forgotten all the fun we had last time.'

Interest flickered briefly in his eyes. 'Listen, I've got guests. You stay here, and I'll see what I can do.'

He left the room and she smiled triumphantly. It was amazing what a fabulous body could do.

He was gone for a long time. The manservant came in with a drink and left her some magazines. She leafed idly through them, waiting, because eventually he would be back, and then tomorrow morning, enter Claudia Star!

15

From the day he walked out on Claudia. David felt depressed. It wasn't that he had wanted to stay. the situation was impossible.

Claudia had turned out to be an out-and-out slut. She lolled around reading magazines all day. only bothering with her appearance if they were going out. She stayed in bed until noon, never tidying the apartment. The only thing she seemed capable of was incessant lovemaking. and whereas before he had lived with her he had always been ready. now he just couldn't do it. She was insatiable and demanding, never getting enough. David had always prided himself on his sexual appetite. but this was ridiculous.

He was pleased to have an excuse to get out. But depression followed, because instead of dismissing the whole mess from his mind and going home to his wife and children. he was an outcast, with nowhere to go except the coldness of a hotel room. No home comforts, just four impersonal walls; an empty bed, and a Do Not Disturb sign.

He returned to work with a vengeance and brooded on the possibilities of getting back together with Linda. He reasoned that she *should* take him back. After all. there were the children to consider. *They* wanted him back. Everything could be like it was before, only this time he wouldn't be such a fool and get hooked up with a tramp like Claudia. He would be more careful, pick and choose, short casual affairs, nothing that Linda could discover.

He phoned his ex-home and the maid informed him that Linda and the children were in the country with her parents. He was pleased. Give her more time to get over it. She was a sensible woman. She would know it was right for them to be together.

The first Saturday he was free he drove down to see her.

She looked surprisingly fresh and well. although her attitude was cold toward him. It was only to be expected.

He told her about leaving Claudia. Her reaction was strangely negative.

Give her time. he thought. she'll come around.

He was charming to her parents. He knew they were back on his side.

Later he drove back to London and called an old girl friend. She was giggly and a bit stupid but had a great body.

They went to a movie and then back to her place. She was lousy in bed. She had none of the franticness of Claudia or the calmness of Linda. He left after an hour.

On Sunday he woke early with nothing to do. An impulse took him to his office. He had a backlog of letters and other work he never found time for during the week.

He really needed his secretary to be around. Poor. plain Miss Field. Maybe she *was* available. she looked the sort of person who never made any plans. He phoned her.

Her voice was timid. 'Hello.'

'Miss Field. Mr. Cooper here.'

'Oh!' Her voice became a startled squeak. as if she had been caught doing something she shouldn't have been.

'Miss Field. how do you feel about working today?'

'Oh. Mr. Cooper—oh. really?'

'It's all right if you can't manage it.'

'Oh. no—Oh. Mr. Cooper. of course I can.'

'Good. Get here as fast as you can.'

She was there within the hour. pale and nervous.

'You look very nice today. Miss Field.' he said politely.

She had brushed her thin stringy brown hair down instead of pulling it back. and she wore a harsh scarlet lipstick on her thin usually colourless mouth. Sunday clothes consisted of a brown dress and blue woollen cardigan. She was a picture of plainness.

They worked efficiently through the day nonstop, until the light began to fade and David suddenly realized it was getting late.

'I suppose we'd better quit,' he said, yawning. 'You must be hungry.'

'Mr. Cooper'—her voice was hesitant, nervous—'perhaps you would care to have a little dinner with me.' A bright red flush was spreading up into her hairline. 'I make it my business to always prepare a *cordon-bleu* dinner on Sundays—one of my little hobbies, and I would be only too delighted if you would sample it.' She added quickly, 'Boeuf Stroganoff, with fresh green salad, followed by lemon meringue pie.'

It sounded good. Besides, he had nowhere else to go. She kept blushing, and he felt sorry for her. 'What a good idea, Miss Field. I'd be glad to.'

She lived in a tiny one room apartment. The couch, neatly festooned with crochet cushions, obviously did double duty as the bed.

She produced a half-bottle of sherry—too sweet—and he sat and watched television while she pottered about in the kitchen.

She prepared a delicious dinner with which they drank cheap Spanish wine. 'I brought it back from my holiday last year,' she said proudly.

After dinner she was obviously a little tipsy. 'I don't usually drink,' she said with a giggle.

He was also slightly drunk, having consumed half the bottle of wine and most of the sherry before dinner. His attention was riveted to the television screen. The Beauty Maid commercial was on, and there was Claudia in her bath. Familiar sharp pull in his groin.

'Oh, Mr. Cooper, our commercial.' Miss Field sat quickly down beside him on the couch.

He felt the nearness of a leg beside him and rested his hand on her thigh. She shrieked, and before he knew it her arms were around his neck and she was pulling his mouth toward the thin red line. They kissed, and as Claudia vanished from the screen so his desire vanished with her. But it was too late. Miss Field was already in action. All in the space of seconds, she leaped up, turned the light off, wriggled out of her cardigan, and was back beside him. 'My dearest, I am yours,' she said. 'I have waited for this moment too long.'

He couldn't believe it. The whole thing was ludicrous.

She lay back expectantly, quivering.

What should he do? She was a good secretary. He didn't want to lose her. He didn't want to hurt her feelings.

She was getting impatient. 'David, my dearest, come to me. I am not afraid.'

He took a deep breath and ran his hands tentatively across her bosom. There was no bosom!

Coyly she said, 'I know I am not well endowed, but there is fire in my loins.'

Oh, my God! he thought. What am I getting into?

Tired of waiting, she locked her hands behind his head and pulled his mouth down on hers.

This is a bloody nightmare, he thought. But as her tongue worked on his mouth so his body started to respond, and soon he was ready.

She was angular, bony, and surprisingly strong. She managed to get his pants and shorts off and then her mouth was travelling down his body and she was kissing him, and suddenly it was all over for him in a huge shaking furious bout of passion. He screamed, but she didn't stop, sending him into a frenzy. A shudder enveloped her and at last she was still.

They lay in silence—his body sprawled across her at an angle. He could hardly believe what had just taken place. Placid, timid Miss Field Mouse certainly knew what she was doing.

He went and locked himself in the bathroom. His body was covered in red weals where her fingers had dug into him. She was a hot bitch!

When he returned to the room her cardigan was back on, and she was primly clearing the dishes. She avoided looking at him as he stepped into his shorts and pants.

'Would you like coffee before you go, Mr. Cooper?' she said. Her voice was controlled, only a slight flush across her cheeks indicating what had just taken place.

'Er, no thank you, Miss Field.' He took his cue from her. 'I really must be on my way.'

'I do hope we can do this again,' she said evenly.

'Yes.' He hesitated. 'Well, good-bye, then. See you at the office tomorrow.'

'Good-bye. Mr. Cooper. see you tomorrow.'

Out in the street he heaved a big sigh. He would have to get rid of her. To have her working with him at the office every day would be a horrible reminder. Next time he would get a pretty secretary—just on the chance he should ever be thrown into an experience like this again.

.He thought about Linda with wry longing. He was ready to go home.

'Linda, darling! You look positively stunning! So slim. so young! This divorce business certainly agrees with you.' Monica led Linda into the living room. 'It's an interesting crowd tonight. no married couples; Jack and I decided it would be more fun. Now let me introduce you.'

There were perhaps twelve people sitting and standing around. Linda recognized Monica's brother. a dress designer. He was with a short. squat woman wearing a very unsuitable silk pajama suit.

'That's Princess Lorenz Alvaro with Rodney,' whispered Monica. 'Exciting. isn't it?'

Linda had never heard of Princess Alvaro. and she didn't see what was so exciting about it. as Rodney was gay.

She was soon chatting quietly to a doctor. A tall and pleasant man. Before they had finished one martini he had invited her to dinner the following evening. and she thought. why not? So she accepted. He was fairly attractive and seemed most taken with her. Definitely a nice man. not a David type at all.

More people arrived. and Linda found herself wedged in a corner. while the doctor told her a long involved story about a patient of his with yellow jaundice. It was rather boring. She smiled politely and wished she hadn't accepted his dinner invitation. Doctor or not. he had a severe case of bad breath.

Idly she glanced around the room. Then she saw Jay and she straightened up. smoothed down her dress. and touched her hair. He hadn't seen her. He was talking to Rodney and Princess Alvaro. and then he was joined by the blond girl who had been in the lobby of the Dorchester the day they had lunched. The blond looked even prettier now in a crisp white pant suit. her hair tied on top of her head with a white ribbon. Jay put his arm around her, and she smiled up at him.

Linda looked away. The doctor droned on.

Monica announced that a cold buffet was being served in the other room.

'I *am* hungry,' Linda said pointedly.

'Good heavens,' said the doctor, 'I must have been boring you stiff. Let's go and eat.' He took her possessively by the elbow and steered her into the other room, where she bumped straight into Jay.

He balanced two plates of food which almost fell. 'Linda!' He sounded pleased.

'Jay,' she said, affecting the same tone.

'Where have you been?'

'In the country with the children.'

'You look terrific.'

Did I look so terrible before? she wondered. 'Thank you.' She couldn't help grinning stupidly.

They stood and smiled at each other, and then the doctor's grip tightened and he said, 'We'd better get our food.'

'Oh, yes.' Linda's heart was beating fast.

'See you in a minute,' Jay said. He winked and imitated an English accent. 'We'd better get our food!'

When Jay was out of hearing distance, the doctor said, 'These American film types are all the same.'

'Oh?'

'You know—brash, vulgar, full of themselves.'

'Do you know Jay Grossman?' Linda asked crossly.

'Let's say we have a mutual friend.'

'Who?' she asked rudely.

'Name no names, hear no pack drill.'

'What?' Suddenly she hated the doctor.

He smiled secretly. 'As a matter of fact, it's one of his ex-wives.'

'Oh.' She tried to sound disinterested.

'A lovely woman,' the doctor continued. 'I believe she had a terrible time with him. She just remarried.'

'Lori?' Linda asked coldly.

The doctor looked surprised. 'Yes. Lori is in London with her husband. He's extremely wealthy.'

'How interesting,' she said sarcastically, and quickly helped herself to food before rushing back into the other room. The doctor followed her closely.

There was nowhere to sit.

Jay was with the blond on a sofa. 'Linda,' he called. 'Sit here.'

'Excuse me,' she said to the doctor.

Jay stood up and she sat down. The blond glanced at her, annoyed.

'Susan,' Jay said. 'I want you to meet a very good friend of mine, Linda Cooper.'

'Hello.' Susan's smile was limp.

The doctor squatted on his haunches in front of them, eating from his crowded plate hungrily. Jay drifted away to the other side of the room.

Susan suddenly got up and said to Linda, 'Perhaps your friend would like to sit down.' She moved across the room to join Jay, and the doctor quickly sat beside Linda. She was well and truly stuck as he obviously had no intention of leaving her side.

'Can I drive you home later?' he asked.

'I'm sorry. I have my car with me.'

'Pity.' He shook his head. 'Maybe I should follow to see you get home safely.' He chuckled.

She could have screamed, he was such a bore! She didn't even bother to reply just jumped up. He got up too.

'Excuse me,' she said firmly. 'I have to go to the ladies' room.'

It was quiet upstairs in Monica's bedroom. She sat at the dressing table and rearranged strands of her hair. Would Monica think her rude if she left? She didn't really care. She looked for her jacket among the coats on the bed. What a waste buying the new black chiffon dress she was wearing.

She found her jacket, went downstairs, and slipped out quietly. She would call Monica tomorrow and explain that she had a headache and had thought it better not to bother with good-byes. Monica would probably be insulted, not invite her again, but so what? It was much more fun staying at home with the children.

Back at home she undressed slowly, wondering why on earth three hours previously she had painstakingly applied such a careful makeup and looked forward so excitedly to Monica's dreary gathering. What had she expected? Prince Charming, not a boring doctor with bad breath.

She felt depressed. Girls like Susan set the pace now with their lithe bodies. Face up to it, Linda, she thought, you've had your best years, you gave them to David. You've got two children. You're divorced. You have to settle for second best now.

She was lonely at night. Once, briefly, it had crossed her mind to phone Paul, but common sense had prevailed. Maybe she had made a mistake divorcing David. Maybe she *should* have given him another chance. But no, she was right, this was better than living a lie with David.

She fell into a troubled sleep.

An hour later the phone woke her.

'Hello.' Her voice was sleepy.

'Are you trying to avoid me?'

'What?' Her mind was still sleep-filled.

'I leave messages for you, you don't return my calls. You ignore me tonight, and then just run off. I want dinner with you tomorrow night, no excuses.'

'Yes, Jay.' Her voice was weak.

'I'll pick you up at eight, and no calls to say you can't make it. I've phoned you three times.'

She didn't know what to say.

'All right, tomorrow at eight,' he said after a short pause. 'And wear that black dress you had on tonight, it looks great.'

Suddenly everything seemed bright again. Jay Grossman was certainly not second best.

Eventually Conrad returned. He had been gone an hour and a half, and Claudia, bored with the magazines and being kept waiting, was a little testy. She covered her irritation with a smile.

He was drunk. He grabbed hold of her, his fleshy hands feeling her body through her thin dress.

She wriggled away. This wasn't the way she had it planned.

'Aren't we going upstairs?' she asked.

His breath. a mixture of strong garlic and Scotch. enveloped her as he replied. 'Sure—sure Just want a little preliminary.' He forced his hand inside the neckline of her dress, grabbing her breasts with rough fingers.

'You're hurting me,' she complained. and then, 'Hey—you're tearing my dress.' She pulled away from him again, furious at the torn dress. but still smiling provocatively. 'Let's go upstairs, lover.' she cooed. 'Let's have a great scene upstairs.'

'Take your clothes off first—I want to take a look at the goods I'm getting.' he said urgently.

It was obviously no use arguing with him. She'd fix him when she got him in the sack.

Slowly she peeled off sensuous folds of white jersey. Underneath she had on only a wisp of garter belt, and pale sheer stockings, her long legs emphasized by the exceptionally high heels she was wearing.

He lunged at her, falling to his knees and grabbing her around the waist. He sunk his teeth into her stomach and bit hard.

She screamed with pain and kicked him away. 'You son of a bitch!'

He laughed, hollow loud rumbles.

She rubbed her stomach, her eyes glinting dangerously, her mouth a tight smile. So he wanted to play games, huh? Well, she knew a few of her own.

'Come on.' He lumbered to the door. She followed him. He pushed her up the stairs ahead of him, stroking her legs, trying to feel between them.

They reached the bedroom. It was very dark, she could hardly see a thing.

'Get on the bed,' he commanded.

She climbed onto a large circular bed, grimly thinking things were going to be different in the morning, when this big slob was sober.

He switched on the lights—bright glaring lights that hit the bed at a hard angle. She noticed a huge mirror above the bed.

He climbed on top of her, not even bothering to remove his clothes, just unfastening his trousers.

'Open up, baby,' he said, 'let's have some action.'

He used her brutally—slamming and grinding into her, and afterwards wanting it different ways, making her do it to him at every conceivable angle.

She worked hard. This was something he had to remember It was funny, really. When she became famous, everyone would say she was an overnight discovery. How right they would be!

At last he was finished. Her body ached from his pressures. She was bruised and worn. She lay spread-eagled on the bed, too limp to move.

He was surprisingly full of life. 'Got a little thrill for you,' he said. 'Just stay where you are.'

He got off the bed and pressed a switch by the door. The mirror above the bed parted and slid easily in two, leaving a gap in the ceiling. A ring of smiling faces peered down at her from the gaping aperture.

She sat up, horrified.

'Just a few of my friends,' Conrad said easily. 'These two-way mirrors are a great gimmick for making a party go with a bang!' He guffawed. 'Pick out who you'd like next.'

A woman's face, grotesquely made up and old, said, 'How about me, Conrad? Can I have a turn with her? She seems to know what it's all about.'

A man's voice said, 'No, me next, let me give her a real fucking.'

'Oh, God!' Claudia jumped off the bed.

'What's the matter?' Conrad asked. 'Don't you want to be in my movie?'

She stared at him, every instinct warning her to get out.

But to leave now—what use was that? That wouldn't get her on the silver screen.

'All right,' she said at last. 'All right. I'll stay, but this time you'd better mean it.'

'I mean it,' he said blandly.

16

David managed to get through the early part of the next week without trouble. Miss Field was, as usual, the perfect, quiet, unobtrusive secretary. Neither of them made any reference to the previous Sunday. Indeed, it was as if it had never happened.

David felt that maybe it had all been a bad dream, but some grim sense of foreboding warned him that it was true. The sooner he was rid of Miss Field, the better. Meanwhile, their relationship was exactly the same as before.

He decided to wait a couple of weeks, then get her transferred to another department, maybe with a raise. She wouldn't object to that.

Mr. Taylor of the Fulla Beans account was in town. David didn't relish the thought, but as usual he was elected to entertain him. Did these poor out-of-towners *never* get tired of the inevitable clip-joint nightclub and the pathetic, blowsy hostesses? It seemed not. Once more David had to fix him up, this time with a big redhead called Dora. Dora laughed a lot and suggested that it would be a lot of fun if Burt Taylor *and* David accompanied her back to her bed.

Neither of them liked the idea. Burt, because he didn't want to share. And David, because he didn't want to know.

She was very insistent, and when Burt Taylor, eyes bulging at the thought of the show she was offering, started to think it wasn't such a bad idea after all, David became really fed up.

He managed to finally persuade them to go off on their own. How he hated this sort of entertaining. These nightclub scrubbers weren't for him. He returned to his hotel room and went to bed.

The week dragged. Wednesday afternoon he phoned to speak to his children. They had just got home from school and were having tea. Ana told him Mrs. Cooper was out.

He was sure Linda wouldn't mind if he dropped by to see them. Maybe she would let him stay for dinner. It was all a question of time with Linda. Eventually she would realize the only sensible thing was to take him back.

He told Ana he would be right over. She mumbled something in Spanish. He could hear the children's excited squeaks in the background.

He left the office in high humour, and went to Hamley's store, and filled his arms with toys. He stopped at Swiss Cottage and bought flowers. By the time he arrived at the house it was two hours later.

Linda answered the door tight-lipped and furious. She stood in the doorway. 'The children are being bathed,' she said coldly.

'All right, I can wait.' He offered her the flowers.

She ignored them. 'David, we have an agreement that you only visit the children at the weekend.'

'What difference does it make when I come? Are you going to penalize me because I want to see my kids?'

She stood back wearily. She didn't want to be unfair as far as the children were concerned, after all, he *was* their father. 'Come in, but please don't do this again.'

'What do you mean? Don't visit my own children again?'

'No, David, I mean please keep to the agreed times.'

'You surprise me.' He shook his head. 'I never thought you would use Janey and Stephen as a weapon against me.'

Her eyes filled with tears at the injustice of what he was saying. 'But I'm not. I'm just trying to do what's best.'

He looked at her coldly. 'And you think it's best that two innocent young children should not be allowed to see their father.'

'You're twisting what I'm saying.'

'I'm not twisting anything. I'm just repeating you.' He thrust the flowers at her. 'Take these—or perhaps you would prefer to throw them out like you would me.'

She accepted the flowers. 'I'll see if bathtime is finished.'

'Can I have permission to go upstairs and see them in the bath?' His voice was acid.

'Of course.'

Stephen stood at the top of the stairs, scrubbed and clean in striped pyjamas. 'Daddy!' he yelled.

Linda heard the cry of joy downstairs. She glanced at her watch. It was six o'clock. Maybe she should call Jay and tell him she couldn't keep their date. She felt so confused. David's attitude toward her was so unfair. He acted as if the whole thing was her fault.

He came downstairs, Janey cuddled in his arms, Stephen clinging to his hand. He fetched the packages from the car, and the children yelled with excitement.

Linda shut the door of the living room and left them all together. She went upstairs and lay down on the bed. She had thought the most painful part of divorce was over, but when you have children it's never over. there's always a small questioning voice—'Why doesn't Daddy live here anymore? When can Daddy come back? Do you love Daddy?'

She tried to contact Jay. He was out.

After an hour she went downstairs. With a forced smile she said, 'Come along—time for bed. School tomorrow.'

Stephen glared at her, 'Oh, Mummy!'

Janey started to cry.

David said, 'How about ten more minutes?'

'Please, Mummy,' Janey begged.

'Oh, O.K.—but no longer.' She glanced again at her watch. It was past seven, and Jay was due at eight. She didn't want him and David to meet. She wished she could find Jay and put him off. Not that she wanted to, but she really didn't feel like going out now.

After another twenty minutes the children were at last safely in bed with David reading them stories. By the time he came downstairs it was a quarter to eight. His mood was cordial. 'I could do with a drink.'

She was nervous. She had a perfect right to go out on a date, but she instinctively knew David wouldn't like it.

He poured himself a Scotch. 'You know, Stephen's a very bright lad. We must have a serious talk about his future.'

She pulled herself together. 'Yes, we must, but not now. I

have to get changed.' Her voice became defiant 'I'm going out.'

'That's nice 'There was a silence. then he added. 'Pretty cushy life you've got.'

Her voice was controlled. 'I beg your pardon?'

'Well. you know. no worries. nice house. I foot all the bills, and you can just run around doing what you like.'

'I don't run around. and you know it.'

'Come off it. You're an attractive woman. a divorcee. Any man know's he's on to a good thing—a free lay is always popular. You must have dozens of offers. Why I bet—'

Her cheeks blazed. 'Get out! Get out of here!'

He put his drink down calmly. 'What's the matter? Don't try to tell me you're not getting it.'

'Please go. David. Right now.'

He sauntered to the door. 'All right. all right, don't get excited. I won't hang around to mess up your date. I'll get back to my hotel room—don't worry about me. just have a good time.'

When he reached the front door she slammed it in his face.

He climbed into his car angrily. Thoughtless bitch! She was as bad as Claudia. They were all the same. all bitches trying to grab you by the balls and squeeze everything out of you.

He drove around the block and then came back and parked a few houses away. May as well wait and see who she was going out with.

Jay was a few minutes late. but hardly enough for Linda to recover. He found her in tears.

'I can't go out.' she sobbed.

He put his arm around her. She leaned her head against his chest and told him a jumbled account of what had happened.

He was sympathetic. 'You must talk to your lawyer first thing tomorrow. You can get a court order to stop him bothering you—he has set times to see the kids. and he'll have to stick to them.'

'I just thought it would be so mean of me not to let him see the children.'

'That's how he *wants* you to feel. He's probably had enough screwing around and decided to come back. His only way of getting at you is through the kids.'

'Do you think so?'

'Sure, listen, Linda—I'm experienced in these things. He blew a beautiful setup with you. You're not some little ding-a-ling—you're a lovely woman, and I bet he wants you back.' He paused and then asked casually 'How do you feel about him?'

She was thoughtful. 'I don't know. I don't love him or anything like that. It's just that in spite of his insults, I do feel sorry for him. After all, I have the house and the children, and what does he have?'

'Hey, whoa, baby, you're starting to think like he *wants* you to think. He chose, didn't he?'

She nodded. 'You're right.'

'Good at least you're starting to realize I'm always right!' He laughed. 'Now, go upstairs, powder your nose, put on your black dress, and let's go.'

She smiled. 'Yes, Jay.'

He took her to Annabel's. They dined elegantly. Jay entranced her with amusing stories about the film and the location in Israel. He told her about his children—there were three of them, one by his first wife and two by his second.

'Beautiful blond Californians,' he said wryly. 'I don't get to see them too much. Lori hated children.'

'How old are they?'

'Caroline's the eldest, she's fifteen—a real cuckoo kid. Lives in San Francisco with Jenny, my first wife. Then there's Lee, he's ten, and Lance, who's nine. They've got a great stepfather now, and I see them whenever I'm in L.A.'

'I've never been to America. Is it as glossy as it all looks on the screen?'

He laughed. 'I guess you could say Hollywood is pretty glossy—personally, the only thing I really like there is the weather.'

After dinner they were joined by friends of Jay's, also in the movie business.

It was a lovely evening. Jay took Linda home in his chauffeured studio car and kissed her on the cheek.

'How about Saturday?' he asked.

'Yes,' she replied quietly.

'I'll call tomorrow. And don't forget, get on to your lawyer first thing.'

'I will.'

They smiled at each other. She let herself into the house and watched him through the window as he climbed back into the car. She liked him a lot.

Claudia buried herself in bed at her apartment. She huddled beneath the covers, bruised, used, and frightened to face anyone.

The day after the debacle with Conrad she called her agent and told him everything was fixed, and that he would be hearing from the studio. Then she took a variety of pills and slept, or tried to.

Claudia was not naïve, there had been many men, many different scenes, the blue movies. But never anything so degrading as the evening at Conrad's house. When she closed her eyes, visions of evil, smiling faces swept before her. All the things they had made her do raced through her thoughts. She could still feel their hands. Her body screamed from the aches of sexual misuse.

She stayed beneath the covers, not eating, ignoring the telephone, inert and numb for several days.

Nobody cared, nobody came. If she died it would probably be months before they discovered her. Where were all her so-called friends?

At last she forced herself to get up. She was thin and white. She dressed and went out. The people in the street disgusted her. She went to see Giles. He was away in Majorca. She returned home and hacked off all her tawny glorious hair with her nail scissors. Then she slipped back into bed, and this time slept.

When she woke the next day she felt much better. She opened some cans and ate. She was horrified to see what she had done to her hair, it stuck out at all angles and looked a mess. She read the papers and magazines that had piled up by the front door, and called her agent.

No, he hadn't heard yet. Had she read that Conrad was getting married?

She grabbed the papers again. There it was—Conrad Lee, sixty-two years old, famous producer, to marry twenty-year-old model and ex-debutante Shirley Sheldon.

Shirley Sheldon! Claudia gasped in amazement. Shirley Sheldon! Ex-fiancée of the Honourable Jeremy Francis, ex-stripper. It couldn't possibly be true. Shirley was a phony debutante only interested in getting on in life. She had only hooked up with Jeremy because he had a title.

Claudia supposed she was going for Conrad's money and fame. But what on earth could *he* see in *her*? She wasn't *that* pretty, she had a lousy figure, and she was a dreary bore. The old schmuck must reckon she really was a debutante. What a laugh! Why, she had introduced them. She remembered Shirley coming to her party and having that great suntan. She must have got it in Israel. What a cow! Where had she been the other night? Didn't he involve his fiancée in his orgies? And if not, why not?

She read the article again. The wedding was set for that same day. She just couldn't believe it. Thin Shirley Sheldon, certainly not an ex-debutante, certainly not twenty.

'Ha!' she snorted. It was all too much.

On sudden impulse she raced to the phone book and looked up the Honourable Jeremy. She found his number and dialled quickly.

He was home, stammering and unsure as ever. 'I s-s-say, Claudia, how nice,' he said, after she announced herself.

'Are you going to Shirley's wedding?' she asked bluntly.

'I should jolly well s-s-say so, wouldn't want to miss that—w-w-hat?' He chorted happily.

'I thought we might go together,' she said casually. 'It's about time we saw each other again.'

'I say, what a good idea. S-s-shall I fetch you?'

She smiled. It was too easy. 'Terrific—what time?'

'If the reception s-s-starts at s-s-six, I think I should come for you at five-thirty.'

'Marvellous, Jeremy.' She gave him her address and hung up. What an idiot he was.

She spent the afternoon at the hairdresser and emerged with a whole new look. Her hair, short like a boy's, sleek, with long sideburns. Fortunately it was the look of the moment. Anyway, all the top models were wearing it. It went well with the ultra-short, skimpy gold shift she chose to wear.

Jeremy was impressed. 'I s-s-say, old girl, you look absolutely super!' he said, when he called for her.

She fixed him a strong martini and noticed his bad complexion was still the same. She resisted a strong temptation to ask him if he ever got laid.

'So good old Shirley's finally making the wedding-bells scene,' she said, sipping her martini and exhibiting a great deal of leg as she sat in the big armchair opposite him.

His eyes bulged. 'Yes, I'll s-s-say.'

'Whatever happened with you two?'

'Well'—he waved his long skinny arms about—'she's a s-s-super girl, great fun and all that, but she s-s-said she needed someone more mature.' He took a few gulps of his drink, his Adam's apple bobbing rhythmically. 'We're s-s-still great pals,' he added lamely.

'Just as well,' Claudia said briskly. 'After all, she's so much older than you.'

'She is?' Jeremy looked surprised.

'I don't want to give away any secrets, I mean she looks after herself so well—but after all, how long can she go on fooling everybody?' Claudia shook her head wisely, and Jeremy stared at her, his mouth hanging open inanely. 'Shall we go?' she asked brightly, jumping up and smoothing her dress down.

'Er—yes.' Jeremy got up too.

He was very tall and ungainly – a real chinless wonder, Claudia thought. It was no surprise Shirley had ditched him for Conrad. At least Conrad had a certain grotesque style.

Jeremy drove a shiny red MG. It was very uncomfortable, he had to cram himself behind the wheel.

'Why don't you get a bigger car?' she asked. After all, his parents were supposed to be loaded.

'Oh, this little bus really gets me around,' he said proudly. 'Wouldn't s-s-swap this one in.'

He drove badly, jerking the clutch, cutting up other drivers without even noticing, and racing cars at the traffic lights.

Claudia felt sick by the time they arrived. She needed a fast drink. What a joy it would be to see Shirley's and Conrad's faces when they saw her. *Quelle surprise!*

David sat in his car smoking a cigarette. He didn't have to wait long before a sleek black chauffeur-driven limousine glided to a halt in front of his house—well, Linda's house. A man emerged. David was too far away to recognize him. He swore under his breath and edged his car a little nearer, but it was too late, the man had already gone inside.

Well, Linda was certainly doing all right for herself. The man, whoever he was, obviously had money.

Women were such schemers. They couldn't wait—here they were divorced only a few weeks, and there was Linda going out and living it up. She probably had this sucker all lined up! Bitch! She was no better than Claudia.

He waited impatiently for them to come out. They were certainly taking their time, probably having a quick one in the living room. He contemplated going in and punching the man—whoever he was—on the nose. But she probably wouldn't let him in anyway.

She would pay for this when he took her back. At the rate she was going, maybe he wouldn't even want her back.

He sat, immersed in his thoughts, until they finally came out. The man, the bastard, had his arm around her. The chauffeur jumped out and opened the door for them. They climbed in, the chauffeur got back in the car, and they slid off.

David set off in pursuit, keeping a discreet distance between the cars. It was unfortunate for him that at Swiss Cottage the chauffeur decided to skip through a yellow light, and David, following him on red, was stopped by a policeman on a motorcycle. He had to produce his licence and insurance, and the policeman gave him a lecture on dangerous driving. Of course, by the time he was free to go, their car had long vanished into the night. Pangs of hunger didn't help his mood. He hated eating on his own, but at this hour there seemed no alternative. He decided to go somewhere cheerful, and he headed for Carlo's.

It was packed, as usual. Lots of bright-looking females in their most startling outfits, and the actors, photographers, and men about town who were their escorts for the night.

The headwaiter told him with a phony sad shake of his head that it would be at least two hours before he could squeeze a table for one in. David slipped him money, and the waiter became a little brighter about his prospects. He asked David to wait at the bar, and he would see what he could manage.

David ordered a Scotch on the rocks and surveyed the scene. He couldn't help thinking about the last time he had been here with Claudia. He wondered what she was doing now, but found he didn't really care. If it wasn't for her, he would be at home with his wife, now.

A woman was staring at him. He stared back. She had mounds of silver-blond hair piled on top of her head, and she wore a white mink coat. Her face looked familiar. She was with two men who were in deep conversation—loud old Americans—one was wearing cowboy boots.

She sat very still. Cool, beautiful, and remote from her companions.

Suddenly David remembered her. It was Lori Grossman. He put his drink down and went over to her table. 'Hello, Lori,' he said, and then by way of jogging her memory, 'David Cooper. Remember me?'

Her smile was small, sensuous as she extended an elongated whiter-than-white hand. 'David. How nice.'

The two men stopped talking. She introduced the elder one—he must have been all of seventy—as Marvin Rufus, her husband.

David looked surprised. Whatever happened to Jay?

'Sit down—have a drink,' Marvin said and immediately resumed his conversation with the other man.

Lori slipped off her white mink coat, revealing black lace, cut to a low V. She had small but perfect breasts. She was wearing no bra.

'I ditched Jay,' she said in answer to his unspoken question. 'He was a real cheap bastard.' She adjusted a fabulous diamond bracelet clamped around her thin wrist. 'Marvin knows how to treat a woman . . .' She trailed off, her pale, frosty, aquamarine eyes staring hungrily into his.

This one was ready! David congratulated himself on being so attractive to women. She was eating him up with her eyes! 'Linda and I are divorced,' he said. 'It just didn't work out.'

'Yeah, I know,' she drawled.

'You know?' he said, surprised.

She smiled. 'A little birdie told me, and I suppose *you* know that my darling peachy ex is dating your ex. Isn't that cosy?'

'Jay is taking out Linda?' He couldn't believe it.

'That's right, honey.' She moved closer to him, and he felt a sudden pressure from her leg under the table. His hand touched a silky thigh. She couldn't wait!

Marvin and the other man talked on, something about market prices in London, and would the pound be devalued.

'How long are you here for?' he asked.

'Just a couple of days,' she drawled.

That would be long enough. If Jay was knocking off Linda, he might as well grab a piece of Lori. She was obviously ready, willing, and able.

Under the table his hand crept farther up her leg, reaching smooth skin above the stocking top.

'Are you meeting someone?' she asked.

He shook his head.

'You must join us then. Marve won't mind. He'll be talking business for hours.'

In a few minutes their table was ready. True to what Lori had said, her husband continued his marathon conversation with the other man, barely pausing to eat.

Lori ate like a sparrow, nibbling small pieces of steak, picking at a salad. Then the music started, and David asked her to dance. She was very tall, her bird's nest of hair making her even more so.

'Well?' he said when they were on the dance floor. The prospect of messing up this spectacular piece of aloofness was exciting him.

She felt his excitement and pressed closer.

'Marve will want to go gambling when we leave here, I'll say I'm too tired, and you'll offer to take me to the hotel. We have separate suites. He won't disturb us.'

He gripped her to him hard. He could feel her bones, as she ground her body to the sound of the music.

'What if it doesn't work?' he asked.

'It will work.' She gave a low laugh. 'It always has before.'

Jay called Linda on Thursday and Friday as he had promised. Hearing from him each day gave her a feeling of well-being. He made her feel alive and attractive again.

She rushed around the shops searching for a suitable dress to beguile him with on Saturday night. Everything seemed to have been made for flat-chested seventeen-year-olds. She finally settled for a very simple white crepe shift, much too expensive, but beautifully cut. She spent the day absorbed in her children, taking them for a long walk on the heath and letting them ride on the donkeys. She loved the kids, and with Jay in her life she seemed to love them even more.

She took her time getting ready for him—long, hot scented bath, white crepe dress, few pieces of good jewelry. She couldn't stop herself from thinking about him making love to her. Did he want to? He obviously liked her a lot. Would he make a pass at her tonight?

Make a pass—what a juvenile thought. She was a divorced woman with two children, not a teen-ager on a second date.

Would he want to sleep with her tonight? That was more like it. She wanted him, she needed him. It had been a long time. Finally she was ready, and he was, as usual, on time.

'You look lovely,' he said. 'You don't mind if we stop at a party for a few minutes? Business.'

The party was in Belgravia, an elegant pre-Victorian house, complete with butler and maid at the door.

Linda was immediately intimidated. She glanced around the luxurious living room and recognized several well-known faces. The place seemed to be filled with stars and beautiful young girls. Jay knew everyone He moved around. greeting people. while she trailed miserably behind him. feeling out of place and suddenly plain.

To top it all, a gorgeous blond whom she recognized as Susan Standish put her arm around him intimately and whispered loud enough for her to hear. 'You bastard! How dare you leave before I woke up this morning!'

Jay pushed the girl away. laughing easily

Linda turned and walked across the room. Nobody seemed interested in talking to her. It was one of those parties where everyone was a 'somebody' in the film industry. and unless you were a 'somebody' or a beautiful young starlet. nobody wanted to know.

She found a chair and sat down. What a fool she had been. Jay wasn't interested in her. he was probably just sorry for her. She sat brooding. After all. he was a big director. he had the pick of all the girls in London. What could she offer him that he couldn't get more brightly packaged elsewhere?

He was heading in her direction. She turned on a bright smile, mustn't let him see she was upset—embarrass him. what for? There was nothing between them.

'Why did you rush off?' he asked. his eyes faintly amused. 'You left me in the clutches of a female would-be star—always in hot pursuit of us poor old directors. Why didn't you stay and protect me?'

She felt like saying. 'You slept with her last night. what do you expect?' Instead she just smiled and said, 'I don't know. I thought I'd sit down for a while.'

'We can go in a minute. I had to put in an appearance, otherwise Jan would never let me forget it.' He pointed to a striking woman in her forties. their hostess.

They left soon after and dined at a small French restaurant in Chelsea. Before they were halfway through their meal he asked her what was wrong.

Linda was bad at concealing her feelings. and her manner with Jay had become almost stilted. 'Nothing.' Inexplicably she found her eyes filling with tears.

He changed the subject. 'Let's take the kids out tomorrow.

I'm looking forward to meeting them.'

She couldn't think of an excuse. 'All right.' She nodded numbly. 'Would you mind if I went home now? I've got a headache.'

He looked surprised but didn't question her. He paid the check and they left.

Conversation was sparse travelling back to Finchley. Linda found the presence of the chauffeur sitting faceless in the front a deterrent.

At the door she offered Jay her hand and he shook it gravely. 'I'll see you and the kids about twelve tomorrow. We'll take them to lunch,' he said.

She nodded listlessly. In the morning she would phone and cancel.

The wedding reception was crowded.

'Steer me to the bar, *I* need a drink!' Claudia said at once.

'I s-s-say, shouldn't we try to find them first?' Jeremy stuttered, looking vacantly around.

'No, let's get a drink.'

They headed for the bar. Claudia had a fast glass of champagne and felt better. She surveyed the crowd, a lot of Shirley's pseudo society friends, and a group of American film people.

'Dreary-looking bunch,' she commented sharply.

Jeremy looked at her vaguely.

A waiter passed with a tray of canapés, and she grabbed a few. 'Ugh—lousy food!' she exclaimed. 'A bit of dried-up old sausage meat, sort of like the bridegroom!' She giggled and gulped down some more champagne.

Two tall, thin, slightly less acne'd replicas of Jeremy approached them. 'J. Francis, old chap,' one of them announced loudly, clamping his hand firmly on Jeremy's shoulder and surveying Claudia. 'How are we, then?'

'Oh, h-h-hello, Robin.'

Robin released his grip on Jeremy. 'Who's your lovely lady?'

Jeremy waved his arms about. 'Er, Claudia P-P-Parker—this is Robin Humphries.'

'Lord Humphries, old boy. Let the girl know who she's talking to.' He smiled at Claudia, revealing a line of crooked nicotine-stained teeth.

She smiled back. She was sipping her fourth glass of champagne.

The other young man pressed anxiously forward. 'I'm Peter Fore-Fitz Gibbons,' he said.

'I say, C-C-Claudia'—Jeremy edged between her and Robin and Peter—'we really should go and look for S-S-Shirley and her h-h-husband.'

'Whatever you say, lover.' She winked at the two young men. 'See you later. Keep it up.'

They exchanged puzzled looks.

'Funny girl, eh?' Robin said.

'Must be funny to be out with old Jeremy,' Peter agreed.

They watched her as she swayed across the room.

'Wouldn't mind a slice,' Robin said.

'Yes,' agreed Peter.

Claudia spotted Shirley. She made her way over fast. 'Shirley! You dark horse!' She stood firmly in front of her, one hand balancing a glass of champagne, the other holding onto Jeremy.

Shirley didn't bat an eyelid. She smiled politely. 'Claudia, darling, such a surprise! So glad you could make it, and Jeremy poppet.' She stood on tiptoe while he placed a sloppy kiss on her cheek. 'Divine to see you both.'

'Where's the bridegroom?' Claudia asked, her words slurring slightly.

'He's around somewhere,' Shirley said brightly. 'Love your hair style, darling, wish I could get away with such a harsh cut.'

Claudia smiled. 'I'm sure you could.'

Jeremy stammered. 'Jolly good show, this whole thing.'

Both girls ignored him.

'Conrad was telling me about the fun you had the other night,' Shirley said, her voice sugary.

Claudia gave her a sharp look. 'Yes, I thought *you* would be there.'

Shirley giggled softly. 'Why be there, when I can see the film.'

'What film?' Claudia's voice became harsh.

'Oh, Conrad always takes a film of those evenings.' Shirley

smiled triumphantly 'Didn't you know. it's his hobby. actually. You must come over one night. and we'll show it to you.'

Claudia stared at her. a horrible sinking feeling in her stomach. She knew Shirley wasn't lying.

'Well. darling.' Shirley continued. 'you did say you wanted to be in his movie.' With a tinkling laugh she turned away to greet another guest.

Claudia stood there. furious and burning. That son of a bitch!

Jeremy said. 'I say. old girl. everything s-s-super?'

She snatched her arm away. 'Shut up. asshole.'

'What.' he spluttered. looking hurt.

'Nothing.' She finished the last of her drink and handed him the empty glass. 'Get me some more. will you?'

She had seen Conrad. He was joking and laughing with an elderly couple.

She swayed over. 'Hey. man.' she said in a loud voice. '*Con-grat-ulations.*'

His piercing eyes swept over her with disinterest. Shirley walked over and attached herself protectively to his arm.

Claudia smiled at Shirley. 'He's a lousy lay—but then. I hear you are too. so that makes it cosy.'

The elderly couple exchanged glances and edged away. Jeremy appeared at that moment with a fresh glass of champagne.

Claudia took it and held it up to them. 'Here's to a couple of beat-up old fucks!'

People nearby were turning to stare.

Conrad said in a low. controlled voice. 'Get the hell out of here. cunt.'

Claudia smiled. 'My pleasure. cocksucker!' She took hold of a startled Jeremy's arm. 'Come on—let's split from this wake.'

A scarlet Jeremy exited with her.

Outside she started to laugh. 'Wasn't that funny? Wasn't that too much?!'

Jeremy stood there. his face a bright embarrassed red. 'I s-s-say. Claudia. how could you—'

'How could I what. man? It was only a giggle.' She suddenly flung her arms around him and kissed him. forcing his stiff lips open with her tongue. 'Come on, let's go back to my place and have some fun.'

Jeremy was reluctant to go, secretly wanting to return to the wedding reception and apologize. But Claudia insisted. 'I'll show you what it's all about, baby,' she whispered. 'I'll give you a trip you'll *never* forget.'

Back at her apartment, she fixed strong drinks and turned on the record player full blast.

Jeremy sat rigid and unsure of himself, while she danced around the room undulating her body and peeling off her dress.

She didn't take much notice of him as she got carried away with the music. She danced and caressed her own breasts, then suddenly, ready for him, she came over to where he sat and began to pull his clothes off.

He started to object.

'What are you—a faggot?' she screamed.

He got up and bolted for the door, running down the stairs like a startled rabbit.

Claudia followed him, and yelling insults, but he didn't come back. In her drunken haze she was amazed. It was the first time a man—well, whatever he was—had turned her down. He had to be gay, those chinless-wonder types usually were.

She went back into the apartment and swigged from the Scotch bottle. Lousy faggot! How dare he refuse her. Probably couldn't do it. She giggled, and then her eyes inexplicably filled with tears. What was her life all about? Where was she getting? It didn't seem to be very far. All she wanted was to be a star. Was that asking so very much?

Tears rolled down her cheeks. She turned the music even louder, then lay on the floor by the speakers. The volume of the music excited her. She started to manipulate her own body—if that crazy skinny fag couldn't satisfy her, then she would just have to do it herself.

Before she could complete the job she fell into a deep drunken sleep, her snores mingling with the sound of John Lennon singing 'I'm a Loser.'

True to what Lori had said, after dinner Marvin immediately

announced he wanted to gamble. The four of them stood in a huddle on the pavement in front of the restaurant.

'Wanna come and be my lucky charm?' Marvin asked Lori.

She wrapped her mink coat tightly around her and shook her head.

Cowboy Boots, anxious to be off, stamped around.

'Well, I guess I'll just play a little craps, then,' Marvin said.

'I'll see Lori back to the hotel if you like,' David quickly seized the opportunity.

'That's mighty nice of you,' Marvin boomed. He kissed Lori on the cheek. 'All winnings for you, sugar.' And with a brief handshake to David, he and Cowboy Boots were away in a cloud of cigar smoke and resonant Texan drawls. He was obviously a trusting husband. Either that or he couldn't care less.

Lori laughed. 'Didn't I tell you?'

They walked around the corner to his car, and Lori whispered to him. 'Are you big? I only like big men.'

In the car she acted like a bitch in heat, grabbing for him immediately. He was proud of what he had to offer. Quickly he drove to the hotel.

Lori swept through the lobby, haughty and imperial, her white mink drawing envious stares from women. She stopped and greeted an actor she knew. The man gave David an amused look.

Her suite was on the sixth floor, very luxurious, furnished in opulent blue and silver. She threw her mink casually over a chair. 'Make yourself a drink, honey,' she drawled. 'I'm just going to put on something more comfortable.' Her dialogue was straight out of a Hollywood movie! He opened a bottle of champagne conveniently on ice and poured two glasses. This was the life! A beautiful woman in beautiful surroundings, champagne, what more could a man ask?

She came back soon—wearing a sheer black negligee, her hair still piled high. He handed her a glass of champagne and she took a small sip, then lay down on the sofa, the negligee falling back slightly, revealing milky-white thighs.

He didn't feel quite ready. She held out her arms to him. 'Come to baby, honey,' she drawled.

He put his drink down and went to her.

'There's a silk robe in the bathroom.' she purred. 'Why don't you get out of your clothes and be comfortable like me.'

He did feel a bit restricted. and the setting seemed too perfect to start struggling out of his clothes all over the floor.

He kissed her on the mouth. tasting her lipstick and then went to the bathroom and put on the robe she had suggested. It was paisley silk. probably her husband's. He admired his masculine figure in the mirror. not bad for forty!

She was waiting for him. draped across the sofa. looking like a *Vogue* advertisement. He took her in his arms.

She put her hands inside his robe, scratching his chest gently with talonlike fingernails.

He stroked her body. She was very thin. with small hard breasts and extended large nipples. An exciting body—not soft and warm like Linda. nor curvy and exciting like Claudia. But very sensuous. all the same. Like a smooth white snake.

He parted her negligee. Her legs were exceptionally long. crowned at the top by a small mound of silver-blond hair. matched perfectly to the hair on her head. She opened them slowly, her hands moving around his back. digging her nails into him. pulling him closer.

With surprise he realized he wasn't yet ready. To distract her from this fact he moved his head to her breasts and started to kiss them.

She moaned softly, digging her nails even harder into his back. After a few minutes she grew impatient. and her hands traveled down his body. Her eyes were closed. but they snapped open suddenly when she felt him.

'What's the matter. honey?' she purred. a slight edge to her voice. 'This is real Georgia pussy!'

Embarrassed. he said. 'It's nothing. just give me a moment.'

Annoyed, she closed her eyes again. this time her hands working on him. pulling. stroking. kneading.

'Come on, sugar.' she pleaded. 'this little snatch is waiting for you!'

His physical reaction was nil. This was a nightmare. something that had never happened to him before. He grew panicky, conjuring up every erotic picture he could think of.

Nothing. absolutely nothing.

He tried to remember the last time he had had sex. Mousy Miss Field. his horrifying secretary. Desperately he thought of the evening he had spent with her.

Suddenly it was all right. he felt himself swelling. growing big, bigger.

Lori sighed with pleasure. 'That's beautiful, honey.' She wrapped her long pale legs around him as he started to enter her, forcefully. powerfully. He would show her!

He drove into her Strong. brutal thrusts.

She squealed with delight. 'Ooh—ooh—that's great honey—that's wild—ooh—don't stop—don't stop.' Her voice changed. 'Why have you stopped?'

He didn't reply He was too overcome with embarrassment. He had heard about this happening to other men, but not to him.

She was getting angry. Her sleek. sexy drawl turned shrill. 'What's the matter with you? Are we going to ball or not? If I want this sort of action. I can get it with my husband!'

He rolled off. 'I'm sorry.'

Furious. she sat up. '*You're* sorry' She stood up too. her hard breasts and exotic nipples staring accusingly at him. 'Get the hell out of here. I've got to find myself a *real* man.'

Humiliated. he went to the bathroom and dressed.

When he came out she was on the phone purring. 'Sure, honey. in ten minutes' time will be fine.'

He let himself out feeling ashamed What a terrible thing to happen. and why? He had fancied her strongly It wasn't *her* fault. Although maybe it was. She made no secret of the fact that there were many men other than her husband.

He went to the bar and ordered a brandy By the time he had finished it he had convinced himself it was *all* Lori's fault. Lousy bitch! She had castrated him with thoughts of all the other men. They were all the same. women. They all wanted to render you impotent in one way or the other.

On impulse he decided to give it another try that night. Not with Lori, of course. But what about Miss Field Mouse? She was quiet and inoffensive. and he was going to get rid of her anyway. so what harm. one more bash?

He didn't even fancy her. so it would be real proof if he could make it with her.

He vaguely remembered where she lived. She was sure to be home. so he had another brandy and set off.

Hammering on her door. he found himself as hard as a rock.

She got out of bed to answer the door. clutching a woollen dressing gown around her. Lank brown hair. sallow pinched face. 'Mr. Cooper!' she exclaimed.

He pushed past her. taking his clothes off and dropping them on the floor. 'Get undressed.' he commanded.

Averting her eyes. she obeyed him.

He took her savagely. pinning her puny body to the floor.

There was nothing wrong with him!

17

Linda never did phone and cancel Jay the next morning. He arrived, took them out to lunch, and the children were captivated.

He told them stories, played with them, and then they all went to a movie.

In the evening he stayed at the house for a bacon-and-egg supper and Linda found herself unable to break off the relationship. She put Miss Susan Standish to the back of her mind and continued going out with Jay. She liked him, the children liked him. Janey especially. He was wonderful with them.

It became a routine to spend every Sunday together. Jay always thought of new things for them to do, and they looked forward to their day out eagerly. It was a good thing, because since David's last visit he had not been heard from. Linda was furious. It was a pleasure as far as she was concerned, but she thought it selfish and mean of David to completely ignore the children. They were constantly asking, 'When's Daddy coming?' 'Where is he?' If it hadn't been for Jay at weekends she was sure they would have been even more upset.

'Doesn't Daddy love us anymore?' Janey asked sadly one afternoon.

'Of course he does, darling,' Linda replied, hugging her little girl to her. 'He's just very busy.'

'I love Uncle Jay,' Janey said solemnly. '*He's* not too busy.'

So their relationship flourished, and at the end of a few weeks Linda found herself firmly in love with him. They went to the theatre, small intimate restaurants, large exciting parties, movies. In fact, they spent almost every night together, and regularly every weekend. They went to the zoo, the park, museums and drives in the country.

He was amusing, attentive, interested in everything she did, but he never attempted more than a brief—almost brotherly—good-night kiss.

It started to drive her mad. Her body screamed out for some sort of attention. Whenever they danced she would have to hold herself in tight check to prevent herself pushing her body intimately against him. When they kissed she was in suspense waiting for him to go further. But he remained the perfect gentleman. Never touching her.

It reached a point where she decided she could go on no longer, and she resolved to bring it up at the next suitable moment.

The opportunity came sooner than expected. There was an end-of-film party at the studio. Linda was chatting to Jay and Bob Jeffries, the assistant director, when up marched Miss Standish. She was wearing the same white pants suit Linda had seen her in before. It suited her, complementing her glowing skin and tumbled blond hair.

'Jay, darling,' she murmured. 'Can I have a little word with you?' She had sly eyes, a secret smile always present.

'What is it, Susan?' His tone was pleasant.

'Privately.'

Jay shrugged his shoulders at Linda and Bob and walked away with Susan.

Linda said, 'Is she in the film?'

Bob laughed. 'At the moment she is, but I've got a feeling she's going to land on the cutting-room floor.'

'Oh.' Linda quickly changed the subject. She didn't want Bob to think she was jealous.

Jay returned quite soon and didn't mention the incident, but Linda knew that as soon as they were alone she was going to bring it up.

After the party, joined by Bob Jeffries and his wife, they went to Annabel's. It was impossible to talk there, and on the drive home there was the ever-present chauffeur.

'You're very withdrawn tonight,' Jay said, his tone light.

She nodded.

'What's the matter?' He was concerned.

'I don't want to talk now.' she said. looking toward the chauffeur. 'Come in for coffee if you like.'

She had never invited him into her house when he took her home before, perhaps she should have.

She left him in the living room and went into the kitchen. Now that she had him there, what was there to say? It was all so difficult. There were no words that could really express the way she felt.

Absently she placed some chocolate biscuits on a plate and fixed coffee.

He was sitting reading the evening paper. She felt at a complete loss for words as she handed him his coffee.

He solved the problem for her by speaking first. 'I have to go back to Los Angeles in two weeks.'

'Oh.' She felt deflated.

He hesitated and then said, 'How about coming with me?'

'With you?' For a few pleasant seconds she considered the possibility, then reality hit her. 'That's impossible, Jay. I can't leave the children.'

'Bring the children. They'd love it.'

She shook her head. 'I can't take them out of school, anyway—'

He cut her short. 'Linda, I'm not very good at this sort of thing. I've only ever said it to idiots before.' He got up nervously. 'Linda. I'm asking you to marry me.' He rushed on. 'I guess I love you. You're the most wonderful, warm, giving woman I've ever met. I know you've been burned once, and I know how you feel—but believe me, I'll try to make you happy. I'm not perfect. I've been involved with a lot of stupid broads—I've got a weakness for tall blonds I can't deny—but if you'll marry me I think everything will work out, and I think we could make a wonderful life together.' He paused. 'Well?'

'Jay.' She whispered his name. 'Yes, Jay, yes, yes.'

He kissed her. 'Let's do it soon, like tomorrow. I can't wait for you much longer.'

She felt tears stinging her eyes. 'I love you.'

He stroked her hair, then let her go. 'Go to bed. I'll call you first thing. I'll arrange everything. The sooner the better, huh?'

She nodded. 'The sooner the better.' she murmured.

Claudia spent the days after Shirley and Conrad's wedding in a drunken stupor She drank a full bottle of Scotch a day. occasionally cramming her mouth with sleeping pills or tranquillizers until she reached a sort of happy oblivion. She didn't eat. wash, or dress. just wandered around the apartment in sordid naked splendour.

The phone rang but she never picked it up. One day the door buzzer rang so insistently that she was forced to answer it.

It was Giles. 'Christ!' He was aghast at her appearance. He bundled her into a dressing gown and made her drink black coffee until her eyes started to focus and she could talk.

'What kind of a trip have *you* been on?' he demanded.

She shook her head. 'I feel terrible.'

'You *look* terrible.'

'What day is it?'

'God. you've *really* been away It's Monday.'

'Monday: I guess I went on a little bender.'

He surveyed the room. empty Scotch bottles. broken records, overturned furniture. 'I guess so. Who was the guy?'

She shrugged. 'No one. Just felt like getting stoned alone. What are you doing here anyway? Thought you were in Spain.'

'I've come bearing glad tidings. Your tits are world-famous.'

He produced a copy of *Man at Play*, one of the biggest-selling men's magazines in the States.

He opened it and showed her the centre foldout. There she was in solid colour standing on her terrace with London silhouetted in the background. wearing the pink shirt which Giles had hosed with water. her perfect rounded breasts standing out firm and full. the nipples rigid and pointed.

He turned the page There she was lying on her bed. black negligee. breasts escaping. mouth half-open. eyes half-closed.

The next page and the next page were all of her. The caption said BEAUTIFUL LONDON MODEL AND ACTRESS CLAUDIA PARKER SHOWS US SOME OF THE BETTER SIGHTS OF GREAT BRITAIN.

'You're a big hit.' Giles said enthusiastically. 'They want us to do a whole new series of photos. They'll pay a bomb. Want us to fly to New York. Want you to meet Edgar J. Pool—owner of the magazine. This is your big chance, baby. *This* is successville.'

She studied the magazine. Why, oh why, had she cut her hair?

'When do we go?' she asked, her face lighting up.

'As soon as we get you into shape. You look scrawny as hell, and that hair—we'll have to get you a wig. Here, sign this.'

He thrust a paper at her which she signed without so much as a glance.

'I'm going to book you into a health farm for a week. You really need it. I reckon about ten days from now we can go. I'll let them know. They're really wild for you—want you to be Miss Playmonth of the Year. Baby, you and I are going to be rich!'

Was it the fifth or sixth night David had spent with Miss Field? He couldn't remember. He only knew it had become a habit to leave the office, eat dinner, have a few drinks, and then go hammering on her door.

She held a sort of morbid fascination for him. What was it that made sex with her so overpowering and exciting? It was certainly the most erotic experience he had ever had. She always crept to the door clutching her woollen dressing gown around her. He had to command her to undress. Then she took her clothes off reluctantly, revealing a thin, white, undernourished body. She was flat-chested, with flaccid nipples that didn't even harden to the touch. However, when he was in her, pounding away, she held him in a grip of steel, squeezing and pumping the life out of him. Giving him no rest, holding him in her like a vice.

He hated her, but he couldn't stop returning night after night.

During the day at the office neither of them mentioned it. She crept around quietly going about her business, mouselike as usual.

He wanted to break the habit.

A busty provocative-looking girl called Ginny was doing an ad for his company. He manoeuvered an introduction, found her very attractive. She reminded him of a much sexier, more obvious version of Claudia.

He invited her out to dinner. She turned up in an almost topless, startling red dress. She had pink-and-white English skin, and full pouty lips.

This was going to be all right, he decided.

During dinner she drank frozen daiquiris and giggled a lot. They danced, and her body was warm and bouncy. All the men in the restaurant were watching her, which made David feel good. At one point, during a vigorous dance, one full pink-and-white breast popped completely over the top of her dress, giving a delightful view of a pale brown nipple, pert and generous. She tucked herself back into her dress with an inane giggle.

David felt the time had come to take her back to his hotel. She put up little objection, and once there it was an easy job to peel her out of the red dress.

She was wearing frilly pink panties and her body was ripe. Her breasts were so big and bouncy and unbelievable that he had a sneaky suspicion that they weren't breasts at all, just a lot of silicone injections put together.

He couldn't do anything. There was no excitement.

Still giggling, she was given money for a taxi and sent home.

He went to bed, couldn't sleep, until at last he was forced to get up and visit Miss Field. By the time he got there his excitement was at such a peak that he hardly made it on top of her.

She had a strange power over him.

He tried with several other women, but each time the same result. His life began to revolve around Harriet Field.

He found out about her. She was thirty years old and had been with the firm for twelve years, working her way up from the typing pool to become his private secretary. There was no gossip about her. She kept herself to herself. She was the office nonentity.

When he went to her at night they never talked. He just told her what to do and she did it, whatever it was.

Sometimes, after sex, she asked him if he would care for coffee or tea. He would always say no, and as soon as he could summon the strength, get up and go.

He wondered what she thought about it all. Why did she never say anything? The whole thing was unnatural.

The next time. of course. was later that same evening. He arrived earlier than usual. and she was still up. clutching a skimpy cardigan around her nonexistent bosom. Automatically she started to undress.

It was the first time he had ever seen her get out of her clothes: Usually it was just a nightgown and dressing gown.

There seemed to be layers of them. Skirt. cardigan. sweater. a vest (one of the most unattractive garments he had ever seen). salmon-pink bra. a slip. long woollen drawers. and thick stockings. Shivering slightly. she stood before him.

She was certainly a randy bitch. he thought. always prepared. Always creamed up and ready to go. Probably been frustrated for years.

Maybe he should make her wait for it tonight. She was already lying on the floor. opening pale. sluggish legs.

He couldn't make her wait. The burning desire he felt wouldn't let him. He ripped off his clothes hurriedly and crouched on top of her.

She heaved a big sigh and they were away.

Afterward she put on her dressing gown and started to tidy his clothes. piling them neatly together. ready for him to put on.

He lay watching her. She really was plain—it wasn't that she made the worst of herself. it was just that there was nothing one could do to improve her.

She noticed him looking and flushed. 'Tea or coffee. Mr. Cooper?'

'Both.' he said abruptly.

She turned to go into the kitchen. and he had a feeling she would bring him both if he didn't stop her.

'Sit down.' he said.

She sat hesitantly. crossing her feet at the ankles. clasping her hands on her lap in front of her.

'I want to talk to you.' he said.

They sat silently. After he had said he wanted to talk to her. he suddenly realized he didn't want to talk to her at all. he just wanted to go.

'It doesn't matter,' he said abruptly.

'Is something wrong, Mr Cooper?'

'For God's sake, don't call me Mr Cooper.'

She lowered her eyes. 'Yes, David dear.'

Christ, she acted like the vestal virgin. She became so coy and retiring.

He stood up, decisions filtering through his mind. He would fire her on Monday, and this was positively the last time.

Maybe he should hammer it into her once more since this was his last visit. 'Get across the table,' he said wearily.

Linda and Jay were married a week later at Hampstead registry office. Quietly, with no fuss.

Linda's parents were present, surprised but happy. The children, dressed in their best clothes, were strangely subdued. A few friends of Jay's and a few of Linda's attended the ceremony.

Afterward they all went back to Jay's hotel suite and ate wedding cake and drank champagne. It was very small, very informal!

Soon Linda's parents said they should be starting the drive back to the country. They gathered together the children, who were going to stay with them, and said their good-byes.

Linda hugged Janey and Stephen to her. 'Mummy won't be away very long, and then we're all going to live together in a beautiful big house with a swimming pool in America.'

'Wow—a swimming pool!' Stephen said delightedly.

Janey was fighting back tears, her innocent chubby face concerned and worried. 'I hope the plane doesn't crash, Mummy.'

Linda laughed and hugged her. 'Don't be a silly baby.'

Jay picked up Janey and kissed her. 'You be a good little girl, and Mummy will be back before you know it.'

Janey looked at him with big brown eyes. 'Are you my new daddy?'

He nodded solemnly. Janey kissed him and scampered off to her grandparents. Soon the rest of the guests departed and they were alone.

Linda took off her hat and sighed. 'I hate leaving the children.'

Jay laughed. 'It's only for a couple of weeks. You don't mind if I have a little time alone with my wife?'

'No. I don't mind.' She smiled at him. 'I love you.'

There were several telegrams. one from Conrad and Shirley Lee. honeymooning in Mexico: *Congratulations. English wives are best. They don't want so much alimony. Love, regards, Conrad and Shirley.*

A sarcastic one from Jay's fifteen-year-old daughter, *Best wishes, Daddy, on your fourth wife. Caroline.*

'She's a fresh kid.' he said grimly.

'Why do you say that?' Linda asked.

'I don't know.' He shrugged. 'I guess it's my fault, really. She's a tough little cookie—takes after her mother. I never spent any time with her. and Jenny didn't remarry, so I suppose it's affected her, not having a father around.'

'I'd like to meet her.' Linda said quietly. 'Maybe when we're settled she could come and stay with us for a while.'

'Forget it.' he laughed brusquely. 'Her mother would never allow it. Anyway, she's not a child anymore; it's too late for me to start stepping into the picture.'

'She's only a teenager. I think we should try it.'

He kissed her. 'You're sweet.'

She smiled and changed the subject. 'I hope I've brought the right clothes for Jamaica. It's all been such a rush.'

'Are you sorry?'

'Sorry? What a ridiculous thing to say. Of course I'm not.'

'Let's have dinner up here. The car will be picking us up at six in the morning. We'd better get an early night.'

'That's a wonderful idea.' She yawned. 'I'm going to have a bath now.'

'Leave it to me. I'll order you something special.'

She went into the bathroom. Her two suitcases and make-up case were stacked neatly on luggage racks.

She hoped she wasn't going to be a big disappointment to Jay. He was used to such beautiful women. She remembered elegant, cool Lori.

Quickly she bathed, then unpacked a long blue silk nightdress and matching robe. It flattered her, plunging between her heavy breasts and swirling down to the floor clingingly. She brushed her thick auburn hair: It was growing, and reached to her shoulders. Her body and face were by no means perfect, but she was an attractive, sensuous-looking woman.

Jay had ordered more champagne, a delicious fish course, and thin slivers of perfect white chicken in a creamy mushroom sauce on a bed of rice. Then strawberries Romanoff and large goblets of Courvoisier brandy.

After dinner Linda felt gloriously happy. Jay made everything perfect. In the bedroom he undressed her slowly, and made love to her beautifully. Nothing frantic, nothing rushed. He caressed her body as though there was nothing more important in the world. He took her to the edge of ecstasy and back again, keeping her hovering, sure of every move he made.

She floated on a suspended plane, a complete captive to his hands and body.

He had amazing control, stopping at just the right moment. When it did happen it was only because he wanted it to, and they came in complete unison. She had never experienced *that* before, and she clung to him, words tumbling out of her mouth about how much she loved him.

Afterward they lay and talked.

'You're wonderful,' he said. 'You're a clever woman, making me wait until after we were married.'

'What?' She snuggled closer to him.

'I wanted you so much. But I knew if I made a wrong move I'd become just another guy on the make. I laid Lori the first time I saw her. She came for an interview, we locked the office door, and made it then and there. Can you imagine marrying a broad you screwed as soon as you met? That's what kind of schmuck I was until I met you, and realized what a real relationship could be.'

She kissed him. 'But weren't you worried if we'd—well—like each other in bed? I mean, why *didn't* you try before?'

'Because I wasn't about to take no for an answer.'

'But I might not have said no.'

He agreed. 'No, you might not have, but you're not the sort

of woman to have an affair. You would have regretted it, and I would have become the bad one in your mind.'

'Oh.' She was amazed at how well he knew her. He was probably right. 'What about Susan Standish?' she asked accusingly.

'I'm a man, Linda,' he said simply. 'Don't expect me to make excuses. She was a nice girl, and I couldn't have you.'

Her eyes were closing. 'I love you, husband,' she murmured, and soon she was asleep.

The health farm wasn't too bad. It was a place to relax, to think and take stock. Claudia submitted her body to the care of experts, and within a few days her physical appearance was back to normal.

She spent her days between massage and therapy, sunning herself beside the luxurious swimming pool in the grounds. The early English sun was weak but restful. She daydreamed a lot of the time, imagining herself a star, a success. That was all she really wanted out of life.

Giles came to visit her. 'You look great!' he said enthusiastically. 'Just like the girl I used to know.'

He had correspondence from the magazine, eagerly waiting her arrival.

'You've really made a big impression on *someone* there,' he said cheerfully 'They can't wait. Planning promotions for you all over the place. They want to feature you big, kid.'

She was delighted. Maybe this was the opportunity she had been waiting for.

Soon she was ready to leave the health farm. Giles took her back to his studio flat in Chelsea. 'I've moved all your things out of the penthouse,' he told her. 'It's not a good scene for you. You'll stay with me until we go.'

She was pleased. Giles was taking her over, and she liked it. They slept in a big sprawling bed like brother and sister, and during the day Giles took her shopping for new clothes. She bought a fabulous shiny ash-blond wig to cover her own cropped hair until it grew back.

He paid for everything. 'An investment,' he told her airily.

Eventually he decided they were ready to go, and he cabled the magazine.

He received a lengthy reply which stated that they had already sent the tickets. And, *Be Prepared Big Welcome For Future Miss Playmonth. All Press Alerted. Party Planned for Your Arrival.'*

Claudia was delighted. New York awaited her.

It was just no good. David could not break the habit of Harriet Field. He found it absolutely impossible to get an erection with any other woman.

He tried religiously, even going so far as to take a girl to a pornographic movie, in the hope that that would excite him enough. The result was the girl got so worked up, that when he couldn't satisfy her she called him every filthy name she could think of.

He felt if he could only make it with someone other than Harriet Field, the spell would be broken. But it remained an impossible feat, and sex with Harriet got better and better.

He took to staying at her apartment all night, for now he found he had to have her in the morning too.

She became even more white and insipid-looking. Slowly she seemed to be draining the strength from him.

He would wake up in her cramped apartment, bad-tempered and uncomfortable. It was obvious that if he was going to continue this relationship he would have to make other arrangements about her living quarters. He didn't want to set her up in an apartment, but it seemed the only answer.

She never said anything to him when they weren't having sex; just kept well out of his way.

Usually he drove her to the office, dropping her a block away. She would huddle in her seat mouselike and silent.

He hated her, but he couldn't leave her. Was it never going to end, this mad animal desire he had for this wretched creature?

He hadn't seen his children for a long while. Too long. Somehow he felt ashamed to face them.

His life became one long round of work, into which he threw himself wholeheartedly. And sex with Harriet. He looked thin and haggard.

It's got to end soon, he reasoned. I'll just keep going until I've had so much of her it will be over.

He ignored everything else and concentrated on getting Harriet out of his system. This involved sleeping with her at every possible opportunity, and now, even at the office he would sometimes lock the door and take her quickly on the floor or across his desk. It didn't help. It just seemed to make her more exciting.

He plodded on, determined to finish the affair.

At London airport Claudia was besieged by photographers.

'Look this way.' 'Over here Claudia.' 'Pull your skirt up, dear.' 'Let's see some leg.'

Claudia obliged. She was wearing a very short skirt with matching coat and clingy silk sweater.

Giles stood by watching. He knew he had made a smart move getting her to sign the personal management contract. Now he had fifty percent of her, and he had a hunch that fifty percent was going to mean an awful lot of money.

The Americans were about to discover a new sex symbol. She would bowl them over. In England she was just another little starlet. In America she had the potential to become a big star. Giles was sure of this. With the right exposure and the right publicity, she had it made.

Of course he would have to watch her closely, see she didn't drink too much, didn't get laid by the wrong people.

She smiled sexily at the photographers, head thrown back, lips parted, slanty green eyes shining. She blossomed even more in the limelight. Her bosom strained to escape the thin confines of her sweater, her legs were long and shapely.

'Come on, baby, we'll miss the plane,' Giles said at last.

She gave the photographers one last provocative pose, then took his hand, squeezing it firmly.

'This is a ball!' she exclaimed. 'I love it, baby. *Love* it!'

In another part of the airport Linda and Jay sat in a V.I.P. lounge sipping coffee. Jay's was laced with a good stiff shot of whiskey. He hated flying and found the only way he could climb on a plane was to be mildly drunk.

Linda admired her wedding ring, a thin band of perfect diamonds. She could hardly believe how much she loved this man. After David, the thought of being able to pick up the pieces and start again had seemed impossible. Now, the ten years with David seemed almost nonexistent.

Jay took her hand. 'You look beautiful today.'

She smiled. 'Thank you.'

A stewardess arrived and told them it was time to board the plane. A lone photographer stopped them in the hall. 'Is it possible to have a picture, Mr. Grossman?'

'Sure.' Jay smiled amicably and put his arm around Linda.

She was surprised. 'Why do they want your picture?' she whispered.

'The studio usually arranges it. Another plug for the movie.'

'Oh.' She nodded wisely.

They sat in comfort on the plane, Jay taking furtive swigs out of a silver hip flask. Then the great engines began to roar, and the plane taxied gently off down the runway.

One morning David woke up in a particularly foul temper. His head ached, and the room smelled of stale sex—Harriet never seemed to open any windows. He reached for her at once, his physical feelings overcame anything else.

After satisfying himself, he felt even worse.

She made him coffee and gave him the morning paper. He smoked a cigarette and glanced at the paper. On the front page was Claudia. She faced the camera three-quarters on, bosom thrust out, hair long and wild, amused knowing smile. She looked gorgeous, shapely legs disappearing into a short skirt.

BEAUTIFUL MODEL AND ACTRESS CLAUDIA PARKER (21) LEAVES FOR NEW YORK TODAY. MISS PARKER PLANS TO DISCUSS FILM OFFERS. SHE IS TRAVELLING WITH GILES TAYLOR, WELL-KNOWN FASHION AND SOCIETY PHOTOGRAPHER. BOTH DENY A ROMANCE.

David felt anger that she should look so good and appear so happy. After he had left her he had imagined she would go to pieces, vanish from his life. But here she was on the front page, off to America, without, apparently, a care in the world.

Bitch! She had ruined his marriage.

He turned the page in a fury. Why couldn't she just have faded into oblivion?

There, on the next page, was a small picture of Linda with a man. She looked calm and smiling. The man held her arm protectively.

MR. JAY GROSSMAN, WELL-KNOWN HOLLYWOOD DIRECTOR, AND THE NEW MRS. GROSSMAN LEAVE FOR A HONEYMOON IN JAMAICA. MR. GROSSMAN HAS JUST FINISHED MAKING *BESHEBA* HERE AND ON LOCATION IN ISRAEL.

Mrs. Jay Grossman—it was impossible. How dare she! He studied the picture intently, searching her face for signs of unhappiness, but there were none—she was serene and confident and very attractive.

How could she do it without telling him?

Then he remembered. Last week she had left three messages at the office for him to phone her, and he hadn't bothered to return her calls.

'Goddamn!' He swore angrily. He had always imagined that Linda would be available when he *did* decide to settle down. She would take him back. Harriet Field had delayed his thoughts about getting back with her. He had drifted into a sordid affair and everything else had been neglected. He hadn't even thought about seeing his children.

He felt trapped. What could he do? There was no Linda to save him now. The time had come to run.

Desperately he thought of the words of a children's song—*Run Rabbit—run rabbit—run run run*—and they repeated in his mind with an insistent monotony.

There were retching sounds coming from the bathroom. Soon Harriet came into the room. Unusual for her, she hadn't dressed yet, but was clutching her faded woollen robe around her.

She stood in front of him, white and wretched-looking. 'We are with child,' she stated blankly.

He stared at her in a panic. And slowly he realized it was too late to run—the trap had closed.